Lancaster Burning

TRILOGY

LINDA BYLER

Lancaster Burning

TRILOGY

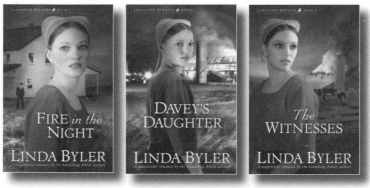

Three Bestselling Novels in One

Good Books
New York, New York

Good Books books may be purchased in bulk at special discounts for sales promotion, corporate gifts, fund-raising, or educational purposes. Special editions can also be created to specifications. For details, contact the Special Sales Department, Good Books, 307 West 36th Street, 11th Floor, New York, NY 10018 or info@skyhorsepublishing.com.

Good Books is an imprint of Skyhorse Publishing, Inc.®, a Delaware corporation.

Visit our website at www.goodbooks.com.

10 9 8 7 6 5 4

Library of Congress Cataloging-in-Publication Data is available on file.

Cover design by Abigail Gehring
Cover photo credit: Thinkstock/David Cloud

Print ISBN: 978-1-68099-062-1
Ebook ISBN: 978-1-68099-115-4

Printed in the United States of America

TABLE OF CONTENTS

A suspenseful romance by the bestselling Amish author!

LINDA BYLER

FIRE *in the* NIGHT

LANCASTER BURNING • BOOK 1

CHAPTER 1

THE FLANNEL CLOTH AROUND HIS NECK KEPT
bothering him that night. It smelled of the Unker's salve
that was slathered all over the cloth and was supposed
to soothe his sore, dry throat. He put two heavy fingers
between the cloth and his neck and struggled to turn on
his side before a cough tore through his sensitive throat—
burning like fiery sandpaper.

Fully awake now, he turned his large, ungainly body
and struggled to sit up. Lowering his legs to the side of
the bed, he extended one foot, searched for his *schlippas*
(slippers), and muttered to himself.

His room on the first floor used to be an enclosed
porch, the place Mam and Sarah did their sewing and
quilting. The spray-painted coffee cans lining the windows held blooming geraniums of various ages.

His single bed was one from the hospital with wheels
on it and a crank. Whenever he was ill, they would make
him comfortable by turning the handle at the foot of the
bed to lower his head or to raise it when the coughing
started.

A white doily with a small brown pony embroidered
on it and crochet work binding the edges covered a nightstand next to the high bed. An insulated carafe of ice
water occupied a cork coaster next to a plastic tumbler
with a blue bendable straw. A small battery-powered
alarm clock sat invisible except for its illuminated numbers. A box of Kleenex, a bottle of Tylenol, and a tall
green bottle of Swedish Bitters completed the assortment
of necessities.

Levi Beiler was born with Down syndrome and gained
weight easily, which was the reason he was a large man.
He was the oldest of ten children, born to David and
Malinda Beiler in the winter of 1977 when the snow-
plows opened the roads from Ronks to Gordonville in
Lancaster County, Pennsylvania.

It had been a shock when their firstborn appeared different—the eyes so small and unseeing, the tongue so
oversized and uncontrolled, the hands and feet square
and without muscle tone.

"*Siss an mongoloid, gel?* (He's a mongoloid, right?)"
she had whispered.

For some reason, it had been harder for David to
accept—his firstborn son's defect a dagger to his heart.
What had he done to deserve this? Was it a curse?

As was the Amish way, he examined his heart. He
must have done something wrong for God to send them a
"retarded" son. As always, the community rallied around
them saying that God only sends special children to special couples, recognizing their outstanding abilities to
care for them.

What a cute one! Grandmothers clucked and swaddled
and gave advice. Grandfathers clapped David's shoulder
and said He would provide strength for the coming days,

and He had—far beyond anything they could imagine.

Levi was thirty-one years old now and still in reasonably good health. Except for his fiery throat.

The house was dark—no switches on the walls, no lights flicking on with the push of a finger, devoid of electricity. The small flashlight he normally kept under his bed was not in its usual place, so he turned to go to the kitchen, holding onto the doorway and then the wooden desk with his slippers sliding across the spotless linoleum.

A movement caught his eye. Something white.

Turning clumsily, he watched but could not see clearly without his glasses. Holding onto the brown recliner, he peered past the maple tree, its budding branches hanging just above his line of vision.

Well, that was a *dumba monn* (dumb man). Why would a white car drive past the house with no lights?

Moving to the window, he gripped the oak trim. Lifting the green blind slightly, he watched, his eyes narrow and brown and cunning. It was a small car, he thought. But with only a half moon to provide a little light, he couldn't tell for sure.

He held his breath and waited. A cough tore through his infected throat, and he squeezed his eyes shut tightly, struggling mightily to swallow.

Should he wake Dat? Maybe they were *schtaelas* (thieves).

Ach (oh), now he needed to use the bathroom. Turning away, he shuffled carefully through the darkened house with a small yellow sliver of light from the half-opened bathroom door to guide him.

Mam kept a small kerosene lamp burning all night for Levi, and now its soft, golden glow was a sign of her love and caring. He was glad he had a good Mam.

When he was finished, he washed his hands and dried them on the brown towel that hung by the sink and decided to go back to bed.

Likely someone turning around, he thought. He put the car from his mind, replacing it with the missing flashlight.

A white form appeared at his parents' bedroom door.

"Levi, *iss sell dich*? (Is that you?)"

"*Ya.*"

"Are you alright?"

"*Nay.*"

"Do you need help?"

"No, I'm going to take Tylenol."

"Where's your flashlight?"

"Lost. *Ich bin aw base* (I am mad)."

Smiling widely in the dark living room, Mam made her way across it, touched Levi's shoulder with one hand, his forehead with the other. She clucked and then shook her head.

"You have a fever."

"I know."

Mam reached beneath Levi's pillow, retrieved the missing flashlight, and clicked it on, waiting while he poured the water and opened the pill bottle. He removed two pills and swallowed them, grimacing and moaning, watching his mother's face for any sign of sympathy, which was there, of course.

"Poor Levi. That throat of yours just acts up now and again."

"I need to eat more ice cream."

"Yes, you do."

Mam went back to bed, rolled onto her side, pulled up her knees, and fell asleep, listening to Levi settling himself in the night.

Upstairs, Sarah had left her west window open just a sliver, the crisp, spring air freshening her room with its fragrance. Her windows were covered with sheer beige panels with scarves of darker hues entwined on a heavy rod above them. So when a flickering light played across her pretty features, her wide, green eyes fluttered, squinted, and then opened completely.

At first she thought it was the swaying branches of the maple tree playing tricks with the light of the half moon. But the sheer beige panels hung still. Blinking, she watched the light. Chills crept up her arms and across her shoulders. Was she being visited by some heavenly spirit? God didn't send angels now the way he had in Bible times.

The light was intensifying. In one easy movement, her tall form sat erect, her eyes wide. A crackling!

Chills ran over her entire body; her nostrils flared. When her feet hit the floor, she was already running and pushing aside the curtains. She knew before she actually saw the grim spectacle before her. Through the branches of the large tree, a hot, orange light on the barn's east side danced, the mocking tongues of flame daring her to do something about them. She could only think of demons, of hateful, vengeful destructive devils in the form of licking flames, greedy in their intent to destroy.

A scream, primal and hoarse, tore from her throat. She backed away, a hand to her mouth, as if to stop that awful sound, that implication of horror.

She was aware of the floor creaking. She wasted no time, her hands on the walls to steady herself as she descended the stairs. She called out, or thought she called, but in reality it was another hoarse scream.

"Fire! Fire!"

Her mother reached her first, a hand at the neckline of her homemade nightgown, her eyes wide with terror. By the light of the crackling flames, the kitchen had taken on an eerie, orange hue, with shadows that pulsed and danced.

Dat came to the bedroom door, his hair and beard wild in the undulating light. He yelled, then dove back to retrieve his pants, buttoning them as he reappeared.

There was a high shriek from Levi's bed. Instinctively, Sarah rushed to his bedside, telling him to stay calm. The barn was on fire, and she needed to make a phone call.

Dat was incoherent. Mam was shoving her feet into her barn shoes, crying out about dialing 911. Sarah pushed past them both, ripped open the *kesslehaus* (wash house) door, flew down the steps, and dashed across the lawn to the phone shanty beside the shed.

She tried to turn the knob three times, but it was stubborn. So she turned in the opposite direction, and the door flung inward. Turning her head, she gasped in terror as the voracious flames licked their way to the barn's rooftop.

The horses screamed. The high, intense sound scattered Sarah's senses for a second. Summoning all her strength, she focused on the telephone on the wooden shelf.

She had no flashlight. Her hands scrabbled wildly now, searching desperately for a source of light. She felt the smooth roundness of a small Bic lighter. Thank God.

Instantly, she flicked it with her thumb and held it steady. A tiny orange flame rewarded her with a small circle of light—ironically so necessary when only a few hundred feet away the same element was now destroying their livelihood.

Lifting the receiver, she jabbed hard at the 9 and then hit the 1 twice. Instantly, a dispatcher on the other end of the line spoke in clipped, precise tones. Sarah gave him articulate directions and then replaced the receiver, a terrible dread seizing her as she kicked open the door.

Acceptance would have been easier if she hadn't had to listen to the desperate cries of the horses. They thrashed and kicked, completely beside themselves with fear. Cows and heifers bawled, their raw fear transforming ordinary moos into sounds of frightful proportions. Sarah barreled straight through the stable door as flames roared overhead, the haymow fully engulfed.

Dat was a dark tragic figure now, so human and pitiful, somehow so unable. Mam, so small and helpless, shoved open the barnyard door.

With a cry and a yank, Dat released the cows from the iron locks around their necks, the lever opening them in perfect unison. Each cow backed over the gutter and turned, bawling, as Dat waved his arms. He yelled and yelled, the sound of his voice futile now, as the roaring and crackling became louder.

The horses! Oh, please!

The floor above them broke—the hissing, tearing sound a knell of doom.

"Priscilla! No!"

Sarah dashed after her sister, whose sole purpose was to reach her riding horse, Dutch. Grabbing her by the shoulders, Sarah screamed and pointed to the break in the floorboards, the sparks raining down on the dry hay stacked by the stone wall. Priscilla wrenched her body from Sarah's grasp, flung herself along the corridor, and wedged beside the horse, desperately searching for the chain fastened to his halter.

It was then that the dry hay burst into flames, the sparks turning into blazing flares. One landed on Dutch's back. He screamed and pawed the air, but he remained tethered to his death by the chain. Sarah fought to contain Priscilla, who was crying out and babbling like a mad person, her need to save her beloved horse dispelling all common sense and thoughts of her own safety.

Choking on the thick, black smoke, Sarah tripped and pitched headlong toward the concrete corridor, the eerie flames consuming the rolling, tumbling smoke above them. As wailing sirens broke through the night, she thought this surely must be the hell written about in the Bible.

Clutching Priscilla, her knees torn from falling, Sarah crawled out of the barn to the stoop beside the cow stable and fell sideways onto the dew-laden grass. The night hissed black and orange as the menacing fire continued to swell. There was no time to rest.

"*Komm*, Priscilla!"

Jumping up, Sarah ran to safety—a sobbing, terrified Priscilla on her heels.

"Stay here. I'm going to help Dat!"

Sarah was vaguely aware of Suzie and Mervin huddled together on the porch of the farmhouse, their faces white in the glow of the fire. Red fire trucks were screaming their way toward the barn, silver flashing on the wheels and sides of the huge vehicles. As the men in fire gear jumped down and wielded hoses, Sarah knew her help was now completely useless.

She turned to go back but felt Mam beside her and reached out a hand as Mam's arm slid about her waist. The cries of the tortured animals pushed Sarah's hands to her ears, where she clamped them as though her life depended on ridding herself of the terrible sounds.

"It's awful, I know. Oh, it's terrible," Mam kept repeating, over and over, as if her banal speech could fix it all.

Sarah was glad when Mam went to the porch to comfort Mervin and Suzie. Dropping down beside Priscilla, she pulled the younger girl against her lap. Pricilla lowered her head and shuddered from the force of her sobs.

They both cried out in high-pitched despair when the diesel fuel tank exploded, sending rockets of flames roaring high into the night sky, increasing the heat and velocity of the fire. That was when the animals' cries ended, each creature mercilessly engulfed and burned to death.

Sarah lifted her face to the night sky and found friendly white stars shimmering in the heavens, as if nothing out of the ordinary was happening. She wondered if God cared that their barn had turned into a raging inferno and trapped the innocent animals in its fiery maw.

Cars arrived, some with blue lights flashing on their roofs. Neighbors—Amish and English—appeared in the line that separated the light from the dark. They were like creatures emerging from a strange other world, their faces grim, their straw hats and camouflage caps all pulled down as if to shield their minds from the horror of it.

Sarah watched the line of men, most in black wearing wide hats, a silhouette of sameness and brotherly love. As neighbors, they stood by Dat, not saying much, their silence a better comfort than words. Words would be about as useless as their blazing barn, Sarah reasoned, so that was how the men likely viewed the situation.

Great streams of water continued to shoot from the expertly controlled hoses. The trained firemen on duty went about their business saving what they could, which

Sarah knew wasn't much. The flames hissed where the water rained down on them, sending up plumes of white steam that were immediately swallowed up by rolling billows of black smoke. And still sirens wailed as more fire trucks rumbled to the scene.

The flames crackled, hissed, and steamed. The fire engines idled, and pumps roared to life as firemen swarmed about. The police arrived wearing dark uniforms with pistols and gold braids and an air of authority. Dat looked old and a bit humpbacked, his homemade Amish clothes drab and ill-fitting, his beard wagging as he told the officers what he knew. Sarah guessed it probably wasn't much.

The night burned into a weariness after that. As Priscilla continued crying, everyone crowded around Dat, the darkness taking back some of the light as the water quenched a fraction of the flames.

Looking down at her sister, Sarah bent her head and whispered, "Hush, hush."

Priscilla nodded, rubbed a forearm across her face, and said, "Let's go in."

Together they walked across the yard and up to the porch, where Sarah thought she heard a soft sound, a calling, but she couldn't be sure. Opening the door, she heard Levi crying out for assistance. Mam had already heard him and, after putting the smaller children back to bed, was a step ahead of Sarah.

"I can't find my flashlight!" Levi said indignantly.

"It's under your pillow, Levi. You don't need it. The house is bright from the fire," Mam assured him.

The loss of his flashlight, coupled with his fever and pain and the terror of the fire, was the small frustration that threatened to send him into one of his seizures. They were frightening to watch, the way his eyes rolled back in his head and his body became rigid, his head jerking and flopping. It was then that he could slide out of bed and fall on the floor with a terrible crash. They always worried about a broken hip or shoulder.

"I want my flashlight!" Levi bellowed.

Sarah quickly thrust a hand deep under his pillow and sighed with relief when an object hit the floor on the other side. She retrieved it, handed it over, and Levi grasped it greedily to his chest. He immediately quieted himself, the object a solace to him and his safety.

He sat, a large lump of a man, his hair disheveled, his beard uncombed, his eyes watering with the fever. Morose but calmed, he watched the barn burn.

Sarah found Levi's glasses, washed them in hot running water, and dried them with a clean paper towel. She brought them back and placed them on his face gently so he wouldn't get upset.

"You know *an dumba monn* drove his car in here." He said it flatly, without expression, his voice gravelly with the infection in his throat.

Mam looked at Sarah and raised her eyebrows.

"You were dreaming."

"Oh, no, I wasn't. I had to get up and take some pills. A car. It was white. He had all the lights off."

"Get the police," Mam whispered. She stroked Levi's shoulder and massaged his back while Sarah hesitated.

"I don't want to go out there—all those men."

"You have to. Priscilla won't. I think they need to hear what Levi has to say."

Obediently Sarah went, slowly calculating which group of men looked the most approachable. Good. There was Dat. Walking on, she tapped his arm and said,

"Dat," very quietly. He didn't hear her, so she tugged at his sleeve.

He turned, smiled, and said, "Sarah."

"Dat, Levi—Mam thinks the police should talk to Levi."

"Why?"

"He said there was a white car in here. Without lights."

Immediately Dat left in search of the officers. Sarah went back inside, away from the hissing and crackling, the mud and blackness, and the stench of rolling smoke.

The propane lamp sent the orange glow of the fire away, its yellowish white light restoring a sense of normalcy to the farm kitchen. Levi shuffled gratefully into its warm circle and settled into the well-used brown rocking recliner with the cotton throw across its back. He looked up with fear and respect when the officers walked through the door.

He told them he was Levi Beiler and politely and quite solemnly shook hands with the officers, peering up at them through his thick lenses. As they introduced themselves, Sarah stood nearby knowing that Levi would never forget their names.

CHAPTER 2

As the fire continued to rage, the streams of water that spurted from the long, snaking hoses turned the barnyard and the macadamed driveway into a brown sluice of debris and charcoal-laden liquid. Firemen in professional gear, their training now being put to use, aimed the nozzles for the greatest efficiency as the night wore on.

Inside the house, Levi gazed in wonder at the stern figures before him—Jake Mason and Brian O'Connell. Awed by the sheer splendor of their uniforms, he filed the men's names away in his sharp, efficient memory.

"How are you, Levi?" asked Jake, the older one, his hair graying at the sides, his stomach snuggly filling the heavy black shirt like a large sausage.

Levi watched the officer's stomach, noticing the absence of wrinkles in his shirt.

"Good. I have a sore neck, though."

He looked questioningly at Sarah for reassurance, knowing the English language remained elusive for him.

Sarah stood by Levi, put a hand on his pajama-clad shoulder, and bent to whisper, "Throat."

Squinting, looking at them, he pointed to his throat.

"Sorry to hear it. Now tell me what you saw."

Levi knew he was important and had an audience, so he played it for all it was worth.

"I need a drink," he said, waving his hand, a kingly motion that sent Sarah to his nightstand. Mam cast a knowing smile in Dat's direction.

He drank from the straw, grimacing mightily, rubbed his hands, pursed his lips, and said, "A white car drove past the house with no lights on it."

Giving no sign of acknowledgment, the officer scribbled on a pad and resumed questioning Levi.

Yes, he'd been awake.

No, he hadn't seen the car here before.

The only person he knew with a white car was Fred Dunkirk, the guy who sold Watkins products, and he hadn't been here since September twenty-third.

The officers shook Levi's hand, thanked him, and turned to Dat, leaving Levi with a beatific grin and stars in his eyes—to think he'd shaken the hands of real policemen.

"You have no reason to believe this was an act of revenge, someone acting out against you? No past grudge, perhaps?" Jake asked.

Dat shook his head, bewildered.

Sarah watched his expression with love for her father flooding her heart. He was an ordained minister, carrying the burden of being a servant of the Lord, striving to keep peace and unity among his people—the small district of twenty-some families—protecting his flock from "the wolf," the ways of the world.

Yes, of course, he had not always said or done the right thing. But so far as he knew, he had no reason to believe anyone would take such hateful revenge, allowing innocent animals to meet horrible deaths like that.

In Sarah's eyes, at the tender age of nineteen, her father was a wise and godly man, temperate, slow to speak, and above all, kind and gentle. There was pain in her large gray-green eyes when she met Dat's, also the color of restless seawater, a distinct feature handed down from Grandfather Beiler.

"I certainly have no reason to believe someone would do this against me," he said quietly.

The policemen nodded.

Dat lowered his head and thought of Jonas Esh's Reuben, who'd been excommunicated for a time—for sins he had brought on himself by his own rebellion. But Reuben did not have the ability, the meanness of heart, to react in such a way. He believed in Reuben, knowing the Esh boys all went through their rebellious phases because of questionable parenting. But when treated with patience and kindness, they all came around to see the folly of it.

What had his father said? You can accomplish more with honey than vinegar.

So when he lifted his head to meet the eyes of the policemen, these thoughts had brought a softness, a peace, to his own.

"No," he said firmly. "No."

As one officer nodded, the other's hand went to his belt as a device chirped and crackled.

Sarah was startled and restrained a giggle, thinking how closely the sound resembled the chirp of a blue jay at the feeder. She mentally formed a picture of a large, aggressive bird attached to the policeman's glossy black belt.

For the remainder of the night, the family huddled on sofas and recliners, covered with various afghans and cotton throws. Levi was taken back to bed after the policemen left. There he mumbled and coughed, the light of the dying barn fire playing across his features.

Mam stood at the sink staring out the window at the horrible reality of the loss. The acceptance drew her shoulders forward in a hunch of despair, her hands clenching the Formica top as if she could fix everything as long as she stayed erect, watching.

Sarah sat by Levi's bed, where the windows were low. Her knees were drawn up, her hands clasping them, her head resting against the cushion of Levi's blue La-Z-Boy. She watched the silhouettes of Amish men and English ones, of firemen and fire trucks, the smoke and the steam and the mess. Wondering how they would ever recover from this completely insurmountable financial loss made her sick to her heart.

"Mam!" she called suddenly, the need to rescue her mother from her pitiful stance at the sink rising to her throat.

"What, Sarah?"

"Come sit down. You can't stop the fire by standing there hanging onto the countertop."

Mam turned her head, looked sheepish, and then sank into the nearest hickory rocker, murmuring and shaking her head in disbelief.

"Try and get some rest, Mam. Morning will come soon enough."

Mam nodded, but Sarah knew she would only shut her eyes and remain wide awake beneath the closed lids, her mind churning with questions tumbling over each other as she planned the upcoming day. The children needed to go to school. Their lunches needed to be packed. Mervin had brought home his arithmetic workbook with red check marks all over one page. Had he done the corrections?

There would be breakfast to prepare for these men. She counted the dozens of eggs in the propane gas refrigerator in the *kesslehaus*, where she stored the extra eggs from her fine flock of laying hens.

As if she read her thoughts, Sarah called, "There are plenty of eggs, and we have canned turkey sausage."

"Yes, Sarah. Bless your heart."

Sarah was warmed and rejuvenated by the sound of her mother's voice. Dear, dear Mam. At a time like this, when tension ran high, she remembered to appreciate her daughter's help. By the light of the flickering flames, she smiled.

The Beiler farm, as always, had been immaculate, the level black-topped driveway lined with maple trees, the lush green grass beneath them mowed twice weekly, in the spring especially. The white fence beside it contained the herd of clean black and white Holsteins, the clipped and well-fed brown mules, Dutch, the riding horse, and George, Charlie, Pansy, and Otter, the driving horses. The stone farmhouse stood off to the left, a proud old house that had weathered centuries of rain and sunshine, arctic temperatures and tropical ones, humidity, drying winds, thunderstorms, and the dark of night.

Dat had just renovated the shingle roof, replacing it with more expensive standing seam metal that was pewter gray, almost black, and complemented the ageless gray and brown stone. The porch had been expanded and stretched across the entire front, except for Levi's enclosure with its tall windows shaded by the maple trees and the boxwoods adding a thick, green skirt.

There was a new addition built on the side, a *kesslehaus*, the hub of Amish farm life. Against one wall stood the wringer washer and plastic rinse tubs. Against another wall were a deep sink, countertops, and cupboards containing canning supplies. The cupboards also held Sevin, Round-Up, insecticides, Miracle-Gro, Epsom salt, and pickling lime.

That was also where they stored the extra-large matches called barn burners used to light the fire for the *eisa kessle* (iron kettle). The huge cast-iron pot rested on the cast-iron top of a brick enclosure. Heavy pieces of wood, along with newspaper and kindling, were fed into the enclosure and lit with a barn burner through an opening on the front that was then sealed with a cast-iron door. The door was securely shut to contain the heat that was necessary to heat the water in the kettle for cold packing hundreds of jars of fruits and vegetables.

The floor was cemented and painted with at least three coats of a light brown oil-based paint—the color of mud. The man at the paint store had tried to persuade Mam that nowadays the water-based paint was as good. But she pursed her lips and shook her head. Her eyes flashed as she said, no, it wasn't. She knew what held up under the countless comings and goings of a large family. Only her oil-based paint would protect the floor against kicked-off boots, endless baskets of laundry, bushels of corn, peaches, and apples, cardboard boxes, and stainless steel buckets.

Adjacent to the *kesslehaus*, the kitchen was large and homey. Golden oak cabinets were constructed along two walls in an L-shape. The large gas refrigerator, an EZ Freeze from Indiana, fit snugly beneath two small cabinets built above it. On the other side of the room were the gas stove and the canister set containing flour, sugar, tea, and coffee running along one countertop.

The kitchen table was large. Two leaves extended it to the required size for seating the seven of them. At one time, when the married boys had all been at home, they'd had as many as four leaves. The brawny sons had needed elbow room as they shoveled heaping mounds of mashed potatoes, beef, beans, and corn into their mouths to nourish their craving stomachs.

The seating area was like an extension of the kitchen, a circle of sofas and chairs, propane lamps housed in oak cabinets, magazine racks containing the *Botschaft*, the *Connection*, *Keepers at Home*, and the *Ladies Journal*—all periodicals about Plain life. Mam looked forward to reading them when Mervin brought in each day's mail on his scooter.

Levi's room was off to the left, facing the front lawn and the white dairy barn that was added on to the older barn structure in 1978 and now housed much of their livelihood. They'd added the cement manure pit, the new barnyard, and the large shop and implement shed the year after they remodeled the house.

Mam had been guilty, plain down guilty, when Ammon King's work crew started gutting the dear old house. What had been good enough for her mother-in-law all of her life should have been good enough for her. But Dat squeezed her shoulders and said they'd been blessed and were now financially able to make the renovations. Though she beamed and smiled and her eyes twinkled as she secretly anticipated her wonderful "new" house, she always kept her head bowed and tried to be humble—but she really wasn't.

They made do in the buggy shed during the renovations that summer. Now Mam grew pots of ferns and fig trees and African violets on the new wide oak-trimmed windowsills. She hung the required dark green window shades in the living room but made pretty cotton curtains in plain beige for the kitchen.

She was, after all, a minister's wife, and her house needed to be in the *ordnung* (within the rules) as befitted the wife of a leader in the church. But, oh, how she adored it! She scattered hand-woven rugs made from cast-off clothing, enjoying the charm the vibrant colors added, and went about her days with a song in her heart, surrounded by the things she loved.

Sarah must have dozed. There was a knock on the door followed by a rustling sound. She realized that someone was in the house. Sitting up and squinting, she carefully lowered the footrest of the blue La-Z-Boy, glancing at Levi's form beneath the covers, and stood up.

"Hannah."

At the same time, Mam's head rolled across the back of the hickory rocker. She gasped, "*Ach* (oh), my!"

Hannah, the wife of Elam Stoltzfus and the mother of several married daughters and two boys, Chris and Matthew, was their closest neighbor. "Don't be scared. Stay there. *Ach*, Malinda!"

An old sweater was slung across her purple dress, a black apron pinned around her rotund form. Gathering Sarah and Malinda in a massive hug of sympathy, she bore enormous amounts of goodwill, kindness, and *an mit-leidich's g'feel* (understanding). She shed a few discreet tears as she spoke, trying in vain to contain them. Stepping back, she kept a large hand on each of their shoulders.

"Oh, I told Elam, of all the folks in Lancaster County, Daveys are the least deserving of this tragedy. Your whole barn! In one night? Do they know what happened? Was it the diesel? *Gel* (right), that was probably where the fire started. You know, I would have come up, but to tell you the truth, I was afraid I'd get smashed flat by a fire truck. Those sirens give me the woolies. *Ach*, Davey."

Leaving Mam and Sarah, she went to greet Dat, his eyes red rimmed, his face streaked and blackened.

"Davey."

She shook his hand as firmly as a man might, then pulled her upper lip over her lower one, ducked her head, and blinked. In the morning light, her dark hair gleamed under her white covering, a shroud of motherliness.

"Good morning, Hannah."

"Oh, you look awful tired, Davey. What a night! What a dreadful night. Elam came up here right away. He said you got the cows out. That's good. But the horses. Oh, I can't think of the horses. I thought of Priscilla's Dutch."

Mam lifted a finger in warning, her eyes rolling to the couch where Priscilla lay sleeping, or appeared to be.

"Well."

Hannah turned to the cardboard box she'd been carrying and carefully extracted two large jelly-roll pans containing her famous breakfast pizza.

"*Gook mol* (look here), Malinda."

Where cooking was concerned, insecurity was completely foreign to Hannah. There wasn't a shred of humility in her. She knew the firemen would be complimenting the huge pans of breakfast pizza as they reached for second helpings. She knew, and she was glad.

Hannah took charge, telling Mam and Sarah to freshen up as she had breakfast under control. Matthew was bringing French toast in her stainless steel roaster.

Mam looked as if she might cry. Instead she laughed with eyes that glistened too brightly.

Sarah went upstairs, her legs cramping with fatigue. She entered her room and held the curtains aside, watching the scene below. It looked like the end of the world— the apocalypse—only all in one spot. Twisted, blackened metal lay jumbled among horrible, charred timbers, once so strong and useful and sweet-smelling from centuries of supporting a roof with the harvest stored below. Now all was reduced to nothingness.

Patches of determined little flames kept breaking out, defiant and rebellious against the dousing torrents of water that had extinguished them. The smoke was unrelenting, groping its ghastly black way into nothingness. The very maw of hell, Sarah thought.

Dat had often expounded on heaven's wonders, but he also spoke of an awful place of fire and brimstone, where torment is never quenched. Well, this earthly fire was quenched. *Kaput* (done). All the power of the devil, and that's exactly what it was, could not prevail against the human spirit of kindness, sympathy, and the goodness that made a community pull together.

In her mind, Sarah pictured their whole church district with ropes held taut over their shoulders, their backs bent, pulling large cut stones to build a wondrous Egyptian pyramid, like the Israelite slaves in a Bible story book. As the knowledge that good triumphs over evil seeped through the fear and doubt, sealing off the conduits of worry and anxiety, Sarah knew she had nothing to worry about.

Hannah was the first one, lifting Mam's burden of breakfast. During the restless night, while they had dozed, uncomfortable, unable to sleep, Hannah had been mixing flour and yeast and sugar and oil, spreading the dough to each corner of the large pans, her heavy fingers repeating motions she'd done hundreds of times. Fried, shredded potatoes were next, then crumbled sausages and large bits of bacon that were applied with a liberal hand. The egg beater had been put to work mixing dozens of eggs that were then poured over it all with a flourish. After sprinkling shredded cheddar cheese on top, Hannah had popped the preparation into a hot oven before tackling the dishes.

She'd wake Matthew early. He was the cook.

Sarah smiled to herself. Matthew Stoltzfus. Tall, dark, and built like a wrestler, and happily dating the sweetest, cutest girl in the group of Sarah's friends.

She shook herself and peered to the right as she heard the grinding of a tractor-trailer's gears. Surely they weren't bringing the bulldozers already.

Incredulous, her eyes popping in disbelief, she watched as the large truck bearing a yellow earth-moving machine came slowly up the drive. A line of buggies followed, the horses tossing their heads impatiently, champing bits in frustration.

"Sarah!"

"Yes?"

"You better hurry up."

She dashed to the bathroom, pulled out the steel hairpins, and ran a brush through her long, curly hair. Opening the silver faucet, Sarah cupped her hand beneath the streaming water and wet her hair. She used a fine-toothed comb to help tame the silken, brown curls and then applied hairspray liberally, her fingers working the pump of the lime green bottle of Fructis. Satisfied, she carefully placed a neat white covering on her head, sliding the straight pins along each side to hold it in place.

She decided to stay in the green dress she'd donned in a panic. It was the color of grass. She yanked a black apron from the closet, slid it over her head, and tied the strings behind her back. She pulled on warm socks and ran down the stairs.

She was surprised to see a line of weary men already waiting to fill their plates. Dat hurried by with clean towels as they washed up at the sink in the *kesslehaus*.

"Pour grape juice," Mam instructed curtly, the strain of the night showing in her eyes.

Quietly, Sarah opened the refrigerator door, found the gallon pitchers of chilled homemade juice, and began to pour, her eyes downcast.

"Matthew, what took you so long?" Hannah said, her voice rough with irritation.

"It takes a while, using up all that bread," was his jovial answer in the gravelly voice that amazed Sarah.

They'd gone to school together. All their years, they had stood in singing class and played baseball and volleyball and Prisoner's Base and King's Corner. He was in fourth grade when she entered first grade, a scared, sniveling little girl who cried every single morning that first week. She couldn't imagine her life without Matthew Stoltzfus in it, albeit in a detached way since he'd started dating Rose Zook.

They were the perfect match, and Sarah was happy for Matthew. So happy, in fact, that she cried great tears of happiness that puddled into a rushing river of misery. It wasn't safe to sit on its banks and observe the way the water took away all her peace and comfort and hope for the future.

But she was happy for Matthew. Really happy.

He stepped up to the table and set down a steaming hot roaster piled high with French toast, looked sideways at her, and said, "Hey, Sarah." She looked back at him, saw the sympathy in his eyes, and knew she'd be sitting by that rushing, roiling river again. Her voice came out a bit choked and shaky when she said, "Hey, Matthew," and she went right back to pouring grape juice as if her only interest in life was how accurately the liquid came to within an inch of the top of each glass.

CHAPTER 3

THE MEN WERE RAVENOUS, AND THE FOOD DISAP-
peared as Hannah's stack of Great Value paper plates
from Wal-Mart were filled one by one. English men with
caps, mustaches, and long shoulder-length hair or no hair
at all—their heads shaven cleanly, shining in the early
morning light—lined up with Amish men, their straw hats
removed, their hair and beards trimmed and cut in almost
identical fashion.

The thing was—English people didn't have an *ordnung*. They could dress as they pleased. If they wanted
to wear something, they could, and if they didn't want
to, they didn't have to. Mentally, Sarah wondered what
Elmer King would look like if he shaved his head like the
one firefighter. He'd probably look very English, at any
rate.

How long would it take a whole head of hair to grow
back?

"Good morning, Sarah."

She started, looked at Elmer King, smiled, and
answered politely. She shouldn't think things like that,

she told herself. But you couldn't help what you thought, could you? She'd never say what ran through her mind; she just thought it, which never hurt anyone.

She was aware of a wet smell—a stench, actually. It smelled like a campfire doused with water, sending up a stinking steam.

Eww. Someone smelled bad.

She saw Mam looking at the firemen's boots, the black ashes mixed with mud making great tracks on her clean kitchen floor. But she stayed quiet, of course.

Old Sam Stoltzfus was already in line, Sarah noticed. Bless him, so eager to help at an age when many men would have been glad to stay at home. Sarah knew, though, that his balding, gray-haired head housed vast knowledge about rebuilding barns, a veritable treasure of unforgotten skills honed by a lifetime of experience. Somehow, the sight of the well-known member of the community was an immense comfort.

Another comfort was the arrival of the womenfolk who came before breakfast was over bearing casseroles and cake pans and Wal-Mart bags. After the others were served, Sarah was fortunate enough to have a slice of the French toast for herself with a cup of good, strong coffee. The sweet toast was thick and spongy, heavy and perfect doused with maple syrup. How could a twenty-one-year-old guy cook like this? She shook her head and hoped Rose would appreciate him. Wow!

Sarah packed Suzie's and Mervin's lunches, making sandwiches with Kunzler sweet bologna and provolone cheese. She added chocolate whoopie pies, wrinkling her nose at the sticky Saran Wrap. The whoopie pies had to be a week old, but she guessed school children never really noticed what they ate. She grabbed a handful of stick pretzels from the bag of Tom Sturgis pretzels, added red, juicy apples, and snapped the lids closed.

Hurriedly, she pushed Suzie into the bathroom, wet her hair, and brushed out the tangles amid silent grimaces. Ignoring the ouching and complaining, Sarah wasted no time getting her sister ready for school.

"I don't know why we have to go if our barn burned down," Suzie said, unhappily adjusting a hairpin.

"You have perfect attendance, don't you?" Sarah asked.

"Yeah."

"Well, then. Careful on your way out."

Casting a worried look out the window of the *kesslehaus*, Sarah decided to walk to the road with them, grasping reluctant little Mervin's hand firmly in her own.

"Not so fast!" he protested.

"You always stalk along like a big old goose," Suzie added, still not quite accepting of the fact that she was being trundled off to ordinary school with all that excitement at home.

"Hey!"

"Well, I mean it."

"Think of the story you'll have to tell the other children!"

"Maybe Teacher Esther will let you come watch!" Mervin shouted.

Sarah watched them go, waved, and turned to go back to the kitchen. Suddenly, she noticed how strange the farm seemed without the big white barn beside the house where it belonged. Is that really how fast a barn can simply disintegrate into a jumbled, stinking mass of blackened timbers?

She couldn't think of the horses and hoped they were turned to ashes, the way bodies were when they were cremated. The calves had died, and a few of the heifers. The wagon parked in the haymow, the diesel and fuel tanks and bulk tank and milking machines—so many things she never thought of were gone.

The trucks and bulldozers and men swarmed around the remains of the barn as the smoke continued to billow, changing from black to gray to white before it was absorbed into nothingness by the atmosphere.

Suddenly she stopped, horrified. Oh, no! She couldn't watch, but she couldn't look away.

The men had found a great, black skeleton, or pieces of one, with large chunks of charred flesh dangling from it like a steak that had burnt on the grill too long. The men rolled, shoved, and then lifted it. When the head dangled, Sarah uttered a strangled cry, turned to lean across the white fence, and retched, heaving up her breakfast. Reeling and sliding to the bottom of a fence post, she willed herself not to faint.

Sarah had never seen anything so grisly, so unnerving. The smoke now appeared as a grinning specter of death, and she had to look away, unable to let her imagination conjure up the evil she felt.

When the insistent whining of the diesel engine in the dozer suddenly stopped, Sarah swiftly lifted her head to witness a sight that would remain locked in her mind forever. Priscilla, a blue wraith with her thin limbs flailing helplessly in the throes of her agony, pounded desperately on the great yellow monster that was taking away her beloved pet.

Sarah heard the screams, the wails of denial, through the film of her own tears. A black form, Dat surely, retrieved Priscilla gently as the dozer operator hopped off his machine and also went to her.

Sarah pressed her fist to her mouth. As tears streamed down her cheeks, her chest heaved painfully, the weight of her sister's grief squeezing the breath from her. She walked slowly, her head bent. When she reached the yard, she noticed the well-manicured lawn that had been so perfectly maintained now contained deep ruts where fire trucks and countless other vehicles had sunk their heavy tires into the sodden soil. Was there no end to the devastation?

Surely the fire had been an accident. If it wasn't, she thought she might not be able to deal with it. Who could be so ruthless, so completely lacking in mercy? She desperately hoped there had been a smoldering spark in the diesel shanty. Didn't that happen sometimes?

Sarah reached Priscilla and took her shaking form from Dat's arms where his filthy, smoke-blackened hands had held her as if he willed her to gain strength from him. Looking out over Priscilla's head, his eyes— dry but so filled with pain and devastation—appeared black.

Reaching out, Sarah said, "*Komm*, Priscilla."

As before, Priscilla went, obeying her sister's voice.

The bulldozer operator's brown Carhartt sleeve reached across Dat's back as they turned away, the English man's coat in stark contrast to Dat's homemade black one. It was human sympathy, man to man, English to Amish, with no difference at a time such as this.

When they reached the *kesslehaus*, Sarah supported Priscilla as she reached to open the door and then turned her to look squarely into her eyes.

"Priscilla?"

It was a question, but her sister knew the meaning of it. She nodded, met Sarah's eyes.

"Sarah, don't be mad, okay? I'm alright. I just knew it was Dutch, and—I shouldn't have acted that way. He just couldn't take him away. I know it's dumb."

Before Sarah could answer, the door opened, and Elmer King *sei* Lydia (his wife, Lydia), a young woman of the community, came out to the girls and wordlessly took Priscilla in her arms, caressing her back as the sobs returned.

"*Siss yusht net chide* (It just isn't right)," she kept saying. "Priscilla, don't cry."

Priscilla took a few deep breaths, steadied herself, and offered to help in the kitchen, bravely facing her loss. Dat came in repeatedly, his eyes soft with care, and inquired about his daughter's well-being without her being aware of it. Mam cried softly but soon lifted her gray apron, removed a rumpled Kleenex, and blew her nose in one hard snort. She sniffed again, put the Kleenex back, and resumed her organizing.

The food arrived steadily all forenoon: doughnuts from the bake shop at Weis on Route 30, boxes of canned fruit, plastic bags of potatoes, cakes, puddings in plastic ice cream containers, stews in blue granite roasters, and endless amounts of meats and cheeses. Some went to the refrigerator in the basement after being carefully recorded on a notepad to help them remember who had brought what and where it was stored.

That was Mam. She was the best manager in Lancaster County, Hannah said.

Sarah watched, amazed at her mother's ability to deal with the responsibility of the day's demands after only a few hours of sleep.

Ruthie and Anna Mae arrived, shock and sympathy written all over their faces, carrying the little ones. Mam swooped in to extract her beloved grandchildren from her daughters' arms.

Ruthie had two children, Sarahann and Johnny, the baby. Anna Mae had little Justin, only three months old. Mam had had a fit when Roy and Anna Mae named their son Justin. She didn't know what they were thinking, she said, giving their son such a worldly name. But Dat smiled ruefully and said they'd better stay out of it before they stepped on toes they had no business stepping on. Anna Mae had always been inclined toward fanciness, Mam said. A real handful.

So they accepted and loved little Justin, and Sarah thought it was a nice name. She was glad Anna Mae had a Justin, so she could have one, too. A namesake was never frowned upon.

After the food was mostly *fer-sarked* (taken care of), they planned dinner. Definitely the roaster full of beef stew. They'd do a sixteen-quart kettle of corn and one of green beans and potatoes. Three heads of cabbage would make *graut* (coleslaw).

The women bustled about. They sliced heads of cabbage with wide knives and energetically scraped them across hand-held graters, keeping time with talk punctuated by bouts of genuine laughter or teasing. The boys — Abner, Allen, and Johnny — arrived with their wives and a horde of little ones who raced around the house, running underfoot the way little cousins do, the excitement high when Doddy's barn burns to the ground.

When Dat was surrounded by his three married sons, his spirits were lifted, energized by their unfailing support. The boys had all chosen to buy homes and start their roofing and siding business in sister communities, where land prices were inexpensive. Now they had a nearly two-hour drive to their parents' farm. Nevertheless, Dat was encouraged by the presence of his sons and their families, greeting each one with a special light of welcome shining from his tired eyes.

The dinner was set up on plastic folding tables in the *kesslehaus*. Great platters of cakes and bars and cookies were placed on another table with lemon meringue, pumpkin, and cherry pies.

Sarah laughed when Hannah hid a particularly high chocolate shoofly pie in the pantry, saying she knew that was one of Amos *sei* Sylvia's (his wife, Sylvia's), and no one made them like her. What the men didn't know would never hurt them.

Sarah stood, her arms crossed, listening to the men as they sat on the porch, their heads bent as they ate hungrily. Talk had started, as Sarah knew it would. The speculation, the blame, the endless questioning.

David Beiler was a meticulous man. No greasy rags in his diesel shanty. Haying season hadn't started. It was too early for hot, green hay. The FBI would be coming. Just watch. Something like this isn't let go in this day and age. Arsonists don't get away with it. Too much technology. Too many smart people. Nobody can light a fire these days and get away with it.

Levi sat in the middle eating vast quantities of the good food, his black sweater gaping open at the front. While he insisted his sore throat was worse, he explained in great and vivid detail his night vigil before the fire.

The men listened kindly, laughing uproariously. Levi laughed with them, his small brown eyes alight with the happiness he felt at being one of them, knowing he had seen that white car and that the Watkins man hadn't been there since September twenty-third.

That really tickled his brothers, who roared in unison, and Sarah laughed out loud, too.

Helping himself to another slice of pumpkin pie, Matthew Stoltzfus turned and watched Sarah laugh. She went to Levi and wiped his mouth tenderly, the light catching the blonde highlights of her glossy, rippling hair, and he wondered at it.

All day lumbering trucks carried away some of the wet debris, but many of the smoldering remains were simply pushed out of the way to prepare for the monumental task ahead. The cows had been dispersed to neighboring dairy farms, where helpful neighbors, who felt they were doing their duty, each took on a few extra ones.

Old Sam Stoltzfus and Levi's Abner sat in the shed beside the buggy with papers spread before them, making a drawing, sketching roughly. Sitting close to the telephone, they would soon be ordering lumber and metal.

In the house, Mam finally sank into Levi's blue recliner and slept for almost an hour.

The daughters-in-law, Maryann, Rachel, and Emma Mae, were all eagerly waiting for the van to take them to their parents' homes. Living so far away, they missed Lancaster County, their birthplace. They were glad to spend time with loved ones in spite of their in-laws' loss.

"Whew!" Priscilla sighed after the last noisy little people had followed their mothers out the door.

Sarah was already drawing water, to which she added soap and a rag, preparing to get down on her hands and knees for the task of washing away the dirt that had been tracked all over the linoleum.

"This is the biggest mess we've ever had," Suzie complained from her place at the sink, where she was washing endless dishes. According to her, dishes multiplied while sitting on a counter, so you never really finished.

The girls worked together late into the evening and then sat at the table, so weary they hardly knew what they were saying but too tired to take their showers. The boys, Abner, Allen, and Johnny, had decided to stay to help Dat with the decisions about roofing and siding, offering to make phone calls, helping to calculate the vast amount of concrete that they would need to pour in the morning.

As they caught up on the news of the community and other concerns, the conversation was woven with tales of other barn fires in previous years. What about the barn fires in Belleville? Folk lore or truth?

As they spoke, a mist of unsettling sensations hovered in the air. Sarah tried to shake off a foreboding feeling of evil that meant to destroy them. Why them? Why a family of ordinary people who went about their everyday lives? Nothing in Sarah's memory had ever evoked this sense of uneasiness.

Before the fire, she had always gone to bed trusting, innocent, knowing that in the morning Dat would be at the bottom of the stairs calling her to do the milking. She'd never even thought of a fire destroying their barn. Now she could never return to that innocence.

The fire marshal had come, hadn't he? Suddenly, Sarah sat bolt upright and inquired loudly about the fire marshal's appearance. What was the verdict?

David Beiler lowered his head, a look of pain crossing his features yet again.

"I just hoped you would forget to ask," he said quietly.

Priscilla's eyes opened wide with fear, and Sarah was frightened for her as well as for herself.

"Was it—did someone light our barn on purpose?" she asked, gripping the arm of her chair.

"I wish I could spare you the truth, but I can't. We have to deal with this strange and troubling fact. It was the work of an arsonist."

"Really?" Sarah gasped.

"So Levi was right."

"Afraid so."

"There are about a million white cars in the state of Pennsylvania, so it doesn't seem to be very helpful—what Levi saw," Johnny said somberly.

"You mean he may as well have seen Santa Claus swooping out of the sky with his reindeer?" Allen asked.

They all laughed, which helped ease the fear. Sarah knew Priscilla had heard enough. It was time to go to bed.

Upstairs, she flicked the small pink lighter and lifted the glass chimney, holding it at an angle. Rewarded with a steady orange flame, she settled the chimney back on the head of the kerosene lamp.

Priscilla was rooting around in Sarah's drawers. That was strange.

"What are you doing?"

"May I wear your nightgown?"

"Why?"

"Oh, just because."

"Don't you want to take a shower?"

"No!"

"Priscilla, what's wrong? You're acting strangely. Why don't you go to your own room?"

"It's dark over there."

"You have a light."

Sarah stopped and looked at her sister, annoyed. She stood gripping a rumpled nightgown to her chest, as if the power of her clenched hands could hold the dark and the evil away from her body. Her eyes were large, too wide open, filled with a sort of wildness now.

When Sarah met her eyes, she dropped them, but her hands remained clenched. Going to her sister, Sarah held her hands in both of her own and whispered, "Priscilla, are you afraid?"

Instantly, Priscilla's pent-up sobs rose to the surface, the culmination of terror and loss and all-encompassing fright. Her innocence forever taken away, she was unprepared to deal with this new and awful thing that wedged its way into their life.

The crumpled nightgown fell to their feet and covered them as Sarah pulled her sister's shaking form into her arms and held her, willing her touch to comfort the girl and bolster her courage.

"It's okay," she murmured over and over.

Finally, Priscilla took a deep breath and nodded her head.

"It's just that... Sarah, if a person so intent on hurting animals did that, lit the barn, burned Dutch, what's going to keep him from lighting the house and killing us all? I'm afraid to go to bed."

Suddenly defiant, she reached for a Kleenex from the box on Sarah's nightstand and shook her head.

"Go ahead, say it. I know you think I'm *bupplish* (childish)."

Sarah sighed and assured Priscilla she was not *bupplish*. But Sarah also felt as if a giant hand was squashing her down so tightly that there was danger of her life's breath being taken away.

Was this just the beginning?

CHAPTER 4

IT WAS ONLY FIVE O'CLOCK WHEN MAM WHISPERED Sarah's name at the door of her room. Sarah moaned groggily and snuggled deeper into her pillow. But the sudden remembrance of the fire and what the day would bring quickly propelled her out of bed. Hurriedly, she dressed, instructing Priscilla to grab the sheets from her bed. There was lots of laundry to be washed before breakfast.

It seemed funny to hear only the soft swish-swish of the agitator. It made only a quiet hum instead of the usual sound of the air motor. The diesel tank, the air tank, and the fuel tank had all been rendered unusable by the heat of the flames, so they were using a generator and a Maytag wringer washer with an electric motor as a temporary set up.

The heaps of clothes at her feet were piles of everyday comfort, the smell of the Tide detergent and Downy fabric softener a solidifying thing. Their essence was something dear and familiar, and no arsonist could touch it.

While the first load of whites swirled in the sudsy water, Sarah went to the kitchen, sniffed, and smiled appreciatively.

"Mmm. Coffee ready?"

Mam nodded, her cup steaming on the table. Pouring herself a cup, Sarah went to the refrigerator, bent to retrieve the Coffee-mate French vanilla creamer, and splashed a generous portion into the steaming brown brew. She took a sip and closed her eyes.

"Did you sleep well?" Mam asked.

"I did. But Priscilla slept with me. She's...."

"Is she alright?"

"I think so."

Mam smiled a sad, knowing smile, one that slid sideways and evaporated as her eyes clouded over with concern.

"Priscilla has always been so soft-hearted. She's so attached to her pets, has been all her life. We should have gotten Dutch out before any of the cows."

Blaming herself as always, Mam fretted about her daughter, who was at the tender age of fourteen.

"We'll just have to get another horse as soon as the barn is done. The sooner one appears, the faster she'll heal."

Mam nodded.

She admitted to Sarah, then, that she knew how Priscilla felt, having lain awake grappling with the onslaught of "why" and "whodunits," the fear of the unknown raising its ugly head. One couldn't escape it. Besides, she didn't really know what was expected of her on this day. Mam felt as if all her pillars of support had been knocked away during the fearful night.

How could she manage a meal if she wasn't sure who was bringing what, how many women would arrive to help cook and serve, and how on earth she'd ever get her laundry room floor clean again?

Sarah blinked, aghast. Her own mother! She always had a firm hold on every situation, a step ahead of her husband, fussing like a capable little biddy hen.

She told Sarah she'd prayed during the night, but her anxiety meter ran so high it seemed as if her prayers bounced off the ceiling. She was sure God was not happy with her for being so afraid.

Sarah pictured her mother lying flat in bed with a pressure gauge attached to her head, the red needle pointing all the way to the right as steam rose from her ears. She giggled, a hand over her mouth.

"What?" Mam asked, perturbed now.

Sarah told her, and Mam had a good laugh, then wiped her eyes and said that was better than a shot of vitamin B.

"You and your imagination, Sarah. Now you better get the washing done. You know Hannah's going to be up here first thing."

When Sarah stepped out with the first load of whites, she recoiled from the heavy, stagnant air, rife with a wet, smoking stench, the early morning darkness a reminder of what had occurred such a short time ago.

As she hung up tablecloths, pillowcases, sheets, and towels, she imagined the driver of the white car hunched over a small pile of newspapers and kindling with a lighter or a propane torch or a book of matches. What exactly did one use to bring down an entire beautiful Lancaster County barn?

As it had been, their barn had been special. The original section was built in 1805 with good limestone laid meticulously by their staunch German forefathers, who were hard working and smart, fiercely brave and determined to thrive in this new land. They certainly had done so, raising amazing crops in the Garden Spot of America

with its fertile, productive soil bearing fruits and vegetables to feed their well-kept animals. They prospered
beyond their imaginations.

Gott gibt reichlich (God giveth richly). They had laid
the foundation of thankfulness, stressing gratitude with
each load of hay, their faith as firm as the enduring stone
walls of each family's barn. But now the seemingly indestructible stone was crumbled and blackened, severely
damaged. Would their own faith withstand this ogre of
evil intent?

Sarah shook her head, showers of foreboding ruining
her day like a quick squall that hindered the drying of
the laundry.

What did the man in the white car look like? Was he
young? Old? Smart? Cunning? Rich or poor? Why had
he done it? Perhaps he was mentally ill. If he drove a car,
he was not physically handicapped, like Levi.

She shivered in the cool morning air, a vivid picture
of the devil himself driving that car entering her mind.
Enough now, she told herself, and stood, watching the
shades of peach and pink and gray spread across the east.
Another day was at hand. What would it bring? She did
not have long to wait.

Men and boys began arriving in vans and buggies and
on foot. Huge tractor-trailers carrying stacks of clean,
raw-cut oak timbers, pine siding, and sheets of metal
belched smoke from their exhaust pipes as the drivers
throttled down to make the turn into their driveway.

The previous day, clacking yellow bulldozers had
crawled and pushed while a knot of able men considered
the damage to the concrete and stone. What was worth
salvaging and what needed to be replaced?

Old Sam Stoltzfus, Dat at his side, had moved among the bulldozers, tablet and pen in hand. His gray and white beard moved gently as he spoke, his wide-brimmed straw hat pulled low over his eyes, his shoulders still held erect, even if his back remained bent.

The order had been placed as soon as possible. Now the great saws bit into sturdy oak logs as they cut the stoutest beams for the new building.

They decided to replace the stones with modern poured cement walls. Dat's eyes had not remained dry as he watched the blackened stone and crumbled mortar being hauled away on whining dump trucks. They'd be used as fill somewhere, an unseen foundation for another hotspot where developers paid phenomenal prices for squares of valuable farmland that were sure to turn a hefty profit.

It was the way of the world, and the sadness of it brought a lump to Dat's throat. He thought of those stones, the heritage of hard work, simplicity, and a frugal lifestyle. It was all being encroached upon by the lust for profit and the promise of a softer, easier, better way of life, the goal being idleness and free time.

Was it a healthy objective by Amish standards? David Beiler knew the answer and concealed his own private mourning.

Would future generations know the fulfillment of a hard day's work, when sweat flowed from a brow that was content? Would they find peace in doing without earthly wants and desires? Would they recognize that true happiness springs from self-denial? Would the will to do for others motivate their days? Or would the Amish church eventually weaken with the fires of the world, seeking after earthly possessions?

As a minister, David Beiler made the comparison in his mind. He sent up a prayer asking God to give him strength for the work in the years ahead.

Then didn't that Samuel *sei* Emma and all her sisters, some from clear below Kirkwood in Chester County, get a driver and start making doughnuts at one o'clock that morning? She was something else, Mam said.

They carried in huge plastic trays of plain and cream-filled doughnuts, some covered with powdered sugar and some dunked in big, plastic Tupperware bowls of glaze (even some of the ones that had cream filling on the inside). The women all smiled and nodded, their coverings white and neat, their dark hair combed sleekly. Their dark brown eyes were alight with interest, looking as if they'd had a good night's sleep and hadn't worked at all.

Oh, it was a fine coffee break, and it bolstered Mam's spirits.

There was tray after tray of these doughnuts and containers of chocolate chip cookies and Reese's peanut butter bars and oatmeal bars with a white glaze crisscrossed over the top. There were blueberry muffins, pecan tarts, and fruit bars that oozed cherry-pie filling.

Hannah, of course, had breezed into the house soon after six o'clock. She came bearing a bag filled with milk filters containing coffee grounds that bulged comfortably after the ends had been sewed shut. She set huge stainless steel kettles of cold water on low burners, placed two filters of coffee grounds on top, and left them to brew. It shouldn't boil, just heat to a high, rich coffee temperature until shortly after nine o'clock, when the forenoon *schtick* (break) was served.

Henry Schmucker called to the men to take a break—the concrete crew, the men still cleaning up the blackened debris, and those building the oak walls on the ground. The rich odor of freshly cut wood was pleasant after the smell of the hovering, wet smoke.

Henry was Mam's brother and a good foreman at a time such as this. Dat said he was a mover and a shaker. Things got done when Henry was around, he said.

The men filed past the long, folding tables picking up large Styrofoam cups of good, black coffee, grabbing napkins with a doughnut or two plus perhaps a bar or a cookie. They stood in jovial groups, talking and laughing, the air permeated with the purpose of the day.

A barn raising was something, now, wasn't it? English men wearing jeans, t-shirts, and baseball caps worked alongside Amish men wearing varying yellow straw hats.

The dreaded photographers, the bane of every Amish barn raising, arrived with their large black and gray instruments of intrusion slung jauntily over their shoulders or around their necks. Sarah knew their air of assured professionalism and superiority raised the ire of peace-loving folks.

She was the first to see them as she walked to the mailbox with the letter for the gas company Mam had given her. How could she know the cameras would instantly begin whirring and clicking? The photographers eagerly captured the long, easy, stride of the tall, young Amish girl clad in a rich shade of blue. The black of her apron, the green maple trees as a lush background, the white letter in her hand, the early morning light a natural wonder—it was irresistible. Sarah was an added bonus to the barn raising.

Returning to the break area where the food was being served, she helped herself to a filled doughnut, bit into it, leaning forward as the powdered sugar rained down. Even with a napkin, eating a powdered doughnut required a certain skill, especially when wearing black. A small breeze could waft the airy sugar straight onto an apron, where it would cling and then multiply by five as it was wiped off.

"Mmm," she said around a mouthful of doughnut.

Samuel *sei* Emma caught the praise, acknowledged it with raised eyebrows, and then laughed good-naturedly.

More women arrived bearing dishes of food. They hurried to place it in the kitchen before moving swiftly toward the coffee and doughnuts. There was plenty to go around, and the women rolled their eyes with guilt as they tried to be delicate while procuring a second doughnut.

Aaron *sei* Lydia told Sarah there is only one way to eat a filled doughnut—in two bites while letting the filling go squooshing off wherever it wants.

Outside, the noise and yells of the men began in earnest when they began to set the massive timbers in place.

"*Noch an tzoll* (Another inch)."

Men heaved, their brawny strength pushing and pulling the oak beams and posts into place. When the first wall was finished being assembled on the ground, they attached heavy nylon ropes to either side of it. With strength provided by sheer numbers, black-clad men swarmed across the timbers and pulled the wall up and onto the new foundation. They fastened the structure with massive bolts, and dozens of hammers rang out as they pounded heavy nails into place to secure the huge oak six by sixes.

On the ground, the other walls were already finished and ready to be put into place. Sam Stoltzfus and Henry Schmucker were the captains of the great endeavor called a barn raising. It was literally that. A barn being raised in front of your eyes, Sarah thought.

"If you blink, there's another wall in place," she told Priscilla, who was standing beside her. Priscilla laughed, and there was a joy in her laugh.

The raising of those walls boosted their spirits in a way that was hard to explain. It just seemed secure and safe and hopeful all at the same time, this coming together of all these good folks to help lift David Beiler's family out of its fear and sadness.

Sarah watched warily as a photographer approached her. He was of average height, with sandy hair cut close to his head and glasses with thick lenses, which made his eyes appear smaller than they actually were.

"Hello," he offered.

The greeting wasn't spoken with a Lancaster County accent. It was spoken more like a "Hel-loo" as in "loop."

His smile was genuine, and Sarah had no reason to dislike him as long as he kept that camera lowered.

Sarah smiled. "Hi."

"Can I ask you a few questions?"

Sarah nodded carefully.

"Why can't I have a doughnut?"

The question was so surprising, so not what she was expecting, that she burst out laughing in her musical way. His sandy eyebrows went up, and he laughed with her.

"Maybe if you'd say 'may I,'" Sarah said shyly.

"May I?"

"Yes, of course."

"May I take a picture?"

"Of the doughnuts?"

"No, you."

"Oh, no. It's not allowed. I'd get in trouble."

"Why?"

Just in time, Sarah saw Matthew Stoltzfus walking across the yard with Rose Zook beside him. In broad daylight! At a barn raising!

Sarah was surprised but glad to see them and excused herself from the impertinent questioning. She turned away and missed seeing the puzzled photographer shrug his shoulders in resignation, then help himself to three glazed doughnuts.

Rose Zook wiggled her fingers prettily and trilled, "Hey, Sarah!"

Sarah greeted them warmly.

"Boy, I'm glad to see you. I was ready to get away from the photographer."

"Was he nosy?"

"Just a bit."

"Rose, I'm going to help now. I'll be ready to leave about three this afternoon. See ya. Good to see you, Sarah."

"See you, Matt."

Rose looked at him, and they exchanged an intimate look, one that excluded Sarah completely. She said nothing, waiting until Rose was ready to go. They stood together, watching the great walls being hammered into place.

It was a true visual feast. Men in black and navy-blue broadfall trousers topped by shirts of every color of the rainbow, wearing golden yellow straw hats, black felt hats, or no hats at all. They were set against the yellowish brown of the fresh cut timbers with the blue sky in the background, the verdant growth of trees and pastures, the dark loamy soil tilled and waiting for crops to be planted.

To Sarah, it was more than visual. It was a feast for the heart as well. Nothing could chase away the gloom of fear and uneasiness like this picture before her. It was the sunshine of brotherly love and caring, standing together through anything and everything that God handed to them.

Like the soaked but still smoking pile of black debris, the dread had to sit on the sidelines like an injured player as the game went on, played out by the goodwill of all these men who had come because of their caring, heartfelt willingness to help.

When the first rafter went up and was fastened in the way of the forefathers, with mortise and tenon, Sarah swallowed. How often had she seen the wooden pegs firmly pounded into the holes drilled into the heavy beams?

They were holes and pegs, so solid and indestructible. But to Sarah, it was a part of her life, her childhood. When she and her siblings had swung from the great old rafters, sitting on the black rubber tire attached to the heavy jute rope, it had never once entered their minds that the centuries-old beams joined by those wooden pegs would give way.

As a teenager, Sarah had helped stack the heavy, prickly bales of hay, so pungent and sweet smelling, clear up to the rafters. She'd reached out a hand and touched the mortise and tenon, wondering at the craftsmanship.

Who had built this great barn? Did the people in the 1700s and 1800s look just like us? Was there, perhaps, a handsome young man, married to his first love, who had pounded the peg into place?

It was enticing, this imagining and wondering. Somehow, the hay stacked so tightly, the alfalfa rich in nutrients for the milk cows below, spoke of the agelessness of this great old barn, housing the fruits of the earth, the animals, a way of life.

The barn had held through the howling winds and snows of winter and the claps of thunder and sizzling lightning during welcome summer thunderstorms that sent them to seek shelter. They threw open the great doors to let the moist, cool air rejuvenate their tired and sweating bodies. The elements were friendly, even in their extremes. Who could know that one tiny flick of a lighter would bring this majestic barn to its destruction?

So Sarah was thrilled as each rafter was firmly pegged in the old way. She was comforted by the sight and gathered hope to her heart.

Rose sighed, a dramatic expression intended to evoke questions. "Oh, that Matthew is something else. He's so cute!"

She clasped her hands rapturously as she watched him, steadily keeping her eyes on his dark, muscular figure. "Look at him, just hanging onto that timber, pounding away! Supposing he'd fall? Oh, I can't stand it!"

Clearly, Rose did not see the barn or the men or feel the emotions Sarah felt. But then, Rose hadn't experienced the night of horror and the ghoulish fear threatening to overtake common sense.

"It does look like he's barely hanging on," Sarah agreed, laughing.

"I hate barn raisings. They're so dangerous."

Sarah bit down on her lower lip, staying mercifully quiet. She watched the men, heard their shouts, observed their willingness to obey, and marveled at the scene before her.

Chainsaws whined and buzzed, their biting teeth sending fountains of sawdust spraying upward. Tape rules snapped as men measured and then set into place another heavy beam, an accurate piece of the huge jigsaw puzzle unfolding before their eyes.

It would be nice to have a special friend in her life like Rose did, Sarah thought. She yearned to have the sense of belonging Rose had. Sometimes she felt as if, at age nineteen, there was a void in her heart that only a true love could fill.

Yes, Mam had warned her. Go slow. God comes first. He's most important.

So she yearned, said nothing, spoke of a love only to herself, and hoped someday, somewhere, God would have mercy and fulfill the want she harbored.

CHAPTER 5

INSIDE THE HOUSE, SARAH DECIDED THAT MAM might as well forget about a clean floor, today or any time soon. She walked delicately around boxes of food, toys, and mashed doughnuts and Cheerios.

A baby screamed from the old high chair Mam kept for feeding the grandchildren. Usually there were two or three babies who needed a high chair, so one of the mothers had to hold her infant while she spooned yogurt into its mouth.

What a gigantic beehive! Sarah stood, uncertain. What to do?

Mam was everywhere, and so was Hannah, barking orders, opening oven doors, checking huge kettles of bubbling food. There were women breading chicken, rolling it in beaten eggs, then seasoned flour and bread crumbs, arranging it on trays to be taken to the neighbors to bake in their electric ovens.

An oversized woman Sarah didn't know was slicing a ham at the table, and by the alacrity with which the woman kept sampling the succulent slices, Sarah felt she'd be fortunate to taste any herself.

She jumped when the woman said, "Hi! *Bisht die Sare, gel?* (You're Sarah, right?)"

"*Ya.*"

"*Vitt dale? Siss hesslich goot* (You want some? It's really good)."

"Thank you."

Sarah reached for the steaming portion, popped it into her mouth, and said appreciatively, "Mmm."

"*Gel? Gel?*"

She was so delighted with Sarah's verdict that she laughed heartily and clapped a pink, greasy hand on Sarah's forearm.

"We could just simply eat it all, you and me!" she chortled, her round face shining with happiness.

Sarah still didn't know the woman's name, but she felt a definite kinship. The woman's goodwill and happy chortling came from the heart, showering Sarah with blessings that rained down like jewels. She'd never need to be afraid again, ever.

That's what happened when people helped each other in times of need. Love multiplied and grew so fast you couldn't even begin to count the vast supply.

All over the kitchen, the women were smiling, patting backs, and supporting one another's decisions about how much butter to brown for the noodles, when the browning process was finished, when to mash the potatoes, and which was better—sour cream, cream cheese, or just plain butter.

There were lima beans and peas and corn, macaroni salad and potato salad, cole slaw and three-bean salad, deviled eggs and red beet eggs, and tiny, dark green, seven-day sweet pickles.

The women put Sarah and Rose to work, carrying

the food to the trestle tables covered with heavy white tablecloths. Loud groans from the sink caught their attention. The women had become enveloped in steam as they struggled to mash the potatoes with the hand masher.

"We need the air drill. Sarah, go get Matthew," said Hannah, who was keeping one eye on the clock.

Rose stepped forward.

"I'll go."

Hannah nodded assent.

Sarah continued her work, carrying out great plastic bags of Styrofoam trays, plastic cups, plastic utensils, napkins, and salt and pepper, as well as applesauce and dishes of fruit. She looked up to see Rose with Matthew in tow, dragging an air hose and a drill.

The beaters were soon attached, and a loud whirring sound followed as the potatoes were whipped into a frenzy. Hands were raised in the air amid cries of "*Geb acht!* (Be careful!)"

Matthew grinned, his dark hair falling over his eyes as the loud noise continued from the whirring of the air motor. Mam threw in the cream cheese, Hannah the butter, and Elam Zook *sei* Ruth insisted on the sour cream.

They gathered round, teasing Matthew, then Rose, who blushed as pretty as the flower she was named for. The boiled potatoes turned into a great vat of whipped mounds laced with so much butter and varieties of cream that the women all proclaimed them better than wedding potatoes! In short order, two more kettles were done in the same manner and were also fussed and talked and exclaimed over.

"*Ach*, my gravy! Somebody get the gravy!" Mam called, waving a hand as the rich ham gravy bubbled over the top of the kettle and all over the gas stove.

Sarah reached it first, flicked the burner off, and moved the kettle off the burner in one fluid motion, spilling a substantial amount of gravy across the top of her hand.

She yelped, flew to the cold water spigot, and let it run across the now flaming burn. Instantly, a row of faces peered into the sink, clucking, asking for B & W salve.

"Comfrey salve," said one.

"Oh, no. You can't beat B & W. Specially with burdock. Do you have burdock?"

"I'd put chickweed salve on it."

"Flour and honey."

"No, not flour and honey. That leaves infection."

"Not in my book."

Sarah was in pain, the babble of voices a sea of irritation, but she tried not to let it show.

No one could seem to agree. Mam did have a jar of B & W on hand but no burdock leaves.

"You likely don't have any weeds," someone said.

"Burdock? Oh, I'm sure there is burdock in a fence row somewhere."

Matthew offered to go, Rose accompanying him, as the women returned to their work stations, finishing the final preparations for the huge dinner that would be set out under the maple trees.

The pain was unbearable when Sarah lifted her hand from the cold water, so she let the water run across it, wondering how it would ever heal. Why now, of all times? She berated herself, gritting her teeth to keep from crying out.

When Matthew returned with the burdock with its large velvety leaves and firm spines in the middle that reach across the leaf diagonally as well, Sarah instantly recognized them.

"That's what I'm supposed to use?"

"Yeah, I'll steam one. I've done burn dressings before."

"There's a stainless steel saucepan to the right of the sink. Here. Bottom drawer."

Matthew found it. She moved over so he could add a small amount of water and set it on the stove.

"It has to boil."

Sarah nodded.

There was no sound except the running water on Sarah's hand until the lid rattled on the saucepan. Matthew lifted it and plunked the heavy leaf into it.

"Are you sure about that burdock leaf?" Sarah asked.

"Course."

"It's not poisonous?"

"No."

"Where's Rose?"

"She wanted to help outside."

"Oh."

Matthew lifted the now limp, brightly colored leaf from the boiling water, laid it carefully on a clean paper towel, then brought the jar of B & W salve, a homemade herb-infused aid for healing.

Standing by the sink, he reached out and turned off the cold water.

"How does it feel?"

Sarah didn't say what she wanted to say. She just nodded her head grimly and kept her eyes averted, desperately trying to keep from shivering because of the pain.

Gently, he patted her hand dry, watching her face, and asked if she was okay.

Again, she nodded, her mouth a determined slash across her white face as she moved to sit on the couch.

"You sure?"

"Yes."

He swabbed some ointment on a piece of paper towel. Then he smoothed it gently onto the burn.

Matthew was bent over, concentrating, extremely intent on his job, so Sarah's eyes wandered across the contours of his face, his eyebrows like two dark wings above his downcast eyes, the nose with a wide bridge, straight and chiseled, perfection. He straightened.

"Does it hurt?"

She looked up, the sting clouding her vision, as he looked down into her pain-filled eyes. It wasn't her fault that he didn't look away, she chided herself later when she felt so guilty and brash and so bold and so…well, stupid.

It wasn't her fault that as he had laid the burdock leaf across her hand, his hands were shaking more than a little. When he wound the sterile white gauze around it to ensure the air could not reach the burn, she couldn't help it that he gazed at her hand. She wondered why.

When she stood up, he was much too close, and she wished he'd move away. When he didn't, she sat down right away, and he looked at her hand again, and said he'd better go on out or he wouldn't get anything to eat.

She said, yes, he'd better.

"Thanks," she added, in a strangled voice full of misery and want and denial.

He blinked. He clenched his lips, opened his mouth, closed it again, and looked at her. Then he went outside, quickly, leaving Sarah sitting in an abandoned kitchen filled with open oven doors and empty kettles, sticky aluminum foil, flies, and dirty dishes.

She guessed this was how it was before you found a person who would be your special friend. You were just too vulnerable. Well, it wasn't right. Matthew was just her neighbor, dating Rose, the perfect couple. Rose was so sweet, blonde, and so right for him.

Deep shame crept across her features, misery so intense on its heels that she lowered her face into her hands and stayed that way until Mam bustled in for a few large spoons. She was so intent on her mission that she failed to see Sarah huddled on the couch.

The burdock leaf miraculously took the pain away. If only there were a plant she could pluck from a field or fence row and tape it across that mysterious region of the heart, she thought ruefully. Stepping outside, she walked slowly to the huge maples with the kaleidoscope of activity beneath them.

There was plenty of food, as Mam figured there would be. Hungry men piled their plates high. They sat together on folding chairs or benches or cross-legged on the ground, their heads bare now, having removed their hats for silent prayer before the meal. Children raced around the perimeter of the trees. Some upset plastic cups of water as mothers hurried to correct their behavior.

Sarah stood uncertainly, hungry but reluctant. Why did she feel as if she had done something wrong? She wanted to walk out the field lane and just walk and walk and walk, across highways and around houses and places of business and people's gardens and keep walking until she was rid of this senseless thing that had happened in the kitchen.

She hoped Matthew and Rose would be married in the fall, and she'd find a special friend and begin her dating life right after that.

"Hey, Sarah!"

It was Levi, sitting on a folding chair, holding court as usual, his brothers teasing him unmercifully.

"I want cake and vanilla pudding and strawberry tapioca," Levi called loudly.

Heads were raised, smiles given generously, as Sarah waved, hurried to the food table, and began to fill his order.

"Not quite so much," Mam whispered, and Sarah nodded, removing some of the vanilla pudding.

Levi's weight was an ongoing battle they never overcame. His love for food filled his days with joy and anticipation. Sarah just never quite had the heart to deprive him of dessert in spite of his widening girth.

What else did Levi have to look forward to, besides his cards—the football and baseball cards he shuffled constantly?

Carefully she walked to Levi with the loaded plate, setting it on the small folding table directly in front of him.

"There you are, Levi."

There were no words of gratitude, just a suspicious look and a concentrated narrowing of his eyes as he held his head to one side. A remarkable amount of time passed as he examined the plate of desserts, leaving Sarah a bit uncomfortable, standing in full view of so many men and boys, who were politely averting their eyes, busying themselves with their own plates of food.

Pressing his lips in a thin line, Levi decided to speak. "You took some of the cornstarch pudding off."

"Just some."

"Why?"

"Levi."

Embarrassed, Sarah bent and said, soft and low, "Mam said."

"Why?"

"Just because. Shhh, Levi."

Clearly upset, Levi's eyes turned dark with pain and disappointment. He opened his mouth, choked, and started wailing loud sobs of hurt. Many faces turned to watch. Tender looks of pity followed before heads bent to their plates.

David Beiler, masterful in the art of comforting his oldest son, stepped over, laid a hand on the heaving, over-weight form, and told him softly that Sarah would put more cornstarch pudding on his plate, his eyes telling Sarah how much—a minimal amount.

Her face turning a shade of pink, her discomfort pain-fully obvious, she stepped up to the dessert table and waited her turn behind a tall, wide-shouldered youth she didn't recognize. His hair was blond, cut in English style. But he wore broadfall denims and a pair of gray suspend-ers, his shirt a decided plaid pattern, not the usual plain fabric that was in the *ordnung*.

She thought nothing of this. The "worldly" haircut was common among the liberal youth. The years of *rum-springa* (running around) produced young men who tried their wings—experimenting in fashion, sometimes driving cars, as well as being active in organized sports. Experi-mentation in forbidden "things of the world" like alcohol and tobacco was not uncommon, resulting in a certain sadness as parental authority was undermined by the lusts of the flesh and the eyes holding court over a young soul.

Families bore it with *gaduld* (patience) and always with the expectation that the young people would eventu-ally tire of these things and seek a more lasting peace—a way of life that spoke of obedience, sameness, a love for parents and God, and a return to the fold. This return was hopefully followed by dating, marriage, and raising a family in the same way their parents had.

It was always a joy to behold when a "wild" youth made the decision to start the instruction class in the church. Heads would be bent, and furtive tears would be wiped away. Fathers and mothers were grateful that the sleepless nights, the anxiety and fear, had brought this reward, one they were not worthy of, their spiritual humility a beautiful thing.

Parents of a youth who did not conform, meanwhile, carried a certain shame buried deep in the heart, an uncomfortable thorn that varied in its ability to cause pain but always there.

The line moved forward. Sarah watched as this unknown youth bent to lift a slice of chocolate cake, promptly dropped it, and watched helplessly as it rolled beneath the plastic table.

"Shoot."

"Don't worry about it," Sarah said.

He turned and smiled easily, unself-consciously. The humor on his open face was genuine, a magnet that drew her eyes to his. The smile on her lips reached her eyes, turning the gray green seawater color to one flecked with gold.

His eyes were very blue. She wasn't aware of it until later, though, when she recalled their interaction.

He plunked a larger slice onto his plate. Sarah added a small amount of pudding onto Levi's plate, caught Mam's eye, who smiled ruefully and shook her head, only a bit, then followed the tall blond youth until she came to Levi.

"There. Now eat."

Levi looked up at Sarah and drew a deep breath—one that quivered, like a small child.

"Are you angry with me, Sarah?"

"Of course not."

She reached out to ruffle his hair. Dat smiled at her, and Levi beamed as he lifted his spoon, happiness and anticipation shining from his florid face.

"*Ich gleich dich* (I love you)."

"I love you, too, Levi."

This exchange was not lost on the blond youth, who watched Sarah and forgot to eat his cake. He'd never seen eyes that color. They reminded him of the ocean but only when it was stormy, not when it was calm. When she moved, he thought of the antelope that roamed the plains of Wyoming. Why had he never seen her? Who was she? He never did eat his cake.

After the plates of food were consumed, large garbage bags were filled and taken to the pile of smoking debris, where they disappeared, the intense heat consuming the plastic.

Women and girls moved from table to kitchen, *fersarking* leftovers, planning tomorrow's meal, complimenting. They were relaxed now, the crowning point of the day achieved.

And it had gone well, hadn't it? It surely had.

Hannah sat smack down in the middle of the riotous mess and folded a fresh slice of whole wheat bread around a large portion of the succulent ham. She poured a glass of ice cold meadow tea and said the young generation could do dishes, which drew a mixed response.

Out in the *kesslehaus*, Mamie Stoltzfus said Hannah sure hadn't changed now, had she? Always running the show, being the boss, and then the minute the real chores started, she sat there in all her glory. It just irked Mamie.

Barbara Zook agreed, but shrugged her shoulders and said that was just Hannah's way.

But still, Mamie said.

Sarah moved to the sink where Rose had begun scrubbing the pans with dried food clinging to their sides. As Rose finished with the pans, Sarah took them and dried each one as if her life depended on it. In reality, her thoughts were far away.

Through the kitchen window, she watched the beams being put into place. Agile men clung to the precisely cut lumber, the hammers flailing. But she was not really seeing anything. What was wrong with her?

She felt guilt about Matthew, and the stone in her heart was now an unbearable thing. There was Rose, beside her, washing dishes at a rapid speed, chattering happily, her blonde hair and beautiful blue eyes adding another stone marked "Shame" to the one that had "Guilt" inscribed on it.

Who did she think she was? Why had Matthew been the one to dress her hand? Why not Mam, or Hannah, or anyone else?

Silently groaning, she half-heard Rose. The men on the new yellow lumber swam together like colorful fish, but her unfocused gaze obscured the sunlight-infused picture before her.

"Sarah, you're not listening to me!"

Rose was emphatic and then looked perplexed as Sarah's hands—bandages and all—stopped their motion and tightly gripped the edge of a large roaster.

"What's wrong with you?" she asked, her bright blue eyes inquisitive, innocent.

Everything's wrong with me. Your boyfriend, Matthew, is an elusive rainbow in my life. I want him. I'm terribly guilty, my mind is so jumbled I can't see straight. How can I get out of this?

"Nothing," she said.

"Well, Sarah, of course there is. You've been through a lot. It can't be easy, knowing someone lit your barn on purpose. It would really give me the creeps."

"It does."

"Of course it does.

Sarah met her friend's eyes in a sort of half-slant. Seeing the blue gaze of love and concern, the childlike honesty and trust, only multiplied her guilt.

It was time for everyone to go home. Then she could sit in a clean, quiet kitchen and have a genuine old-fashioned talk with Mam.

She needed advice. She needed Mam.

How desperately now she wanted Mam to tell her that it was alright to let yourself love your best friend. No. Mam would never.

Sarah dried the roaster viciously and avoided Rose's eyes.

CHAPTER 6

THE NEW BARN STOOD LIKE A BEACON OF RENEW-
al, a proud sentry of fellowship, caring, and love admin-
istered to those in need. Yet the weeks following the barn
raising taxed the good humor and energy of the whole
family.

It was the rain. The constantly scudding gray clouds
containing inch after inch of rain persistently rolled in
from the east, slowly eroding the optimism of even the
most encouraging member of the family.

Even Mam, who usually refused to spend needless
money to dry clothes, gave in and hired a driver to take
the mounds of laundry to the Laundromat over along
Route 30. She muttered to herself as she dumped out the
gallon jug with its heavy accumulation of loose change
and counted her quarters feeling as blameworthy as
someone who had just committed a crime.

The thing was, those great, gleaming washers that
spun her towels and tablecloths and the broadfall pants
and dresses would simply disintegrate her clothes one
of these times. She placed no trust in anything electric.

Who knew if she wouldn't be shocked—simply sizzled to death the moment she reached out to grasp that handle to extricate what was rightfully hers? Sitting and sewing all those clothes wasn't just anything, after all.

And how many times had she pressed the wrong button accidentally, setting the heat on the dryer to high, ruining her good dresses and capes and aprons, wrinkled completely beyond repair? It was risky, going to the Laundromat.

Sarah adjusted the white covering on her head, hurriedly sticking the straight pins through the thin organdy. She ran down the stairs when Jim Harper, the driver, tooted his horn, jangling her nerves the way it always did. He was the only driver who did that. All the others sat in the driveway, waiting patiently if the family wasn't immediately aware of their arrival, although they turned their heads occasionally, to see if anyone was coming out the door. But they didn't put the palms of their hands on the center of the steering wheel to let their impatience be known.

Sarah helped Mam lug the heavy plastic hampers and totes to the small navy blue van. She arranged them in the back, slammed the door, and went around to the side.

Mam said hello, but Jim just grunted and said, "Seat belts."

They complied, and he moved off, complaining about the weather and that he couldn't see what was wrong with driving a horse and buggy to the Laundromat. He was clearly unhappy with the few miles he would be able to charge.

Mam humored him, saying with a choking sound in her voice that the horses had burned. Jim placed a hand on Mam's shoulder and apologized profusely, saying he didn't know. He was sorry, he said.

Mam assured him and told him she wouldn't drive a buggy to Route 30 and through all the stoplights, even with the safest horse. Too much traffic, too many tourists gawking.

Sarah groaned aloud when she saw the occupants at the Laundromat. Oh, no.

"Mam, look!"

"Oh, we'll be busy. She'll let us go."

Sarah knew better about Fannie Kauffman, the most inquisitive, anxious woman in at least a fifty-mile radius.

They had no sooner settled themselves after filling the hungry machines with Mam's precious quarters than she bustled over, the pleats in her ill-fitting black apron shelving over her hips, pinned much too tightly between layers of overeating.

"Malinda!"

"Fannie."

"It just rains, doesn't it? I told Elam that if it doesn't stop raining, we won't get the tobacco in until June, which will just make it late for market, and we won't get our price. But then, who am I to complain? You losing your barn and having that loss. My goodness. I said to Elam, I guess the Lord chastens whom He loveth, *gel*? *Gel*? You have to wonder what you did to deserve this, *gel*? David likely did nothing. He's such a perfect man."

There was really no nice way to answer that hailstorm of words, Sarah thought, so when Mam smiled a bit rigidly but made no comment, it only increased Fannie's velocity.

"But then, you have Levi too, you know. A retarded boy. Well, you do good, though, you do good. You know

I wasn't at the barn raising, not that I didn't want to, but my sciatica was acting up. Pain! Oh, Malinda, I was in mortal pain. My lower back, down the back of my legs. I had Davey's Rachel to do my work every day that week."

There was a shrill beep, and Fannie erupted from her chair and lunged across the gleaming waxed tiles to reach the stopped dryer. She grabbed the handle of the large machine and gave it a tug before extracting the armfuls of clothing.

Mam sighed, a deep, tired, very relieved sound. She cast a weary look at Sarah when Fannie wheeled her cart over to the plastic table beside them and started shoving hangers into the shoulders of Elam's shirts.

"How's the barn coming? Are you milking yet? Are you? Good. That's good. But you know how much your cows will drop back in production? Way far. I told Elam that family has no idea how great their loss will be yet, even if you have Amish fire insurance. It never covers it all."

She stopped for breath and then bent to pick up a stray dryer sheet, holding it to her nose for a quick sniff.

"These dryer sheets don't work."

Mam raised an eyebrow, enough of a reply for Fannie to keep up her verbal onslaught.

"Have you heard about Junior's Melvin? Our Junior? He had such a stomach ache...."

Sarah watched a young girl slumped in a blue plastic chair near the door, her legs sprawled in front of her. Her light brown hair fell over her cheeks like a curtain of privacy, a signal, along with her drooping shoulders, to leave her alone. She was thin, almost painfully so, and her hands picked restlessly at a thread along the bottom of her beige shirt.

Sarah felt a tinge of pity, then concern, when a small white vehicle pulled up to the front window. A young man hopped out and tore open the steel framed door, almost colliding with the girl in his haste.

She pulled her legs in and wrapped her arms around her middle. Her shoulders squared as she turned to face him with large, dark, defiant eyes. She recoiled as he lowered his head and hissed something quiet but deafening with a menacing force.

Sarah turned away. This was none of her concern. She watched though, unable to turn her eyes away as he hooked a hand beneath the girl's elbow and clawed at it, forcing her to stand and follow him, her head bent, the fine brown hair falling over her cheeks.

A white vehicle.

Well, no sense in making the comparison. There was none. Who could ever find the person in a white vehicle that supposedly lit their barn a few weeks earlier?

Sarah half-heartedly listened to Fannie and watched the small red light on the washer, the suds banging up against the glass and churning the clothes inside to a clean maelstrom.

The rain fell relentlessly as lines of traffic hissed past, water streaming off them. The stoplights, signs, store fronts—everything was wet and shimmery with water.

Sarah tried to imagine Noah's flood in Bible times. It would have rained a hundred times harder. Then the springs of the earth would have opened, water gushing from the ground in a way no one had ever seen before and wouldn't again, ever. The water would have covered the streets, then the vehicles, the signs, the stores, the stoplights. People would be drowned by then, or clinging to treetops or high buildings. She shivered, thinking of it. Water everywhere.

Fire was the opposite of water but just as destructive.

Already, Sarah missed the barn. It was on days just like this that, as a child, she had played in the haymow with her brothers, the clamorous rain drumming down and sometimes drowning out their voices. The only thing between them and the sound of it was the old sheet metal and a few wide lathes.

It was safe and cozy and crunchy with hay. They piled bales to make perfect houses, brought lunch and had dinner in it, spitting out the prickly hay seeds if they dropped onto their sweet bologna sandwiches.

Allen claimed people could eat hay if they chewed it long enough and then promptly inserted a long strand into his mouth and chewed furiously. Abner told him to get that out and quit it—cows had two stomachs, humans had only one and weren't supposed to eat hay.

The washer clunked and then stopped. The red light went off, so Sarah got up, opened the door, raked the wet laundry into a large, wheeled basket, and pushed it to a dryer.

Fannie came rolling over. Rolling was the only way to describe her—rounded and tipping from side to side, like a child's plastic ball that bounced along.

"Sarah, don't you have a *chappy* (boyfriend) yet?"

From behind the door of the dryer, Sarah shook her head, "No, I don't."

"What are you? Twenty? Twenty-one?"

"Soon twenty."

"My girls all married before twenty. What are you waiting on?"

Fannie snapped a dishcloth and folded it meticulously, without looking at her.

"There's no hurry."

"Sure there is. A girl blooms like a rose at age sixteen, and it's all downhill from there." She laughed ridiculously, becoming hysterical at her own joke.

Sarah smiled weakly, and decided one ill-mannered person could erase weeks of gratitude for the wonder of human companionship. She decided to stand her ground.

"I have dreams of becoming an old maid and having my own dry goods store."

Her words carried well, reaching Mam's ears as she ducked behind a washer to conceal her wide grin and jiggling shoulders.

Fannie finished and left hastily, splashing clumsily through the rain in her large black Skechers, her bonnet stuck haphazardly on her head, no doubt flattening the questionably white covering beneath it.

Inside, Mam shook a finger at Sarah.

"Now, Sarah!"

"Well. She could have stayed quiet. She's simply so nosy. It's ridiculous."

"Her heart's in the right place, though."

"You sure?"

Mam didn't bother answering but asked Sarah if she really wanted to be an old maid.

"You should say 'single girl.'"

"Or leftover blessing? No. I don't want to be alone all my life. Of course not. I want my own house and yard and garden. Just like you. But...well, Mam, you know how it is."

"Is it still?"

Sarah nodded, which produced a drooping of Mam's kind features.

"You do try and let him go? Out of your thoughts?"

"Yes, Mam. I do. Seriously, the harder I try, the worse it gets."

Sarah launched into a colorful account of her burned hand, the way Matthew reacted, Rose's innocence, her guilt. But she stopped the story there, reserving the attractive blond young man and hiding him from her mother's scrutiny, knowing disapproval was forthcoming.

They folded soft towels, the clean-smelling linens, and were careful to test the heat in the dryers containing the dresses and black aprons.

"Well, Sarah, you know I'll always tell you the same thing. This time is no different. Pray, pray, pray. Always. You will discern God's will for your life once you have given up your own will, and I'm afraid Matthew is simply that. Your own will—wanting something you can't have. You know how much human nature tends to run along those lines. Just like Aesop's fables. Remember the story of the fox who wanted the grapes that were out of his reach?"

"And when he finally acquired them, they were sour, and he wondered why he'd wanted them in the first place," Sarah finished for her mother, nodding good-naturedly.

Jim, the driver, was gruff and short with them on the way home. He required a twenty-dollar payment, saying he had insurance to pay, and he sure wasn't making any money hauling people to the Laundromat.

Mam handed over the twenty-dollar bill, but her eyes sparkled too brightly, and she slammed the front door with plenty of muscle behind it.

Sarah ducked her head and splashed through the rain with the hampers of laundry, happy to put it all away in the drawers and closets, thankful to have clean, dry clothes, for now.

Surely the rain would stop soon. She paused by the window of her room and saw the muddy churning waters of the lower Pequea Creek had risen way beyond its banks. She shivered, a foreboding clutching her reason.

The new barn was stately, built solidly in the old pattern. The exterior's new ribbed metal siding was white, the color of the old barn. New cupolas proudly straddled the peak of the roof, the weather vanes turning as the wind changed direction, guarding the Beiler farm with their resilience. Look at us, they seemed to say. We're new and better, here for the next hundred years.

Sarah smiled and was glad.

The old stones and timbers were gone, but good had come of it as well, Dat said. The new barn was better. The ventilation design, the materials—everything was better, especially the diesel and the air system. It was the sadness of lost history that kept him humble, the ruined painstaking work of his forefathers.

He said the Amish church had seen changes in the past two hundred years, and they weren't all bad, same as the new barn. Some things were good, like milkers and bulk tanks and pneumatics, battery lamps and fiberglass carriages and nylon harnesses that were lighter and more durable. Better.

And still it rained, day and night.

Dat slogged through the mud to accomplish even the smallest task. Mud was everywhere from the way things had been churned up around the barn by the dozers and lifts and other equipment. Dat said if it continued raining, the roads would be closed due to the high water. He hoped no one would try to cross the creek where it overflowed; that was downright dangerous.

Priscilla stood by the window in Levi's room, chewing alternately on the inside of each cheek. Or she chewed the nails of her right hand, her eyebrows rising taut above her large, anxious eyes, watching the green maple leaves dripping water.

Levi sat at his card table, laying out the football cards, the sequence in his head followed to perfection. He looked up, considering his sister.

"Go away, Priscilla. You bother me."

"Hush, Levi."

"I mean it."

Dat looked up from the German *Schrift* (scripture) he was reading. His glasses were perched on his nose, allowing him to peer over them, and he smiled. This would be interesting, he thought.

Priscilla didn't answer. She just reached out to ruffle a few cards.

Instantly, Levi's hand came up, his eyebrows came down, his shoulders straightened, and his voice burst out in one big bellow.

"*Ich tzell dich schimacka!* (I will smack you!)"

Calmly, Priscilla bent over to retrieve the stack of football cards, holding them at arm's length, a smile teasing him.

"Give them."

"Say, 'Please.'"

"No."

Priscilla walked away, holding the cards, still teasing.

Levi didn't feel like getting out of his chair, so he yelled at the top of his lungs for help from Dat.

Dat looked up.

"What, Levi?"

"Priscilla has my cards!"

"She does? Well, I guess you'll have to come get them."

"I don't want to."

"Why not?"

"I'm tired."

Dat thought he heard the wail of sirens in the distance. On a night like this? Surely a fire would not survive this deluge.

When Levi continued his howling, Dat hushed him and curtly told Priscilla to give him his cards. Then he told everyone to listen. He thought he'd heard sirens.

The cards forgotten, Priscilla stood, a statue of fright, the color draining from her face, remembering the fire. She moved slowly, as if in a trance, and placed the cards on Levi's table, never hearing his resounding "*Denke* (Thank you)."

In her mind, the barn would soon be burning.

Dat saw Priscilla's fear, slowly laid his German Bible aside, and went to her. Gripping her arms, he looked into her terror-stricken eyes and gave her a small shake.

"Priscilla!" His voice was kind but firm.

As if roused from a faint, she blinked, looked at Dat, then fell against him. As she sobbed out her pain and anguish, his arms came around her, his head laid on her hair. He sent a prayer to the Father to protect his vulnerable daughter.

Mam came, lifted a hand, and caressed her back, saying the siren was likely only the medic for someone who needed assistance because of the high water.

After she cried, Priscilla could always pull herself together and talk about her fear. Tonight her words came fast and low. She said she missed Dutch so much, she hardly knew what to do. Would she be allowed to get a job somewhere—to save up money for a new horse? She knew it was too much to ask.

"See, Dutch was important to me in a way that even people aren't. With a pet, like dogs and cats and ducks and chickens, it's different. They need you. People don't really, because they have other people."

Dat listened and nodded, deeply moved.

Then the high insistent wailing grew closer and much more resounding.

Sarah was reading the cousin circle letter, one that circulated among her cousins and kept them all in touch with the news in each other's lives. She heard the sounds around her in an absentminded way as she sat away from the others. But when the siren's wails became louder, she laid the circle letter aside, rose to her feet, and asked hurriedly if there was another fire.

"It's only the twelve o'clock *pife* (whistle)!" Levi shouted.

Dat said, no, it was after suppertime.

The light was gray, the day heading into evening. The chores were done and the dishes washed. It was the time of day when every member of the family wound down and relaxed.

Mervin and Suzie were playing shuffleboard in the basement, obviously having heard nothing as the game continued with the sound of the thumps from below.

Everyone was ill at ease. Dat put his Bible away, and Mam gripped the countertop as she watched the dreary evening through the kitchen window, wondering, hoping.

Sarah merely paced, slowly moving from window to window, stopping to pick up a magazine, dusting a bookshelf with the hem of her bib apron, filling Levi's water pitcher for the night—anything to keep from holding still. The wailing, that rising and falling sound, always meant something was wrong—a person was hurt or a building was burning. Or now, with the rain and the creeks overflowing their banks, was someone injured, lost, or worst of all, drowned in the brown roiling, rushing water? At times like this, Sarah wished for a telephone in the house.

Mam was listening by Priscilla's side again, and Dat joined her, concern mapping out the love he so plainly felt for his troubled daughter.

The sirens came to an abrupt stop. Should they sigh with relief or hold their breaths for the bad news that might follow?

"We didn't used to be like this," Sarah said suddenly.

"What do you mean?" Mam asked.

"Well, look at us! Priscilla crying, Dat too nervous to study, me unable to hold still. We're just a family of nervous wrecks."

Dat nodded soberly. "With good reason, Sarah. We've just come through a terrifying night, followed by unanswered questions in the weeks that have followed. Now when a vehicle pulls up to the barn, I'm instantly on edge, wondering if the driver will bring harm. I'm suspicious, always alert to unexpected danger. Before the barn burned, it never crossed my mind to be afraid. We have lost an innocence."

Mam nodded, her agreement evident in her eyes.

"Are you alright, Priscilla?" she asked, her arm sliding across her younger daughter's shoulders.

"Not as okay as I will be a year from now," she answered, wisely recognizing her own ability to rise above the frightening circumstances that had assailed her life.

Sarah hoped she was right.

CHAPTER 7

In THE MORNING, LOW CLOUDS HUNG LIKE DREARY curtains, hiding any chance of happy sunshine. The Beiler family woke and went about the morning chores, slogging through the slippery mud and rivulets of water, carrying feed and water to the calves, feeding the rowdy heifers that bounced around stiff-legged, splattering mud and water as they vied for dominance.

In the new cow stable, the cows had created a wet path from the wide, rolling door to their separate stalls, their hides slick from the night's rain, their legs caked with the slop from the barnyard.

It was Sarah's turn to milk, so she moved among the cows changing the heavy milkers, listening to the rhythmic chukka-chukka sound from the compressed air pulling the milk from the cows' udders.

Everything was so new, yet so much the same. The windows tilted open to allow the misty air to circulate. The firm contours of the new cement permitted the brand new feed cart to be pushed around with ease.

Not everything was finished. Some doorways still didn't have their wooden doors. Some of those that had doors needed a doorknob here or a few hinges there. But all in all, it was overwhelming that, even with the amount of labor involved, so much had been accomplished in such a short time.

Dat lifted an especially heavy milker from one of his best milk cows, his eyes wide with surprise, his muscles bulging against his shirt sleeves. He looked at Sarah and said, "Well, goodness! Looks as if the cows are feeling right at home again. She's really producing."

And then, because David Beiler was a man filled with gratitude in all things, his eyes watered and ran over behind his glasses. His mouth wobbled just enough for Sarah to see he was filled with emotion. And she was glad.

In all things, Dat would say, good can come of tragedy, to those that love God. Loving God was elusive, since you couldn't see Him. You could love God best by loving other people, and this was the one virtue Dat stressed, his family being recipients of his own love and forbearance to his fellow man.

If you point a finger in accusation, three more on your own hand point straight back at you, he'd say.

No question, God sent disappointments and setbacks to each person, and of all the undeserving people in the world, Dat was the one. But Sarah also knew that His ways are not our ways; His thoughts are not our thoughts.

As he poured the good, rich milk into the gleaming new Sputnik, a stainless steel vat on wheels, he blinked back tears at this undeserved blessing. David Beiler knew his view of God and the church had been illuminated by a higher and better light.

Surely, God had dug, mulched, and applied fertilizer so his fruits would multiply. This barn fire had been painful, indeed. But hadn't He designed the agony that separates the dross from the gold?

The family sat at the breakfast table. The propane gas lamp, hissing softly, cast a cozy light into every corner of the kitchen in spite of the low-hanging clouds outside. The rain had stopped for now, but as the water drained from hills and slopes, the creeks and rivers continued to rise, filling them with a brown, butterscotch color, swirling and churning, murky and threatening.

Mam brought a platter of fried eggs and set it between her plate and her husband's. She sighed and looked to Dat. He nodded, and they all bowed their heads for the silent prayer, Levi's loud whispers rising and falling as he thanked God for what he was about to receive.

They lifted their heads after Dat. Some reached for their glasses of orange juice, and a few began buttering toast as they passed the egg plate from one to the other. They spooned stewed saltine crackers, slathered with generous portions of homemade ketchup, onto their plates alongside small sections of rich sausage. It was a bountiful breakfast for a hungry family that had already done a few hours of work.

Mam's eyes twinkled as she set a cake pan in the middle of the table, waiting for the praise that would surely come.

"Overnight French toast!" Levi yelled, his eyes alight with anticipation.

"Yum!" Mervin shouted simultaneously.

Levi turned to his youngest brother, lifted a heavy hand, and cocked his head to one side like an overgrown bird. Mervin caught his eye, grinned, and slammed Levi's hand with one of his own in a cracking high five. Levi laughed out loud. His day was starting out right.

Dat said it was getting late to plant corn, but he guessed it would clear up and dry out. It always did.

Mam poured his coffee and asked what his plans were. Dat smiled and said he'd been thinking during the night that a very important thing had not yet been accomplished since the fire. When Dat said something in that tone of voice, everyone listened, knowing it would be good.

Looking at Priscilla, he announced, "I think it's time we replace Dutch, if you're willing to accompany me."

The only way she knew to express herself was to clap her hands and let her eyes shine into the light of Dat's.

"Can I go?" Suzie asked, hopefully, already knowing the answer.

"Sorry, Suzie. You have school."

Mervin cried and kicked his chair. Levi told him he could go along, but in the end he had to go to school. However, he went with the promise of a waterer for his rabbit pen, which was sold with other pet supplies at the New Holland Sales Stables.

"A good day to go!" Sarah said, enthusiastic as ever. She loved a good horse sale, and today's would be doubly exciting, helping Priscilla try to bond with another horse.

Mam opted to stay home, saying an empty house and her sewing machine were a wonderful way to relax and catch up on her much needed sewing.

Levi didn't ask if he could go. He just took for granted that he would. He hurried to his room to choose a brightly colored shirt, so he wouldn't get lost. His muttering was punctuated by loud bursts of happy laughter, followed by serious admonishments to himself.

"Now Levi, you are not allowed to have ice cream first. You have to eat a cheeseburger. Or maybe a hoagie.

See what Dat says."

When Dat brought the carriage and the new horse, named Fred, to the sidewalk, Sarah was ready and helping Levi into his "gumshoes." Priscilla dashed out and clambered into the back seat, a flash of blue and black and a whirl of eagerness after the fear and heartache of losing her beloved pet.

Levi needed help to get into the buggy, so they tilted the front seat forward the whole way, allowing easy access to the back one.

Dat helped Levi, steadying him, encouraging, as Sarah held the bridle. The new horse had a good look about him. His eyes were calm and sensible, with no white showing in them. A steady flicking of his ears was the only sign of his mindfulness.

The buggy tilted to the side as Levi lifted his bulk up one step, with Dat supporting his waist. He lifted the other leg up and into the buggy, gripping the silver handle on the side.

He plunked down heavily beside Priscilla and said loudly, "Cheez Whiz!"

"You're too fat, Levi!" Priscilla said, laughing at his expression.

"I am not. I'm a big man."

"Yes, you are, Levi. You're a big man," Dat said, grinning.

"I can smack hard too, Priscilla," Levi said soberly.

"You better not."

"Then you have to be nice to me."

"Come on, Fred," Dat said as he clucked and pulled gently on the reins. The new horse moved off as if he'd done this thousands of times, trotting nicely past the maple trees dripping wet with morning moisture. He turned left on the macadam road, perfectly obedient, the picture of a good sensible horse.

"Boy, must be that Samuel Zook knows his driving horses. I think we got ourselves a winner."

Dat closed the front window carefully over the nylon reins, protecting them from the cold, swirling mists. He had no more than clicked it into place when a feed truck came around a bend in the road with its slick blue tarp flapping on top and its engine revving after maneuvering the turn.

Down went Fred's haunches, and up came his head. With a swift, fluid motion borne of raw fear, the horse reared, shied to the right, came down running, and galloped off across a neighbor's soggy alfalfa field. The buggy swayed and teetered as Dat fought for control. Levi yelled and yelled and wouldn't stop, increasing the horse's fear.

They came to a stop in the middle of the squishy alfalfa field with Fred snorting and quivering. Everyone was thoroughly shaken up. Levi's yells changed to incoherent babbles of fear.

"Well, here we are," Dat said calmly. They all burst out laughing except Levi, who said it wasn't one bit funny and Dat should not be so *schputlich* (mocking).

So there they sat, the steel wheels of the buggy firmly entrenched in the sodden earth. Fred decided this was the end of his journey and refused to move.

Patiently, Dat shook out the reins, clucked, chirped, and spoke in well-modulated tones. It did absolutely no good. The horse stood as firm as a statue carved in stone, the only sign of life the flicking of his ears and an occasional lifting or lowering of his head.

Dat opened the door of the buggy and leaned out to

evaluate the situation. The wheels were partially sunken into the muck and sprouting alfalfa.

"He's probably balking because it's hard to pull if he lunges against the collar. It could be too tight."

Sarah glanced down at Dat's shoes.

"No boots?"

"So we just sit here?" asked Priscilla.

"Probably."

Levi said they wanted to go to the horse sale, not sit here, and Dat better start smacking this crazy horse.

Dat said, "No, Levi, sometimes that only makes it worse. He'll go when he's ready. Horses that balk are often confused."

Priscilla made no comment but then said, "Let me out, Dat."

"It's too muddy, Priscilla."

"I can clean my shoes when we get there."

"Alright."

Dat got out and stood tentatively in the soft field. Sarah sat forward, allowing the back of her seat to lower, so Priscilla could scramble over it.

Going to Fred's head, Priscilla rubbed his nose and spoke to him like a petulant child. She told Dat to get in, then tugged lightly on the bit. Her answer was an angry toss of Fred's head. She kept up the repetitive stroking, adjusted the collar, and loosened a buckle on one side of the bridle, her fingers searching expertly for any discomfort from the harness or the bridle.

"Alright, Fred. Come on now. We have to buy a horse to live with you."

Priscilla coaxed, tugging gently, and Fred decided it was time to go. He veered to the left, almost knocking her off her feet, before gathering his hind legs into a lunge and taking off in great leaps, mud flying from his hooves as well as the buggy wheels.

Inside the buggy, Dat lifted a forearm to protect himself from the chunks of mud that found their way through the window as he struggled to control the horse. Then he slid back the door of the buggy to see what had happened to Priscilla. He was rewarded by the sight of her dashing across the soggy alfalfa field.

Sarah breathed a sigh of relief when the buggy clunked over a small embankment and down onto the welcome macadam where Dat pulled Fred off to the side, waiting for Priscilla. She lost no time running to the parked buggy, her breath coming in gasps.

Pricilla's hair curled every which way from the moisture in the air. Her covering sagged and slid off the back of her head. She didn't look at her shoes; she just slid them off, put them under the front seat, and plopped down beside Levi.

"You're wet!" he yelped

Priscilla grinned, gasped for breath, and rubbed a wet hand against Levi's cheek. She was rewarded with a resounding smack, his favorite way of dealing with life's outrages.

His famous smacks were never hard, never hurtful. His nature was much too affable to be taken seriously, so they were accepted without reprimand and just considered a part of their good-humored Levi.

Fred stepped out and trotted willingly the remainder of the way to New Holland, stopping at the one red light obediently, stepping out when asked.

When they arrived, Sarah helped Priscilla clean up in the large well-lit bathroom, supplying a fine toothed comb for her hair, pressing and shaping her organdy covering as best she could.

A few English girls gave them a not-so-friendly glance when they cleaned Priscilla's gray Nike's with wet paper towels, but there was nothing to say, so Sarah averted her eyes while the other girls washed their hands and rolled their eyes at each other. Well, they'd just have to think what they wanted. Not everyone had a car that always did exactly what was required of it. Especially not the Amish.

Priscilla glared after them, sensitive to these things at her age.

"They were mean."

"Not really. It isn't very sanitary, cleaning your shoes in here."

"You want to go back and sit in the field again?"

Laughing, Sarah clapped an arm around her younger sister's shoulders and thanked her for saving all of them.

"Thanks. Dat is so—well, he just doesn't have it," she answered.

The large arena where the horses were sold was filled with a solid wall of people stacked in diagonal layers in the stands. Every color imaginable reflected from the electric lights against the white walls, the metal railing, and swirls of dust. Far below the cavernous roof, an auctioneer and two seated clerks took up positions at a podium. A horse was brought in, pawing the sawdust, his eyes rolling with fear.

"We need to find Dat," Sarah said loudly above the din.

"That will be a job."

"Let's go to the pens."

Priscilla hesitated.

"Why not?"

"There's so many men."

"Come on!"

They ran down the steps and through the alleyways until they arrived at the long row of riding horses tethered to a board fence, patiently switching their tails. Some of them appeared high strung, others docile. Others were too thin and misshapen, their coats scraggly.

"They'll go for killers."

"Likely."

As Sarah had guessed, Priscilla found no extraordinary horses and finally said they may as well go back.

Men in plaid shirts with seed-company logos across the fronts of their caps lounged along the fence, respectfully dipping their heads. Children ran and shouted, weaving through alleyways and much too close to the horses' hind feet. They dashed about chattering like excited little squirrels, eating Skittles and Starbursts and M&M's. It was great fun to be at a horse sale.

The girls said hello to Reuben King and Lamar Stoltzfus, two boys from Sarah's youth group, and then moved on to find seats, with Dat and Levi, if possible.

So many straw hats and black coats! They simply stood, their eyes searching the crowd as the auctioneer prepared to open the sale.

Priscilla's eyes darted from row to row, but Sarah's had stopped, resting on Matthew Stoltzfus sitting with his brother, Chris.

Ah. He was here. Why hadn't she dressed better?

She should have worn the new rose-colored dress. She hated the sweater she was wearing. It would look better on Mam. And here she was, her covering gone all flat and frumpy because of the morning's heavy fog and humidity, even if it wasn't actually raining.

Oh, he looked so good. His already tanned face and dark hair set him apart, way apart, from the rest of the crowd. Her heart was hammering in her chest. Her mouth went completely dry. She swallowed, choked, and tried desperately to hide all this from Priscilla.

"There! Right there they are."

Of course—the opposite end of the arena.

Sarah turned, her sense of loss so complete the whole crowd may as well have been stripped of color as her world changed to black and gray. She followed her sister numbly, looking neither left nor right.

Dat looked up, grateful to see them arrive, and patted the seat beside him. Priscilla bounced into it, a rapturous smile lighting up her pretty face. Sarah sat down on the remaining seat, apologizing to the large woman next to her who was wearing an inexpensive pink cowboy hat and brilliant red boots, her belt completely hidden between her jeans and too-tight shirt.

"That's okay, honey. You make yourself comfortable."

She leaned sideways to accommodate Sarah and smiled, a genuine wish of good humor on her painted red lips. Sarah smiled back and settled in, the smile sliding off her face as she glumly assessed her situation.

Here she was, still in the hold of whatever in the world you called the emotion that controlled her whenever she caught sight of Matthew Stoltzfus, and he was happily dating her best friend. Since the barn raising, her river of misery had grown simultaneously with the rising creeks. Her mental agony, like the non-stop rain, was almost unbearable at times.

This had been going on since she was fourteen and in vocational class. Only when Matthew spoke to her was her day colored with a vibrant shade of yellow, like the sun or a rose—the flower of love—or blue, like the great clean wondrous sky. It was always Matthew, in her dreams, in her waking hours. How could he deny her now, after what happened at the barn raising?

Then guilt and shame intensified the hovering shapes of depressive thinking, and Sarah knew for certain this had to stop. With great effort, she turned to the sight before her, the horses, the men and boys riding them. Occasionally, a lithe English girl rode one, too.

The loud voice of the auctioneer rose and fell, its staccato rhythm giving her an intense headache. Sarah wished she hadn't come.

Just when she thought she couldn't sit there one more minute, a rider entered the ring on a black and white paint. The horse had a fine small head and curved ears, the flowing mane and tail neatly brushed, the coat sleek and gleaming from good grooming. His rider sat with easy grace, bareback, holding the reins loosely.

The horse didn't really trot or gallop—he flowed. His hooves lifted and set down easily, as if there were springs in his legs that moved them without effort.

Priscilla leaned forward, the knuckles on her hands white as she clenched the armrests of her seat.

"Dat!" she whispered.

Dat saw and winked broadly at Sarah. He knew.

Sarah winked back. Then a strange hiccup jumped in her chest, and she realized she was crying. What a precious father! She knew that he wouldn't stop bidding until he had procured the one object that would successfully erase the hurt and the pain the arsonist had inflicted with a small rasp of his lighter.

The bidding started at five hundred dollars. Priscilla sat back, her hands gripped in her lap.

"Five hundred! Five! Five! Who'll gimme fifty? Five hundred fifty! Yes! Six hundred!"

Sarah watched Priscilla, whose pulse was beating against the side of her neck where her sweater had fallen away. The pupils in her large green eyes dilated as she gripped her hands more tightly.

When the bidding escalated to one thousand, she put her hand on Dat's arm and said it was okay to let him go. Then she turned confused eyes to Sarah, pleading, unsure.

The horse pranced and stepped lightly, tossing his head in excitement, and still the rider sat easily, a tall, blond youth who appeared to have been riding horses since he was six years old.

Levi sat on Dat's right side, a can of Mountain Dew in one hand, a large bag of buttered popcorn in the other. His face shone with happiness. He was completely unaware of Dat's subtle nodding of his head. The popcorn was more important.

The bidding escalated. The rider pulled the horse to a stop and then cantered him slowly around the ring.

Dat paid eighteen hundred dollars for Priscilla's horse, and not one person at the New Holland Sales Stables thought it was a penny too much. The poor girl had suffered plenty at the hand of that arsonist, who still ran loose, they said.

When Dat smiled at Priscilla and said, "Let's go!" she burst into tears. Sarah had to help her find her way out between the seats, apologizing with multiple soft expressions of "Excuse me" and "I'm sorry." They finally made it out the side door. When they led Priscilla to the horse, he lowered his head. Priscilla cupped her hand beneath his nose and laid her forehead against his. The tears dropped off her face and ran in little wet rivulets down the horse's face. She whispered brokenly, "Hello, Dutch."

Dat got out his red handkerchief and blew his nose hard, then dried his eyes, and squeezed Priscilla's shoulders.

Levi reached deep into the popcorn bag for another handful and slowly blinked his eyes.

CHAPTER 8

SARAH STOOD IN THE MIDDLE OF THE GARDEN and leaned on a hoe watching Priscilla ride Dutch, circling the pasture. They were in perfect tune with one another, a sight to behold. Sarah never tired of it.

It was the middle of May. The rains had stopped, and the soil had dried. The warm bright sun shone from a blue sky alive with scudding white puffs of clouds. Sighing, she turned, picked out a few cucumber seeds from the small packet in her hand, and dropped them in the hole she had made with the hoe.

With all the rains and the flooding, the planting had been late this year. Sarah was grateful to be able to plant the "late" seeds—corn, cucumbers, lima beans—crops that wouldn't push their way up from the soil if the earth was not properly warmed by the sun.

Chattering barn swallows, daring little acrobats of the air, wheeled and turned, grabbing insects as they executed their aerial show. From a distance, she heard the clanking and squeaking of Dat's corn planter, the mules walking at a rapid pace, their nodding heads and flopping ears never quite in harmony.

She knew Dat would be on the cart, watching the planter, his thoughts on his sermons, the congregation, the troubles and concerns as well as the joys. Last night, though, he'd talked plenty, for Dat. He wasn't a person of excessive speech, but he needed a listening ear, he'd said.

The barn fire had occurred, yes. Someone had lit it, with intent to destroy, provoke, excite, whatever. Who knew for what reason they did this? And now the men were sidling up to him at church and saying that he needed to do something about this. Some seemed to think he was not doing his duty as a minister to let this all go on as if nothing happened. He could at least cooperate with the prosecutors. The church members thought Dat was too compliant and said he had to do what he could.

Every Sunday, Dat would develop a headache and a tic in one eye. Apparently, no one in the congregation had gotten a decent night's sleep since the fire.

Take Amos Fisher. He said he slept in his own bed, or tried to, until all kinds of images encroached on his thoughts. Here he was, with forty head of cattle, beef cows, all housed in his new ventilated barn. What if someone snuck in and just got a big bonfire going?

He'd taken to sleeping on the couch in his kitchen, so that he could at least hear a car if it drove by. The sleeplessness was making him groggy, and his arthritis was flaring up in his thumbs. It would be different if Sylvia cared. She just rolled over on her good ear and slept like a rock. Amos didn't know what would happen if his new barn burned.

Dat tried to explain to Amos how difficult it was to pin down this arsonist, and the police weren't even completely sure it was an arsonist. He didn't get very far after that, the way Amos flew off. So what could he do?

Softly, Mam asked what his own personal feelings were.

Dat gravely stroked his beard and shook his head from side to side as he contemplated the question. Arriving at a decision, he sat up straight, his far-seeing eyes not really aware of his surroundings.

He said he looked on the situation as a spiritual chastening, a call to be a better person. In the Bible, hadn't Job suffered tremendously? For Dat to poison his own life with unforgiveness was unthinkable. Yes, the loss had been great, but the aftermath had been rich in blessings.

The sight of those caravans of men arriving to help was one blessing. He'd simply wanted to kneel before them all and wash their feet as a sign of humility, the way Abraham did in the Old Testament.

In view of the tremendous caring and love poured out on his family, who could stand if he didn't forgive?

Suddenly, Dat's face took on a silly grin. "And besides, now my cow stable has plenty of new and modern things, for an old preacher."

Mam laughed with him, knowing how happy he was with the new barn and appreciating his resilience.

So, Sarah had thought, no matter how overwhelming the flood of kindness had been, someone always managed to insert a prickly note of dissension. Like Fannie Kauffman.

In the garden, Sarah tramped down the last of the soil, straightened her back, and went to find a small wooden stake for the cucumber-seed packet to mark where they'd been planted.

She reached up to the top shelf in the garden shed, her hand searching for a stake. Something smooth and round came into contact with her fingertips. A lighter. Hmm.

Why was a white Bic lighter on the top shelf in the garden shed? Slipping it into her pocket, she decided to tell the family. It was extremely odd.

She found a stake, attached the seed packet with a thumb-tack, and stuck the marker into the ground. That was really cute.

Mam hurried out to the garden, saying it was time for the pea wire to be put up. Those pea vines were growing faster every time she checked them.

Sarah had just emerged from the garden shed with an armload of stakes when a gray car came slowly up the driveway and rolled to a stop beside the garden.

Two policemen extricated themselves from the unmarked car as Mam dropped her roll of wire and went to greet them. They exchanged pleasantries, Mam's voice low and careful, the way she was with strangers.

"This the new barn?"

"Yes."

"No information? Nothing unusual? No sightings? No media?"

"Um, excuse me. What is media?" Mam asked, clearly ashamed that she didn't know.

"Photographers? People asking questions? Reporters?" Mam shook her head.

Sarah's heart pounded. Should she come forward with the lighter? But it had been in the garden shed and likely had nothing to do with the fire at all.

She decided to keep her peace and went back to pound stakes into the loose soil.

The policemen asked for Dat, and Mam pointed to the team of mules pulling the corn planter.

Quite suddenly, the white lighter felt red hot, like a small plastic conscience burning a hole in Sarah's pocket.

Stumbling across the garden, she was surprised that her hand wasn't burning, that the lighter was smooth and cool.

The officers looked up.

"H...hello," she stammered.

"Yes, young lady?"

She held up the lighter, explained how uncommon it was to find a lighter on the top shelf in the garden shed.

The tall, heavy officer asked quickly if there were more children around. Was there a possibility that one of the younger children had hidden the lighter?

It was terrible to see the color drain from Mam's face and the raw dread in her eyes. Surely not Mervin or Suzie? "Get Dat," she ordered, her voice quivering.

Sarah handed the lighter to the police and ran swiftly past the strawberry patch, white with blossoms, past the raspberries, the compost pile, the woodpile, and over the small wooden bridge built over a cement drain pipe. She stood at the edge of the field, waving her arms, although she remained quiet, until he came closer.

"*Komm*! *Komm rei*! (Come in!)"

Dat waved in acknowledgment, finished the row, and then turned the mules toward the house. He left them standing by the garden without tying them and went to greet the officers, tipping back his straw hat to wipe the dirt from his brow.

"Yes. Mr. Beiler."

"Hello. Good to meet you."

"I'm supposing each member of the family has been thoroughly questioned?"

"As far as I know."

"You have no reason to believe any of your children would have been playing with this lighter?"

The officer held it up, and Dat's face blanched, quiet confidence replaced with confusion.

"Well..."

"Your daughter found it."

Sarah answered Dat's questions and turned to find Suzie and Mervin scootering home from school.

"Here are the little ones."

Dat's voice tried to be confident, but the bravado held a tinge of doubt.

What if? Sarah thought.

What if Mervin had been playing with the lighter, became afraid, and hid it? Or Suzie? It was unthinkable, Suzie being so timid, so conscientious. Still, one never knew.

The children were called to join them. Priscilla came from the barn, her face glowing from her ride, but she swallowed, wrapped her arms about her waist, and scuffed her sneaker into the dirt.

The police questioned them, not unkindly, but so seriously it seemed as if they were threatening.

Mervin shook his head no. So did Suzie, pure innocence shining from her untroubled gaze, a clear testimony of her genuine goodness, a repeat of Priscilla.

Then Mervin began to cry. Dat looked sharply at Mam, questions clouding his eyes.

Speaking in hiccups, his English broken and mixed with Pennsylvania Dutch, the way little Amish children do, Mervin said he'd found it.

"When?" the officer asked intently, bending low.

"When the barn burned."

"Which side of the barn?"

"Over there. Where the heifer pen was."

"You're absolutely sure you weren't playing with the

lighter?" Dat asked, his face stern and serious.

Mervin nodded, his blond hair wagging over his ears. His guileless eyes stared straight into Dat's, which was not lost on the officers, who were acquainted with every trick humankind could imagine, and then some.

"Then why did you hide it?"

"You mean, in there?" Mervin pointed to the garden shed. "I was afraid you would think I started the fire, and I didn't."

Marvin lowered his head, the silky blond, brownish hair falling over his eyes, a curtain to allow him time to compose himself, to decide to be forthright.

"Dat, I just crumpled some old newspapers and—I wanted to see how high the fire goes, how fast it spreads."

Lifting his head, he stared wild-eyed at the officer standing closest to him.

"I didn't do it," he burst out.

The officer nodded, his eyes liquid and kind.

"Well, we could take the lighter, get the fingerprints," said the other, "but I doubt if it would tell us much. Arsonists always wear gloves of some sort. Or almost always."

"Is there anything we can do to make the community safer? Members of the congregation are sleeping very little, if at all, imagining this arsonist on the loose, afraid they'll be the next victim."

"As far as you personally doing something to help? No. If someone has an old, especially prized barn, or lives close to the road with the house a good distance away from the barn, yes, there is something they can do. They can always sleep in the barn. It's the only sure way to hear anything. Or get an extremely good watchdog, trained to bite intruders, which is questionable. What if a person stops and gets out of a car during the night for reasons other than lighting a fire?"

Dat nodded soberly. "So we'll have patience. Wait. See how it goes, right?

"About the only thing we can do at this point."

Priscilla turned to go back to Dutch, but Mam called her back. Pea wire was cumbersome, unhandy, and Dat had corn planting to do. It was late in the season.

Sarah smiled and said goodbye to the officers.

No one like Mam to bring you straight back to reality, plunk you down in the middle of it, and put you to work.

Dat was the kindhearted one, the dreamer who colored your days with different shades of jokes, laughter, smiles, little sayings, or poems. Mam was a hard-core realist.

Grumbling to herself, Priscilla walked slowly to the roll of pea wire. With her foot, she sent it rolling slowly across one of Mam's prized geraniums.

"Priscilla Beiler! Now look what you did!"

Mam almost never shouted. When she did, it was stentorian, fierce in its power to bring the offender straight to their knees in repentance.

"Sorry, Mam."

"I should think so."

Bending, Mam plucked off pieces of the broken geranium, held them tenderly in her cupped hands, and scuttled to the house. An air of righteous indignation hovered over her white covering, its wide strings flapping behind her.

Sarah stood, her hands on her hips, surveying the damage.

"One geranium gone," she said, wryly.

"Boy, she got mad."

"Well, you need to be careful."

"I didn't try to roll that wire over the geranium."

"Dat spoils you, Priscilla."

"I know. I love my Dat."

Sarah smiled and continued pounding wooden stakes into the ground, remembering when she was fourteen years old, riding horses, swimming in the creek, going to Raystown Lake during the summer at Uncle Elam's. Life was one happy chunk of solid uncomplication, as sturdy as a cement block, and as simple. And it was supposed to stay that way.

Turn sixteen, date Matthew Stoltzfus, marry him, and live in a small white house under a maple tree—a house with a porch, two small dormers on the roof, and ruffled white curtains at the upstairs windows. She'd grow zinnias and lavender and daisies in the garden, and Matthew would help her pull ears of corn that they'd freeze in small bags tied with red twisties.

They'd go to an island somewhere, to a beach, and swim. She had never seen the ocean, and she planned to some day. With Matthew.

She had turned sixteen, alright, but everything had gone wrong after that. Everything. Matthew treated her the same way he had always treated her. He just didn't seem to think there was anything wrong with that. He liked her a lot. She was his friend, Sarah, still as easy to get along with as always.

It was Rose who bowled him over eventually. Sarah remembered exactly where she was standing when Allen told her Matthew had asked Rose Zook. She had almost fainted from an acute sense of shock, followed by a gloom as thick and impenetrable as the hide of an elephant.

Mam had stood by her side. They'd talked, reasoned, shared their feelings, and grew close. But at the end of the day, she still had to sit on the slippery banks of the muddy river called misery—and simply deal with it.

Every weekend, she saw him. Them. Sometimes on Saturday evening if there was a volleyball game or a skating party or a hockey game. Always on Sunday evening at the supper, when the Amish youth groups gathered at designated homes of parents or siblings, and a large supper was served to as many as a hundred or two hundred of them.

Volleyball games, or baseball for the boys, were often in action at the suppers, followed by hymn singing. They'd all assemble along lengthy tables, the girls on one side, the boys on the other, hymn books scattered along the tables with pitchers of water and plastic cups, dishes of mints.

They sang many hymns, and sang well, the parents chiming in as they sat along the walls on folding chairs.

And always, there was Matthew. He would smile at her, genuinely pleased to see her each weekend. She lived for his smiles. They were like a benediction, a scepter held out for her to touch, blessing the week that stretched out empty and arid without them.

Eventually, when Rose became his constant companion, Sarah had given up in a way. But only sort of. The thing was, he'd single her out, go out of his way to say, "Hey, Sarah. How's it going?"

Or the funny, "S'up?"

He knew she'd laugh when he said that. So many reasons to believe that someday, somehow, they'd be together.

Until they weren't. Now he'd been with Rose for a

year. A whole year and they'd grown closer and closer. Rose beamed and smiled and related every incident of their personal conversations to Sarah, including the times she loved him best. Sarah had hidden all of her own feelings securely away, despising the dishonest person she'd become. The incident at the barn raising had been her undoing, again.

Well, life went on, and that was that. But just thinking about it made her so angry that she pounded the wooden stakes for the pea wire so hard that she sank them in too far into the ground, and Priscilla had to pull them up a bit.

"Stop being so *rausich* (aggressive)."

"Get the job done!" Sarah grinned.

"Why don't we just let the pea vines crawl around on the ground, and pick the peas from there?"

"They don't produce as many peas. The sunlight can't reach them very well."

"Who says?"

"I don't know. I guess Mam."

Sarah straightened her back and gazed at the horizon, where storm clouds were gathering at a rapid rate. To the east, the white light of the brilliant late spring sun was being chased away by a threatening darkness rolling steadily along the horizon.

A rumbling, soft and low, brought the uneasiness that accompanied an approaching storm, so Sarah increased the pounding, wanting the pea rows to be finished before a spring deluge turned the soil into a quagmire.

The cows in the pasture lifted their heads. Crows flapped their dreary way across the sky, their hoarse caws preceding them. Sarah stopped pounding and watched the straight line of the crows. She shivered.

"I hate crows."

"Whatever for?"

"They're evil, like a premonition of something bad."

"No, they aren't. Duh, Sarah. My favorite book in third grade was *Blacky the Crow*. Shame on you. You know what? It's your imagination going way overboard again. I never saw anyone who could imagine stuff the way you do."

Sarah laughed and brought the mallet up and over her shoulder in a mock stance. Priscilla shielded her face with her hands and begged for mercy, laughing.

The crows wheeled back, their sizable black wings flapping faster as they lowered themselves into an oak tree behind the shed, their garbled crowing accompanying them.

Sarah watched as the mighty, dark birds shuffled from branch to branch, quarrelsome as they vied for position. The leader raised his wings, flapped them ominously, then settled down, a strangled caw his last attempt at frightening them.

Sarah turned to watch the approaching storm and heard the distant rumbling. As the air around them became quiet, only the crows' squabbling broke the humid eeriness.

She became rigid with—what was it? Apprehension? Leftover fear? For reassurance, she turned to the new barn, a large, well-built monument of hope and goodwill, evidence of what a band of men could accomplish in the face of evil.

Still, she shivered.

Priscilla pounded in the remaining stakes. Together they stretched the wire between them, then pulled up a few spring onions, peeled off the outer layers, broke off the hard growth along the bottoms, and crunched them between their teeth without bothering to wash them.

Next Sarah pulled gently on the prickly radish tops, exclaiming at the size of the large, red orb attached to it. She rubbed it across the black bib apron she wore, twisted off the top and the small root growing on the underside, and popped it into her mouth.

Her eyes watering, Sarah exclaimed loudly and ran for the water hose wound on the bracket by the *kesslehaus* door. As she bent over gulping large mouthfuls of water to cool her fiery mouth, Priscilla howled with glee.

The crows squawked their sinister calls of warning. Sarah stood, the hose in her hand, water spurting unnoticed, as they flapped their wings, exploding from the tree and wheeling on the still air. The rolling black clouds moved and changed their appearance in the background.

CHAPTER 9

THE STORM BENT THE ENORMOUS MAPLE TREES, the wind whipping the branches into helpless, skinny arms, flailing and twisting madly. A plastic bucket went skidding drunkenly across the porch floor, banged into a ceramic flower pot, and fell off the porch into the newly planted petunias below. The wooden porch swing creaked on its chain, pushed by the force of the approaching storm. Barn cats ran stiff-legged, their tails aloft like furled sails, slipping to safety through the small hole cut along the bottom of the barn door.

Dat came clattering up to the forebay, the brown mules leaning back to stop the corn planter after they trotted through the door. Dat's eyes were wide beneath the flopping brim of his straw hat. Just in time, he yanked down the wide garage door, lowering it behind him, before lunging to the windows to watch the fury of the wind. He'd never seen darker clouds or ones that churned like these. He hoped the rest of the family was all safely in the house.

The two maple trees bent and twisted, the small leaves whipped furiously, and the hail began to pound on the metal roof with a deafening clatter. Inside, the girls huddled by the windows, recoiling as the darkness exploded into a blueish slash of sizzling lightning, followed immediately by an earsplitting crack of thunder.

"Get away from the window," Mam warned.

Obediently, they stepped back, gasping as the hail pelted down, bouncing around in the green grass like cold, icy toads, hopping and careening all over the place.

"*Siss an schlossa*! (It's hailing!)" yelled Levi from his swiveling desk chair by the row of windows.

"Good thing Dat made it to the barn," Mam said, so grateful her mouth quavered with emotion.

Then she asked, "Where are Suzie and Mervin?"

Sarah wheeled, wide eyed.

"They're...they were right here in the kitchen. They came in with us."

"No, they didn't. They went to the barn."

"They came in when it became windy, I thought," Sarah said, suddenly alert, searching the dark kitchen for any sign of them, their shoes, a tossed head scarf, Mervin's little straw hat.

"They're in the barn," Priscilla said again.

The rain followed the pelting hail, coming down in gray sheets of windblown water. It sluiced down the driveway, poured out of the downspouts, and ran down the windowpanes, obliterating the barn and outbuildings in its force.

Mam's eyes became large with anxiety, and she chewed her lower lip without realizing it.

"I just wish Suzie and Mervin were here."

"Mam, it's okay. I'm pretty sure they're in the barn."

"I hope."

Sarah went to the door leading to the upstairs and called their names, receiving no answer. She went to the

basement, searching, knowing they would be in the kitch-
en with Mam and Priscilla if they were in the house. But
she searched anyway to ease her mind.

The lightning flashed through the small rectangular
window, illuminating the whitewashed stone of the old
part of the cellar. Sarah winced as the intense clap of
thunder followed.

They had to be in the barn.

Upstairs, Levi whimpered with fear. He told Priscilla
that God was mad at them, for sure. The barn burned,
and now this.

It was raining too hard. It rained five inches in an hour
and thirty minutes. Ninety minutes of water dumping
and blowing from the sky, the likes of which they had
never seen.

Dat remained in the barn, helpless but glad everyone
was safely in the house. He fed the mules and horses and
swept the loose hay and dirt from the forebay, frequently
going to the window to watch the rain in disbelief.

The small creeks and waterways of Lancaster County were already running full. The butterscotch-colored
water had returned to its normal gray-green, but it was
still rushing swift and high even before the storm struck.

An alarming amount of water rode in on the great
gray wings of the storm, releasing the deluge in a thirty-
mile-wide swath of wind and moisture. The creeks rose at
an alarming rate, churning and bubbling over the banks
into pastures, flooding newly planted cornfields and new
alfalfa pushing its way into a hearty growth of verdant
strands of nutrition for the many herds of Holstein cows
scattered throughout the county.

In a few hours' time, many motorists became stranded. Cows bawled from the safety of higher ground, as

small meandering creeks turned into vicious, dangerous torrents that swept away anything in their paths.

When Dat bent his head and splashed his way into the house, he found Mam white-faced and bordering on hysteria. Her rapid words pelted him, and he felt anxiety rising within him.

"Where are Suzie and Mervin?"

"Aren't they with you? In here?"

Sarah didn't think anything out of the ordinary could possibly happen. Their barn had burned so recently. They'd spent one night in pure terror and now lived in fear and uncertainty. God didn't do things like this. Not tragedies in pairs.

"They're probably in a shed somewhere—the garden shed," Mam said, her voice only an octave lighter than anger.

Dat wheeled without a word and went out through the rain, searching everywhere as Mam breathed rapidly, brokenly. She put up her hands and took out the pins in her covering. She pulled it off, put the pins back in it, and laid it carefully on the countertop. She tied on a navy blue headscarf and a black sweater and left the house without another word.

Sarah and Priscilla were mute with fear.

"*Selly glaenie hausa*! (Those little rabbits!)" Levi growled. "Always making trouble." He bent his head, shaking it from side to side, making clucking noises, as if that alone could bring them safely into the house.

The rain still came down steadily but with less force, as Dat and Mam splashed from haymow to implement shed, garden shed to corncrib and back to the garage, calling, calling.

When Sarah could not stand another minute of

waiting, she joined her parents, dashing senselessly after them shouting, "Suzie! Mervin!"

There is nothing emptier than the emptiness of a missing person. The very atmosphere is depleted of rationality when someone cannot be found.

Sarah's mind absorbed this emptiness, this wet, watery world without Mervin and Suzie in it. She imagined them, soaking wet, stranded behind the Stoltzfus barn where the road turned sharply upward. She imagined them sitting beneath Hannah's porch roof, safe and warm and dry. She'd give them a cupcake with white frosting on top. She imagined the small winding stream of water between them, so small it didn't even have a name. Surely they wouldn't have tried to go to the Stoltzfus place in that rain?

After searching every corner of every building, there was nothing to do but huddle under the porch roof and begin meaningless suggestions born of raw fear.

No, not the police. They didn't need to know.

There was a certain unwillingness to let their neighbors find out. Not us, again. It's embarrassing.

These words were not spoken, only thought, but they were thought together—a bond of understanding encircling them. As long as they didn't know for sure, why trouble anyone?

It was when Mam began to cry that Dat sprang back to reality, put a hand on her shoulder, and said everything would be alright. Mam jerked her shoulder away and yelled at him in a voice tinged with craziness.

"We have to find them, Davey!"

Sarah thought of the crows cawing from the oak tree and felt the hopelessness, the first slice of dread cutting into her heart.

Suddenly, a thought sprang into her mind. Why had God kept the knowledge of the fishing poles from them? She knew before she went to see, the fishing poles would not be there.

They had told only Levi. Levi remembered everything, didn't he?

Sarah rushed at him, grabbed his shirt front, hauled his big head around, and glowered at him.

"Why didn't you tell us?" she hissed, overcome with dread.

"I couldn't remember. I couldn't say if I forgot."

Levi cried. He begged Sarah for mercy.

Sarah stormed to the porch, a weeping Priscilla in tow, and in a terrible, hoarse voice told Mam and Dat.

"No! No!"

Mam sank to her knees pleading to her God to spare her little ones, please, please. Dat looked across the porch, seeing nothing, his straw hat dripping dirty water, his beard beaded with rain. And then they moved as one, back out into the rain, knowing their search must go on.

As Sarah opened the gate, she saw the slippery mud and the fullness of the cow's udders as they stood patiently by the barnyard. She knew they should be milking. But she and Priscilla, Mam and Dat followed the cow path in the dripping aftermath of the storm, stumbling over tufts of grass as they spread out, unwilling to see, unable not to.

Ah. The creek had risen to a heart-stopping muddy flood that tumbled and churned behind the wild rose bushes and tall weeds immersed by the rising waters. They ran up and down its length, calling, calling, calling.

"Mervin! Suzie!"

They were wet, their shoes sucking the mud, their throats dry with apprehension, and still they called. Finally they stopped and looked at each other.

"We need help," Dat said calmly.

They cried together but differently now, a sort of acceptance settling itself over the hysteria, quenching it. Their heads bent, they walked back to the house. Dat moved to the phone shanty like an old man, bearing the weight of his missing children.

The medics were the first to arrive in their red and white vehicle equipped to save people's lives and a driver and an assistant blessed with helpful knowledge to relieve the pain of people in accidents, old people in cardiac arrest, or stroke victims. In this situation, they could only wait and talk into squawking devices or cell phones.

Many vehicles followed. Large green SUVs with blue lights rotating on their roofs, fire trucks, black and white police cars. Again.

Amish folks arrived, on scooters, walking, with umbrellas. Elam Stoltzfus and Omar Zook from across the pasture. Hannah came, sloshing through the rain, her flowered umbrella a bright spot of color in the gray evening.

Someone started the Lister diesel, its slow chugging a comfort of normalcy. Men were milking, doing Dat's chores, as others formed an organized search party.

The light was gray as the storm wore itself out in small showers and slivers of light to the west. It seemed the world had been scrubbed and tossed about, then righted and patted dry, as if the countryside had emerged from a huge washer.

Sarah stood with Priscilla, numbly watching the scene with eyes that were still clouded with refusal to believe.

They couldn't have been swept away. That creek was not high enough. Suzie could swim. She was quite good at diving and swimming at their cousins' pond. She would have made her way safely across, even if the creek was rising fast.

All that evening they searched. So many men. Why couldn't they find anything? At least a fishing pole, a tackle box.

Panic became a constant foe, successfully fought back only to advance again with reinforcements of alarm, trepidation, and horror.

It was the failure to know for sure, the overwhelming doubt, that was hardest.

Hannah, her daughters, Matthew and Rose, women from neighboring homes and businesses all came and went, their voices reassuring the family with genuine kindness.

Mam remained in her hickory rocker by the stove, a figure bent with restrained panic, her eyes wild, showing white. The frightened look stung Sarah's heart.

In the gloom, they sat. Mam's lips moved as she prayed. Someone wiped a furtive tear.

Hannah brought her forest green container of coffee. Sylvia Esh contributed a stack of Styrofoam cups, a tall plastic container of creamer, a glass sugar shaker, and some plastic spoons. An English woman dressed in a pants suit brought a large white cardboard box containing doughnuts from the bakery in Bird-In-Hand. Hannah promptly opened the lid, chose a custard-filled one, cupped her hand underneath it, and turned her back to take the first bite.

She should turn her back, Sarah thought. Then because she was guilty of spiteful feelings, she began to weep softly, wiping her nose furtively when no one was looking.

Priscilla glanced at her sister, bowed her head, and wept quietly with her.

Outside the commotion heightened with those milling about on the porch, an increased flurry of activity, and Mam shot out of the hickory rocker, her mouth open as if to cry out, but no sound emerged. The hand she lifted to her mouth was shaking so badly she could not keep it there, so she clenched both hands at her waist, the nails digging into each palm.

What was it?

Sarah got up and moved stiffly to the screen door. In the near darkness, a great shout went up, an exultation of humankind, a victory over fear and anxiety.

A burly fireman, his brown canvas raincoat dripping, his large face wreathed in smiles, carried a form wrapped in an orange blanket.

Suzie!

Sarah rushed to her, clawed at the blanket, and found a white-faced, wild-eyed Suzie, her hair matted to her head with silt and mud and water.

Mam grabbed Sarah by the sleeve, pushed her aside, and murmured incoherently as she tore the child from the fireman's arms with a wild possessiveness. She sat down on the porch chair and let the blanket fall away, touching Suzie's face and dirty hair as she checked for injuries.

"Suzie. Oh Suzie," she said over and over.

Dat and Priscilla and Sarah crowded around, reached out, touching, reassuring, as Suzie burrowed her head into the rough, orange blanket against her mother's shoulder. She cried and cried, then said she was thirsty.

Thirsty! And all this water.

Only forty-five minutes later, they found little Mervin's lifeless form washed up against the large culvert that went beneath Abbot Road, about a mile downstream.

He had been carried to an eddy, where dead leaves and stalks swirled and caught against the side of the large, concrete culvert that was normally more than sufficient to let the meandering little stream run through.

With Suzie on her mother's lap, sipping hot mint tea with sugar, and the women crowding around the scene of deliverance, the arrival of Mervin's body was a hard blow of cruelty.

Another fireman, another orange blanket. But this time, no cry of victory, no shouting, only a solemn handing of the small still form to his father, who lowered his face, his straw hat hiding it, the only sound a paroxysm of loss and love for his small young son.

Mam bore it stoically, although her tears would not stop flowing all through the evening.

Dat carried Mervin in and laid him tenderly on the kitchen sofa. Slowly, reverently, they folded the blanket away, revealing the face of their beloved Mervin, his features perfect, showing no signs of suffering or struggle. Sarah gazed on the sweet face of her brother, so angelic in death. She cried as if her heart would break.

Why? Always the questioning, the constant chipping away of faith.

When Suzie was strong enough, she began to talk. She and Mervin had told Levi but left quickly, knowing it was soon chore time. They'd only wanted to catch a few of the fallfish that swam in small creeks in spring.

They had waded to the other side, then decided to follow the bend in the creek. They probably went farther than they thought, catching fish. When the storm came, they were scared. Afraid Dat would be angry, they had waited too long. They hid beneath some trees, then panicked, and tried to cross. A wall of water caught them, tumbling them about.

She did have Mervin's hand. When she realized the situation was dire and the brown water had much more power than she expected, she struggled to save herself and her brother. When she crashed into an overhanging tree and Mervin was whirled away, she figured she'd probably drown, even though she so badly wanted to live.

She had caught the low branch of the tree, but she didn't know she'd have to cling to it as long as she did. The water rose fast. She had to continually creep her hands up the branch to keep her head from going under.

She knew Mervin had been torn from her grasp, but hope kept her outlook bright. She talked to herself, telling herself to hang on, another five minutes, then another, and when the huge spotlight shone on her face, she thought she yelled. But in reality, she could only make weak mewling sounds, like a kitten. Her hands were scratched and broken open, her fingers stiff with cold and fatigue, but she was alive.

The coroner came, a small portly man who gravely performed his duty, nodded, and left.

They took Mervin away, still in the orange blanket, wearing his black trousers and gray suspenders over the blue shirt with two buttons missing. Dat and Mam felt him all over, as if to remember every inch of him. They kissed his beautiful, cold face.

"Goodbye, Mervin," they said and then turned away to hide their faces, their shoulders shaking with the force of their sobs.

Quietly, Hannah produced a box of Kleenex from the light stand, letting her hand rest on Mam's shoulder.

The boys came again from Dauphin County with their wives and children, crying, hugging, saying, "Thy will be done."

They sat around the kitchen table and talked, while Mam, seemingly stabilized by these motherly duties, helped organize blankets and air mattresses, extra pillows.

Suzie had a hot bath, shampooed her hair, and reappeared, dressed in a clean flannel nightgown, her eyes still wide with fright. They plied her with chicken corn soup and a toasted cheese sandwich.

Hot chocolate? Shoofly pie? No, she could not eat.

Finally, she asked if God could forgive her for letting Mervin drown in that awful brown water. Everyone shook with sobs.

Mam gathered her up in her arms and held her as if she would never let her go. Dat hovered over her and said she was not responsible, little Mervin's time to go had come, all designed by the Master's hand.

She cried then, in great, shuddering sobs, a tremendous healing balm for a young child of ten.

"Well," Dat said, blowing his nose. "Well, there's no use asking why these things happen. It seems harsh, one chastening gone and another bitter one arriving so soon after. But we want to accept, examine our hearts, and repent of any wrongdoing. Hopefully, from this we will learn lessons, have our views and values widened, and our spiritual needs fulfilled. In all things, there is a purpose, and we don't question."

Sarah listened, frustrated. We don't question? How could he say that?

Dat was a good, kind person, and so was Mam. They lived righteously and worked diligently at home and in the church, striving to secure the love that binds. And this was their reward?

Nothing went right, not one thing. How could God look down from his throne and call this fair? He must be strict, she thought. And besides, she prayed and prayed and prayed for Matthew, and He never answered her. Her yearning heart was now filled with grief.

CHAPTER 10

IN THE MANNER OF THE AMISH, THE HELP BEGAN
to arrive immediately the next morning. Neighbors came
to do chores at five o'clock, just as Dat was holding a
lighter to the propane lamp.

It was Elam, wishing him a good morning, inquiring
about his night's sleep. Yes, he'd slept, Dat assured him
but didn't elaborate about the long sleepless hours when
his heart had cried out with the voice of Job. "For the
thing I greatly feared has come upon me.... I have no rest,
for trouble comes."

Oh, he could exhort, lift up the weak, talk of reason
and reward. But in the still of the night, he'd wrestled with
his own personal angel. Where have I failed that all this
trouble comes upon me? he silently asked. Where have
I gone wrong? Perhaps I am puffed up, self-righteous. I
have not given to the poor as I should have.

"Those poor Daveys," they all said. "And him a minister, yet. You'd think he'd have enough on his mind, *gel?*"

Hannah was in charge, producing a breakfast casserole made with eggs, bread, cheese, and ham. She'd added
parsley, peppers, and onion.

The men cleaned the barn and prepared the machine shed for funeral services, moving equipment and power washing. Dat and Mam sat with the *fore-gayer* (managers), the three couples from their church district who were chosen to organize everything over the next few days.

Elam and Hannah, of course. John and Sylvia Esh, and Reuben and Bena King. They were all in their forties or fifties and had experience with funerals. They would do well, Dat knew.

They sat together at the kitchen table and made a list of those they would "give word" to come to the funeral. Who would carry the coffin?

Grandfather Beiler arrived, leaning heavily on his walker, his knees wobbling as he let go of it to place a kind hand on his grieving son's back. He knew well the throes of grief, having lost Suvilla two years prior.

Grandfather Kings, Mam's parents, arrived, white-haired, thin, and capable for their age. Mommy King went to her daughter, her arms embracing the grieving form. They stood weeping, the one a solace to the other, as mothers tend to be.

Levi sat in his chair and told their neighbor, Elam, that Mervin had drowned in all that water. He told him people drown when they breathe water instead of air. It rained too much, but not quite as much as Noah's flood.

Elam nodded and gave Levi a York peppermint patty. Levi asked if that was all he had; he wasn't so *schlim* (fond) of peppermint patties.

In the new part of the basement, the women cleaned and scoured, washed windows and arranged long tables. The men set up gas stoves, and other women arrived bearing boxes of food. The fire company donated the sliced roast beef, the meat traditionally served on the day of a funeral. Dat said it was too much, and Mam shook her head and said that was for sure, but they wiped their eyes.

Aunt Rebecca sewed new black dresses for Suzie and Priscilla in one day. Mam said she was so talented on the sewing machine.

They all had to wear black now for a year, whenever they put on their Sunday best. It was a sign of mourning, of respect and tradition, and it was taken seriously. They did it gladly.

Aunt Rebecca sewed the black dresses, capes, and aprons with the summer's heat in mind. She chose the fabric wisely, using lightweight rippled fabric that had a bit of body. Priscilla was very happy to wear the dress, as Aunt Rebecca was a bit fancier than Mam.

Sarah had two black dresses, one almost new, so she wore it on the first day of preparation. Since there was not much for her to do, she wandered to the basement, eager to see who was causing all the friendly chatter, the sounds of much needed fellowship.

Hannah grabbed her in a firm hug, shed a few tears with her, and asked how she was doing.

"Okay, I guess. As okay as I can be," she answered.

Sylvia and Bena gripped her hands, patted her shoulders in the motherly fashion of older women, and then began asking questions, their eyes friendly, without guile, bright with curiosity.

Sarah related the drowning in Suzie's words, while they clucked and sympathized.

"I never saw anything like that storm!"

"I hope I never have to experience one like it again!"

"It wasn't *chide* (right)."

A large woman Sarah did not know brought two cake pans covered with aluminum foil. Hannah reached for the cakes, thanked her, and then wrinkled her nose in distaste when she saw all the horsehair clinging to the aluminum foil.

"You almost have to put your food in a plastic garbage bag. You know, the kind you pull shut. These hairs get into everything. Especially in spring, like now," Sylvia complained.

Bending her head, Sarah huffed, breathing out sharply, trying to rid the aluminum foil of the offending hair.

"Ick," Sylvia said.

"A little horse hair won't hurt you," Bena laughed.

"Amish people grow up on it!" Sarah said, smiling widely.

The women planned lunch, preparing a kettle of chicken corn soup with homemade noodles that Bena had brought and canned chicken pieces from Omar *sei* Ruth.

Someone had brought ground beef; another had brought sausages. There was plenty of bread and applesauce and pickles, so that was what they prepared for the family, the relatives, and the many people who came to help.

In the late afternoon, the men from the funeral home brought the small, embalmed body back to the house. Tears flowed afresh as they prepared the little body for burial. They sewed a white shirt, vest, and trousers, a sort of half garment, draped over the body, appearing neat and very, very white. Mervin's blond hair was so clean, his skin so perfect, his eyes small half-moons of dark lashes laid permanently on his cheeks.

Sarah choked, thinking of the hateful, clawing flood waters reaching up and over his sweet face, squeezing the warm loving life completely away from him at such a tender age.

How could God allow it? She cried silently with Priscilla.

She couldn't bear to watch Mam lovingly dress her small son one last time, caressing the sweet face before tearing herself away and slumping against Dat, her grief almost more than she could bear.

The vanloads of people arrived then as the viewing was being held that evening. Relatives and friends, both English and Amish, came to grieve with David Beilers.

Da Davey und die Malinda. Sie hen so feel kott. (Davey and Malinda. They had so much.)

Parents brought Mervin's little classmates, all dressed in black except for the light blues and greens of the boys' shirts. Their faces paled with various stages of anxiety, wondering if Mervin would look different when he was dead. They peered into the plain wooden coffin set on wooden trestles in the emptied bedroom and were too scared to cry, except for the older girls, who sobbed quietly into their handkerchiefs.

And except little Alan. He and Mervin weren't just friends. They were real buddies. They scootered to school together, traded half their lunches with each other, and shared every bit of accumulated wisdom they had learned in each of their six years. They both thought the teacher was fat and grouchy, but they weren't allowed to talk about it at home, so they talked plenty to each other.

Children were supposed to respect the teacher, whatever that meant. They just knew that it was no fun to color the best you could and then still get scolded for going out of the lines when you barely did ever. Or have your ear pulled if you got out of line at singing class, which wasn't one bit your own fault either, the way Mandy pulled the songbook in her own direction.

Poor little Alan stood there in his lime-green shirt and black vest and trousers and his black Sunday shoes and blinked his eyes rapidly. And then because Mervin really was dead, he turned his face into his father's side and cried and hiccupped with pain. His mother handed him a Kleenex and patted his thin, heaving shoulders. Death was very real, then, for six-year-old Alan.

Sarah sat with the family, shook hands solemnly with countless well-wishers. She held the grandchildren, helped her sisters-in-law with their rowdy little ones and crying babies, and shook yet more hands as the rooms became steadily warmer.

She was tired, her eyes red with fatigue and emotion, and she thought the night would never end.

Then Matthew and Rose appeared, dressed in the traditional black. Rose's hair gleamed blonde beneath the propane lamps, and Matthew stood tall and dark and attentive behind her, his face already so tanned by the May sun.

And here I am wrinkled and tired and sweaty, holding this fussy baby. And here he comes, of course.

She received Rose's hug graciously, their tears mingling. Sarah was truly in awe of her sweet, beautiful friend. When Matthew gripped her hand, she looked down at his vest and refused to meet his eyes.

The contact with his hand meant nothing at all. It was merely a handshake, same as everyone else. Then why did her eyes follow him as he moved across the room, the yearning in them unknown to him? She could tell herself anything she wanted, but her yearning was there, always.

She longed to get away alone, sink into a soft bed, and sleep for a whole long night and part of the following day. She longed to get away from here, this community, these people. Somewhere far away. Away from Matthew and the river of hopelessness. Maybe, just maybe after the funeral, she would.

The day of the funeral service dawned a perfect day, the kind where the humidity has been lifted by the force of a storm, the air so clear it intensifies the green of trees, hills, and crops to a heartbreaking hue. Now it reminded Sarah so intensely of heaven. Purple and lavender irises took on a brilliant new color, the light of the sun coaxing all of God's majesty from them. The late tulips waved their red and yellow banners of comfort and encouragement to the mourners who attended the services.

The driveway and surrounding areas were covered with gray and black buggies, horses of black and brown obeying their drivers, stopping when asked, and moving on when it was time. Young men from David Beiler's church district moved among the teams, numbering the sides of relatives' buggies with a piece of white chalk.

It would all be done in order, the parents riding in the first buggy behind the specially built carriage that would carry the plain wooden coffin. The remaining family members would follow in buggies marked with the number 2, then 3, and so on, until the cousins, uncles, and grandparents were all in line, moving slowly to the graveyard.

But first, hundreds of people gathered in the clean implement shed, squares of carpeting laid on top of the stained concrete, the glossy benches in neat, parallel rows. The mourners were directed to their allotted spaces by the kindly *fore-gayer.*

In the house, a close relative led a special service for the immediate family. It was an hour spent grieving together, the coffin in their midst, before the actual service.

After that, they filed solemnly behind the pallbearers into the large shed containing hundreds of their friends and relatives, all dressed in black except for the men's white shirts and the women's white coverings. The clothing was an outward sign of inner peace and love, the weaving of lives in a simple black and white bond of unity. They were all there together, all believing in the same God, their souls redeemed by the same Jesus, their views and values not always identical but always tempered by the fires of surrendering to one another, bending to each other, acquiring a level of unity by love.

The sea of black and white spoke to Sarah's heart, the tremendous impact of generations of a people who strove to live together. They believed firmly in holding their neighbors in high esteem, in loving their neighbors as they loved themselves. This love was built on the foundation of Jesus Christ.

Oh, it wasn't perfect, she knew. Views and values were often solitary, each individual deciding what was right and wrong for them, shifting like sand. The winds of change and self-will constantly worked against this solid foundation. But the *ordnung* provided a guideline, a coming together, a rope on life's pathway to heaven.

When Isaac Stoltzfus, an uncle to the family and a minister, stood up, the funeral became starkly real. Sarah bowed her head. Isaac spoke of heaven's joy at receiving a small child who was innocent and had not yet trod life's sin-cluttered path. In her mind, Sarah saw Mervin with a small white robe around his heavenly body and wings of sparkling gossamer. He would have lovely blue eyes, his open mouth smiling, singing, his hair as gold, as heavenly as anyone could imagine. Happiness was all about him, a giant bubble of perfect love that no one on earth could begin to fathom.

Sarah cried. It was the parting, the agony of his death, the way he had died, the murky brown water entering his nose and mouth. How terrified he must have been. How alone. That was the hard part.

A second minister spoke of God's love, the love He had for Mervin, and how much further along he was now. Meanwhile, those left behind battled on, courageously meeting Satan and his allies on life's road to heaven.

When the service was over, each person filed past the open coffin. Many shed discreet tears, then left the family to view the beloved face of its youngest member before the lid of the small wooden coffin was closed.

Sarah looked at Mervin one last time and etched his features in her heart. She lifted the soaked Kleenexes to her nose one more time, her head bent, and told him goodbye.

In the buggy that was marked by a 7, there was a plastic bottle of water and two sandwiches in a Ziploc bag. She rode with her cousin, Melvin, with Priscilla and Suzie in the back seat, the youngest in the family, riding behind their parents and older brothers and sisters and their wives and husbands.

Melvin took up the reins, and thanked Dan, the young husband of her friend, Anna, who had tended the horses. Melvin looked at Sarah, grinned, and asked if she trusted him to drive.

"Of course," Sarah said, grinning back.

Bending, she retrieved the bottled water and the sand-wiches. She asked her sisters if they were hungry, then handed them a sandwich to share.

Melvin watched out of the corner of his eye. Sarah handed the remaining sandwich to him.

"You take half."

"I'm not hungry."

"It'll be really late, Sarah."

"That's okay. You eat it."

"You sure?"

Sarah nodded.

Appreciatively, Melvin ate half of the diagonally cut sandwich in two bites. He reached for the other half before noticing the line of buggies was moving.

"Oops. Better mind my business."

He stuffed the remaining bread into his mouth, his cheeks bulging. Unable to cluck, his mouth filled with bread the way it was, he took up the reins and shook them.

Melvin was already twenty-five years old, a member of the church, his hair sort of cut in the *ordnung*. But he was a bit of a rebel, a free thinker who did things by his own standards. When he could get away with his antics, he would.

He was Mam's oldest brother's son, tall, powerfully built, a hard worker who was a foreman on his older brother's roofing crew. He had a pleasant, if not handsome face, brown eyes that could be as sincere as a puppy's and sparkle with his own ribald humor or flash with anger.

Mam said he was sadly spoiled, but Sarah always said if spoiling did that to a person, then she hoped all of her children would be spoiled. Melvin was by far her favorite cousin. He never failed to lift her spirits and encourage her.

The sandwiches were a special favor from the *fore-gayer*, a kindness for the burial and return trip to tide them over till the actual meal was served after the services.

Swallowing, Melvin clucked now, his horse still waiting for that certain sound before stepping out. It pulled impatiently on the bit and bumped into the back of the buggy ahead of them.

"Boy, this is going to be a real pain," he muttered.

"Why?"

"Oh, this crazy Buster."

"Well, maybe if you didn't name your horse Buster, he'd behave," Priscilla said from the back seat, where she was watching the line of teams snake slowly up the road.

"What's wrong with Buster?"

"It's a dog's name."

"Nah."

Sarah loved Melvin, watching his profile now—the way his nose looked as if he'd banged it against a wall, and it had stayed that way ever after. She loved him more as he launched into an entertaining account of a dog's name, the one he'd given his German shepherd, which certainly did not look like a Buster. His horse resembled a Buster. Sarah smiled.

When they neared the graveyard, the white fence gleamed in the sun around the plain gray gravestones that dotted the well-manicured lawn inside it. The mound of fresh earth beside the rectangular hole in the ground, surrounded by the trees and fields of Lancaster County in springtime, brought the onslaught of unaccustomed grief once more.

Would they actually lower poor, drowned little Mervin into that gaping hole?

Melvin said it didn't seem real. His brown eyes filled with tears as he ran a forefinger beneath his crooked nose.

He leaned over in Sarah's direction, pulled out a white Sunday handkerchief, and honked his nose loudly.

"He'll make a real cute angel," he said, sniffing.

Sarah wanted to hug him, hard, but she knew it would only embarrass him, so she didn't.

They opened the coffin at the graveyard, giving them all one last opportunity to view little Mervin, his face so waxen in the sun, his hair so white blond. When they closed the lid that last time, Mam seemed to shrink into herself, the black bonnet on her head hiding the intense sadness of the moment.

The young men worked hard to fill the opening, their shovels scooping the soil over the small coffin after it was lowered. As they worked, a resignation, a softening, moved across Dat's features. He knew and accepted that one of his own was safely at Home, and in this he rejoiced, the spiritual side of him winning as always.

Back at the farm, everyone sat at the long tables, where the thinly sliced roast beef was layered on platters, accompanied by Longhorn and Colby Jack cheese. Bowls of mashed potatoes, thick brown gravy, and coleslaw completed the funeral meal. Dessert was simple canned fruit and platters of cake with coffee. It was good, sustaining the entire family in a tradition kept for generations.

The kindly folks stayed until everything was spotlessly cleaned and put back in order, the leftover food *fer-sarked*, benches and carpeting hauled away, and the milking done. They gave their final condolences, and the family was alone.

"Alone, but not alone," Dat said. God was right there with them, and He would stay in the days and weeks ahead.

They had weathered the fire, hadn't they? They'd come through this together as well.

CHAPTER 11

S UZIE WENT BACK TO SCHOOL ALL BY HERSELF
and cried her heartache to Priscilla when she got home.

Company began to arrive, the living room filled with
well-wishers every evening and every Sunday. It was
another tradition, a gesture of love and caring, a kindness that even Mam finally admitted was a bit overwhelming.

Her garden was becoming overgrown with weeds, and
no one was weeding it. The yard looked hairy, she said.
The radishes and onions needed to be pulled. The things
that had been damaged by the hail and rain needed to
be replanted. But always, there was company, and Mam
sat politely, said the right thing, and cried quietly while
her eyes darted longingly to the garden or to the sewing
machine as she tried not to think of the piles of fabric that
needed to be cut and sewn.

They went to Mervin's room and packed his clothes in
boxes and then carried them reverently to the guest room
and the cedar chest, where moths wouldn't enter and the
heat of the attic would not fade the colors. Mam cried
when she found a pair of underwear and two filthy socks

in his drawer. He would change clothes fast and furiously, the clothes hamper against the wall completely forgotten as he dashed down the stairs again. He was not allowed to chuck the dirty clothes under his bed, so throwing them back in a drawer was not really disobeying.

They found a blue jay feather, two rocks, some fishing line, a red and white bobber, three birthday cards, and five dimes in the little chest on top of his dresser. Bits of paper, scotch tape, and markers sat on his desk. A picture of Jesus stuck on his mirror beside one of Donald Duck and Goofy, cut from a birthday card.

So typical of a six-year-old boy. So Mervin. And so final.

Time moved on. The Beiler family accepted and did not question, courageously going about their lives in the traditional Amish fashion. There were moments when the memory of the storm, the disappearance, the horror overtook them, sinking its claws of discouragement deeply into their shoulders. But with time, the despair became less and less.

Among her people, Sarah knew accepting death was another way of accepting what God had wrought. To question it, to become bitter, to fight or rail against His will was wrong. They believed death was His will, no matter how hard it was to understand. And so the healing process began, the wonder of each new day emerging once more.

It was in August, the month when everything in the garden seemed to ripen at once, that Sarah noticed a change in Levi. He lacked his usual good humor and often displayed fits of temper. It was surprising because he had been perfectly manageable at the time of Mervin's death, the funeral service, and the weeks after.

Sarah was in the garden with a plastic bucket of ripe tomatoes half full at her side. She bent over to grasp another sun-ripened red orb, wondering if they wouldn't have an entire bushel basket full today. The sun was already hot, the intense heat warm against her back, as she picked tomatoes.

Glancing at the lima beans, she noticed the heavy pods bulging where the ripened beans pushed against the sides. She straightened her back and sighed. So much for asking Mam if she was allowed to get a job. As long as there was Levi to look after, cows to milk, and the large farmhouse, garden, and lawn to care for, she'd be here.

She was increasingly restless and unsure if that Levi wasn't terribly spoiled. She wondered if she would ever get over Matthew. She was completely sick of going to Saturday night volleyball games and Sunday suppers and hymn sings when always—always, like a gigantic fly buzzing on her shoulder—his presence agitated her.

She knew when he arrived with the beautiful Rose, and when they left. She knew where he stood on the volleyball team. She knew when he filled his plate, where he stood in line, and where he sat at the singing table.

She knew when he was happy, hilarious, or quiet. She watched the features on his face like the captain of an ocean liner follows his computer—carefully watching the display to chart her own happiness.

If he appeared moody, her spirits rose. Yes! There was a chance that he wasn't happy and wanted to break up with Rose. Perhaps, oh, just perhaps, please God, let it be, he was becoming bored with her perfect beauty, her immaculate ways.

If he was bubbling over with smiles, his face lit with an inner happiness, her spirits plummeted to the depths, hope quenched, the "ztt" of a tiny flame plunged into water.

Every Monday morning, she showed Mam her plastic mask of untruth, happily talking of Rose and her other friends, Lydiann and Rebecca, and Josh and Abram. She told Mam all about them having had a good weekend.

She had no idea Mam knew. Mam saw the strained smile and the increasing despair, but she decided to let Sarah busily weave her web of unhappiness until she was ready to talk.

As Sarah suspected, there was more than a bushel of tomatoes to pick. The lima beans were ready, and the peach peddler had come the day before with a bargain Mam could not turn down: twenty-two dollars a bushel. My. Oh, my, she said.

Abner's wife, Rachel, was not well, so Sarah left her a message and offered to do a few bushels for her. That was why the *kesslehaus* floor was covered in newspaper, piled with ripening peaches. Sarah quartered tomatoes, digging out the green tops with a vengeance. Her mood was as black as the dresses flapping tiredly in the tepid breeze with the rest of the day's laundry hanging on the wheel line.

"Sarah!" Levi's loud, whining voice sent an arrow of impatience straight through her.

"What do you want?"

"I want pretzels and Swiss cheese."

Sarah looked at the clock.

9:37.

It was time for his snack, but he'd eaten three eggs for breakfast.

"No."

"You're being mean, Sarah."

"You're too fat."

When Levi began to cry, Mam scolded her, drops of sweat beading her upper lip, her face red from the heat.

"You sure are not yourself these days, Sarah. Why would you talk like that to Levi? Bless his heart," she chided quietly.

"He is too fat."

"Sarah, he's always been that way. What is wrong with you?"

"Nothing."

Dutifully, she laid down her knife, went to the refrigerator, and searched for the cheese. Taking up a block of the fine cheese made in Ohio, she shaved off a few thin slices, put it on a napkin, and added a small mound of Tom Sturgis pretzels.

"He'll need a drink," Mam instructed.

Woodenly, her anger just below the surface, she yanked out a two-liter bottle of Diet Pepsi, poured a glassful, added three ice cubes, and took it over to his card table, where another puzzle was half finished.

"You have to help shell lima beans later this afternoon," she informed him curtly.

Levi looked up at Sarah, his beady, brown eyes as sharp as a hawk's. "You old grouch."

Sarah smiled in spite of herself. Her lips widened into a genuine laugh, and she clapped a hand on his shoulder.

"You're the one who's a grouch."

"You know why? I don't feel good. My stomach hurts. You're a grouch because you can't marry Matthew. He likes Rose, and you can't hardly stand it."

"Now watch it, Levi," Mam said. She was not smiling.

As the tomatoes bubbled on the stove, sending their aroma throughout the house, Sarah got down the Victoria strainer and prepared to attach it. She adjusted the part that clamped onto the countertop and held the bowl. She attached the roller and handle, checking to make sure it was properly fastened. Then she turned to her mother and said, "Mam, why can't I get a job the way the other girls do?"

"Oh, Sarah."

It seemed as if that statement alone punctured Mam's sense of well-being as efficiently as a pin stuck in a balloon.

"Mam, I'm always here, working. I don't get to experience the outside world the way my friends do. I need a break. Why can't I get a market job? Or a cleaning job? Anything to get out a bit."

"You should help Anna Mae more. She has her hands so full."

"So does Ruth. If Anna Mae would stay home instead of running to every Tupperware and Princess House party, she'd get her work done. Ruth has two little ones and quilts!"

Sarah's voice rose to a frustrated squeak. The tomatoes bubbled over, turning the blue gas flame to orange, so Mam flicked it off with a quick twist of her wrist. Then she turned, put her hands on her hips, and said firmly, "Sarah."

"What?"

Sarah looked up, her eyes pools of misery, and Mam knew the time had come.

Carefully, she laid her dishcloth on the countertop and said quietly, "Sit down."

"No. The tomatoes are ready."

Sarah knew Mam was very serious, so she obeyed, her heart beating rapidly as she sat down.

"Sarah, I know how desperately unhappy you are. You can't always be so false on Mondays."

Gathering her last fortress of defense, her last hope of regaining her pride, she burst out, "I'm not!"

There was a decided snort from Levi, who sat at his card table, observing all of this.

"Levi, now you be good, and stay out of this."

"Yes, you are, Sarah. And I know it's Matthew. You have never once let him go the way you should. He is dating Rose, and hopefully he will marry her."

Sarah shot a look of complete disbelief at her mother.

"How can you say that?"

"What do you care if you don't want him?" her mother countered. "Sarah, it's very wrong of you to want him. Thou shalt not covet. Matthew is Rose's boyfriend. You are not a part of his life, Sarah. He loves Rose very much. You can easily see that. You see, often when we are blinded by our own will, we see only what we want to see, not what is reality. Your frustration is making your life miserable. Just miserable. You try to keep that happy face on, and it's not working. Accept God's will, Sarah. Let Matthew go. Pray for God's guidance in your life. We had to do that over and over when Mervin drowned."

Sarah bent her head, hid them in her hands.

"I can't," she whispered brokenly.

"You can."

"It would be easier if he died," she said with so much misery that Mam's heart quaked with the fullness of her motherly love.

"Sarah, I want to promise you Matthew. I want to promise you many things that would make you happy. That's a mother's instinct—to keep her children happy. Dat and I want to give you your heart's desires, always.

But sometimes it isn't possible, and we realize life is made up of choices and difficulties. The greatest gift we can give our children is courage, the will to do what is right in the face of adversity."

"Matthew isn't always happy." Tenaciously, a bulldog of resolve, Sarah clung to her love, to the terrible, hopeless yearning, the river of misery she chose to visit far too often.

"Well, Sarah, if you're going to be stubborn, we'll just give this a rest, okay? I can talk, but you are the one who needs to see. Let's get started with the tomatoes."

"But Mam, listen to this."

Shamefacedly, her eyes blinking back tears, Sarah related the incident at the barn raising, the intense feeling of love, and the way Matthew had reacted to the bandaging of her burned hand.

Mam held very still, her white covering well over her ears, her hair falling away on each side of her *schaedle* (part) and smoothed back firmly in the way of a minister's wife. Finally, as Sarah stumbled to a halt, she reached out a hand and placed it on Sarah's forearm.

"And that, Sarah, is precisely why I hope he marries Rose." Puzzled now, Sarah lifted her eyes to her mother's. "Matthew had no business bandaging your hand. He does that with more girls than you. Half of Lancaster County's girls want him, and he knows it."

Sarah was shocked as Mam's nostrils flared. Mam's voice carried a certain quality she had never heard. Her own humble mother, speaking in this manner!

"Seriously, Sarah, you have to listen to me. We all like to think that we're good Christians who don't decide our love by a handsome face, but we both know that is often the case. Almost always the first attraction. And Matthew has held you in his gaze seemingly always. I wouldn't trust him farther than I could throw him."

Mam's words were firm and rock solid with meaning.

Wow. Sarah mouthed the word silently, then slid down in her chair, and gazed at the ceiling.

"Do you want me to tell you another motherly quality? We want the best for our children, and we're secretly proud if our sons and daughters have 'a catch.' You know what I mean? But it's all pride, the world's way, even if we get caught up in it at times. We're painfully human, and not so perfect."

"So what should I do to change things?" Sarah asked.

"Stop thinking he wants you. He doesn't. He's dating Rose. He's a flirt."

Like rocks thrown at her, Mam's words hurt, and Sarah winced, now painfully aware of her mother's honesty. This was so unlike her soft-spoken mother.

Mam lifted the lid of the tomato kettle, and Sarah's life stretched out in front of her, a long, dry, windblown desert without a road or a map to guide her survival without Matthew. Or the hope of him.

With fresh resolve, Sarah dressed carelessly in the usual black that Sunday afternoon. Melvin would be by to pick her up with, of course, the trusted Buster. He was almost an hour late, and in the heat of August, her hair would not stay in place, springing from the hold of the hairspray, free to look awful, she thought.

Well, who cared? She had pondered Mam's words carefully, or so she chose to believe. No more Matthew for her.

When Melvin finally did arrive, he tied Buster to the hitching pole, went to talk to Dat, and had a glass of mint tea and a handful of pretzels. Eventually he got up, poured himself a drink of water from the pitcher in the refrigerator, took a long look at himself in the mirror over the sink in the *kesslehaus*, and told Sarah he was ready.

The crickets, katydids, grasshoppers, and cicadas were all trying to outdo each other, their symphony reaching a deafening crescendo in the tired dusty weeds by the roadside as Buster walked slowly up the hill.

"I love the sounds of the insects at the end of summer," Sarah said suddenly.

"Why?"

Melvin's brown eyes searched her face, his serious expression a magnet for the humor his face always evoked.

"Oh, I don't know. I love fall and winter. Weddings coming up, Christmas, cooler weather."

"Why would you look forward to weddings? I only go for the roast and mashed potatoes."

"And taking a girl to the table in the evening?"

"No, Sarah. You are so mistaken. You are so mistaken it's not even funny. I do not enjoy taking a girl to the table. You know why? Because I'm old and a member of the church, and the brides are always so glad I'm there. Then they can pan off any homely, unpopular girl on me, because they know I'll be agreeable and talk to them. Usually they're my age or older, fat or…"

Melvin's eyes became sincere, liquid with goodwill.

"Sarah, you know I don't think I have to have some beauty queen to take to the table, but last year about took the cake. I was given every odd-looking girl in Lancaster. I'm sure they're all precious in God's sight, and every one of them would make me a good wife. But give me a break. That last wedding at Jonas Esh's, I hardly knew what to do. I don't even remember her name, but every time she said something, she sort of shifted and banged her shoulder against mine. She'd go, 'Yes, me, too!' Bang! Or she'd say, 'Did you know Davey Beilers? The ones whose barn burned?' Bang! It went on and on all evening. I was never so glad to leave the table in all my life. I'm not sure she was all there."

By then, Sarah was laughing, silently shaking with mirth, listening to Melvin's one-of-a-kind description.

"But, Melvin, maybe she just liked to be close to you."

"Evidently."

After that, Melvin launched into a colorful description of the place they were re-roofing—the shrubs, the lawn, the swimming pool, the gated community—until Sarah realized they had already arrived at the home of her friend, Rachel.

Would she ever forget that evening when Matthew and Rose arrived happier than she'd ever seen them? Could she ever remember a time when they had arrived and she didn't bother wondering if they were happy in their relationship, or if they were having a weekend together that was not so good?

She ate the meatballs with barbeque sauce, the scalloped potatoes with cheese, the salad, and the corn but tasted nothing at all. She smiled and talked and went through the movements of every Sunday. And she hurt so badly somewhere in the region of her heart, or wherever it is that emotions are kept, that she thought she surely could not go on.

When a tall, dark, good-looking figure stopped and lowered himself down on the grass beside her, looked into her eyes, and said openly and unselfconsciously, "Hey, Sarah! S'up?" she looked into Matthew's eyes and laughed with a happiness so intense she thought she couldn't handle it. She knew she hadn't even started to take Mam's advice.

Over by the volleyball net, a tall blond youth with his hair cut in the English fashion leaned against a buggy wheel. He quietly watched that girl whose curly hair always invoked in him a desire to smooth it back with his hand. He thought her eyes were like a restless sea.

So. That was how it was with her. This Matthew guy.

He'd bide his time. There was no hurry. He had checked the Fisher book, that thick manual of Amish people's names, birthdates, and addresses. He'd asked his mother.

Yes, she had said, she believed that was the minister David Beiler's girl. They lived near Gordonville. She knew her mother's family. Why did he ask?

He had shrugged his shoulders and left the room.

After supper, Sarah leapt like an agile cat and spiked the heavy volleyball as solidly as any guy, winning the game point. She turned, graceful, her eyes alight with the competition, holding up a slender brown hand to receive the high fives of her teammates, but he didn't have the nerve to push his way through.

When the guy named Matthew ducked under the net and teased her, the look of raw adoration she gave him cemented his resolve to stay in the background.

How, then, could he explain what soon followed? She was yelling, "I got it," and moving quickly toward the sideline, her hands together in perfect volleyball form. Suddenly she tripped over her feet and collided with him, her weight slamming him to the ground, the volleyball bouncing off as the opposing team sent up a great whoop of victory.

Blushing furiously, the seawater eyes stormy with defeat, Sarah looked at him and apologized. Before she had a chance to leap to her feet, he was on his, extending a hand.

"Sorry. I really slammed into you," she said before accepting his proffered hand.

Close up, the wonderful eyes were rimmed with thick dark lashes that accentuated their myriad of colors. Her skin was so tan and flawless, the hand so slim, yet bearing a certain power. Her black dress only served to remind him she'd lost her little brother, making her vulnerable still. He wanted to hold her in his arms and smooth her rebellious hair.

But what he did was say, "It's okay."

She certainly had slammed into him, both physically and emotionally. Maybe even miserably.

CHAPTER 12

The August night was unusually hot. A sound woke Sarah from a deep slumber, the aftermath of a restless tossing earlier, the heat making the night unbearable. It was either that or her thoughts.

Hadn't she impressed Matthew with that spike! He'd shown in his eyes how much he admired her, the way they had glistened with approval. So close he had been, too, standing right there in front of Rose, and he didn't care.

Now if that didn't mean something, she didn't know what did.

But then what a klutz she'd been, falling over that blond guy. He was nice, but she could never date someone who wasn't, well...Matthew. She wondered if that was the reason no one ever asked her for a date. Perhaps it was as if she walked around with a sign on her back that said, "Don't touch me. I'm waiting for someone else. Still."

The blond guy had jumped up and offered his hand to help her up. Not very many boys were so thoughtful. He was also very good-looking, in a blond, non-Matthew way.

A sound broke through her deep sleep, and her eyelids quivered, shaking her dark lashes. When the wail of fire sirens hit a high note, her eyes flew open. In one flash, her hand raked back the thin sheet, her feet hit the floor, and she flew to the window, her heart pumping, her teeth already chattering with fear.

Thank God.

The barn stood in the hot August night, a great white sentry of safety, the silver roof gleaming in the waning moonlight, the cows scattered like black dots across the undulating green pasture, now grayish-silver, their shadows black strips.

No flames leaping. No smell of choking black smoke. But the siren's wails drew closer.

Grabbing a robe, she felt her way down the stairs, finding Dat awake, wearing only trousers. His arms and shoulders gleamed white and strangely unprotected in the moonlight. She had hardly ever seen her father without a shirt. He seemed younger and more vulnerable.

"Dat."

Turning, he said, "Sarah."

He went to the bedroom, where she heard a drawer opening and closing. He reappeared wearing a white t-shirt with Mam following close behind. Together they went out on the porch, their eyes searching the horizon for any sign of a fire.

The night was still, the leaves hanging as quietly as if they were in the house. The only noise was the tired trilling of the insects, having now rasped and rubbed and sung their way to exhaustion. The stars hung from the blackness of night, winking and twinkling, the moon's dim light casting over the earth in shades of dull gray and white.

Dat paced the lawn, lifting his head to watch in all directions, the memory of his own barn fire still fresh in his mind. Mam was the first to see, gasping as the small pink glow turned to orange.

"Dat!" she called. "Look to the east."

Sarah looked, a dagger of fright following as she watched. Dat leaped up on the porch, his eyes wide as the orange light intensified.

"It has to be close to Ben Zook's," he said. "I'm going over."

"Walking?" Mam called, not expecting an answer the way Dat ran, hatless and wearing only his t-shirt and trousers. And him—a minister.

There was no use going back to bed. It was just after two o'clock. Mam and Sarah sat together on the wooden glider listening to the sirens, watching the night sky, and waiting anxiously for Dat's return.

After a few hours, they went to the living room and stretched out on the recliners. They knew there would be lots of work ahead of them, and they needed to rest. Finally they dozed off but slept only fitfully.

When Dat had not returned at five o'clock, they dressed, tied men's handkerchiefs over their hair and called the cows in. Sarah washed their udders with a disinfecting solution while Mam began to attach the milking machines. The friendly hissing of the gas lanterns that hung from nails on the walls was comforting, but they watched them warily now with, presumably, a barn burning somewhere.

When dawn broke across the farm, the rooster in the henhouse crowed raucously, the hens began their silly "be-gawks," the heifers mooed hungrily, and still Dat had not returned.

Priscilla woke then stumbled wide-eyed to the barn looking for Sarah, Mam, anyone. She said Levi was crying of a stomach ache. Mam hurried back to the house while Sarah and Priscilla finished milking. They fed the horses and chickens, poured milk in the cats' dish, washed the milkers, swept the milk house, and still Dat had not returned.

Sarah decided to check the messages on their voice mail and was relieved to hear his voice.

"Mam, this is David. The barn at Ben's burned to the ground. They didn't save anything. They think it was an explosion. I'll be home soon."

Mam's eyes filled with quick tears. She shook her head in thought, murmuring as she broke eggs into a bowl.

"It's awful. Just awful, girls. What a loss! It's unbelievable. How long can this go on before someone catches up with these people?"

Her words fell in a hard rhythm as she beat the eggs with a fork. Still muttering and shaking her head, she added chunks of fresh tomato, parsley, peppers, and onion, throwing in bits of leftover cheese and sausage.

Sarah fried potatoes and poured juice, while Priscilla hunkered on the floor, waiting until the toast was finished in the broiler. Suzie stumbled sleepily down the stairs, but Levi wouldn't leave his bed, saying his stomach pain was so bad he hadn't slept all night.

They told him about Ben Zook's barn, and he became so excited he forgot all about his stomach. He hurried, shuffling to the table, exclaiming that the man in the white car was at it again. He ate three slices of toast with butter and peach jelly and fried potatoes with homemade ketchup spread liberally all over them. Then he asked for shoofly pie to dip in his coffee. He burned his tongue on the coffee and said it was Sarah's fault. She should remember to add cold water.

Mam told Levi quite firmly that Sarah had nothing to do with it and to stop being so quarrelsome. Levi said that if he had to go to the hospital for his stomach ache, Mam wasn't allowed to go along.

When Dat finally arrived, his face was gray with black streaks where sweat had mingled with the ashes and smoke. His eyes gave away his feelings of helplessness in the face of another monstrous fire, flames crackling and leaping, destroying the centuries-old handiwork of another Lancaster County barn.

He sank into his chair, lowered his elbows to his knees, and hung his head, a gesture so unlike Dat. A dart of quiet fear pierced Sarah's mind. It was the defeat, the undoing of one who had always been so brave and capable of meeting adversity head on.

His gray hair was matted, stringy, the scalp showing on top where the hair had grown thin. The odor of smoke clung to him—a bad vapor of premonition.

No one spoke. The clock on the wall ticked away, unaware of the scene around the kitchen table. Levi slurped his coffee and drained it, carefully swallowing the last of the shoofly crumbs. Then he rubbed his face across an extended sleeve.

Sarah silently handed him a napkin, raised her eyebrows, and smiled. He returned the smile and punched her forearm with affection.

Dat lifted his head then, and met Mam's searching eyes. He found the caring and support he sought, his own eyes conveying gratitude without words. Then he began to talk, quietly at first.

"It's a mess. It's just a horrible thing—the cows tearing

at their stanchions, bawling out their terror, the desperate bleating turning into cries that were intolerable, the hay that burned as swiftly as any flammable substance, the shrill, high shrieks of the horses as they banged around in their stalls. The fire engulfing them was actually merciful. We tried. We tried to loosen a few cows, but I've never seen a fire like that. It was like a cannon blasting through the barn."

Dat shook his head.

"Not that I've ever seen a cannon. I imagine the ball of fire to be like one."

"Ball of fire? Was it lightning?" Priscilla asked, her face ashen with memories still vivid.

"No. It wasn't lightning. They're all talking, talking, on and on."

He lowered his head into his hands, the work roughened hands now streaked with the soot and ashes of his neighbor's barn. A stupendous burden weighed on her father, and Sarah knew it was not the fire, not entirely. He sat up suddenly, his eyes weary but filled with a solid light of knowing.

"It's so hard to take. Ben is so angry. He is demanding that something be done now. They're like a clamoring mob. They say, Amish or not, we can't sit on our hands and take this. Someone started this fire, and he needs to be brought to justice."

"But...," Mam began.

"That's just it, Malinda. It's not our way. It's not. We are a nonresistant people. Or used to be. To my way of thinking, we do not fight back. God allowed the arsonist to accomplish this. He could have stopped him, but he didn't. It is a chastening, and in everything, some good can come of it. We need to adhere to our way of forgiveness. But Ben is like a madman. He's stomping around, making threats, shaking his fist."

"But for him to have to listen to those innocent animals' suffering..." Sarah said gently.

"Oh, I know. I know. It's almost more than any man can handle. And Ben's barn was rich in history, valuable way beyond mere dollars. It was an old German bank barn, built in the late 1700s. You can't replace that workmanship. It's just...well, sickening. They're bringing in trained dogs to sniff out certain chemicals. And the media will go wild about this. With Ben's anger, we will not be a light to the world. I shudder to think of what he'll tell reporters. It'll be a real jolt to the community. I hope all of you stay home as much as possible. We don't want our pictures in any newspaper or magazine."

Quietly, Mam got up from her chair. She broke a few eggs into a bowl, turned on the gas burner beneath her frying pan, and added a dot of butter. She took Dat a cup of steaming hot coffee and then laid a gentle hand on his shoulder.

"You'll feel better after you eat," she said softly.

Dat reached across and patted the hand on his shoulder, saying quietly, "*Ach*, Mam. What would I do without you?"

The day was bright and hot and humid. In spite of the heat, Mam kicked into high gear, urging everyone else along. They would pull the corn they had planned on freezing and take it to Ben's, along with the lima beans.

"Sarah, take Priscilla with you. Pull the sweet corn in the garden, the early patch of Incredible. Keep it in the shade. Pick the lima beans. We'll take them over to shell them. Suzie, is your breakfast eaten? Hurry up. You can pick tea. I'll make concentrate. Get the woolly tea and all the spearmint. David, what time are you going back?"

"I need a shower and some clean clothes. Girls, now please don't forget. Watch out for the cameras. Don't talk to the reporters. Keep your faces hidden if they try to take your picture."

In the garden, Sarah and Priscilla bent their backs obediently, holding the heavy lima bean bushes aside as their hands searched for the ripening pods. There was no sound except the dull thunk of the hard pods hitting the plastic buckets. The sun was already on their backs like a giant toaster, showing no mercy for the girls' comfort level.

Sarah straightened and wiped the back of her hand across her forehead, where beads of sweat had accumulated.

Priscilla groaned. "Whose idea was this—to plant these endless rows of beans? Nobody likes them, except Dat."

"Levi."

"I could easily live without lima beans."

Sarah shrugged her shoulders. "You know how Mam is. A garden without lima beans is just unthinkable. It would be like making a dress with a *leppley* (the small fold of fabric sewn into the waist on the back of the dress)."

Priscilla giggled. Then she said seriously, "I think Ben Zook has every right to be angry. I hope the same person lit his barn that lit ours and that the police catch him, and he dies in jail."

Sarah gasped.

"Priscilla! Seriously. We are not allowed to talk like that. Not even think it."

To Sarah's disbelief, Priscilla began to sob hoarsely. A sort of feral anguish tore from her throat in great heaves, a sound Sarah had never heard from her sister.

As Sarah placed a hand on her sister's heaving back, Pricilla moved away quickly saying, "Don't. Don't." Sarah stood helpless, holding the corner of her bib apron, pleating it with her fingers, not knowing what else to do.

Priscilla sank to the soil between the lima bean bushes. She lifted her tormented face, her eyes streaming, and shuddered before catching her voice.

"Sarah, you don't know how it is to lose a horse. You were never like me. I know Dat meant well, and my new Dutch is all I could ever dream of. But that arsonist took away my real Dutch, and I'll never love another horse the same way. It's not just the barns burning—it's the loss of heartfelt love for the animals. They didn't ask for some... some...."

Priscilla was at loss for the proper word to describe the total disgust she felt.

"Don't say it. Priscilla. Don't. You can't hate. It will consume you, and you'll become spiritually unhealthy."

Viciously, Priscilla yanked off a lima bean and threw it angrily into the bucket. With a sneer, she said, "What do you know about it, Sarah? Huh? Nothing. Not one thing."

Sarah blinked. She started to say something but just looked off across the garden and down to the orchard, where barn swallows wheeled in the sky, their sharp jabbering a sound of home.

No, she didn't know. Or did she? Did she hate Rose deep down inside? Did she just frost her hate with a sweet icing of falsehood, going about her life intensely longing for the one thing she couldn't have? Could she stand here and show her sister the path of righteousness, when in truth she was decaying spiritually by the power of her own obsession?

She imagined herself covered with sticky, sweet, cream-cheese frosting, her stomach a carrot cake, spoiled, the gray-green mold growing, growing, taking over her health and happiness.

Was she hating? Did she wish Rose well? And her impatience with Levi. She'd always loved her handicapped brother. But of late....

Dear God. You have to help me. I can't do this alone. Oh, I can't. I love Matthew, helplessly, hopelessly. I can't get away from it by myself. Give me courage. Give me strength.

It took her breath away, knowing the truth. Roughly, Priscilla brought her back to reality.

"Come on, pick beans. Don't just stand there as if there was a spook in the orchard."

Numbly, like a manipulated marionette, Sarah bent her back and started to pull off the lima beans, a mighty battle beginning in her heart.

Her love for Matthew Stoltzfus was as all-consuming as the fires that had devoured the barns. He ravaged her whole life, like a disease that would eventually annihilate her.

Well, obviously, the barns were being started by a person who meant evil, who wanted to harm someone or something, who possibly held a grudge against the Amish and their Plain way of life.

Her love for Matthew was from God, pure, cleansing, bringing happiness. Or was it? Mam's warning flashed through her mind. Well, another obvious thing—what did she know? Mam wasn't at the suppers and singings, the volleyball games. She didn't know how Matthew admired her, talked to her, made her laugh. He didn't do that to the other girls at all. She was the only one.

Soon they'd break up. Soon. Rose was too beautiful, too perfect. He'd tire of her, and he'd be all Sarah's.

And so her thoughts tumbled and twisted, first in one direction, then in another. But always, tenaciously, she clung to the love of her life.

Priscilla attached herself just as firmly to a total disdain of the person who had taken her precious Dutch from her. The barn fires had spawned the works of the devil in all their masked forms.

Upstairs, the girls showered and then dressed in the customary black, with dear little Mervin gone only a short time. They wore no capes, it being the middle of the week, but they pinned their black aprons neatly around their small waists. Leaning over their dressers, they combed their hair back sleekly, adding mousse or hairspray, anything to tame the unruly hair.

As always, Sarah dressed for Matthew. He was sure to be there, as were all the able-bodied men of the community. So she combed, patted, combed again, sprayed, stood back, frowned, then took it all down and began again.

"What is wrong with you? Your eyebrows are arched straight up, and you look as if you could explode or something."

Priscilla was ready to go, covering pinned neatly, her blonde-brownish hair pulled sleekly back, her flawless face tanned, her eyes, well, yes, she was turning into a very pretty young girl.

"It's my curly, crazy, dumb hair!"

"You always did have that."

"It's the humidity. It turns my hair into corkscrews. They just spiraling wildly off my head."

"Well, go ahead and use the whole bottle of hairspray. Plaster your hair down hard as a board. You know the Fructis stuff isn't cheap."

"Who buys it? You or me?"

"You."

"Well, then."

Sarah lifted the green bottle, working the pump madly, while Priscilla plopped down on the bed, leaned back on her hands, and rolled her eyes.

"Go load the corn and lima beans a while. Dat got the spring wagon out. Go. Go on!"

"Your hair isn't the only thing out of control!" Priscilla shot back and started for the stairs.

Laughing, Sarah could hardly see to comb her hair, so she leaned on the dresser, giving in to the mirth, and was shocked to find herself crying and laughing at the same time.

Alright. This was enough of this stuff, as dear Mommy Beiler would say.

She raked her hair back once more, plopped her covering on top, pinned it, and without another look, ran down the stairs, through the empty kitchen, and out to the spring wagon, where Levi and Priscilla sat waiting.

Dat stood at the horse's head. "My, Sarah, we've been waiting." But he was friendly, smiling. If he felt impatient, he'd never show it, his emotions about such minor things always on an even keel.

"It's my curly hair."

Dat laughed and leaned sideways to look through his bifocals at the now severely plastered hair.

"It looks pretty straight to me."

Sarah laughed. "*Ach, shick dich* (Behave yourself)."

It was nice to have that reprieve of normalcy before the mile and a half to Ben Zook's farm, or what was left of it.

They arrived to the stench, the smoke, the milling about of people with stiff, numb movements, eyes full of dread or horror, caring, or disbelief. They arrived to the fire trucks, the engines and hoses, the black water draining away, carrying flakes of ash and the remnants of this proud old German barn that had been destroyed by a flick or two of a lighter.

Fire and water—two life-giving elements that humans needed to survive. But in out-of-control quantities, both devastated unlike anything else. Sarah saw the muddy flood waters churning over Mervin's head. She shivered and heard Dutch's screams as the raging fire overtook him.

And when Matthew Stoltzfus walked over to help Dat with his horse, she heard the distinct cawing of the crows.

CHAPTER 13

"MORNING!"

"Good morning, Matthew. Good to see you. Hey, if you don't mind, I'll get the horse if you help the girls unload. Would you see that Levi has a comfortable chair somewhere? Maybe here by the fence?"

"Morning, Matthew," Levi chortled.

"How's it going, old boy?"

"Good. I'm real good."

"Hey, Priscilla," Matthew said, grinning down at her.

She didn't bother answering, intent on rescuing Mam's cakes from beneath the seat.

"Hello, Sarah."

"Hi, Matthew."

She smiled and looked gratefully into his brown eyes, so glad to see him, her whole world lit by his smile.

"Only Mam would bake a layer cake. Black walnut with caramel icing," Priscilla mumbled.

"Something wrong?" Matthew asked, bending to put his face close to Priscilla's to hear her better.

"Oh, nothing."

Matthew's arm went out, for only a second, a half circle about her waist. Blushing furiously, Priscilla yanked at the cake, grasped it, and pivoted out of his way.

Matthew laughed and looked down at Sarah. "Boy, your little sister is growing up!"

He whistled, watching her retreating form.

Sarah giggled and thought how kind Matthew was, always thinking of others, and of someone like Priscilla, who had been so saddened by the loss of her horse.

"She'll likely take this barn fire hard."

"Matthew! I want down!" Levi yelled.

"*Ach*, Levi. I forgot you, talking to Sarah."

Oh, what hope! What a true cemented hope sprang in Sarah's heart, hearing those words. He had just admitted that she was a distraction. She mattered so much that he forgot about Levi! Imagine. The morning was now filled with pure, unadulterated sunshine, birdsong, monarch butterflies, grass as green and flowers as pink and blue and purple as Sarah had ever seen.

The scene of devastation at the barn faded into the background. Sarah shucked the corn all by herself in Ben *sei* Fannie's garden. She threw the husks across the fence to the three pigs they were fattening, about the only animals they had left.

As her hands ran swiftly across the ears of corn, removing the silk with a stiff bristled brush, she thought of Matthew. When she carried the first dishpan full of golden ears into the kitchen, her smile was dazzling, her face glowing.

She wasn't even aware of the cluster of women at the kitchen window watching her sister. Priscilla stood, still as stone, gripping the picket fence with white-knuckles.

The color drained from her face as she relived the horror of her own personal barn fire, the one that had trapped Dutch in its fiery claws, making him suffer as no horse ever should. Her Dutch. Priscilla smelled the burnt bodies of the cows, the huge draft horses, and she remembered.

Levi sat a few feet away, his straw hat pushed back on his head so he wouldn't miss a thing. Men shouted as trucks moved among the gigantic black hoses. Cameras flashed as reporters skulked about, knowing they would soon be asked to respect the Amish men's wishes.

Flames still broke out in the charred wreckage. Blackened stone upon stone—the mortar that had held them together for centuries now crumpled by the intense heat—was all that remained of what the forefathers had built by the sweat of their brows.

"That girl is going to have to go for counseling."

"Not Davey Beiler's girl. He's better than any counselor."

"She looks awful."

"Somebody should go get her."

"You can't help her."

"Oh, my heart goes out to her."

"Where's Malinda?"

"That poor woman has had enough. She doesn't need to be here."

"Priscilla brought two cakes in. She made a black walnut cake."

"*Ach*, that Malinda. She is something else."

"Her caramel icing is a tad too sweet, though." This comment came from the owner of the community's top roadside bakery, Henry *sei* Suvilla, completely uncontested by any other.

Amos *sei* Leah stuck a skinny elbow into Danny *sei* Becca's ample side, causing her to jump with an almost inaudible little squeak. Two eyebrows shot up, and when Suvilla glowered at them, Leah quickly brought a hand to her mouth as she turned away.

Well, no wonder. Suvilla may have quite a business at her roadside stand, but nobody made walnut cakes with caramel icing the way Malinda did. And her being so genuinely humble.

Half these tourists didn't really know what good shoofly pie was. They bought Suvilla's dry old things and thought that's how shoofly tasted.

"Oh, my! No! Here comes a reporter. Straight up to Priscilla!"

"Oh, *siss unfashtendich!* (This is just senseless!)"

"Somebody go get her."

"Where's Sarah?"

A flurry of searching followed but to no avail. It was too late. The reporter, carrying a whirring black contraption on his shoulder with straps dangling, bore down on the unassuming Priscilla.

She was completely unaware, lost in her own sad world of memories and loathing of anyone evil enough to murder these faultless animals. They had never done anything except serve their masters—giving their creamy milk, pulling the plow or the hay rake or the balers— servants that made a living, a way of life. Wasn't that check in the mailbox because of them? Wasn't the milk possible because of the horses' hard work, their beautiful heads nodding, their harnesses clanking, doing what God designed them to do?

So the fortunate person with the camera captured the innocent young Amish girl and all the horror mirrored in her eyes and sold the picture to the prominent Lancaster newspaper with Priscilla's own words in the story.

"No, I do not forgive him. I hope he spends the rest of his life in jail."

The repercussions were terrible. Amish people all over the United States gasped in disbelief—except for a handful who felt the same, Ben Zook among them. The Beiler family knew nothing of it, unaware that day at the barn raising.

The next day was different. Priscilla stayed home with Levi and Suzie, who had both come down with a stomach virus. Mam said it was the dog days of August, what else could you expect?

She didn't understand the politeness, the cold distance between her and the good womenfolk until Hannah, bless her heart, drew her aside and whispered, "Did you see the paper?"

"Which one?"

"Here."

Hannah shoved the article under Malinda's face. Sarah leaned over to see, and both of their faces blanched.

"Oh, my goodness," Sarah said, slowly.

Mam lifted tortured eyes to Sarah. "Why? Why was she left alone?"

"I was probably shucking corn."

Malinda compressed her lips and stared out the window as tears sprang to her eyes.

"And David thought to warn them all. The children." She sighed, then squared her shoulders.

"Well, it is what it is now. We can't undo it. We'll just have to take the beating, the humiliation that will follow this article."

"It's because of Dutch," Sarah said wildly.

"We know that. But the world doesn't," Mam replied.

And where was I? Sarah thought miserably. I didn't even see her. I had my head in the clouds the whole blessed day, thinking of Matthew. And what had he done on Sunday? Nothing. Not one solitary thing. He never said hello or smiled or anything. As far as he was concerned, Sarah may as well have fallen off the face of the earth.

She stood in Ben Zook's kitchen, picked up one chocolate cupcake after another, and spread chocolate icing on each one before placing them in a Tupperware container, seeing nothing.

Her heart ached for her parents. Priscilla had said the wrong thing, sparing no one. Those words were not her upbringing, not the Amish way. No doubt Dat would be accosted, over and over.

The yellow, pine-scented skeleton of the new barn grew beneath the hot, August sun. Once again, men clad in black joined forces with men in jeans and plaid shirts or t-shirts, wearing shirts out of respect, when, anywhere else, they might have gone without.

Hammers pounded, chainsaws whined, men shouted, tape measures snapped shut. Women moved back and forth, keeping the large orange and blue Rubbermaid coolers filled with fresh ice and water, with plenty of paper cups beside them.

It wasn't more than midmorning before David Beiler's neighbor, Sammy Stoltzfus, grabbed Dat's sleeve as he hurried by on his way to get a box of nails. He shoved the distasteful newspaper clipping under Dat's nose.

"Your Priscilla, *gel?*" he asked, in a voice oiled with sarcasm.

Dat stopped, searched his pocket for his handkerchief, and mopped his dripping face before tilting his head to look through his bifocals.

As Sammy peered shrewdly up at David's face, searching eagerly for signs of outrage, another man, Levi Esh, came on to the scene and stopped, curious.

David Beiler's face remained inscrutable. He might as well have been etched in stone, that was how still he stood, reading the article slowly, taking his time.

Before he'd finished, Sammy couldn't take the suspense a second longer and blurted out, "Is that what you teach your children?"

Still Dat stood unmoving, reading. Slowly, he folded the paper and handed it back.

"It's a pretty poor light, for the Amish, don't you think?" Sammy asked intensely.

Dat looked at the ground, moved his foot, then lifted his gaze beyond Sammy. "Yes, it is," he said finally.

"I thought so!"

Sammy fairly bounced in his aggressiveness.

"So. What will give?"

Levi Esh extended a hand to Sammy, and he handed over the evidence.

"I don't know. She's only fourteen."

"Well, somebody should have to confess."

"She's young, Sammy. Her horse burned in our fire. She's having a hard time getting over it."

"So now you stick up for her. That makes you every bit as bad as her. I hope you know this is being talked about all the way out to Wisconsin. My brother's out there. He left a message. Said he hoped I'd *fer-sark* this."

Levi Esh lifted his head, pursed his lips, narrowed his eyes.

Dat took a deep breath. "Sammy, I'm sorry. This is not what we teach our children. But she's hurting. She was very attached to her horse. He was a pet. She'll get over it, but give her time."

"Girls shouldn't be allowed to have horses. They didn't used to, in my day. You need to show better leadership. God didn't spare your Mervin, you know."

Sammy sniffed indignantly and rocked back on his heels, his hands clasped behind his back.

Then Levi spoke. His words were modulated but carried a certain authority. "I think we need to be careful here, Sammy. This newspaper article alone is punishment enough for David. It's unfortunate, yes, but we know why Priscilla said that. She's only fourteen. A child. Her pet was brutally burned. Don't you think your measuring stick should reach a bit farther?"

"What do you mean?"

"Just that. Go home and read it in the Bible."

Sammy knew what Levi's words conveyed, but he had the bit in his mouth and wasn't about to give up.

"Well, I told Ezra I'd take care of this. You know as well as I do it can't be forgiven until someone confesses."

With that, Sammy stalked off, dead bent on doing the right thing no matter what. Levi Esh placed a hand on David's shoulder and wished him well. The days and weeks ahead would be turbulent.

When the nine o'clock coffee break was announced— actually closer to ten o'clock—David was stopped again. This time it was by a well-meaning elderly lay member who was completely disturbed by the photograph and accompanying words.

"The world and her ways are encroaching on the young generation. God help us," she lamented.

Dat agreed and tried to explain, but he was rebuked with a stern warning to heed his role as a leader.

Dat had no more than taken up a cup of coffee and was reaching for a warm cinnamon roll when Henry King unfolded the same article, inquiring about Dat's knowledge of it. Dat nodded again, and again he bowed his head as pious judgmental words pelted him, hurting every bit as much as jagged rocks.

He was not doing his duty as a father—and certainly not as a minister of God—if he didn't have a better hold on his children than that. This came from a man who had three sons who had deserted the Amish way of life and chosen to live their own lifestyles.

Over and over that day, as he pounded nails, the sweat flowing freely in the ninety-degree heat, Dat prayed for the power to forgive those who were well-meaning but unkind in their rebukes. Yes, Priscilla had done wrong. But oh, how his love for his daughter throbbed in his heart!

Priscilla had always been emotionally frail, crying all the way to school that first day. Tears had dripped from her face as she wrangled her way through her first poem at the Christmas program. To be subjected to two great tragedies at the tender age of fourteen was almost more than he could bear on her behalf.

Dat struggled mightily against the urge to lash out in words of self-defense. Pushing back thoughts of Jesus' words to the scribes and Pharisees, he persevered in his work and self-control.

In the house, Mam stirred the corn and lima beans, added a stick of butter, and told Hannah she could take over. Mam wanted to walk home. Hannah told her she couldn't in this ninety-degree heat, and Mam said she'd be better off melting away down the road than staying here fuming. Hannah laughed good-naturedly and let her go.

Mam told Sarah to tell Dat, and then she walked the whole way home. When she arrived, she slammed the *kesslehaus* screen door as hard as she could. Kicking off her shoes, she sat down in the hickory rocker by the stove, lowered her face into her hands, and cried and cried, releasing all the humiliation and the disappointment in human nature.

Priscilla found her mother there, shocked to see her tear-stained, swollen face. They unfolded the newspaper article, pored over the story, cried, laughed, then cried some more.

Levi wanted to see, so they showed it to him, and he shook his head, grimly prophesying a sad future for Priscilla for letting someone take her picture.

"I didn't know, Levi!"

"Yes, you did. You were looking straight at him."

"Not on purpose."

"Yes, you were."

"No."

They let Levi have his say and then started making supper. Mam cut open a succulent watermelon and a warm cantaloupe, while Priscilla apologized, saying she hadn't thought.

"But is that really how you feel?"

"Yes."

"But you know, you must forgive others or our own sins cannot be forgiven."

"I'm being very careful until I decide to forgive."

"Priscilla!"

"No, I mean—how can I say this right? I know I have to forgive the arsonist. I plan on doing that. I actually have started the process. I'm not as mad as I was. But Mam, it's so awfully hard to move on. Especially now, since it happened again. How many more fires before we all...." She stopped. "I may as well admit it. I'm not sure about our belief in being nonresistant. Are we just going to stand by and let that man or men or whoever just go along and burn barns?"

"It's only happened twice. Perhaps it will stop."

"And what if it doesn't?"

"We'll have to wait and see."

Priscilla shook her head.

Five days after the fire, Ben Zook had a new barn. The red barn was trimmed in gray with a gray roof, fancy by Amish standards. It did not complement his white house, but it was another beautiful symbol of fellowship and hard work.

By the last week in August, when the children traipsed eagerly back to school, a new diesel engine purred in the sturdy shanty attached to the back milk house wall. The only thing that kept them from milking was waiting for the new bulk tank. Once that was in place, they could purchase a new herd and get back to business.

With his horses and buggy gone, Ben Zook jogged or ran everywhere, his thick hair becoming steadily woollier as the days went by. His straw hat sailed off his head all the time. His anger had subsided, but he remained huffy, wary of anyone who tried to convince him to forgive and forget.

Sarah offered to help Ben *sei* Anna with her peaches and apples, scootering over the Thursday after school opened. Anna was short and as round as a barrel, with a pretty face—a match for her husband with her unbridled energy.

Her house was fairly new—they'd remodeled—but with nine children under the age of fifteen, there was a lot of wear on the new linoleum, she said.

"I'm not much for mops," she said. "The only way to clean a floor is on my hands and knees."

"Your house is always so clean."

"Puh!" Anna waved her hand, dismissing the praise. "My sisters say I have OCD, but I don't," she said, looking over her shoulder as she washed her hands. "Here, come wash your hands before we start to peel the peaches— Emma! Pick up the Legos. They don't have to be all over the floor."

As they peeled the soft, juicy fruit, Anna talked about the fire, explaining in minute detail the explosion that had woken them, the burst of terror, the feeling of desperation, followed by acceptance after the knowledge of helplessness.

"There is simply no feeling quite like it. To stand by while your whole means of making a living sizzles and flames and roars its way to total destruction. It's just unreal. You know, I told Ben, I was literally heartbroken. I was so upset I threw up that night. But, you know, God giveth us richly all things to enjoy, and I suppose he thought it was time to take some back. I don't know. Why does bad stuff happen? You can't figure it out. Ben got so mad, it wasn't funny. He says this is just going to go on and on, unless someone tries to stop it. He says he's going to sleep in the barn. Huh! That won't last long."

All morning, she talked, her words punctuated by another pretzel or cookie or peach stuck in her mouth. At eleven, she shrieked and said she forgot her brother, Lee, was here for dinner, and she had nothing ready.

"Well, he's not hard to cook for. I'll make chili and cornbread."

Cupboard doors slammed, pots sizzled, the can opener cranked, and plates crashed onto the kitchen table with alarming force.

"Oops! Here they come. And Ben's in a hurry. He hops, like a rabbit, when he's in a hurry. Shoo, I hope he likes chili. He's sorta picky. Come, children. Mary, come. Wash your hands."

Sarah helped little Mary wash her hands, then emerged from the bathroom, wiping her hands on her bib apron. She looked up—straight into the eyes of the person she'd toppled at the volleyball net.

"You're?"

"You?"

They both laughed, she blushed, and he looked tremendously pleased.

"You know each other?" Anna asked, her head swiveling from one to the other.

"I think we met once," Sarah said, smiling at him.

And he thought he had never been so close to ecstatic as when she looked at him and parted her lips in that perfect smile. It was not lost on Anna, who looked from Sarah to Lee and promptly stuffed a slice of cornbread into her mouth to ease the stress.

CHAPTER 14

COUSIN MELVIN PICKED SARAH UP EARLY SATUR-
day evening. She wore the customary black. She also wore
sneakers, as volleyball became a bit competitive on Saturday night, although she knew she'd play barefoot most
of the evening.

In addition to her traditional garb, Sarah wore an air
of disquiet. Her eyes seemed haunted from lack of sleep,
and a certain unhappiness, a subdued quality, hovered
just below the surface.

Melvin greeted her with the usual, "Hey, Cuz!"

"Stop calling me that."

"I wish you weren't my cousin. I'd marry you right
off the bat."

"I know you would."

"Seriously, there aren't many girls like you."

"Yeah. Well…"

Sarah stopped, turned her head, and blinked back the
hated wetness that rose too easily to her eyes.

"Well, what?"

"Nothing."

"What?"

"Nothing, I said. It's nice if you think I'd be okay to marry. Nobody else does, evidently."

"Ah-hah! I knew something was wrong. Your eyes were too flat when you climbed into the buggy."

"Too flat! What does that mean? Duh!"

"You know, Sarah, I'm going to stop right up there at the Tastee Freez, and we're going to eat ice cream and talk. I have a hunch that you and I are in the same boat, paddling like crazy with one oar in opposite directions, and we're so hopeless. Whoa, Buster!"

The light stayed red for too long, so Buster pranced and bucked and tossed his head, rattling his bit. But Melvin said not to worry. It was all harmless, and Buster just did it for fancy.

They pulled up to the hitching rail beneath a spreading crepe myrtle that was blooming profusely and humming with honeybees. Melvin declared it completely unsafe. He made her get back in the buggy and waited through the red light again with Buster acting as crazy as before. Melvin tied him to a tree on the opposite side of the street.

"Give me your hand to cross the street. People will think we're a couple," he said, grinning at her.

Who could be unhappy in Melvin's company?

He ordered a banana split with two spoons, and they sat outside in the waning summer light. The ice cream melted and dripped while he went back for napkins. He met a friend and talked so long that Sarah had to keep scraping the melting ice cream into her mouth.

When he finally sat down again, Melvin paused for a long moment of indecision about which side would be his, the strawberry or the chocolate, and wondered which one she liked best. He didn't include the vanilla with the chocolate syrup as he hoped he could eat that all by himself. He finally reached the conclusion that she could have the strawberry side; it was girlish.

"You know, like Strawberry Shortcake. That coloring book and doll character. It's for girls, so you have the strawberry."

"You know what? I wouldn't tell just anyone this, but I love strawberry ice cream. Mommy buys it all the time from the Turkey Hill down the street. Their ice cream is the best—better than Schwan's."

Clapping a hand to his forehead, Melvin squinted and rocked from side to side with pain in his eyes. He said he didn't know why, he never got a brain freeze no matter how fast he ate ice cream. And he also just remembered he had forgotten his volleyball.

Sarah watched him and then burst out laughing. She spluttered and pointed her plastic spoon at him and said he could just quit that.

Melvin laughed and laughed and said yes, he had a horrible case of brain freeze. They finished their banana split and ordered French fries, loading them down with ketchup and salt. They ate every last one and even dipped the tips of their fingers into the white cardboard container and licked off the salt.

They talked until the lights blinked and wavered and cast their steady blueish glow into the night. Clouds of insects swarmed around the hypnotic light, smacked madly against the hot bulb, and fizzled to their deaths.

Melvin said she could hide nothing from him—that she never got over Matthew. She said no, she didn't, that she was exactly like one of those insects and Matthew was the pole light.

Melvin snorted and said he wished Matthew was a pole light. He'd smack his bulb out.

"You know, Sarah, I can hardly stand it. Every little thing he does, you take as sincere. He knows it. He just keeps you dangling. You're always thinking that around the next bend, he'll break up with Rose. You know he won't. She is as sweet as she's beautiful. I don't think she has a mean word in her vocabulary. Is that how you say vocabulary?"

Sarah lifted her face to the night sky and laughed a laugh of genuine amusement. Here was a person who was completely straightforward. He was as simple to read as a child's book—uncomplicated, nothing hidden, content to be who he was, thinking he was quite cool and handsome when he really wasn't. Not much, anyway, and so lovable because of this rare trait.

Too many people, especially youth, were so desperate to be someone they absolutely weren't. In the process, they lost their genuineness, the only thing that actually was real.

Melvin was so real.

"Okay. So now you figured out my life. Let's start on yours."

"Ah, no."

"Come on. Who is it?"

"She's dating."

"She's dating? No wonder you said we're in the same boat."

"Yep. We are."

"Let me guess."

Sarah lifted her face, rubbed her nose, and hummed. She threw a covering string across her shoulder then remembered to tie it before tossing it back.

"Not Lavina?"

Melvin pursed his lips and nodded, his brown eyes

liquid with sincerity.

"Yep. Her."

"But..."

"I know exactly what you're going to say. Eggs-zackly! She's too cute for me."

Aghast, Sarah stared at her cousin in disbelief.

"Too cute? But...Melvin!"

"Don't you think so?"

"Well, yes, of course. If you do. I just can hardly believe you would consider Lavina Esh."

"Not Esh. Not Lavina Esh. She's..."

"Well, Melvin, I wondered."

They laughed, the sound of understanding. When he said Lavina Fisher, from below Christiana, Sarah couldn't picture her.

"I don't know her, do I?"

"You do."

The calm night was ripped in two by the wail of a fire siren. Instantly, Melvin's head came up, and he grimaced.

"You know," Sarah said. "It doesn't matter where we are or what we're doing. That sound will never be the same for us. We can no longer think it's someone else. Someone English who we don't know."

"It totally gives me the shivers."

Sarah nodded, then confided in Melvin about the newspaper story of her sister.

"Yeah," Melvin agreed. "It's tough for your dat. That poor man has had more than his share of late. It's hard to understand, a family like yours, and Mervin's death. Why does God allow these things?"

"Melvin, we're not perfect. I can write a whole list of ways we could improve. Other people don't know, can't see, but we have many faults. A whole bunch, to be exact.

I truly think God chastens those He loves, to make us better, more loving, kinder, *mit-leidich* (understanding)."

Melvin nodded soberly. He wiped his mouth very carefully, adjusted his collar, brushed imaginary crumbs from his trousers, and sniffed.

"See, Sarah, I wish you weren't my cousin. You're such a treasure."

Sarah laughed and watched the insects' wild flight around the hypnotic pole light, but she said nothing.

They left the Tastee Freez and arrived late at the volleyball game. Dozens of buggies and a few vehicles were parked in the lower pasture, the horses contentedly chomping hay from a flat wagon. There were three nets set up. Huge battery-operated lights illuminated the night. Color-infused movement pushed back the soft, velvety curtain of darkness.

As always, her face tightened searching for Matthew. She was not content to enjoy her evening until she knew he was there. As always, he was front and center, his height a great asset to his ability. As usual, Rose stood beside him, dressed in the lovely color of the flower for which she was named, her blonde hair sleek and gleaming in the strong light.

Sarah sighed, a tiny sound of resignation, like the flutter of a despondent moth. Why did she stand here with her older cousin Melvin, putting herself through this week after week? The futility of her longing loomed before her, an impenetrable wall without end. She could not climb over it, or dig beneath, it, or walk around it to the right or to the left.

He didn't know she had arrived, and if he did, would it make a difference? How did one go about extricating one's self from a spider web so effectively spun? She was as helpless as a dead fly.

Melvin, beside her, glanced at Sarah's face as Matthew successfully spiked the ball. Rose squealed and turned to him for a congratulatory high five. Melvin watched the pain and jealousy move across Sarah's features in a numbing wave. It was a shame.

As usual, the life of the evening was partially extinguished for Sarah. She half-heartedly entered a game on the side that needed players, which was not Matthew's team, of course.

She spoke to her friends, smiled, laughed, greeted others in a daze of sorts, her gaze constantly going to Matthew's game.

"Hey, watch it!"

A girlish yell broke in on her incompetent play, and she whirled to face the admonition.

"Sorry," she murmured miserably as the ball bounced away unheeded.

"You want someone else to play?" the girl asked, not completely without anger.

Sarah turned and sized up her challenger. She was tall, wide in the hips, tanned, freckled, with hair that should have been red but looked like it was toasted. She had a full, generous mouth, a prominent nose, and at the moment, she was not completely thrilled to have Sarah on her team.

"No, I want to play."

"Well, then, keep your mind here, and stop watching the other game."

Sarah was humiliated beyond words. She blinked rapidly to dispel the hot tears of frustration. She glanced again at the tall freckled girl and decided she knew exactly who she was.

That's Lavina. Lavina Fisher. The one Melvin wanted. But she was dating someone else.

Hmm. Sarah's eyes narrowed, watching her. Lavina played aggressively, pounding the volleyball with solid "whumps," moving quickly, shouting her moves to the other players. If she was English, she'd likely go far as a volleyball player, Sarah thought. Whew. Melvin better think about someone else.

After that, she forgot Matthew and played, putting her heart into the game. She kicked off her sneakers. She'd show that big bossy Lavina.

When the evening was over, Sarah had pushed her way into Lavina's good graces. She had whirled and twisted and dove, fists extended, helping their side win two straight sets. When the last game was over, they found themselves seated side by side on the ground, propped up by their hands, legs extended, as they talked about the game.

"You're Lavina Fisher, right?"

"Yes. I am. And I know you—Davey Beiler's Sarah, right?"

Sarah nodded.

"You just lost your little brother. I'm so sorry. It must be very hard. And didn't your barn burn too?"

"Yes."

"It must be tough."

"It is."

"Little brothers are so precious. I have three, and they're the delight of my life. I teach school, so naturally, they're my pupils. And what a challenge, teaching them!"

Sarah laughed.

"You hungry?"

"Not really."

"Oh, come on."

"No, I just had a banana split at the Tastee Freez with Melvin."

"Melvin? What Melvin?"

"My cousin."

"That older guy who lives alone with his widowed mother?"

"Yes. That's him."

"He's your cousin?"

"Yes. My mother's oldest brother Alvin's son."

"I know who he is."

This was spoken in haste, the words hard, pelting. Sarah raised her eyebrows and turned her head to look at Lavina.

"Why does that make you...whatever?"

"What?"

"Why did you get mad, thinking of Melvin?"

"I didn't. Well, maybe. I didn't want to let it show. It's just that...if you wait for someone for so many years, you finally come to the long overdue, sane, conclusion, that he doesn't want you, doesn't even know you exist. And so, you move on. I moved on. I'm dating happily now."

Sarah tried hard to hide the incredulity she felt. Oh, my goodness.

"I'm glad you're happy," she said but only as a soothing message, a sort of space between them until she had time to absorb the power of Lavina's words.

So. Is that how it was with Matthew? Is that why the attraction was so powerful that day? What if Matthew was like Melvin and wanted her, but he was too shy to ask? That was how it was with Melvin. And Lavina had wanted him all that time.

She drew up her knees, smoothed her skirt over them, and shivered with happiness.

So when Matthew dropped down beside her and said, "S'up?" Sarah turned to him with a shining face, her hope renewed, and asked how he was doing. When he said, "Fine and dandy," she fell in love with him all over again. Especially when Rose remained standing beside the table loaded down with homemade pizza, grilled hot dogs, cookies, bars, and whoopie pies and continued talking to Elmer Zook.

Sarah would be patient, bide her time, unlike poor Lavina, who hadn't waited long enough.

Should she speak to Melvin about this?

"You're not even listening to what I'm saying," Matthew said.

"Oh yes, I was. You were saying it's Rose's birthday."

"Mm...hum. Now. What would be a good gift? If you were my girlfriend, what would you like?"

Oh, the radiance of the night! The unbelievable thing he had just spoken of! Sarah giggled.

Lavina watched her, shrewdly, her eyes missing nothing.

"Well, I've always wanted one of those oak tea carts. Or a clothes tree. Both of them make nice gifts for someone who has been dating a year or so."

"A clock. I can't wait to give her a clock."

Sarah's radiance was dashed to the ground by a black hand—a hand so large and so capable of ruining all her hopes. She could not answer, could not think of a word to say.

A clock, Matthew. No. A clock was an engagement gift—the Amish version of a diamond ring. The hoped for, long-awaited gift of commitment desired in every

young girl's heart. Please don't say that, Matthew. She
looked into his face, startled that she hadn't said the
words out loud.

"Why? What's wrong with a clock?" Matthew asked.

It took every ounce of willpower to recover, to speak
normally.

"Nothing. Of course. Nothing. It's perhaps a bit soon.
That's all."

"Yeah."

Lavina jumped to her feet and said, "Come on, Sarah.
I'm hungry."

Sarah sat, refusing to go, until Lavina reached down
and grabbed her hands and pulled her to her feet.

"I don't want to go alone."

There was nothing to do but leave Matthew, so she
did.

They filled their plates, although Sarah thought she
might as well have scooped a nice pile of sawdust onto
hers, so unappealing was the thought of any food at that
moment.

Lavina led her away from the groups of girls, away
from the glare of the unforgiving lights.

"Sarah, I know I don't know you very well, but…is
that Matthew your friend, or…."

"Friend," Sarah broke in, hurriedly pulling the curtain
of oblivion abruptly between them.

"A bit more?"

"Look, Lavina, you don't even know me. Stop asking
impertinent questions that are none of your business."

With that, she flung the white Styrofoam plate to the
grass, sprang up in a quick movement, and walked quickly away, the mind-numbing events of the battered evening
spurring her on. When Lavina called after her, she ran.

Sarah ran the whole way through Elam Lapp's lower pasture, stumbling over rocks until she found the field lane that led to the large white barn. Her breath was coming in ragged gasps as she approached it, her heart pumping out her despair.

When she reached the road, the narrow macadam country road to Ronks, she noticed how the enormous white barn stood close to it, only a strip of well-manicured lawn between the road and the building. This was the kind of setting the fire marshals had warned about. In a few short minutes, barns like this could easily be ignited by the occupants of a vehicle stopped along the lonely road on a dark night.

Sarah shivered. And then—because their barn had burned that awful night, and because Mervin had died, that dear, innocent, tow-headed little soul—she began to shake uncontrollably. She sank to the dew-laden grass by the barn, overcome by the power of the tragedies coupled with Matthew's disclosure of his desire to present Rose with a dumb clock.

Suddenly, she hated Matthew with an alarming, powerful sense of revulsion she had never thought possible. He had been her captor far too long, holding her hostage, her whole life held in his hands. His hands—when it should have been God's hands.

Well, let him give Rose a clock. She hoped he'd be happy. Suddenly the knowledge that he would be happy brought a hoarse cry to her throat, and she buried her face in her hands, her body shaking, dry sobs escaping her.

That was where Levi Glick, known as Lee, stumbled across her as he walked home, envisioning Sarah sitting with Matthew again, her eyes vivid, her features animated.

"Oops. Oh."

He jumped back, apologizing and alarmed.

"I'm sorry. I didn't see you. Who...?"

He bent, and she twisted away from his gaze, swiping a forearm viciously across her face, then using the hem of her apron, as she breathed hard, struggling for control. It was too dark to see who sat before him until yellowish headlights on the road suddenly appeared, starkly illuminating Sarah, her face swollen from the effects of her painful realization.

Lee stood, waiting for the car to pass. It was a small white one, traveling only a few miles an hour, and they both thought it would roll to a stop. Seemingly, the driver spied the two figures, accelerated smoothly, and continued on his way, leaving them enveloped in the still, hot August night.

Awkward. That's what this is, Sarah thought, grimly. Lee made the transition smoothly.

"Do you want to go back?" he asked kindly, completely ignoring the fact that she had been distraught, knowing how mortifying this chance encounter must be.

She shook her head but then realized he couldn't see her and whispered, "Not really. Melvin won't know where I am."

"Who's Melvin?"

"My cousin. He brought me."

Lee said nothing, just stood beside her, gazing off into the summer night sky, and waited.

"Will you be okay? I don't want to leave you here by yourself. It is the middle of the night, after all."

"I'll be alright."

Indecisive, he remained. The sense of loss was too great if he left, but to stay might pose a whole set of new problems.

What had caused her to become so upset? What was the puzzling aura about her? This girl fascinated him. All the turbulence in her green-gray eyes was drawing him—but to what?

Resigning himself to what he knew was best, he walked away.

CHAPTER 15

IT WAS ACTUALLY HANNAH, MATTHEW'S OWN
mother, who was the next to completely wreck Sarah's
fresh new resolve. She came breezing in on a tempest, the
winds of October bringing gusts of hurricane force. They
sent maple leaves skidding wildly across the porch and
smacked them up against the wire fence in the pasture,
shoving them through the white picket fence in the front
yard.

Hannah wore a headscarf over her white covering,
smashing it flat against her hair, which wasn't far from
its usual appearance as she had no time for a matter as
unimportant as a covering. Her heavy sweater was buttoned down the front, and she pulled off a light pair of
gloves as she walked into the kitchen.

"Chilly out there."

Mam looked up from her pie dough, or rather, the
flour and Crisco she was mixing into pie dough.

"Hannah! What brings you?"

"The wind. It blew me straight up the road. I can't
imagine getting ready for a wedding. Just think of all the

plywood and plastic being nailed into place. I bet a bunch of men are chasing after their hats," she said, chuckling.

Lifting her glasses, she peered into the bowl containing the pie crumbs.

"Crisco or lard?"

Mam laughed, a good-natured, relaxed chuckle of comfortable friendship, of years of having Hannah living just down the road.

"You know which one."

Hannah laughed with Mam, and Sarah smiled to herself.

"Matthew wants me to try and make those fry pies. Some people call them moon pies. But why go to all that bother if one large pie gives you the same exact taste? He says Rose's mother makes them. She dips them in glaze, like a doughnut. Well, whatever she does, you know, is how it's done."

She rolled her eyes, a gesture of impatience.

"And now... *ach*, I don't know why I start. I was always hoping he'd see the light, and...well, you know what, it isn't nice, but Rose will not always be easy. He'll have to take care of her, no doubt. He's talking of giving her a clock, and they've only just been dating a year."

Her voice rose on a panicked note, ending in a squeak of desperation. Immediately, Sarah listened closely, now keenly aware of Hannah's wishes.

Mam remained quiet, the sun and clouds changing the light in the kitchen as they played hide and seek with the wind. Mam's covering was large and very white, her face small and serene, the blush in her cheeks a sign of her healthy way of life. Her navy-blue dress was cut well, the neckline demure, the black apron pinned snugly around her waist. Mam's strong arms turned the lump of dough.

Sarah could not picture her mother being like Hannah, their differences so obvious. Yet they remained true friends, the bond of love between them as strong as steel cable. They defended each other fiercely. And yet, where Matthew was concerned, Mam would not speak her mind, and Sarah knew why: she did not approve.

In her wisdom, she kept her peace. She knew every Monday morning Sarah had subjected herself again to a useless struggle, like a trapped sparrow beating her wings against a window, when all she had to do was turn away and escape through the wide-open door.

A small smile played on her lips as she scooped some flour from the container, scattered it on the countertop, pinched off the proper amount of dough, and patted a small addition on top. Taking up her rolling pin, she plied it lightly over the dough in an expert circular motion. Hannah shrewdly observed over her shoulder.

"You know your dough wouldn't crack like that if you used lard?"

"Now, Hannah!"

Hannah poked an elbow in Mam's side and laughed.

"You know, Malinda, Mommy Stoltzfus always said the beginning of the end of all good pies and doughnuts was the exclusion of lard."

"Our generation will live longer, thanks to good, clean arteries."

Hannah sniffed indignantly.

"Who wants to live 'til they're a hundred? Folks caring for you, helping you in and out of a carriage, being a burden to your children. See, that's another thing. I cannot

imagine that *piffich* (meticulous) Rose taking care of me
when I'm old. Matthew always says he would be the one
to care for me, and he would, bless his heart. He's such
a sweet boy."

Mam discreetly waved a bright warning flag of caution, but Sarah's eyes turned to pools of yearning, imagining Matthew caring for his aged mother. Mam knew the
tightrope that extended between sons and their wives.
It was a balancing act to be negotiated with great pru-
dence. And wasn't that Matthew a spoiled one? Ah, but
the consuming jealousy one would battle. How well she
remembered those days.

Many Amish lived double—one might call it. An
addition to the house accommodated the son and heir,
who would farm the home place. The new bride he
brought home would start out optimistic, so in love,
convinced her Daniel or John or Sam would love her
unconditionally. But she only became bewildered, then
hurt, then angry, when she found her young husband
visiting with his mother, when his rightful place was with
his wife.

Hadn't Mam and Dat navigated those treacherous
waters themselves and counseled many troubled newlyweds since they were called to the ministry?

Oh, Sarah.

Mam rolled her pie dough expertly, her old wooden
rolling pin clacking at both ends. She draped the round,
flattened orb across the pie plate with the ends hanging
unevenly and took up a dinner knife and sliced them off
so fast Sarah could hardly see her turning it.

Sarah finished peeling apples, set aside the peelings,
and began cutting the apples in small slices, filling the
pastry. Mam stirred the pie filling of brown sugar, butter,

milk, vanilla, and water as it bubbled to a caramel-like consistency. Then she poured just the right amount over the freshly sliced apples.

"That does look good," Hannah observed. She watched Mam roll out the lid, the pie's top crust, which had small indentations cut into it to allow the steam to escape. She flipped it neatly on top of the filling, and Sarah's fingers worked the dough into an even crimp.

"Boy, Sarah, you sure can *petz* (pinch) pies, for someone as young as you are."

"Thanks," Sarah murmured.

"Did you know my sister Emma needs a worker?"

Sarah's head came up. "Where?"

"Her bakery in New Jersey. That farmer's market there. You should apply. You'd make an excellent worker."

"Oh, Mam! Why can't I? You could manage. Levi is doing really well. Priscilla is home."

Her eyes pleaded with her mother. Hannah looked from Mam to Sarah. Mam pursed her lips.

"Oh, Sarah, I depend on you so much. It's not just the work. It's the companionship, the support. You've always been here."

"Now, Malinda, that's not fair. Maybe it's Priscilla's turn to support her mother. I think Sarah needs to get out and see the world a bit."

"Maybe you're right."

At the supper table, Dat ate two hefty slices of warm apple pie with vanilla ice cream, telling Mam between mouthfuls that it was the best pie she'd ever baked. Mam smiled back, and her cheeks flushed slightly. Levi whooped and hollered and raised his fork and said she shouldn't have sent a pie to Elam's.

"Hannah doesn't need our apple pie. She's big enough!"

Dat pushed back his chair, his eyes twinkling merrily at Levi.

A resounding crack came from the front yard. Suzie dashed to the window and gasped when she saw the heavy limb lying across the driveway.

"It must be terribly windy out there."

Dat's face became sober.

"I certainly hope there is no fire tonight. A barn would be gutted almost immediately, with the power of this wind. It seems that once you've gone through it yourself, you're just never quite the same. I shiver to think of a fire tonight. I have half a notion to sleep in the barn, just to be safe."

"You'll do no such thing!" Mam's voice was terrible, and they all turned to stare at her, shocked.

"Davey, you know what a sound sleeper you are. You'd never wake up. You know better!"

Dat nodded. "Perhaps you're right."

Silence remained after that, its presence calming, comfortable, as each member of the family remembered the night of the fire, the storm, the horror, the grieving, as if it had all happened yesterday. Only a short summer season had passed since then, but they had all learned so much. Like gleaning sheaves of wheat, the knowledge of others' suffering and loss felt ten times keener now.

Dat's hardest trial had been the laymen's bickering, each one convinced his opinion was the one with which Dat should agree. The disturbance over the newspaper story had subsided to wary muttering about Davey Beiler protecting that girl. It was, after all, only a horse.

Sammy Stoltzfus called his brother in Wisconsin and

left a message telling him that if Levi Esh dealt with him in this manner one more time, he may as well start looking for a farm out there. After all, the closer the end times came, the worse people would become, and if Davey Beiler knew what was good for him, he'd take that daughter firmly in hand.

After the second barn fire, a decided change had blown in. An unwelcome fog of suspicion shrouded the congregation. Dat desperately tried to turn a blind eye to it, but it was there nonetheless. On one hand, the fires had united them in love and brotherly concern. On the other hand, unsound theories pervaded the community that had formerly been innocent and childlike in its trust.

Mannie Beiler put padlocks on all his barn doors, and Roman Zook bought a Rottweiler, a huge slobbering beast with a massive head and wide paws. It barked and growled and muttered to himself all day. Eli Miller slapped his knee and laughed uproariously, thinking of an arsonist caught by the seat of his pants by that dog.

And David Beiler was saddened by all of it. There was no use being touted and admired by the world if the truth was decaying, a spoiling mold growing unobtrusively within two members of the church and spreading among the others as the weeks went by. Where was true forgiveness?

Each and every time he stood up to minister to his people, David exhorted the truth. "In our hearts we are a peaceful people, so let us be very careful, not boasting of revenge, not assuming something we are not truly sure has occurred."

He also knew human beings were often doing the best of their ability, and he overlooked many things, measuring each person through eyes of love.

The story of John Stoltzfus's Ivan was repeated time after time and never failed to bring a smile to Dat's face. Ivan was only eight years old, but he was determined to protect the family farm and his small flock of sheep. He unfolded his sleeping bag in the haymow, a powerful Makita flashlight beside him, a Thermos bottle of water, and the latest Bobbsey Twins book.

Why his parents allowed the courageous little third-grader to sleep there in the first place was beyond Dat's comprehension, but that was beside the point. The poor little chap had been awakened by the cruel wail of fire sirens. He panicked and ran through the sheep pen in his underwear, terrifying the creatures to the point that one of them got hung up on the barbed wire, and they had to call the veterinarian.

Other stories and questions—and the attitudes behind them—were not so humorous. There were those who believed the Amish way of forgiving did not apply when one's livelihood was in danger.

"Yes," David said, "Yes. You're right. But what will you do? Does unforgiveness and threat bring back the barns, cows, and horses? The balers and wagons and bulk tanks?"

Each evening he prayed for wisdom to weave a thread of unity and peace in a world that was slowly unraveling through suspicion and fear.

That evening, Sarah said evenly, "Dat, Hannah's sister, Emma, has a bakery at a farmer's market in New Jersey. She needs help. May I go if they ask me?"

"I guess that would be up to Mam."

Priscilla looked up, her eyes alight. If Sarah was allowed to go, perhaps she would be too eventually.

Mam shook her head ruefully, then admitted to her

own selfishness, wanting Sarah with her. "But, of course, she may go. Let's wait and see first if Emma actually needs someone. You know Hannah."

It was said fondly as her friend's fussing and stewing about life was a great source of humor in her life. Dat nodded, understanding softening his eyes.

"Oh!" Priscilla gasped.

"What?"

"I forgot. Ben *sei* Anna left a message last night. She needs you to help with applesauce on Wednesday, which is tomorrow. Sorry, Sarah."

"It's okay. I guess I can go. Right, Mam?"

Mam nodded, already gathering the dirty dishes and drawing the hot water to wash them.

"Wouldn't know why not."

Through all of this, Levi sat somberly, making no effort to include his own opinion, which was highly unusual. He remained hunched over his card table, shuffling his Rook cards, his large head swinging from side to side as he talked to himself. Finally tears began to roll down his cheeks, and he dug in his pocket for a red handkerchief, which he used to blow his nose repeatedly.

At bedtime, as Mam helped him with his pajamas, he told her that she'd likely never have to do it again.

"Levi!" she said, shocked.

"No, you won't. I'll just pass away now. I'll go to heaven to be with Jesus and Mervin."

"Don't talk like that, Levi. We'd miss you too much. We couldn't bear it, after losing Mervin."

"Well, my time's about up—especially if Sarah goes to market. That will be hard for me to bear."

"*Ach*, Levi."

Mam patted his shoulder. She made a big fuss about his ability to dress himself and brush his teeth and said they'd be just fine without Sarah.

The next morning, Sarah scootered the mile and a half to Ben Zook's and was shocked to find ten bushels of Smokehouse apples in the washhouse. Anna had her breakfast dishes already washed, the Victoria strainer attached firmly to the tabletop, and the first apples cut and on the stove.

"Morning, Sarah!"

"Morning!"

"Didn't you get cold, scootering?"

"I dressed warmly."

"Did you have breakfast? I saved some casserole for you. Let's have a cup of coffee before those first kettles are ready to put through the strainer."

"You put your kettles through?"

Anna laughed, her stomach shaking. She moved with surprising speed, her round form fairly bouncing with energy as she poured two mugs of coffee, lifted the creamer bottle, and raised her eyebrows. Sarah nodded.

She set a glass dish between them, steam rising from a deep, delicious looking casserole that was covered in buttered corn-flake crumbs. Taking up a spatula, she cut a huge square, slid it expertly on a small plate, and handed it to Sarah.

"Oh, I had breakfast, but it's been an hour. I can always eat some more."

She laughed, helped herself to a generous serving, and took a hefty bite. She rolled her eyes and said this recipe could not be beat, now could it?

Little Mary climbed on her mother's lap and promptly became the recipient of a nice sized mouthful of breakfast casserole.

"*Gute, gel?*" Anna chortled happily.

The door banged shut, and in walked Anna's brother, Lee, who was taken completely by surprise, his reaction to Sarah's presence a complete giveaway. He was holding his forearm firmly as he nodded in her direction.

"What's wrong with you? You look terrible!"

Anna rose to her feet, dumping Mary unceremoniously onto the floor.

"Cut myself. It's pretty deep."

"Let me see."

As he slowly lifted the clamped hand, blood spurted from a wide cut on the underside of his arm. Immediately, Anna's face blanched. She made small mewling sounds and sagged back into her chair, then slid to the floor below.

"She's fainting!"

Sarah stood, helpless. Lee said she'd be alright, she always did that. He seemed completely at ease with his sister crumpled to the floor.

Sarah looked from him to his sister, then moved quickly to the medicine cabinet in the bathroom. She found all kinds of salves, gauze, and adhesive tape. She grabbed them all and hurried back to the kitchen.

"I think the most important thing would be to get the bleeding stopped. You sure you didn't cut a vein?'

"No. Just wrap it tightly."

"With what?"

"A small towel would work."

Sarah grabbed a towel and pulled it as tight as possible, watching his face for any sign of discomfort.

"Still okay?"

"Yeah."

But he sat down, his face contorting.

"Does it hurt?"

"A little."

Mary began crying, so Sarah scooped her up and sat facing Lee, who lifted the towel and peered underneath.

"Shouldn't you go have that stitched?" Sarah asked.

"I doubt it. We'll stop the bleeding, put butterfly bandages on it. That should fix it right up."

Sarah was relieved when Anna muttered and coughed, and raised herself to a sitting position, still mumbling to herself.

"She's coming around."

"You sure don't worry about it," Sarah said.

"It's normal. I told you."

Fully awake now, Anna said, "Shoot, I passed out. Boy, I hate that. It happens so easy. *Ach*, my. Now I'm sick to my stomach. Shoot."

She lifted herself from the floor and wobbled dizzily to the bathroom. Lee shook his head.

Sarah bent and removed the towel, astounded by the size of the cut.

"You'd better go have that taken care of," she said.

"You think?"

"I do."

"Ah, just stick a few of these on. It'll heal." He grabbed several butterfly bandages.

"It's going to leave a scar."

"That's alright. It's just my arm. No problem."

So as he held the cut together, Sarah concentrated on applying the bandages just right, holding the edges of the cut uniformly. She held her breath and bit her tongue as she did the best she could, then straightened.

She looked at him fully for the first time ever, the blue of his eyes taking her completely off guard. His eyebrows were perfect, like wings. His nose was stubby and wide but somehow also just right.

He looked back and saw clear eyes of green flecked with gold and gray and bits of brown. At the lowering of her eyebrows, her eyes clouded over with a hint of bewilderment. Her breath came in soft puffs as her heart beat a notch faster.

Over and over, she relived that moment and chided herself. What was God trying to show her? That she was simply swayed by close proximity to any available man? Or was it the beginning of the end of her whole world being wrapped up in Matthew Stoltzfus? Would Lee provide the freedom she so desperately needed?

Ten bushels of apples later, she still had no clue.

CHAPTER 16

THE COOLING OCTOBER WINDS MUST HAVE BEEN host to a serious virus. Levi came down hard with a temperature of 102 degrees, his large body lying as still as death, his breath coming in great gasps.

The rasping sound from his bed in the enclosed porch aggravated Sarah's nerves as she did the Saturday morning breakfast dishes. Her arms covered in suds, she scrubbed the black cast iron pan that was caked with bits of cornmeal mush and grease.

The wind had died down, but scattered puffs still blew leaves half-heartedly across the driveway. The strong winds left a residue of straw, bits of hay, a Ziploc bag, bits of paper, plastic, and cardboard strewn around the yard. The day would be busy with the weekly cleaning, Mam hanging out two days' laundry, and cleaning up the messy yard.

Already Priscilla was upstairs, wielding the broom and dust mop. By the sounds from above, Sarah hoped she was cleaning underneath the beds. Priscilla was only fourteen years old, so her cleaning was done only well enough to get away with. This usually meant that Sarah had to spray the bathtub again or remove every object on a hastily swiped dresser and dust it again.

Today, with Levi breathing like that, Sarah became impatient. She whirled away from the dishwater, took up her apron, and dried her hands. Going to the stairs, she told Priscilla to clean the bathtub right this time and let the cleaner on the tub walls while she did the rest of the bathroom.

Priscilla mumbled a reply, the banging resumed, and Sarah could picture the few jabs of the dust mop, leaving disorderly trails underneath the beds.

Turning, she approached Levi's bed and bent to crank his head a bit higher to ease his breathing. He started, his swollen brown eyes opened to a slit. He coughed painfully then asked for a drink. Sarah checked the pitcher on his nightstand and found it empty. She took it to the kitchen to refill it, adding mostly ice cubes.

She lifted the blue straw to his mouth, watched as he swallowed a small amount, and then set the tumbler back on the nightstand. She arranged his pillows to keep his head from sliding to the side, put a hand on his feverish head, and asked if he was alright. Wearily, Levi shook his head.

"Do you want Swedish Bitters?" Sarah asked.

Again, he shook his head and fell asleep.

Sarah brought the broom, a bowl of hot vinegar water, the window cloth, and a bucket of sudsy Lysol water to begin cleaning his room. She set the geraniums aside and washed the shelves, windowsills, and windows, rubbing the glass panes until they shone.

She picked off the yellowing leaves from the geraniums, the dead blossoms following them to the floor, then set the plants back. She stepped away to view the result of her work and decided anew that she would never, ever, have one painted coffee can in her house and certainly not one that was covered in floral contact paper.

Mam was frugal. She viewed every empty tin can as a new flower pot. She bought all her Maxwell House coffee in tins, not the new fangled plastic containers, just so she would have another flower pot to keep her beloved geraniums through the winter.

Mam couldn't imagine paying five dollars for a geranium. Anna Mae and Ruthie were of the younger generation, and they refused to keep a single geranium in any tin can. They kept theirs in the cool part of their basements, in the same pots that had contained them in the summer. They brought the geraniums back up in the spring, clipped them back, and had beautiful new plants.

It had escalated to an all-out geranium competition, albeit an unspoken one. Ruthie had a large new deck built onto her house with pretty pots distributed across it, many of them containing geraniums bursting with healthy pink or red blossoms.

When Mam spied them she said, "My, oh," but that was all. She didn't question the method of keeping them "over winter" or ask which greenhouse Ruthie had gone to. She just said, "My, oh." Ruthie and Anna Mae laughed heartily about it but never approached Mam or asked her to change her geranium habits.

Sarah now questioned herself. When will I ever have the chance to clean my very own house? I'll be twenty years old next month and don't even have a boyfriend (or a special friend, as her mother would say).

She'd had chances. Boys had asked her on dates, but accepting was unthinkable. Even though it was one sure way of allowing Matthew to fade from her life, she couldn't do it.

She often wondered why he'd asked Rose instead of her. Obviously, if he was attracted to her beauty, that was the whole thing right there. Sarah couldn't even come close to that blonde perfection.

She took all the things off Levi's nightstand and wiped it well with the Lysol water and then replaced the items.

Well, Rose was so good-natured and amiable—as sweet as she was pretty. So Sarah guessed that it all made sense. But she had immediately picked up on the way his mother sniffed and disapproved. If he listened to his mother, he wouldn't date Rose; he would date Sarah.

But what could Hannah really do? She couldn't go around telling her children who to marry like they did in some cultures.

Sarah swept the dust and dirt and bits of geranium residue out of Levi's room, then dropped to her hands and knees to scrub the floor. Levi's breathing rose and fell above her.

Perhaps Matthew had no idea how she felt. Was that it? Or maybe, and this was very likely the truth, he had never felt the same thing for her—not when they went to school and most certainly not when they had each turned sixteen, joined the group of youth, and began their *rumspringa* (running around) years. She was just Sarah, his buddy. The thing was...

Miserably, she sat back thinking of her burnt hand. That incident had only cemented her longing firmly into place. Likely he'd just been nervous, wanting to get out of the kitchen, afraid Rose might find him alone with her.

Viciously, Sarah wrung the soapy water from the cloth and resumed her cleaning. Reasoning, wondering, she remained caught up in the subject that occupied her thoughts most of the time: Matthew Stoltzfus.

But now there was the disturbing intrusion of that Lee. Uh-huh. She had resolved on the weekend of Matthew's first date with Rose that she would never marry until he did. That was the one and only thing she had never told anyone, not even Mam or Priscilla.

So Lee, who she had now decided was most definitely attractive, may as well not even try. Not that he had. He was always at Ben's when she went to help Anna, who was fast becoming a close friend and confidante. They could easily talk a whole day about any subject, bushels of apples and peaches disappearing beneath their conversation.

She didn't know Lee at all, but she smiled to herself remembering how unconcerned he'd been about his sister sliding to the floor in a faint, looking for all the world like a soft teddy bear thrown against a kitchen chair.

Sarah got up and surveyed Levi's room with satisfaction. Turning to get the brush and dustpan, she saw a dust mop come bouncing down the stairs in a shower of loosened dust followed by three knotted Wal-Mart bags filled with a week's worth of trash can waste.

"Priscilla!" Sarah yelled at the top of her lungs, indignation coursing through her veins. She knew better. Nobody threw that mop down the stairs.

In response, Priscilla called, "Bring me a bunch of plastic bags!"

"No!"

"Come on. You old grouch."

"No. I would if you hadn't thrown that dust mop down the stairs."

"You know I didn't clean the stairs yet. What's shouldn't I throw it?"

"The dust flies all over the house, not just the stairs."

"Girls! Come," Mam called. "Do you want a few cookies? I'm so hungry from the washing."

The girls put aside their differences and joined Mam at the kitchen table. She heated the coffee and got out a container of cream-filled molasses whoopie pies and one of chocolate chip cookies.

Sarah unwrapped a whoopie pie, took a large bite, and said nobody had ever come up with a better recipe.

"You're getting fat," Priscilla said dryly.

"What?" Sarah shrieked.

Mam chuckled as she poured the coffee. Then she laughed outright as Sarah made a mad dash for the bathroom scales.

"135!" she wailed a few seconds later.

"I told you!" Priscilla said jubilantly.

"It's that job at Ben Zook's. Anna eats all day long. Mam, you know how much she weighs? 208. She said so herself."

"Well," Mam laughed. "She has always been that way. I remember her as a little girl, her round little body covered with that wide, black apron. She's never been different, but she had no problem catching a good husband."

"That's for sure.'"

Dat entered the kitchen with Suzie in tow, their faces flushed with cold air and hard work.

"We're hungry!" Suzie said, her voice low.

Since Mervin's death, Suzie had seemingly found solace in becoming her father's right-hand person, the way Mervin had been. Whenever she could, she accompanied him from barn to workshop, from cow stable to haymow, handing him tools, always asking questions.

Dat seemed to appreciate this, his former little companion stolen from him by the cruel flood waters. Suzie, in her childish way, remedied that theft the best she knew how.

"I'm going to finish the cow stable, then Suzie and I are going to go to Intercourse to the hardware store. You need anything?"

"Clothespins."

"Alright. After that, I'll bring Suzie home before I go help Ben Zook. He still needs help finishing up doors, and he said his diesel shanty could still use some work."

They sat dunking their cookies in coffee, lost in thought, until Levi's raspy breathing broke through to them. Dat looked up.

"Is that Levi?"

"He's pretty sick this time."

After they finished up their snack, Sarah resumed her cleaning. Priscilla sprawled across the sofa with the daily paper, which was every bit as annoying as Levi's breathing.

Sarah was aggravated. She weighed 135 pounds, couldn't eat whoopie pies, was almost twenty and still single, and had one annoying fourteen-year-old sister and a brother with Down syndrome who was a lot sicker than even Mam knew. Everything irked her this morning. Melvin hadn't called all week, and she was sick and tired of those stupid volleyball games anyway. What was the point of batting that ball back and forth across the net?

"Get off the couch," she growled.

Priscilla obeyed but promptly sat on the recliner, the newspaper held in front of her face.

"Priscilla!"

"What?"

They were interrupted by the sound of hoarse coughing, which turned into a wheezing of mammoth proportions, as Levi struggled for breath.

Mam hurried into his room, Sarah following.

"Levi."

Mam called his name tenderly, as Sarah smoothed the covers over his shoulder.

"He's so hot, Mam."

Mam nodded, held the digital thermometer to his ear, and lifted it, mutely, for Sarah to see: 104.3.

"Time to call someone," Mam said briskly.

Sarah nodded, grabbed a sweater, and went to the phone shanty with the speed she felt was necessary.

It was Saturday, so the health center was closed. She dialed 911 and calmly told the dispatcher the situation. Inside, Mam was trying to relieve Levi, who was now awake, crying in pain, his massive chest rising and falling as he struggled for breath.

Levi's condition was not out of the ordinary for the Beiler family, so their movements were not panicked, just calmly efficient. They sat him up, offering a drink of cold water, their eyes speaking volumes as they knew it was bad this time.

Levi was whisked away to Lancaster General Hospital. Dat was notified and joined Mam there while the girls finished up the cleaning and prepared to work outside.

They'd call around three o'clock.

The autumn sun had warmed the air, and Sarah soon shed her black sweater, raking the front lawn with long even strokes. The wash flapped in the sky high up on the wheel line, a colorful picture of motion, the green, blue, purple, and pink colors waving back and forth, whichever way the wind sent them.

Priscilla used the leaf blower. Suzie ran in circles, flopped into the piles of leaves, and then helped rake them onto the plastic sheet before they dragged them away to be burned.

The crisp air lifted Sarah's spirits, and she reveled in the perfectly raked yard. She leaned on her rake and admired the brilliant red, orange, and yellow of the chrysanthemums planted in a row along the garden's edge, the cover crop already producing a thick, green lushness.

Another season had come and gone, and the shelves were well stocked in the cellar. Applesauce, peaches, pears, five varieties of pickles, tomato soup, spaghetti sauce, and red beets—the variety of colors a sight to behold. Corn, lima beans, peas, green beans, cherries, and raspberries occupied the freezer in labeled boxes, ready to be cooked or made into pie fillings.

It was a wonderful way of life, and the rich gratitude that flowed through Sarah's veins brought a renewed zest for life, for the Amish way. No doubt it didn't make sense to the English world, and it certainly didn't have to. Sarah knew her people were not out to prove anything or live self-righteously. They weren't looking down their noses with the attitude of the scribes and Pharisees in the Bible.

It was an appreciation of heritage, a rich experience of lives lived before theirs—the stories, the respect for birth, life, and death, for marriage and raising children. It was continuing to live upright humble lives and existing in harmony amid a world filling with more and more confusing and unwanted technology.

Here in the heart of Lancaster County, with all its sprawling development and tourism, Sarah could see the physical results of her labor and enjoy the same house, yard, garden, and outbuildings as her mother, grandmother, and great-grandmother before her.

Except for the barn. She turned and eyed the sturdy new building, and a sadness coupled with appreciation enveloped her. The barn was resplendent. A change had come into their lives, and they had to accept it. She could picture the old barn, so timeless, so beautiful, but it was gone now. A new one took its place, and it was okay.

Missing Mervin was not. How he would have run and leaped into piles of leaves, scattering them untidily all over the yard. Sarah would have chased him, caught him, tickled his sides, rolled him into the leaves until they both fell back, breathless, laughing, his eyes alight with the little boy mischief she loved.

But *so iss is na* (so it is now). Mam's words were tapped into her mind like old Morse code.

Geb dich uf (give yourself up). It was a full time job, giving herself up, but anything else surely led to misery and kicking futilely against walls of restraint. She could kick and pummel that wall with a fist and get absolutely nowhere. It only bruised and battered the spirit, the soul.

Little Mervin was not here to spend his days growing up with them. It was so final—and so real.

Sighing, Sarah turned, called to Suzie, and went to the phone shanty, leaving her rake leaning against its front wall. She spoke to Dat, who told her Levi had a serious infection in his lungs, a bad case of pneumonia, and was in the ICU.

Sarah gasped, tears of pity welling in her eyes. Did she want to come stay with Mam, or would she rather do chores? She'd milk, with her sisters' help.

Dat thanked her and said it meant so much. Mam would be glad if he could stay, at least until Levi was stable.

Sarah soon found herself in the cow stable with a navy-blue men's handkerchief tied over her hair, pulled down almost to her eyebrows, and sturdy Tingley work boots on her feet. She wore an old purple dress and no stockings. She lifted her arms as she called to the plodding cows, their heavy udders dripping with milk.

Priscilla wheeled the feed cart along the alley, dumping scoops of nutrient-rich cow feed on the tiles beside her, the eager cows curling their long, rough tongues greedily around it.

Suzie was feeding the chickens, the sheep, and the two pigs Dat had bought from his neighbor, Elam. They would be fattened for next winter, he said. Suzie loved the pigs, and Sarah told her that if she wasn't careful, she wouldn't be able to let Dat butcher them. She said the cute little pigs would turn into big lazy hogs. Then she wouldn't be attached to them.

Sarah tapped the first cow's hip and was rewarded by a polite lifting of one hind foot, then another. The cow moved over to accommodate her, allowing her to dip the udder in the disinfecting solution, then attach the gleaming stainless steel milking machine.

As the diesel purred in the shanty, the sun began its descent toward evening. The cows rattled their locks, a horse whinnied, and another one answered. The steady chugging of the milkers brought contentment to Sarah, and she smiled happily at her sister.

Priscilla smiled back and gave the feed cart a shove, sending it crashing against the chute. She turned, dusting her hands by clapping them against each other.

"Now what?" she asked, grinning cheekily.

"You better watch it. That's a new feed chute, you know. You probably put a good sized dent in it."

In reply, Priscilla spread her arms and twirled, a pirouette executed perfectly, the lime scattered on the aisle assisting her movement. Sarah stood between two cows, an elbow on one's back, watching as Priscilla leaped and twirled again, just for the sheer joy of it.

Well, you were only fourteen once, she thought, smiling to herself. That time when you were still enough of a child to spontaneously whirl around a cow stable, not yet having to worry about the *rumspringa* years.

Sarah was startled to hear a clapping sound. She looked toward the door of the milk house and saw Matthew Stoltzfus watching Priscilla, his dark eyes alight with enjoyment.

"Bravo! Bravo!"

Priscilla came to an immediate halt, her cheeks flaming, her eyes blinking miserably.

"Keep going!" Matthew shouted, boisterous to the point the cows drew back on their locks, causing them to clank loudly.

Priscilla shook her head, her eyes downcast.

"Hey, Priscilla, you need to come to the..."

"She's only fourteen!" Sarah spat out forcefully.

"Whoa!"

Startled, Matthew looked at Sarah, whose eyes were flashing with outrage.

"I didn't see you, Sarah. S'up?"

As usual, the anger dissipated, and as usual, the greeting brought the response he knew it would—a smile returned, a gladness in the green eyes.

"Oh, not much. Levi's in the hospital, so we're doing chores this evening."

"Poor old chap. What's wrong with him this time?"

"Pneumonia."

"Yeah, well. One of these days the old boy will kick the bucket. Mongoloids don't often live to be forty, do they?"

Sarah opened her mouth in reply but was stopped short by Priscilla's clipped tones.

"He's not a mongoloid, Matthew. That word is out-dated, taboo. He has Down syndrome. We hope he'll live to be a hundred. You have no idea how much our family enjoys him. He's the star of the household. But you wouldn't know, because he doesn't look nice to you."

"Whew! What a speech!" Matthew clapped a hand to his forehead, and then took off after Priscilla in mock pursuit.

She gave him no chance, standing her ground as obstinately as a pillar of iron, her eyes flashing defiantly. He stood grinning, his hands on his hips, but his eyes fell first. He turned away, the grin slipping away, embarrassed but desperately trying to hide it.

He walked the length of the cow stable, then turned back, and said, "I almost forgot what I came for. Can we borrow your croquet game? Sisters and husbands are coming."

"Sure!" Sarah smiled too brightly, stepped out too quickly. "I can show you where it is."

"You're milking, Sarah. I'll go."

With that, Priscilla ushered Matthew out the door, and Sarah felt the life-giving air leave her body in a whoosh of defeat. He left and never looked back, sending her heart plummeting into another week of lost hope and despair.

When Priscilla returned, she was not smiling, just talking fast and hard and with meaning. She told Sarah that Matthew was about the last reason she could think of to act the way she did. What was wrong with her? He was arrogant, a flirt, and not even worth her time. Furthermore, he was dating, and it was about time she got over him. If she kept this up, sure as shooting she'd be an old maid. She was halfway there already.

She finished with a grand, "So go ahead, ruin your life. He knows everything he's doing to you. You're just another one on his string of starstruck young ladies. It's disgusting."

Sarah was speechless as she watched her younger sister stand her ground, amazed at the resolve she was displaying. When had she managed to acquire this attitude?

And then Sarah realized it was a necessary virtue birthed out of her loss. She had weathered a terrifying episode, dealt with waves of grief, been tossed about by winds of change. But she had clung to her little life raft of prayer and newborn faith. She had come through with flying colors. Bravo, Priscilla, Bravo.

CHAPTER 17

LEVI WAS IN THE HOSPITAL ALMOST A WEEK. SIX days, to be exact. He was everyone's friend, a favorite. He spoke in broken English, his droll sense of humor the talk of the third floor, where he had been transported after the infection in his lungs was under control.

He felt so important, being wheeled down the wide, gleaming corridors of Lancaster General, as he referred to it. His narrow brown eyes beamed brightly as he smiled, turning his head this way and then the other, trying to check out the occupants of each room they passed.

"What is he doing? Why is she here? What's wrong with her?" Over and over he voiced his curiosity, the nurse's aide at his side answering in monosyllables that were just enough to satisfy Levi.

In his room, Sarah adjusted pillows and pulled a warm blanket over him. Exhaustion crept over his pale features.

"Try and get some sleep, Levi." She patted his shoulder, smoothed back the thinning hair, and wished he could have a good, hot shower.

Levi nodded, his eyes already drooping. Turning his large head, he said, "I can sleep having you here with me, Sarah. I know you'll watch out for me."

He sighed, turned his head, and fell asleep almost instantly. Good. Now she'd find something to eat.

She found the elevator and located the hospital cafeteria, where she selected scrambled eggs, bacon and pancakes, orange juice, and coffee with cream. She paid and found a table, collapsing gratefully into an upholstered booth.

She'd done the milking that morning with Priscilla. It was several hours of hard work, and there had been no time for breakfast. The driver had arrived at eight. She was barely out of the shower and dressed in time.

The cafeteria was crowded with people holding trays and jostling their way to and from tables. Red-eyed doctors, nurses in scrubs, anxious visitors—they all sought a moment's rest and some food to sustain them. She looked up when someone stopped at her table.

"Do you mind if I sit here? The tables are all full."

A shy, nervous young girl, probably about the same age as Sarah and dressed as a volunteer, stood hesitantly at her table.

"Of course. Sit down."

"I'm sorry."

"Don't be. There's room."

"My name is Ashley. Ashley Walters."

"Good to meet you. I'm Sarah Beiler."

Ashley smiled, hesitantly, unsure, and sat down.

That was the one nice thing about being Amish in an area that was the hub of, well—being Amish. The English people around them accepted their way of life and their dress without staring or being rude. It was not unusual, then, for an Amish girl to be asked by a local English girl to share a table. The differences between them were accepted, comfortable, a part of life, as were the farms and the horses and buggies traveling briskly along the country roads.

After Ashley sat down, an awkwardness developed at the table. Ashley began eating, buttering her toast after she'd tasted it, and salting her eggs before realizing Sarah might want to pray.

"Oh. Oh. Excuse me. I..." Her drawn features looked even more pinched before she hastily laid down her fork.

Sarah shook her head and reached for her napkin.

"Don't worry about it. Go ahead. We don't always say grace in public. My father says it can be done in silence."

Smiling, she took up a slice of limp bacon and consumed it in two bites. "I'm so hungry," she remarked.

Ashley smiled. "Did you have chores to do?"

"I sure did." She explained the milking, the driver arriving at eight, and Levi.

Ashley nodded, sympathy showing in her brown eyes.

"Poor guy. How old is he?"

"He has Down syndrome. He's approaching thirty-two—old for someone with Down syndrome."

"Oh my!"

She asked where they lived, and Sarah told her. The recognition in Ashley's eyes was followed by an inquiry about their barn.

Sarah nodded and said it was April when it burned.

Ashley nodded. Her eyes clouded with sudden emotion, and she crumpled her napkin tightly and threw her silverware on the blue tray, the eggs uneaten. She whispered, "I...I have to leave now. Bye."

"Bye," Sarah said, but she knew Ashley hadn't heard as the other girl rapidly wove her way through the crowd, turning sideways to squeeze between tables, apologizing, her tray held high. She disappeared as quickly as she'd arrived.

Shaking her head in bewilderment, Sarah buttered her pancakes liberally and then soaked them well with syrup from a small, glass pitcher. She cut a substantial square and shoved it into her mouth, chewing appreciatively, and followed it with a long swallow of coffee.

Mmm. She was hungry, 135 pounds or not, and she planned on eating this whole stack of pancakes all by herself.

She wondered if the mention of barn fire had anything to do with Ashley's swift retreat. She doubted it. And yet. . . . She shrugged her shoulders, cut another buttery, syrupy chunk of pancake, and chewed contentedly.

Back in Levi's room, the nurses were trying to find a new vein on the back of his hand for his IV, so Sarah stepped back out into the corridor, wincing as Levi began to cry pathetically. *Ach* my, Levi.

Two nurses worked—the one as short and round as Hannah, the other one tall and angular—talking nonstop. "She's drawing into herself, I tell you. She can't get worse. She doesn't talk."

This was followed by a thumbs-down gesture and a vigorous nodding of her companion's head. "I got her to volunteer here just so I can keep her near me when I can. I'm just going crazy. I don't know what to do."

They smiled at Sarah as she entered the room again.

The nurses had taped the IV needle to Levi's arm and said he could soon have his breakfast. He dried his eyes clumsily and sniffled. Then he told Sarah that the nurses about killed him with that long needle.

"You'll be okay, honey."

The largest gray-haired nurse adjusted the IV bag and said that if that needle was not in his hand he wouldn't get better. Levi watched her face, his features inscrutable, and then announced loudly that if he didn't get something *chide* (right) away for breakfast, he wasn't going to make it anyhow. They laughed in delight, both nurses chuckling together, and promised him pancakes.

"I want shoofly!" That really got them laughing, and Sarah laughed with them. "I mean it. I'm terrible hungry for shoofly."

When his breakfast finally did arrive, Sarah watched Levi's face as she lifted the heavy lid on the steaming plate—a small mound of lemon-yellow eggs of some questionable origin, a slice of dark wheat toast, a small pot of fruit cocktail, and black coffee. Poor Levi. It was only a fourth of his generous breakfast at home, and he began crying in earnest.

"*Vill net poshing* (Don't want peaches)."

Sarah glanced nervously out the door toward the nurses' station and explained hurriedly that he could have fried mush and shoofly when he got home, but would he please be good and eat this?

"*Vill chilly* (Want jelly)."

Relieved to find a packet of grape jelly, Sarah spread it on the wheat toast, which seemed to placate his despair. Levi ate the toast and all the eggs, but he refused the fruit, saying nobody eats peaches for breakfast. They are only for supper with chocolate cake and cornstarch pudding.

The small amount of food did seem to lift his mood somewhat, and he drank his coffee obediently before drifting off to sleep. Thankfully, he forgot about the promised pancakes.

Sarah settled herself in the enormous plastic-covered chair as best she could and opened an issue of *National Geographic* she'd brought from home. Dat said it was an expensive magazine but well worth it, with knowledgeable articles from around the world. Sarah loved it and read it carefully from cover to cover.

She immersed herself in an article about the Inca culture and then drifted off to sleep before waking with a start and reading on. Machines clicked and beeped, the voices of nurses rose and fell, carts wheeled past, clanking and whirring.

She was startled to see two doctors enter Levi's room wearing ties and expensive, perfectly pressed shirts beneath their open white coats. Sarah stood up, extended a hand, and answered their greeting. Then she listened politely to their diagnosis.

Levi's pneumonia was the result of his weakened immune system, which went with his declining heart condition. People with Down syndrome often have weak hearts. He would be given the best blood pressure medication and another pill to keep his heart rhythm as steady as possible, but exercise and diet would help as well.

Sarah's heart sank, imagining Levi on a restricted diet. Hoo-boy.

She nodded, answered their questions, and thanked them, relieved to see them disappear. Doctors were intimidating. They were smart, wealthy men who were held in high esteem by the Amish, or most of them.

Sarah could never quite grasp the exact meaning of their medical jargon, which made her feel insecure or embarrassed, sometimes both. She was not well-informed about medical terms. She was just an Amish country girl with an overweight brother who had a bad heart, evidently.

Oh dear. Would Dat and Mam be able to pay all Levi's medical bills as time went on? Well, one thing was sure: in these matters, when medical expenses climbed out of control, the alms of the church were always there with the deacon kindly offering assistance wherever it was needed.

Her people did not believe in insurance, choosing instead to place their trust in God and the support of the church, as in times past. But as medical costs continued to escalate to exorbitant levels, the Amish had developed their own aid plan—Amish Aid. Sarah knew that church members made monthly payments into the plan's fund. When a family faced a medical issue requiring hospitalization or extensive care, Amish Aid stepped in to help with covering the costs. Sarah also knew that the Aid plan was somewhat controversial. While it was a necessity for some families, it was shunned by others.

Dat had been a man of means, but now? The fire damages had exceeded his Amish fire insurance and put Dat into an unexpected financial free fall. And then there had been the funeral expenses.

Well, Sarah would get a job, that's all. She was still waiting to hear from that Emma. Likely Hannah had made it all up. She had said she needed someone to work at her bakery, but where was she now?

Levi whimpered and burrowed into his pillows. Immediately, Sarah leaped to her feet, afraid he'd pull on some needles or tubes. She watched over him carefully.

Sarah looked up with surprise when she saw Ben Zook *sei* Anna come breezing through the door, her brilliant lime green dress certainly doing nothing to hide her size. Her face was alight with interest, her pretty eyes smiling pleasantly, her white teeth gleaming evenly.

"Sarah!"

"Anna! What brings you in here?"

"Oh, that Lee. He... I couldn't tell him a thing. Mind you, that arm is so infected, he plum down has blood poisoning. He could have died. He cut himself with the blade he used to..."

She stopped and looked at Levi. "Oh my, he looks so sick. Is he any better at all?"

"Yes. Oh yes. He was moved from the ICU."

Anna bustled over and put her arms around Sarah. She gave her a squeeze, patted her back, and said she had to be off as they were taking Lee to his room from the ER.

"He has a temperature of 102 and everything," was her parting line, her bright green dress disappearing with a swish.

Sarah sat back in her chair. She was staying here at the hospital until morning, which now seemed a bit unsettling somehow. Should she go see Lee? Say hello? She supposed she could walk into his room and say, I told you so, but as far as she knew, no one likes to hear that, especially men.

Oh, she'd stay right here. She wouldn't go. It would be too bold of her with him lying in a hospital bed. He'd be ashamed of the fact that he was there, and she had no business visiting him. No, she wouldn't go.

The day slowly wore on, the clock hands moving to the noon hour. Levi awoke grumpy and hungry, asking for shoofly pie or at least a bowl of Corn Flakes.

Sarah told him he had to wait till lunchtime, when they'd bring his dinner. The meal eventually arrived. On his tray they found steamed fish—unsalted, of course—bilious green beans, and macaroni and cheese. He threw a fit of rage, and Sarah had to call the nurses to adjust the IV tube in his hand.

Overwhelmed and tired of the too bright room, the green paint, the slippery chair, Sarah scolded him with words of serious rebuke, telling Levi if he didn't behave she was going to call a driver and go home. The scolding left him in such a state of repentance that he ate every bite of the healthy food on his dinner tray, drank all the ginger ale, belched loudly, and said he wanted to watch TV.

"No, Levi."

"Why?"

"It costs something, I think."

"You can pay."

"Dat wouldn't approve."

Levi's eyes narrowed, and he told Sarah that Dat wasn't there, that if he walked in, he'd turn it off as fast as he could. Sarah laughed but remained adamant.

The telephone by his bed rang, and Sarah answered. It was Mam, and she wanted to talk to Levi. He grabbed the receiver and proceeded to air all his grievances about the food, and how mean Sarah was, and could she bring shoofly pie in the morning?

Well, he didn't know. Surely, Sarah could ask the doctors, he told Mam.

After Mam promised to bring him food, Levi handed the receiver to Sarah. Then as she turned her back, he pressed the call bell attached to the rail on his bed. Sarah hung up quickly when a nurse appeared inquiring about Levi's needs.

"I want to watch TV."

Patiently, the nurse brought the remote, showed him what buttons to press, and how to change the channels before she left. Sarah decided to keep her peace and see how well Levi would follow instructions.

First, he pulled himself upright as far as possible, then clutched the narrow, black device, and began a laborious process of selecting the button that "made it go," muttering to himself. When nothing happened, he asked for his glasses, perched them on his nose, and bent over the remote once more. After he located the proper button, the TV flashed to life. Another round of muttering, another painstaking attempt at "something else," and then he found a channel about wild animals.

What wonders flashed before his eyes! It was a story-book come to life, the elephants of Tanzania roaming the plains, their leaf-like ears flapping in slow motion.

He chortled and pointed and said, "*Gook mol!* (Look here!)" over and over until he simply wore himself out. He fell asleep with the remote clutched firmly in his hand.

He told the nurse later that afternoon that he had seen elephants. He hadn't known their ears were so busy. She told him he should have ears that big to keep the flies away. Levi considered what that would be like and then told her that if his ears were that big, his wool hat wouldn't fit to go to church.

Oh, the nurses loved him alright, and Levi enjoyed every minute of their teasing, always coming back with sharp answers.

By five o'clock, Sarah was still making up excuses for herself for not going to say hello to Lee. She was not combed. Her hair was a mess. Her covering wasn't neat. What would she say? She didn't know him. He didn't know she was there. Or would Anna have told him? Probably.

She was ravenous, having skipped lunch. Levi would be alright until she returned, so she told him she was going to get a sandwich and that she'd bring it back as soon as possible. He barely heard her, engrossed in another animal show.

Sarah hurried down the hall with her purse slung over her shoulder. She looked neither left nor right on her mission the cafeteria.

Again she saw Ashley Walters, who was evidently now intent on avoiding Sarah, and ducked into an elevator with an open door. Sarah wondered why Ashley suddenly seemed so afraid. She wasn't at first, when she sat down at Sarah's table at breakfast. Perhaps she had become ill at ease with Sarah being Amish and all.

Still. Sarah pondered Ashley's hasty retreat after she had confirmed that their barn was one of those that burned down last spring. Did Ashley have some connection, some knowledge of the barn fires? Surely not this sweet, hesitant girl.

Levi came home from the hospital with his ego greatly inflated. His knowledge of wild animals had grown to the point that he took it upon himself to educate every member of the family about lions, giraffes, and just about every other creature that roamed the African grasslands. Suzie was intrigued at first, and Priscilla pretended to be bored, but she actually listened in her own sly way.

So life resumed its normalcy again. Mam finished the housecleaning, and Sarah sewed new dresses for the upcoming wedding season.

When Sunday arrived, Dat's face became drawn, worry clouding his keen eyes. He sat reading his German Bible, his mouth moving as he memorized and prepared for the sermon he would be expected to preach.

The truth was that his ministry had never weighed heavier on his shoulders. It seemed to drain his life's blood. He was tired from the lack of support from the members of his congregation.

Davey Beiler's *ihr* (own) Priscilla had done wrong, and it was not easily forgotten. Now their Levi had been in the hospital again, Mervin was dead, and the barn had been burned at the hand of an arsonist. It seemed God was concerned about the family. Well, no wonder. Look at his sons, the way they carried on with that roofing and siding business, showing no interest in taking over the family farm.

Although that was the thinking of only a handful of people, to David Beiler it was a handful too many. The intricate pattern of love and fellowship was unraveling, destroying the age-old heritage of one for all and all for one, a beautiful design only God could have woven.

David felt the loose threads when he stood up to preach, and his throat constricted with fear, with failure looming on the horizon like a midsummer hailstorm. The black cloud to the west was predictable, but the strength and fury of the storm was not.

So he wavered, the crumbling of his spiritual post a genuine threat. His knees shook, his hands clenched and unclenched, and he stood wordless.

Mam, seated in front of him on a folding chair, bowed her head even farther, her lips moving in prayer. Nervous members of the congregation shuffled their feet as the ticking of the plastic clock on the shop wall became deafening.

Someone cleared his throat, which seemed to jolt David back to life. He began speaking, choked, and stopped.

Anna Mae, sitting in the women's row, watched her father's face, and quick tears of sympathy formed. Her Dat had had too much. Sarah was horrified. Please, please. She silently begged for help without forming the actual words of a prayer. Priscilla sat like stone, her face blanched of color.

Then it seemed as if God supplied his needs, and he spoke, softly, lovingly but with power. He left nothing back. He told them of the heaviness of his heart, the silent, cunning way the devil was weaving a pattern of his own, destroying the perfect will of God. There was evil among them, but that evil could not enter into the fold unless they allowed it.

Two barns had burned by the hands of someone who meant harm. A young child had died. Let it not once be named among them to berate, to gossip. Instead, they needed to hold themselves accountable, one to the other.

Small human minds cannot think as God does. Where there is suspicion, hate, backbiting, and bickering—the devil's own handiwork—the church community needed to replace it with love and forbearance, brother to brother, supporting, upholding, forgiving. God is not mocked.

The conviction that fell was terrible, weighing down guilty members as David Beiler bared his soul. They had never heard anything like it. Old Sylvia Riehl said it was time the poor man spoke from the heart, as she cut a piece of snitz pie at the table later in the day.

For now, God had triumphed.

CHAPTER 18

MAM STOOD AT HER IRONING BOARD AS THE LATE
November sun slanted through the kitchen window. Her
right arm moved rhythmically, pressing the new black
cape and apron she'd finished that afternoon.

The maple leaves were gone, and the trees looked
unclothed, exposed to the chilly winds that warned of
snow but were unable to produce it. The brown, dried up
remnants of leaves that clung bravely to the cold branches
of the oak trees rustled in the steady breeze, as if their
perseverance allowed the Beiler family a tenacious hold
on autumn. It was wedding season.

Mam suppressed a sigh of weariness. Every Tuesday
and every Thursday, starting the last week in October,
after communion services were over, the weddings moved
along in full swing. Fifteen of them this year. That meant
invitations to fifteen weddings for David Beiler, who was
invited along with Malinda for any number of reasons—
as a minister, an uncle, a friend.

Monday mornings for Mam meant laundry. During
wedding season that task included cleaning the black
mutza (suit or coat) and woolen hats, ironing extra

coverings and white shirts, polishing black Sunday shoes, and making sure there were plenty of snowy white handkerchiefs pressed and in the top bureau drawer for her husband. Priscilla's job was to wash and polish the buggy.

Sarah had been called to go with Hannah's sister, Emma, and her husband, Amos, to work at their large, bustling bakery at the farmer's market in New Jersey, about a hundred miles away. Every Friday and Saturday morning, the market van picked up Sarah at three thirty and returned her at eight o'clock in the evening. She seemed to float on pure adrenaline now, dashing down the stairs, banging the front door so the picture on the wall rattled, eager to be a part of the new world she had discovered.

Secretly, Sarah felt pretty in her white bib apron. When she learned to ring up orders on the electric cash register, she felt very worldly indeed. A real career girl. She loved the atmosphere of the huge farmer's market. There was a constant rush to mix, bake, wrap, and display the pies and cakes, the bread and cookies, the cupcakes and cinnamon rolls—the list was endless. Sarah rose eagerly to the challenge.

She was a farm girl, her arms rounded, strong, and muscular. So the fifty-pound bags of flour and sugar were no problem, the endless rolling of pie crusts no big deal. She smiled easily and was always friendly and helpful to the other workers. Emma watched and noticed. She wondered why she hadn't asked Sarah to be a bakery girl before.

The only downside was the lack of sleep, which often caused her to doze off during the three-hour church service on Sundays. She also had trouble staying awake late on Saturday nights with her girlfriends.

But she had money in her wallet now and a savings account at the Susquehanna Bank without her parents' names on it. If she wanted to purchase a framed piece of art from the craft shop, she could. Or if she wanted to surprise Levi with a new trinket or game, she could do that too. It was absolutely liberating, this new job.

Now the weddings had arrived, and Sarah found she could exist on very little sleep, returning home late every Thursday evening for just a bit of sleep before the alarm rang in the middle of the night—or so it seemed at three o'clock.

The family was wearing black at every wedding this year, since they were still in mourning for Mervin. Sarah had sewn not one, but two new dresses, capes, and aprons, so she still felt as if she was dressed in wedding finery despite their somber color.

She went to Mam at her ironing board to ask if the coverings were ready for tomorrow's wedding. Mam shook her head.

"That's next."

"What should I do?"

"Well, you can make Levi's bed. Just use the clean blue sheets in the bathroom closet. I doubt if the wash is dry yet."

"I'd rather put on the fresh ones, from off the line."

"Alright with me."

Sarah sat on Dat's chair, leaned back, and watched Mam lift and inspect the new apron. She nodded with satisfaction, folded it in half, then again, and hung it carefully on a plastic hanger.

Sarah opened her mouth then closed it as she gazed through the kitchen window at the brown oak leaves. Finally she said, "Mam."

Absentmindedly, Mam said "Hmm?" as she resumed her ironing.

"Rose and Matthew broke up."

"Did they?"

Mam had not really heard Sarah, her own thoughts preoccupying her. Suddenly she stopped the rhythmic movement of the sadiron and asked, "What did you say?"

"Rose and Matthew broke up."

"Oh, my goodness! Who did it?"

"Rose."

Mam's face went pale, her thoughts whirling, stirred to hurricane force by the ensuing tragedy that was sure to follow. She was scared of the torrential rain, the spiritual and emotional blast that could sweep away her daughter in its terrifying grip. Her lips pale, compressed, she asked flatly, "Why?"

"We talked almost all night, Rose and I. Mam, I feel so sorry for her. She has no real reason. He's everything she always imagined her boyfriend to be. Yet she feels empty and drained, she said. She wants to stay away from him at least a month to see if her feelings change."

Mam pursed her lips, folded the black cape, and hung it neatly on the same hanger. "Oh, they all say that."

Sarah was astounded and looked sharply at her mother's pale face, the too-bright eyes. There was a sharp edge in her soft voice. "She wants someone else. You know that," Mam added.

The words were flung at Sarah with a strange intensity before Mam turned, walked swiftly into her bedroom, and closed the door with a firm "thwack" behind her.

"*Die Mam iss base!* (Mam is angry!)" Levi shouted gleefully from the sofa, where he lay with a stack of catalogs, looking for horses.

Sarah felt a warm flush rise on her face. She knew. She knew with a sickening certainty what had upset her mother. It was the idea of Matthew being free. Free to ask her. Free to be hers!

Unable to stay seated, Sarah jumped up, ran up the stairs, and flung herself on her bed, her chin in her cupped hands, her feet in the air, the old house slippers dangling as she dreamed.

God had answered her prayers! He had put her through the fire, brought her patience, and now he was delivering her into a brand new day, one of hope, one rosy with the glow of a new future. Her whole room was infused with the light of her love for Matthew, a golden yellow halo that transformed the very color of the walls. Her world had come crashing about her, righted itself, and turned to its original color.

Then the dark form of her mother appeared in the doorway. "Sarah, I'm asking you to listen to me, this one time. I know it may not make a difference to you, but I don't feel right saying nothing at all."

Sarah rolled over, sat up, and pushed her feet into her slippers. The sun disappeared behind a gray November cloud, bringing a sense of unrest and dread into Sarah's bedroom. She looked at the ratty old slippers and wondered why she'd kept them so long. Dropping to the recliner in the corner, Mam squared her shoulders, folded her hands, and began to speak.

"I know how it is for you. You fancy yourself in love with Matthew. You always have. My soft mother's heart wants to tell you that you can have him. God has answered your prayers, and this may be so. I hope it is. But you must face reality. It was Rose that broke up, not Matthew, which means nine chances out of ten, he's heartbroken, and he wants her back."

"You don't know!" Sarah's voice was raw with fierce denial.

Mam remained silent, holding Sarah's intense gaze with the kindness in her own. Sudden confusion caused Sarah to lower her eyes.

"No, I don't." Mam said softly.

The wisdom Mam had gleaned through her years of experience helped her accept the truth: Sarah had built an impenetrable wall of fantasy around herself. She stood up, brushed imaginary dust from her apron, and said, "I wish you God's blessing, my daughter." She walked softly to Sarah's bed and held Sarah in her arms. The moment was warm with love put firmly in place, because it never failed.

Patting the shapely shoulders, Mam stepped back and quipped, "So, if the waters get rough, I guess I'll sit beside you in your little rowboat and row for dear life!"

Sarah smiled hesitantly at her mother, and they laughed together softly. Why, then, did she flop back on her bed and stare at the ceiling? She didn't know she was crying until something tickled her ears, and she recognized the wetness sliding down each side of her face. Immediately, she sat up, grabbed a Kleenex, and went to the window, gazing out through the gray branches of the maple trees, seeing nothing.

She had never dressed with more care or anticipation. She combed and patted, moussed and sprayed her hair, until finally she achieved the perfect sleekness she sought.

Black it would have to be, but a new black, the fabric full-bodied with a bit of a ripple, not too fancy, not too plain. She successfully pinned the cape after three or four tries, satisfied that each pleat was just the right length down her back. Then she pinned the apron snugly about her waist.

She had just pinned and tied her new white covering on her head when she heard the obnoxious air horn on Melvin's buggy. He had attached it to the twelve-volt battery beneath the floor of the buggy in its own box, riding low above the road.

Dabbing a small amount of her favorite fragrance on her wrists, she grabbed a few Kleenexes and ran downstairs, where Levi sat with his coffee and shoofly pie, yelling lustily that Melvin was there.

"Bye, Levi. You be good for Priscilla!" She grabbed his arm, kissed his forehead, and left him swabbing the spot with his red handkerchief and a smile on his face.

Priscilla didn't respond. The longing in her eyes was too intense. Weddings were off-limits for fourteen-year-olds, except for cousins or close friends, so her lot was to stay home with Levi, get Suzie off to school, and sometimes babysit her nieces and nephews. That was fun for a while until the day wore on, and they became tired and cranky, and Levi teased them without mercy.

When Priscilla complained to Mam, Mam said Ruthie and Elmer were extremely sociable, staying at weddings until the last song was sung, and yes, Ruthie could be more considerate of Priscilla's long day with the children.

Levi shook his head after the *kesslehaus* door closed behind Sarah. "Boy, the flies shouldn't bother her today," he mused before cutting off a large chunk of shoofly pie with the edge of his fork.

Melvin was in a sour mood, scolding her for being late and saying, "Watch out for the heater, there."

Sarah pressed her knees together and clasped her hands in a grip that gave away her eagerness. Melvin watched from the corner of his eye. Buster trotted briskly, his ears forward in a perfect circular shape, his tail lifted, his steps high.

Sarah smiled to herself. No use wasting it on vinegar-infused Melvin. Sour old bachelor. It wasn't her fault he hated weddings.

Silence pervaded every inch of the buggy. Not a good, comfortable silence, but one ripe with unspoken thoughts. Well, she'd wait. Melvin could never stay quiet very long, and she knew the subject that he'd tackle the minute he put his prickly pride behind him.

The air was damp, the skies overcast, but there was a telltale line of blue to the west, emerging as the thick gray blanket of morning clouds moved on.

Sarah was glad to see the pretty blue sky approaching. Susan and Marvin deserved a beautiful wedding day. They were both only twenty years old, so young, but they had been dating for more than two years, almost three. The parents had given their consent, saying it was better to marry young than to be dating too long.

They would occupy the small Cape Cod on the Miller farm, paying minimal rent, a favor Dan Miller presented to young couples to give them *an guta schtart* (a good start).

Susan would be so happy, decorating and painting her cute little house and cooking supper for her beloved Marvin with the brand new stainless steel cookware her mother had purchased from the traveling *Kessle Mann* (cookware salesman).

Sarah inhaled happily, then exhaled quietly, warily watching Melvin from the side. Yes, her chance of marriage fluttered a victory flag on the horizon. Soon. Oh, just soon.

Melvin's voice broke into the silence. "I guess you feel like the cat that got all the cream."

"Why?"

"You know why."

"Why?"

"You know."

Sarah laughed, elation rounding out the happy giggle that rolled from an overflowing heart.

"Well, I can't help it they broke up."

"It was her, Tub said."

"Yeah."

"So, that could mean he's still in love with her. Likely he's heartbroken, his pride shattered. He probably won't be at the wedding, if I know Matthew right."

There it was again. This dark prediction, a pressing insecurity flung about her shoulders by someone she loved.

Instantly, a quick retort rose to push back the cloak of doubt. "You don't know, Melvin. He may not be heartbroken at all. Perhaps he's...well, sort of glad it's over. Maybe he was bored with Rose. Her...her...perfection, or whatever."

Melvin snorted so vehemently he had to lean over so he could extricate his white handkerchief.

"He never once got bored with her!" he burst out.

"You don't know," Sarah countered forcefully.

Then, neither one having the wisdom born of experience, their youth rolling the losing dice, their barbed conversation turned into an argument, albeit a polite one, as cousins tend to do. Buster trotted up to the Reuben Stoltzfus farm pulling a gray and black buggy with an invisible cloud of dissension hanging above it.

Yes, Matthew was there. Sarah watched the long row

of boys file in, her fevered gaze latching onto the sight of him with much the same intensity that a drowning man grasps a life preserver. See, Melvin.

Her lips curling with her own sense of victory, she lowered her eyes, afraid to look up, afraid not to. When she dared, she peered between heads and shoulders until she found him, gazing at the floor. Oh well, she had a whole wedding service ahead of her to try to gauge his mood. Hadn't she become quiet adept at it over the years?

There was, however, one thing that troubled her. Rose. She'd been so wan and pale, her face aged with the trial she'd gone through, her beautiful eyes clouded with indecision, or fear, or... what? Sarah didn't know. What if she wanted him back now that he was no longer hers?

The opening song was announced, and great waves of the ageless plainsong rolled evenly across the clean, painted woodworking shop as the approximately four hundred invited guests joined their voices in the wedding hymn.

Chills chased themselves up Sarah's spine. She joined in, reveling in the opportunity to be one with the group of singers. She loved to sing in church, and weddings were even better. So many voices blended in song were *himmlisch* (heavenly), and she could easily imagine a host of angels singing as they did.

Then she looked up, straight into Matthew's eyes, which confused her so much, she stopped singing. Goodness. What in the world? What was wrong with him? Surely it couldn't be that bad. His eyes were dark pools of misery, so bad, in fact, that she hardly recognized him.

Well, she'd remedy that, as soon as she was able.

After dinner, the single girls stood outside against the shop wall, waiting for the single young men to choose

them to accompany them to the long tables to sing wedding songs and have cold punch and pizza or soft pretzels or some other special treat. Sarah was afraid, truly
terrified, her breath coming in gasps, quick and hard.
She could feel the warmth and color leave her face. She
became quite dizzy, her head spinning, but sheer willpower righted it and kept her feet solidly on the ground.

Then they came, led by a young married brother of the
bride, who was teasing and laughing to put the nervous
young men at ease.

From beneath lowered lashes, she saw a few boys each
pick a girl. They walked away together to spend the afternoon seated next each other at the long wedding table.
She watched Lee approaching, surprised to feel a rush of
companionship. Merely friendship though.

Through a blur, her heart hammering in her chest, she
saw Lee approach Rose, his eyes questioning her. With
a small smile, she moved away with him. My, what a
couple they'd make! A ripple of teasing and good-natured
calls of praise rose from the crowd, and Lee ducked his
head, smiling.

Matthew! Swaggering just a bit, desperately trying to
conceal his self-consciousness, he strode up to Sarah and
extended a hand. She grasped it with fierce possessiveness.

No words formed thoughts, no thoughts could
describe her feelings as she followed Matthew to the table
and sat on the long bench beside him.

He looked at Sarah, said, "S'up?"

She giggled, shamelessly, gladly, unreservedly.

Oh, just look away, Mam. Just look away right now,
with all the senseless fear and doubt in your troubled
eyes. Nothing, not Mam, not Melvin, not the tides of time

would remove Matthew from within her grasp. Not now. Please. Not now.

They sang together, they talked, they shared a butterscotch sundae, they ate soft pretzels dipped in melted cheese. And all the years of yearning, the prayers, the patience had finally come to fruition for Sarah.

Somewhere, in some distant corner of her mind, a persistent little voice kept interfering, an unwanted dose of reality that she couldn't completely ignore. This thing of going to the "afternoon table" was not very promising, after all. Often young men would choose a friend, someone who was easy to spend time with, an acquaintance. So, for that reason alone, Sarah could not become overconfident. Still, he had chosen her. That knowledge alone overrode the reality, which she put aside easily.

"So," Matthew was asking. "What do you think of me and Rose breaking up?"

Surprised, Sarah looked at him, but his eyes gave nothing away.

"I...I don't know."

"Yeah, me either."

The words were dull, flat, weighted down with bitterness.

"She says a month. I told her if she broke up with me I was going to go English. I mean it. If I can't have Rose, I'm not going to stay Amish. There's no point in it."

Babbling incoherently now, Sarah tried to make him see that he couldn't leave his family. He'd break his mother's heart. And mine, Matthew, and mine. It's pulverized already. How could I bear it?

Her thoughts wove themselves painfully into her mind, her mouth speaking the accepted words, her mind thinking the unaccepted ones.

The pain of his words was too great to bear. He was still in love with Rose. Her mind refused to comprehend it. But maybe he only thought he was still in love. Sarah could change him. She could win.

Lifting her shield, adjusting her armor, she prepared herself for the battle of her life, knowing she must be brave and courageous. She resolved to pray without ceasing, and God would bless her. Wouldn't He?

She lifted miserable pools of stormy seawater green eyes and found the blue of Lee Glick's upon her, his blond hair shining like the sun about him. In that blue, there was rest and comfort. She wanted to stay there in that calm. It was mesmerizing, a cascade of pure, clear, no, blue water. She had to tear her eyes away.

And Lee did not know it was possible to feel what he felt for Sarah on that sun-infused November afternoon. It was far more than he imagined love to be. It was a sweet and tender pity, a cradling of her troubled head to his chest, coupled with the wonderful knowledge that God, who was fairly new to him, would do what He would. Lee only had to bow his head and accept it.

Unknowingly, he laid his sacrifice on the altar.

CHAPTER 19

"ASHLEY!"

"Sarah!"

Again the two girls met, this time in the middle of the crowded farmer's market. People milled about them, shoving, moving from one stand to another to buy fresh produce or cheese or a pound of freshly butchered grass-fed organic beef or eggs laid by hens who pecked about in pure grasses free of pesticides.

Restaurants at the market catered to every taste—Italian, Chinese, Amish home cooking, American cheeseburgers and fries—a vast melting pot of ethnicity. The flea market stands sold leather goods, jewelry, and antiques. Others sold furniture crafted who knows where but labeled "Amish." The whole market was a wonderful place to walk aimlessly and enjoy the smells, the sights, the people.

Sarah didn't think Ashley would stay to talk, but she lingered long enough to exchange pleasantries. Ashley's father had a flea market stand where she worked. She inquired politely about Levi's well-being but then said she must be on her way.

"We'll likely keep running into each other, won't we?" she asked, backing away, waving.

Sarah gasped as Ashley backed straight into a large column and slid down to the floor, her legs crumpling without resistance. Lowering her head she giggled uncontrollably, her stringy brown hair hanging stiffly on either side.

Sarah hunkered down, pulled her skirt over her knees, and asked if Ashley was alright.

"Oh, yeah, yeah. Jus' fine."

Still laughing, Ashley got to her feet and wandered off with a haphazard wave of her hand. Puzzled, Sarah shrugged her shoulders and went on her way, already five minutes into a half-hour break. She hurried to the Kings' restaurant, where Rose served tables, found an empty spot, and hoped Rose would be the one to wait on her.

Here, in this crowded place with the homey, checkered tablecloths, she could get a twelve-inch hoagie loaded with anything she wanted and a glass of water for five dollars (Pepsi cost two dollars). She rarely spent more than that on her break. She'd eat half of the delicious sandwich, mayonnaise squeezing from the sides of her mouth, pickle juice soaking the crusty home-baked wheat roll, and then take the remaining half in a Styrofoam container to eat later, usually in the van on the way home while she elbowed the other girls away.

Rose came bustling over, clapping a hand to her forehead while sliding into her booth. "I'm beat!"

"Busy?"

"Just run ragged. Where do all the people come from?"

Sarah shook her head.

"You want your usual hoagie?"

"I'm starved. Put plenty of ham on it."

Rose hurried off, her small frame neat and compact, her sky-blue dress and white apron giving her a celestial quality.

When Rose returned with the oversized sandwich and a tall glass of ice water with a thick slice of lemon, Sarah squeezed in the lemon, added a few packets of sugar, and stirred as she half-listened to Rose's encounter with an extremely harried boss.

"So, how are you? For real," Sarah asked.

"I don't know. Okay, I guess. One day I feel sorry for Matthew, the next I miss him. I'm all mixed up."

"Do you want Melvin and me to pick you up Saturday night?"

"No."

"Why not?"

"Oh, I don't know. I'll find someone to take me."

"Whatever."

"Yeah."

With an awkward wave, Rose moved off, her eyebrows lifted a few notches too high in Sarah's opinion. So, she was too good for her and stodgy Melvin. Well, that was fine with her. Melvin acted too bizarre around Rose anyway, trying to impress her with his stretched truths and weird rambling on and on about nothing. But then, most young men did that around Rose. Melvin was only being normal.

After a long Friday at the bakery, the two-hour ride home was a welcome reprieve. The market girls slouched in various positions, pillows stuffed into any available corner, and tried to gain back a bit of sleep. The van moved along with the four lanes of traffic, the lights stretching out from the fast-moving vehicles in an unbroken line, until they reached the darkness of the country.

The back roads of Lancaster County were always tedious, heads sliding, bobbing, as the driver maneuvered the van as efficiently—and as swiftly— as possible.

Half-asleep, Sarah jostled against Rachel Zook, who jabbed her elbow into Sarah's arm.

"Look! What is that?"

"What?"

Sarah blinked, sat up, and peered out the window. She could see nothing out of the ordinary. She kept watching and saw a few lights, some buildings, the night etched in black and gray. Absolutely nothing unusual.

"There it is again!" Rachel hissed.

Sarah pulled back, grimacing. Whew, Rachel must have had Italian food for lunch. A strong garlic odor was escaping from her mouth in great, steaming billows.

"There!"

Rachel pointed, and Sarah turned her head, more to avoid the garlic than to concern herself with the horizon. A grayish, almost white line hovered above the horizon, so nearly the same color as the rest of the night. Suddenly, a reddish glow burst up, like northern lights, and then disappeared.

"I see it!" Sarah whispered.

The van rolled to a stop at an intersection and allowed a car to pass, before continuing on the way home.

"Hey, Ike!" Rachel called, sending the rich odor of garlic wafting across the occupants of the back seat.

"Ew! Rachel, what in the world did you eat for lunch?" Rose grumbled, half-asleep.

Sarah burst out laughing, holding her stomach as tears of mirth squeezed between her eyelids. That was the best thing about market jobs—the companionship in this fifteen-passenger vanload of girls along with a few older people, all contained together in an oblong box of steel and metal hurtling through the night. The close proximity produced a bond of sisterhood.

Only sisters would be so honest as to blurt out about garlic breath, or so Sarah had thought when she first rode to market in that van. She soon learned differently. They fought for doughnuts, scrambled across seats for bits of soft pretzel, pinched, punched, pulled sleeves and coverings and hair, yelled and teased and hooted with joy, then one by one, they all fell asleep. The driver was usually a long-suffering individual who tried to be strict but enjoyed the antics as much as anyone else.

"Hey, Ike!' Rachel screeched again, causing Rose to turn her head and wave a hand furiously in front of her nose. "Look to the left!"

Sarah could see Ike's silhouette leaning forward, alert.

"What is going on?" he said finally.

The van slowed, the driver also craning his neck for a glimpse.

"It almost looks like northern lights," he observed.

"That's close to Bird-In-Hand. Or Monterey. Somewhere along 340."

The van rolled to a stop, heads popped up like corks, eyes blinking, the girls muttering questions. There— another finger of pinkish red, a gray sky stained by a color that was not really supposed to be there.

"Somepin's goin' on!" Ike observed, the driver's jargon rubbing off on him.

They all held their breaths as a sharp whistle stabbed the night somewhere behind them. Quickly, the driver turned the wheel to the right, and they drifted off the shoulder, the van leaning toward a ditch filled with cold, black water. A gleaming red and silver mammoth, flashing the power of its presence, plunged through the night, roaring past them and leaving the van rocking in its wake.

"Has to be a fire!" Ike said decidedly.

The driver pulled back onto the road and asked if they wanted to see what was going on. There were exclamations of agreements and some grumbling went up, but they had little choice—riding in the van being guided by their driver.

Sarah's heart began a frantic hammering as the light steadily grew more orange in color.

"It's another barn, I bet."

"I mean it, seriously."

"If it is, we're moving to New York."

"They can light fires in New York, too."

"You think?"

"Hey, be quiet. This isn't funny."

"Hush."

But only Sarah understood the terror of another barn fire. It was a stake driven through her heart, producing memories of their fateful night. She began to shake uncontrollably as more fire trucks zoomed past, their engines whining and sirens screaming, bringing back memories of the smoke and flames, the charred dirty water after it had soaked the burning timbers and hay and straw. The fire had cruelly licked at the docile cows, annihilated the living, breathing horses, and thrown the gently, obedient creatures into a living hell of pain and fear.

When they came upon the scene, they stayed back, away from the red-faced, shouting fire-police volunteer who was whipping his green fluorescent flag in frenzied circles. The barn behind him had turned into a massive inferno of pain and torment. The flames whipped away from the barn toward the house, which stood close to the barn, separated only by the driveway and a small block of lawn.

The market workers decided to get out of the van. But Sarah could not move, her eyes pools of horrified memories. A great cry arose from the crowd as the small flames rolled along the asbestos shingles, the house clearly in grave danger.

"Sarah, come. We're walking across the field for closer look."

"Come on!"

The girls took off across the field as Sarah slowly got up and moved to the van door. Her heart pounding frantically, she gripped the vinyl handle and lowered herself slowly to the ground. Her intentions were to follow the small flock of girls, led by Ike and the driver, but the nausea rose swiftly in her throat and gagged her.

The whole world tilted dangerously to the right, then whirled recklessly around her. She lifted her hands to steady herself, but there was nothing to hold her up. She was being spun into a black vortex, the hot bile rising in her throat. She was as helpless as the brittle, brown leaves whirling through the cold November air. She was aware of making hoarse sounds, then mewling helplessly before she was gratefully erased to oblivion.

She thought she was at home, being sick in her bed, so she leaned over, her hands searching for the small wicker wastebasket with the Wal-Mart bag in it. She retched miserably over and over and tried to lift her head, but the dizziness was too severe.

When the rough stubbles of the alfalfa plants pierced the skin on her cheek, she became half-conscious and confused as someone held her head, stroked her back, and murmured words of comfort.

"It's okay, Sarah. Don't feel bad. It's okay."

A long shudder passed through her, and she turned her head away, ashamed, aware of some person here with her, with these vehicles, these cars, on this dark, windy night. The dancing orange light across someone's head reminded her of why she had become ill and passed out like some eighty-year-old person with a weak heart.

"Oh my. I'm so sorry," she whispered.

Two hands slid beneath her arms, and she was lifted to a sitting position. She struggled to stay upright but kept leaning to the side until two arms held her firmly, a clean men's handkerchief wiped her face as she kept whispering apologies.

It was when he produced a stick of gum and the sharp smell of the Dentyne was held to her face that consciousness returned fully. Focusing through the haze of her blurred vision, she said, "Melvin!"

"No."

Confused, she gave up, accepted the chewing gum, and sagged weakly against her rescuer.

"It's me. Lee."

She blinked. Who? Lee who? Oh, him. Here she was, held against him by his own strong arms in this cold alfalfa field with the fire blazing uncontrollably beyond them, the now-distant forms of the other market girls silhouetted against the flames.

"I understand why you...why you were sick. Please don't feel bad. Your own fire hasn't been so terribly long ago."

In answer, she burrowed her face against his corduroy coat, which smelled of woodchips and steel and shaving cream. She burst into harsh, gulping sobs that tore from her throat, and he held her close and blinked back his own emotion.

"I am so sorry," she said, finally spent of the horror and sadness the night had invoked.

"It's okay."

"Can I get up now?"

"Do you want to?"

"I think I can."

She turned away, and he let his arms fall away obediently. A small cry followed as she teetered crookedly away from him. So he did the most natural thing in the world and reached out with both arms, pulling her against him. He held her there, leaving her with no choice but to apologize.

"The whole world is just spinning so crazily," she gasped.

"Yeah, well, so is mine," Lee answered.

"What? Are you getting sick too?"

She looked up into his face.

Yes, he was, he said, giving a small laugh.

"Sarah."

She was startled by the sound of his voice, the deep emotion that rose from his throat.

"I'm sick about that Matthew guy. And you."

Her face was only inches away, her eyes unfathomable, so large and dark and tortured with...

With what? Lee's courage failed him, his speech slid away, and silence replaced it. She bent her head. His arms stayed around her. When she lifted her head, she spoke the truth in a soft, quavering voice, the humiliation so heavy, it broke his heart.

"Lee, you have to understand. It's always been Matthew. Through school, through *rumspringa*, and now through Rose. I can't help how I feel about him. I have to wait."

Slowly, she pulled away, out of the unsettling circle of his arms. She turned her head to watch the roaring inferno beside them—the clanking of hoses, the voices of men, the roar of engines—and shivered.

Then she did something so surprising, he carried it in his memory for months. She stepped right back into the circle of his arms, grabbed the lapels of his work coat, and said, "But, Lee."

He had to bend his head to hear her voice. "I won't admit this to myself, hardly. But you...you are making this whole Matthew thing easier. Can you understand that?"

As he had never known the depth of his feelings for her, so had he never known the steely resolve, the desperate control he now needed to exercise over his desire to pour out his long-awaited love in a crushing embrace, just once touching his lips to hers, to allow her to feel his love. Just once.

When she stepped back, he gripped his hands behind his back to keep them from reaching for her, the emptiness unbearable now.

"I'll be honest, Sarah, okay? If you say it makes it easier, do you mean I may have a chance someday?"

She was going to say, "Don't wait for me, Lee." She really was. What she said was, "Your eyes are so blue. They remind me of a...a... This is dumb, Lee." She gave a low laugh. "Your eyes make everything easy. They're calm."

"Thank you, Sarah."

He decided he'd never care much for Ike Stoltzfus from that night on, appearing from nowhere like that, followed by a gaggle of market girls wanting to witness the latest devastation in their community.

The farm was owned by Reuben Kauffman. Everyone called him Reuby. He was a short, rotund fellow with vibrant blue eyes set in a ruddy, glowing face and a benevolence toward his fellow men creating a kind aura about him.

He lost everything. The house was almost completely ruined in addition to the barn.

The vinyl siding had buckled and crumpled as windows shattered into thousands of pieces from the heat of the gigantic tongues of flame. The force of the late autumn gusts that had brought the first serious cold from Canada down to eastern Pennsylvania propelled the fire. They said the plastic pots containing African violets melted down across the shelves straight onto Reuby *sei* Bena's clean, waxed kitchen linoleum. It was an awful mess.

They should have let the house burn to the ground, Mam said. They'd never get the smell of smoke out of the furniture, the rugs, and the clothes.

The following week, Sarah and Priscilla sat on either side of Levi, and Mam sat beside Dat in the spring wagon on the way to the Kauffman farm. The air was calm, harmless, almost an apology in its stillness. As Fred, the family's new driving horse, trotted briskly, the heavy woolen buggy blankets kept them warm against a late frost. They smelled the dry, dusty odor of corn fodder being baled in Jake King's corn field—or what remained of it.

The spring wagon hauled cardboard boxes and bags full of food from Mam's shopping spree. She had been busy visiting her favorite stores, and she beamed with the charity that bubbled from her heart for Reuby *sei* Bena. Poor woman. The poor family, losing everything like that, and they'd never hurt a flea.

Mam bought towels and sheet sets at JC Penney because they ran the best sales. She bought fabric and housewares at Country Housewares and a set of cookware at Nancy's Notions in Intercourse. She wished she'd known the children's sizes, but she bought black coats and bonnets of various sizes at Teddy Leroy's shoe store.

This would all be carried discreetly into the shop, placed quietly with the mound of charitable contributions, and no one would ever know that Davey Beiler *sei* Malinda had spent the more than eight hundred dollars her husband had given her, his heart overflowing with sympathy, driven by the need to help poor Reubys.

Hadn't they been through the same terrifying ordeal? How could they close their hearts or their pocketbooks now, when yet another family suffered an even greater loss? And most unsettling, what new troubles would this barn fire stir up?

David Beiler's heart quaked within him. A twitch began in the corner of his right eye when he drove past the knots of Amish men talking intensely, their beards wagging and hands gesticulating.

A horde of trained personnel came to the family's assistance. State police, some in unmarked police cars, the fire marshal, and the press were all trying yet again to make sense out of an unthinkable deed.

The arsonist, who had now struck three times in less than a year, was determined to create significant damage. He—or they (perhaps it was a group of individuals)—had swept a storm of fear, chaos, and havoc across the Amish community. Anyone starting a fire on a night like that, the wind howling and screaming through the darkness, meant serious harm.

David got down and put the reins through the black ring in the harness. He was not surprised that his hands were shaking. Sarah and Priscilla, surveying the damage, inhaling the smells of leftover smoke and soaked debris, remained seated until Levi said he wanted down off that spring wagon, even if they were going to sit there all day.

CHAPTER 20

Eager helpers had walled off and insulated a corner of the implement shed. They would eventually install water lines and lay sturdy carpet over the power-washed cement. Reuby and his family would live there until their new home was built.

The women hosed down the furniture and washed it with a solution from the fire company. Then they washed it again with Pine-Sol or Mr. Clean or whatever the ladies of the surrounding area had brought. Then they polished it, but some of it would have to be refinished. They washed all the dishes, but very few of the fabric-covered items, clothes, or curtains could be salvaged.

The men had deliberated, but in the end, Reuby waved an arm and said, "Bring it down!"

It was hard for Bena to give up her home and possessions, Mam said. She'd hoped they could salvage the house and more of the belongings, but Reuby said the dry wall was wet, and the two-by-fours were charred and weakened, even if they were standing. There wasn't a window they could use.

So Bricker's Excavating had gone to work. Bena, short and squat, stood with her children gathered around her like homeless peeps, their faces aged with childish concern. They watched as immense yellow dozers with deafening diesel engines razed their home. Bena lifted her apron and found the white handkerchief she kept tucked away, held it to her nose, blew efficiently, and blinked back the small number of tears she allowed herself. She sniffed then turned, replaced her *schnuppy* (handkerchief), and herded her flock of children toward the implement shed. It was time to get to work.

Sarah, Priscilla, and their sister, Anna Mae, worked with Ben Zook *sei* Anna sorting half-burnt items still dripping from the water of the fire hoses. A large blue barrel marked "trash" stood to their right and cardboard boxes marked "kitchen" or "closet" or "bedroom" to their left.

One of the women filled a wringer washer with steaming hot water and powdered laundry detergent. Another filled the rinse tubs with warm water and Downy. They washed and rewashed the salvaged clothes only to raise them to their noses, sniff, and shake their heads. It was hopeless, so they sent for Reuby *sei* Bena.

"It's just so hard to part with some of these things," she said dully as if she was far away, in a world where she knew nothing of that terrifying night of howling wind that had sent dragons of flames onto her good sturdy house. She had imagined the house would always stand, keeping them safe and protecting them against the elements. She used to think nothing could destroy those four walls and the shingled roof.

Repeatedly, then, the women tossed wet items into the mouth of the blue plastic barrel marked "trash."

Anna looked up from the charred remains of a wooden toy box, the remaining toys lying soaked and blackened, a pile of innocence destroyed.

"Come here."

Sarah went over, looked into the toy box, and shivered. There were the usual plastic rings, trucks, a few Matchbox cars, and a stuffed horse, all shifted to one corner, blackened and gray with soot and soaked with water. A doll stared up at them, one eye opened, another one closed, in an eerie wink, the hair blackened and dirtied by the water, the little Amish dress and black pinafore apron sodden.

Sarah shivered again.

"It plain down gives me the creeps!" Anna said forcefully.

Sarah nodded then gazed out toward the steaming remains of the barn. Small pockets of blames continued to break out, stubbornly refusing to be quenched. In that moment, Sarah realized the Amish community was under siege and needed help from the English world. The danger had been grave before, but now, it was grim. Her beloved Dat could not sort this out alone. A whole band of Amish ministers and laymen could not keep this evil at bay.

Yes, they would pray and place their trust in God, the way they always did, but God was in heaven, and they were down here. And unlike the sparrows, they couldn't just sit on the fence. They needed to use the wisdom that God would provide.

Sarah wondered if this was how people felt in Iraq or Afghanistan or wherever it was that the war was still being fought. It was the falling away of normalcy, the community thrust into uncertainty by the power of barns burning at the hands of an arsonist, a monster without mercy who did not value human life or the lives of fault-less animals. Someone who wanted the Amish people to experience horror and fear, ridding them of the only safety they'd ever known: God and each other. For, really, how could God be trusted, if He allowed such tragedies one after another?

"Sarah, come on. Stop standing there like a statue with your eyes bulging out of your head!"

Anna Mae grabbed her arm. Sarah turned and shook free of the whirling mass of fear and doubt.

Ben Zook *sei* Anna straightened her ample body, rubbed her lower back, and asked if there was going to be a coffee break today or what. She was starving. They'd had a fresh cow that wouldn't accept the little bull calf, and she'd had an awful time of it, trying to get the silly thing to drink out of a bottle. Then she had no time for breakfast except a few potato chips while she was pack-ing lunches.

"I'm so hungry I'm going to fall over," she announced, her eyes mirroring her genuine distress.

"*Maid!* (Girls!)"

Anna whirled eagerly to the sound of Hannah Stoltzfus's voice.

"*Kommet, maid!* (Come, girls!)"

Anna dropped everything immediately, slid one arm through Sarah's, and propelled her along. Anna Mae and Priscilla followed, laughing at the round Anna with her arm through Sarah's, tall and thin beside her.

They waited politely as the men served themselves first, grabbing large Styrofoam cups of steaming coffee and a handful of cookies or doughnuts or a granola bar or a chocolate whoopie pie or a slice of coffee cake.

Anna was beside herself with glee. She planned what she would eat long before she could actually help herself to all the baked goodies spread in wonderful array on the plastic table, a dream come true, calories without worry. She'd have a blueberry doughnut first. Dipped in coffee, they were absolutely the best thing ever. But she would have to use a plastic spoon, the way they went to nothing so fast.

Then, after the doughnut, she would have a chocolate whoopie pie. She knew who made them, and she was talented. Not everyone made good whoopie pies. Nudging Sarah, she asked if she'd ever tasted Elmer Lapp's whoopie pies. The ones they sold at their produce stand? Well, she guessed if those tourists from New York City, the ones in the big buses, if they thought that's what whoopie pies were supposed to taste like, no wonder you couldn't buy them in their big city.

Anna was the first in line, chortling and smiling, stirring creamer into her coffee, when someone approached Sarah from the right, a large being hovering at her elbow.

Turning, she was pleasantly surprised to find Hannah, or Matthew's mother, as she always thought of her.

"Sarah, can I have a word with you?"

"Sure!"

They stepped away, Sarah trying desperately to hide her eagerness, her complete willingness to comply with any of Hannah's wishes.

"Sarah, did you talk to Matthew this weekend?"

"A little. Why do you ask?"

Hannah's eyes were feverish in their intensity.

"How did he seem?"

Sarah could not give her the answer she sought, knowing instinctively what Hannah wanted to hear, so she shrugged, turned her face away.

"Sarah?"

She was alarmed to hear the unprotected panic in Hannah's voice.

"Was he happy? Was he himself? He doesn't seem a bit heartbroken, now, does he? Huh? Does he?"

Without saying a word, Sarah shook her head from side to side, supplying the answer Matthew's mother wanted to hear, which wasn't really lying, just helping to soothe the poor woman's worries. How could she tell her of the devastation in his eyes? How could she stand here and tell his mother of the misery he carried like a shroud, enveloping himself against any overtures even she attempted?

Her face flamed now, thinking of the subtle ways she'd tried and failed. For without a doubt, Matthew was clearly heartbroken, the youthful exuberance gone, replaced with a lethargy, a sick pallor on his normally tanned face. He was hurting far more than Sarah had imagined.

"Well, if he's alright, then, I doubt if he'll ask her again, do you?"

"I don't know."

When Sarah spoke, it felt as if her tongue was covered with a woolen fabric that had thoroughly dried out her throat, and her words croaked, like a frog.

Hannah looked at her sharply.

Sarah cleared her throat.

"You're not telling me the truth," she hissed.

In response, Sarah turned and walked away as fast as she could, her eyes seeing nothing, her face revealing everything. She grabbed a cup of coffee, the array of baked things sickening her now, and rejoined Anna, was too busy dunking another blueberry doughnut to see the expression on Sarah's face. Looking up, she caught only a glimpse the fading anger.

"What got into you?" she asked in the forthright manner Sarah had learned to appreciate.

"Oh, Hannah."

"Hannah? Matthew's mam? Oh, I can only guess why, huh?"

Sarah nodded.

"She's probably hurting with poor Matthew. *Ach* my. That's so sad. I hate breakups. Hate them. They're mean and cruel and dumb."

The passion in her voice surprised Sarah. Turning, Anna went back to work, forgetting her heavily creamed coffee with the blueberry doughnut crumbs floating on top. Reuby's daughter, who was only two years old, ambled up to the cement block where Anna had left it, lifted the cup to her mouth, and drank every drop. She took the cup back to her mother and said very clearly, "*Ich vill may coffee* (I want more coffee)."

Anna remained closemouthed, her nostrils distended enough that Sarah knew she was still upset. Why would she be so worked up about Rose and Matthew's break up? What was it to her?

Her mind was taken off the prickly subject by the sight of her father standing with a group of men, his head bent in submission, as he listened to the voices around him. Sarah knew he wouldn't say much. It was her father's way. He'd listen, cultivate what he'd heard, think it through, and talk it over with Mam.

On the way home, the November sun seemed weak and ineffectual as it neared the line of trees to the west. The air was cold, and it would likely be colder tomorrow. She winced as a huge tractor trailer roared past, sending in a draft of frigid air that crept up under the woolen buggy robes, causing Priscilla to shiver.

"Poo!" Levi exclaimed.

"We're almost home," Mam answered calmly.

"They want to hold a meeting," Dat said quite unexpectedly.

"Who does?"

"The men of the surrounding districts."

"What about?"

"The barn fires."

"What are they going to do?" Mam's voice rose an octave, and her bonneted head turned toward Dat, who stared straight ahead, avoiding her intense gaze.

"I don't know. Something, they said. They think we should fight back."

"How?"

Dat shrugged.

"Oh my, Davey. This is very upsetting. How can anyone fight back? There is not much we can do."

"Levi's Abner wants to hire private detectives."

Mam lifted both hands and slapped them down in complete disbelief, sending up a few puffs of dust.

"But even an English detective wouldn't know where to start."

Dat nodded in agreement.

"I'll go to the meeting, likely. I just hope enough of us can come up with a peaceful solution to win over the hotheads."

He pulled on the left rein, an unnecessary maneuver, as Fred leaned toward the driveway without being told. They rode the remainder of the way in silence, then climbed off the spring wagon and walked into the house, each one separated by their own thoughts.

Levi's cough returned after the ride in the cold air, so Mam decided to stay home from the barn raising on Thursday. Emery Fender, the lumber-truck driver, would pick up Dat, so Sarah decided to drive Fred by herself.

Levi was terribly upset about staying home because of his cough. He cried, threatened, and pleaded with Mam, who stood her ground and said there was no way he was allowed to go, and that was that. To ease the pain, she promised him a pumpkin pie if he'd drink his tea with lemon and honey in it.

That evening Matthew walked up to the front door and asked Sarah if she wanted to ride with him the next day. After this unexpected piece of good fortune fell in her lap, she sang, smiled, and whistled her way through the rest of the evening.

Priscilla would go along, but she'd be in the back seat, and that was alright with Sarah. Oh, again, God had smiled down on her and blessed her with Matthew's presence, she thought the next morning as she combed her hair, hovering within inches of the mirror.

Mam asked both girls to mind their business, watch to make sure the men had enough water to drink, and to please stay away from photographers and reporters. She sized up Sarah's hair and covering, her eyes narrowing.

"Sarah, do you have on your good covering?"

Caught, Sarah thought resignedly. "Afraid I do," she trilled, trying to lift her mother to a lighter mood.

"Afraid you'll leave it here," Mam said dryly.

"Please, Mam. My other one fits so stupid. One side leans forward, no matter what I do with it."

"Sarah."

Oh, so she was going to treat her like she was still in

first grade, then. Instant rebellion sprang to life, like boiling water poured on coffee granules. "Mam," she said, fast and hard, "You are just mad that I'm going with Matthew. That's the only reason you don't want me to wear my best covering."

Mam opened her mouth, a sharp reprimand on her tongue. But she knew Sarah was right, and she knew she'd been caught red-handed trying to steal the small amount of courage Sarah had outfitted for herself by wearing the Sunday covering.

Wisely, Mam turned away, swallowing the sharp retort. She said no more, allowing Sarah the upper hand. She wisely guarded the open door that led to the complicated world of mother-daughter relationships, viewing the days that stretched both behind her and ahead of her.

How could daughters see right through you like that? How? It was annoying and maddening, all at once. Of course she didn't want Sarah to go with Matthew. She didn't trust him, didn't trust him one bit.

Then, because she was tired from having lain awake until all hours of the morning with her thoughts whirling about her—tormenting her, rendering her unable even to say a decent prayer, the state she was in—she waited till the girls ran out the door. Then she sat down on the old hickory rocker and covered her face with her apron and had a good long cry.

The string of barn fires, the insecurity they had brought, her Davey being so troubled, the loss of Mervin, her worries about Sarah and Matthew—suddenly and unexpectedly it all took its toll on Mam.

The ride with Matthew was less than comfortable. The buggy had no back seat, the way Matthew had it filled with sports equipment and clothes and all kinds of other stuff. Priscilla had to perch on the door ledge, leaving the cold wind pouring in the open door.

Matthew said if Sarah sat back, Priscilla could fit on the seat between them. But she refused, so she was cold the whole way. Matthew teased Priscilla and spoke only to her, looking at her entirely too much.

Sarah may as well have been a log or a length of stove pipe propped up in the corner, for all the attention he paid her. To make everything much worse, Priscilla continually giggled and smiled but also responded with an intelligence that seemed to intrigue Matthew.

After a few miles of this, he seemed to notice Sarah's lack of input, so he said, "Why so quiet, Sarah?" illuminating her world with the power of his kind, dark eyes.

Oh, Matthew. His eyes made her knees weak with the knowledge of her love. Never would she leave him. Never. She would always be here for him, waiting, hoping, and yes, praying that God would allow her to be his wife someday. His eyes were pools of kindness, of uplifting, of support, a wonderful boost to her faltering hope.

Could she help it, the waves of longing, the repressed love and devotion that held her in its unwavering grip? When she was with him, there was no doubt in her mind: It was always Matthew, and it would always be.

"I wasn't quiet," she said now, breathlessly, in spite of herself.

"Yeah, you were. But that's just you, anyhow. You're not as talkative as your sister. Hey, Pris, when will you be sixteen? When's your birthday?"

"November."

"Really? Wow! You'll be sixteen this month?"

"Fifteen."

"Aw, come on. You mean I have a whole year to wait?"

Priscilla blushed and became flustered. She looked into Sarah's eyes. Finding misery so raw, she did exactly the right thing and asked Matthew what he was thinking. He was way too old for her, seriously. And she no longer giggled.

Cold, disenchanted, her hopes dashed for the thousandth time, Sarah waited until Priscilla stepped down from the buggy before following her.

"Hey, don't I at least deserve a thank you?" he called after them.

"Oh, of course."

Sarah stopped, walked back, and thanked him, looking directly into the deep brown of his eyes, shoring up her resolve for the uncertain days and weeks and months ahead.

As if in another world, she heard the truck engines and the shouting voices, smelled the sharp odor of the new yellow lumber, as the many men dressed in black trousers and coats swarmed around the building site. They had already erected the main beams.

She guessed her love for Matthew was a lot like the barn fires, wasn't it? Dashed hopes destroyed by something so much larger than herself, only to be rebuilt, started anew, and continued on. But there was a growing uneasiness, a cold and dreadful realization, circling, circling, like wary wolves intent on their prey. She was keenly aware of Matthew's disinterest. She just couldn't let that control her hope. She had to keep moving. Fresh courage was her shield, her weapon, against the circling doubt. All was not lost.

The sound of hammers ringing against steel, the high whine of the chainsaws, the voices calling to one another—was it really happening again? The only thing that seemed real to her was the sound of the women, talking and laughing as they bent over the folding table with the dishpans containing potatoes and water, paring knives flashing as they peeled.

A stainless steel bucket piled full of potatoes fed a hundred, wasn't that right? Or was it two? And the same old spirited argument, paring knifes versus those Tupperware peelers. Or were the Pampered Chef ones best?

Aaron Zook *sei* Mary said what did it matter, a peeler is a peeler, and none of them work. A great clamoring of voices ensued, and Sarah smiled. She began cutting peeled potatoes and put her troubled thoughts to rest.

Here she was at home.

CHAPTER 21

THE ACTUAL SPEED WITH WHICH THE BARN TOOK shape was unbelievable this time. The women stopped mid-morning to observe. There were more men than usual, they decided.

This third barn fire was attracting a lot of attention. Concerned members of the Old Order from as far away as Ohio and Indiana wanted to help, share their views, extend their charities.

The house was cleared away for the most part, but Reuby and Bena were still planning, knowing that if they rushed through that stage, it would spite them later on, Bena said.

The barn must be rebuilt first; Reuby's livelihood came from milking a herd of cows. By the time dinner was served, the metal sheets were being screwed into place on the lower end of the forebay.

"My oh," Grandmother Miller said from her vantage point at the stove, waving the great wooden spoon and causing quite a stir among the women and girls.

Someone observed flatly that it was no wonder the new barn was going up so fast, with all the practice they'd had since early spring. It was sobering, all agreed.

Grandmother Miller shook her head, saying, "*Die lenga, die arriga* (The longer it goes, the worse things get)."

They made dire predictions. The end of the world coming any day now, according to the Bible. Mankind was going awry, and evil was prevailing. Mind you, the world is in such a state of sinful activity.

Sarah drew into herself. Yes, there was a certain truth in their words, of course. But what about the overwhelming response among the Plain people when tragedies did occur? Didn't that count for something? But she stayed quiet, being only a young single girl and outnumbered by her older peers.

Amid their prophesying, the women mashed the potatoes, which they kept warm and ready to serve along with gravy, ham, meatloaf, and chicken.

Kentucky Fried Chicken in Lancaster had donated twenty large containers of their chicken, with its distinctive taste—the best, in Dat's opinion. He called it Lucky Fried Chicken because he felt lucky every time someone brought some home or he got to eat at one of the restaurants. Sarah smiled, thinking of Dat.

No doubt, all the Amish would be touched by this generous gesture from the English people. The support from *die ausrie* (the outsiders) was indeed phenomenal, and it humbled the Plain people.

At a time like this, Sarah thought, the line between the English and the Amish was blurry. There really was no line. All over the world, every culture, every religion, understood loss and tragedy, horror and fear. There was always the good in man to combat the evil of men, and so it was this time. After a triple dose of disaster, the good poured in over and over, endlessly. It was truly an indescribable feeling.

Wolf Furniture brought two La-Z-Boy recliners with brown upholstery. Poor Reuby *sei* Bena told the driver he had the wrong place. He showed her the address on the delivery sheet, but she said, no, he had it all wrong, and he may as well take them back; they couldn't afford them.

He said, "Ma'am, I think they're donated."

She burst into tears and wiped her eyes with the corners of her *kopp-duch* (head scarf). Reuby came on the scene and shook the driver's hand so powerfully that the man had to keep taking it off the steering wheel and flexing his fingers the whole way back to Reading.

After dinner, they washed kettles and bowls and cleaned up as best they could. The temporary living quarters in the shed were almost impossible to keep clean, with the mud and the cold and the number of people stomping around.

The girls grabbed their coats and sat on the sunny side of the corncrib to watch the men, refilling the water jugs whenever it was necessary. The frame of the barn was all but completed, rising like a yellow skeleton into the blue November sky.

In the east, a wall of gray was building, rolling across the blue, changing the atmosphere slightly, as if the sun wasn't quite sure of itself. A wedge of geese honked their tardy way across the sky, like schoolchildren who knew they were late but kept hurrying along. Inexplicably, the hammering slowed as the men and boys watched the formation of Canadian geese, then pounding resumed.

Matthew walked by with Amos "Amy" King, one of his friends, and asked Sarah when they'd be ready to go.

"Whenever you are."

"In an hour or so? I have to feed heifers tonight."

"Sounds good."

Matthew smiled at her, then at Priscilla.

"How are you?" Amos asked.

"Good. I'm good."

"This your sister?"

"Yes. Priscilla, this is Amos."

"Hi."

Clearly flustered, Priscilla smiled up at Amos before quickly and shyly averting her eyes, as most fourteen-year-old girls do when introduced to a young man who was old enough to be *rumspringing*.

Sarah was glad to see this shyness in Priscilla. It spoke well for her character, and Sarah hoped she'd keep that sweet trait, even when she was sixteen. Too many pretty girls lost their shyness after receiving too much attention from the young men. And Priscilla was certainly notice-able, with her blond-streaked honey-colored hair, blue-green eyes, and round features.

She had a calming quality about her, an aloofness actually, that seemed attractive to some, like Matthew, Sarah admitted in spite of herself.

Watching Amos now, she could see the admiration, the way his eyes lingered on her face. And Sarah was glad— for a short time, anyway, until Matthew stepped over to Priscilla, reached down, and tweaked her ear.

"Yeah, Amy. Sarah's little sister, huh? She's not even fifteen yet. Not quite."

He lowered himself beside her, as close as possible, turning his head to watch her face. Amos smiled and watched Matthew, wondering what Sarah would say.

She said nothing, just stared straight ahead, her fea-tures inscrutable, as the November sun took on a dim quality and the gray bank of clouds moved in from the east.

The men were moving in double quick time now. Some pulled out cell phones and checked the weather. Yes sir, ice coming. Ice and rain and about anything you could expect, they said. Well, they'd have this barn under roof by tonight.

There was quite a buzz about the weather. With renewed effort, friendly banter, bets called on and off, the men quickened the work pace.

Sarah watched and saw Dat, proud of his ability to straddle a beam with the best of them. Then she saw Uncle Elam and Paul Stoltzfus, the roofer, pulling steadily on a sheet of metal.

A gray truck pulled up to the barn, dispatching two young men who hurried to the side of the truck, extracted leather tool belts, buckled them on, and adjusted them, looking steadily up at the barn the whole time. Sarah guessed that men buckled tool belts the same way women put on aprons—easily, without really looking, having done it so many times.

One young man threw his cap into the truck, his blond hair gleaming in the cold sunshine. She wasn't aware she'd drawn a breath sharply. It was Lee.

He had no time to look around, intent on getting up on a beam and helping. Together, the two young men sprinted to the back of the barn, ran up the ladder, and were lost among the dozens, the hundred other men. Sarah sighed.

Matthew was still busy showing off his knowledge of Priscilla to his friend, Amos, with absolutely no help from her. Suddenly, a bolt of anger shot through Sarah, and just as suddenly, she concealed it.

What was Matthew doing, sitting right there like a spoiled school boy, flirting shamelessly with poor Priscilla, who by now looked as if she didn't really know what to do with him? Why didn't he get up on that roof and help? Or why didn't he go over and offer help to the men on the ground? There was so much he could be doing.

But, of course, when he was attentive and charming on the way home, Sarah's heart melted within her all over again. Her love for him was real and steadfast. Priscilla stayed in the background, quiet, watching their faces, wondering if Sarah would ever attain the love of her life. Only time would tell. But with the wisdom of her fourteen years, almost fifteen, Priscilla decided she wouldn't waste a week's worth of Fridays on that loser. He was a charmer, and she'd almost been under his spell that day, but no longer.

How could she help Sarah best? She couldn't believe her ears when she heard Matthew ask Sarah if she wanted to go along to Ervin Lapp's on Saturday evening.

Sarah's face turned from its normal color to a pasty white before a spot of color reappeared on each cheekbone. She stammered a bit but said, "Why, yes, I'd be glad to go with you," and he said, "Good, good."

When they walked into the warm kitchen, Levi was coughing, and Mam's eyebrows were arched at a 45-degree angle, the tension heavy enough to cut with a knife.

Priscilla was dismayed to hear Sarah tell Mam about going with Matthew on Saturday evening, cringing as Mam gave her a tight smile and said, "Oh, did he?" Mam then turned away and began folding clothes with a vengeance. Sarah ran upstairs as fast as she could and flung herself on her bed and breathed a deep sigh of complete happiness that could only come from a dream fulfilled, at long last.

Yes, it was not a real date. And yes, he was just offering her a ride. But it proved to Sarah that he enjoyed her company, wanted to spend time with her, and would just maybe show Rose, who was bound to be there, that this was what he'd wanted all along.

The heights she rode on wings of joy! Over and over, she thanked God for His deliverance from the river of misery. He set her feet firmly on higher ground, where the view was infused with stardust and the birds sang in harmony with the praise that poured from her soul.

She read her Bible in English, the words of comfort and praise in the Psalms more meaningful than ever. God was so good, so kind, to help her rise above the doubts that had been her constant companions for far too long.

Her elevated reverie was broken by her mother's voice, calling her rather urgently, saying there was someone on the phone for her.

Instantly, Sarah slammed her Bible onto the nightstand, slid off the bed, and raced downstairs. Shoving her feet into a pair of boots, she grabbed a sweater off the hook, and kicked open the screen door as she pushed her arms into the sleeves before racing across the lawn to the phone shanty.

The black receiver lay on its side beside the telephone, and she picked it up swiftly and breathed, "Hello?"

"Hey, watcha doin'?"

Melvin.

"Oh, not much. I just got home from the barn raising at Reuby's."

"Oh, you were there? How'd that go?"

"Really amazing this time. It's like the women were saying—it's sad to have to admit it, but practice is in good supply. I mean, think about it, Melvin. Three barns since April."

Melvin's voice was serious, intense.

"Well, since no one seems to care about the arsonist, he'll just keep it up, thinking he's doing something right. We need to do something, get organized, get moving."

"How Melvin? Do you have a legitimate plan?"

"Sure. If you have a barn full of expensive milk cows, then sleep out there. Every night. Equip the barn with some first class smoke detectors. Call the police every time anything out of the ordinary happens. Anything at all. Whatever happened to Levi seeing that white car the night your barn burned. Did anyone ever see another one? Did anyone think to ask?"

Sarah sat down on the cracked vinyl seat of the old steel desk chair, tipped it back, and gazed at the ceiling as Melvin rambled on.

She had to admit, he was a mover and a shaker, and he got things done. He was smart and ambitious—too much so, Dat said.

When she could finally get a word in edgewise, she said she'd ask Dat to invite him to the meeting that would be held the following Monday evening. Instantly, Melvin drew back, saying he was the youngest in the bunch, unmarried, and his theory would mean nothing.

But Sarah would hear nothing of his attempt at being modest. He wasn't humble, and she knew it. Any effort of modesty was completely invalid, where Sarah was concerned. She knew Melvin well, and humility was not one of his attributes. He knew he wanted to be at that meeting, and he also knew the thought of speaking out there was extremely challenging.

So she let him talk, adding an mm-hm, okay, or yes, whenever she felt they were needed. She got down a lined tablet from the shelf, crossed her legs, and wrote "Matthew Ray Stoltzfus" over and over, with hearts and daisies and other doodles portraying her happiness.

Finally Melvin's subject of the barn fires ran dry, and he quickly asked what she was doing Saturday night.

"Matthew is taking me to Ervin's."

The line went silent with his inability to respond appropriately, so Sarah waited, her lips curved prettily with the victory that was so securely in her possession.

Finally, "Matthew?" It was an awkward sound, a squeak, a balloon releasing the air.

"What's wrong with that?"

"Oh, nothing. Nothing."

"Well, then?"

"But, they just broke up."

"It's not a date."

"I know."

Strangely, then, silence returned, the line quietly humming in their ears but sizzling with the unspoken instruments of hurt wedged between them—truth unable to be spoken on Melvin's side, defense rearing its shield on Sarah's.

His voice drained of any bravado, Melvin finally said, "Well."

"What?"

"Well, I guess that makes you happy."

"Yes, it does."

"Good for you."

"You don't mean that."

"But I do, Sarah."

She laughed, a short expulsion of disbelief. "No, you don't."

Melvin hunkered down on the hay bale he was sitting on and decided the fat was in the fire now. If she was going to act like that, then he'd just tell her, swimming along in her total blindness, swept away by that current named Matthew.

"Alright, Sarah. I'm only telling you this because I care about you. I worry about what will happen to you. You're my favorite girl in the whole world. You know that."

He stopped, allowing the dramatic statement to claim her.

She wiped her mouth with a thumb and forefinger and grimaced. Thinking what a complete professional Melvin was, she felt the first twinge of unease.

"Matthew is a nice guy, but he's likely using you to make Rose jealous."

The truth in his words came down on her like a whip, slicing through the inner most region of her conscience, that place that vibrated with tiny blue, pulsing lights, so irrelevant they were once easily covered up by her own beautiful words of love and longing, the yearning piled safely on the entire mass of her own security. Now a hot anger shot through her, alarming in its resonance. She almost hung up on him, but the training in good manners she had received from her parents restrained her.

"I'm sorry you have to feel that way, Melvin."

Melvin shook his head. Her words were as artificial, as slyly sweetened, as deplorable, as any he had ever heard. Enough was enough. Touché, Sarah.

"Well, I'll see you there, okay? I'm looking forward to it. You know the oldies team is going to win, don't you? We're going to whip everyone!"

This was pure Melvin, enthused, back on track in his unbridled zest for life, the competition of the upcoming ping-pong games erasing all the bad feelings between them.

Sarah smiled, then laughed, shoving back the ill will, and they chatted happily about ordinary, mundane things, the darker subjects of Matthew and the barn fires behind them now. As always, friendship prevailed, and theirs was a rare and precious thing, too valuable to shatter with the resounding click of a receiver slammed down in anger.

Sarah shivered, drew the sweater tightly across her chest, and leaned forward to warm herself. She glanced at the lowering sky, the world turning from a white gray to a darker gray as the sun set behind the heavy layer of restrained ice and rain or whatever would be released on the cold, brown earth lying dormant now, awaiting its cold winter cover.

Melvin was still talking, but her mind was on the solidness, the new stronghold of Reuby's barn, just put "under roof" today. How grateful he must be! The ice and snow could assail it now, pound it, and bounce around on it, and the men would have a protected place to complete the job.

She thought of Bena's reaction to the La-Z-Boy recliners and smiled, remembering her short, round form, her purple *kopp-duch* (head scarf), her misshapen everyday sneakers of questionable origin, her sagging black socks, the way she dipped her head in true humility after acknowledging that the recliners really were given to them, delivered by this English man.

"You're not listening." Melvin whined.

"Yes. Yes, I am."

"What was I saying?"

"You were talking about this new schoolteacher at the school across the road from your house."

"But what did I say?"

"That she's from Perry County."

"No, she's not. That's not what I said. See, you weren't listening at all."

"Oh, you said Dauphin."

"Well, yeah."

"Don't act like I'm two years old, Melvin. You know I hate that, when you sound so condescending."

"I didn't know you knew what that word meant."

"Smart, aren't I?"

"Not so much."

Sarah laughed and told Melvin she was freezing. There's nothing colder than sitting in an unheated phone shanty.

"I'm in the barn. I'm not cold."

"Well, lucky you. See you Saturday night, Melvin."

"Bye."

She could hardly open the door fast enough or race back to the house with enough speed, hurling through the kitchen door and moving swiftly to the coal stove in the corner. She shook her hands above it, as chills raced up and down her spine.

Levi observed all this from his chair, where he was patiently waiting on the casserole to come out of the oven.

"You were out there over an hour," he said dryly.

Mercifully, Mam had her back turned, putting carrots in a dishpan to peel and cut. She pinched her lips into a grim line, her eyes dark pools of worry and hard-earned restraint.

"Yeah well, Levi, you know how Melvin talks."

Levi nodded, smiled.

So, it was Melvin. Mam relaxed visibly and turned to ask Sarah to peel the carrots. Sarah moved obediently to the kitchen sink. She told Levi about Melvin wanting to be at the meeting and that he should be questioned more thoroughly about the white car.

Levi lifted his shoulders, shifted in his chair, and cleared his throat with great importance. "I'd be glad to go to the meeting. I can answer questions if they put them to me."

Sarah smiled, noting the *gros-feelich* (proud) cadence of his words.

"I'm sure Dat will want you to go, Levi."

"I think Monday night would suit me alright," he answered, looking across the kitchen at the calendar, his eyes glistening.

CHAPTER 22

THE PREDICTIONS FROM THE WEATHER FORECAST proved deplorably accurate. Tiny bits of ice mixed with cold, wet rain drove in from the east, relentlessly battering the new metal siding of Reuby Kauffman's barn. It fell on the half-frozen debris-filled troughs of mud and water blackened by the charred bits of wood, twisted nails, corkscrewed metal, and chunks of blistered tile and drywall and concrete. It swirled and eddied around potholes in the broken macadam and pooled in deep ruts left by the fire trucks and bulldozers, creating a slick, glistening other-worldliness by the time Reuby awoke the following morning.

David Beiler was one of the first people to arrive, his old wool hat bent and dripping, the droplets hovering on its brim as if undecided about whether to freeze or slide off. He threw the leather reins across the horse's back, reached for the *shtrung* (leather straps connecting the harness and buggy), clicked the backhold snap, and looked up to find Reuby striding through the mud.

"Morning, Davey."

"How are you, Reuby?"

"Good. Good."

Dat looked out from beneath his hat brim, his gaze warm with the compassion of a person with *aforeung* (experience). He was shocked to find Reuby's normally vibrant eyes clouded with fatigue, defeat—and what else? Dat shivered, shaken to the core by the gray pallor on Reuby's face.

"Reuby, are you sure you're doing good?"

In answer, Reuby half turned, his mouth working, as he fought to gain control over the debilitating despair that threatened to squeeze the life from his veins. He swallowed, nodded.

Dat came around to Reuby's side and placed his gloved hand on the wet black shoulder, a gesture of pleasant understanding, of deep sincerity, and compassion.

"Reuby, it seems impossible now, but it isn't. You'll receive help. God will provide. He always does."

Deeply moved, Reuby's shoulders began to shake, as the control he held onto so firmly slipped from his grasp. Dat's hand remained on his shoulder, the other held the bridle of his unquestioning Fred, who stood obediently in the cold wet rain until his master would lead him to shelter.

Reuby's head came up then. He shook it back and forth, produced a red, wrinkled handkerchief, and blew lustily. He placed it quickly back in his pocket, as if the disappearance would hide his shame at crying when he was, after all, a man who viewed the whole world through rose-colored glasses of love and charity.

"How can a person go on?" he mumbled brokenly.

"God will see you through."

"But I'm already deeply in debt. So deep, in fact, I don't know if it's wise to rebuild. The Amish fire insurance will never cover it all. I feel perhaps I should just give up, rent a small home, get a day job."

"In the Old Testament, God told the children of Israel to be patient, to stand by, that he would show works of wonder for them. If you rebuild in faith, God will bless you, like Abraham of old. His belief in God was rewarded many times over."

"I'm not Abraham."

There was a tinge of bitterness in Reuby's words, so Dat told him to come to the meeting on Monday evening. A group of men were assembling to figure out a solution of sorts. They would talk about finances as well. Already, there were trust funds established at two different banks, the generosity of the people reaching unbelievable levels.

Reuby nodded and yawned. He peered at Dat with bleary eyes and said, yes, he'd be there. Then he yawned mightily once more. Dat knew Reuby had barely managed an hour's sleep, the enormity of his situation keeping him awake long hours as the icy rain pelted the shambles of his home and pinged and clattered against the metal roofing of the makeshift quarters in the implement shed.

"The sun will shine again, Reuby. God never makes us suffer more than he gives us the strength to bear."

Reuby nodded and watched dully as more teams appeared. Dat knew he was tired, discouraged, and moving in a fog of disorientation and would be for a while longer.

"Be thankful no lives were lost," he said.

"I know, I know. You lost young Mervin, and nothing can replace that kind of loss."

"Absolutely," Dat said.

Far from the site of the barn raising, Sarah shivered as she sat uncomfortably in the back seat of the van, wedged between Ruthie Zook on her right, and Anna Mary Fisher on her left. Both were sound asleep, their pillows stuffed haphazardly into the corners of the back seat, their mouths hanging open in the most unattractive manner.

The ride to market was risky, unnerving at best, the driver hunched over his steering wheel, staring into the night at the slick and dangerous roads. Massive dump trucks crawled along, their beds lifted as they swirled salt, calcium, and cinders onto the roads for the edgy motorists trailing behind.

If Ike Stoltzfus would close his mouth for one second, Sarah thought. As if the driver knew he had support from the back seat, he turned and told Ike to keep his opinions to himself. He was the driver and he would decide the speed. It was no big deal to be late; the market wouldn't exactly be booming with customers in this weather anyway, so just shut it. Ike slouched back in his seat, crossed his arms, and began to brood, glancing balefully at the streaks of ice and rain in the glare of the headlights.

The van veered crazily as the driver swung the steering wheel to the left, then right, but they stayed on course, the speed significantly reduced yet again.

Ike yelped but remained quiet, his eyes sliding to the tense profile beside him.

Anna Mary's head swung back against Sarah's shoulder. Her eyes fluttered open, and she gasped. Ruthie's head slid forward, she righted it awkwardly, and went right on sleeping.

Sarah sipped her lukewarm coffee from the tall travel cup. Anna Mary leaned over and asked if she could have a swallow of it. Handing it over, Sarah grimaced as she engulfed the lid with her heavy lips, slurped, and handed it back.

End of the coffee for me, she thought.

"You can have it."

"You sure?"

"Yeah."

"Thanks."

The ride was stretching into its fourth hour when they finally rolled up to the vast brick building on Progress Street. The Amish had turned the obscure old train station into a bustling, friendly market full of life, sounds, and smells that enticed consumers to buy something from each stand.

Sturdy posts and a mock shingled roof framed Amos Fisher's produce stand. Piles of fresh tomatoes, green, yellow, and red peppers, towers of cucumbers, zucchini, summer squash, carrots, garden lettuce, and new onions created a feast for the eyes. The bonus attraction for modern shoppers was the organic label boasting that no pesticides or insecticides had been used to grow the vegetables. Customers from the big city paid the price, placing their trust in the bearded fellow and his helpers wearing white bib aprons and coverings on their heads.

Despite the numerous meat counters, some customers only bought from the stand run by a Jewish family. Their meats were kosher, prepared according to the requirements of the Jewish law in the Old Testament. Kosher or not, he had the best salami in the market, and a lively mix of customers, both Jewish and English, Amish and Mennonite, bought from him.

Sarah always viewed the Jewish family with a certain mix of awe and curiosity. What she really wanted was to sit down and compare their beliefs. How different or similar were they? Like the Jews, the Amish derived many of their highly esteemed traditions from the Old

Testament. She supposed belief in Jesus separated them, but still. Both groups seemed to have a common love of tradition, and that interested her, although she doubted she'd ever have the nerve—or the time—to start a conversation with them.

The largest stand in the sprawling market was the Stoltzfus bakery, where freshly made pies, bread, rolls, cakes, cookies, and cupcakes rolled off the shelves as fast Sarah and the fourteen others who worked there could restock the spotless white shelves. They covered cinnamon rolls with Saran Wrap before they were properly cooled. But the goods sold rapidly just the same. Sarah chuckled as an overweight lady happily snatched up the fresh buns and scuttled to a nearby table before peeling off the plastic and tucking into the first heavenly mouthful, rolling her eyes blissfully at her companion.

Sarah mixed huge vats of yeast dough and put large mounds of it into the proofer, a machine that produced just the right amount of warmth and humidity to raise the dough to the required size. Then she turned it on a large, floured surface and began forming the quota of bread, rolls, and sweet rolls. Her arms became rounded and well-muscled from plying, rolling, and turning the dough, sprinkling it with brown sugar and cinnamon and walnuts.

There were five sit-down restaurants and many booths where customers could eat food they bought to take out. Leather supplies, a craft stand, and outdoor furniture—all at reasonable prices—catered to many different preferences.

Sarah truly loved her job now, and her devotion showed in her willingness to take on any task. But she was mostly restricted to the "yeast crew."

Now, because of the inclement weather, they cut down on the amount of dough they would mix for the day. And the workers were allowed a forty-five minute break instead of only thirty. At one o'clock, Sarah still had not taken her break, allowing the other girls their turns, saying she wasn't that hungry.

Then quite suddenly, she felt dizzy, her stomach caving in on itself. A half hour later, Ike told her to go on break, just when she wondered whether to collapse or eat dough. Of course, she did neither.

Hurrying along the aisle, her purse slung over her shoulder, Sarah sat down heavily and waited at her usual booth for her friend, Rose, who was having a slow day and came over almost immediately to sit with Sarah. As always, she was beautiful, her hair gleaming in the electric ceiling lights, her skin flawless, her robin's egg dress reflecting her perfect blue eyes.

"Sarah!" She reached across the table, grasped both of Sarah's hands, and squeezed. "I miss seeing you! I could hardly stand not going to the supper on Sunday evening!"

"Where were you, Rose?" Sarah asked, concerned now.

"Oh, I don't know." Rose removed her hands and looked away and then back. She cupped her delicate chin in one hand and shrugged.

"Sometimes it's hard to go to the supper crowd. I mean, I'm happy. Don't get me wrong, it's just that...I don't know."

"Well, you've always been dating," Sarah said too quickly and much too easily.

"I guess. I don't know." She brightened then and leaned forward and said, "You know who is just so attractive? That Lee Glick. See, the reason we never knew of him is that he used to be with the Dominoes, that other youth group, and now he moved down here with his sister, that Anna and Ben. Their barn was the second one that burned. Anyway, I went to the dinner table with him. I was surprised he went in to the afternoon table. He picked me, remember?"

Rose giggled, then looked away. "Oh, what can I get you? It's almost two o'clock. Haven't you eaten anything at all?"

Sarah shook her head. "Bring me a bowl of chili. Fast!"

Rose giggled again and hurried off, waving a hand behind her.

The Dominoes? No, he wasn't.

The Dominoes was the name of an Amish youth group. Because of the many youth in Lancaster County, they were divided into groups with different names, like the Dominoes or the Drifters—any name to mark them as a specific group.

The largest was the Eagles, a parent-supervised group attempting a cleaner, better way of *rumspringa*, without the smoking and drinking of past days. Concerned parents and ministers, alarmed at the moral decline among the youth, were attempting a new *rumspringa*, where the *ordnung* still applied. This caused quite a bit of controversy among Amish wary of anything untraditional. A peaceful truce had been reached, although problems still broke out. But as Dat told Sarah, the problems could be solved when each placed the emphasis on giving in to the other in humility and brotherly love.

Rose didn't know that Anna had told Sarah that Lee had been with the Drifters, the older group, not the Dominoes. Sarah was peeved, intimidated by Rose's knowledge of Lee. What would Rose say if she knew about last week at Reuby Kauffman's?

Her face flamed suddenly. When Rose appeared with a steaming bowl of thick chili, a dollop of sour cream and cheddar cheese on top, she looked anxiously at Sarah and asked if she had a fever. Blinking nervously, Sarah said, no, no, she was fine, and lifted the soup spoon to her mouth.

Rose seemed satisfied with Sarah's reply, then asked if she'd seen Matthew this week. Sarah nodded and told her about the barn raising, offering nothing more.

"Well, how does he seem to you? Is he himself? I mean, you know, getting on with his life?"

Rose was nervously folding and unfolding a napkin, the toe of one foot bobbing furiously, her eyes too intent.

"Well, he teased Priscilla a lot, but—you know—that's how he's always been. He seems happy, yes, at least as far as I can tell."

Rose said nothing, folded the napkin again. "Well, I better go. We didn't finish making some of the soups. In this weather, it'll take a lot, later on in the day. Hey, see you at Ervin's."

Sarah nodded.

"How are you going?"

Sarah cringed inwardly, wishing with all her heart that Rose hadn't asked her that one question. Why did she have to know?

"Matthew."

"Oh."

Rose lifted her chin, scowled, turned on her heel, and hurried off, moving faster than she had all day.

Well. So be it, Rose. You're the one that broke off the friendship.

Before long, the chili was gone, so Sarah paid, wandered two aisles down, bought a chunk of chocolate walnut fudge (she'd save some for Levi, his favorite), and was slowly walking past the leather goods stand when someone called her name.

Surprised, Sarah turned. "Oh, Ashley. Hi."

"What are you doing?"

"Eating fudge."

Ashley giggled, then looked ashamed and ill at ease, fingering a key chain, her eyes averted.

"How are you?" Sarah asked.

"I'm okay."

"Good."

An awkward silence followed, and Sarah wasn't sure if she wanted to keep the conversation going or move off. Ashley's thin, fine hair somehow looked hacked off, and her face was white and riddled with acne. Her eyes clouded with anxiety or shyness, Sarah wasn't sure which. She was painfully thin, her gray sweatshirt hanging as if on a coat hanger.

Suddenly, she lifted her head, as if in desperation. "Did...did you know those people whose house burned, like, last week? Did they...are they okay? Like, what happened?"

The words were a torrent, unleashed by the force of her curiosity, raining on Sarah so that she could hardly meet her troubled gaze.

"Reuby...Reuben Kauffman's?"

"I dunno. I guess."

"Yes, their barn and house—both were destroyed by fire. They're doing about as well as you'd expect. They're good people and are hurting at the loss, of course, but they'll be okay in time."

"But no one was hurt? Or, like, killed?"

"No, nothing like that."

"Oh." Then, "Are...are these people going to try and find out who, like, did it?"

"Oh, I don't know. We're having a meeting soon, at my house—my dad's a minister—to try and figure out a way to keep the barns safe. I don't know how we could actually find the arsonist."

"Yeah. Well, I have to go."

She disappeared behind a wall of elaborately tooled leather belts without giving Sarah a chance to say good-bye. So Sarah shrugged her shoulders and moved on, letting the whole conversation go for now. There was too much to see, too many people to greet and talk to, even if only for a minute.

"Hey, Sarah!

Ray King waved a hand across his cheese display, a beaming elderly woman at his side, her hair parted like the white wings of a dove, crowned by a large white covering. Ray was a big man, larger than Levi, his round face florid, his beard bristling with good humor. A white butcher's apron stretched loosely across his round stomach.

Sarah smiled and moved over to their stand. She stretched on tiptoes to see what free samples they had today.

"Havarti. Swiss. Aged cheddar," she read aloud.

"What? You can read?" Ray boomed, and his mother gave him a resounding smack on his arm, which was as big as a log.

Sarah laughed, sampled them all, and made a face.

"What? My cheese is no good? Don't let my customers see you pull that face."

"No, it's not your cheese. It's eating anything after that extra sweet chocolate fudge."

Ray laughed and said he hadn't eaten any fudge for while. He was going to buy some, and he left the stand hurriedly, his large frame rocking from side to side.

His mother shook her head, saying *"Eya braucht's net* (He doesn't need it)."

Sarah moved on. She waved to Rachel Fisher at the fish stand, the rich aroma of frying fish whirling around her. The warm, full-bodied seafood smell made her inhale appreciatively.

"Sarah!"

She stopped and waited as Rachel handed her a small cardboard boat with red crisscrossing on it. It was filled with broiled scallops.

"Taste these. Tell me what you think. Too much lemon? Not enough? It's something new."

Gingerly, with thumb and forefinger, Sarah attempted to lift one of the succulent orbs, which was broiled crisply and coated with a clear sauce. Instantly, she pulled back her hand.

"Ow! They're hot."

"Here. Use a plastic fork."

Sarah jabbed a scallop with the fork and blew on it repeatedly before taking a tentative bite. She chewed, held her head to one side, and rolled her eyes before pronouncing them awful, just awful.

Rachel let out a devastated sigh.

"No!"

Sarah laughed and told her she was joking. They were simply the best thing ever.

"Oh Sarah, thank you so much! You really mean it? We got this great buy on fifty pounds of them, and we have to sell some scallops this week. And just look at the weather out there! It's driving me plum crazy."

Sarah said calmly, "You'll make it." She waved and moved on.

Leon and Rachel Fisher were some of the most successful market people and lived in one of the nicest homes in Leola. She'd heard through the grapevine that they sold thousands of dollars worth of seafood each week, although they always complained of the high cost of their lease, the fish, the help. But it was all done in humility, not flaunting their actual success.

The farmer's market was a great part of Sarah's social life now. She made new friends, comfortably joked with other vendors, and became close friends with her coworkers.

As she returned to her work station, her thoughts went back to the timid Ashley, her fevered questions, and wondered at the mysterious traits she displayed. She was obviously not comfortable with who she was. But who could know what her life was like? What had been in her past to create this sense of imbalance?

Dat often told them not to judge anyone unfairly, before actually knowing what their circumstances were. Be slow to judge, slow to pass opinion of someone, and be patient with each other's shortcomings. Mam lived this advice largely by example. She remained kind in situations others probably could not, her uncomplicated manner a healing balm in more than one prickly situation. So Sarah gave her shy, new friend the benefit of the doubt and felt peaceful, at ease, and only curious to get to know her better.

As she thought of that evening, a new joy rose within her, and she hummed along with the beat of the mixer.

Matthew coming to pick her up! Imagine!

She hoped Mam's feathers would remain unruffled, but she'd be glad to escape out the front door. Mothers were unpredictable creatures.

CHAPTER 23

By early Saturday evening, the ice and rain had moved on. The wind blew strongly, and a weak November sun melted the ice on the south and west sides of buildings, trees, cars, or whatever had been covered by the thin coat of freezing water.

It was the kind of day when it was easier to stay indoors, the wind a bit too belligerent for skirts and dresses, the ground either muddy or covered with thin sheets of cracking ice like broken glass underfoot.

Priscilla, however, chose to ride Dutch, his hooves sinking into the mud and smashing the thin ice that stretched across puddles. It was all the same to him.

When Sarah came home from market, Priscilla came running across the driveway from the barn, her cheeks ruddy with the cold and the wind, her eyes dancing beneath her honey colored hair that had been tossed in windblown tendrils about her face. She was shouting as she ran, oblivious to the curious faces pressed against the tinted glass of the fifteen-passenger van.

"Sarah! He cleared the creek!"

"What?"

The wind whipped her skirt about her, tore the single syllable from her mouth, and whirled it away.

"Dutch! He jumped the creek!"

"Priscilla Beiler! How?"

"Oh well, you know. If you go fast enough, he has to do it."

They bent their heads to the wind and moved rapidly to the front porch, bursting through the door, glad to feel the heat and homey aroma of the kitchen.

Mam looked up from the kitchen sink and said, "Hello, Sarah. Home so soon?"

"Yes, Mam, the market was slow."

"I would imagine people are reluctant to leave their houses in this unpredictable weather."

"He jumped the creek, Mam!"

"Your horse? Priscilla, I seriously fear for your safety."

But Mam's eyes shone, and just the smallest hint of pride asserted itself. It was there in the way a small smile played around her lips and made itself at home, the lifting of her rounded shoulders, and her quick movements as she whirled to the stove.

Was it some remembered time of her own? Did she accomplish a neat, heart-stopping leap on the back of a favorite horse, a pleasure forgotten that was now revived by the antics of her daring young daughter?

"Whoo!" Priscilla fist-pumped the air.

Suzie giggled from her side of the card table, where Levi sat facing her, the game Memory between them. Levi viewed his sister with flat eyes and said she was *grosfeelich* (proud), pressing his lips together in righteous indignation.

Priscilla pulled back on his wide, elastic suspenders and let them snap gently against his back. He swiped at her clumsily, almost upsetting his rolling desk chair.

"*Denk mol* (think once), Levi! Here I come, galloping full tilt, and I don't know if Dutch will do it, so I have to prepare myself to stop. But I can feel it this time. His speed increases, he bunches his muscles, and I can tell he's going to attempt it this time. I can't tell you how thrilling it is."

Levi contemplated his sister's words, before saying calmly, "*Du bisht net chide* (You're crazy)."

Priscilla laughed happily and with abandon. "I knew he could do it!"

"Levi, go!" Suzie commanded.

Levi lowered his great head, swung it to the side, hummed, then reached down with his wide, stubby fingers and picked up two cards, blue ones with orange fish imprinted on the heavy squares and said, "Yep! Got it!"

Suzie growled and eyed his stack of cards that was so tall it leaned crookedly. She counted her own meager five sets. "Levi, you cheat!"

"Hah-ah, I don't. I remember stuff, that's what I do. I remember a lot of things in my life, Suzie."

Filled with the knowledge of his amazing memory, Levi puffed out his chest, snapped his suspenders, and chortled to himself.

Suzie overturned a card with a small pink doll carriage on it then hovered over the cards undecidedly. Finally she swooped down, turned one right side up, squeezed her eyes shut, and howled with disappointment.

"I know exactly where it is!" Levi shouted.

Mam walked over to watch, resting a hand on the back of his chair as he pounced dramatically on the two cards that created a set, fairly yodeling in his excitement. Suzie was a good sport, shaking her head at the end of the game. Levi had twenty-three sets to her nine.

Priscilla ate three chocolate-chip cookies with a tall glass of milk. Sarah handed the chocolate fudge she had bought to Levi, who thanked her rather stiffly, completely bowled over by his good fortune.

Mam seemed to be relaxed and accepting of Sarah leaving with Matthew, so Sarah said that, if it was alright, she'd better start getting ready to go to Ervin's. Mam looked at Sarah, smiled, and said yes, maybe she'd better, and inquired politely what time he was arriving.

Well, you had to hand it to her, Sarah thought as she wound her way up the steps, her hand clinging to the smooth wooden railing.

It was already pitch dark, the bony branches of the maple tree scraping across the porch roof creating unsettling sounds. It was not a good night to be going anywhere. But with Matthew at her side, who would notice the wind or the cold or the leftover spitting rain?

The all-important moment of choosing the perfect dress came first. Slowly, she leafed through the multiple colors of sleeves, hanging side by side in a neat row.

Not red. Sleeves too tight.

Brown. No. Ugly color. Or wait. It was November, brown was a fall color, the color of acorns and dry leaves.

Nah.

Lime green. Sick color, no.

Blue. Too much blue. Always wore blue.

Green. Sage green. The color of her eyes. Hate the fabric. Makes me look fat.

Teal. Oops. Sleeve torn at underarm.

Beige. Too blah.

Navy blue. Too plain.

On and on, then back again, Sarah fingered the empty sleeves hanging before her, dissatisfied with every single one.

She would wear black every Sunday until May, but on Saturday night, she was allowed to wear anything she wanted.

Going to the bedroom door, she called for Priscilla.

"She's outside!" Mam answered.

So much for moral support, Sarah thought. Well, she'd shower, wash her hair, clear her head of indecision, and then perhaps choose randomly, like a game of pin the tail on the donkey. But it was important that she look just right, so that probably wasn't a good idea.

In the end, she put on the brown dress but was absolutely put off by the pallor it cast on her anxious face. Instead she chose the brightest dress she owned, a magnificently colored red.

Her hair refused to cooperate, as usual, and she finally had to let the right side be ruled by its disgusting cowlick. Her apron didn't fit right, and all her shoes looked stupid. Every pair was either too big, with the toes pointed skyward, or too old and worn, too tight or too cold. She should have gone shoe shopping.

So then, because her best sneakers had gray and green stripes in them, she shed the red dress and donned the lime green one. She grabbed her favorite coat and ran down the stairs just as two headlights approached the front yard.

Mam smiled and said, "Bye, Sarah. Be careful."

Priscilla, glued to a chair with a book in front of her face, said nothing, paying Sarah as much attention as she would a fly. If it wasn't Priscilla, it was Mam, or the other way around. She thought they must plan together who would disapprove. It was only a minor annoyance, which completely disappeared when she climbed into Matthew's buggy.

"Hey, Sarah." He smiled at her warmly, his white teeth illuminated by the brilliance of the headlights. Her knees went weak with a happiness beyond anything she had expected.

"Hi, Matthew." What a wonderful way to begin this idyllic evening.

Matthew was talkative, entertaining her with vivid accounts of his job and the dinner he had cooked the evening before. Sarah smoothed back her hair and answered smartly, trying to be witty and worth his company.

She was disappointed when they arrived at Ervin and Katie's house, having to share Matthew with everyone else. She didn't let it show as she jumped gracefully off the buggy, politely helped him unhitch, and handed him the halter and neck rope before walking away.

She stopped, undecided now. Should she wait until he tied the horse? Should they enter as a couple? Did he want the crowd of young people to know he had brought her?

The wind whipped her lime green skirt, pulled at her hair, and tugged her covering away from the pins that were holding it. So she decided to move up to the porch at least, before her hair and covering were a complete wreck.

The door was flung open by a squealing Rose, who was in a high state of excitement from having just beaten that Lee Glick at a game of ping-pong. There was a spot of color on each of her cheeks, her smile was wide, her face already glowing.

Sarah always felt her confidence slip away the minute Rose was within sight. Like a ship tossed by one hard wave, Sarah was knocked off course, but she quickly righted herself. She regained her composure, ready to snap on her confidence and enjoy the evening, remembering that God had made her this way. God had endowed Rose with a more startling beauty, and it was acceptable, Sarah thought, remembering her mother's kind words that to base confidence in beauty was like building a house on quicksand.

Quietly, Sarah entered the basement, led by her hostess, Katie, who followed behind the whirling Rose. She bent to say hello to those who were seated, but she entered the crowded, well-lit room without Matthew.

Lee Glick leaned against the paneled wall, his hands in his pockets, his dark, forest green shirt turning his complexion to an olive hue. He watched Sarah.

The grace with which she moved! Not very many girls could carry off this unconsciousness of themselves, an innocence born of a good upbringing. She was like a calm pool of water in a hidden corner of a forest—ethereal, transparent, cool, and untouched.

CHAPTER 24

THE BASEMENT WAS WELL LIT, WITH PROPANE GAS lamps at both ends and battery-powered lights illuminating the two ping-pong tables. Groups of young men stood against the paneled walls waiting their turns to play, cheering or egging on the other players.

They wore brightly colored button-down shirts, some with stripes or a soft plaid, an occasional t-shirt showing beneath an open collar. And they wore black broadfall trousers with narrow waists and loose suspenders. If a mother complied with her son's wishes, the waist of his trousers fit snugly to allow the exclusion of suspenders altogether.

There was Melvin, dressed in a shocking color of teal, his face red with exertion, doing his level best to "whip" everyone. His hair was beginning to show that gleam of scalp, a dead giveaway of balding. He was yelling much too loudly, moving with reckless abandon, evidently having a hard time "whipping."

He didn't see her arrive, so she sat down on the arm of a sofa, beside Rose, and watched. After numerous exertions of arms and legs, his face turned an alarming shade of red and he finally managed the game point, raising his paddle high, lifting his face, and yelling a shrill cry of victory before bowing low and then straightening and stomping both feet.

The girls found his display quite hilarious. Rose laughed loudest of all, which pleased Melvin so much that he repeated the whole procedure.

Sarah laughed out loud, helplessly. That Melvin. What an individual!

A girl Sarah had never seen placed a hand sideways across her mouth, giggled, leaned forward, and rolled her eyes at her companion, Arie Beiler, an older girl who had been in Sarah's group of youth as long as she could remember. The new girl seemed to know Arie well, so Sarah wondered if she was the new schoolteacher Melvin had spoken of.

She was dark-haired, and wore glasses with heavy black frames, giving her an edgy, career-girl look. Her mouth was wide with full lips, her dress a charcoal gray, with shoes that were almost sandals but not quite. She was not thin, although she carried the excess poundage well, her hands large and capable, her shoulders wide.

Hmm, Sarah thought. An interesting character, this one.

Later in the evening, she made a point of introducing herself, shyly, but with so much curiosity, she had to carry it out.

"Hi. I'm Sarah Beiler. I should know you, likely, but I have no idea who you are."

"Hi, Sarah. I know who you are. Minister Davey Beiler's daughter, right?"

Sarah nodded, suddenly speechless.

"I'm Edna King from Dauphin County. They had a problem school, near Ronks, so they asked me to teach this year. This is my eleventh term. I do art classes as well—at different schools."

Her eyes were bright with curiosity, her words spoken clearly, no humility in sight, so far as Sarah could tell, but she liked her immediately.

"Yes, I'm Davey's daughter."

No credentials, she thought wryly. No career, no boyfriend, not getting married, just Davey's girl.

"You lost your little brother shortly after the fire, right?"

"Yes."

"Well, that's so awful. It must have been a hard, hard time."

"It was."

"You have my deepest sympathy."

Sarah lowered her eyes, feeling a bit out of her league. This Edna was so well-spoken, so learned, so...so English. Sarah felt like some country bumpkin who could hardly speak.

"So, are you healing? Time does help the grieving process."

"Oh, yes. We miss Mervin, especially these winter evenings. But he was so innocent, and he's in a better place now."

"Certainly. Oh, absolutely."

"Winner's pick!"

The call was from Lee Glick, who stood, tall, relaxed, his hair very blond, surveying the crowd, taking his time choosing someone to play. He was wearing a navy blue polo shirt, his shoulders pressing against the seams. Sarah turned her eyes away, to Matthew, who was slouched on a recliner laughing.

"Sarah?"

It was a question but a calm, assured one, sending a stab through her stomach, creating a tumultuous feeling near her heart, as if her ribs had closed in on its regularity. She looked up and acknowledged the warmth in his eyes, then rose to the challenge, moving fluidly, with unconscious grace. Taking up the red paddle, she smiled at him.

"I never played ping-pong with you. Are you any good?" His question was for her ears alone, and she blushed painfully.

"Of course."

"Alright, then. Here we go."

His serves were atrocious, but Sarah had played enough ping-pong with her older brothers to have acquired the skill of the return. Lee raised his eyebrows, whistled, and realized this was no ordinary girl playing ping-pong.

Lee was an extraordinary player, but so was Sarah. Mid-game, he put both hands on the table, palms down, leaned forward, and asked, "Where did you learn to play?"

"I have four older brothers, remember?"

"I didn't know that."

"They were, shall I say, exacting teachers. Mean, too!"

He laughed, his blue eyes sparkling, and she joined in.

At the end, she won by one point. The score had been tied at twenty, the youth mostly on their feet, cheering. Melvin was completely beside himself, the veins in his neck protruding to the point that Sarah thought he might pop one.

"I should have warned you, Lee. She's a mean one."

Lee laughed and shook his head, breathing hard.

Sarah sank onto the sofa, shy now that the game was over, suddenly disliking the attention.

As if Matthew wanted to share the glory, he sat down beside her, his gaze never leaving her face, saying he'd play this next game. And because his eyes were so dark and compelling, and he was Matthew, the love of her entire life, she said of course she'd play. She got back on her feet and picked up the paddle.

As usual, Matthew was no contest. She beat him handily, without too much effort, but she knew Matthew wasn't much interested in sports. He'd rather be cooking or reading, he always said.

She remembered sitting beside him in school, doing anything to gain his attention, even dropping a wad of crumpled paper in the aisle so she could bend over to retrieve it. But his nose was in yet another book, and she may as well not even have been there at all.

In the end, Matthew threw down the paddle, hard, and turned away with no further ado. All the spark left Sarah's eyes, and her smile melted into trembling insecurity before she lowered her head and walked away, misery creeping into her eyes.

Lee had to clench his hands until the muscles rippled beneath his shirt to stop the anger, the overwhelming feeling of helplessness. Sarah, my love.

"Sarah! Pick me!" Edna King raced around the table, and Sarah's face was filled with light again.

Lee's hands unfolded, and he turned away casually, so that no one was aware of the intensity of his emotion.

The evening was ruined for Sarah, however. She had upset Matthew, so the snack that was set up on the side tables may as well have been sawdust and chicken bones as the dryness in her mouth created a sour despair.

Katie had decorated the table with a ping-pong theme using a green tablecloth with a ping-pong net dividing the food from the drinks. She stuck tiny plastic paddles into white icing on top of chocolate cupcakes, and dusted cookies formed in the shape of ping-pong balls with powdered sugar.

Sarah sipped disconsolately on a lemonade, her face a mirror of remorse, until Rose slipped an arm through hers. She leaned close and whispered, "Matthew was a poor sport."

So. She had seen. How well Rose must know Matthew!

"It's okay," she muttered. Rose nodded then giggled when Melvin sat beside her. He leaned across and hissed, "Sarah, introduce me to the schoolteacher."

Sarah examined Melvin's red face and unkempt hair. She wanted to tell him to go outside, stand in the cold wind, cool off, and fix his hair. But what she said was, "Now?"

"Course."

Ach, Melvin. She cringed but stood and moved to touch Edna's elbow.

"Edna, I want you to meet my cousin, Melvin. I think he lives just across the road from your school."

Edna turned, her face alight with interest. Showing her good manners, she allowed herself to be led to the sofa, where Melvin reclined with Rose, in all his red-faced glory.

Thankfully, he stood and shook her hand, very politely. He didn't hold Edna's hand too long or too hard, and this is what he said: "I've been wanting to meet you for a long time. I often watch you play baseball with the children."

Much to Sarah's complete surprise, Edna seemed to lose all her composure. Her face changed color, and her well-modulated voice slid away into a stammering squeak.

"I...Yes. How are you?"

She blinked, adjusted her glasses, sniffed, and then, much to Sarah's chagrin, lifted her apron, found a Kleenex, and blew her nose. Oh my goodness, Sarah thought.

Melvin must have found that whole display of discomfiture a pure delight. His eyes took on that light of familiarity, that cunning beam that was a prelude to a full show of every one of his charms. In his own eyes, Melvin would be the benevolent knight in shining armor, ready to rescue his damsel in distress, that lucky girl who would now be subject to his personality.

"I'm well, thank you! Your name, though?"

Edna may as well have been in the presence of a king, the way she became tongue tied, clearing her throat, stammering, and finally saying, "Edna. Edna King."

"Edna? Oh, I love that name. It's so different. Not many Ednas around. Too many Sarahs and Rebeccas and Suzies. Sorry, Sarah."

Sarah punched his arm. Edna smiled and picked at her dress front, her nervousness only producing more confidence in Melvin, who went way overboard in his introductions. He told Edna his great-great-grandfather was a blacksmith from Switzerland, and Sarah figured it was another one of his stretched truths, feeding off his heightened emotions, laid out for the sole purpose of impressing the worldly Edna King.

She was led away by Matthew, then, who said he was ready to leave, as it was getting late, and they had church tomorrow.

Without a moment's hesitation, Sarah said goodbye to Melvin and told Edna it was a pleasure to meet her. She hurried up the stairs for her coat and purse, thinking she had to dig up enough nerve to help Melvin with his shirts.

Who in the world made those shirts? He'd look so much better in store-bought ones. He always picked a fabric and color that would be truly lovely stitched into a dress for a girl. And with that Edna! Now she had good taste. Understated, but classy. Not out of the *ordnung*, she dressed respectfully, but...well, differently.

Why were her thoughts carefully assessing Melvin now? She wondered at this, as she located her purse and shrugged into her coat.

Matthew was hitching his horse to the carriage to take her home, an unbelievable occurrence, a dream come true, and here she was, thinking about Melvin's shirts. What an old maid!

She was stopped at the door by Rose, who was breathing hard.

"Is...is Matthew taking you home?"

"Yes. He brought me."

"Oh. Yes, well. That's...well. Okay. Have a good night."

"Night, Rose."

Matthew's horse was prancing, so Sarah lost no time running out to the buggy, swiftly getting in, and firmly closing the door. When he released the reins, they were off with a hard jerk, the gravel pinging against the buggy as the horse's speed increased.

Matthew was busy controlling the eager horse, so he said nothing, and Sarah watched his profile, the perfect downward slope of his nose.

She'd go shopping with Melvin. She'd ask him to go

along to Rockvale Square to visit a few men's shops. Oh, he'd protest. There would be nothing harder for Melvin to swallow than being told he needed help with his clothes. In his own eyes, he was quite dapper, but if that Edna turned out to be interested, he'd better get a few shirts. Maybe gray, or almost black. A pinstripe wouldn't hurt.

Perhaps that was the reason Edna was in her eleventh year of teaching. She was almost thirty years old. And she became as flustered as someone Priscilla's age meeting Melvin in his brilliant teal colored shirt.

"What did Rose have to say tonight?"

Matthew's voice split apart the reverie, and she had to shake off the image of Edna before replying.

"Oh, not much. She seemed thrilled to play ping-pong with Lee Glick."

Intended barbs like that fired much too quickly. They were completely untypical of Sarah, and she knew it. Where they borne of desperation?

Matthew's voice was low and harsh. "Yeah, well. It might be a good idea to eliminate the girls playing against the guys, and you know it."

There was no answer to this, so she remained quiet, afraid she might upset him again.

The night was moving around them, the horse's mane and tail blowing, the weeds shivering beside the road, bushes shaking thin branches at the wind's command. Distant pole lights seemed to blink as branches raked across their beams, and the buggy swayed just a bit as they rounded a curve.

An oncoming buggy dimmed its headlights, and Matthew clicked the dimmer switch on the floor with his foot.

"Old Dutchies are out late tonight," he muttered.

Sarah laughed, hoping to elevate his mood. He smiled in return, which encouraged Sarah to bring the evening to a better note with happy chatter of her week at the market, launching into a vivid account of her new acquaintance, Ashley.

"I didn't think you were the type to make friends with English girls. Especially not someone like her."

"Oh, but she's so nice. She seems genuinely interested in the barn fires that have been going on all year. She's so caring. I think it really bothers her that we're all going through this together."

Matthew nodded. "You better be careful, Sarah. She might know more than you think. Don't trust anyone, as long as these fires are being lit."

"Alright. I'll be careful."

They turned into the Beiler lane, and too soon, Matthew tugged on the reins, stopping the horse at the end of the sidewalk.

Just when Sarah could hardly bear to lift her hand to tug on the door handle, Matthew's voice stopped her.

"You don't have to go in right away."

Slowly, slowly, her hand slid down, and her breathing almost stopped. The wind whipped the branches of the maple tree. Somewhere a gate clanked against the chain that restrained it. A heifer bawled from its enclosure, a small plastic bag whirled away, causing Matthew's horse to lift its head suddenly, and he tightened the reins.

Then, "Sarah, do you think Rose is unhappy?"

"No." Too quickly, too decisively, the word was placed between them.

"She doesn't miss me?"

"No."

"How well do you know her?"

"We've been friends forever. I know her very well. She is after Lee Glick now."

After the words were out, she felt as if she was sliding uncontrollably into a world where there was no safety, no restraint. Her heartbeat fluttered and accelerated, until she became lightheaded. Oh, but, please God. I'm so close. Please don't take him away.

She wasn't lying. She just wasn't including all the facts. She took a deep breath, steadied herself, and told Matthew that Rose was doing just fine, was happy now, whereas after the break-up, she hadn't been. Matthew listened quietly and nodded speculatively.

There was a space of silence that prickled uncomfortably with unspoken feelings, words that hung in the balance, deciding Sarah's future. If Matthew did not come to a decision tonight, when? Oh, when would he ever?

A gentle nod of her conscience reminded her of the timeframe, that it was too recent that Rose had ended the relationship. But Sarah was afraid that if Matthew didn't commit now, he might never.

Finally he sighed. "Sarah, you know how it is. I'm still not really moving on. I miss her terribly. But if I know that it's absolutely hopeless, once I find out for sure, will you be my girl?"

"Oh, yes. Yes, Matthew! Of course I will."

Too quickly, too exuberantly again, and she knew it. But like the wind howling outside the buggy, her caution was caught up and whirled away.

With Matthew, all thoughts of right or wrong were confused, the line blurred into a fuzzy gray that her conscience could never quite completely touch.

Why then, when he pulled her roughly against him, his face lowered as his mouth found hers, did she pull back? Was she afraid, with the thought of Mam's warnings forced between them?

"Matthew."

"What? What's wrong now, Sarah?"

She heard the urgency in his voice and succumbed, allowing herself the privilege of being in his arms, blindly erasing the overwhelming feeling of something being not quite perfect.

How many years had she imagined this? How many months had she wondered how it would feel to be in Matthew's arms?

It was Mam—that was all.

A sob rose in her throat, as unexpected as a beam of light on this stormy night. She stumbled into the house, her covering disheveled, her hair windblown, her heart and mind caught in a sweet but indefinable misery.

As she lay sleepless, the branches creaking outside her window, she choked back the mysterious lump that kept rising in her throat. She was tired, that was all. That, and Mam's dire warnings.

Well, Mam knew a lot, but she didn't know Matthew, so she'd get over it eventually. No matter that she was clearly second best. She would be first in his life.

She flipped on her side and was shocked to find tears sliding across her nose. She swiped viciously at them, a fingernail slicing into the skin below her eye. She winced, squeezed her eyes shut as tightly as possible, and tried to give praises to God for Matthew's love. But she found that not quite possible either, like a harmonica with one stuck key, just one note short of perfect.

So Sarah pushed past the mysterious tears, the image of Mam, the warnings, the stuck note that stubbornly refused its song. She prayed the prayer of too many young girls whose hearts and wills are not in complete sync with the will of a loving heavenly Father.

God, please listen to my prayer and give Matthew the love I feel for him. I want him so much. Not my will, but thine, Lord, you know that. All things are visible to you, including my thoughts. Please, bless me with Matthew.

In time, it would all straighten out, she knew. Even if it wasn't perfect now, God would provide. Placing her trust firmly in his hands, she fell into a troubled sleep. But she woke up crying, thinking Mervin had called her.

All this, however, was tucked into a hidden recess of her mind, and the face she presented to her mother at the breakfast table was one of sweet and unconfused innocence. Except for the lurking shadows Sarah was completely unaware of.

Mam watched her daughter and knew how much wisdom and patience it would take to keep her peace.

CHAPTER 25

By Monday evening, the wind had died down and the air had turned crisp and cold. Dat spread clean, yellow straw in the horse stable, preparing for the horses that would be tied in the stalls.

As he fluffed up the clean bedding, his lips moved in prayer, putting this meeting of minds into God's hands. He knew well how meetings could turn disastrous, with everyone voicing their own opinions, each one different, and sometimes espousing views that were poorly thought out and coupled with passion and self-will.

But it was good they could come together like this, and he walked through the barn with an optimistic outlook. He was glad old Aaron Glick would be among them, and he was pleased that there remained a measure of respect for the older generation.

Levi was in fine fettle, dressed in a blue shirt, his hair shampooed and combed with slow and deliberate care, his glasses polished, held to the light, and polished again. He knew this was a matter of importance, and he knew the fact that he had seen that white car would finally be noticed.

And the biggest highlight would be his mother's warm cinnamon rolls, frosted with caramel icing. She said he'd be allowed coffee, although it had to be decaffeinated. Decaf. That's what people said when they ordered breakfast at a restaurant.

Levi loved to drink coffee with the men. He didn't particularly enjoy the bitter taste. But if he put lots of creamer into it and had plenty of cinnamon rolls on the side, it made him feel like one of the men, sitting there, grimacing that certain way, to show he could drink it hot, like a man.

So when the men began to stream through the door and take their seats around the kitchen table, Levi sat at the end, reaching up a heavy arm to shake hands enthusiastically, so glad to see Omar's Sam and Abbie's Ben's Amos, Davey Esh, and Sammie's Reuben, for he knew them all. Levi rarely forgot a name or a face, usually connecting the two within seconds.

Dat opened the meeting with a moment of silence, and Levi looked very grave when the men's heads were lifted. He knew who God was, and he knew that it was important to include that invisible chap at times like this.

Dat spoke first, as minister as well as a victim. He spoke of the fact that they had no clues at all about the arsonist, other than his son Levi's description of a white car, and he'd let Levi tell them exactly what had occurred that night.

Levi cleared his throat, looked around the length of the table to make sure he had everyone's attention, and then drew his eyebrows down behind his glasses. He sighed with resignation when Melvin appeared at the kitchen door and said, "Come in, Melvin. You should have come earlier." There was friendly chuckling as Melvin slid unabashed into the remaining chair.

Levi waited, then began, his voice low and strong, his demeanor one of pure enjoyment.

"As you know, the night the barn burned, I was sick with *hals vay* (sore throat). I was up and around."

Dat hid a smile, his son so obviously holding court and his choice of words so clearly premeditated.

"I thought it was so strange that a white car would come in the lane at such a late hour."

Here, Levi's eyes narrowed, and he achieved that perfect cunning look of his, the one he assumed when he played Memory with Suzie.

"I went to the bathroom, and when I came out, the car was going past the house already."

Dat's head lifted, his gaze became intent. "You mean going back out?"

"*Ya. Ya.*"

"You never mentioned that, Levi."

"Well, I'm not done, Davey. Maybe you'd want to stay *sochta* (quiet)."

The men exercised great restraint then, no one wanting to upset Levi, but they found it hilarious that he had called his father by his given name. Oh, he was a character, they said after the meeting.

"The shape of the tail lights was sort of round and down low, so I remembered them. I have a whole pile of football cards, you know, and then I started collecting car cards. Vehicles, you know. *Scheena. Mascheena.*"

He had everyone's attention now, the roomful of faces turned toward him.

"Suzie, I need a glass of water." Suzie, seated in the background, blushed and looked frantic, reluctant to be seen by all the *freme* (strangers). So Melvin got up and poured him a cold drink from the pitcher in the refrigerator and handed it to him.

As wily as a small bird, Levi's eyes twinkled up at Melvin, "Is your name Suzie?"

With that, Levi slapped the tabletop with great hilarity, and no one could keep from laughing as he took his time drinking the water, for all the world an imitation of his father when he preached. He then looked around for a place to set his tumbler even though the tabletop was clearly in front of him.

Dat thanked God silently for the gift of his son with Down syndrome and the way he spread humor and goodwill around the table. Just stay with us, Lord, he begged.

"So," Levi resumed, "as close as I can get to it, I think it was a little Volkswagen. An older model from 1978. Like this one."

Taking his time, he pushed back his chair and turned, his wide back bent at a slight angle. Reaching into a drawer, he produced a card with a vehicle showing the distinguishable features of a 1978 Volkswagen.

"It's a punch bug," he said, grinning widely. "I believe the car the arsonist drove was an old punch bug."

Murmurs broke out, but resonantly above the others, Melvin said, "Boy, that would really narrow it down!"

Heads nodded assent. Without being aware of it, Melvin took the floor, Levi listening with a resigned expression. He wasn't finished yet.

"Well, if it is an old Volkswagen the way Levi says, I bet we could eventually find the driver. That wouldn't be impossible. Hard but not impossible, if we get the cops in on this. And in the meantime, we need to take every precaution to stop this arsonist from becoming bolder yet. He obviously isn't worried about anyone catching him setting fire to a barn, or he wouldn't do it anymore. It's just a matter of time till the next one goes up."

"Ah, come on! He's not going to have the nerve," Abbie's Ben's Amos said confidently.

"That's what you think," Melvin shot back. "What's going to keep him from it? We just sit here like a *glook* (hen) hatching peeps, doing nothing, so what else can we expect?"

There was a ripple of assent, but no one spoke up.

"I suggest, if you live close to the road, your chance is about 75 percent higher of having your barn lit. If you don't, it could be lit anyway. So, if I had a barn, that's where I'd sleep."

Voices of disagreement broke through.

"I ain't sleeping out there."

"No way."

"In winter?"

"Nobody could pay me to sleep out there."

Now Melvin's face turned red, his eyes glistening with the need to express himself.

"Well, be that way, then. If your barn burns, don't come crying to me."

At these hotly spoken words, Dat's warning flag waved silently.

Old Aaron Glick was bent, thin, his hair and beard a banner of white in his old age. But his eyes were bright with wisdom and experience.

"I think Levi here is on to something. The Bible says a

child shall lead them. Well, Levi is a man, of course, but we would do well to heed his words. However, Melvin is right. If you want to join the community effort to stop the fires, either sleep out there or spend hundreds — maybe thousands — of dollars installing some smart smoke detectors."

Merv Zook, who was somewhat ill-tempered too much of the time, cut him off. "By the time a smoke detector went off, the barn would be half burnt to the ground."

"Well, then, sleep out there," said Abbie's Ben's Amos, who was still annoyed that Merv had never fully paid him for the last load of straw, the money from which he wanted to spend on a new patio for his wife. The look Merv gave Amos was sadly lacking in brotherly love, but the meeting righted itself and kept moving forward.

Elam Stoltzfus, soft-spoken, ill at ease in a crowd, and never one to voice his opinion, came up with the most workable solution so far. "Could we install a bell attached to a wire that runs across the driveway?"

But without electricity? How would they work?

Inverters. There was a way.

Someone suggested putting an article in the daily paper, warning the arsonist of these three precautions the Amish people would be taking.

Dat shook his head no. "That would not be our way. We don't want to appear as if we're going to battle. I think each idea that has been offered is a good one. Each man must decide for himself. But I do agree with Melvin. We need to wake up, become more aware. No one knows the horror of a night like that unless you experience it firsthand. Let's do what we can to avoid it. Melvin, you're a young man with time on your hands during winter when roofing's slow. Would you be willing to take the responsibility of talking to the police?"

"I could do that."

Sarah was seated in the living room crocheting a white afghan. She looked up and smiled when Melvin spoke, noting the lack of humility, the joy of his elevated position.

"So," Dat continued, "We have agreed to take Levi's words seriously, right?"

Levi nodded vigorously, and Dat smiled at him.

"The rest of us will decide to cooperate with either a bell or a smoke detector or we will leave our good warm beds to sleep in the barn."

Laughter broke out, but everyone was seemingly in agreement. Then Ez Stoltzfus said that if everyone trusted in the Lord with all their hearts, the way the Bible says, there would be no need for any of those costly solutions. An aura of shame arose, and no one had anything to say.

Finally, when the silence became uncomfortable, Dat spoke again, saying that was true, and if Ez's faith was great, then it would be alright for him to do nothing.

Melvin, however, was visibly sputtering.

They exchanged ideas and solutions for another hour, until Levi said he believed he smelled coffee. He turned his head and wiggled his eyebrows at Mam and Sarah, who hurried to the kitchen to serve the men cups of coffee, fresh cinnamon rolls, stick pretzels, and sliced Longhorn cheese.

Levi was so clearly in his element, and it touched a chord in Sarah's heart to see the kindness of these men around him. They knew he was special and treated him as someone who deserved just that. Special treatment.

Abbie's Ben's Amos's wife, Lomie, had sent a package containing a new Sunday handkerchief, two packages of Juicy Fruit gum, and a pair of brown jersey knit gloves for Levi. He was beside himself, since it wasn't even Christmas yet.

Mam served quietly, nodding her head at comments, smiling in that discreet way of hers, always showing good manners, living her life by example. Dat was confident in his wife's dutiful maneuvers. It was clearly a blessing watching her parents interact with the men of the community, Sarah observed in silence.

What set a minister's wife apart? Nothing, and yet a great deal depended on her support. She needed to supply quantities of it, always striving to build her husband's confidence and his service by *guta-rote* (sound advice) as the lesser vessel. At the same time she was a powerful ally, and Sarah knew the power of her mother's prayers better than anyone.

All she wanted from life was a marriage like her parents' marriage, and Rose had told her not everyone could say that, after she sighed dramatically and rolled her eyes.

Melvin caught Sarah's eye, beckoned her over, and then rose to go to the *kesslehaus*, where a dim kerosene lamp shone from its black wrought iron holder on the side of the oak cabinet.

"So, how's my Sarah?" he asked, grinning cheekily.

"Your Sarah?"

"Yeah. Hopefully not Matthew's yet."

Sarah sighed and let it go. So now there were three of them. Genuine roadblocks. Mam, Melvin, and Priscilla.

"No, not yet," she said quietly with restraint.

"Tell me about Edna."

"Edna King? Oh, she's great! Melvin, she is!"

They stood in the *kesslehaus*, two cousins who shared a rare and beautiful friendship. Under the cold December moon, in a world that had been fractured by three horrifying barn fires, the assembly of men in the kitchen, each one looking out for the well-being of the others, enjoyed warm cinnamon rolls and coffee as they tried to patch together a workable plan.

For Sarah, her personal world was no different—torn with indecision, doubt, and above all, the yearning to be Matthew's wife. It was all she had ever wanted. Now it seemed so near and yet so completely unsure. Was anything ever certain in life?

Now it seemed every barn roof that gleamed in the moonlight on this night was in danger. The Amish men of the community knew this. They had formed a plan of sorts, but ultimately their faith ruled, and they knew it. So nothing was certain, nothing was worthy of confidence, at a time such as this.

It was faith, as stated in the book of Hebrews, that sustained them all: "Faith is the substance of things hoped for, the evidence of things not seen."

Sarah could only rely on her fledgling faith, as she chose to think of it. Her father's faith was like an eagle, soaring on powerful wings, so many years ahead of her in the wisdom and learning she hoped to achieve someday.

Outside, the moon touched each carriage top with a dull gleam, spidery branches etching a pattern across them. Somewhere in the old apple orchard, an owl called, and another one answered, its hushed cry a warning to all the small creatures of the night, burrowed in their warm hollows and caves in the ground.

The warm yellow light shining from the kitchen was a small beacon of life, love, and caring. But the splendid light of human charity was the new barn, perfect in its entirety, the symmetry a banner of God's gift to man—the serenity to accept the things they could not change, the courage to change the things they could, and the wisdom to know the difference.

And somewhere, a white older model Volkswagen puttered along the rural roads of Lancaster County.

The End

A suspenseful romance by the bestselling Amish author!

LINDA BYLER

DAVEY'S DAUGHTER

LANCASTER BURNING • BOOK 2

CHAPTER 1

SARAH BEILER, DAVEY'S DAUGHTER, BENT OVER, grabbed the back of the stubborn boot, and yanked as hard as she could. She groaned and threw the offensive footgear into a corner of the *kesslehaus* (wash house). Priscilla had worn them again and gotten them wet. Would she never learn?

Resigned now, Sarah found her old Nikes, undid the laces, shoved her feet into them, and tied them again—more roughly than necessary. She'd just have to tiptoe through the snow, unless Dat had shoveled a path to the barn, which was unlikely considering how precise he was with the milking time.

Grabbing a navy blue sweatshirt, she pulled it over her head, tied a men's handkerchief low on her forehead, and plunged through the door, bracing herself for the cold and snow of December.

Sarah quickly lowered her head to avoid the stinging flakes, then lifted her face to the sky, which was dark and gray but alive with the swirling whiteness of the first snowstorm of the year. Christmas was only a week away.

They'd have a white Christmas!

Already, the snow was drifted against the corner wall of the new cow stable, where the wind created eddies, same as a creek when it rounded a bend.

Excitement pulsed in her veins at the thought of an early snowstorm creating a wonderland for Christmas. It was just more festive with snow. Holly was greener, berries were redder, cookies more Christmasy, gifts wrapped in red and green glowed brighter when there was sparkling snow.

Sarah's early morning grumpiness had dissipated by the time she pulled on the door latch to the milk house, where the glass steamed from the hot water Dat had already used. She entered and set to work assembling the gleaming stainless steel milking machines.

The diesel in the shanty purred to life as Dat prepared to begin the milking.

When Sarah walked into the newly whitewashed cow stable, the two rows of clean black and white Holsteins were already being fed, jostling their chains, lifting and lowering their heads, impatient to taste the richness of their twice daily portion.

"Good morning, Sarah."

"Morning."

Dat went on with his feeding as Sarah prepared the first three cows for the milking machines and then turned to fetch them from the milk house.

She still appreciated the barn, the cow stable, and the milk house in a way she never had before their barn burned to the ground only eight months prior. It had happened one April night when the buds were bursting open on the maple trees in the front yard.

The whole family had suffered a night of terror,

standing by helplessly as innocent animals, family pets, faithful workhorses, and driving horses had suffered horrible deaths. The battle against real fear occurred after the local police called it arson.

Davey, as a minister of the Old Order Amish who had lost his own barn, could freely sympathize with Ben Zook and Reuben Kauffman after each of their barns was also set on fire. He became a pillar of support for both of them.

His leadership in the community was thrown into question, however, when Priscilla, his daughter who had been deeply traumatized by the terrible, fiery death of her riding horse, Dutch, was questioned by a local reporter about the fires. She answered the reporter in a way that was considered inappropriate for the Amish, saying she hoped the arsonist would go to jail and die there.

Levi was the oldest of Davey's children and had Down syndrome. He was thirty-one years old, overweight, and clumsy, but he was the character of the family and was known and loved by everyone around him. He enjoyed a life of love and compassion, feeling pretty sure that he was an important part of Lancaster County, especially since the last meeting between prominent members of the church, when he was called upon to describe what he had seen the night of the Beiler barn fire as he had been up and about the house with a sore throat.

Levi had an exceptional memory and was astonishingly observant. He had informed the men at the meeting that a white car, maybe a Volkswagen, had driven by the house.

Sarah was now twenty years old, tall and lithe, with curly hair that never lay as sleekly as she wanted. Her seawater green eyes changed color with her emotions—gray and stormy like waves tossed by the wind when she was upset, dancing yellow lights like sunshine on rippling water when she was happy. She had grown up with a constant yearning for her neighbor, Matthew Stoltzfus, whose brown eyes never failed to melt her. He had always been the object of her affection, and she had never dreamed of marrying anyone but him. But when she turned sixteen years old, the time when she entered her years of *rumspringa* (running around), Matthew suddenly began dating her friend, Rose, a sweet and beautiful girl.

Their relationship had thrown Sarah completely off balance and stretched her faith to its limit. Now suddenly, a few years after they had begun dating, Rose called off the relationship with Matthew, which put him in an awkward situation as he strove to hide his emotions with pride and hurt battling for control. He had given Sarah enough reason to believe that he would now pursue her, and she now lived in constant suspense waiting to see what would really happen.

"Sarah!"

"What?"

Dat's call was urgent, so Sarah set down the milker she was carrying and hurried toward the sound of his voice.

"Is Priscilla up yet?"

"No."

She came upon an unforgettable sight. In the early morning dimness, the sputtering gas lantern swayed on its hook from the new, yellow post that had been erected by hundreds of men eager to show their charity by helping Davey back to his feet, lifting his spirits to new heights by erecting a new barn in only a few days. In the lantern's light, Dat's eyes were pools of shadow, the wide, black brim of his felt hat hiding the emotion on his face as he stood, helpless, in the face of the scene before him.

Sarah reached her father and grasped at the oak post, rough and splintered but a support as she beheld the horror. She let go of it then as both hands went to her mouth, and she uttered a long moan of denial.

In the light of the unforgiving lantern lay Priscilla's new riding horse, also named Dutch, a replacement for her first beloved horse. Dat had tied him in the stall with a neck rope—the soft, sturdy nylon rope often used for driving horses—when he was cleaning the box stall the day before.

Dat had intended to finish, but a distraught member of the church had come to seek advice, and Dat left the barn. He figured Dutch would be alright for a while. Then, with his mind filled with his church member's troubles, he had spent a distracted evening and hadn't been able fall into a restless sleep until after midnight.

Now Dutch's sides bulged, and his legs curled helplessly. But the real horror was his twisted, elongated neck, where the rope buried into his flowing mane, strangling the life from his veins as he had desperately struggled to free himself. It appeared as though his own panic had been the cause of his death.

"He's dead!" Sarah cried, her voice cracked with fear. Dat shook his head, his lips a grim line of resolve, but he did not utter a word. Slowly, he reached into his pocket, extracted his old Barlow knife, moved in beside the already cold form, and cut the nylon rope with a few precisely executed movements.

Dutch's head flopped to the floor with a "whumpf," and bits of shavings wafted upward, clung to the beautiful mane, and shuddered, as if attempting to give some sort of life back to the dead horse.

Dat did not look at Sarah, his voice like gravel pouring over stone when he said, "Go get her."

"I can't."

Dat was suddenly crushed by the emotional weight of too many barn fires, too many men bringing their petty disagreements, too many sleepless nights. He turned on Sarah, his large, work-roughened hands clenched, his eyes bulging, and he yelled in a voice Sarah had never heard before.

"*Harich mich* (Listen to me)!"

Her breath coming in harsh sobs, Sarah ran, slipping and falling to her knees, her bare skin exposed to the wet iciness of the snow. She got to her feet and kept going, blindly. She slipped again on the wet floorboards of the porch, righted herself, and fell through the door, her breath coming in ragged gasps.

Mam was sorting laundry on the floor of the *kesslehaus*. The safe, ordinary odor of moist, used towels, soiled socks and dresses and shirts and aprons brought Sarah back from the shock. Her mother straightened, looking at her in surprise.

"Sarah! *Voss iss lets* (What is wrong)?"

"Mam! Priscilla's horse! He...he hung himself."

"Oh my," Mam replied with complete hopelessness, a defeat so raw she could not utter another word, unable to draw the breath needed to say anything more.

Leaving her mother, Sarah moved heavily, numbly, up the stairs and found her way to her younger sister, Priscilla, who lay snugly under the warm comforters, sweet and innocent. Her hair was light brown with streaks of blonde running through it, and her green eyes were closed in trusting slumber.

Sarah reached out and shook her shoulder, then sat

on the edge of the bed and whispered, "Priscilla. Cilla!"

Alarmed, Priscilla sat up quickly, her large eyes blinking.

"Sarah! It's your turn to milk."

"I am milking. Priscilla, listen, you have to be strong. Dutch...he...your horse is dead."

"What?"

It was plain she had not understood Sarah's words. She was sure she just hadn't heard right.

"He hung himself by his neck rope."

"No, he didn't. He couldn't have. He's not in a tie stall."

Priscilla was certain there was a mistake, so there was no reason for her to become upset. She remained calm and carefully explained it all away in her still somewhat groggy state.

Sarah persuaded her to get dressed and come to the barn, where they found Dat, grimly lifting full, heavy milkers and dumping them into the stainless steel Sputnik vat on wheels. Wearily, as if he had suddenly aged far beyond his years, he told his daughter what had happened, flinching in the face of her inability to accept what had occurred.

"He'll be alright," she said and moved away toward the horse stables to find her beloved pet, still and cold and unmoving, her second precious horse now as dead as her first.

"He did," she whispered.

Broken, she fell on her knees beside him, her hands fluttering to his chest, reaching out to feel for just one steady heartbeat but defeated already.

"Why?"

She lifted her head, seeking an explanation.

Dat spoke reassuringly, taking all the blame, saying he should not have left him in a tie stall.

"But why?" Priscilla asked, struggling to understand how a horse as smart as Dutch could have panicked as the rope tightened.

"Well, it happens. Some horses just lose all common sense and keep jerking and pulling until their breath leaves them."

Priscilla remained quiet, her hands stroking the still, lifeless form of her horse. She was weeping but calmly, resignedly.

Sarah searched Dat's face, and he shrugged his shoulders.

"I'll finish milking," Sarah said.

Dat nodded, then looked past her as the figure of his wife came through the door. He was visibly lifted by the appearance of his unfailing supporter.

Mam did not go to Priscilla. She just put a hand on the side of the cow that was being milked and took over, instinctively handling the heavy milking machines and helping Sarah do what had to be done.

They left Dat with Priscilla and Dutch.

The cold and the snow whirled outside the rectangular blocks of yellow light at the windows. The purring of the diesel was muffled by the storm and the drifting snow as the milkers ka-chugged along, extracting the rich milk from the cows.

There was no singing, no humming, no whistling this morning. There were only two women who had once more been assailed by adversity and were now gathering the strength and resolve they would need yet again. They silently went about their duties, knowing that this, too, would pass, and the sun would shine again, for Priscilla, for them all.

In the horse barn, Dat stood, his head bent. Then he fell to his knees beside Priscilla, an arm going around her thin, heaving shoulders.

That was all.

But is there greater human support than that of a father's love? Feeling the undeniable strength of that strong arm across her back, a heart filled with compassion and caring propelling it, Priscilla turned her head and buried it in her father's coat as his other arm came around and held her close to his heart. He willed her to be strong, to be able to rise above this loss one more time.

"*Noch ay mol* (One more time), Priscilla," he murmured, his tone as cracked and broken as his heart.

Priscilla nodded and sniffed but remained in the circle of her father's comforting arms.

"God does chasten those He loves. Don't feel as if you did something bad to deserve this. You didn't. Perhaps He just allowed this to see what we make of it."

Sighing, he reached for his handkerchief, stood up, and handed it to her.

"We'll get another one, okay?"

She nodded.

"At least it's not one of us, Priscilla."

She nodded again. "Yes, Mervin was...so much worse."

The memory of his youngest son's drowning remained an ache in Dat's heart, one that would never leave him, and one he cherished, strangely. The memory of six-year-old Mervin served as an unfailing source of empathy and understanding when folks around him were hurting or grieving, grappling with their own losses.

"Yes, it was," Dat agreed.

"Well," Priscilla began. Her voice broke as she let out a long, unsteady sigh, and the soft weeping resumed as Dat stood by, his presence a support.

She rubbed the wrinkled, red handkerchief fiercely across her eyes and shuddered. Then she pinched her lips together in an attempt to show strength and steady her emotions.

"Well," she began again. "I should be glad maybe, Dat. You know he was going blind in one eye, don't you? The whole eye was clouding over, and when I went around barrels, he didn't always know what he was doing. So maybe...I don't know. I'll probably want another horse, eventually."

Dat nodded. "Yes, I'd noticed he had trouble in that one eye, but I figured it might not amount to much."

"It would have."

Dat knew Priscilla was probably right. She knew so much about horses, so he nodded.

She looked down at Dutch, lying so still and cold, and she squared her shoulders and said, "Will Benner have to take him?"

"Do you want him buried here on the farm?"

"Yes. I'd rather. I can't stand to think of him being used for dog food. Could we bury him beside the remains of the barn?"

"Of course."

When Dat and Priscilla reappeared, Sarah could tell by the set of her younger sister's shoulders that everything would be alright. Priscilla would rise above this. Hadn't she already weathered so much?

Mam headed back to the house with her arm around Priscilla's waist and sat her down at the kitchen table. She made a cup of strong mint tea with cream and sugar, brought her daughter warm slippers, and stoked the coal fire in the stove. Then she banged the big cast iron frying pan onto the gas stove and added a generous glug of canola oil. She turned to the refrigerator and removed the blue granite cake pan of cooked cornmeal mush. With an efficiency born of habit, she sliced it and placed the pieces in the sizzling oil, talking all the while, reliving disappointments of her own, and calling Suzie, all in one breath.

Suzie was the youngest daughter and was still in school. She was a miniature replica of Sarah, except for her straight, honey blonde hair and her love of dogs. The goal of her life was to own a Lassie dog, her name for collies.

Mam opened one of the oak cupboard drawers, pulled out an old beige, doubleknit tablecloth made with her own hands, and spread it quickly across the kitchen table. Then she thumped six Corelle plates and six clear plastic tumblers, her *vottags glessa* (everyday glasses), onto the table.

She set a jar of homemade ketchup, a dish of butter, one of homemade strawberry jelly, salt and pepper, the honey bear, and Levi's vitamins in the middle of the table.

She turned to slice bread for toast when Levi's voice cut through the comforting sounds of breakfast preparations.

"Malinda!"

So it was Malinda this morning, not Mam. She caught Priscilla's eye, and they lifted the corners of their mouths in unison.

"*Du mochst an hesslichy racket* (You make a big racket)!"

"Come on, Levi! Time to get up."

Levi's bedroom was on the main floor in the enclosed porch facing the driveway and barn. The many low windows were filled with tin cans containing colorful geraniums, Mam's pride and joy.

His hospital bed, a nightstand, dresser, recliner, and a few bright, woven rugs made up his pleasant bedroom. It was his area of comfort and belonging in the old stone house that had been remodeled over the years to accommodate a family of ten children.

Three married sons and two married daughters completed the David Beiler family. Anna Mae and Ruthie were each just a few years older than Sarah and already had babies and homes of their own that were filled with the aura of completion and contentment that seems to permeate young Amish homes.

They had a fit about Sarah and her senseless yearning. Although they usually kept their thoughts to themselves, occasionally a snippet of their indignant views would slip out, allowing Mam to glimpse the discordant note between her married and single daughters.

Well, Anna Mae and Ruthie had better watch out, she would think, setting her jaw firmly as she drove Fred home from sisters day. Those two had had pretty uncomplicated courtships.

"Malinda!"

"Levi, what is wrong now?"

"*Ich hopp ken hussa* (I have no trousers)!"

"*Yoh* (Yes)."

"*Nay* (No)."

Priscilla got up from her misery to help Levi find a pair of trousers, which were not in the usual drawer but folded neatly and stacked on top of his dresser, where she had put them the day before.

"You have to look, Levi."

"That is not where I look for my trousers, and you know it. You just didn't want to open the drawer and put them in. I know how you are. Always in a hurry."

Priscilla managed to laugh and tweaked his ear. He lifted a large hand to slap it away, but he was smiling, the crinkles beside his deep brown eyes spreading outward.

Breakfast was subdued but not without encouragement, as they heaped their plates with the crispy, golden slabs of cornmeal mush, fried eggs, stewed crackers, and chipped beef gravy. The plastic tumblers were filled with the orange juice made from frozen concentrate that Mam bought by the case from Aldi.

Levi's weight was a constant challenge. Some meals could turn into a battle of wills, but the first meal of the day was normally not restricted, so he was a cheerful person at breakfast, happily dabbing homemade ketchup over his stewed crackers and spreading great quantities of strawberry jelly on thick slices of toast.

Priscilla ate very little, and Sarah noted with concern the look of suffering in her eyes as she watched the snow swirling against the kitchen window.

Mam poured mugs of fragrant coffee and brought a fresh shoofly pie from its rack in the pantry. Sarah cut a fairly large wedge for herself and one for Levi, smiling at him as he thanked her over and over.

Dat said he'd have to ask Ben Zook to use his skid loader to bury Dutch. Then they had to explain to Levi what had occurred that morning, and he listened with great interest.

Wisely, he shook his great head. "Well, I didn't make it up then. A car drove in here. I was up during the night and walked to the bathroom. I saw it. I bet there was someone in the barn."

Dat slowly set down his mug of coffee, the color leaving his face. Mam turned, her mouth open in disbelief, her eyes wide, alarm clearly visible.

But it was Priscilla who began to shake uncontrollably.

CHAPTER 2

DAT QUESTIONED LEVI EXTENSIVELY, AND HE answered with calculated precision.

No, it wasn't snowing then.

Yes, it was a white car.

White shines in the dark. It's a lot lighter than the darkness. The lights were round, down low, just like the time the barn burned.

Clearly, there was only one choice. The police had to be notified. The story made it into the *Intelligencer Journal* the next day. It was just a short strip with no picture, which was Dat's wish.

The police had urged the Amish people to invest in dogs. Big dogs trained to attack, but Dat was slow to be convinced, saying if they did get an attack dog, was it really worth the injury to another person? What if an intruder was accidentally killed?

As they discussed the article and the issue of the dogs, Sarah suggested allowing Suzie to get her Lassie dog, and Mam's face softened as she looked at her youngest daughter with so much affection that Sarah could hardly watch.

Then Sarah caught Priscilla's eye and smiled, encouraging her to smile back.

Priscilla had been brave the day before, Sarah thought. Very brave. In fact, so courageous, it had broken her heart to watch her sister standing in the snow, a black figure, her head bent, her shoulders slumped, her eyes downcast.

Priscilla had been braver than she had been herself. For one thing, why did they have to send that Lee Glick with the skid loader? Dat could have driven Fred over to Ben Zook's and left him in the barn while he came home with the piece of equipment to bury Dutch himself.

Furthermore, wasn't it about time that Lee finished up his stay at Ben Zook's? Sarah thought he would have returned home months ago, but now he had a job and everything. Had he decided his home was now here in this community?

The thing was, Lee always unsettled Sarah—not really unsettled, but he left her feeling as if she wasn't quite getting it or didn't understand something he understood.

Or was she just remembering the night of Reuby Kauffman's barn fire, when she…. Sarah lifted cold hands to cheeks that turned warm at the thought. Oh, he was just being kind, she told herself. He would help anyone. But would he help anyone in such a…thoughtful way?

At any rate, who showed up driving that skid loader but Lee Glick with his blond hair covered by a gray beanie? His gloved hands quickly dug a hole, drug out the sad black and white carcass with the skid loader, and rolled the great horse into the yawning, cavernous hole before covering it neatly and packing it down by running over it repeatedly.

Sarah could have stayed inside, she supposed, but Priscilla needed her support, so she stood beside her, watching the snow drift across the landscape creating a vast whiteness interrupted only by jutting buildings and trees and telephone poles, drooping wires hanging between them.

When the skid loader stopped and Lee hopped off, Dat reached into his pocket for his wallet, but Lee waved it away and stood talking to Dat for the longest time.

Lee was taller than Dat, something Sarah hadn't realized. As they turned, Priscilla waited, her eyes never leaving Lee's face. She was mesmerized, Sarah could tell, and was surprised to find herself suddenly irritable, cold, her feet wet inside the soft lining of her snow boots.

When the men reached the girls, Lee looked only at Priscilla, and she lifted her eyes to thank him.

"Hey, no problem. Glad I could help. Must have been hard, losing another horse."

"It was."

"I feel really sorry for you. I sure hope the police can help."

"We talked to them this morning already."

"Really?"

Priscilla nodded.

Dat gave Lee more details, and he whistled low, then shook his head. And he continued to ignore Sarah as if she had all the charms of one of the apple trees behind them as he asked Priscilla questions and listened closely to her replies.

Just when she was ready to walk away, Lee turned to Sarah and asked how she was. His eyes met hers with so much blue it was like a streak of lightning blinding her for a second before she could see clearly.

"I'm fine," she said curtly.

"You get home okay Saturday night?"

"Yeah."

Defiantly, she met his blue eyes, eyes that seemed to mock her now. She felt as if he knew everything that happened that night between her and Matthew Stoltzfus.

She felt the warmth rising uncomfortably in her face, and she lowered her eyes and kicked at the loose snow, her composure sliding away in a free fall along with the whirling snow.

Dat stood comfortably, his hands in his wide trouser pockets, his black coat bunched up above them, his wide black hat protecting his face and shading his eyes as he observed this exchange with seasoned perspective.

It wasn't Dat's way to say anything serious about matters of the heart. That was Mam's domain, but a small smile played around his lips as he noticed Sarah struggling to regain her air of aloofness.

So that was how it was with Sarah. Well.

The remainder of the day she thought of Matthew, his warm brown eyes, the way he had asked if she'd consider being his girl. She thought how it would feel to have finally attained the long awaited goal of being exactly that— Matthew's girl. Oh, the thought of buying and wrapping a gift for him! She'd dreamt about it for years but knew couldn't happen this year, but the next one, likely.

As she mixed the butter and sugar for a batch of peanut butter cookies, she planned what she would buy. When she burned the first sheet of cookies, Mam was not happy, her cheeks a brilliant shade of red, her hair almost crackling with frustration, clucking and fussing, saying she'd never been so on behind with her Christmas baking, and goodness knows she still had nothing for Anna Mae's baby.

"Sarah, stop being so dreamy. It upsets me."

Sarah watched her mother running around,

accomplishing nothing. She told her to calm down—she was acting worse than Mommy Beiler ever had.

"Humpf."

It was a huge insult. Mam esteemed her work ethic far above that of her late mother-in-law's, but she was used to navigating the surprising waters of mother-daughter relationships, and so she drew her lips to an uncompromising line and remained silent.

After about a hundred Hershey's kisses had been pressed into as many peanut butter cookies, Sarah felt uncomfortably warm and nauseous, not to mention completely irritated by Mam's silence, so she said loudly, "I don't know what you're so mad about."

Mam burst out laughing, sat down, and slid low in her chair, her feet wearily stretched in front of her. She pushed up her white covering, extracted a steel hairpin from her bun, and scratched her head before replacing it.

"Huh," she sighed. "One of these years, believe me, I'm going to skip Christmas altogether. I'll just sit in a corner somewhere and read a Bible story about the Baby Jesus and let it go at that."

She stretched her arms over her head.

"Levi, get away from there!"

Mam sat up and leaned over, her eyebrows lowering as Levi tried to make off with yet another cookie.

This was when Sarah loved Mam best. When she was completely herself—just Malinda, humorous and comfortable and not taking things quite as seriously as usual.

"These peanut butter cookies make me sick after the chocolate on top gets cold," Levi said, as wily and slick as any thief trying to convince a judge of his innocence.

"They do not!" Priscilla retorted.

The door burst open, and Suzie exploded into the

house with her bonnet tied haphazardly over her head scarf, her boots covered with snow, and her coat buttoned crookedly.

"Hey! The English people's school bus is stuck on the hill past Elam's!"

"Oh my goodness. Is it still snowing? *Ach* (oh), it is. Well Suzie, I hope you were careful coming home. My goodness."

Suzie reached for a cookie. She watched Levi's hand snake out and grab one, too, before shuffling back to his card table and the display of cards spread on out it.

"Levi, put that cookie back," Mam said without turning around.

Levi stopped in his tracks, facing away from Mam, and said, "What cookie?"

"The one in your hand."

Quickly, Levi inserted the cookie in the gap between the buttons on his shirtfront and answered glibly, "I don't have one."

"You don't?"

"No."

"Okay then."

That was the most entertaining part of the entire day, aside from the hole being dug for Dutch, or rather, that chap driving the skid loader, Sarah decided.

Why did he do that to her? It seemed as if he kept planting his blond head into her thoughts when she did not want to think about him at all.

It was Matthew she loved, and it was Matthew she planned on marrying. It was just that....

She wished that she'd never gone to Reuby Kauffman's barn fire. All it had done was bring back the terror, the memory of the screaming animals, and all the helplessness their own fire had brought into her life.

And then Lee had held her securely in his arms as she struggled to recover from her fainting spell. Of course, he would have helped anyone. That was how Lee was.

He was the one who buried Dutch. And he was helping his brother-in-law, Ben Zook, finish the details in his barn, working every evening after work for months. He was always one of the first ones on the scene at barn raisings, one of the last to leave. It seemed as if that was all he did—work for other people and help them out.

Was that how someone was measured? Sarah didn't know. She just wished she'd never met him, the way he made his way into her thoughts like an uninvited intruder.

Sighing, she thought about making supper and doing chores. The usual routine suddenly felt like an insurmountable burden. All she wanted to do was roll into her bed and cover her head with the quilt to block out the snow and Christmas and Dutch and Priscilla and, yes, Lee.

That evening, Sarah walked to the barn and halfheartedly helped Dat with the milking. Her thoughts were a million miles beyond the cow stable, Lancaster County, or anyone around her. She missed Mervin and wished she could see him again, touch him, tousle his blond hair, just one more time.

When a cow lifted a heavy, soiled foot and kicked her shin hard, she yelped in surprise, then pain. She began howling in earnest, bringing Dat to her side as a dark bruise started forming beneath her woolen sock.

"Boy, she socked you one, didn't she?"

Grimacing, Sarah laughed ruefully, nodding her head. "She has a secret hatred for me."

Dat laughed heartily and agreed with Sarah that she

was an ill-tempered cow. He had seriously considered turning her into steak and hamburger. Now he said he just might have to.

"Nothing broken, is there?"

"No, it was just enough to make me good and angry."

"You weren't too happy to begin with."

Sarah nodded. "Yeah, well. Sometimes you just aren't yourself," she said, making an enormous effort at cheeriness.

Dat watched Sarah and then took the golden opportunity to ask her if she had prayed for God's guidance in seeking a life companion.

He was shocked to hear the rebelliousness in his daughter's voice.

"You make it sound like one of those better-than-thou books. Of course I pray. The Lord showed me a long time ago that His will is for Matthew and me to be together."

The words were explosive, forceful.

Dat's eyebrows raised of their own accord.

"Alright, Sarah, alright. You know I'm not the one you talk to about matters of the heart. I get embarrassed talking to you about...."

"Say it," Sarah said harshly, unkindly.

"Sarah."

The tone in his voice stopped her downward spiral into a stream of hurtful and useless words.

"You don't want to be this way."

"How do I want to be?"

Dat didn't answer. He just turned to the cow being milked and bent to retrieve the milker. He poured out the warm, creamy milk and placed the machine on the next cow.

Straightening, he watched Sarah's face and said, "All

I want is for you to be honest with yourself."

"I am."

"Alright. If you are, there is no need to defend yourself."

That sent Sarah into a miserable state of confusion. Dat had never mentioned Matthew's name, so what was all that supposed to mean? Now thoroughly confused, she walked out of the barn into the cold evening that was just headed toward dusk. The sun was spreading a pink and apricot glow beneath the remnants of the snowstorm, infusing the stone house with an other worldly brilliance as the snow piled in glistening heaps on the shrubs and bushes reflected the same beautiful radiance.

Well God, she breathed, her prayer a whispered need, a small cry of confusion from a bowed spirit. You're going to have to come through if....

She couldn't finish, somehow unable to lay her sacrifice on the altar, afraid to think or pray about what was hidden in the recesses of her heart, that delicate balance of her own will, God's will, and Matthew.

As if in immediate answer to her troubled spirit, a dark figure cut into the Beiler driveway, the black horse easily pulling a two-seater sleigh—a cutter—painted a glossy black. Her cousin, Melvin, waved wildly. He was wrapped in a ridiculous pile of outerwear, his prominent nose rising above his gaudy, plaid scarf.

"Sarah! Good! You're home! Come on. Let's go for a ride before every back road is cindered."

"Give me a minute!"

And that was all she needed. She washed her hands, donned clean socks, boots, a sweater, coat, head scarf, and warm gloves before limping and slipping out to the sleigh and the impatient horse.

"Here we go! It's unreal how quiet this is. There is not one sound except for the horse's hooves, and even they're muffled."

He talked as if he had invented the sleigh and the horse and created the snow, the sun, and the clouds himself, Sarah thought, knowing Melvin as well as she knew herself.

They sped through the waning light, the cold invigorating her, dashing all the confusing thoughts from her head. Like cobwebs, they were swept away with an unseen broom.

Melvin chattered away, and Sarah listened, nodding her head or saying, "Mm," or "Okay," or some other fitting word to assure him that she was listening.

When she did have the opportunity to tell him about Priscilla's horse, asking if he had seen the paper, Melvin's mouth opened, his eyes widened, and he shook his head in disbelief.

That was all it took to start another of his verbal explosions, his head nodding and hands gesturing as he spoke of the very real danger of someone losing yet another barn or more livestock.

"It's just a matter of time. I bet you anything that horse reared back out of fright, seeing someone sneaking into the barn. But the nerve! Can you imagine someone doing this again? Still driving the same car? He can't be too smart, or he'd drive a different vehicle. For Pete's sake, Sarah. What a loser!"

Sarah reminded her agitated cousin that Levi may not have been completely awake or was imagining things, trying to create drama, enabling him to have the top spot at meetings.

Melvin disagreed vehemently, turning the sleigh at the

end of Irishtown Road, skillfully handling the reins with one gloved hand as the other one waved in the air for emphasis.

That was the end of the conversation as the wind picked up and whirled their words away in its fury.

Sarah's shin throbbed painfully beneath the heavy blankets, and her face was numb with the piercing cold. She pulled the blanket higher, hiding her face behind it until they slowed to a stop back at the house, and Melvin jumped out.

"Come in for hot chocolate," Sarah said.

"You know I won't turn that down."

"Good."

Limping, her leg causing her serious discomfort, Sarah made her way into the house and hung her wet, snow-covered things by the coal stove to dry.

Levi was getting ready for bed, taking his blood pressure medication and his vitamins and minerals. He was dressed in flannel pajamas, navy blue ones with the white pin stripes. He had on brown slippers, and his hair was clean and wet from the shower.

"Melvin's here," Sarah told him.

Levi shook his head, slowly gathering the small pile of pills in his hand.

"I'm going to bed."

"But Melvin wants to talk to you."

"No, I don't feel good."

"But Levi, he's worried that our barn isn't safe, the way Dutch died."

"No, I'm sick to my stomach."

With the words spoken forcefully, Sarah knew his mind was made up, and he would refuse to cooperate at all.

Levi turned away and shuffled heavily to his room. He sat on the edge of his bed and muttered to himself before turning off the battery lamp and swinging up his legs, grunting with the effort of settling his large body comfortably.

Mam appeared out of nowhere, clucking, bringing an extra comforter to spread over Levi's great bulk. She tucked him in, worrying about the roaring wind outside as the snow blasted against the windows. She returned to her bedroom and opened the lid of the cedar-lined chest that had been her great-grandmother's and had the initials A.M.K. inscribed on the front.

She pulled out homemade comforters, pieced with blocks of fabric cut from remnants of fleece. They were knotted securely with brightly colored yarn from leftover skeins from afghans she had crocheted.

None of the colors matched, but that was not the purpose of the comforters to begin with. As long as the fleece patches were sewed firmly and the yarn was pulled through twice and securely knotted, they were well done and served their purpose.

Those comforters stayed in the cedar chest all year except for the coldest part of the winter, which had come early this year.

Mam bustled up the stairs, Suzie in tow, distributing the necessary comforters. She spread them over the beds, tucking them between mattresses and box springs, saying, "*Ach* my. *Siss kalt do huvva* (It's cold up here)."

She clattered back down the stairs, a cozy light shining from her kindly eyes, *fer-sarking* (taking care of) her children on a cold winter night, the way she had done ever since her firstborn lay in his crib in a corner of the bedroom in the old stone house.

She'd bustled then, and she bustled now and was fulfilled by her motherly duties.

"Just listen to that wind!" she exclaimed to her husband and her nephew, Melvin, who had followed Dat into the kitchen.

Dat shook his head, saying he'd watched those gray clouds just as the sun left that red slash in the sky. He figured a real wind would be kicking up.

Melvin looked around for Levi, clearly wanting to have him describe in detail what he had seen during the night.

"Where's Levi?"

The question was inevitable, and Sarah knew he'd be disappointed, knowing once Levi refused to talk, it was like trying to budge a two-ton rock. Impossible.

"He's in bed."

"Well, ask him to get up. I want to talk to him."

As always, Melvin's voice was clear and precise, and it carried well, producing a rumpus from the hospital bed.

"Melvin, just go on home. I'm not well."

"*Ach*, come on, Levi!"

"No."

"I'll give you some gum."

"No."

Melvin looked to Dat for assistance, then to Sarah, saw the futility of his attempts, and sank resignedly into a kitchen chair. Sarah served him hot chocolate and peanut butter cookies, and they talked far into the night.

The fear wrapped itself around Sarah, an unsettling cloak of mystery, the unknown a burden as Melvin's words rang in her ears.

"Mark my words, Davey. There's more trouble to come. If he thinks we Amish are all going to turn our backs and let him terrorize all of us, he has another guess coming."

Maybe we're the ones who have another guess coming, Sarah thought to herself.

CHAPTER 3

THE WIND WAILED AROUND THE EAVES, SENDING A section of loose spouting clattering down the side of the stone house with a metallic crash that woke the whole household. Levi cried out in alarm, and Suzie called from her bedroom in hoarse terror.

Sarah jumped out of bed, grabbed her woolen robe, and hobbled painfully down the stairs, meeting Mam already halfway through the kitchen, her small flashlight slicing a path across the darkened room.

No one went back to bed before Dat dressed warmly, lit a gas lantern, and searched the barn and the outbuildings, holding the lantern high, before finally coming upon the indentation in the snow left by the section of spouting. He carried it triumphantly to the porch, his great relief visible.

Mam sighed, the tension leaving her body, and told them they could now go back to bed. Sarah took two Tylenol tablets and swallowed them at the kitchen sink. She cowered at the window as a mighty gust bent the great, old maple trees in the front yard, erasing the vast bulk of the new, white barn for only a few seconds.

She shivered.

The cold lay around the baseboards along the walls and crept along the windowsills, where the coal stove's heat could not quite keep it at bay. Little swirls of chills shivered up Sarah's back as she turned to Mam, who was warming her hands by tentatively touching the tips of her fingers to the top of the coal stove. Mam pulled Suzie close against her when Sarah came to join them.

In the dark and cold, they huddled, the warmth a comfort, creating an aura of normalcy. Though they didn't say it, they all knew this whole scene contrasted sharply with the way they would have reacted previously to a noise in the night.

The truth hovered between them, driving them into isolation with their own thoughts. The shame of their fear, or the admission of it, would have to remain unspoken, a denial of the fact that it existed.

They were people of faith, weren't they? Christian folks of the Old Order who placed their trust in God. They were blessed by Him as seasons came and went, with the rain and the sun and the good, brown earth sprouting the seeds they planted and the barns bulging with the abundant harvests as the leaves turned colors, signaling winter's approach.

So what were they doing now, cowering around this stove and casting furtive glances over their shoulders, peering into the dark corners that had become hiding places for strange men, Bic lighters flicking as they terrified good, strong, sensible horses into a state of deathly panic?

Barns that stood tall and stately had crumpled and burned to useless black piles that no one could ever fully erase from their minds. The memories left apprehension lying thick and suffocating over Lancaster County.

"Go back to bed," Mam said curtly.

Everyone obeyed, silently padding their way up the staircase, knowing that in previous years, they would all have remained in their beds and later laughed about the great crash the spouting had made during the night. But that was before the ongoing mystery was wedged into their lives. Now, they would need to adjust, over and over, to overwhelming waves of fear.

In the morning, Leacock Township already had the great, rumbling snowplows shoving walls of snow to the sides of the roads. Heavy chains were secured around the big tires, and the machines clanged and banged as they scraped along, yellow revolving lights warning passing vehicles—if there were any—of their approach.

The wind remained stubbornly stiff and unrelenting, so Sarah helped Dat shovel paths to the barn and every-where else anyone would need to go on the property. The wind had their walkways blown shut again in a few hours, so they kept at it. The sun was shining, however, and Sarah preferred the outdoors far above being cooped up inside with Levi.

His stomach pained him terribly as a result, of course, of his over-consumption of peanut butter cookies.

Mam was at the phone half the morning. She was in quite a stew about Ruthie's two year old who had the croup. She worried he'd have to be taken to Lancaster General Hospital *ivver vile* (soon).

Suzie couldn't go to school, so she sang the same song over and over as she sharpened her colored pencils with a battery-powered sharpener that emitted a high whir as each pencil was poked into it.

"My Lord, my King, you're my—WHIRRR—every-thing—WHIRRR—Glory sing."

Sarah could only take about two minutes of that until the cold and the wind looked positively inviting. Back outside, she looked up to see her sister, Priscilla, wading through the snow on her way to find a sled, no doubt.

As Sarah turned in the opposite direction, she saw another familiar tall figure wading through the snow, coming over the small hill from Elam's.

Matthew!

As usual, her breath caught in her throat, and her heartbeat, thought it was already elevated from shoveling snow, accelerated to an even faster rate. And, as usual, she felt her confidence slip away, afraid that this time she would need to accept that he was back together with Rose, the relationship resumed, and this time, they would remain together, inevitably being married the following year.

She was surprised to see he was waving, his arm swinging wide with enthusiasm as he caught sight of her. She stood still, awaiting his approach, a smile playing around her lips.

"Hey, whatcha' doin'?"

She lifted her shovel and turned her face to smile at him.

"Shoveling?"

She nodded. "What does it look like?"

"Shoveling snow?"

She reached out to hit his forearm playfully, and he smiled at her, his teeth dazzlingly white in his dark face, his black beanie pulled low on his forehead, his eyes warm and brown and inviting.

"Hey, Sarah. I walked the whole way up here through

the cold and the wind and the deep snow to ask you to go to the Christmas singing with me. Want to?"

There was no shyness, no hesitation with Matthew, and she answered quickly and maybe a little too loudly with a resounding, "Oh yes!"

Her eyes were shining, her face glowed, the tendrils of her curly, brown hair swirled about her forehead, and she could not take her gaze away from him.

"Good. Good, then. I'll pick you up Sunday evening. Around six, six-thirty."

"I'll be ready."

"You have a Christmas dinner that day?"

"Yes, of course. Though it's a little strange with Christmas on a Sunday this year."

"Well, we have Monday off, too, Second Christmas."

"We have the Lapp Christmas dinner that day."

"Your mam's side?"

"Yes."

"That's cool."

Matthew stood, relaxed, unwilling to leave her, so she leaned on the shovel and watched his face, taking in the way his nose turned down just perfectly, the two black wings for eyebrows.

He said, "Your hair's a mess," as he reached up and lifted off his stocking cap. He set it firmly on Sarah's head, pulling it down well below her eyebrows, then stood back and laughed aloud.

"You look really cute like that."

Sarah pushed the beanie up, a warmth spreading over her face.

From the kitchen window, Mam's paring knife slipped, wobbled, then stopped completely, her jaw sagging in disbelief as Matthew put his cap on Sarah's head. Her mouth compressed, her eyes sparked, and her nostrils distended only a millimeter as she brought the paring knife through the potato with a new intensity.

Did that boy have no shame? In broad daylight, traipsing right in their driveway to flirt openly with their daughter, who he knew was an easy target. In her day, in her *rumspringa* years, that was completely unthinkable, and here he was, larger than life, without a care in the world of what she or Davey thought.

A sharp pain shot through her thumb as the knife slipped again and cut a nasty slice into the skin. Quickly, she bent and opened the cupboard door, ripped a paper towel off the roll, and wrapped her it around her thumb.

She wanted to cry. She wanted to bang her fists against the window and chase him away like an unwanted starling at the birdfeeder. Instead she walked calmly to the oak medicine cabinet, got out the box of Band-Aids, and applied one with all the concentration she could muster, avoiding looking out the windows as much as she could.

Taking a deep breath, she steadied herself and sat down heavily. She knew this was not right. So she bowed her head, the part in her hair perfectly centered, her hair sleekly falling away on each side. Her hair was graying but still retained most of its dark color under her large, snow-white covering with its wide strings falling down her back.

Her lips moved in prayer as tears hovered between her eyelashes and quivered there before dropping onto the gray fabric of her apron, creating dark splotches while her cheeks remained dry.

Mam had reached her Waterloo. It was such a maddeningly futile situation, and she knew she must let go, give up her own will, and replace it firmly with God's will.

How could her own precious, beloved daughter be so blind when the dashing Matthew was so obviously still in love with the beautiful Rose?

Or was she, herself, blind to God's will? She didn't know, so she gave herself up to God, following the advice handed down from generation to generation, the sound principle of the ages for every Amish wife and mother. You could never go wrong by giving yourself up.

Mam had just resumed her potato peeling when Sarah bounded into the *kesslehaus*, yanked open the door to the kitchen, and charged over to Priscilla at the sewing machine.

"Did you see Matthew?"

Priscilla looked up.

"Where was he?"

"Here. He came to ask me to go to the Christmas singing!"

"He did? What did you say?" Priscilla ducked her head and giggled as Sarah swatted her shoulder. "You said no, right?"

But Sarah was already on her way up the stairs, taking two steps at a time before bounding back down.

"Mam, may I go to Lizzie Zook's store?"

"Why?"

"I have to have a new Christmas dress. I have to."

Resigned, Mam turned, her face inscrutable. "Why?"

"Matthew was here. He asked me to go to the Christmas singing with him. I only have my burgundy dress from last year, or that homely looking dark green. I look sick in that one. Please, Mam?"

What Mam wanted to say and what she did say were two entirely different things.

"I suppose you can. How would you go? Surely not

Fred and the buggy on a day like this?"

"Of course!"

Priscilla was elected to accompany her in spite of Suzie's protests. Levi came to the rescue and promised her a game of Memory, and Sarah promised her a new book.

The town of Intercourse was digging itself out of the snowstorm, but as it was only a few days before Christmas, plenty of cars crawled along Route 340. Horses and buggies clopped along the roadside. Pedestrians hurried along swept sidewalks and ducked into shops frantically looking for last-minute gifts. Trucks carrying fuel oil or tanks of milk geared down for the red light at Susquehanna Bank as the girls neared their destination—the fabric shop in the heart of the village.

Bolts of fabric stood upright along low shelves, an endless display of colors and patterns making it difficult to choose. Sarah remained indecisive till Priscilla began tapping the toe of her boot and looking at the ceiling, accompanied by a hum that grated on Sarah's nerves. Her sister's impatience distracted Sarah and scattered her resolve to settle for the red that was not as pretty as a more brilliant shade—one that would be completely unacceptable to Mam.

Mam was so strict, Sarah thought. She never changed with the times. Well, not never. But not very often.

"Priscilla!" she hissed.

"Hmm?"

"Would you get this one?"

"You're crazy," Priscilla said flatly.

"Why?"

"You just are. You know Mam will never allow it. Don't even think of letting Dat see you in that orange red."

"They'll hardly see it."

"Not at the singing?"

"Oh, I forgot."

Her shoulders sagged with defeat. Well, it would have to be the dull red with the barely discernible stripe. That was all there was to it.

She took it to the counter to have it cut, paid for her purchase, and returned to the buggy, stowing the white plastic bag beneath the seat.

On the way home, they ate broken pieces of Fifth Avenue candy bars from the plastic bag they had purchased at a reduced price from Nancy's Notions. They examined the Christmas wrap and bows Sarah had purchased for her gifts, and Sarah launched into a colorful account of the elaborate gifts she would buy for Matthew once they were dating. She shrugged off the look she was receiving from Priscilla.

"You don't like Matthew," she said out of the blue much later.

"I like him okay. I just don't want you to get hurt. I'm sure you know as well as I do, he likes every girl in a hundred mile radius."

"But he will like me best, once we're dating."

Priscilla pretended to read the new children's book she'd purchased for Suzie and shrugged her shoulders with an air of disinterest.

"Yeah. Could be."

The subject was over almost before it started, and nothing more was said.

On Christmas Day, the sky was a spectacular shade of blue, crowning the white snow, creating crevices of blue and gray where the shadows lay beneath the drifts.

Sarah was up early, helping her mother arrange all the

wrapped presents in a large pile on the drop leaf table in the living room. It was overflowing with gifts beneath and beside it as well, the way it always was.

The forest green of the roll-down blinds behind the sofa blocked the bright glare of sunshine on snow. The cushions on the couch had patterns of brown and red and, with the green blinds, created a scene of Christmas colors.

There were no other decorations for the holidays except for a few red and green candles scattered throughout the house. Since Dat was a minister, it was expected that their family would have a plain house, to lead by example, without worldly displays of expensive artwork or fancy curtains.

Not that Mam didn't think about it, she always said. But she had a nice, new house and nice furniture, so she was content and wanted to stay within the rules.

Anna Mae and Ruthie gave Mam nice things, saying what did it matter, but invariably the ceramic figurines and fancy candleholders and dried flowers ended up in the bedroom, out of sight.

The turkey was in the oven, the stuffing bursting out of its cavity, and by mid-morning the smell of celery and onion permeated the house. In the *kesslehaus*, the ham cooked in ginger ale and pineapple juice, moist and succulent, causing Dat to inhale mightily as he walked through the door.

Sarah was peeling potatoes at the kitchen sink when the first vanload of brothers and sisters-in-law arrived, followed by a team and buggy containing Ruthie and her husband. The chaos officially began.

Dat hurried into the bedroom in his stocking feet, tiptoeing, telling Mam to welcome them in. He hadn't changed clothes yet, and Mam's cheeks flamed red as she said, "*Ach* Davey, what were you doing till now?"

She opened the door, stood aside, and smiled as she waved her offspring inside and kept on smiling.

She cuddled babies, kissed toddlers, shook hands, and looked deep into her grown sons' eyes. She saw they were alright, life was good for them, and they were glad to be here.

"Where's Dat?"

"Oh, he's still changing clothes."

"What a loser!"

"Hey! Watch what you're saying!"

Dat emerged from the bedroom carrying his black Sunday shoes, his black socks in the opposite hand, and his hair uncombed. But a wide smile of genuine holiday welcome was shining from his face.

"Barefoot!"

"What's wrong with you? It's Christmas!"

Dat's eyes shone with a bit more than their ordinary moisture as he wrung his strapping sons' hands, telling them it was just wonderful to see them again. He shook hands with the daughters-in-law and gently held the grandchildren and marveled at their growth.

Mam's eyes sparkled, her color remaining high as she whirled between the stove and the long table, which was now extended with twelve leaves, allowing twenty-four people to be seated at once.

The tablecloths were green, the paper plates a patterned red, the plastic tumblers clear. These paper products were all Anna Mae and Ruthie's doing, Mam had lamented as she placed them on the table early that morning. She should be using her Sunday dishes, she said. Sarah told her times were changing, and she'd be thankful when it was time to do dishes.

Ruthie had made the Christmas salad in Tupperware molds, two of them, but told Mam she hadn't the slightest clue how to get them out of there. She knew they'd flop the minute the molds were inverted.

Mam's eyes sparkled as she filled the sink with hot water and lowered the molds into it for about a minute before turning them on a plate and slowly taking off the lids. She was rewarded by a sucking sound, and a perfect ring of red, green, and white Jello stood perfectly on the plate as Anna Mae's family and another vanload arrived.

The house was full, too warm, and extremely noisy. Levi held court by the drop leaf table, taking gifts as each new family presented them and thanking the givers repeatedly.

It was a wondrous Christmas dinner. Mashed potatoes heaped in Melmac serving dishes, puddles of browned butter pooled on top and running down the sides. Gravy—thick and salty—in Mam's best ceramic gravy boats. Wide homemade noodles swimming in chicken broth. Carrots and peas seasoned with a pinch of salt and plenty of butter. And coleslaw, deviled eggs, applesauce, and, because it was Christmas, cashews and the best olives in cut glass dishes with dividers down the center.

Dat had Abner believing he had cured his own ham and had a good laugh before he told him it was a John Martin ham. Allen said he probably raised the turkey, too.

No, Dat admitted, the meat was bought at the grocery store. Raising pigs and turkeys for meat was just not profitable, unless the farmer had a couple thousand of each and a good contract from the feed company.

"Sad, isn't it?" he said. "It used to be that my

grandfather could make money keeping a few hens and pigs and milk five cows by hand, but no more, as the price of feed eclipsed the price per pound of beef."

This led to a discussion of times past, including the boys' antics growing up on the farm.

Sarah was careful, eating very little, knowing Matthew would be picking her up at six. She'd have to look her best and being stuffed with holiday goodies was not an option.

Allen leaned across the table. "Don't you have a boyfriend yet?"

Sarah shook her head and busied herself feeding little Ruthanna.

"What are you waiting on?"

"Oh, till I'm thirty."

"You already are."

They all laughed uproariously at Sarah's expense. She laughed with them, so glad the secret in her heart was not visible, her joy a hidden treasure from prying eyes.

"Hey, you should come to Dauphin County to teach school. Next year three of our teachers are getting married. You haven't taught school yet, and that might fit you perfectly," said Rachel, Allen's wife, her voice carrying a seriousness that Sarah knew was not just banter, like her brothers.

"Maybe I should."

But, oh, I won't. I won't, she thought, exhilaration infusing her mind and heart. Next year, I might very possibly be married to Matthew.

Gifts were exchanged, the children wiggling in their seats, anticipation coloring their cheeks. They squealed with delight at the books and Legos, the dolls and coloring books.

Levi unwrapped his gifts with a great deal of show-manship, folding the wrapping paper and telling Mam to keep it with a gruff commanding voice. He was simply speechless when he received a brand new air hockey game from his brothers.

That was what they played the remainder of the day, as they nibbled on the homemade candy and cookies, the leftover ham and turkey, the fruit and nuts and punch.

Dat watched from his seat on the brown recliner, a child on each knee, and whooped and laughed and forgot all his troubles for one blessed Christmas Day.

He remembered to thank God especially for Levi, who continued to bring them many moments of pure and unabashed humor. Lord knew, there were plenty of concerns to level it all out these days.

CHAPTER 4

TRUE TO HIS WORD, OR ALMOST, MATTHEW arrived at a few minutes before seven. Amid much loud teasing and banter, Sarah managed to get out of the house unruffled, a smile on her face.

Matthew greeted her warmly, kept a lively conversation going, seemed genuinely interested in her family's Christmas dinner, saying he couldn't imagine having a family that size.

Sarah laughed as she leaned back against the seat. Matthew asked if she was wearing a new coat.

"Yes."

"It's pretty cool. "

"Thanks."

She became shy then, wondering if the new coat was trying too hard. Well, she'd needed one, so she guessed he'd just have to think what he wanted.

"You didn't buy the new coat on my account, did you?"

The question took her completely off guard, and she floundered, red-faced, caught in a hard place. If she said no, he'd think she didn't care, and if she said yes, it would appear a bit desperate. She just couldn't come up with a coherent answer.

Matthew seemed to enjoy her discomposure, a half smile playing around his features, his confidence allowing him to relax and remain at ease, even when Sarah was so obviously nervous. That was the only rough part of the whole evening.

He unhitched his horse, asking her to help and then wait until he could accompany her to the shop where the parents and youth were assembling.

The youth sat around a long table with the girls on one side and the young men on the other. The parents sat around the walls of the shop, and propane lamps hissed gently from their cabinets.

The singing had already started when they arrived, a sea of green and red and black dotted with white coverings, as everyone lifted their voices to sing the old German and the newer English Christmas carols.

Many faces turned to watch their arrival. Acquaintances' hands went to their mouths, and eyebrows lifted. Well, he hadn't waited long to move on, they thought.

Mam stared straight ahead, and Dat lowered his head. Matthew's mother, Hannah, watched them like an exultant hawk sure of its prey. Her husband, Elam, didn't care one way or another as he was sound asleep beside her.

"How'd you get here so fast?" Sarah whispered to Mam.

"The boys dropped us off."

"Oh."

"Rose!" Sarah turned to greet her friend, who was also dressed in red, but to Sarah's chagrin, the red she'd wanted so badly before deciding to take Priscilla's advice.

Oh, she looked like a Christmas flower, her blonde hair shining, her face glowing, catching the red of her dress. Her large eyes were luminous, her white teeth so perfect as she caught Sarah's arm.

"Come with me!"

Together, they made their way to the bathroom, giggling nervously, and then collapsed on the rug and talked as fast as they could, catching up on local news. They chatted about the farmer's market in New Jersey where they both worked and what a madhouse it always became over the holidays, when they were absolutely run off their feet.

Then, the inevitable.

"I didn't see you come in. How'd you get here?"

"Matthew."

"Is he taking you home?"

"Yes. I...I think so."

Rose said nothing after that, the silence thickening around them. Suddenly she blurted out, "Sarah, how does he...I mean, like, how does he seem to be? Happy? Sad?"

"He's...he's just Matthew. Sort of the way he always was. Normal. The way I've always known him."

"Is he going to ask you?"

"No."

Her answer came too loudly and forcefully, and Rose knew it as well as Sarah.

Sarah's face felt burning hot, she reached both hands up to cool it, her icy fingers bringing their temperature back to normal.

"Rose, please don't be suspicious of me."

"Well, the thing is, I miss him, and I'm torn with horrible indecision. Are break ups ever okay? I mean, here

I am, rid of what really bugged me about Matthew. His selfishness, his....I mean it, Sarah, don't you ever tell anyone this, but he's sort of lazy sometimes, and yet I find I miss him so much. His good qualities do far outweigh his bad ones. Love is so weird. Sometimes I wonder if I know what it is. Now that I don't have Matthew, part of me wants him back. It's so hard to know what is right. I'm afraid to go back, because what if I don't want him after all—after we're back together?"

She leaped to her feet, leaned across the narrow counter top, and checked her image very carefully in the mirror. Then she turned, taking a deep breath and clasping her hands in front of her small waist, the one-sided conversation obviously over.

"Well."

It was an ending, and Rose had pulled the lever of control on the conversation, her blue eyes infused with a sweetness that comes in a packet, Sarah thought, Sweet and Low and awfully artificial.

Obediently, Sarah stumbled clumsily to her feet, so ill at ease she could not meet her friend's eyes. She felt gawky, unkempt, only a shadow of Rose. Yes, she was a shadow. A darker version of the true Rose.

As they walked into the room, the singing was already going well, rising to the rafters of the shop where members of the Amish community had gathered for an evening of praise on Christmas.

Many of the songs were sung in the old German language, timeless old Christmas hymns that reached back to the homeland in the Emmenthal Valley of Switzerland. There the forefathers had come to a decision to move to the New World, and they had settled in Berks County but ultimately became cloistered around Lancaster, where the soil was dark, loamy, and very productive.

The German hymns were beautiful and easy to sing. The youth sang mindlessly as they waited for the more catchy English tunes that were allowed after the traditional ones had been sung.

Children were lined up in small groups on the benches along the walls, trying their best to behave. They were so stoked on sweets, they could barely hold still, so they swung their feet, wriggled, pinched each other, giggled, and laughed out loud. Then they clapped their hands over their mouths, their eyes rolling above them, before a stern father or harried mother came to straighten up their erring offspring, which also served as a reprimand to all the children for a while.

After all, it was Christmas. Tomorrow was another holiday and another Christmas dinner or get together or hymn singing, so the children remained in high spirits.

Sarah, however, remained subdued, singing without her heart or her mind in the music.

So, that was how Rose felt. She wanted Matthew if she couldn't have him, but if he was available, she was not so sure. What in the world was wrong with her?

For Sarah, there was no question, no doubt, no wondering. She would always be happy to be with Matthew, second best or however he wanted her. As long as she might have a chance to be his wife, to share the remainder of her life with him, she would be senselessly happy.

That was all she wanted from life. Wasn't that real love?

That dry-mouthed, heart-thumping sensation the moment she was fortunate enough to be in his company? Everything he did, everything he said seemed so right and fine and wonderful, and that was how it would remain after they were married.

Marriage problems were completely out of the question for her and Matthew, as they would be the perfect epitome of God's will.

And so Sarah's thoughts went swirling about here, rampantly wandering there, her will level with God's, she was sure. After all, wasn't He a loving benefactor who gave richly of all things to enjoy? Dat spoke of God's love every single time he stood up before his congregation.

In the Old Testament, if God was with the children of Israel, they were given the victory over opposing armies. Nervously, Sarah stole a sideways glance and figured if that wasn't a formidable foe, she sure didn't know what would be. She watched Rose singing prettily in her showy Christmas dress, knowing all eyes were upon her. She had to know.

A swift dart of anger found its mark in Sarah's heart, thrown skillfully by the one who deceives. Her countenance fell as she lowered her head, and the singing paused for a bit.

She'd approach Matthew. She'd ask him fair and square about Rose.

Immediately, she knew she couldn't. She would not be able to build up the nerve, the sense of self to ask. Nor would she have the strength to accept if his answer was a disappointment.

She'd just clothe herself with God's righteousness, as the men of old had done, and He would be on her side, so who could come between them?

These thoughts came to her rescue on the way home, when Matthew remained silent. The horse plodded through the drifts that kept blowing stubbornly across the road in spite of the frequent runs made by the snowplows.

It was when they were stopped by the barn that Matthew turned, looked at her in the light of the headlights, and asked, "What would you say if I asked you for a date?"

There were no words anywhere for Sarah, her mind scrambling to catch what Matthew had just said.

"Did you hear me?"

"Yes. You mean, what would I say?"

"Yeah."

"How do I know if you're serious?"

"Oh, I'm serious."

"Then, I guess it's a yes."

"Good."

Sarah sat, looking straight ahead, a statue of fright.

"Aren't you going to look at me?"

She did, slowly, always obedient to Matthew's voice no matter what he asked. It was Matthew, the love of her life, and she would do whatever he asked, if it meant being his.

So when he leaned towards her and found her lips, there were none of Mam's urgent words of warning to keep her from joyously yielding to his passion.

It was much later when Sarah ran up to the porch, opened the door silently, and tiptoed across the kitchen and up the stairs with stars in her eyes.

Sleep completely eluded her now. With her eyes wide open and her thoughts so scattered she could only retrieve bits and pieces of them, she lay in bed and smiled into the darkness.

He loved her!

He hadn't said the words, but oh my!

Over and over, she relived the evening and the intimacy with Matthew. And knew she had conquered.

Matthew loved her!

His mother would be so happy, the circle so complete now. Mam would be alright with time, wouldn't she?

She thought of telling Hannah and Elam, knowing her position in their family would be cemented from the start. Hannah had always wanted this.

She thanked God over and over, her heart singing an old song of love.

In the morning, she was allowed to sleep in, if half past six could be called that, rising from her bed after being awake most of the night.

Nothing, however, could now dampen her outlook on life. Her wide eyes and bright smile gave her away completely before the family even sat down around the cheery breakfast table.

"My, you're happy this morning!" Mam observed.

"Yes, Mam, I am. Matthew asked me last evening."

She couldn't stop the heat rising in her face nor could she meet her mother's direct gaze, creating a sense of caution between them.

There was a moment of silence as Mam struggled with her emotions, unknown to Sarah, of course, the way she busied herself with the pancake batter. Eventually Mam said brightly, "Good for you, Sarah. I'm happy for you, if this is what you want."

"It is."

At the breakfast table, the steaming dishes between them, their hunger slowly satisfied, they spoke of Matthew and Sarah. Dat succeeded at hiding his surprise, and Levi slid his gaze slyly to the side and announced that there would be a wedding soon. Sarah laughed happily and said yes, there might be, but not till next year.

Priscilla watched Sarah's face and kept her innermost

thoughts to herself. She congratulated her with as much genuine honesty as she could muster, but all was lost on the jubilant Sarah.

Suzie was the only one to remain silent, keeping her eyes averted, pouring syrup on a buttered pancake with great concentration.

"Suzie!" Levi tapped her arm. "Aren't you going to say something to Sarah?"

"Yes, of course. I just guess my teacher will be disappointed. Matthew comes down to school almost every evening," she said.

Mam's eyes met Dat's, and both raised their eyebrows, their faces completely rearranged seconds later, although there was no need as Sarah was oblivious to their exchange.

"Who is your teacher?" Levi asked quickly.

"You know."

"No, I don't."

"Her name is Naomi Ann."

"Who?"

"Oh, you don't know her." Suzie waved a hand, eliminating the need for further questioning.

Soon the Monday that had begun so favorably was clouded when Sarah caught sight of her mother sitting alone in the middle of little Mervin's twin bed. Her shoulders sagged with the weight of her grief as she held a pair of his flannel pajamas to her face and inhaled their smell, her *zeit-lang* (longing) for her youngest child encompassing her spirit yet again. Sarah stopped as she passed the door of his room and then went in to sit silently beside her mother, her hands in her lap, her head bent.

Finally, when a broken sob rose to the surface, she slid a comforting arm around her mother's heaving shoulders and said, "Don't, Mam. Please don't."

There was no answer, only small pitiful sounds coming from the pajamas.

Sarah's own eyes filled with tears, but something— what was it?—kept her from feeling deeply sympathetic. Did Mam really have to be like this, now?

Choking, Mam dropped the pajamas in her lap, wiped her eyes with the always useful corner of her apron, and took a deep, shaking breath.

"Sometimes, on days like this, when I'm not really pushed to get a lot of work done, I come up here to Mervin's room, just to remember. It helps to hold his clothes, feel them, inhale the odor of him. Or I guess what's left of him."

Sarah nodded, unable to form the words expected of her.

Sniffing, her mother straightened and reached for the small cedar chest containing his treasures, her fingers lifting each one—a steel sinker, a pencil sharpener, a bit of paper, two quarters, a dime, a spool of white thread. Then she replaced them, closing the lid, a finality, once more grasping for strength to sustain her.

"Oh, he was just so small. The water so horrible and strong. It must have thrown him around like a rag doll. I always hope he bumped his head and passed out, that he didn't suffer, swallowing that awful water. He was so little, so alone, and I wasn't there to help him."

Lost in the throes of her agony, she stared, unseeing, at the opposite wall, unable to rise above the bitterness of her small son's drowning.

"Why do you still feel this way, Mam? It's almost eight months since he died."

"I know. Time passing by helps, but I still need my

personal time to grieve every now and then. He was my baby."

Mam turned her head then, taking Sarah completely by surprise, and said, "Let's talk about you now."

"Why me?"

"Oh, I'd think you'd be so very excited about dating Matthew."

"I am, Mam. It's every bit as unreal as you imagine."

Mam nodded, flipped a covering sting behind her back. "So now we need to have the talk about dating, too."

"What do you mean?"

Mam watched Sarah's face, the color spreading across it, the averted eyes, and knew suddenly why she had felt this sense of sadness, the grieving for her lost son, which had to be faced as well as this talk with her daughter.

Her voice fell firmly on Sarah's ears.

"You know that I cannot be untrue to you, Sarah."

Groping for words, Sarah's mouth opened and closed again.

"I want you to be happy."

Mam watched Sarah's profile, the bowed head, the way the curls sprang from her forehead like they had done when she was a little girl. Mervin's age.

How precious these daughters had been arriving in succession after four boys! Little Sarah, her hair a riot always, the mothers clucking and exclaiming, saying that the paternal grandmother had given her that wavy hair— that's what.

Here she was, concerned about Sarah but grieving for Mervin when, after all, Mervin was *fer-sarked* now, wasn't he? But what about Sarah?

"You know I have my concerns about Matthew. He's

always been a magnet for girls, and I'm just so afraid...."

"Stop it, Mam," Sarah's voice cut in, sharp, frightened. "You don't want me to be happy, or you wouldn't talk to me this way. Matthew really does love me, Mam. He...he kisses me. He...he likes me much more than other girls. I know I can keep him happy. I can be his girl, and he will not want anyone else."

Mam thought of backing down, of trying to believe her daughter. She thought of putting her up on the same pedestal where she'd perched Allen, thinking he was so much more than he was. In her eyes, in those days, Allen had done no wrong. Whatever he thought, Mam thought. Whatever he did, Mam thought was just great as well.

That, she knew now, was the surest, fastest path to a very real tumble off the pedestal, hurting more than one person in a clumsy plunge seen by everyone who had predicted it.

Mam had learned her lesson when Allen had moped around the house, sighing and crying after his beloved Katie broke off the relationship. He lost his position as foreman of his uncle's framing crew soon after.

To exalt one's offspring, to esteem them with pride, was not the way of the fruits of the Spirit, the humility and love of Christ's way, she had learned and learned well.

"Sarah, you stop." Mam's voice was terrible, cutting through all the assurance Sarah had piled around her sleeping conscience.

"First of all, young lady, he kisses you? And how much do you think that has to do with real love? The kind that lasts."

"Everything!" Sarah burst out passionately now.

Mam shook her head in disbelief. "Have I not taught

you anything?"

"Why would you have? I never dated. That should be reason enough, don't you think?"

"Sarah, you must listen to me. You said he asked you for a first date and yet he has already kissed you? More than once? I am having a fit, seriously."

"Well, you'll just have to have one then."

With that, Sarah propelled herself off the bed and strode purposefully into her room, closing the door with more force than necessary.

Up came Mam's head. She stretched both arms high, got off the bed, and followed her daughter's footsteps. She yanked open the door and stood there, her feet planted firmly, her eyebrows lowered, her fists on her hips.

"You will not slam a door in my face!"

"I didn't."

"Of course you did."

Then Mam talked, really talked. She warned Sarah of the dangers of confusing love with want or need. She said it was the confusion that follows the heels of living by your own will, tricking yourself into believing that God approves of your will.

Sarah calmed under Mam's words, spoken with authority, although not without kindness. Mam assured her she would stand by her choice, and only God knew what the end result would be.

"I think you are old enough to make sensible choices, Sarah, but this is not one of them, allowing yourself this intimacy with him before you are dating. It's just not good, and I'm afraid nothing good will come of it."

Sarah said nothing.

"I'll have to ask you to promise me you'll speak to Matthew about this."

"I can't, Mam!" Sarah wailed.

"Why not?"

"It's asking too much. It's...it's all I have."

Sinking down beside Sarah, Mam realized from this statement just how great the danger really was, and she quaked in her shoes.

Oh my dear, small Mervin! I grieve for you when you are so safe, in a much better place with the Heavenly Father and all the angels. Here on earth, we are faced by this real adversary. How should she go about this?

In her wise way, Mam decided to wait. She needed to talk to Davey. They had a Christmas dinner to attend, and Sarah must have a bit of time as well.

So she held her troubled daughter in her arms, rested her forehead on Sarah's cheek, and told her to be very careful and to pray. God always answers the prayers of the humble, and she had so much more to offer Matthew—a good personality, a sweetness of character, and, of course, she was pretty, if that meant something.

Sarah laughed softly. She shook her head, but she knew without a doubt that she could not do what Mam required of her. It was too much.

CHAPTER 5

BY MARCH, THE CUSTOMERS AT THE FARMER'S market in New Jersey were always impatient for the arrival of new spring onions, red radishes, and asparagus from Lancaster County. Sarah worked at the bakery, which took up one part of the huge brick building where many vendors plied their wares.

Today, Sarah was in a sunny mood, laughing at a heavyset matron who asked her why anyone could ever be anxious when these warm cinnamon rolls were so delicious and available the whole year round.

She stood behind a plexiglass wall, rolling a strip of soft dough for the cinnamon rolls, the wooden rolling pin making a clacking noise as she bore down on both handles, her arms rounded, muscular.

"Do you have a moment?"

Sarah looked up, surprised to find her friend, Ashley, from the leather goods stand. She was a thin, pale girl who seemed as if her world was filled with anxiety.

They had more than just a passing friendship now. Sarah felt sorry for Ashley and was often unable to put her large, frightened eyes out of her mind.

Sarah asked for permission to take a break, and the two girls walked together through the market. They slid into a booth close to the soft pretzel stand, where the warm, yeasty smells made their stomachs rumble.

"Did you eat?" Sarah asked.

"No."

"You want to?"

"It's okay. I don't have any money."

"I'll buy you a pretzel."

"No."

Ashley had never allowed Sarah to learn much about her, other than the fact that her father owned the leather goods shop. But she was a nice girl even if she was timid and shy. And she had shown an interest in the survivors of the latest barn fire, where the house had burned as well as the barn.

Ashley wore a dull, washed-out sweatshirt, not quite green and not gray, her hair hanging thinly on either side of her face, and a....

Sarah gasped.

"Ashley! What happened to your eye?"

"Oh, it's nothing. It...I...like...I hit the corner of a cupboard door. At night. It was dark. Dumb."

Ashley bent to retrieve her purse, winced, then let it go, placing both hands on the table before picking at her fingernail, examining her hands very closely.

"Ashley. Is something wrong?"

"No."

The word was emphatic, followed by a swift shaking of her head. Suddenly, she gripped the table's edge, her eyes opened wide, and she met Sarah's eyes with intensity.

"Well, not really. But..."

Sarah waited.

"Since you're dating, do you, like, know your boyfriend really well? Do you know where he goes and what he does?"

Catching the inside of her lip with her teeth, Ashley's eyes were pools of raw concern.

Sarah laughed softly.

"Well, Ashley. I can't always compare some things with you. Our people live very quiet lives, in a way. Usually Matthew goes to work, comes home, reads, helps his mother, or plays baseball or volleyball sometimes. Just ordinary, dull stuff. So I don't feel as if I need to know where he is or where he goes throughout the week."

"Oh," Ashley said softly. "So, if my, like, boyfriend, disappears sometimes, would you worry if you were me?"

"Disappears? You mean he leaves for weeks or months?"

"Weeks...sometimes just days."

"He doesn't tell you what he's doing?"

"If I ask, he says he's just working or going to school or visiting."

"Well, then I guess he is."

"Yeah."

Sarah smiled reassuringly at her friend, bringing a warmth to her eyes, which crinkled at the sides as a smile spread across her wan face.

"Well, yeah, whatever," she said, trying to reassure herself.

"I mean, if you love him, I think you should be able to trust him. It seems those two sort of go together."

"You're right."

Ashley looked off across the market at the lights, the signs, the milling customers, her eyes wide, unseeing.

"How's...those people?"

"You mean Reuben Kauffmans?"

"Yeah."

"Good. They really are strong people."

"That's awesome. I have to go."

Ashley slipped away, disappearing into the crowd, the way she often seemed to do, leaving Sarah to shrug her shoulders and move off in search of something to eat.

Sarah never tired of the market's wide array of foods. She tried something new almost every week, when she was working on Fridays and Saturdays.

She bought a bowl of creamy potato soup, ate it with a dish of applesauce, and started back to work. She was suddenly stopped by the sound of voices behind the crowded display of leather products.

"You can't go around asking questions!"

There was a murmured reply and a louder voice, threatening, angry.

Sarah shivered as she hurried on, looking back over her shoulder after she passed. Something just wasn't quite right.

The spring peepers kept Priscilla awake that evening, so she got up to close her bedroom window on the east side of the house, figuring the bit of fresh air could be sacrificed for some peace and quiet.

She was bone weary after helping Mam with the Friday cleaning, helping Dat with the milking, and washing the carriage for church on Sunday. She had begun to think she was about as handy as that Robinson Crusoe's man Friday, doing everything and anything no one else had time to do.

She could hardly wait until the year passed and she would turn sixteen years of age. Then she would be allowed to work at the farmer's market with Sarah. Life was just so boring at fifteen.

Priscilla pushed aside the curtain, and a flickering, orange light entered her line of vision only a second before she screamed and screamed, a long, drawn out, shrill cry of alarm that brought a yell of response from the bedroom below.

"Fire! Fire! Dat! Dat! It's a fire!"

She couldn't move. She stood rooted to the spot by the window, her hands grabbing the windowsill, her nails digging into the varnished wood. She could see the flames already, beginning to leap wickedly in the night sky, illuminating the billows of smoke.

Sarah rushed into Priscilla's room, confused, having just fallen asleep after her long day at market.

"Oh no!"

Her hands went to her mouth, as if to keep the words from escaping. They heard Dat. He was running, opening the kitchen door. Levi bellowed from his room, a cry of alarm asking for someone to tell him what was going on.

"It's...it's at Elam's!"

"No! It's up the road."

"Surely not at Lydia's!"

"Oh no!"

The girls dressed hurriedly, grabbed sweaters and headscarves, and followed Dat out the front door. They walked quickly, the sound of the fire sirens a comfort now, assuring them that help was on the way.

They hurried past Elam and Hannah's, whose house was dark, which seemed unbelievable, but Sarah didn't want to alarm them. Besides, she looked terrible and didn't want Matthew to see her like that.

"*Ach* my."

Dat said the only thing he could think to say, the pity so overwhelming.

Yes, it was the barn belonging to the struggling Widow Lydia Esh. It was a rather large, old one, the paint peeling like white fur down its sides, the roof in good repair even though the metal was mismatched.

She kept a respectable herd of cows, and her oldest son, Omar, a square-shouldered, responsible seventeen-year-old, managed the animals with surprising expertise.

"There's no one awake!" Priscilla gasped.

With no thought other than the poor widow asleep in her bed, the girls ran, their speed increasing as they rounded the bend, hurtled down an incline, and raced up to the porch, their breath coming in gasps as they pounded on the front door.

The night their own barn had burned was still fresh in their minds. They opened the screen door and banged harder, yelling with all their might, the cows bawling in the background.

"Get the cows!"

Leaving the porch, they evaluated the distance from the licking flames to the cow stable. They might be able to save some of them.

Priscilla was yelling, crying, spurred on by a sense of duty borne of her own heartbreaking experience. She had no thought for her own safety, only that of the very necessary cows, the widow's livelihood, her bread and butter.

They raced through the door and searched for chains, snaps, anything that would give them a clue as to how the cows were tied.

"Snaps!" Priscilla shouted.

Sarah fell and started to crawl along the floor but bumped into the large face of a cow that was clearly terrified. She groped along its neck, found the collar, then the chain and the metal clasp, and clicked it open.

Bawling, the cow backed out, followed by four or five more.

Silently, a dark form joined them, unsnapping the cow's restraints, his arms waving, shooing them out.

Omar!

"Do you have horses in here?"

"One!"

"It's getting hot!"

"I'll get him!"

The youth plunged into the far corner of the barn, only to be met by a determined Priscilla, hanging on to the halter of a magnificent Belgian.

"I got him. Get what you can from the milk house!"

Sarah had already headed that way and was met by a stream of firemen, their great pulsing beasts already parked, men swarming everywhere, shouting, organizing.

Lydia Esh was also in the milk house, blindly throwing out buckets, milking machines, water hoses, anything she could fling out the door, her mouth set grimly, determined to survive.

The night sky was no longer dark, lit by the roaring flames of yet another barn fire, and it wasn't quite April, the month of their own fire.

Sarah heard strangled crying and looked to the old farmhouse, where she saw a cluster of shivering, frightened children cowering against the wooden bench by the door.

Quickly, she wound her way between the fire trucks, saw Dat and a few neighbor men backing a wagon away from the barn, and went to the children, herding them inside, lighting the propane lamp, assuring them they would be safe there in the house.

Anna Mae was Priscilla's age, a dark-haired girl who was terrified senseless with the shock of the fire. She stood by the refrigerator crying, unable to help with the younger ones.

Sarah steered her to the couch, covered her shivering form with an afghan she found on the back of a chair, and then sat beside her, rubbing her back and speaking any word of comfort she could think of.

"Are we going to die?"

The quavering little voice came from a small boy. There was a hole in his pajama top, his hair was tousled, and he was hanging on to a raggedy teddy bear with one of its button eyes loose and dangling from a white thread.

Sarah scooped him up quickly, smoothed his hair, and assured him they would certainly not die. The firemen were there now, and they'd keep the house safe.

The neighbors poured in, standing in the yard, white-faced, disbelief stamped on their features. This time something would have to be done, their faces said.

To start a barn fire was one thing, but to take from a poor widow was quite another. It was a slap in the face to a community already downed by previous fires but a brutal blow for a woman who had already endured more than her share of grief and hardship.

The flames leaped into the night sky, but the steady streams of water sizzled and sputtered, battling the tongues of fire far into the night. The water from the great nozzles was not used sparingly. And the haymow contained less than a third of the year's hay, so that helped.

In the course of the night, they soon realized there was more saved and less damage done because of the fire company's timely arrival. Who had called?

Dat testified to hearing the sirens when they were barely out of their own driveway. And Elams hadn't even been awake yet. Someone English? Some Amish on the road late at night?

Lydia Esh stood by the old tool shed, her work coat pinned securely with a large safety pin, and watched with hard resolve as the firemen worked to save whatever they could.

In the light of the flames, the cows stood, backed up against the peeling board fence, and watched warily. A neighbor man had taken the Belgian stallion home to his barn, away from the terrifying blaze.

Elam and Hannah came walking together, their faces grim with fear and—was it only weariness?

Hannah came into the kitchen, clucked and fussed. She told Sarah that this time it was completely senseless. A widow.

She praised Sarah effusively, saying of course she'd be the one here. But didn't she have market tomorrow? Sarah nodded, but she'd probably take off with an emergency like this in the neighborhood. She was willing to sacrifice a small portion of her wages if she could be of help to Lydia.

The widow seemed so alone, so gaunt, so determined. She had no husband to lean on, standing alone by the tool shed, and Sarah wondered what must be going through her mind.

Self-pity? Defeat? Prayer?

She moved to the kitchen window, still holding the small boy, in time to see Omar walk over to stand beside his mother. She turned her face to him, then slowly reached out and clasped his hand, before releasing it quickly as if that small gesture of love embarrassed her.

Then Priscilla also moved to her side, slid an arm beneath Lydia's, and laid her head on her shoulder. Obviously moved, Lydia laid her cheek on top of Priscilla's head, and they stood together, an example of shared experience, heartfelt *mitt leidas* (sympathy), a statue of neighborly love.

But what really moved Sarah was the figure of Omar, the oldest son, who stood with his wide shoulders held erect, mature beyond his years, holding heavy responsibility before his time.

As if Priscilla read Sarah's thoughts, she moved to his side shyly but touched his arm and spoke. He inclined his head and answered, and that was where Priscilla stayed as the fire burned steadily into the night—at Omar's side.

Sarah turned and opened a cupboard door to look for a kettle to heat water for coffee. She found one and filled it, then searched for coffee with Hannah's help. Quietly, trying to hide the truth from each other, they slowly closed door after door before settling back on the couch, their eyes speaking. There was no coffee. There was only a scant amount of flour and sugar, a bag of oatmeal, a box of generic Corn Flakes.

"*Siss net chide* (It's not right)," Hannah breathed finally.

Sarah shook her head dully.

Hannah got up, saying she'd go get coffee and wake Matthew. It was embarrassing, the way he slept.

Sarah had no idea Matthew was still in bed. My, he was quite a sound sleeper. Perhaps he was up, already starting the French toast he'd made on the morning of their own fire.

A smile of belonging played around her lips, and she cuddled the small Rebecca close. Always, Matthew's love sustained her, lifted her spirits, no matter what.

When Hannah returned, she was pulling an express wagon laden with groceries. Sarah helped carry them in, amazed at Hannah's "extras."

The children were falling asleep again, so Anna Mae carried a few of them to her mother's bed, emerging white-faced but helpful as reality sunk in.

They made coffee and then sliced bread for sandwiches. Lydia came into the house and said, oh no, they shouldn't go to all that trouble, but she said it softly, as though if she spoke too loudly, her voice might break into tears, and she could not display weakness now.

Sarah spread mayonnaise on one piece of bread, mustard on the other, then layered the sweet Lebanon bologna and Swiss cheese between the slices and cut them diagonally while Hannah finished the coffee.

They put bags of pretzels, cans of beans and peaches and applesauce in the pantry. A large round container of oatmeal cookies and one of chocolate chip were stored away beside them.

Lydia watched and apologized. She said she was a bit short this month, but the milk check was due tomorrow.

Hannah was kind, telling her she'd get a lot more than that before this was all over, chuckling in a way that meant well for Lydia.

When the men slowly trooped in for refreshment, Sarah couldn't help watching for Matthew, who remained maddeningly absent.

Hannah sidled up to her.

"He wasn't feeling good last night. I think he took too much Tylenol for a headache."

So that was it. Good. Sarah was relieved now, and she stopped watching the line of men. Matthew would be here if he felt well, that was one thing sure. He was so good-hearted, so neighborly.

The last one to come in was Omar, his face streaked and black, his eyes weary. Lee Glick walked with him, his own face darkened, highlighting the electric blue of his eyes. They were talking seriously but stopped when they reached the light of the kitchen.

Lee thanked Sarah for the coffee, but she did not meet his eyes, finding a certain safety in avoiding them.

Lee stepped to the side of the kitchen with Omar following him the way a stray dog follows his benefactor, a look of adoration on his young, traumatized face.

Priscilla tried to be discreet, but her ears were tuned to everything Lee was saying, her eyes opening wide, snapping, alert. Finally, she just gave up and joined in the conversation. Whatever it was they were discussing, it was apparently an interesting subject for her as well.

Weariness overtook Sarah soon after the refreshments were served, and she looked around for Dat, caught his eye, and gestured to the clock.

He nodded. Relieved, Sarah moved to his side.

"Ready?"

"I'm falling asleep."

She told Lydia they'd be back in the morning after a few hours of sleep. She told Priscilla to come, they were going home now.

"Hey, thanks. You...you saved the cows," Omar said, talking mostly to Priscilla.

"You're welcome."

"Thank you, Sarah."

"You're welcome. You know we experienced the same thing, so we know exactly how you feel."

He nodded shyly.

"Good night, Sarah."

She looked up and met Lee's blue eyes and immediately wished she hadn't. The light in them questioned her, mocked her, put her on guard, as if she needed to explain her position in life, for being here, for dating Matthew, for...so many things.

She decided then that he was *gros-feelich* (proud) and she had chosen well, being with Matthew.

"You could at least have said goodnight to him," Priscilla grumbled as they wound their way between the throbbing fire trucks.

Sarah said nothing.

"Did you hear what he was telling Omar?"

"What?"

"He's interested in raising Belgians for profit. Lee is. He doesn't think Omar knows the value of that big stallion. Oh my goodness, Sarah! That horse could walk right over you and not even know it."

Sarah plodded along beside her sister as Priscilla babbled on about Omar and his Belgian and how kind that Lee was. Sarah's head spun, and she wished Priscilla would just be quiet.

"Where was Matthew?"

"He didn't feel good."

"Poor baby."

Sarah didn't feel the remark deserved an answer, so she walked on under the early spring sky, the night air still sharp with cold. But she could hear the sweet sounds of the earth waiting to burst into new life. The peepers were still persistent, their shrill mating calls stirring some old, bittersweet memory for Sarah. She became nostalgic, thinking back to when life was less complicated, soft and innocent, the way the years of her youth had been for so long.

The stars twinkled down from the black velvet sky as if to remind Sarah of their steadfastness. They were a guiding light, a trusting age-old light that God had planned the same way he had planned the spring peepers, the changing seasons, and, above all, the design He had for her.

Unbidden and mysterious, two tears emerged, quivered, and slid slowly down her soft cheeks, lit only by the light of a waning moon and about two million stars.

CHAPTER 6

Dat said if Lancaster County had responded well to disaster in the past, the caring was doubled, tripled, quadrupled for the poor widow after Hannah spread the word effusively and colorfully about the under-stocked pantry.

Even conservative members of the Old Order Amish voiced their outrage now. Something had to be done about all the fires. Old Dannie Fisher talked to the media, a vein of anger threaded through his dialogue, and no one blamed him. His old, bent straw hat was the focal point of the photograph on the front page of the Lancaster paper.

Ya, vell (Yes, well), they said. Enough is enough.

That poor Lydia Esh.

She's so *geduldich* (patient).

Aaron had passed away after a long and painful battle with lung cancer. The medical expenses had climbed to phenomenal heights. Always she'd accept the alms and the deacon's visits with a bent head and a strong face, any sorrow or self-pity veiled and hidden from view. She expressed gratitude quietly, showing no emotion, and no one could remember seeing her shed a tear at her husband's funeral.

And now, with hundreds of men swarming about her property, vanloads of people arriving daily from neighboring counties and states, her situation spoken to the world through the eager media, she showed no emotion— only a certain clouding of her eyes.

Sarah was in the small wash house, sorting through boxes of groceries—tin cans of fruit in one box, beans, tomato sauce, and other vegetables in another, and cereal, flour, sugar, and all the other dry staples in another. Many friendly faces she did not know assisted with the pleasant work.

The day was sunny, as if God knew they needed good weather to begin building the widow's barn. The mud was the biggest hurdle. Great deep pools of water had turned the already soaked fields into a quagmire. Load after load of stone was poured around the barn foundation, and still vehicles became hopelessly embedded in the wet ground.

Men called out, hammers rang, trucks groaned through the dirt and the mud and the gravel, and the sun shone as folks from all over came to the aid of Lydia and her children.

Someone had the idea to paint the interior of the house after noticing the stained, peeling walls and the lack of fresh, clean color. They'd buy paint after the barn was finished. They'd organize work days for different districts, have frolics to paint and clean, freshen the entire house. They'd plant the garden, mow the grass, plant some shrubbery, and build a fence.

Sarah approached Lydia that Monday, her eyes bright

with the plans the women had devised. Lydia sat at the kitchen table, her angular frame so thin, her black apron hanging from her waist. Her hair was combed neatly, dark and sleek, her eyeglasses were sparkling clean, her covering clean but limp with frequent washings.

It was her eyes that concerned Sarah. They were veiled with a cloudiness, yes, but the inner light that everyone's eyes contained simply was not there.

Sarah hesitated to let the word enter her mind, but Lydia's eyes looked dead, lifeless, as if the spirit in them had left.

"Lydia."

"Yes?"

She turned her head obediently, and Sarah shivered inwardly at the darkness—that was it—the darkness in her gray eyes.

"What would you say if we painted your house?"

"Oh, I guess that would be alright."

"Are you sure?"

"Yes."

"We'll wait till the barn is finished. Wouldn't it be nice to have a fresh, clean house?"

"Yes."

Lydia was speaking in monosyllables, dully.

"Lydia, are you alright?"

Sarah leaned forward, put a hand on Lydia's as a gesture of comfort, and was appalled when Lydia pulled her hand away from Sarah's touch. Her lips drew back in a snarl, the darkness in her eyes became blacker, and she hissed, "Don't touch me."

Sarah gasped and turned her head as tears sprang to her eyes.

"I'm sorry."

Immediately Lydia rose to her feet and left the room.

The remainder of the day was ruined for Sarah. She felt as if she had inadvertently overstepped a boundary, been too brash, too....she didn't know what. She had only wanted to help.

She assisted the other women by mashing the huge vats of potatoes. She poured water into endless Styrofoam cups and washed dishes, but her heart was no longer in the duty she had previously performed so cheerfully.

Lydia moved among the clusters of people and did her tasks swiftly and efficiently, but alone.

When Sarah noticed Omar watching his mother, she decided to speak to him. She moved to a position where he could easily see her motioning to him with a crook of her finger to come outside with her.

"Omar, do you think your mother is alright?"

Omar was frightened by Sarah's question. She could tell by the swift movement of his head, the wide opening of his eyes—so much like his mother's but with a shock of dark hair falling over his forehead above them.

"Why do you ask?"

"She just seems to be half aware of...of everything."

Omar said nothing. He just turned his head, his eyes searching the crowd, before speaking.

"She's strong. She'll be okay. It's not like she hasn't weathered a lot more than this."

"Yes, of course. Your father's illness. I realize that. As you say, she'll be alright."

Priscilla came out of the house to stand beside Sarah, and Omar's eyes brightened immediately, the gray dancing with flecks of blue.

"Hey Priscilla."

"How's it going, Omar?"

"Alright, I guess. I just can't keep up with everything. Or everybody. Sometimes I get the feeling this barn is taking on a life of its own, building itself."

He grinned, his wide mouth revealing his perfect teeth, his face alight with a new energy.

"Oh, it's wonderful, Omar!"

Priscilla spoke eloquently, and he looked away from the undiluted eagerness in her eyes. Lowering his head, he kicked at an emerging tuft of grass, then looked up, revealing the veil that had moved across his own eyes, darkening them—just like his mother's.

"Yeah, well, we don't deserve any of this."

The words were harsh and imbedded with irony, self-mockery.

"Don't say that, Omar."

"I know what I'm saying. We're not worthy."

He turned on his heel and disappeared into the crowd, melting into it as if to find safety in the numbers. Sarah and Priscilla stood numbly, watching, keeping their thoughts to themselves.

The long lines of men snaked toward the house. The men filled Styrofoam trays with the good, hot food that had been donated and cooked by people from many different denominations or no denomination at all. All kinds of human hearts had been touched by the need of a poor young widow, and her situation had served to remove any fences of superiority or self-righteousness.

A need was being met, quite simply. More than one minister stood in his pulpit, or just stood without one, as was the Amish way, and spoke of the goodness of the human spirit in a world where pessimism is often the norm. Hadn't the loaves and fishes been distributed and twelve baskets left over?

Stories circulated about groceries being stored in the cellar and every available cupboard, even the attic, at Lydia's home. A brand new EZ Freeze propane gas refrigerator from Indiana also arrived out of nowhere.

Lydia hadn't had a refrigerator all winter, but she said she was thankful for the ice chests on the front porch. Sarah knew she probably didn't have much to put in them anyway.

Lengths of fabric, buttons, spools of thread. Coats and shawls and bonnets. The donations were endless. It was enough to make a person cry, Mam said.

The Beiler family hummed with a new purpose—that of making a different and a better life for the Widow Lydia. Dat had dark circles of weariness under his eyes from lack of sleep, and Mam was way behind with her housecleaning. March was coming in like a gentle lamb, just right for opening windows, airing stuffy rooms, turning mattresses, and sweeping cobwebs.

Sarah missed another week at market, and Priscilla traipsed over to the Esh family farm with any weak excuse. Sarah had a feeling her visits were more about Omar, Lee Glick, and the Belgians than anything else.

Then another bolt shook the community. Lydia Esh simply disappeared.

A frenzied knocking on the front door of the Beiler home was the beginning. Dat stumbled to the door in the dark, his heart racing, his mind anticipating the sight of the familiar orange flickering of someone else's barn burning yet again.

Instead, he found a sobbing Omar, completely undone, his mother's disappearance stripping away all the steely resolve that had upheld him after their barn burned.

Davey steered him into the dark kitchen with one hand

and buttoned his trousers with the other before going to the propane lamp cabinet and flicking the lighter that hung from a string below the mantles.

As a yellow light flared across the room, Omar sank into the nearest chair. He covered his face with his torn, blue handkerchief, shaking his head from side to side, the only way he could think to show Davey Beiler, the preacher, how bad it was.

"I'm not surprised. I'm not surprised," he repeated over and over.

Dat remained calm and said nothing. Then he looked up to find his loving wife and steady helpmeet—dressed with her apron pinned on and her white covering in place—padding quietly across the kitchen in her house slippers.

When Levi called out loudly, insisting that someone tell him what was going on, Mam spoke to him quietly and said he must stay in bed, which seemed to comfort him. He obeyed, grunting as he turned on his side and muttering about "*da Davey Beila und all sie secrets* (that Davey Beiler and all his secrets)" before falling asleep.

Omar spoke quickly. He couldn't seem to stop, his seventeen-year-old voice rising, cracking, falling, telling a journey of pain that had been repressed far too long.

"It wasn't the way you think it was in our family," he began.

A story of such magnitude had never before assailed Dat's heart. How could the children have appeared so normal? Omar was saying his mother had always been abused.

"Abused?" Dat asked.

"Whatever you call it. He called her horrible names. He hit her across the face, across the back. He pushed her into the gutters when they milked and laughed when the manure surged around her legs. He seemed to hate her and wanted to make her cry. But he couldn't stand her crying either. If she didn't cry, he quit easier than if she did."

"What about you children?" Dat asked grimly.

"It wasn't us. He was good enough to us. Not always nice, but he never laid a hand on any of us—just her."

"Why?"

Omar shrugged, wiped his nose, and then fell into a silence steeped in abject misery.

"I don't know what to do."

"Was your mother....How shall I word this? Did she do anything to deserve your father's behavior? Did she fight back? Treat him miserably so that he retaliated? Was it just a bad marriage?"

"Mam always did the best she could. She finally got to blaming herself, assured us she just hadn't tried hard enough, spent too much money, overcooked his eggs, threw away some food. Whatever trivial thing he accused her of, she believed him and took the blame."

He began crying uncontrollably then, unable to form coherent words.

Mam came to stand beside Dat. She placed a warm hand on the worn, white t-shirt covering his shoulder and massaged it, a gesture born of habit, telling her burdened husband she was there for him and supported him always.

"I'm so afraid. I'm afraid to look for her. I'm...."

Omar looked up, the terror in his eyes a palpable thing.

"She....What are we going to do if she...killed herself?"

Dat spoke. "Omar, she wouldn't do that. She was not mentally ill. Your mother is a strong, good woman. She may have gone to her parents for advice or to a minister."

Vehemently, Omar shook his head.

"No, she didn't."

"Why do you say that?"

"Her parents blame her for the abuse. She told me."

A shadow moved across Dat's face, and he swiftly rose to his feet.

"Call Sarah, Malinda."

His voice was terrible in its purpose.

"Come, Omar. We must find her."

"Why...why are you in a hurry now?"

"She may be like a trapped animal. We need to search."

Together they moved out the door, Dat shrugging into his old, black work coat and setting his straw hat firmly on his head.

Sarah was awakened by the urgency in Mam's voice. She dressed quickly and ran down the stairs, followed by Priscilla.

Mam's face was pale, grim.

"Go help look for Lydia. She just disappeared, late this evening. Omar talked. It's frightening."

Sarah shivered, thinking of Lydia's aversion to being touched.

"God, please go with us now."

The prayer was simple but sincere as she grabbed her sweater and ran down the porch steps and out to the road, her long legs propelling her easily, her breath coming fast but comfortably. She was fit and young, strong with the physical labor to which she was accustomed.

Dat had a lantern, Omar a powerful flashlight. They gave the girls a battery lamp and instructions, their faces tense with the reality of this night.

"We'll stay within the farm's boundaries. If we don't find her, we'll have to call 911. You girls search the house first."

Priscilla whimpered, an almost inaudible sound, but Sarah heard it and reached out to take her hand.

"Do you....Would you rather go back home?"

"No. I want to stay with you."

Quietly, not wanting to wake the children, they tiptoed down to the basement, holding their breaths. They held the lantern high, the white light casting weird shadows on the aged walls. The paint was peeling, and greenish mold grew along the bottom of the stone walls.

A pile of empty potato bags almost stopped their heartbeats. Sarah kicked them aside, relieved.

The basement produced nothing. There was no sign of anyone having disturbed anything at all, so they tiptoed back up the dusty staircase. They searched the kitchen, living room, the main bedroom, even beneath the unmade bed. Then they inched their way upstairs.

"We can't wake the children."

"I know."

"The attic?"

Would they be strong enough to face something as horrifying as....? Sarah refused to think the word. She wouldn't.

Turning the old, porcelain knob on the attic door, Sarah grimaced as it squeaked loudly. Then she stepped cautiously on the first old stair tread, which groaned forcefully. Hoping for the best, they made their way steadily up the stairs, every step sending out a new and strange squeak or groan, until they reached the top where they stood together, their breathing inaudible.

Sarah held the battery lantern up and sighed. Boxes, bags, old furniture, torn window blinds. There was nothing of value, but the huge jumble of things could hide a person well. The rafters were low and dark with age. Nails had been pounded into them, no doubt having held hams and onions and strings of dried peppers in times past.

"You hold the lantern," Sarah whispered.

Priscilla obeyed and held it high as Sarah moved boxes and bags and got down on her knees to search beneath the eaves. Priscilla's large, frightened eyes searched the rafters, thinking the unthinkable.

Suicide.

God, we've come this far. Please stay with us.

When Sarah yelped in alarm, Priscilla clapped a hand over her mouth to stifle the shriek behind it, but it escaped around her fingers. She couldn't hold back the high-pitched scream.

No matter now, Sarah thought resolutely. They'd have to know. Her hand had made contact with a thin form lying behind an old quilt frame. She was on her back, her face turned to the side, her skin translucent, her eyes closed.

Sarah crawled closer and put an ear to Lydia's chest. She raised exultant eyes to Priscilla, who was now trembling.

Muffled bumps and cries from below told them of the children's rude awakening by the awful sound in the night.

"She's warm! She's breathing. Lydia!"

Sarah shook the limp shoulders gently.

"Beside her," Priscilla said.

Sarah's eyes took in the bottle of ibuprofen. The cheap

brand from Walmart. Equate. Suddenly it angered her, and her mind refused to accept this bottle of pills lying empty, the cap carefully replaced.

"Get Dat! Tell the children to be quiet."

She guessed anger was a good replacement for fear. It could get her through the worst of times if it had to. Sarah was braced up by it, strong because of it, as Dat and Omar pounded up the stairs, their eyes wide, the fear mixed with relief, and, yes, anger.

"Let's get her down," Dat barked.

"Omar, call 911. Now."

"On my cell phone?"

"However."

In his moment of terror, he wasn't thinking straight, Sarah knew. It was only later that she allowed herself a small smile, thinking of Omar asking her dat, the minister, if he should use his cell phone. Cell phones were forbidden instruments of encroaching technology, but they were used by many of the youth and some older people as well.

Grunting, Dat reached for Lydia's still form, pulling her away from the eaves and instructing Sarah to hold her below her knees. He'd take the shoulders.

Sarah was not sure she could carry this poor creature down the attic stairs. Even a thin woman was dead weight in that state.

She hesitated.

"I…I don't know."

"You can do it, Sarah."

Together, they inched their way down the creaking attic stairs. Lydia's head rolled to the side awkwardly, her legs flopping on either side of Sarah's hands and her feet slapping randomly against the steps.

"*Kinna. Bleivat drinn!* (Children. Stay there!)" Dat called, his voice loud with authority. They were crying, asking questions, and Anna Mae refused to obey, charging through the doorway of her bedroom, crying uncontrollably.

"She's sick," was all Dat said.

"Come, Anna Mae. Come with me. The ambulance is coming."

Priscilla slid an arm about Anna Mae's shoulder, explaining, consoling. Her sobs turned to sad, hiccupping whimpers.

By the time they'd finally reached the living room on the main floor, the high, wailing sirens were already audible.

Sarah met Dat's eyes, visibly relieved. They both looked at Lydia, her frame swallowed by the old green sofa, the holes torn in the upholstery covered by a crocheted afghan, discolored from frequent washings in the old washing machine.

A sadness spread through Sarah's heart as the knowledge of this pitiful situation spoke to her. Lydia looked so young, her skin pearl white, her wide eyes closed, her mouth still determined, strong.

How old was she?

Omar was seventeen years old.

Please let her live, dear God. Just let her live. Sarah wasn't aware that she was praying until she saw Melvin come charging through the front door, and she burst into tears of shock and relief all at once.

Sarah had forgotten that Melvin belonged to the fire company now. Since the barn fires had started, he was determined to be of value to the community. But nothing had ever prepared him for this sight, and he had to step aside, grappling with the overwhelming emotion, and let the trained personnel take over.

Lydia was hospitalized, and the deadly quantity of ibuprofen removed from her stomach by the greatest invention, the stomach pump. Her parents were at her side, the beginning of a deep remorse entering their hearts.

Sarah and Priscilla stayed with the children, and they talked with Melvin and Omar for hours. Anna Mae hovered around the conversation, her face white with fear and disbelief.

Melvin listened, dumbstruck for once in his life. It was an uneasy situation for him, being cornered by an unbelievable situation and rendered helpless without knowing what to say. He had never in his life felt the kind of pity that swelled up inside him and took away every other emotion. Even his bravado was gone and his skill of planning, of moving and shaking. He simply did not know what should be done, except maybe get down on his knees and admit to God that he didn't understand how he felt, and He'd have to make it plain.

CHAPTER 7

IN THE MORNING, WHEN SARAH WAS FRYING CORN-meal mush for the children and Priscilla was helping Omar do chores, there was a soft knock on the door, and Matthew entered.

Sarah was giddy with happiness to see him. She lay down the spatula she was holding, her eyes weary with the events of the night, and said, "Good morning!"

"Sarah!" Matthew greeted her as joyfully. Without a thought of the children, she flew into his arms and was held, secure in a haven of comfort.

Her Matthew. Still unbelievable, after these months of dating.

"Tell me what happened," he said, his face alight with interest, his eyes soft and kind, such a rich brown and filled with caring.

Sarah obeyed. She spoke quietly to protect the children from more fear, then turned to the stove to finish breakfast.

Matthew listened and then responded kindly but with a sort of petulance, inquiring about her having to be there.

"Oh, we're neighbors, Matthew. Omar came to our door."

"Every time there's a scene, and that seems to be happening with a certain regularity, there you are in the middle of it. Why?"

His tone was high, anxious, mocking.

Sarah remained at the stove, her back turned, and she stood very still, breathing slowly, gathering control.

Turning, she said levelly, "It's my duty. My parents always stress that."

"Well, mine don't."

There was nothing to say in response.

As if he had suddenly been given a new license, he began to barrage Sarah with his ideas about the barn fires.

Quite clearly, these fires brought out what was in the Amish, which wasn't very much, he said. He rambled on about this woman who was so worldly she'd attempt suicide and how Mervin was drowned by the devil's hand.

"I mean, Sarah, look around you. God is trying to say something here. All this isn't happening to the Mennonites or the other churches around us that are much more spiritual."

A dagger of fear shot through Sarah, but she quickly gathered her composure and calmly broke eggs into a pan. She bent gracefully to lay slices of bread in the broiler of the old gas stove.

"I think the Amish church is way out of line. All we think about is *ordnung* (rules). There's a reason for these barn fires."

Sarah slid the door of the broiler shut with her foot and gave it a small kick to make sure it closed all the way. Then she slid a spatula beneath a sizzling egg, still remaining quiet.

"Well, aren't you going to answer?"

"Yes, Matthew. You have a point. Of course."

He came over and stood a little too close to her. He whispered in her ear about how he wanted to kiss her, but there were too many eyes around. Then let himself out the door with a silly wave, leaving Sarah smiling foolishly at the eggs. She kept on smiling as the children sat around the table and ate their breakfast.

Oh, that Matthew was something. She sure hoped he wasn't going to get some idea about leaving the church into his head, just because of the fires.

She watched as the teams began to arrive, the kindly women entering the kitchen, asking questions, clucking, caring. The police and private investigators came, asking questions, interrogating Omar, Priscilla, and Dat as well as herself.

They tried to remain as truthful as possible but knew, ultimately, that the real reason for the attempted suicide would have to come from Lydia herself.

The news reporters and journalists went wild with the nature of this story, the barn fires projected on TV screens across the nation, sensational half-truths filling the members of the Amish community with dread.

Where would it end? How much was simply too much?

At home again together, gathered around the kitchen table, Dat spoke at length, sparing his family nothing. He said these were hard times, spiritually as well as emotionally, and they would all need to remain steadfast in prayer and supplication and draw close to God to ask his guidance.

Levi said God was angry at Lancaster County, and everybody better sit up and take notice. Dat reprimanded

Levi sharply, something so unusual even Mam looked surprised.

"God is allowing this to draw us together. Look at poor Lydia. A family in dire straits, robbed of a chance to have...." He stopped and broke down, his eyes filled with so much tender pity, Sarah imagined his eyes looked like God's somehow.

Sarah, however, kept the small tidbit of Matthew's attitude hidden. He was likely just going through a bad time, unable to do anything about these fires continuing and feeling helpless because of it. Bless his heart.

Despite the somber topic, Priscilla was beaming and smiling, unable to contain her excitement about the new barn Abner Fisher had just designed for the horses, those Belgians. She said if Omar didn't mind, she'd like to work with them, and if she was allowed, she wouldn't need another horse to replace Dutch.

"Priscilla," Levi said forcefully.

"What?"

"You can't go over there and work with Omar. He's a boy."

"I know. But his sister, Anna Mae, is there."

"You're not going," Levi said.

Dat smiled widely and winked at Mam.

"We'll see," was all he said.

The Widow Lydia came home from the hospital. Sarah and Mam walked through the tender spring sunshine, carrying a freshly baked carrot cake made with pineapple, nuts, and raisins and covered with cream cheese frosting.

Lydia was propped up on pillows, the fresh, white pillowcases framing her thin, tired face. Without her glasses, she appeared so young. The light in her eyes was genuine now, a small flame of hope burned there, the deadness gone.

Her mother and father were both present, hovering about, finding her glasses, arranging her pillows, asking if she was cold, bringing a blanket, quietly wiping their own tears.

The outdoors hummed with activity, as usual, the projects still going on but with a difference since word had circulated of Lydia's illness.

Tight-lipped wives packed their husbands substantial lunches, saying enough *ga-mach* (to do) was enough. They'd cook a good hot supper in the evening, but a packed lunch was enough for today.

At the end of the day, many of the wives raised their hands in dismay after finding all the food still in the Ziploc bags. The men sheepishly admitted that the dinner had been catered again by the folks at Kentucky Fried Chicken.

There was no contest between a cold lunch or that chicken. All this, however, was spared the Widow Lydia. She remained in bed and talked, shared, and cried with her parents asking her forgiveness over and over. They had no idea it had been so bad, they really didn't, and Lydia believed them. They made an appointment to go for extensive counseling at Green Pastures in Lebanon County, at David Beiler's request.

Mam and Sarah left the cake, their hearts immeasurably relieved to see the healing in Lydia's eyes. Again, the Amish folks as well as many of their English neighbors had rallied around the poor, the needy, the hurting, and the wounded in spirit, and life resumed its normal pace.

The trust fund at Susquehanna Bank grew to mammoth proportions, but Lydia did not know. She went back to her duties slowly, but she sat and cuddled little Rebecca and her thin, small Aaron most of the time. She thanked God for David Beiler, though he did not know that he had done anything at all.

The wind was a bit chilly when Mam asked Dat to hitch up Fred. She wanted to pick up her sister and go to Ez *sei* Mamie's (Ez's wife Mamie's) quilting, over along Route 897.

Dat did his duty, and Mam sat happily on the driver's side of the preacher's *doch veggley* (carriage), took up the reins, and thanked her husband.

"Be careful," Dat said. It was the same thing he always said, and Mam smiled.

The preacher's carriage had no front, just a heavy, black canvas duster that those in the front seat pulled up over their laps. There were doors on either side to slide closed when the weather was inclement, but today Mam kept them open and enjoyed the brisk little winds that flapped the gum blanket and swirled about her face.

She wondered if all Amish carriages had been preachers' *doch vegglin* in times past. Probably, the way most things changed over time, the storm fronts (windows with a sturdy dash) were a new and modern addition at one time. That had probably followed on the heels of the market wagon, the heavy, versatile carriage used to haul produce or baked goods—wares of all kinds—to open air markets in Lancaster City.

Mam adjusted her black bonnet and was grateful for her shawl. The black, woolen square of fabric pinned securely around her shoulders guarded against the chill in the wind.

Turning into her sister's driveway, she noticed the new growth of her hostas. The wide green leaves pushed the mulch away, new life springing from the earth everywhere, although Davey had told her it was still plenty wet

to plant peas. She had the cold frame filled with early lettuce, onions, and radishes. She had checked them herself
this morning and was surprised at the growth.

"Whoa."

Fred stopped obediently and then pulled on the reins
to loosen them. Mam watched the side door, eager to see
her sister, Miriam. She emerged, pulling the door shut
behind her, one hand going to her covering. As usual, she
wore a black sweater, but no shawl or bonnet.

Lifting the gum blanket, Mam exclaimed, "Where's
your bonnet?"

Miriam plopped down on the seat, wiggled her shoulders, and said, "Boy, we fill up this front seat pretty snugly."

Mam smiled and thought, you mean you do.

Miriam weighted a bit over two hundred pounds and
frankly stated that fact to any who inquired. She'd been
heavy all her life. She was who she was, she carried it
well, and tough if someone thought she was fat.

"Where's your bonnet?" Mam repeated.

"You know I hate bonnets."

"Now, Miriam."

"Sorry, Malinda. But I'm not a preacher's wife."

No, you're not, Mam thought wryly, knowing her sister was undoubtedly not cut out to be one.

"Well, alright. I like my shawl and bonnet on a chilly
day."

They had gone a few hundred yards when Miriam
said, "Poo!" and reached for the gum blanket, pulling it
up well above her waistline.

"Should have worn your shawl and bonnet."

Miriam shrugged and said the good, thick buggy blankets would keep her warm.

Fred trotted briskly. The two sisters talked nonstop, catching up on community news, family gossip, the highs and lows of raising large families, clucking, lending listening ears, always sympathetic, understanding. It was the way of sisters everywhere, confiding in each other, the trust so complete, so cushioned with unconditional love, that conversation flowed freely, unrestrainedly.

"How's Sarah doing with her Matthew?" Miriam asked.

"Fine, I guess."

"You don't sound too enthused."

"I'm not."

"*Ach* Malinda. Come on. He's quite a catch, and you know it. You're just trying to be humble. Duh!"

"Miriam, I think looks is about as far it goes with that one."

She held up one hand to hush Miriam.

"Let me have my say. I can't talk like this to anyone else, not even my husband, who is always a pushover where Sarah is concerned."

Mam stopped, looked at Miriam.

"Isn't a pushover a baked item?"

"You mean a popover?"

They laughed heartily, rich chuckles of shared humor. Then Miriam told Mam if she didn't watch her horse they were going to have a wreck, and she meant it. Mam said no they weren't, she was a good driver, but Miriam didn't really think she was. She just didn't say it.

"Anyway, you were saying?"

"Oh, Matthew Stoltzfus."

"Yes."

"You know I think the world of Hannah. She's my best friend. But she had those two boys long after her girls, and..." Mam's voice became strong, forceful. "They're both spoiled rotten!"

Miriam gasped. "Malinda! I can't believe you said that!"

Mam sat up straight.

"Yes, I said that, and it feels good to be completely honest. She caters to those boys. She thinks they can do nothing wrong. And Matthew is less than ambitious. He flirts with any girl who will look at him, and there are plenty of them. I'm not convinced he loves Sarah at all. She's just second best because Rose doesn't want him."

"Wow!" Miriam mouthed.

"Yes. It's that bad."

"Are you sure you're not being too hard on Sarah?"

"No."

"Boy, Malinda. You sound like someone I don't know."

"Well, don't know me then. I'm just so sick of tip-toeing around Sarah and turning a false face decorated with an artificial smile. I know it's not going to make a lick of difference what I say. She fancies herself in love with him."

"Malinda! She is! That poor girl has always wanted Matthew."

"Wanted and loved are two very different things."

Miriam nodded.

"You are absolutely right."

"I know I am."

"Let's not talk about this anymore. It makes me sick to the stomach. Your Sarah is such a nice girl. I know she deserves genuine happiness with an extra nice guy."

Mam flicked the reins across Fred's back, urging him on. They'd be late for the quilting, and Mamie made the best filled doughnuts in Lancaster County.

Ez *sei* Mamie had pieced the plum-colored quilt by herself, a new design, she thought, until the contrary Emma Blank informed her that the Courthouse Steps pattern was as old as her grandmother's grandmother.

"Well, it's new to me."

So began the day at an Amish quilting. The colors of the quilt in question were called plum and sage, whereas years ago, they would have been called green and purple. They still were by the older generation.

The fact that Mamie made the best filled doughnuts was widely discussed and finally accepted, after weighing the pros and cons of using doughnut mix or stirring up batter from scratch.

"You can't beat the ones made from fresh ingredients. And you have to have real mashed potatoes in the dough, not potato flakes," Mamie said, her cheeks like ripe apples, her eyes popping. The overwhelming pressure of having all those talented women in her house automatically cranked up the volume that was loud to begin with.

"I don't believe it," countered Emma Blank.

"Me either! We make thousands and thousands of them for bake sales and auctions. Every single one of our doughnuts comes from a mix. We buy it in fifty-pound bags," another voice chimed in, "And they are amazing."

Mamie's eyes snapped, but she smiled and, with a grand gesture, set a beautiful glass tray of perfect filled doughnuts in the middle of the table, surrounded by carafes of coffee and *vissa tae* (meadow tea).

Much oohing and aahing followed. Eyes rolled, and exclamations of *"Siss net chide* (it isn't right)" and other approving statements mingled with giggles and outright laughs of appreciation. Hands repeatedly reached for more doughnuts, everyone knowing full well that they were unbeatable.

Miriam whispered to Malinda that she guessed she'd have to stick a bag of pretzels in her pocket to keep that cloying sweetness from staying on her tongue till lunchtime. Then she admitted she'd eaten three doughnuts.

"Not three!"

"Three."

The women set to work. Their needles were plied expertly, up and down, in and out, the sturdy off-white thread pulled between the layers of fabric and batting.

Thimbles flashed, silver or gold. Occasionally *naits* (thread) was called for across the frame as the spools lay in the middle of the large quilt out of everyone's reach.

Someone would quickly press down on the quilt, allowing a spool to roll toward a hand where it was snatched up and thrown to the person asking for it.

Inevitably, the conversation turned to the barn fires and the latest victim who had been unable to face her life anymore. It was spoken of quietly, reverently, and without malice. Mam knew the most. She knew the truth as the well-informed minister's wife. Yet she spoke only what was necessary and then passed out post-it notes with Lydia's address written on them.

Women blinked back tears of sympathy, blew their noses surreptitiously, and avoided eye contact, each one bearing the news stoically. The poor, poor woman. Oh, it hurts to hear it, they said.

Mam assured them all that healing was well underway, and her counselors were well pleased with her progress.

"You know she always was quiet. I suppose we just accepted her as that. She hid so much."

"What do you think became of Aaron?" Emma Blank

asked, her words falling like rocks on macadam.

No one answered.

Mam finally spoke in a quiet voice, reminding Emma of his long and painful battle with lung cancer, the suffering that provided opportunity for him to repent.

Miriam said nothing but thought her sister had such a nice way about her, always soothing ruffled feathers, looking for the good in people, no matter what the circumstances.

That's why she was more than a bit surprised by her dislike of Matthew. Well, time would tell.

The men of Leacock Township held another meeting about the fires, this time speaking at length about the need to either get large dogs or sleep in their barns. It had to be one or the other. Mastiff. German Shepherd. Doberman. Whatever it would take.

Some farmers installed alarms with wires encased in durable rubber stretched across their driveways, but they needed electricity, so only a few actually used them.

Dogs were acquired, or sleeping bags and air mattresses. But sleeping in the barn lasted for only a few weeks for many as the meticulous housewives turned up their noses every time the well meaning boys of the household came in the house after spending a night in the barn.

Men tilled the fields as the sun shone and birds wheeled their ecstatic patterns in the sky. Tulips pushed the soil aside and grew tall and stately, tossed about like hula dancers in the spring breezes.

Women bent their backs in their gardens, purple, blue, green, and red skirts tossing about them as they planted fresh, new onion bulbs and wrinkled, grayish peas, tiny radish seeds, and lettuce seeds so fine they threw them in slight indentations in the soil and figured at least half of them would grow.

Children skipped through the fields, holes in their school sneakers, longing to go barefoot, but their mothers remained adamant. The earth was too cold. They must wait for the first bumblebee.

The children searched the fence rows for new dandelion growth and picked the greens joyfully. They carried them to their mothers, who washed and steamed them. Then they fried a good bit of fat bacon, stirred flour into the cooked and crumpled bacon, added chopped hard-boiled eggs and the steamed greens, and had a fine supper.

The Widow Lydia walked carefully among her new shrubbery, unable to take it all in. She marveled at the bulbs that had produced wonderful red tulips, a gift from Royer's Greenhouses.

And then because they were so red, and the leaves so green, and the fresh mushroom soil around them so brown—everything a rainbow of vibrant color—she folded her arms on the new PVC fence surrounding her house and cried.

She cried because she was grateful that she could. She could let great, wet tears flow down her thin, pale cheeks and never once feel any guilt. It was alright to cry. In fact, she was supposed to cry. They said it was healing.

The barn stood at the bottom of the small incline below the house, new and shining, as if it grew from the earth itself, sprouting from a bulb like the red tulips. In a sense, it had. A bulb was a small thing, but with God's power, it grew to a much larger thing of indescribable beauty. The men had been tools in His hands, bearing the ability to wield a hammer, operate a saw, read blueprints, all the while their hearts holding goodwill toward their neighbor.

So the earth bore its new life, and the barn stood solid

and charming, one complementing the other to form a picture of beauty, as hearts that are hidden from sight grow by the Master's Hand, in love, in forbearance, and tender pity.

CHAPTER 8

SARAH KICKED HER BARE FOOT AGAINST THE moist, new grass below the swing by the grape arbor and thought about the words Matthew was saying. She rolled them over in her mind, trying to decipher their meaning, but none of it made any sense at all. He wanted to go away. He wanted to travel, see the world. He needed to get away on a spiritual quest.

Sarah felt herself becoming hysterical, imagining his perfect profile with the dark hair and brown eyes climbing a tall mountain with no trees, just grass and a small, wizened little man sitting on top.

A spiritual quest? He hadn't committed himself to the Amish church yet, as she had done the previous year. But how could he want to seek anything other than the faith of his fathers? She simply could not grasp what he was saying.

He'd be gone for a few months. Months? Not weeks. Or days. Months. The time was too long, the distance too great.

Feebly, she tried to explain that she couldn't allow

this. They'd never make it apart, but she floundered, wallowing in the misery of her useless explanations and refusing to accept his words, hoping her refusal would keep him from leaving her.

He took her willing body into his arms. He kissed her with the usual enthusiasm and promised her he'd be back if she'd be patient with him. She traced his face with her fingertips and tried to memorize the exact dimensions. Her heart was already aching with the pain of missing him.

He was going with a single man from the Charity group, one of the other Amish youth groups, he said just before he left. Lester Amstutz. She nodded dumbly and stood up woodenly. She was surprised her limbs didn't creak and clank, as if made from tin, when she turned to go inside.

She stood with her hand on the doorknob for a long time, unable to face the suffocation her bedroom would subject her to. Turning, she reached out a hand and whispered, "Matthew?" It was a question, as if she was unsure about what he had told her. She wanted to run after him, hold him, keep him from going anywhere without her, but she could only stand on the front porch and whisper his name again.

What was that about loving something and setting it free? If you loved something and set it free, it would return? Or "he" would return. Not "it."

Reality finally reached her senses, and Sarah turned the knob, made her way up the stairs, and lay on her bed, fully clothed. Sleep eluded her and the night stretched out long and black and filled with sorrow.

Somewhere inside, she knew Matthew was trying to be gentle. He did not want to be Amish. He didn't appreciate the heritage of his family, the old linage of conservatism, the traditions, the way of life.

Well, when he returned and had made a decision to leave his family and join a worldly church—was there such a thing?—she'd go with him.

Dat and Mam would get over it, eventually.

Wasn't that the most beautiful verse in the Bible? That part about Ruth going with her mother-in-law? "Thy God shall be my God." But she already had a God.

The old rooster in the henhouse crowed, and through the heavy blackness, Sarah squinted at the alarm clock and rolled out of bed. She surprised Dat by being the first one in the barn at four thirty. She wasn't tired, she said.

That spring, Sarah's world became tumultuous, her mind and spirit tossed about, surging forward, drawing back. The only description fitting of her inner turmoil was the stormy waves of the sea.

It was funny, the way doubt changed her perspective. The kindly people in church, sitting on their hard benches with their attention levels varying to some degree, all made her wonder if it really was the way Matthew had said—unspiritual.

There was Henry Zook, sound asleep, his head rolling to one side, his mouth sagging open slightly. If that wasn't unspiritual, she didn't know what was.

In the kitchen, a group of young women was gossiping, covering their mouths as they glanced around, their eyes stealthy like cats. Catty, that's exactly what they were. Well, perhaps Matthew was right.

She saw the yellowed covering set haphazardly on the head of the aged deacon's wife, a fine dusting of dandruff across her black cape. She thought of the snowy line veils the women in the Charity group wore instead with their hair combed up over their heads in a loose, attractive fashion. They wore pure pinks and yellows and blues. And Sarah suddenly didn't like the sloppy old Amish *ordnung.*

Then she became thoroughly miserable, remembering the day of Matthew's departure, the eagerness in his eyes, the new light of expectation. She would have done anything to keep him.

Lester Amstutz had waited in his sports car, keeping an eye on every move they made when Matthew stopped to say his final good-bye. Lester's head remained turned in their direction, watching shrewdly like a lion inspecting its prey, unsure what the outcome of its stealth would be.

Matthew had not held her hand that day. He only held her eyes with his own, his voice quiet, smooth, like water gliding quietly over oiled rocks, without turbulence. His voice was even, flat, whispery in its reverence. Had he already made a decision?

Fear had clawed at her heart, raking its fiery talons through her, producing a pain so great she had reached out with both hands, her palms upturned, and stepped toward him, a great sob catching in her throat as the words poured from her pain.

"Matthew, you can't! You can't do this to me. Does my love mean nothing to you? Does our God, our way of life, our heritage mean nothing? Don't go. Please, don't go. You'll be enticed into a new belief, to a place I cannot follow."

Matthew drew himself up, his voice quiet, reserved, as smooth as silk.

"I must go, Sarah. I have prayed. I want to become born again. Whosoever cannot leave his father or mother or sister or brother is not worthy."

"Don't, Matthew." Anger consumed her now. "You know better than to spout that verse at me. If you do that, you are clearly calling me an unbeliever. I am not. Neither is your father, or your mother, or…or Chris!" she spat out.

"By your anger, I know you are not born again."

She wanted to draw her arm back and smack him across his face, beat his chest with her fists, rail and cry and break down this new barrier between them. What she did do was draw a deep and steady breath and say, "It certainly has not taken you long to descend into self-righteousness."

A small, sad, smile played around Matthew's lips. His eyes became heavy-lidded, almost sensual. "I found Jesus last night at the revival meeting. I have not, as you say, descended into self-righteousness, but I've been clothed by the righteousness of Jesus."

"So you're not coming back?"

"Oh, I wouldn't go so far as to say that. I'm on a search for the true call of Jesus Christ."

There was nothing to say to such piety.

"I am a new creature, alive in Jesus."

That was the sentence that threw her off balance, hurling her into a vortex of uncertainty, wavering unsteadily on the brink of a precipice as he turned, still wearing the small, sad, conquering smile, and walked placidly away from her.

Would she always have every single angle of his body imbedded in her mind? His dark hair, cut just right, his wide shoulders, the way he swung his arms, his loose gait, even the way he placed his feet, so athletic, so Matthew. Her Matthew. No one else's. Not the world's, not a church's, not a new belief's.

Oh, come back to me, Matthew. Just come back.

And so her spring had turned gray. She no longer enjoyed the beauty of the azure sky, the birds' songs, the smell of fresh soil and newly mown hay, the wonder of a newborn calf. Her life was too full of indecision, longing, fear, and, above all, the strange new way she now viewed the Amish through lenses of doubt.

Was Matthew right? Was not one member of the Amish church born again? Did they all live in ignorance and suppression? She thought she might eventually go mad as the darts of confusion slowly entered her heart, draining the life from her.

Desperately, she hid her turmoil from her parents. They knew Matthew had gone on a trip to see the western part of the United States. That was all. That was all Hannah knew, or Elam. They went about their busy lives, working from sunup to sundown, happy and talkative, their ignorance about their son's travels a blessing, Sarah supposed.

Was it pride that kept her secret intact? Sarah didn't know. All she wanted was for Matthew—the old, happy, genuine Matthew—to walk back up on the porch, take her in his strong arms, say there was nothing out there for him, that he was staying Amish.

She prayed frequently and fervently, with tears squeezing between her stinging eyelids, which were red and swollen from lack of sleep.

Mam watched her daughter, bought allergy medication at her request, and said nothing.

One fine spring evening, when the air was mellow with summer's warmth, Sarah could no longer hide the fact that her life had turned completely upside down. Mam sat on an old lawn chair on the porch, sewing buttons

on a new pair of denims. The thimble on her third finger flashed in the pink glow from the setting sun. Her
face was serene, the dark wings of her sleek hair now
showing an extraordinary amount of gray, her homemade
covering large and snowy white, the wide strings pinned
behind her back with a small safety pin.

Mam's hands were calloused and work roughened
but somewhat softened each day by the same lotion, the
large yellow bottle of Vaseline Intensive Care, which she
applied liberally at bedtime. She was humming softly,
contentedly. Then she stopped, laughed, and said she
didn't even know that song. It just stuck in her head, the
way Priscilla kept singing it around the house.

Sarah smiled. Knowing she would burst into tears and
thereby lay bare her secret, she got up and said she was
walking down to Lydia's to see how she was doing.

Mam nodded assent and then shook her head at Priscilla, when she rose to accompany her sister.

"Better not, Priscilla."

"Why?"

"I'm afraid you're spending too much time with Omar.
You're only fifteen."

Priscilla blushed furiously. The color in her face did
not escape Levi, who watched her with a calculating
expression, pursed his lips, and asked Priscilla if she
hadn't heard that the younger daughter should not marry
before the elder.

"Oh hush, Levi!"

"No. You shouldn't be going to the widow's house."

Mam smiled but said nothing.

"The barn fires made a mess of many people's lives,"
he said, shaking his great head sorrowfully.

"What makes you say that?" Mam asked.

"That poor widow. My, oh."

Mam said, yes, he was right, but there was also much good that had come of it. Every trial, every adversity in life serves the purpose of making people better, whether they are aware of it or not.

She clipped the strong black thread with her small quilting scissors and looked at Sarah, whose eyes became liquid with her own hidden feelings, guarded for so long. She propelled herself off the porch and away from the love in her mother's eyes, the one thing that would bring down the wall of reserve around her.

Sarah found Lydia relaxing on her own porch, the children around her. Omar was in the new horse barn building stalls for the large draft animals.

She waved, and he answered with a hand thrown high over his head.

Sarah grinned and greeted Lydia gladly.

"Such a pretty evening!" she responded.

"Sure is. Hi, Anna Mae. How is everyone?"

"We're doing well, Sarah," Lydia said. "Too good, I'm afraid. It doesn't seem right that we just take and take. It's overwhelming."

"Don't you worry, please, Lydia. I'm sure many families have been blessed by their charity."

"But it isn't really right, is it? I mean, I could take the cost of this."

She spread her arms to indicate the yard including the new white fence and the shrubs bordering it. She could live on the price of that fence for quite some time.

"*Ach* now, Lydia. You must stop that."

Lydia asked the children to see if Omar needed help, and Anna Mae left with them obediently.

Lydia turned her head and looked squarely at her new

found friend. She began to talk, hesitantly at first, then with more conviction.

"It's hard for me, Sarah. Too hard. I talk to my counselors but...."

Lydia stopped and looked away, unseeing, across the yard. Her gaze went down to the hollow where the new red barn stood resplendent in the evening's glow.

Sarah remained quiet, biding her time, allowing the widow the space she needed to gather her courage.

A small vehicle drove by slowly. The occupants turned their heads to peer at the new barns. From the wide door of the smaller building, Omar straightened his back, throwing a friendly wave at the car's occupants.

For a second, Sarah thought it was Ashley, from market, in the passenger seat. Her eyes were wide, her face thin and white.

Must be her imagination.

But when the car returned and slowly made its way past in the opposite direction, she had a full view of Ashley through the front window. Hastily Sarah stood up, waving a hand eagerly, wanting to catch the girl's attention, but her gaze was focused on the barns.

It was clearly Ashley, Sarah realized. Why hadn't she returned her wave?

Like a bolt, the memory of Levi describing the car he had seen the night of their fire came back to her. He had described the taillights as being low, like a Volkswagen's, and this car was certainly a Volkswagen, and light-colored as well.

Was there a connection? Was Ashley involved in these fires somehow? Sarah thought of the girl's fright, her frequent questions. She didn't even hear Lydia ask her a question.

"Hello, Sarah?" Lydia laughed.

"Oh, sorry, Lydia. I just thought I knew the girl in that car, but she obviously didn't see me."

"Well, you probably don't want to hear about my boring, messed up life, anyway."

"Stop it. Please do continue."

"Well, I was just saying that it's hard for me to accept all this. Soon after I married Aaron, I learned life is easier if you kept blaming yourself when things...stuff, you know, goes wrong. That way, you don't see all the bad in the other person. Do you understand?"

"Well, not really. How can you place the blame on yourself for something you didn't do?"

"Well, I could. I wasn't a good wife."

"You weren't?"

"No."

"Why?"

"Oh, there were lots of things. I don't think Aaron would have lost his temper so easily if I would have tried harder to keep things going smoothly. Sometimes I just gave up and didn't try, figuring it would make no difference, and that was wrong."

Sarah shrugged. "I don't understand."

"Maybe I'm not saying this right. When the barn burned, I blamed myself. I figured I must have done something wrong, and God was chastening me for my wrongdoing. You know we can bring a curse on our own heads for not having enough fear of God in our hearts, don't you? Sometimes I feel cursed, Sarah. The night I no longer wanted to live—that was only the easy way out. Not easy, but the only way. A life of wrongdoing, then Aaron's suffering and death, the bills, the children crying, my baby so thin and sickly, never enough money, then the barn, and always, I felt cursed. It's as if God placed a special accountability on my head, and I literally had to pay here on earth for every one of my missteps, known or unknown."

Sarah sat on the wooden rocking chair, her thoughts slowly clicking into place, a typewritten message, easily deciphered. Here were the two opposite sides of Christianity.

The message was drummed into Sarah's mind, and she grasped it eagerly, greedily. The truth was a thing she could hold and cradle and care for with a genuine and sound mind.

There was Matthew on one side, aloof, with great quantities of redemption given to him, but so sadly unaware of the great gift he could not obtain because of his exalted, prideful state.

Lydia, on the other hand, was cowering in fear of her own wrongs, feeling cursed, unable to lift her head and accept as much as one ounce of forgiveness. She was not even able to believe. And both of them were missing Jesus's greatest gift.

Love. The love of their parents, their neighbors and friends, their church. They were missing it all as they grasped for the truth of Jesus. Hadn't He dwelt among sinners and shown His love to all?

With sadness in her heart, Sarah told Lydia the details about Matthew's leaving, revealing that it wasn't what Elam and Hannah thought it was.

Lydia listened, her eyes soft and luminous with sympathy, as Sarah poured out all the misery of the time since Matthew had left.

"He's not coming back?" she questioned softly.

"I am still hoping."

"Why are these revival meeting so *fa-fearish* (misleading)?" Lydia asked.

"I think they are misleading only to the Amish. I don't think the basic content is wrong. It just leads us away from what we have been taught."

"We can't judge others, I know."

"Absolutely not."

"But Matthew is not honoring his parents."

"No."

"Surely that must bother him."

"I doubt if it does. He feels free. He has Jesus now."

Lydia nodded, understanding.

"I would say he'd have more of Jesus by loving and obeying his parents and remaining humble, esteeming others above himself."

Sarah nodded, then asked bluntly, "Are you born again?"

"Oh, I wouldn't talk about that. The fruit of the Spirit is the only way we know. Isn't that what we believe? And I couldn't say I have any fruits at all, or…or all this bad stuff wouldn't have happened."

Sarah laughed softly.

"Well, Lydia, I'd say Matthew is floating somewhere close to the moon, but you're tunneling below the surface of the earth."

"*Ach*, I know. My counselors say I'm getting somewhere, though."

At that moment, Omar appeared, his face lined with fatigue, his shoulders rounded with the weight of responsibility far above his years, a tired smile lighting up his face.

"Hi, Sarah!"

"Hello, yourself. Hard day?"

"Sort of. Trying to do too much during the daylight hours, I guess. I don't know what I'd do without Lee Glick. He's over here every chance he gets. Did you know he's helping me get started raising these Belgians? He claims that with the cows' income and the farming, we can turn a profit. Sometimes though, when I'm tired, like now, I just want to go work for him. By the hour. Less worry. Less responsibility."

He looked around.

"Where's Priscilla?"

"Levi wanted her to stay home."

"Oh."

Omar was clearly disappointed, but he said nothing further. He just smiled and let himself through the door to the kitchen. Anna Mae followed him, clearly idolizing her older brother.

The soft, velvety darkness gently folded its curtains across Lancaster County. The two women sat side by side on the front porch of the old farmhouse, united by the shared calamities they had experienced, coupled with troubles of entirely different kinds. Their personal heartaches brought them together in ways they could never before have imagined.

Lydia was a member of the same church district as Sarah, but she had only been a slight acquaintance, someone Sarah had spoken to only occasionally. Now, however, she had shared her deep and personal secret about Matthew and had lent a sympathetic ear when Lydia shared hers. What a rare and appreciated treasure!

Only time would disclose the real nature of Matthew's spiritual adventure, which is exactly what it was, Sarah decided as she walked home through the mild, dew-laden evening. She walked with her head bowed, her thoughts wandering as she sifted through new information. Was it okay for Matthew to do what he was doing, in God's eyes? Did his parents' pleas and broken hearts mean nothing at all? Who was right and who was wrong? Were they both wrong?

And there was the poor Widow Lydia, unable to lift her head, so burdened by her own shortcomings.

Well, Sarah wasn't going to figure it out in one night, and, very likely, she didn't have to. All she needed to do was allow Jesus to carry her yoke, and she'd be just fine.

That was why she was humming when she walked past Elam's house. For once, the pain wasn't quite as blinding even though she knew Matthew was not upstairs in his room. He was somewhere on God's earth, and where there was life, there was hope.

But there was still one other thing. What was that frightened Ashley doing in a cream-colored Volkswagen driving past Lydia's farm? As Melvin would say, "The plot thickens," she thought and chuckled.

CHAPTER 9

SARAH SHIFTED HER WEIGHT, PULLED UP HER knees, and braced them against the seat ahead of her. She was searching for a measure of comfort to grab a few minutes of sleep before arriving at the market in New Jersey.

"Hey!" Ruthann reached behind her head to tap Sarah's knees.

"Relax. I'm not disturbing you."

With a snuffling sound, Ruthann slouched down and went back to sleep.

Sarah was cold, but she didn't have the nerve to ask the driver to turn the air conditioning off. He was overweight and was drinking his coffee in great, hot slurps, so he probably needed the cool air to stay comfortable. Meanwhile, the group of young passengers was freezing, many of them huddled under the small, fuzzy blankets they'd brought from home.

Sarah couldn't find her blanket that morning. She had scrambled wildly about her room looking for it as the van's headlights sliced through the darkness of the early summer morning. Priscilla had probably borrowed it again. She was always too lazy to go to the cedar chest to get a blanket of her own.

Sarah managed to doze fitfully, but she was glad when the vanload of workers reached their destination. She was happy to jump down out of the van, stretch, and start her day after a quick trip to the restroom to fix her hair and pin on her freshly ironed covering.

She had dark circles lurking beneath her green eyes, and the pasty beige color she was wearing did nothing for her complexion. There was a coffee stain on the front of her white apron, but dabbing at it with a towel only made it worse, so she gave up and went to work, greeting her employers and fellow workers with half-hearted attempts at imitating her usual cheerfulness. Everyone knew Matthew was still away, so they shrugged their shoulders and left her alone.

Sarah measured ingredients and turned on mixers but kept her eyes averted, sending a clear signal for everyone to leave her to her thoughts. As the morning wore on, however, she became steadily caught up in the grinding work of the bakery. Her thoughts were occupied completely by her ability to turn out enough fresh cinnamon rolls, bread, dinner rolls, and sandwich rolls. She also helped out with any other pastries as needed.

An hour after her usual break time, she was exhausted, hungry, and completely fed up with her job. She felt as if no one cared whether she had a break at all. She figured that all the other girls probably had had theirs by this time, but because she was stuck back with the dough mixers, who would even care if she got one or not?

Fighting the waves of self-pity that threatened her, she looked up to find her boss, Emma Glick, handing her a ten-dollar bill and saying Sarah was always the last to go for her break. She said to take an extra long one, and here, use this.

"You're doing an excellent job," she said, patting Sarah's shoulder.

Lifted from her pit of despair, Sarah gratefully accepted the money and thanked Emma. She went and bought the largest sandwich she could find and settled herself into a booth, not caring whether she saw Rose or not.

It was pure bliss—the homemade hoagie roll, browned and crisp from the oven, layers of ham and cheese toasted and melted with mayonnaise. The sandwich was then filled generously with shredded lettuce and onion with fresh red tomatoes peeking out from underneath.

She munched happily, wiped the mayonnaise from her lips, then smiled at Rose when she approached her table.

"Hey, stranger!"

"You hungry?"

"Not anymore."

Their small talk was just that—very small. In fact, it was ridiculous the way they circled around the subject of Matthew.

Sarah finally realized it was only her pride that was coming between them. Swallowing that pride, she slowly revealed to Rose the agony of her heart, knowing she just couldn't hold it in much longer. Rose completely caught Sarah off guard with her gentle sympathy as she lowered her face into a used napkin, smearing mayonnaise across her nose and leaving a thin shred of lettuce dangling from one eyelash. Rose laughed hysterically when Sarah told her and reached to remove the lettuce.

Rose then filled in Sarah about Lee Glick, how much fun they had hanging out together, and how her heart skipped about seventy beats last Sunday evening at the singing, when he loitered around their buggy. She thought sure he was going to ask her.

Rummaging in her purse, she found a small mirror, checked her appearance, batted her perfect eyelashes, and smiled at Sarah.

"I wouldn't get too miserable about Matthew. Lee is much better for me."

"What does that mean?" Sarah asked sourly.

"Well, you'll get over him. Find someone better."

"It's not that easy, Rose. I have always loved Matthew."

"You never told me."

"You knew."

"Not really."

Sarah had no answer for Rose's denial, so she sighed and changed the subject. She told Rose about the vehicle going past Lydia's house.

"You go hang out with that Lydia? She's mentally off, isn't she? She gives me the shivers. I don't know how you do it, helping her."

Sarah was surprised at her friend's lack of empathy.

"She's so pitiful, Rose. You have no idea."

"Whatever. I think it's creepy to spend time with her."

There was nothing to say in response. Wanting to show her disapproval, Sarah left the booth hurriedly, leaving Rose staring after her.

Sarah was seething now. Her day had started poorly to begin with, and now Rose had suddenly made her feel small and inadequate, the way she looked down her nose at Lydia. Sarah stormed past the meat stand, disregarding the friendly smiles of the proprietors and leaving them with raised eyebrows and questions in their eyes.

Her head down, her step quickening, she rounded a corner and hit something solid and immovable. She lurched to the right but was caught by a strong arm. She heard a "Whoa!" as she steadied herself. Then she saw a navy blue shirt, open at the neck, a pair of broadfall denims with a pair of gray suspenders attached.

"Watch where you're going!"

Sarah caught hold of the corner as she stepped back and looked up into the face of Lee Glick. His blue eyes mocked her, but not unkindly.

She rose to the challenge.

"Watch where I'm going? What about you?"

Only for a few seconds, he allowed himself to watch the restless colors dancing in her eyes, completely losing any measure of time. It was a nanosecond, and it was an eternity. It was the most mesmerizing moment of his life, acknowledging the depth of this girl's spirit, her goodness, her sincerity.

"I didn't know you worked here," he said. What he wanted to say was something so much more profound, so filled with longing, questioning, wondering.

"At the bakery."

"You on break?"

"Just finished."

"Let me buy you dessert."

Ill at ease, shy, Sarah turned her head to look behind her, thinking of Rose.

"You don't have time?"

Sarah nodded, incapable of speech now, his blue eyes captivating her.

He bought two raspberry twist ice cream cones and led her outside where picnic tables dotted the narrow strip of grass by the parking lot. Young pear trees were planted at measured distances, their small leaves rustling in the summer breeze and creating a bit of shade across the graying, splintered top of the wooden table.

Sarah sat opposite him, swung her legs beneath the table, ate her ice cream, and was suddenly aware of an all-encompassing shyness gripping her throat. She could not speak.

Lee watched her face intently, following the shadows of the pear leaves as they played across her golden face, her startling eyes, the honey-colored waves in her chestnut hair.

He wanted to paint her portrait, silly as it seemed. He felt he could sit there for the rest of the day and say nothing at all. He could just watch her expressions, the eyes that gave so much away.

Finally she said, soft and low, "Why are you here?"

"We're roofing a house about a block from here."

"You came to see Rose?"

"Rose? You mean Rose Zook?"

Sarah nodded, bit down on the cone, afraid he had, afraid he had not.

"I didn't know she worked here."

"Oh."

Then, without thinking, having already thought far too much about this subject, he said, "How's Matthew? Heard from him?"

He wiped his mouth with his napkin and averted his eyes, too chicken now to meet hers as he was consumed with fear in anticipation of her answer. For a long moment, she didn't answer. When she did speak, her voice was barely above a whisper.

"I don't know how he is. I haven't heard from him."

Lee raised his eyebrows, ashamed of the joy that flooded his very soul.

"He doesn't write? Call?"

Lee drew his breath in sharply when she leaned her
elbows on the table and hunched her shoulders. Her
eyes became almost brown with shifting forces, waves
whipped to foam by the strength of her emotion. She
paused, breathing hard.

"He's on a spiritual journey, he says. He thinks Amish
people are not born again, that these barns are burning
because we aren't who we should be, we aren't really
spiritual. Too much *ordnung*, he says. The thing is he
doesn't even want to be Amish. He's threatened to leave
the church ever since he broke up with Rose."

She stopped, biting her lower lip.

"Lee, what do these barns have to do with it? What?"

She'd said his name!

"I don't think someone lighting fires has too much
to do with the spiritual health of the Amish church. If
anything, the Amish spirituality has only increased....I
don't know. It seems just about everything good there is
to practice is being done even more."

"That's what Dat says."

"Maybe I shouldn't give my opinion. I'm not worth
a whole lot when it comes to Bible stuff. I don't know
a lot about anything. But you only know what you feel,
and if a barn raising isn't the fruit of the right spirit, then
I don't know what is. It's a coming together, everyone,
and the whole reason is to help the poor guy who lost his
barn. I always think the whole thing in a nutshell—as far
as religion goes—is giving a hoot about what happens to
your neighbor, helping out whenever someone needs you,
simply because you care."

Sarah breathed in slowly, blinking her eyes as if to truly grasp the meaning of the words he was saying. She realized that Lee spoke, and thought, along the same lines as her own revered father.

Lee's eyes found hers. There was not a word spoken between them, and yet Sarah felt as if they had talked at length.

Cars came and went, passersby strolled along, carrying purchases, or eager to make them. Despite the bustle of the market, Lee was oblivious to any motion around him, consumed by his strong feelings for this troubled girl.

Suddenly she spoke. "Are you born again?"

"You shouldn't be asking me that question."

"Why?"

"It's not our way."

"It's Matthew's."

His hope was dashed in an instant, leaving scalding burns like a kettle of boiling water dropped to the ground. Sarah's words splashed a dangerous wetness against his heart and left angry blisters of pain. Unable to stop himself, he leapt to his feet, his blue eyes blazing with a new and terrible light.

"If you want to follow Matthew, then go. Just go. Get out of my life, out of my mind, out of my knowing you even exist. Okay?"

He placed both palms on the rough, weathered surface of the picnic table. The muscles of his shoulders strained against the navy blue fabric of his shirt, the heavy veins in his tanned neck bulging as he fought the overpowering emotions that threatened to consume him.

"You seem happily oblivious to the fact that you are already misled, going around asking people if they're born again. Do me a favor, and stay away from me, okay?"

With that, he abruptly straightened, turned on his heel, and stalked away. As he threaded his way between the parked vehicles, his closely shorn blond hair shone like a beacon of sunshine.

Sarah lowered her head into her hands, but her eyes remained dry. She felt cold and barren, windswept like an arid land without rain, without sustenance of any kind. Flat and unemotional. That obviously had not been the correct thing to say.

Well, he couldn't blame her for wondering if Matthew was right. He was, after all, her boyfriend, her fiancé, her intended. Obviously, her intended.

A great weariness enveloped her now. It folded her in seductive arms and whispered words of defeat into her tired ears. Perhaps it wouldn't be a bad idea to leave the Amish. If she was with Matthew, she'd be sure. She would have made a decision, and she would stick to her choice. No more doubting and wondering.

She would know she was born again, have a sure pass into heaven, and she could join the people who thought the same way she did.

Matthew would marry her. She would be forever secure and loved, and she would be knowledgeable, growing in wisdom from the Bible.

Back at the bakery, Sarah burned a tray of sweet rolls and was sharply reprimanded by her boss. She wept furtive tears into a paper towel and wondered if her life would ever right itself. If only Matthew would come home.

Sarah rushed to compensate for her mistake with the sweet rolls and cut her index finger with the dough cutter. She slashed it horribly, and blood spurted from the long gash. Her day's work was now finished except for standing at the cash register, her finger throbbing painfully inside its heavy bandage.

When Sarah stumbled in the door at home, Mam looked up with her usual warm smile of welcome. The smile quickly slid away and was replaced by a lifting of the eyebrows, a clouding of concern.

"How was your day?"

"Fine."

Sarah's tone was short, clipped. The word was hard, like a pellet.

"You don't look fine."

"I cut my finger."

"Did you take care of it?"

"Yeah."

Mam sighed and decided to take action. Enough was enough.

Resolutely she poured cold mint tea over ice cubes in tall glasses. She placed the glasses on a tray along with slices of sharp cheddar cheese, some Ritz crackers, hot pepper jelly, and the soft, raisin-filled cookies she had just baked before supper.

"Let's have a glass of tea," was all she said. She was soon joined by the rest of the family. Levi heaped crackers and cheese with large spoonfuls of the quivering hot pepper jelly.

Sarah joined them reluctantly, her tears on the verge of spilling over. Dat plopped on the wooden porch swing and slapped Levi's knee with a resounding whack.

"Davey Beila!" Levi said, greeting his father and calling him by his given name as he occasionally did.

"How much of that pepper jelly are you going to eat?" Dat chortled, slapping Levi's knee again with affection.

"All of it, Davey. Then you can't have any."

Smiling, Mam handed Dat a glass of mint tea. The humidity produced beads of moisture on the outside of the glass, and a ring of water remained on the tray after she lifted it.

The night was coming on, but it did nothing to lift the blanket of oppressive humidity. The heavy green maple leaves hung thickly, completely still, not a whisper of a breeze stirring them.

"A storm will come up later tonight," Dat observed.

For now, the routine of the evening, the homey atmosphere, the completely relaxed setting surrounded the family. It provided the foundation of their home, a place where each was accepted and loved without having to be told. And it finally broke Sarah's resolve to hide away her doubts and fears about the future.

Hesitantly at first, then with stronger conviction, she told them of Matthew's quest and the real reason he was traveling.

In the fading summer light, Dat's face appeared shadowed, patriarchal. His graying beard flowed across his chest, and his hair lay close to his skull where his straw hat had pressed against it all day as he worked the fields. He looked away across the porch and the neatly cut lawn, past the new barn and the fields beyond. He said nothing to interrupt the flow of words that now rained from Sarah.

Mam clucked, put a hand to her mouth, and shook her head, but she remained as quiet as she could.

"So, I'm no longer sure what is right and what is wrong. Everything is blurred. And my *zeit-lang* (longing) for Matthew to return is almost more than I can bear.

"And what if he's right? What if we Amish are blind, misguided individuals who have grown up in the shadow of the *ordnung* and all the Old Testament stuff that doesn't amount to anything at all?"

The questions vibrated above them, static with a sense of the unknown. Levi smacked his lips appreciatively after a long drink of the icy mint tea. Then he slid forward clumsily, balancing himself by grasping the chain attaching the swing to the hooks above it, and reached for two raisin-filled cookies.

"Levi," Mam said.

"We didn't have much supper, Mam. *Kalte sup* (Cold soup)!"

"Just one, Levi."

Resignedly, Levi returned one cookie, asking Dat if he was full on *kalte sup*.

"We had fish, too."

"I don't like fish too good."

Dat smiled at Mam, knowing Levi would eat another cookie eventually.

"Well, Sarah, you likely asked the most often asked question among the Amish people nowadays. It really surprises me how long you've kept this to yourself."

She hung her head. "I'm sorry," she whispered.

"Don't be. I just hope you aren't planning on following Matthew."

"I want to."

"I believe that."

Then Dat told her that he believed any individual could search the Bible and could pick out verses to justify their own beliefs. But too often, a belief was an attitude, a way of thinking, a way of looking at the world with either an air of superiority or an inflated ego. Call it born again, if you want, he said.

"When Adam and Eve were in the Garden of Eden, the serpent misled Eve by saying if she would eat the forbidden fruit, she would know what was right and what was wrong, like God. To this day, we completely mislead ourselves—and others—by thinking we know who is born of the Spirit and who is not."

Sarah interrupted her father. "But we have to! Matthew said!"

"Let me continue. When a breeze stirs the leaves on the maple tree, as the Spirit stirs the hearts of people, we know the leaves are moving because of the wind, but we don't know where the breeze is coming from or where it's going, in Jesus's words. We really don't. Tell me, Sarah, where does the wind come from and where does it go?"

She shrugged her shoulders.

"That's right. The power of the Spirit is God's, and only His to know. We are mortals. That is our way, Sarah. Yes, I know exactly what you're going to say, Sarah.

"Many *ausre gmayna* (other churches) accept powerful testimonies. They accept the faith of each individual by their moving reports of visitations by the Spirit. They highlight the condemnation, the repentance, the saving of their souls by the blood of Christ. That is all good and right. That is our way as well but with less fanfare, of course. You know that we cannot exalt ourselves by that alone.

"It is only by the fruits that we can know someone. And the fruits of the Spirit are a gift of God. They are nothing we do ourselves. So we choose to remain humble, exalting only the Father above and no mere mortal."

"What about Matthew? He's a new person, in Jesus."

"For awhile. He'll be back down."

"Dat!"

Sarah was shocked, angry.

"I'm serious. An English man told me once that a person who has come to the knowledge of the truth should be incarcerated for a while. They're on fire for the Lord, handing out tracts, just sure they are sent to save mankind.

"Likely they still disagree with their wives, spend money unwisely, and lose their tempers. They are human. Just like us. So our set of manmade rules—the law, if you will, the *ordnung*—serves its purpose, keeping our exalted selves restrained."

"So then, who will got to heaven, the Amish or the… the…others?"

Dat stroked his beard thoughtfully in the light that was visibly fading into the night.

"I think we all have the same chance. It's God's job to separate the weeds from the healthy plants, and not ours."

"What about Matthew?"

"I think he's on a dangerous road, but it's not in my hands at all. It's up to God to judge, to know what he will need in later years to mold him and purify him."

"What would happen if I chose to leave the church and to follow him?"

Darkness erased most of Dat's features, but the silver trickle, the trail of Dat's tears, sliced through her heart, leaving a physical pain somewhere in the region of her stomach.

He breathed in, a long, shaking inhalation of love.

"Eventually, you'd be excommunicated for your disobedience."

"I thought so."

"Are you seriously thinking it over?"
"I'm waiting to see what Matthew will do."
"Then, we'll leave it at that."
"What do you mean?"
"Just that. I can't tell you what to do."

CHAPTER 10

When Matthew's letter arrived, Sarah could not hide the shaking in her hands, so she escaped to the privacy of her room in spite of the sweltering afternoon sun burning through the glass panes of her windows. The screens below allowed only short puffs of hot air, sullenly ruffling the silky panels and barely stirring the air in the room.

A fine line of perspiration beaded her upper lip, and stray curls clung to her damp forehead as she sat on the edge of her bed. She pressed her knees together, her bare heels inches off the floor, the tension distributing her weight over her bent toes.

The envelope was plain white, and the folded paper inside plainly visible. The letter was thin—surely only one sheet.

With shaking hands, she lifted the flap and ripped open the top of the envelope, hurriedly extracting the one folded sheet of lined paper. He had always had good handwriting.

Dear Sarah,

You must come to me. I am leaving for Haiti in two weeks, on the 15ᵗʰ of August. I want you to be with me, flying above the earth.

I think I can make you understand my way. Please come to me. This freedom is unbelievable. The chains that have kept me bound to the Amish are gone.

I'm free!

My cell phone number is 717-555-0139.

Call me!

Matthew

She could not contain the conflicting emotions that surged through her body. She held the paper to her heart, a sob catching in her throat. Her breath came out ragged, edged in pain and suffering.

She would call him. She knew she would.

Rocking forward, then backward, she opened her mouth as if to cry, but only a raw moan of misery emerged. The inner conflict was an unbearable thing. She could never leave Dat. She knew he was a barge of truth, plowing steadily through all kinds of weather, waves crashing around him, and he never faltered. The closest he had ever come to being undone was in the aftermath of their fire and then losing little Mervin in the flood.

But she could not live without Matthew. She loved him. Unconditionally. English or Amish, Mennonite or Catholic, Lutheran or Baptist. What really was the difference?

If the leaves on the trees were like human beings the way Dat said, did they all look alike to God from way up there, and did he love them all the same?

Immediately, she flew down the stairs, burst through

the door, and sprinted across the lawn, the grass crinkly and dry in the late afternoon sun. Her feet only skimmed the ground before she yanked open the door of the phone shanty, bent over the dusty white telephone, and punched in the numbers. The desperate need to hear his voice surpassed every other emotion.

On the fifth ring, his voicemail greeting washed over her aching heart, the sound of his voice a drop of water to a dying soul. Instantly, she dialed again and listened to his message a second time before replacing the receiver and slumping down into the old, cracked vinyl seat of the phone shanty chair.

Should she leave a message for him? No, she'd try later.

With a song in her heart, she went to the wash line and took down the black socks, denim trousers, and red men's handkerchiefs. She tugged on the line to bring in the multi-colored dresses, the black aprons, and pale shirts.

Whistling softly under her breath, she carried the large basket of clothes to a kitchen chair, took up a pair of trousers, and began folding them. Her thoughts raced, hysterical with the joy of Matthew's invitation.

Suzie came into the house, letting the screen door bang behind her, which provoked a snuffling sigh from the recliner, where Levi lay stretched out for his afternoon nap.

"Shh! Levi's asleep!"

"Time for him to come help in the garden. We have about a mountain of green beans waiting to snap, and now Mam says we have to hoe the rows yet today. It's at least a hundred degrees, and I am not kidding you."

Sarah smiled at Suzie.

"Well, see if you can get him awake."

In the evening, the air turned uncomfortably humid, the lowering sky threatening, ominous. Sarah perspired freely, sitting in the phone shanty, unsuccessfully making another attempt at reaching Matthew. She held the receiver to her ear and was amazed to hear the beep indicating a message had been left on their voicemail. Quickly she checked the caller ID panel and found Matthew's number.

With bated breath, she listened to his voice. "Hello, Sarah. This is Matthew." His voice! But it wasn't really Matthew. It was low and smooth and polished, with a hint of a western accent.

"I hope you are well. I'm sorry I didn't answer my cell phone, but where I am, the service is sketchy at best. Call me, leave me a message. I need your answer by the second of August." No goodbye.

Well, the second of the month was today. She couldn't make a choice of such magnitude in a few hours. It would break her parents' hearts. The church would eventually cast her away, shun her. She needed to understand excommunication better.

Sarah looked anxiously around the property. The wind was strangely stilled, the black clouds churning above the barn roof, jagged knives of lightning breaking out of the restless thunderheads. A fear of times past enveloped her. Surely not another flood!

There was another thin, high crackle above her, followed by a distant rumble. Immediately the heavy foliage on the maple trees danced to life as the wind kicked up with the approaching storm.

She couldn't leave a message now, so she turned away from the phone shanty, shutting the door firmly behind her and running swiftly across the lawn.

Mam was on the porch, grabbing the Zip-loc bags

she'd washed and hung on the small clothesline with wooden clothespins.

"Close the upstairs windows!" she called out as Sarah bounded onto the porch.

When she was in Suzie's room, she was surprised to see a team come in the driveway at breakneck speed. She peered anxiously through the window that was already splattered with fat raindrops. She recognized her cousin, Melvin, leaning forward, his eyes searching the sky as he surveyed the oncoming storm. Sarah greeted him in the forebay, just as the hailstones came crashing down on the new metal roof and the wind reached a high crescendo as it whined around the corner of the barn, bringing the hail and rain along with it.

"Melvin! What are you doing out on an evening like this?"

"Oh, nothing much. I was on my way to meet Lee at Lydia's, but I saw that I better find cover immediately."

At the mention of Lee's name, Sarah averted her eyes, her bare toe pushing bits of loose straw across the packed cement.

Dat suddenly burst through the milk house door. He greeted Melvin effusively, wiping the rain from his face with a soiled, wrinkled handkerchief.

"Whew!"

"Some storm. I'd let you know how bad it's going to be, but I can't check my cell phone with you around, Davey."

Dat grimaced and said he shouldn't be so worldly or so outspoken. Melvin grinned cheekily and clapped Dat's shoulder and told him not to worry, that he was raised to be respectful of the ministry.

Dat's eyes twinkled, and he shook his head.

"*Ach* Melvin, you're as full of hot air as you always were. If you were as respectful as you want me to believe, you wouldn't have mentioned the cell phone at all."

Melvin floundered about as his face turned red. He could not come up with a decent reply. Sarah burst out laughing, understanding Melvin and his need to look good wherever he went. Dat laughed, too.

"Probably the weather forecast would say it's stormy with a chance of hail in Lancaster County."

"Southeastern Lancaster County," Melvin corrected him wryly.

They all grimaced as the storm worsened. The sound of hailstones hitting the roof was deafening, like the din of thousands of projected golf balls. Speaking was impossible, so they stood in companionable silence. Each of them winced as the square barn windows turned an electrifying shade of blue for an instant, followed by dull rumbles of thunder. The peals reverberated among the storm clouds as if God had ordained a heavenly roll call in an attempt to catch his mortals' attention.

Finally Dat raised his voice.

"Good way to start a barn fire!" he shouted.

"You betcha!" Melvin agreed, vehemently nodding his head.

As the brunt of the storm abated, grumbling its way reluctantly to the south, they splashed into the house, dodging puddles and low hanging branches dripping with water.

Mam met them at the door, a worried expression erasing the serenity that was so commonplace.

"Thank goodness!" she said. "Sarah, I wasn't sure where you were, and I guess as long as the world goes round, storms will bring back memories of our little Mervin."

Her mouth wobbled visibly, and she blinked back the tears that so easily rose to the surface.

Melvin settled himself comfortably in a kitchen chair, his expressive eyes watching Mam's face, mirroring his own emotion. Mam shook her head, composed herself, and disappeared into the pantry as Levi stumbled from the living room, pure delight written across his face.

"Levi!" Melvin shouted.

"What's up, chap?" Levi said, loudly imitating the English man who drove the large rig that hauled their milk.

Melvin laughed.

"Not too much, Levi. How about you?"

"Oh, I think we got the barn fires stopped. Nothing going on since the Widow Lydia's."

"It hasn't been that long. Don't hold your breath."

"I don't look for another fire. The Amish are more aware of what that guy did. They're sleeping in barns, got big dogs that bite hard, alarms. Everyone has something," Levi said, his voice rising with excitement, aware of Melvin's attention.

"Levi's right," Dat said.

"Yeah, maybe the fires themselves aren't the real danger now. What about that Elam's Matthew taking off like that? Sarah, did you know he's texting the youth all the time? Surely you've broken up with him by now."

With Melvin, there was no tiptoeing around feelings. Everything was blunt, spoken in plain words, his recipients allowed to accept his words or disagree.

Sarah's face colored with misery, and she blushed self-consciously.

"No," she said in a cracked, hushed tone.

"What? Why not?" Melvin asked, his eyes popping

in disbelief.

"Well."

"Well, what?"

"I thought perhaps he'd change his mind yet."

"Ha! Ever hear of that happening? Once they get ahold of their Jesus, they're GONE!" Melvin brought his arm up and swished it through the air, a vivid symbol of the disgust he felt.

Dat's eyes watched Melvin. They were sharp in their disapproval, but his voice was gentle.

"Melvin, it's a good thing for someone to be concerned about his soul, finding Jesus, accepting redemption, any way you want to word it."

"Yeah, but those holy rollers that take their vows and then break them—they'll be surprised on judgment day, let me tell you."

"Be careful, Melvin. It's a narrow and slippery path when we condemn, and when we refuse to try and understand, we do not have the right kind of love in our hearts."

"Well, they're wrong—people like Matthew."

"There's a huge possibility we're all wrong if we fight about Scripture."

"What do you mean? You're a minister, and you're uncertain?"

"Let me explain, Melvin. I don't agree with Matthew doing this to his parents, to the ones who love him, especially Sarah. But we have to be careful. We need to carry our own cross, let Matthew carry his, and leave him to God's hands."

"So, Sarah, knowing you, you'll probably go puddling off after him."

"I doubt if I'll puddle."

Melvin didn't acknowledge the humor. An angry blush

crept across his cheeks, and he became almost belligerent.

"You'll be put in the *bann* (excommunicated). Then you'll slide straight to hell." He addressed Sarah angrily, his face working with suppressed feeling.

"I wanted to ask Dat about the true meaning of excommunication, as I have to make a decision today," Sarah said. "Matthew left a message for me. He invited me to go to Haiti with him on the fifteenth."

Dat's face was a mirror of Mam's with the color receding, leaving only fear and pain. They tried to grasp the fact that Sarah may actually want to leave, thereby breaking parental and godly rules. They knew they would be unable to restrain her if she wanted to go.

Pushing back the urge to cry out or hold back his darling daughter bodily, Dat calmed himself as a thick veil of confusion drew over Sarah's features. Her misery was so apparent, the reason for it so obvious. It drew its strength from the deep root that was her overwhelming infatuation with Matthew Stoltzfus, the single object of her desire.

No one spoke.

The rain still streamed down the kitchen windows, but the wind had died down and no longer whistled around the corners of the house.

Melvin was pouting, his mouth drawn firmly into a line of disagreement. He refused to accept the fact that his favorite cousin just could go skipping off scot-free, leaving his uncle's family with broken hearts. He'd love to have ahold of that arrogant Matthew about now.

The dripping from the faucet turned into a steady trickle, so Mam got up to adjust the handle. She checked the coffee in the stainless steel drip coffee maker, settling the top back with a bang to hasten the hot water dripping through the grounds.

She stood at the sink, her back turned, watching the rain creating a pattern of tears on the window pane. Her mind just could not grasp what Sarah was actually contemplating.

Dat drew a deep breath.

"And you want to go?" he asked, his voice gravelly with pain.

"Oh, of course. I'm just afraid of the *bann*."

"You should be!" Melvin exclaimed, leaning forward with intensity.

"Sarah, it is not fear of excommunication that keeps us together. If the pattern of life is as it should be, your love toward us is what should secure you to your heritage. The whole thing in a nutshell is love. Even the *bann* is a form of love. So many don't understand that, even our own people. But when we place someone outside of our church, we are acknowledging that they need chastening—trials and adversity—to become a better person, so their soul may be saved.

"Sarah it would be wrong for you to go with Matthew, because it would be blatant disobedience. It would be completely without love. In this day and age, we Amish believe in the saving grace of our *Herren Jesu* (Lord Jesus), and you would be turning your back on that.

"In the end, the choice is yours. Of course, you would be welcome to return, to visit. But our spiritual unification would be gone. The freedom from guilt would be lost as well. Matthew promises you freedom, but you would not be free."

Mam watched Sarah's face, the struggle darkening her once carefree face. She missed that face from the years prior to Matthew.

"So, you're saying I have to choose between you and him."

"Yes."

"Why? Why do the Amish have to be so thickheaded? Why can't I go off and do what I want with your blessing?"

Dat never faltered.

"It is not the way of Jesus's cross."

"Why? How?"

"We are taught from childhood to deny the flesh, our own will."

"But I love him!" she burst out.

"I believe you. But he obviously does not love you."

Dat's voice was firm, cemented in true conviction, and Sarah's eyes opened wide in astonishment at his statement.

"You know how it is, Sarah. Sometimes a disobedient youth joins the wild *rumspringa* crowd. But then if he truly loves a girl, he gives up the ways of the world for her. Matthew obviously isn't doing that. He doesn't love you."

"But he wants me to come and accompany him to Haiti!" Sarah burst out.

Far into the night they reasoned. Dat and Mam listened with great patience and forbearance, allowing Sarah to express her point of view. They were considerate, temperate, while Melvin bubbled and hissed with attempted restraint, his eyes bulging with the force of his own emotions.

In the end, Dat conceded wearily with drooping shoulders. He got up, put a hand on Mam's shoulder, and they said good night, leaving Melvin and Sarah alone in the kitchen.

They lay in bed, side by side, the way they had for almost forty years, and they never fell asleep. All night, their lips moved in prayer, two steadfast warriors, their pillows soaked with the many tears that slid down their cheeks. All through the night, their hands remained clasped, symbolic of the strength of their partnership in the face of this spiritual hurricane that blasted their very souls.

Sarah told Matthew she would go.

His voice was still as flat and smooth as before. Without raising or lowering it, he said he was glad.

"Just glad?" Sarah said.

"There is only one source of true joy," he told her in a much quieter tone than before. "That is our Lord and Savior, Jesus Christ."

"Oh," was all she could think to say.

She replaced the receiver with shaking hands and sat alone in the darkened phone shanty, senselessly pleating the skirt of nightgown.

Had Matthew gone a bit overboard or something?

Priscilla had a fit—what Grandmother King called a conniption. Anna Mae and Ruthie were horrified and demanded an explanation. How in the world could Mam let Sarah get away with this secrecy, this rebellion? Why was she allowing Sarah to run after that spoiled Matthew? He always got his own way with everything, and when he couldn't have his gorgeous Rose—the one time he had ever hit a brick wall—he acted like the spoiled brat he'd always been and just left, taking it out on everyone. It was his battered ego, his pride that was driving him.

They were reprimanded sharply by Mam. "Such talk! Such *unlieve* (hatred)!"

Ruthie bit into a raspberry and cream filled doughnut,

leaning over her coffee cup. The cup only caught about half the powdered sugar, leaving the rest to sift onto the black bib apron covering her ample chest. She wiped it off, leaving a white streak, snorted, and told Mam it was about time this family had a healthy dose of telling it like it is. With genuine honesty.

Anna Mae looked directly into Sarah's eyes and told her if she was dumb enough to run after Matthew, all the way to Haiti, where it was hot and miserable and full of missionaries, then she guessed she'd just have to. But don't come running back for pity, she said.

Levi told her a snake would bite her. He had heard that in Haiti they grew long enough to reach from the house to the barn.

They were seated around the old kitchen table having sisters day. The married girls came home for coffee and brunch with a large spread of food. It was one of the events that Levi especially looked forward to, mostly for the food.

Priscilla looked bored with the whole thing. She had already said her piece with no effect. So after she finished her plate of breakfast casserole, she went outside to clean the forebay.

Sarah was crazy, completely nuts, in her opinion, so what was the use even trying to make her see another point of view? She was just stumbling blindly after that inflated ego known as Matthew. He'd just switched from full of himself to full of himself spiritually. Same thing.

In the house, Sarah listened to her sisters. She actually burst into great heaves of laughter when Anna Mae said if she boarded that jet and flew to Haiti, she'd be compelled to hijack it like some whacko.

"You're not going to do it," Ruthie said emphatically.

"But I can't say no to Matthew!" Sarah wailed.

"I'd have no problem in that category. Bye! See ya! Adios!" Anna Mae said, holding little Justin by the forehead as she swiped a Kleenex across his eyes, looking for his nose.

"Watch what you're doing!" Sarah said.

"What? Oh, Justin. Sorry! Here."

He twisted his head, pushed out his round stomach, and howled for all he was worth, so she set him on the floor, his nose still dripping, her attention still riveted on Sarah's plans.

"*Butz sie naus* (Clean his nose)!" Levi yelled. "*Ach my.*"

Anna Mae scuttled after her son and caught him. She leaned over and swiped viciously, getting the job done. Then she turned and went straight back to the table where she again started listing every one of Matthew's major downfalls.

And still Sarah remained unconvinced.

CHAPTER 11

THE DAYS THAT FOLLOWED SISTERS DAY WERE THE kind of days Mam imagined the writer of the "Footprints" poem had experienced firsthand.

Anna Mae and Ruthie were powerful allies, her strength bolstered by their honesty and support. But it was on her knees in her bedroom that she found complete solace, carried through the days by the strength of her faith.

Dat fasted every day, continuing in prayer and supplication, calling at the throne of God without shame. It wasn't only Sarah's leaving of the Amish that bothered him. It was the added concern that Matthew did not truly love Sarah and her willingness to blindly follow him regardless.

Another week passed until the day before Sarah's departure. It was a time of heartache for the whole family, an event so unthinkable producing an ominous foreboding for Dat and Mam.

The evening was mellow, cooler than some August nights, when Priscilla announced quietly that there was a message on the voicemail for Sarah. Surprised but pleased and thinking of Matthew, Sarah walked slowly, her head bowed, watching the way her bare feet broke the brittle, parched grasses after weeks of hot, dry wind and little rain.

Cautiously, she punched the buttons and listened to the message—a great disappointment. It was the Widow Lydia, asking her to spend the night if she could as she had something to discuss with her. Matthew hadn't called at all for at least six or seven days.

Sarah would send Priscilla to Lydia's.

Slowly she walked back to the house, torn between her loyalty and friendship to Lydia and the realization that Lydia knew nothing of her plans to leave the next day to join Matthew.

What would she say?

Guilt washed over her, sensing the betrayal Lydia would surely feel.

Greater love has no man than this: that he lay down his life for his friend. The words entered her mind, a blaze of knowledge, and as quickly, she reversed them. She was laying down her life for her Matthew, denying father, mother, sister, brother.

Mam looked up from her sewing.

"Who was it?"

"Lydia."

"Oh?"

"She wants me to come stay for the night."

"Oh?"

"Priscilla can go."

"I think you should. She asked you."

Reluctantly, Sarah threw her pajamas, toothbrush, and a few toiletries in an old bag. Without saying goodbye, she walked out the driveway, her thoughts in turmoil yet again.

The twilight was fast descending, casting shadows across Elam Stoltzfus's property, darkening the pine trees to black and the white house to a dull blue gray. Hannah had a few rugs on the line, Sarah noticed, and her mop was still propped against the back stoop.

A small car appeared out of nowhere, the headlights' glare blinding. Sarah threw up an arm to cover her eyes. Sensing danger, she stepped sideways. Something was out of the ordinary with a car moving at that rate of speed on this country road.

As she stepped into the thick uncut grass at the side of the road, the car came to a rocking halt, spraying gravel from its skidding tires. A dark-haired youth poked his head through the opening of the lowered window.

"Tell your people to watch their barns tonight."

Before Sarah had the chance to reply or ask any questions, the car took off with another screeching of tires.

Cold chills chased themselves up and down her spine. Should she turn back? Go to her parents or press on to Lydia's? Shaking, her knees weak with fright, she decided to keep going and maybe send Omar to alert Elams and her parents.

There was a light in the new horse barn, but she decided to speak to Lydia first. She found her nestled on a lawn chair in the dusk, her feet tucked under herself, an opened book laid face down on the small table beside her.

"Sarah! Oh, I'm so glad you came! Please tell me all about it."

Confused, Sarah blinked. "You mean the car?"

"No, I don't know anything about a car. I mean Matthew."

"Oh, Matthew. I didn't know you knew."

"Hannah was here all afternoon. You must be devastated. Here, sit down. Aaron, make room for Sarah."

Aaron was only two, but he greeted Sarah with a hearty "Hi!" and a wide smile before tucking himself into his mother's lap.

"What are you talking about? Why would I be devastated? I'm planning on going to Haiti with Matthew. Do you mean deciding to leave my family, or what?"

Lydia's arms fell away from little Aaron, and she turned her head and stared at the floor of the porch. A quiet groan escaped her lips.

"You don't know then?"

"What? What don't I know? I guess not, if you don't tell me."

Sarah was panicking, her voice high and shrill.

"Sit down," Lydia whispered.

Sarah sat, leaned forward, clenched her hands till the knuckles paled in contrast with the healthy tan on her hands.

"Matthew already left for Haiti. He….Oh Sarah, I don't want to be the one to tell you this."

"What? What is it?"

Sarah's throat was dry, her voice ragged. Her breaths were coming in quick succession as the color drained from her face.

"He met someone and married her within a week. She's a…a woman of color. A nurse. She lives in Haiti."

"Noooo."

The word was a sob, a moan, a long, drawn out wail of denial. Lydia rose and gathered her in her thin, helpful arms. The calloused hands that worked side by side with her oldest son now seemed soft, soothing, angelic in their power to still Sarah.

Sarah had never known that a person could feel so much pain and still be able to bear it. How could she be holding up beneath a weight that was crushing her and squeezing the air out of her?

She had no breath left to cry. Her eyes remained dry, her mouth open as a high wail emerged.

Lydia held her, soothed her, but she was afraid for Sarah in those first minutes as the cruelty assaulted her.

"Why? How could he? Why didn't he call me?"

"Hannah said he's so soft-hearted, he just couldn't tell you. He knew you would take it hard. He's just so kind, Hannah said."

Sarah began to shake then. Her whole body convulsed as she rocked back and forth, her arms wrapped around her waist. She hung her head as she mourned with deep grief for a lifetime of loving Matthew, now so completely lost.

"Hannah said he wrote to you."

A hot, blinding anger sliced through the life-taking sadness. Sarah sat up, lifted her head, her face white as the painted railing behind her. She spoke slowly and quietly but with terrible conviction.

"Oh, did he really? Hannah says he did? I doubt if he went to the trouble of finding a pen or spending forty-five lousy cents on a stamp."

Lydia turned her face to hide her relief. Yes! Sarah would survive. Already her resilience was showing through, her anger a sign of normalcy.

Suddenly, Sarah clapped her hands to her knees, got up in one swift motion, and stalked across the porch to look out across the lush, green cornfields of Lancaster County. She unrolled the age-old scroll of a young girl's first rejection as she attempted to decipher her own blindness for the first time. As she did so, the process began to melt away the guilt, the indecision, the awful prospect of leaving her family.

She believed God had made her decision for her.

With each wave and rustle of the deep green leaves on the cornstalks, her heart cried out her pain, but her appreciation of family and friends followed on its heels. With Matthew gone, could peace be a possibility? Her whole life had revolved around him. Now everything was black and white.

Turning, she asked loudly, "What else did Hannah say?"

"A lot," Lydia said, laughing hesitantly.

"Tell me."

As they talked, Omar came up on the porch, his lantern bobbing, followed by his faithful shadow, Anna Mae.

Sarah clapped a hand to her mouth.

"I forgot."

She told Omar about the small car. She watched his eyes widen and Lydia's face turn grim.

"Let's just all sleep in the barn," Lydia suggested.

"Should we?"

"Sure. We'll nestle down in the hay. We can watch the bats fly around and listen to the skunks snuffling in the grass. Let's do it. We'll start a little camp fire and toast some hot dogs and marshmallows. Please stay, Sarah."

Sarah agreed. She left voice mail messages for Elams and her parents, hoping they would check them before turning in for the night. Soon she found herself leaning forward from an old camping chair, gripping a long handled fork holding two hot dogs, one for Omar and one for herself.

Opposite her, Lydia brandished another fork. The two marshmallows she was roasting had caught on fire, and she waved them wildly to quench the flames. The heat left the sweet treat blackened but hot and gooey all the way to the middle.

"Mm. Oh my, I love these things," Lydia gloated. She removed a marshmallow to set carefully on a graham cracker that was coated heavily with peanut butter and topped with a neat square of Hershey's milk chocolate. Adding another graham cracker, she pressed lightly to blend the flavors before taking a large bite, melted marshmallow squeezing out the sides.

Sarah watched the warm, comforting coals as she turned the cold, unappetizing hot dog into a steaming hot, crispy, greasy goodness.

"Roll, please!" she said.

Omar immediately brought a roll, brushed the ashes off his hot dog, and handed the ketchup, pickles, and onions to Sarah. Lydia watched her friend's face, keenly aware of the depth of her pain and the courage needed to put on this front of normality.

They ate, joked, and drank homemade root beer poured from a glass gallon jug into plastic tumblers. All the while, they kept their eyes and ears open for any unusual activity.

Cars passed on the country road, horses and buggies clopped by, and all remained peaceful. The stars appeared one by one as night followed the setting sun.

They noted the absence of bats, who usually made an early evening appearance, leaving their perches in the barn rafters to glide expertly through the night, gobbling up insects at an amazing rate. Omar said they'd be back. They just needed a little more time to adapt and take up residence the new barn. Somewhere in the distance, a fox barked and an owl hooted as the nocturnal creatures began their nightly hunts.

Anna Mae said she was afraid. Lydia rocked little Aaron and told Anna Mae not to worry. They'd be fine with Omar here, and Sarah. Hadn't Sarah showed how fearless she could be in the face of an emergency, releasing cows and saving the Belgian on the night of their fire?

Immediately Omar spoke up, correcting his mother. "Priscilla saved Dominic."

"Oh, that's right. I forgot," Lydia assured her seventeen year old, winking broadly at Sarah.

What a comeback for Lydia, Sarah thought. The poor, tortured soul had taken only timid, little steps of recovery at first, but once she found her stride, there was no turning back. Even her face had smoothed out and her eyes relaxed. Her appearance was completely different now. She was still painfully thin, but she looked almost youthful after her recovery and healing had infused her whole being with a new sense of freedom and purpose.

They laid an air mattress, a new Coleman, on the barn floor and spread a clean sheet across it. They gathered pillows, sleeping bags, flashlights, an alarm clock, bug spray—everything they would need to stay comfortable.

Sarah lay beside Lydia with little Aaron nestled between them. Far into the night, they talked, sharing deepest feelings and emotions that had long been suppressed. They wept together, laughed together, became quite hysterical at times, and still they did not sleep.

Lydia told Sarah perhaps this hard and monumental task of forgetting Matthew would lead to her greatest happiness in years to come. Sarah quickly assured her that seemed impossible now.

"Perhaps," Lydia whispered. "But what if he turned out to be like Aaron?"

"He wouldn't. Matthew was...is kind," Sarah said, immediately sticking up for Matthew as she had always done.

"Aaron was kind while we dated."

There was nothing to say to this, so Sarah remained quiet.

"Did he actually beat you?"

"He hit me, yes. He hated me. I'll never marry again." The words were bitter, dripping with dark, acidic memories.

"I'm not supposed to talk about this, I know. But Sarah, I feel the hand of God has revived my empty existence with your friendship. With Matthew gone, we can be a tremendous help to each other. You'll have much of the same bitterness to overcome as I do."

"I'm not angry with Matthew. Just surprised."

There was a long, companionable silence, little Aaron's breathing lulling them softly to sleep, slowing their own soft breaths with the pungent smell of new hay as a heady perfume.

Omar stirred in his sleeping bag, muttered to himself. Somewhere off in the distance, a dog began an erratic barking. Rolling onto her back, Sarah took up her little travel alarm and checked the time.

12:38.

She rolled back on her side, whispered goodnight to Lydia, and then cried herself to sleep, thinking of Matthew on his trip to Haiti without her. She refused to believe he had married another woman. He probably wasn't married, just dating, she told herself. He wouldn't have wanted her to come to Haiti if he was already married.

And certainly not to a woman of color. That just wasn't Matthew. But then neither was the flat, oily voice with the nasal twang she'd heard on the other end of the phone line.

Sarah had told Lydia she was surprised, her pride rising to the surface. Surprise was such a lukewarm term for the horror of the reality that still had not sunk in. Disbelief was much more possible. She didn't have to believe it, not yet.

With that comforting thought, she fell asleep.

A cow's bawling woke her. She was cold, so she sat up, her hands raking across the slippery fabric of the sleeping bag. As if in the distance, yet somehow close by, she heard the idling of a car engine.

The cow bawled again and rattled her chain. Sarah tilted her head, trying to catch the slightest noise. Above her, the new rafters creaked. The metal roof popped as it cooled in the night air. A truck changed gears out on the Lincoln Highway.

Slowly, the great barn door slid back as if on its own. Sarah stifled a scream. A dark form wedged its way inside, followed by another. Immediately, a piercing wand of light waved from side to side, finding the occupants of the barn floor.

Sarah leaped to her feet just as the figures turned to leave, clawing at the door.

Sarah ran. Omar yelled and caught the one figure by the shirt. Together, they rolled down the incline outside the barn door.

It was complete bedlam. Lydia screamed, and the children cried out as Omar rolled around in the grass, trying to keep hold of the writhing trespasser. Sarah sprinted to keep up with the fleeing figure ahead of her.

Pent up anger lent wings to her feet, and her long legs pumped, her arms swung. A section of the gravel cut into her bare feet, and still she ran. Past the idling car, past Elam Stoltzfus's dark house, beneath the huge maple tree across the road.

She wasn't sure what she'd do if she did catch the person in front of her. She simply wanted him away from Lydia. Away from the new barn. Away from even the possibility of bringing any sort of further destruction to that family who had already suffered more than enough.

She cried out in surprise when the figure ahead of her suddenly crumpled into the tall weeds beside the road, sobbing hysterically as if strained for breath.

"Don't hurt me."

The whimpered cry was barely coherent.

Behind them, the idling car revved to life and spun out of the widow's driveway. The headlights dimmed, but the vehicle moved steadily towards them.

In the glare of the headlights, Sarah cried out as the small, thin figure ahead of her lunged to her feet, still sobbing, and ran crazily, panicked, after the fast moving vehicle, her thin hair flying in every direction.

"Ashley! Wait!"

Sarah ran, trying to catch up, wanting talk to her, but the vehicle slowed and screeched to a grinding stop as Ashley flung herself into the passenger seat. The car took off, spraying dust and gravel and chunks of macadam into the dark night.

Sarah stood in the middle of the road and stamped her foot, her fists clenched in rage and frustration. It had to have been Ashley. Why couldn't she have caught her?

All those questions, that nervous wondering, the pale, skinny girl frightened of her own shadow—it all suddenly

made sense. Ashley was somehow involved in these barn
fires. She knew more than she was willing to admit.

Well, more was accomplished with honey than vinegar, her dat always said, so Sarah's path was clear.

Turning, she strode purposefully back to a disheveled
Omar, a wilting Lydia, and the traumatized children, all
standing in an unsteady little circle of light provided by
a single flashlight.

Everyone talked at once, but no one made any sense
at all. It was four o'clock, the hour when weary farmers,
tired of their night's vigil, relaxed and slept deeply for
another hour before it was time to get up and begin the
morning milking.

After everyone had calmed down a bit, Sarah helped
Omar with the milking. Anna Mae and Lydia fed the
horses, the calves, and heifers.

The birds twittered as the sky lightened, heralding a
new day, the navy blue streaks of night banished by the
approaching orange, yellow, and pink of the sun.

They called the police, after deliberating whether or
not to mention Ashley Walter's name.

If it had been her, and if the police questioned her and
she denied everything, all would be lost.

If they kept the knowledge to themselves for now, perhaps more would be gained.

They decided not to reveal the name.

The police were courteous, listened to descriptions,
and thanked them for the information, but as usual they
didn't supply any concrete promises. They were doing all
they could, which Sarah knew consisted mostly of guess
work so far.

The vehicle had been small and of an indefinite light
color. Omar could supply only the fact that his antagonist

had dark hair and a slight build.

Disheartened, they lingered over coffee, their appetites diminished by the event in the night.

Already, the heat was intensifying, and little puffs of warm air were coming through the window screens.

Sarah picked at the edge of her French toast, swirled it in syrup, then put down her fork.

"I dread going home," she said to no one in particular.

"Stay here and help me do corn," Lydia said quickly.

"No, I should help my mother. She always has so much to do in August. I just don't want to walk past Elam's. What if Hannah stops me?"

"She won't."

With that assurance in her ears, Sarah strode purposefully home only to be confronted by Hannah, her *dichly* (head scarf) sliding off her head, her forehead already shining with perspiration, her apron as wrinkled as if she'd slept in it.

"Sarah!"

She clasped both of Sarah's hands in her large, capable ones, her mouth pursed in a show of emotion.

Wearily, resigned to her fate, Sarah lifted her eyes to Hannah's, waiting, saying nothing.

"It isn't Matthew's fault. He was confused. He's born again now, and he said God guided him straight to this lovely woman who is just the most wonderful thing that ever happened to him. He says she has a heart of gold and is so well versed in the Scripture, same as him. He told me he found his soul mate. Think of it, Sarah. His soul mate. Oh, I believe it."

She stopped, searched Sarah's eyes, then dropped her hands, stepping back.

The slow rustle of the maple leaves above them played

across Sarah's flawless, tanned skin, the light in her eyes changing from yellow, green, and gold to a deep and restless gray, the hurt and sorrow of years of love and trust betrayed in the cruel manner which Matthew had chosen.

Clearly, Sarah spoke, her words precise, well placed, ringing.

"Hannah, in your opinion, nothing has ever been Matthew's fault. His whole life has been spent atop the pedestal you provided for him."

"Sarah! Don't be so....Why, Sarah, I hardly know you like this!"

"Well, you can get to know me if you want. If not, that's fine with me. I have been dragged through the muck by Matthew for the last time, Hannah. And you, too."

"But...."

Sarah lifted a hand. "Perhaps I can find who I really am, post-Matthew."

"What?"

Hannah was left standing by the side of the road, beneath the maple tree in the hot, morning breeze, puzzling about Sarah's words. She didn't know what exactly what Sarah had meant by "post-Matthew."

CHAPTER 12

Word spread swiftly via the grapevine—known as the Amish phone shanty—and Sarah, unknown to her, became a bit of a celebrity.

She has more nerve than common sense, they said. Well, Davey Beiler's girls are all alike. Outspoken. Not afraid to speak their minds. You wouldn't think so, knowing their mother. She's so *tzimmalich* (humble).

Disbelieving individuals clapped work-roughened hands to their mouths, and with each phone call, Sarah's caper got a bit more out of hand, until the folks in Perry County actually believed Davey Beiler's *ihr* Sarah (his own Sarah) had caught the arsonist all by herself.

Well good, they said. Now the poor folks in Lancaster County can relax.

That part, at least, was the truth. Everyone figured after a scare like that, no one with brains in their head would attempt another barn fire for a good, long time. Men returned to their comfortable beds and enjoyed solid nights of sleep. Dogs returned to the safety of the back porch as the hot summer nights gave way to the winds of autumn, the time of harvest, council meeting, and communion services among the Amish.

Sarah muddled through September, half-heartedly performing what was expected of her, nothing more. At market, she made a point of strolling by the leather goods stand, appearing as disinterested as possible, but not once did she catch sight of the elusive Ashley.

The longer the girl's absence continued, the more convinced Sarah became. Something definitely wasn't right with that girl. She was almost certain she had chased her bashful friend that night at Lydia's, but she harbored doubts as well.

Even if Ashley was connected to the arsonist, she would never light a fire herself, Sarah was sure. More than likely, she was committed to a man who was the arsonist, or an accomplice.

As time crawled by on sluggish treads, Sarah became steadily oblivious to any purpose or objective in her life. She was sick of all the flour and the yeast and the shortening, the plastic wrap and endless Styrofoam trays at market. She was tired of the milking and cleaning and other countless chores at home. There was no point in anything, with Matthew gone.

Hannah no longer came to visit Mam, and Elam stayed at home, no longer bothering to walk over for a friendly chat with his neighbor. He carried the true humility of having a son gone astray, but Hannah bore her pride for her son like a misplaced banner, speaking loudly about his missionary work in Haiti without an ounce of modesty in her bearing.

Nevertheless, Mam's loyalty to her friend didn't waver. She assured Sarah over and over that this was just Hannah's way. Deep down, she was really hurting about her son's disobedience to his parents' wishes.

The air was tinged with autumn's smells, that dusty, earthy odor from the corn fodder being baled, the last of the hay put in bags.

In the kitchen, Mam's knife peeled deftly beneath the heavy skin of pale orange neck pumpkins. The garden had produced a gigantic pile of them, and Mam said they couldn't be wasted. They'd cook them down, cold pack them in wide-mouthed jars, and have all the pumpkin they needed for a few years.

Mam's pumpkin pies won prizes throughout all of Lancaster County, due in part to her own home-canned pumpkin. Better than the orange stuff out of a can, she'd say.

Without thinking, Mam remarked drily, "If there's a chance of making a wedding for you within the next few years, we'll have all the pumpkin we need."

"Thanks a lot, Mam," Sarah answered, her voice heavy with sarcasm.

"Oh, I'm sorry. I didn't mean to offend you."

"I know."

They worked in companionable silence, the orange flesh of the pumpkin bubbling on both gas stoves, one in the kitchen and one in the *kesslehaus*, filling the house with its autumn fragrance.

Sarah was washing jars in hot, sudsy water, stacking them upside down on clean towels, when she heard a steady knock on the front door.

She scrambled to rinse and dry her hands, then peered through the screen door at a man of ordinary height. He had no distinctive features, just dark eyes, his hair cut closely to his head, a graying mustache clipped cleanly along his upper lip.

"Hello. My name is Thomas Albright."

"Hello."

"I'm wondering if I could come in and ask a few questions about the barn fires in your area."

Mam appeared behind her briefly, a quiet presence.

"We don't like to talk about them."

"But you will?"

"We'd rather not."

"Why?"

"Too much room to make mistakes."

"Well."

There was a pause. The man shifted his weight from one foot to the other as if to relieve the mounting tension in his mind.

"Is your father home?"

"Why do you ask?"

"Is he or isn't he?"

Sarah eyed the man levelly, still feeling no apprehension. He didn't appear very harmful. Sort of short and soft, babyfaced.

"He's baling corn fodder."

"Where?"

"South of the barn."

In the kitchen, Mam set a kettle of boiling pumpkin on a cast iron trivet, letting it cool long enough to put comfortably through the strainer.

"Could I ask him a few questions?"

"I doubt it."

"Smart cookie, aren't you?"

Sarah said nothing, lifted her chin coolly.

"Tell me, if you're so smart, how well do you know Ashley Walters?"

"She's an acquaintance."

"That's all?"

"Yes. We talk."

The man put his hands behind his back and tipped forward on the toe of his shoes, then back on his heels, surveying the ceiling of the porch, examining each screw holding the white vinyl in place.

"Tell me, did you give chase to her the other night?"

"What are you talking about? Of course not."

"Amish girls don't lie."

So, it was her wits against his. What did this man want from her?

"No, they don't," Sarah countered.

"But you do."

"How do you know Ashley?"

"Let's just say she's an acquaintance."

Sarah nodded.

"Mind if I smoke?"

"Yes."

"You do?"

He mocked her with his eyebrows. "So what will you do if I smoke?"

"Probably nothing."

"Good girl."

Deliberately and taking his time, he made quite a show of extracting a package of cigarettes, finding a lighter by patting his pockets. After he lit a cigarette, be began insolently blowing smoke through the screen on the door.

Sarah didn't flinch.

"Why don't you come out on the porch if you're not going to invite me in?"

"I'm helping my mother."

"She in there?"

"Yes."

He moved up against the screen door, pressing the length of his body against it, waggled his fingers, and said, "Hi, Mrs. Beiler."

"Hello," Mam said politely, then went on washing her sieve, as if he was of as much consequence as an annoying fly.

"Not very friendly, is she?"

"She's friendly."

"Just not to me."

Sarah remained silent, wishing he'd leave.

"So, when you chased Ashley the other night, what were you going to do with her if you caught her?"

Sarah didn't answer.

"I thought you Amish were nonresistant."

"We are."

"You call that nonresistant?"

When Sarah didn't answer, he flattened himself against the screen door a second time, gave a small derisive snort, and told her to stay away from Ashley Walters. Then he added that if anyone in Lancaster County thought they could relax about their barns, they were badly mistaken.

"The worst is yet to come," he growled theatrically.

With that, he flicked the burning cigarette into the shrubbery, turned on his heel, and left.

A brown SUV. There was nothing in particular to set it apart from hundreds of others. Sarah still wasn't frightened as she coolly informed Mam that he reminded her of a little Chihuahua trying to scare someone.

"He may be dangerous. You'd better tell Dat," Mam said, wisely wagging her head in that knowing way of hers.

Six fresh pumpkin pies were lined up on the countertop when Dat came in from baling corn fodder, dusty, his eyes red-rimmed with weariness, his hair clinging to his scalp.

He caught sight of the pies, and an appreciative grin spread along his lips, changing the light in his eyes. "I can't believe my good fortune. What a wife!"

Mam blushed and beamed, smoothed her apron with both hands, and said, "Why, thank you, kind sir!"

There was a happy chortle form the rolling desk chair, and Levi burst out, "*Da Davey und de Malinda sinn kindish* (Davey and Malinda are childish)!"

Dat was wily, and he knew light-hearted banter would mean a generous slice of pie, so he played right along with Levi.

Sarah burst out laughing, and Suzie threw her report card, hitting Levi's shoulder. He bent to retrieve it, leaned to one side, and slid it beneath his backside, sitting solidly on the offending item.

"*Gepps* (Give it back)." Suzie stood in front of Levi, hand outstretched. "*Gepp* (Give it)."

Resolutely, Levi shook his head.

"Young girls have to learn not to throw report cards."

"Levi!" Suzie howled.

"Levi!" he mimicked, lifting his face and howling.

Suzie dove into him, pushing forcefully on his stomach, and, with Levi's feet both resting on the chair legs above the casters, he was sent skimming backward across the smooth linoleum, coming to rest with a clunk against Dat's roll top desk. His head snapped forward, and a great guffaw was expelled from open mouth.

"*Na grickst net* (Now you won't get it)!"

Suzie shrieked and ran after him, shoving him against the sofa, where he spun helplessly in a half-circle, giggling wildly.

Priscilla looked up from the sewing machine, leaped to her feet, put her hands on the back of the rolling chair, and sent him flying away from Suzie, as he shrieked with glee.

Sarah stood against the counter, her arms crossed, caught Dat's eye, and give him a wink. They both knew Levi was one of a kind.

"Davey, die maid sinn net chide (these girls are crazy)," he chortled to his father.

"You enjoy it, and you know it, Levi. But how long do you think we'll have to bug Mam before she'll let us eat pie?"

Levi shrugged his massive shoulders, his bright, brown eyes eagerly scanning Mam's face.

"You'll ruin your supper."

"Come on, Malinda!" Levi begged, so completely in earnest they all burst out laughing.

As it was, they ate more than one pie, sitting around the pumpkin-strewn kitchen, enjoying the perfect creaminess with just the right combination of spices. The tall shivery, custardy sweetness melted in their mouths, completely ruining the appetite that should have been reserved for healthier fare.

Priscilla said pumpkin was a vegetable so they were having a healthy supper. Levi said pie crust was a vegetable, too. Mam laughed so hard that she had to gasp for breath and wipe her eyes.

Dat said after chores Mam could just make bean soup with applesauce. Bean soup consisted of a can of great northern beans dumped into a saucepan of browned butter with some salt, milk, and bits of torn, stale bread. It was best eaten with dried apple pie, but if there was none, applesauce worked just fine.

Spicy red beets made a great side dish.

"*Rote reeva* (Red beets)!" yelled Levi.

There was a new calf in the barn, its white and black colors so much crisper than it mother's. It was so fresh and brand new and wobbly on its thin legs.

Sarah crossed her arms along the top of the pen, watching it struggle to stay on its feet, the mother cow pleasantly licking and nurturing it, establishing a bond between them.

Dat came up beside her to watch. "Cute little one, isn't she?"

Sarah nodded.

"Who was the man at the door earlier?" he asked.

Sarah told her father, giving all the details, and he frowned, his brow furrowed with lines of concern.

"It just doesn't sound good. I don't think we have any reason to relax or feel that the barn fires are a thing of the past. Something is definitely not right among us."

He paused. "How sure are you that it was Ashley that you were chasing?"

Sarah shook her head, her mouth in a straight line of concentration.

"Just about a hundred percent. That poor girl—I don't know, Dat. Something is not right with her."

Dat shook his head again, worry drawing vertical grooves between his graying eyebrows.

That next Sunday as David Beiler stood to preach, he cautioned the congregation about feeling smug, satisfied, full, quoting the verse in the Bible about the man who said to himself, his barns were full to overflowing, he'd build more, and have plenty for years to come.

In a spiritual sense, he cautioned against the satisfaction of feeling full as well as thinking that worldly goods were a blessing, that nothing could touch the harvest, so plentiful, so packed down and running over as it was.

Sarah sat on the girls' bench, her head bowed, perplexed. Dat made it sound so complicated. Sometimes, she still felt confused, thinking of Matthew, but the minute she remembered his sudden marriage, the confusion left.

She wished Dat would just chill. If someone was going to burn more barns, they would. She had her own idea of exactly how Ashley Walters played into this string of fires. And she was sure it was only a matter of time until the next one was lit.

Her thoughts flitted to the night before. Saturday evenings were always hard, the emptiness, the barren land without Matthew stretching before her, year after year.

She'd just be a single, leftover blessing, as old maids were called in polite circles. She'd start her own bakery. She'd told Melvin about it. He said she was too optimistic. The last thing Lancaster County needed was another bakery. There was already one at every fence post.

She and Melvin had walked up to visit with the Widow Lydia, who was already ready to go to bed for the night, her eyes large and self-conscious, her hands constantly going to the belt of her soft blue bathrobe.

Sarah could not understand her discomfiture, until she saw Melvin watching her, standing stiffly inside the front door, tugging at his gray sleeves as if to lengthen them.

Lydia had made coffee, but the evening was stilted, stiff, and uncomfortable, the way her brothers used to describe a new pair of denims.

Finally, when conversation lagged, they'd walked home together. Melvin was strangely quiet, contemplative, a reserved manner creating an aura of distance, keeping Sarah from seeing his true feelings.

He went home early, leaving her alone on the porch in the chilly evening, the crickets still gamely chirping their songs, in spite of falling leaves and lower night temperatures.

She guessed she was like those tired crickets, knowing the end had already arrived, yet chirping anyway.

She laughed to herself, a self-mocking, unattractive snort, sitting alone, wrapped in her old sweater, her feet uncomfortably cold inside her sneakers.

She wondered if the weather changed in Haiti. Was it always tropical? Warm? She rocked forward in misery, thinking of Matthew, so tanned and fit, working hard to build homes for the natives, his wife ministering to the sick, the perfect couple working for the Lord.

Well, I'm just too Amish. Home canned pumpkin, bean soup, white cape and apron pinned to her dress, the uniform of the unmarried woman.

She had still not fully recovered from the wonder of the possibility of leaving, the excitement of actually being able go and do something out of the ordinary.

Ha, she thought again. You know better than even think about it. No, she would not want to leave, truly. It was a lust that had never been fully conceived. A thought, a desire, gone as swiftly as Matthew.

On her knees that Saturday night, she had prayed for direction, for peace, for acceptance of her lot in life, and went to bed with a strong spirit, bolstered by her time spent in prayer.

Just keep on showing me the way, O God. Didn't King David repeat that same prayer many times in Psalms?

How then, could she ever suppose God had heard her pathetic prayer? The hymn singing on Sunday evening was abuzz with the news. Rose Zook was glowing in a dress the color of bittersweet made in the latest fashion, her skin radiant from the joy within. Lee Glick had asked Rose for a date, the beginning of what promised to be a steady relationship.

Sarah sat carved in stone, unable to understand the dead weight somewhere in the region of her heart. Why?

Who could figure out why a person felt the way they did? She'd never been attracted to Lee, had she? Could she help if it he had assumed he loved her?

The songs were announced, the beautiful hymns rose and fell around her, and she sat, hearing nothing, staring at nothing, wishing with all her being she could get off the bench and go home. Home to her bed, where the pillow was soft and yielding, cradling her tired head that churned with all sorts of questions and exclamations, but always ending in commas, without a beginning and without an end.

At the close of the evening, before the snack was served, they all sang the customary congratulations to the new dating couple. Rose dipped her head, blushing and giggling. Sarah was completely taken off guard by the assault of the green monster that had many names but whose only truthful one was jealousy, pure and simple. She felt as if she hated Rose. Almost.

Sarah's cheeks flamed with embarrassment, tears sprang to her eyes, and she kept them lowered, cautiously folding her hands tightly, keeping her eyes trained on the whitening of the knuckles. Best to stay that way. If she kept her eyes on her hands, no one would know the roiling unrest inside of her.

It was only the passing of the trays of cookies, huge bowls of potato chips, and platters of cheese and pretzels that made her lift her head, smile, acknowledge comments from friends.

Oh good, no one had noticed.

Daring a look across the room, her eyes made solid contact with the devastating blueness of Lee Glick's. Instantly, her eyes left his, slid away to safety, before returning, her heart rate increasing rapidly as their gazes held, melded, touched, and understood.

I didn't know, Sarah.

I didn't know you didn't know, Lee.

In a daze, a dizzying, dangerous edge of uncertainty, with a thread of hope woven though the insurmountable, she walked to Melvin's buggy, helped him hitch up his restless horse, and then collapsed against the seat back. She restrained the urge to cry and sniff and blubber her way into Melvin's pity, sharing the whole array of misery that was her life.

"Now that's a cute couple," he observed, as they drove past Lee and Rose attaching his horse to the shafts.

"Yeah."

"She must have known what she was doing, breaking up with Matthew."

"Yeah."

"Smarter than you, maybe?"

His elbow jabbed her side good-naturedly, and she stifled the urge to slap him. She nodded her agreement and watched the stop sign flapping back and forth in the stiff breeze.

"Say something."

"Be quiet, Melvin. Just shut your mouth for one second."

"Oops. Now you're mad."

"No. Just tired and…"

"You wish Lee Glick would not be dating Rose."

"I don't care about Lee Glick. I don't care about Rose. Let them date and get married and live happily ever after. Who cares?" she spat out.

"You love him," Melvin said quietly, and flicked the reins.

CHAPTER 13

"MAM, I HAVE TO GET AWAY."

Sarah flung the statement across the table as they relaxed together with their second cups of coffee before starting the serious scrubbing and polishing, dusting and moving furniture.

Shocked, Mam choked on her hot drink, wiped her mouth, and opened her eyes wide to look at Sarah.

"You mean, away? Leave the church? Or...or what?"

"I just want to get out of Lancaster County."

"Sarah, stop talking like that. You can't. You have your job, and your place is right here with your family."

"How do you know?"

"Why would you question it?"

Miserably, she confided in Mam, always her refuge when things got really serious.

Her mother listened carefully, lent a patient ear, sipped her coffee, cut a cinnamon roll in half, and resolutely set one half on Sarah's plate. She shook her head when Sarah wailed about getting old and fat on cinnamon rolls on top of everything else, then watched as her daughter took a great bite, shook her head, and promptly took another.

"If all else fails, try pastries," Mam remarked drily. She observed the change in Sarah, the tension in her shoulders, the down turn of her usually wide and smiling mouth, the clouded eyes darkened by her own unhappiness.

"Sarah, you need to find joy in doing for others. You're so anxious about the future, and there is absolutely no hurry. Enjoy your time being single. Why panic?

"Matthew so obviously was not for you, and I'm so glad God has been gracious, sparing you the heartache of living with a man who marries for reasons other than true love."

"He loved me."

"No, Sarah, he didn't. I remain firm in that belief."

"Then evidently Lee doesn't, *didn't* either. He asked Rose."

"Your stubborn...."

"My stubborn what?"

"Nothing."

Mam got up, whisked the dishes off the table, barking instructions to Priscilla. She told Sarah to get up off that chair and find the ceiling mop. The attachment was in the top drawer, and she could use Palmolive dish soap since stronger cleaning solutions made streaks on the kitchen ceiling.

Priscilla sang catchy tunes, washed walls, whistled, teased Levi, organized drawers, found old post cards and letters in Mam's cedar chest, chortled to herself about her sister Ruthie's sloppy handwriting. Sarah was left to her thoughts as she plied the mop steadily across the gleaming ceiling, the tiny bits of fly dirt steadily disappearing beneath it.

Mam worked alongside Sarah, wringing a cloth from a plastic bucket of sudsy water, washing down walls, rigorously attacking any stain on the doors or woodwork.

The cleaning of the old house was a twice-yearly occurrence, usually in April and again in October, or the last of September, depending on the weather, which was the inspiration for Mam's rush to get the house cleaned now.

Dat told her he believed all Amish women were born with the instinct to clean house, like monarch butterflies or homing pigeons, drawn to the attic with a sense of purpose, an uncanny direction that sent them straight to the scrub bucket and up the stairs.

Mam chortled and beamed, said nah, no one cleaned the way her grandmother used to. She never lugged bucket after bucket of hot, soapy water up two flights of stairs to the attic and scrubbed that splintery "garret" floor, the way grandmother had. Mam swept, cleaned under the eaves with a brush and dustpan, straightened up, organized, washed windows, but she never once washed her attic floor, no sir.

That was where Mam headed next though, armed with a broom, garbage bags, window cleaner, and bug spray. She had that certain bright-eyed anticipation about her, her nostrils flared just enough to convey the bubbling of energy, and away she went, barking orders, her broom keeping time.

Later Sarah found Mam sitting on her backside beside a plastic tote, her legs stretched in front of her as she pressed a tiny blue sleeper to her breast, her head bent over it, her grief unbearable for only a moment before she got ahold of herself, as she'd say.

They lifted blankets, small white onesies, stained

only a bit around the neckline, but even the stains were precious, knowing little baby Mervin had drooled there when his baby teeth were pushing through his soft, pink gums.

"Mam, seriously, do you remember this? The first time you took him to church?"

Mam nodded, her lips wobbling, a moment of vulnerability she couldn't control.

"Remember how hard it was on my pride, the fact that he wore a dress and white pinafore?" Sarah asked.

"Oh Sarah! I would have forgotten."

"You said you had to lead by example and wear a dress on poor Mervin, but I was so embarrassed!"

"Sarah, your grandmother wore a dress on Dat until he was potty-trained. That was the old way. Now young mothers are horrified to think of putting a dress on their little boys to take them to church just that one first time."

"Some mothers still do."

"Yes, a few. But you know how times change. What was considered Plain years ago, conservative, you know, is hardly practiced anymore, it seems."

They read Mervin's baby book together, remembered the first time he sat alone, crawled, his first tooth, a lock of his hair Scotch-taped into place, but there was not one photograph.

They were oblivious to the lack of photographs. They were not a necessary or customary item for the Amish, so their absence went unnoticed.

The attic was cleaned, Mam's emotions were dusted and swept along with the floors and walls, and all was well once again.

Mam decided Priscilla's room needed a coat of paint, but Priscilla refused, saying she'd be sixteen years old soon, and then she'd decide what color she wanted. So Mam shrugged her shoulders and said alright, and that was that. They worked their way through the upstairs, wiping down the walls, and down the stairway, washing curtains and bedding and rugs. Anything washable in Mam's path was laundered in the wringer washer and hung on the wheel line to dry.

By evening, there were usually two red spots, one on either cheek of Mam's cheeks, her eyes drooping with weariness, but she was still ironing curtains, her fatigue only apparent when she snapped at Levi or answered Dat curtly.

The kitchen was the sticker, she always said. Sarah knew it, too, thinking of moving the gas stove out from its station between the cupboards, egg yolk and grease and dirt staining the sides of it, rolls of dust and dirt beneath it, the oven blackened and speckled with six months of hard and constant use.

Every half year, Mam sprayed the oven cleaner liberally, then stood up, gasping and saying, "That stuff is wicked. It can't be good for you."

But a clean oven won out, always. A few fumes wouldn't hurt, as long as that oven was sparkling, at least till the next apple pie bubbled over, or the next tray of bacon sizzled and splattered grease over the racks.

Doing the bacon in the oven was the lesser of two evils, according to Mam's way of thinking. Bacon splattered everything, but at least it didn't have to be turned in the oven. It came out nice and crispy without anyone having to touch it.

They put Levi to work that day, assigning him to polish the leaves on the fig tree growing in its big ceramic pot in the corner. He stayed at his job for hours, content to be part of the housecleaning, his face pink with the praise Mam showered on him.

Dat ate a bowl of corn flakes and chocolate cake for lunch, saying he'd been hungry for that for a while now. He didn't eat the cereal separately, but plunked a sizable square of chocolate cake right in the middle of a large bowl of corn flakes that had been liberally sugared. The bowl had also been filled with plenty of creamy milk, and it soaked into the heavy chocolate cake.

Levi said that was slop and wanted no part of it, muttering to himself as he buttered two slices of bread and plunked them on the griddle. He eyed Mam hopefully before bending to find the cheese in the refrigerator himself.

He made his grilled cheese sandwich and poured a glass of milk, then got up to make another one, resigning himself to his fate. No use begging Mam when she was cleaning house, that much he'd learned when he was young.

That was why Sarah was glad to go to market the following day. She was thoroughly tired of the intensity of housecleaning with Mam.

She felt energized and took a new interest in her work, doing her best to produce a quality product, whistling softly as she plied the dough with a spoon or the mixer or turned out flaky pie crusts.

She could hardly believe her eyes when Ashley Walters walked directly up to her, the only thing between them the clear Plexiglass that separated the customers from the employees.

"Sarah?"

The word was a question, a frightened, whispered question that hung between them, a butterfly swishing its dainty wings against the glass.

"Ashley!"

"Can we talk?"

"At ten o'clock."

"It has to be now."

"Now? Right now?"

"Yes."

Looking around, Sarah asked Emma if it was alright if she went on her break early as someone needed to talk to her.

"Sure. No problem."

"Thanks."

Quickly, Sarah grabbed her purse, asking Ashley where she wanted to go.

They sat on a bench near the front entrance, the throng of people coming and going providing a wall of privacy, a detraction, which was just what they needed to blend in as part of the life of the market, seen but not really noticed.

If anything, Ashley had only become thinner, her pale cheeks almost translucent, the blue veins in her forehead more noticeable than ever. Sarah looked closer, then drew back in surprise when she realized Ashley's lower lip was split open and partially healed. Her eyes were puffy, her skin blotchy.

As usual, she wore an oversized sweatshirt, torn jeans, and sneakers—curled, creased, and filthy.

When she spoke, her words were slurred. Sarah caught a strong smell of alcohol on her breath.

"Sarah, I have no one else. I'm in trouble. I don't have the nerve to get away from Mike, and I can't tell my dad. He'd kill me.

"There's a lot going on. There's a lot of weird stuff

going on. Mike is my, well, sort of boyfriend. Sometimes boyfriend. But he, well, he's getting worse. He has a problem. I'm afraid for my life now, sort of. Not really, but just, like, sort of. I have to hide so Mike can't find me. If I go to someone Amish, I bet he'd never imagine I was there."

"What about your parents?"

"My dad hates me. My mom is in California now. They aren't together anymore."

"Your dad doesn't hate you."

"He will if he finds out about Mike."

"Well, I don't know what to say, Ashley. I'd have to talk it over with my parents. I don't know how wise it would be to hide you. Are you in trouble with the law, or is Mike? Should we call the authorities? The police?"

"I have nowhere to go!" Ashley's voice rose into a shriek of hysteria before she clapped both hands over her mouth and rocked forward, her thin hair falling stiffly forward as if to hide her somehow.

Passersby eyed her curiously. If they sat here and Ashley continued her theatrics, they would draw too much attention. Sarah got up and turned to tell Ashley to come with her, but she was knocked off balance by Ashley lunging against her, her thin hands grabbing at Sarah's bib apron, her mouth open, mewling like a lost, starving kitten, grotesque, yet so completely pitiful.

"You can't leave me here!"

"I won't, Ashley. I'll leave a message for my mother to call me. We'll decide something, okay? Just find a place here in the market and stay there, until I can tell you what my parents say."

"I'll stay in a booth at the restaurant."

"Alright. Just stay there, till I find you."

Ashley's whole body was shaking now, her lip swollen and purple, her fingers restlessly stretching the wristband on her sweatshirt as she searched Sarah's face.

"Can I borrow a couple dollars to get something to eat?"

"I'll go with you."

Could Sarah trust Ashley to be truthful? She had no idea what was going on in her life, and perhaps they'd all be getting into something far worse than they'd anticipated.

Mam answered the message on her voice mail dutifully, the way she always did, walking to the phone shanty a few times a day to see if anyone had called.

Sarah explained the situation as best she could, interrupted only by Mam's sympathetic clucks or words of warning, placed aptly, an attempt at caution.

In the end, Mam relented, saying she'd speak to Dat, but certainly, there was no way Sarah could leave the poor, frightened Ashley at the unoccupied market later that evening.

Ashley greeted Sarah's acceptance with a nod of her head, eyes averted, bringing a storm of doubt with it. Was she doing the right thing?

A small duffel bag was the only thing Ashley carried with her as she climbed into the market van with her head lowered, her eyes downcast, a whipped animal, afraid of more punishment.

She slunk into the far corner on the back seat, slouched down as far as she could, as if to obliterate herself completely. Then she turned her face to the window and closed her eyes, shutting out Sarah and the world around her.

The usual, noisy banter wasn't completely stilled, but a respectful air permeated the interior of the van, as if the girls knew their loud joking, their fun and laughter, might hurt this sad, thin girl with the stringy, unkempt hair.

When they arrived at the farm, Ashley sat up, her eyes wide with fright, her head turning from left to right, the reality of her situation clearly upsetting.

"Sarah?" Her white hand groped for Sarah's sleeve, found it, plucked at it.

"You sure this is okay?"

"Of course. Come on."

Ashley followed her, apologizing in hurried whispers as she squeezed past the market girls' knees. There was a loud cracking of plastic breaking and a shriek from Sarah, followed by a wail of denial as she stepped down from the van and surveyed a broken plastic container with a thoroughly ruined lemon meringue pie squeezing between the cracks.

"Oh my word! Whose pie?"

"Mine! Did you step on my pie, Sarah?"

Annie, the biggest girl in the bunch, eyed Sarah with a very real sense of loss. Sarah tried unsuccessfully to hold back her laughter, but the occupants of the van heard the spluttering from her and joined in, until everyone was laughing with her.

Still chuckling as the van sped away, the two girls walked to the house, the welcoming yellow light in the windows as homey as ever.

"I'm home!" Sarah called.

Mam was at the sink washing supper dishes, but she turned, wiping the suds from her hands with a corner of her apron, a smile of welcome on her kind face.

Mam's eyes changed from the glad welcome she produced so naturally to one of shock, but she regained her composure just as quickly. She held out a hand warm from the dishwater and said, "Hello, Ashley."

Ashley allowed Mam a wild glance before ducking her head, her hair covering most of her face, the way it often did.

"I hope you can make yourself at home here. I have the guest room ready for you, and there's a bathroom you can share with the girls. Your supper is in the oven."

Turning, Mam bent to retrieve an oblong casserole and set it on the table, sliding a heavy potholder underneath.

She filled two glasses with mint tea, adding plenty of ice from the freezer, and set out a Tupperware container of applesauce and one of bread and butter pickles.

Sarah took a long drink of her tea, sighed, and lifted the lid of the casserole.

Levi appeared at the doorway, clearing his throat and gesturing at Ashley, who sat, terrified, unable to lift her glass or attempt conversation.

Wow. This is going to be rough, Sarah thought.

"Hey, Levi! How's it going?"

In answer, Levi drew his eyebrows down and told Sarah in perfect Pennsylvania Dutch that she could stop being so *gros-feelich* (proud) right now, that just because she had an English friend didn't mean she had to talk like Melvin.

Mam put at hand on his shoulder, sat him in a kitchen chair, and introduced him to Ashley, who barely acknowledged his presence. She merely nodded her head, her eyes trained steadily on the silverware beside her empty plate.

Levi, however, was delighted by the fact that they had English company, so he leaned forward, smiled, his beady brown eyes as observant as always, and bellowed, "Hi, Ashley. I'm Levi!"

Ashley cast him a wild-eyed look and nodded miserably before turning her face away.

"Sees shemmt sich, Mam (She's ashamed)!"

Mam held up one finger against her mouth and
motioned Levi to hush, which was completely lost on
him. He leaned forward, his ample stomach shoving
against the table, turned his head, and told Ashley in
broken English that his name was Levi Beiler and he was
her friend, and he hoped she knew how to play Memory.

Ashley glanced wildly at Sarah, who nodded, smiled,
put a hand on her arm, and said Levi would be a good
friend, and yes, he was a champion Memory player.

That brought a small smile of recognition from Ashley, but she still refused to eat, her fingers twisting restlessly in her lap.

"Can I give you some baked spaghetti?" Mam asked
politely.

Ashley shook her head.

"No?"

"I...don't feel very good. May I...Do you mind if I go
to my room?" she said, her voice low and rough, as if it
hadn't been put to use for a long time.

"Certainly. I just thought you might want to meet
David, my husband, Sarah's father, and her two sisters,
Priscilla and Suzie," Mam said hopefully.

"Okay. If I don't have to eat."

"You don't. Maybe you don't like our supper. Can I
get you something else?"

Ashley shook her head, a pinched look about her nose,
before looking around desperately and asking forcefully,
"Is there a restroom?"

Sarah jumped up, guiding her to the downstairs bathroom, then stopped on her return to the kitchen table as

she listened the sound of Ashley being violently sick in the safety of the bathroom.

Sarah shook her head at Mam's questioning eyes, then slid heavily into her chair, her shoulders bent with weariness.

"*Sees grunk* (She's sick)!" Levi announced.

"Shh!"

"*Sees an cutza* (She's throwing up)."

"Levi!"

Getting laboriously to his feet, he shuffled to the medicine cabinet in his room, returned with a large bottle of colorful Tums, and waited patiently by the bathroom door until it opened hesitantly. A still terrified Ashley slid out between the door and the frame, as if she was too frightened to open it more than a few inches.

"Ashley! Here!"

Levi handed her the peace offering, his face shining eagerly in the light of the gas lamp, his small brown eyes as innocent as a child's and as eager to please.

Ashley stopped, turned her head, and looked at Levi with only a fraction of her guard down, but a small crack appeared in her wall of reserve. She reached out, and Levi placed the Tums in her hand triumphantly.

"Take two," he said, with an air of superiority.

"I will," Ashley said, very low and quiet.

She picked up her duffel bag and questioned Sarah with her wide, startled eyes.

"I'll show you," Sarah said quickly and led the way up the stairs as Levi sat down at the kitchen table and began the long process of presenting his case for a plateful of baked spaghetti, which would be his third for the evening.

When Dat, Priscilla, and Suzie came in from doing

the evening chores, there was quite a flurry as everyone tried to tell them about Ashley at once. The din of the conversation prevented anyone from noticing someone at the front door, knocking, then knocking again, before opening the door and saying, "Hey."

Only Dat heard the greeting, turned, and said, "*Vell* (Well)!"

Surprised, the family's conversation ended, and they turned in respectful silence as three members of their community stepped inside, their faces grave and solemn. For one heartstopping moment, Sarah thought they had come bearing tragic news, a death, another barn fire, until she remembered that kind of news was usually spread through the phone lines.

She never once gave it a thought that they were all members the school board. She picked at the cold spaghetti on her plate, twirled her fork around and around, and ate a few pickles as she thought about Ashley being sick on her first evening with the family. She wondered what actually possessed the poor girl and chuckled to herself about how Levi had immediately taken her under his wing, like a sick kitten or a lame bird.

That Levi was a character, he surely was.

CHAPTER 14

WHEN JONAS KING SAID LOUDLY THAT THEIR
school needed help, Sarah's fork stopped, the spaghetti
slid off, and a wave of shock zipped from her head to
her stomach. The school board! It was October, and the
school board was here?

She leaned back against the kitchen chair, her breath
creating a small puffing sound as it left her body.

"So, we didn't know if Sarah would consider taking
on the school or not."

She heard the words through the rapid pulse in her
ears, but it was followed by a high-pitched ringing that
blocked out Dat's answer.

Then they all turned to look at her, their eyes kind
and curious, their straw hats held politely in their hands.
Their hair stuck to their foreheads, the way Amish men's
hair always does after their hats are removed.

Vaguely, she saw Mam's wide eyes, Priscilla's downcast ones, Dat's questioning.

"Sarah?" he asked.

She focused on the kind eyes of her father, a shyness

overtaking her, the reality of these men's visit too much to fathom.

Jonas broke into the silence.

"We have a real mess. I simply don't know how else to put it. Disrespect, disobedience, pupils simply refusing to cooperate. Mothers, parents, are taking the children's sides. I won't blame you if you refuse to help us out, but we all agree, perhaps you can. We did hear about driving off the…the…those who came into Lydia Esh's barn, and we thought maybe if you could do that, you could handle a roomful of problem pupils."

Sarah smiled shyly and picked at the tablecloth where the hem was wearing thin, leaving strands for her to pull. She didn't want to remember that night, especially not now with Ashley upstairs, so frightened of being here, her future in jeopardy.

"I…have a job," she said, facing the men now, able to warm up to them, inspired by the praise, which was not given easily, she knew.

"You go to market?'

"Yes."

"Well, there are market girls all over Lancaster County, but not everyone can teach a school, especially not this one," Abner Esh broke in, his rotund little form shifting from one foot to the other.

Mam asked the men to be seated. The table was cleared discreetly, Priscilla dutifully washed dishes, and Levi listened respectfully as talk swirled across the table, the problems, the solutions, the task at hand a monumental one by all accounts.

Mam served coffee and a platter of pecan bars. Sarah asked them if it was alright if she took a week to think it over. She would have to let her boss have at least a week or two to find a replacement.

"So you are considering?" Abner Esh asked.

"Yes."

It was a long time before Sarah fell asleep that night. The events of the day crowded out any relaxation as her mind picked up and examined first one obstacle and then another, discarding one solution and then the next until she became quite weary of it.

Ashley was the first problem. She couldn't just hide out here with Mam, spending her days in idleness, worrying Mam. She would have to find a job somewhere, but not in the immediate area. She had no money and no vehicle, and she was clearly more troubled than even Sarah knew.

They would let the teacher go. Fire her. Sarah knew her well. Martha Riehl. She was in the same youth group as Sarah, although not in her intimate group of friends.

She was pretty, dark-haired, very outgoing. What would she say?

They'd remove her from her teaching spot—no doubt she loved her job—and she'd be replaced by Sarah. She'd be angry, feel betrayed. And just how severe were the discipline problems?

Sarah sighed as the short hand on her alarm clock slowly crept past the twelve, and she was expected to go to market again in the morning. Would it be her last week there? She got out of bed to pull the shades down over the windows, the brilliant moonlight annoying now as she tossed restlessly in her bed.

She reached for the bottom of the shade and was just about to pull it down, when, out of the corner of her eye, she caught a slight movement, a weak light, in the barnyard beside the silo.

She stopped, straining her eyes as her heartbeat accelerated. It wasn't dark at all. In fact, everything was awash in a silvery light, illuminating the dark shapes of the cows lying in the barnyard and the pasture beyond.

There! The light was not nearly bright enough to be a flashlight. It was more like a penlight.

Watching closely, Sarah grasped the window frame, her breath coming in short, ragged puffs.

There was no wind, only the silence of the night and the beauty of the silver moon shining steadily from a cloudless night sky speckled liberally with twinkling stars.

Her eyes picked up the weak, yellowish light. It couldn't be a penlight. They had more of a bluish white light produced by LED bulbs, those new ones that used only a fraction of the energy that regular bulbs consumed. What was going on?

Suddenly a thought entered her mind. The cows weren't afraid at all. They lay contentedly, and not one got up or milled around. There was no bawling or any other sign of fright. Whatever or whoever it was, the cows were accepting it.

A dark form bent over a cow and slapped it. Dat!

The cow lunged slowly to her feet, followed by the unsteady little form of a newborn calf, wobbling along in the moonlight, aided by her father's caring hand along its back.

Dat would put the cow in a warm stall with clean straw, protecting the newborn calf from the frost of the night, which was sure to cover the fields and woods before morning.

Satisfied that the weak light was Dat's ailing old flashlight, Sarah left her vigil by the window and fell gratefully to bed, the pulled shades sufficiently darkening her room, enabling her to close her weary eyes and finally fall asleep.

It seemed like only an hour had passed when her alarm began its delirious music, much too loud and way too annoying. She was going to get rid of that obnoxious thing as soon as she could purchase another.

She sighed, weariness washing over her as she remembered the visit from the school board members. How could a person come to a sensible decision without adequate sleep?

Sarah washed her face, brushed her teeth, put up her hair as fast as possible, and threw on her clothes without knowing exactly which dress she was wearing. She pinned on her covering and ran down the stairs, just as the headlights of the market van swept across the yard.

Mam had told Sarah not to worry about Ashley. Priscilla was good at being with people like her, so they'd be fine. Levi would win her over as well.

Sarah slumped against the side of the van, asleep before they hit the interstate on the way to New Jersey, oblivious to the girls' chatter and the roaring of the great trucks moving past in each direction.

The day was long, and her mind weary at the end of it. She packed up a few bakery leftovers without talking to anyone about the school board's visit, collected her pay, and went to the van, suddenly knowing with startling clarity what her decision would be.

She needed to get away, she'd told Mam. Out of Lancaster County, which held Matthew's memory and all the painful details in every road, every field, every farm and house and restaurant and store they'd ever been to.

She no longer wanted to see his house with the spreading maple tree across the rural road, the picket fence beneath it, his bedroom window shaded by it.

If she did go away, could she truly escape? The pictures

would remain in her memory. Perhaps filling her mind and heart with a roomful of boisterous boys and girls would be the perfect answer.

Hadn't the men said those boys were almost uncontrollable? It would take every ounce of her strength and likely more of her patience than she could produce, but she knew she wanted to try.

She imagined Matthew being chased out of Lancaster County by a group of rowdy children from the problem school and shook silently with inward giggles. Well, so be it, Matthew Stoltzfus. So be it.

Saturday evening was always a joyous time with the return home from market, the usual happiness and lighthearted talk, the anticipated end of her work week, and the long awaited opportunity to see Matthew. Now when the market van drove up to the door, the anticipation was replaced by a certain acceptance, a feeling that seemed to signal a better place, although not a perfect one.

Matthew was gone. Over and over, she had to remind herself of this fact, but no time was quite as difficult as the return from market on a Saturday evening.

She was shocked to see Mam's pale face, her lips compressed with restraint, Priscilla sitting on the couch staring into space, her eyes wide.

"What?" Sarah asked immediately, afraid for them all.

"She left," Mam said, her tone anxious.

Levi broke in.

"A white car. A little one. She went to the phone shanty. She did. She called. Someone came."

He was speaking in loud tones, clearly distraught. He had wanted Ashley to stay. She was his friend. She said she'd play Memory.

The real story came from Mam, who said Ashley had

come down the stairs late, about ten o'clock or around there, refused breakfast, and asked for the telephone. She waited on the porch shivering, her coat pulled tightly around her thin frame, talking to herself, until a car pulled into the driveway. She'd gone without a goodbye or thank you. She simply walked down the steps and into the waiting car.

The driver of the car was wearing dark glasses, a cap pulled low over his forehead, and a dark coat, so there was no way anyone could tell who he was or what he looked like.

Sarah was frustrated, afraid for Ashley.

"If I knew where she went, I'd hire a driver and go look for her. But I have absolutely no idea where to start. She never told me anything about her background, her whereabouts.

"One thing is sure, she's afraid of the person she's with. He seems to have some control over her, and she knows much more about these barn fires than we think."

Mam nodded, saying wisely that Ashley held a secret about something, and it was so bad it was making her literally sick.

For now, they could only pray for her safety and hope for the best. God loved Ashley same as everyone else. He had a plan for her life, and she was important to Him.

"Just because we're Amish and have a stable home doesn't mean we're above her in God's eyes. He cares deeply about Ashley and so should we. That poor girl is so pathetic," Mam said, tears rising unbidden.

Sarah ate a slice of sweet baloney and a dill pickle, drank some tea, then poured a glass of creamy milk, and took two oatmeal cookies from the Tupperware container in the pantry.

"You know what I think, Mam? I honestly think Ashley knows who started every one of these fires. I think deep down she's a good girl, one who lives with a conscience that can barely tolerate the guilt, and I think this Mike, her boyfriend, is every bit as dangerous as she says. But I'm not convinced he's the actual arsonist."

Levi looked up from the puzzle he was assembling, his eyes shrewd, narrowing.

"I think you're right, Sarah. You know, the other day I was thinking hard. I remember the small, white car that was here the night of our barn fire, and I think the person driving the car then was much bigger than the thin guy that picked up Ashley today."

"Oh no, Levi," Mam cautioned.

"Malinda!" Levi held up a warning finger, and Mam smiled widely, the way she always did when Levi called her Malinda.

The peace that entered Sarah's life came slowly, in bits and pieces, in times she least expected it.

On her way to church the following morning, when the sunlight glistened on the frost in the hollows, wisps of fog hanging like ghosts above it and the sun so brilliant it hurt her eyes through the glass of the buggy window, she felt peace.

A calm, unhurried feeling of having cares that were not so enormous that God would not be able to handle them. Peace.

It came in many forms—the sound of the steel buggy wheels on the cold, hard gravel coupled with the dull, familiar sound of iron-clad hooves pounding on pavement, the tinkle of snaps slapping against the reigns, the homey clop of another team following them and checking the rearview mirror to see who it was.

It was familiar, home, her life, her culture. This was the only way she understood the accompanying peace.

This peace, however, was shattered by the appearance of Hannah, greeting her effusively the minute she stepped out of the buggy, chilled, eager to get into the house with her friends.

"Sarah! Oh, it's good to see you! I just have to share this with you. You'll be so happy for Matthew. They're expecting! Imagine! The Lord is surely with them, wouldn't you say? I can hardly wait to tell your mother."

Sarah nodded her head and began to walk away, but was stopped by Hannah's voice again.

"Sarah, Matthew called to tell me the good news. He asked about you. He wanted you to be the first to know. He cared very much what you thought. Oh Sarah, I can't tell you how happy he is. I can just hear the joy in his voice when he talks about his work in Haiti. He's serving in an orphanage now. Think of it, Sarah."

Sarah met Hannah's eyes, behind the glasses, eyes that sought her approval, searched for agreement, strengthening the faith she had in her beloved son.

Hannah saw the colors in Sarah's eyes change from green flecked with gold to a turbulent surf of brown and gray and restless green. She stepped back, away from the ongoing reality she saw there.

Only a whispery sigh and a hint of an accompanying smile gave away any emotion. Rachel Zook handily stepping between them, shaking Hannah's hand with a hearty good morning, as Sarah fled to the safety of the house.

She found peace was elusive, especially in the face of adversity. She listened closely as the young minister paced the floor, expounding Christ's life and his lessons, but her mind wandered constantly, thinking of Matthew, his life, his calling, his wife and the child they were expecting.

He wanted me to be the first to know, Hannah? Really?

Sarcasm and rebellion crowded out the morning's peace, and she felt torn, embattled, losing ground, her feet slipping down the dangerous slope of doubt and self-pity wrapped up with remorse and what-ifs until she couldn't concentrate on the long closing prayer in German and the final song.

She blinked back the tears that the rousing melody forced to the surface, checked every youth seated on the boy's bench, and had never felt Matthew's absence so keenly. Would it never go away?

Would his memory dog her happiness all the days of her life, a barrel of darkness she'd drag along with baler twine slung over her shoulder, crippling her, holding her back from her normal, free walk?

Well, if it did, there wasn't too much she could do about that now. She would have to do the best she could.

She dressed carefully that afternoon in a crisp navy blue dress, pinned her cape neatly, was careful about her apron, precisely lining up the two ends of the belt, pinning it securely.

Her hair looked better than she had ever seen it now that Priscilla had introduced her to a new product from Pantene, which helped hold the curls in place even better than hairspray.

She put a new white covering on her head, satisfied with her appearance, for once.

"Think of it, Pris. When I teach school, I'll have to pin on a cap and apron every single morning. And tie my covering, then yet."

"Then yet?" Priscilla mimicked from her perch on the

bed.

"Whatever."

"What's with this Pris thing? I don't want that nickname. You better not start it. I'd rather have Cilla."

Sarah laughed.

"Who's taking you?'

"Guess."

"Melvin?"

"You got it."

"How can you stand riding around with that old Melvin? He's way past the time that he should even be running around. He's not popular at all. You'll never get a husband, hanging out with him."

"Priscilla, I like Melvin."

"I know you do. That's nice. But, seriously, how old is he?"

"I think twenty-eight or twenty-nine."

"Shoo!"

"Yeah, really."

"And every time he comes to pick you up, same thing. He comes in, sits down, eats and eats and eats, talks to Dat endlessly—probably because he's closer to his age than yours—then goes through the ritual of combing his hair, and he doesn't even have any in the front. And there you sit, when I know you'd much rather be on your way to the youth supper."

"Oh well, I'm not sixteen anymore. And Matthew isn't here, so going away on Sunday holds very little excitement. The thrill is simply gone. Which shoes should I wear?"

"The flats."

"Not the heels?"

"No, you're tall enough."

"Giraffe tall?"

"No, just tall."

"Priscilla, I can't wait till you're sixteen. It'll be so fun getting ready to go away together!"

"Yeah, but you have to remember, Omar is going to take me. Melvin won't be in the picture, okay?"

Sarah raised her eyebrows, bumped Priscilla's arm with her fist, and said, "My, my."

"For someone who says there's no excitement in going to the supper, you certainly are being very careful about your appearance, which is just a nice way of saying you sure are sprucing up for someone. Who is it?"

Sarah slapped her sister playfully. Priscilla yelped and ran down the stairs ahead of her. Suzie looked up from the card game she was playing with Levi, sniffed, and went back to her game.

Dat was seated on the recliner, a large ceramic bowl of popcorn beside him, a steaming mug of coffee on the lamp stand, his white shirt and black Sunday trousers making him look younger, relaxed.

He smiled at Sarah, asked who was picking her up, then smiled again, although his eyes clouded only slightly as he watched her walk to the kitchen for a bowl to fill with popcorn.

"Mam, you may as well make another popper of popcorn, if Melvin's picking her up."

As it was, Melvin was late, and they all got into a discussion about Ashley Walter's strange existence, which seemed to escalate Melvin's opinions about the barn fires to zealous heights. Sarah watched the clock and figured the day would soon be past and she'd still be sitting there at her parents' kitchen table.

She agreed it was troubling, but if Ashley made the

choice to go back to her boyfriend, there wasn't too much they could do except be patient and hope no tragedy would come of it.

Dat's eyes filled with tears of compassion, and Levi looked somber, contemplating the loss of a promising Memory player.

When they finally got to the supper at Aaron King's, Sarah found an exuberant Rose beaming happily, waiting eagerly to extol every last one of Lee Glick's virtues to her best friend, who listened, expressed amazement, happiness, disbelief, whatever was required of her.

Aaron King *sei* Anna had done an outstanding job of planning a menu for over a hundred youth. The scalloped potatoes and ham, creamy with onions and cheese, and the green bean casserole were perfect. Sarah balanced her paper plate on her knee, ate appreciatively, talked to her friends, and rose above her heartache once again.

She whipped Rose at an intense game of ping-pong and was surprised when Lee stepped up and asked to play.

Rose acknowledged her new boyfriend coyly but handed over the ping-pong paddle, saying Sarah would never, ever beat Lee, there was simply no way. She followed that statement with a high shriek that drew exactly the amount of attention she'd hoped it would when heads turned, smiled, and watched for a while, before returning to their games.

Caught off guard, Sarah blushed and became flustered, nervous, with Lee towering only a ping-pong table's length away, his blue eyes challenging, alight with interest.

They were a match, one almost as skilled as the other, but Lee was a wicked server and won by three points.

Sarah laughed, her eyes the color of spring water with sunshine dancing on its surface, her hair gleaming in the lamplight. Lee handed over the red paddle as she smiled up at him, guileless, unafraid. Unafraid or released?

He reached for the paddle, his fingers closed over hers, so firm and warm, so compelling, and stayed for seconds longer than was necessary.

On gossamer wings, the breath of attraction dipped and hovered between them, sacred, beautiful, but scarred now by the years of disappointment for Lee, by the doubt that real love could ever be possible again for Sarah.

Without a word, they wondered at it.

CHAPTER 15

SOMETIMES, SARAH THOUGHT, LIFE GOES BY SO fast, and quite unexpectedly a situation arises that would have been unfathomable before.

She put both hands on her desk, clasped them firmly, the fingers intertwined, took a deep breath, and said loudly, "Good morning, boys and girls," to the echoing, empty classroom, then bent forward, laid her head on the desk, and whispered, "You're going to have to help me here, Lord. It's really scary."

Teaching in an Amish one-room school was not a job that required any further studies than the eight grades she had already had. She had finished her schooling at age fourteen and then attended vocational class once a week until she was fifteen, as Pennsylvania state law required.

She remembered the order of school, the work, the way eight grades were managed. This school, Ivy Run, had twenty-three pupils distributed among eight grades, so it posed no threat as far as the number of children she would be required to teach.

The frightening part was the bad attitude, the

disrespect that had run rampant the past few years, the children, or some of them, grieving their teacher terribly with blatant disobedience, among other things.

Ivy Run School was only about four miles from Sarah's home, but she rode to school with a driver rather than by scooter or horse and buggy. The school board offered to make arrangements to save her time.

The board members had been extremely kind, offering assistance, volunteering services, but so far, she had not heard a single word from any of the parents. She hardly knew who they were, anyway, so that was no big deal. She just hoped they'd be able to work with each other when things got out of hand, which Sarah felt sure was bound to happen.

It was Thursday afternoon, which left two days at market, one Sunday, and one early Monday morning, before she would stand at this desk and wish every pupil a good morning.

She wondered if her knees would support her, or if she'd faint dead away.

The school was an older brick school on Hatfield Road, set in a grove of chestnut and maple trees. The roof had been replaced a few years before, and the windows were fairly new, but the old brick structure remained the same, the porch built along the gable end, the cloakroom enclosed on one side.

The floor was a smooth, varnished hardwood, gleaming with years of hundreds of little feet walking across it. The cast iron desks were painted a shining black with refinished oak tops and seats that folded up or down.

A blackboard ran the length of the front with a white border along its top, the alphabet in cursive, print, and German on it. Rolled up maps hung just below the letters, and a row of shelves stood beneath the blackboard.

A gray metal file cabinet stood off to the right, a propane gas heater to the left. Above the heater hung a round PVC ring with wooden clothes pins attached to it with nylon string, a homemade wonder for drying caps and mittens in the winter.

The rows of windows on each side of the classroom were topped with beige, roll down blinds, serviceable when the sun blinded a row of pupils hard at work.

The artwork on the walls had been done by the previous teacher, such as it was, and Sarah could tell that had not been her interest at all as the name charts along the top of the blackboard were colored poorly and coming loose at several corners.

Perhaps, if they had time, she'd make her own name charts, colored brightly, with black lettering.

Sarah sat back, sighed, and then became quite giddy with anticipation.

The classroom was infused with a golden, late afternoon radiance, turning an ordinary room into a warm haven of light.

She stood up from the chair, stretched, and turned to get her sweater, when she heard a grating noise, a clicking.

The door.

Okay. Some was trying to...

She stepped back, both hands going to her mouth to stifle a scream, when the handle turned. The door was yanked open unceremoniously, a head was pushed through wearing a beanie. The intruder's face was dirty, his coat torn in places, soiled, but the eyes as blue as always.

Lee Glick was completely taken aback, his hand going

to his filthy beanie, before shaking his head, laughing ruefully, and saying, "What are YOU doing here?"

"Oh, you scared me!"

That was all they said for quite some time, Sarah standing in the middle of the aisle in the gold light, Lee standing just inside the door, his face streaked with dirt, his clothes obviously having seen better days.

He repeated the question, and she answered with one of her own.

"I came to get Marlin's arithmetic book. He's crying up a storm, because he had a stomach ache in school and couldn't get his work done, he told Anna."

"Your sister Anna?"

"Yeah."

"They come to this school?"

"Evidently. This is where I was told to go."

"I'll be teaching here, starting Monday morning."

"Are you serious?"

Sarah nodded. "They're having a lot of problems."

"Tell me about it. That's all Ben's children talk about at the supper table. You know you're in for it, right?"

"What's that supposed to mean?"

"What I said. Sarah, it's awful the way these kids act. I'm afraid for you. I really am."

"I can't do more than fail, can I?"

"No, you're right."

"I think the biggest problem, from what the guys on the school board said, is two or three families. Probably the first day I can pretty much tell who they are. Then I guess I'll go from there."

Lee grinned, his teeth very white in his darkened face. "So that's your game plan?"

"Yup."

"Good luck. You know you'll need it."

Sarah laughed. "By the way, I didn't know you mined coal for a living."

Lee looked perplexed, then a hand went to his face, and he laughed sheepishly.

"No, not coal mining. Just removing a very old slate roof and replacing it. I've looked like this all week."

"Anna's probably having a fit."

"She is."

Sarah laughed again, thinking of the overweight little Anna, huffing around her house, cleaning, washing, clucking. She missed her and told Lee to tell her hello.

"I will."

There was an awkward silence, which surprised Sarah, their conversation having flowed so freely in the time he was there.

"Guess I should go," he said very quietly.

"Yes. My driver should be coming any minute."

He looked out the south windows, his gaze unfocused, and she looked through the north ones. It was much easier and safer that way.

Sarah took a step backward and saw her driver pull into the school yard.

"My driver's here," she said loudly, nervous now.

His reluctance to leave was apparent when he said, "Sarah, tell me. Tell me something." His voice faded away as his eyes were lifted to hers, held steady.

"Just...How are you doing? Are you okay? How did you feel when you found out about Matthew? I can't explain to you, the agony I experienced at...over the time you...he...."

The questions seemed to release a torrent of emotions as his breath accelerated, his voice rasped and cracked before he stopped, bent his head, and kicked the toe of his work boot self-consciously against a desk.

"I have to go," he said and turned.

"I didn't answer your questions," Sarah said coolly. "I am doing okay. Not fine, just okay. I will be fine." She laughed, a soft sound bordering on hysteria.

"I don't know how I felt when he left without me. Something inside of me died. I was angry, hurt beyond words, but, of course, part of me protected him, and I didn't believe any of it, but only for a short time. Hannah, his mother, is a big help. When I think of being actually married to Matthew, I can't imagine." Her voice faded away, and she shook her head from side to side.

"So, I'll teach school. I'll become a tall, skinny old maid who puts her life into the classroom, and people will call me a leftover blessing for the community. My hair will turn gray, and I'll make coffee at weddings and wait for some old bachelor or widower to ask me."

Lee laughed, tilting back his head. Then he looked closely at Sarah, the smile fading from his mouth as he held her eyes with his.

An uncertainty spread across his face, then determination as he made up his mind and closed the gap between them with two long strides, his hands came up to encircle her forearms. He tugged gently, "Sarah."

The tenderness in his voice was so real, so alive, it brought a lump to Sarah's throat. She could not have uttered a word if she had tried.

"Do you think you'll ever be able to love again? I mean, before you become an old maid?"

Sarah shrugged her shoulders and his hands fell away. He clasped them behind his back, but his face was so close to hers, she could feel his breathing.

She raised her face, found his eyes, and was lost in the blueness of them. He watched the color in hers change with emotion turning them dark with remembered pain, gray and anxious with mistrust, then vibrantly green with longing, flecked with lights of new hope.

"Sarah, I have Rose. I must honor that."

Numbly, her eyelids heavy, covering the display of feelings, she nodded.

"Yes, Lee. You do. And I wish you the best. You two are so perfectly matched. Everyone says."

"She's a nice girl. I am in awe of her in so many ways."

Leaning sideways, Sarah retrieved her new book bag, grabbed her sweater, and said, "Good. That's good. I have to go now. My driver is here. She's been waiting."

They moved as one through the door, suddenly so far apart that any words would have to be shouted in order to be understood.

They didn't look back, neither did they wave, as each one moved in opposite directions in separate vehicles.

Sarah's driver, a neighbor who was close friends with Mam, took one long look at Sarah and asked what happened back there. Sarah laughed and told her not to worry about it.

Lee's work driver reminded him of the arithmetic book and had to pull into someone's driveway to turn around and take him back to the schoolhouse to get it.

Good thing Ben was one of the caretakers and had given him a key.

One last weekend at market, Sarah thought, as the van sped along the interstate, rain hissing beneath the tires, the windshield wipers clicking rhythmically, the fast-moving monstrous trucks spraying the van as they roared past.

The girls in the van were sitting or lying in various positions, half-awake or asleep, oblivious to the rain or the traffic, trying to grab a few minutes of rest before the churning pace of a busy market day.

Rain meant an increase in customers. It was always that way. Sarah didn't know why. Perhaps people didn't want to work in their yards or do any outdoor activities on a rainy day. They thought of a place that was cheerful and bright, filled with comfort food, especially good, hot soups and stews, warm doughnuts and cinnamon rolls and whoopie pies and cupcakes. So they'd be frantically busy today.

She'd try her best to imprint in her mind the many precious memories of the short time she'd been at market, the sights and sounds and smells of this wonderful place, filled with friends and acquaintances, people she had grown to love and respect.

The driver turned up the volume on the radio, and the van was filled with predictions of snow or ice by evening, warning motorists to use caution, especially on interstates leading to higher elevations.

That's us, Sarah thought, but she dismissed the threatening weather as they pulled up to the vast brick wall of the farmer's market.

Sarah measured flour, yeast, sugar, eggs, and salt. The great paddles of the mixer turned, thoroughly mixing the cinnamon roll dough, bread dough, and all the different yeast breads that were placed on the shelves in tempting rows.

Sarah's hands flew. She focused on her work as she rolled pound after pound of soft, delicious smelling dough into long rectangles. She quickly sprinkled brown sugar and cinnamon along the length and rolled the dough to form long pinwheels, before grasping the smooth cutter and severing one cinnamon roll after another from the long lengths of dough. She placed the rolls in foil pains and dotted them with walnuts and chunks of butter.

As she had predicted, the crowds appeared at about ten o'clock in the morning and never let up.

Sarah didn't get her first break until after lunch, her harried boss apologizing profusely. Sarah understood and said she'd be fine, but she was so hungry she bought a soft pretzel and dipped it in cheese sauce to eat on her way to the restaurant to order her lunch.

She ordered the special there, roast beef and gravy, with French fries and coleslaw. She sat down across from Rose Zook, who was slowly spooning the perfect combination of vanilla ice cream and hot fudge sauce into her mouth.

"You know you eat an awful lot," Rose observed after Sarah had scraped her plate clean.

"You ate a bunch of my French fries—probably half," Sarah answered her friend. "But you know I had a soft pretzel on the way here," Sarah added, laughing.

"You didn't!"

"I did."

"Well, that's okay. You can eat. You work hard."

Suddenly, Rose's eyes darkened, and she toyed with her paper napkin, her head bent slightly. She sat back as both hands went to her stomach, then she spoke quietly. "I am eating everything in sight right now. It's stress."

Rose put an elbow on the table, cupped her chin in her hand, her gorgeous, heavily-lashed eyes blue but clouded with worry.

"I hardly know how to tell you, but Sarah, something isn't right with Lee. I just can't describe it. Really it's just…well, weird. He's nice to me, very attentive, actually, but it's like all of him isn't there or something. He seems kind of distracted."

Sarah's own hot fudge sundae now became the focus of her attention. Guilt, coupled with self-loathing and shame so all encompassing it felt like burning fire, washed over her.

"I mean, I know Lee loves me. There was never a doubt in my mind. He just doesn't seem as if he's quite like he was when we began dating. You don't think…I mean, Sarah, do you think he's thinking of someone else?"

Blinking rapidly, her face flaming, she shook her head, avoiding Rose's gaze.

"What's wrong with you?" Rose demanded, suddenly.

"Nothing, Rose. Why?"

"There is, too."

"I'm just too full. My stomach hurts terribly."

"Are you serious?"

Sarah nodded miserably.

Rose laughed, a high-pitched giggle of understanding and friendship and relief all rolled into one burst of joyous sound.

"So, what do you think about Lee?"

"Oh, guys are hard to figure out, Rose. Don't ask me. I have no faith in my ability to understand guys. Look what happened to me. Fine one minute and oh so miserable the next. Who knows what they're thinking? I'm going to be an old maid schoolteacher, living in my own small house, thin and pinched and mean."

Rose whooped with laughter, then smacked the table top with the palm of her hand, turning heads as she did so.

"Sarah, that is exactly why you are my closest friend.

I just love the way you express yourself. Well, good. Then I have nothing to worry about you, right? I mean, Lee sometimes, well, he mentions you. How different you are from most other girls. And...Well, you know, Sarah."

Rose broke off, biting her lower lip.

Sarah couldn't get away fast enough, scuttling down the aisles wanting the floor to open and swallow her.

Shamed, her face flaming now, she knew she was every bit as bad as a traitor, an adulterer.

Oh, she'd wanted Lee to take her in her arms, kiss her, and tell her he loved her, the way men did in all the novels she read, in all the hopes and dreams of her heart. Every girl yearned to be loved, it was simply the way it was.

Solomon devoted an entire book in the Bible to the love between a man and a woman, and God was pleased, Sarah felt sure.

But why? Why was she always the odd person caught in a love triangle with Rose as the prominent character?

She thought of the heart-stopping depth of Lee's blue eyes, the powerful, magnetic attraction she had experienced. His blond hair, the soiled stocking cap, the black dust on his face, the work-roughened hands clenching her arms.

Oh, Lee. It's too late, now. I ruined you with my undying love for Matthew, my stubborn refusal to see what he was. A man in love with Rose, my oldest friend. And here I go again.

And yet. He'd talked of her, to Rose.

It was hard to suppress the pinwheels of joy that cavorted freely and colorfully through her entire being, her heart soaring and swelling with a newfound awe. And yet she wondered if it would ever be possible, and now, so soon, she knew.

Too soon. It was much too soon. Her broken heart had left her vulnerable, and she'd be hurt. Again.

"Hey!"

Sarah stopped and turned, searching for the person who had called her, perplexed.

Harold from the leather goods stand stood at his entrance, his arm waving, motioning her over. He was tall, with wisps of sandy hair combed thinly across the top of his scalp, which showed though easily. His mouth was surrounded by a splattering of sand-colored stubble, a short goatee that was never quite there and never quite gone. His eyes were gray, so much like Ashley's.

Sarah stood before him, lifting her eyes to his.

"Where's Ashley?" he demanded brusquely.

"I have no idea," Sarah answered.

"Well, maybe you're telling the truth."

Sarah decided to offer no information. Perhaps he never knew Ashley had asked to go home with her. She stood quietly.

"You know she disappeared."

"You mean, completely?"

"Yeah."

Sarah bit her lip, said nothing.

"How much do you know about her?"

"Not much. We talked a few times. She's nice."

"Well, I'm going to warn you now. Stay away from her. She's bad news. She's addicted to alcohol. Does drugs. You wouldn't think it, but she's a mess. Can't handle life."

Sarah lifted her chin. "You could help her. She said you hate her."

Harold became a changed man. His face whitened, he stammered, and became extremely uncomfortable. Then he did his best to hide his discomfort by laughing, a rocky snort lacking any kind of true mirth.

"Ah, you know how teenagers are. They all think their dads hate them. She's just a kid."

Sarah faced him squarely. "She's troubled about a lot of things. Her boyfriend, Mike, for one. And for some strange reason, these barn fires that have been cropping up really bother her. She's obsessed with them."

Instantly, Harold began rambling, his words falling over one another in his haste to assure Sarah that his daughter was mentally off with all the substance abuse, and she knew nothing of these barn fires, not one single thing. He finished with another warning.

"You stay away from her. Don't mess with her. She's…"

"Well, if she disappeared, I won't be able to," Sarah said stiffly.

Having spoken himself into a corner, Harold rambled on again, saying she'd come back, she always did, that's what he'd meant in the first place.

Sarah nodded, then moved on without saying good-bye, her head held high, her gaze trained straight ahead.

She'd just brush that Walters family off, forget she even knew they existed. Like a spot on a wall, they would be easy enough to wipe out of her memory, and she would be glad to be rid of them, someone else's concern, none of her own.

What Harold and Ashley Walters did or said was absolutely none of her business, and she'd take his advice and keep it that way.

From the produce stand, a husky, black-haired youth stopped hammering the board he was putting into place as he turned and watched the tall, lithe girl in the star-tling blue dress swing by, her movements swift and easy, reminding him of a deer, so soft, so graceful, and as lovely. He turned, slowly, and went back to work.

CHAPTER 16

WHO COULD EVER HAVE PREDICTED THAT THE arsonist would choose an evening when the roads were slick with freezing rain and snow to bend over his lighter and newspaper and bits of wood and start the diabolical little fire that consumed yet another poor farmer's livelihood?

Enos Miller was young, his mortgage payments on the old Hess place high. But with his wife's frugal spending habits, good management, and careful planning, they'd made it through the first five years.

Annie had born him three children. Blessings from above, he called them. His quiver was well stocked with the three little souls God had *be-shaed* (given) them. His days were filled with hard work, and he enjoyed the fruits of his labor, anticipating the time the children would work side by side with him, building a secure foundation of tradition and trust.

They'd put the baby, Ben, to bed and covered him with an extra blanket, the sound of pinging hail on the north bedroom window calling for warmer covers. Then they knelt side by side by the foot of the high, queen-sized bed and bowed their heads as Enos prayed the German evening prayer and Annie kept her mind on his words, repeating them silently.

Annie had extinguished the kerosene lamp with a quick puff, and together they cuddled beneath the comforter brought from the cedar chest she'd received from her parents, lined with the sweet smelling wood, the flannel patchwork retaining the scent of cleanliness and home.

He kissed her goodnight, told her he loved her, then fell into a deep, restful sleep, the grateful slumber of a weary man after a hard day's work. He'd commented to Annie before he fell asleep what a good feeling it was to be finished cleaning out the box stables just as this rain turned to ice.

It was the baby's coughing that woke Annie, sleeping with her senses alert, the way young mothers do.

By that time, the fire had reached the horse stable, where the driving horses had been tied to keep them warm and dry, out of the harsh elements that night.

Annie was bewildered by the banging at first, then terrified by the high screaming of the panicked horses. She flung the bedroom door open, rushed to the hall window, and beheld a sight she would never forget.

She called to her husband in panic, her voice coming from deep in her throat, hoarse and primal, a cry of complete disbelief.

Enos felt the horror before he saw it, fumbling with his clothes, crying out, croaking words of defeat in Pennsylvania Dutch as he pulled his shoes blindly onto his bare feet. He stumbled, slid on the ice, fell, crying out again and again as he made his way to the barn, yanked open the door, and was met by a wall of raging fire, consuming the air he had given it.

The hellish situation encompassed his senses and imprinted into his memory, the smell of burning cowhide and the black smoke, the screams of his animals in indescribable pain and suffering, the icy rain pelting his back, the red-orange inferno driving him back, away from any attempt at saving even one cow, one calf, one horse.

Still sobbing, he slid across the gravel driveway, his mind clearing enough to propel him toward the phone shanty set halfway out the driveway between the poplar tree and the wagon shed.

Just as he reached the shanty, his feet gave way on the dangerous slickness, and he fell hard on his hip, saved from a mean break by the youthful resilience of good strong bone and muscle. He crawled, then pulled himself up by the handle on the door, wet, shaking, his teeth chattering. He directed the fire trucks, giving the address, 177 Heyberger Road.

Everything moved slower that night.

The cinder trucks went ahead of the fire trucks as the township worked together with the local fire companies to allow them access to the Enos Miller farm, set back on rural roads, around turns, up hills and down, every inch of the roadway slick with ice and snow.

Mercifully, the two oldest children slept through the worst of it, their angelic little faces turned toward each other in the safety of the room at the top of the stairs, covered with a heavy flannel comforter. It was one of the ones Annie's mother, Sadie, had knotted with her sisters that day, after they found out there would be a new baby, at the age of forty-six.

The baby had settled down with his pacifier, and Annie

was grateful for that as she stood inside the front door, alone, crying helplessly. She watched their hopes and dreams consumed by roaring flames, disappearing into the wet, icy atmosphere in great black billows of smoke.

Annie was quick-witted and intelligent. She remembered the last time she'd paid the fire tax. It had come in the mail, stating the amount they would owe, the Amish method of paying for their own catastrophes at times such as this.

Yes, God would provide.

As the flames leaped and danced and licked the night sky, she felt the safety of their heritage, a net designed by caring individuals, their hands intertwined to form a safe haven of care. At the root of it was God's love, the kind human beings could only obtain from a heavenly father and rely on to make life better for one another.

So she remained calm when the fire company could not respond immediately. She opened the door to call Enos and was grateful when he came up on the front porch, away from the pelting ice and rain.

She comforted her husband, fulfilling the duty of all wives, being a helpmeet, a bolster to her beloved in this time of need. He slowly regained his composure before he heard the wail of the fire sirens down on 896.

"*Ess mocht sich* (It will be alright)," Annie said, and he knew he had never heard sweeter words.

Yes, they would make it. Everything would be alright.

That statement, however, did nothing to prepare them for the days ahead, the unbelievable loss buried in the wet, blackened, stinking pile of debris. When the rain finally stopped and the cold, merciless sun shone through the clouds, it illuminated the remains of things that tore at Enos with claws of pain.

The hay wagon had been his grandfather's. His dat had given it to him, smiling, pointing out the heavy oak boards worn smooth by generations of men toiling in the hot summer sun. Now it was reduced to twisted steel wheels.

The feed cart and the wheelbarrow had both been repaired, used long past their primes, but they had served as beacons of Enos and Annie's careful planning, their balancing of a meager budget.

As always, the help arrived with horses pulling gray and black buggies, the iron clad hooves ringing in the icy wetness, the mud splashers hanging between the buggy shafts and catching all the bits of grey ice and mud before they slid off and fell back onto the road.

They disembarked, these men dressed in black doubleknit coats and black felt hats, their black trousers tucked into tall, rubber muck boots, their hands encased in brown work gloves, their ruddy faces alight with kindness yet again.

Women came, too. They turned, reached under seats, pulled out long aluminum cake pans or Tupperware containers of pies or cookies. They brought Walmart bags of crackers and pretzels, cheese and bologna, whatever they could find in their refrigerators or cellars, raiding their own pantries with hands driven by generosity.

They clucked about all the mud tracked into Annie's clean house, asked earnest questions, their eyes birdlike, inquisitive, wondering how the fire had started on a night like that. And Enoses living on a hill the way they did. *Ach* my.

The carpenter crews arrived in pickup trucks, big four-wheel drives with heavy caps on the back, carrying electric tools and portable generators. Youth came wearing stocking caps and dressed almost English, but they had kind, sympathetic faces and respectful attitudes, Enos told Annie later. He had to give them that.

The children had caught the flu. They were feverish, whining their discomfort, as the house remained perpetually cold and muddy with the doors opening constantly. There was no rest for Annie.

She carried on, dutifully performing every task that needed to be done, received boxes of food, cooked along with the women, washed clothes, nursed the baby, rocked her cranky little ones, and tried to look for the good in everything.

Dat heard of the fire in the morning from the milk truck driver.

He was grave, his face lined with the bad news, his eyes concerned, knowing this fire would stir the dreaded pot of loud opinions, determination, the rumblings of retaliation that were always voiced by those who thought along the ways of the worldly.

Over and over, Dat stressed the importance of staying pure from the world, which meant not only dressing modestly and living a simple life but having attitudes and goals that were not worldly. He truly believed there were plenty of worldly men dressed in Amish clothes, secure in their displays of righteousness, but who harbored attitudes of gain and selfishness, even *schadenfreude* (pleasure at the misfortune of others), and were as worldly as if they drove around in Mercedes Benzes and dressed in brilliant hues.

But humans were just that, human, and he offered up patience and forbearance as well, striving to live by example, aware of the immense job at hand, especially at a time such as this.

He ate his fried eggs and sausage, finished his dish of rolled oats and shoofly pie, drank his steaming mug of coffee, and said he'd be glad if Sarah could accompany him, if Mam was busy at home.

Sarah nodded, willing to go, although a bit pensive, sad that her last market day had been cancelled because of the ice and snow. Well, she'd visit occasionally, or substitute if she was asked. She'd now have to accept the market days as a time remembered.

She dressed warmly and put on her new wool, pea coat and wrapped a warm green and beige plaid scarf around her neck. Then she carried out the boxes of food Mam had prepared yet again.

She loosened the latches on each side of the buggy and lifted the back on its hydraulic hinges. She loosed the seat back and swung it to the side, lifted the seat bottom and placed the cardboard boxes underneath. Running back to the kitchen, she picked up her coffee cup, the lime green to-go cup that had been a market favorite. She said goodbye, then dashed out to help Dat hitch up Fred, who was already pawing the ground, eager to get started on the long trek to Georgetown, nearly ten miles away.

How could such a beautiful, glistening world be marred by another tragedy?

Dat remained quiet, his eyes sad, his black felt hat lowered to hide that very question.

Sarah sipped her coffee, remained quiet alongside her father, and was startled when he spoke, his voice gruff and loud.

"It wouldn't be as hard if these hotheads would calm down. And I really am afraid your cousin Melvin is behind a lot of it. He seems to be building momentum, becoming even more verbal and aggressive as time goes on. We may never find out who this arsonist is. Never."

Sarah nodded. "But isn't it dangerous, going on this way?"

"No lives have been lost. When that happens, we'll take action."

"But you don't want to wait that long."

Dat nodded, then turned to smile at Sarah. "Do you have a plan?"

Sarah laughed and stuck her elbow in Dat's side. "Of course not."

In companionable silence then, they rode the rest of the way, enjoying the display of ice and powdery snow melting in the early winter sun. Bare branches were transformed into works of art, red berries on low-growing bushes popping with color among the dark brown branches covered with glowing ice.

Giant yellow trucks clanked past, the chains on the huge wheels rattling, shoving slush and spreading salt or cinders, allowing folks all over Lancaster County safe passage to their jobs or errands.

Fred didn't seem to mind the trucks, and he stayed steadily on course when they passed, although he always picked up his head, his ears flicked backward, then forward.

"Remember George?" Dat asked once.

"Yes. That horse was crazy!"

Dat nodded.

George had been a perfect horse, trotting swiftly, steadily, until he met a truck or tractor, anything large or noisy. Then he shied so badly they often ended up in a field or up a bank, narrowly missing telephone poles or fence posts. Eventually he had to be sold, Dat proclaiming him an accident waiting to happen.

Sarah was sickened by the sight of the smoking remains of the barn, her face losing its healthy color as she struggled to gain some sense of understanding.

It was always the same. How could Dat remain so passive about this? Rage coupled with determination brought two bright spots to her pale cheeks, but she said nothing.

So what if Melvin was worldly? Nobody else was trying to do anything to stop this senseless display of blatant hate.

Sarah didn't know Enos and Annie Miller, but they were young, Amish, and in need. And since their own barn had burned to the ground, just like this one, that was reason enough to want to help.

She was met at the door by a buxom older woman who smiled at her and asked if she needed help. The woman grabbed the cardboard box and lumbered into the house with it, calling over her shoulder that if there was more, she'd help.

Sarah winced as the woman stepped off the porch, wearing no coat, stepping solidly on the slippery steps without fear, her dark eyes alight with interest as she moved along with surprising speed for her bulk.

"Here. Give it. Just put the other one on top."

"It's too heavy," Sarah protested.

"I think not. I got it."

She hurried back, bearing the heavy boxes, and Sarah shrugged, raising her eyebrows at Dat.

"I think she's Shteff's Davey's Sam *sei* Edna."

Sarah nodded, allowing Dat the impression she knew exactly who that was, when she actually had no clue. Dat knew a lot of people.

Sarah met Annie Miller for the first time that day. She

was the sweetest, most loving person she'd ever seen. She was in awe of this cherubic human who moved among the women, quietly instructing, accepting, helpful, ministering to her three whining babies, the way Sarah imagined very few young woman could do, especially given the circumstances.

The young girls who had arrived first were put in charge of cleaning out the implement shed, a workshop of sorts. It was cold and very dirty, a place Sarah could not imagine being hospitable to serving food.

A handful of girls she did not know accompanied her, but they soon introduced themselves, put a straw broom in her hand, and set to work.

A group of young men had moved the plows and baler and a wagon. Shop items were moved against one wall—a table saw, a press, a drill—and covered with clean plastic.

Sarah leaned her broom against the wall, wrapped her arms tightly around her waist and shivered, surveying the dusty mess.

Outside, the revving of diesel engines could be heard in the distance. Men shouted, horses stamped their feet.

A tall, black-haired youth peered through the door. He was handed a shovel by another youth Sarah didn't know. "Come on, Alan. Make yourself useful."

The black-haired one grinned. His voice was deep and low and rough, making him sound much older than Sarah judged him to be. His teeth were very white, his smile wide and attractive. My, Sarah thought, then unwrapped her arms and set to work.

The banter flowed, girls sneezed and coughed, guys set to work cleaning the old cement block chimney. Someone brought in a woodstove, attached a stove pipe, and in no time at all there was a roaring fire to ease the biting cold.

Sarah swept, helped unroll plastic, plied a slap stapler, and became very aware of the black-haired youth's whereabouts. She knew when he left and when he returned, but her face remained guarded and uninterested as she worked in earnest.

They soon had a reasonable space to serve food, so they set up folding tables and covered them with lengths of plastic tablecloth. The women decided to serve sandwiches and soup, since the crowd would be much bigger in the coming days.

Large kettles filled hamburger mixed with onion, ketchup, mustard, brown sugar, salt, and pepper were set on the roaring wood stove, along with kettles of chicken corn soup and one of ham and beans. Cakes, pies, and puddings appeared, as did hungry men, blackened, already showing signs of strain, the usual good will marred by an impending wall of disagreement.

Before the afternoon had waned, Dat appeared and told Sarah he was preparing to leave. Without further words, he nodded to the women and left.

Sarah was puzzled but shrugged her shoulders, went to the house, and grabbed her purse.

She looked around for the youth who had gotten her attention, but he had evidently left as well.

Oh well.

Dat was curt, his eyebrows drawn to a tense line, goading Fred as if he needed to get as far away as possible from Enos Miller's, and fast.

This was so unlike Dat. Sarah felt a wave of dread close its talons around her sense of optimism.

Everything would be alright, eventually. Everything.

"Dat?"

She spoke hesitantly.

He grunted, never taking his eyes off the road.

"Didn't you always feel that everything works together for good to those that love God?"

It was like a knife through her heart when trails of tears slid down Dat's cheeks. He placed the leather driving reins between his knees, leaned to the left, and dug around in his pocket for a handkerchief, before blowing his nose, wiping his cheeks, and replacing it with a solemn shake of his head.

"I have, Sarah, I have. But I'm not sure we can claim that promise anymore. How can we love God if we can't love our own brethren?"

Sarah nodded.

"I'm just afraid the time is fast approaching when the lessons we could learn from these fires are turning into bitter lessons, hard to tolerate. We're headed into a black abyss of hate and fighting."

"That's a strong word, Dat."

"What else is it? Unbelief? Unlove? That's only a nice way of saying the word hate. God cannot bless us this way. I'm deeply concerned, and I blame Melvin. He needs to be stopped."

Sarah cringed, thinking of Melvin. Dear, noisy, outspoken Melvin. Opinionated, yes, that too. Still she felt sorry for him.

Melvin meant well, that was the thing, and he was just sure the arsonist could be caught red-handed, by his cunning, his ability to outsmart anyone else.

Wherever Melvin went, groups of men surrounded him, slowly began nodding, seeing things his way, which, in Dat's opinion, was the world's way—to go after the arsonist, offer no second chance, no forgiveness, just slap him in jail, and let him suffer till he's sorry.

At the supper table, Dat scolded Levi harshly for upsetting his glass of water, Levi cried, and Mam's mouth turned down, taut, her disapproval unspoken but stamped on every feature.

As Sarah had experienced, things that seem so awful often turn into hidden blessings, twinkling little lights set everywhere to lighten the burden of plodding pilgrims, moving forward on the road of life.

Dat had a meeting with Melvin, one on one, which must have created a newly discovered humility in her normally brash, outspoken cousin.

Sarah sat at Lydia's kitchen table early the following evening, feeling lonely, frustrated, and in need of advice, turning once again to the pleasure of having a true friend. She unwrapped her second whoopie pie, a pumpkin one. She had already devoured a chocolate one. She chomped down on it, groaned, and peeled back more of the Saran Wrap.

"Mm! Seriously, Lydia."

Lydia laughed. It was a new sound, like rolling, babbling water, as if the happiness had to tumble over rocks to be released. Likely, it did. Her heart was probably like a rock, but it was finally breaking, softening.

"You need to start a bakery."

"I know. But I couldn't, with the cows. And now the horses. Omar is so busy, and Anna Mae is so attached to him, everywhere he goes, she's there, too. In fact, Sarah, I'm afraid she is experiencing her first dose of attraction to that Lee Glick who spends so much time with Omar. Sarah, he is so awfully nice and good-looking and sweet and good."

"I know."

"Is he single?"

"No. He's dating Rose."

"Matthew's Rose?"

Sarah nodded, finished the pumpkin whoopie pie, balled the Saran Wrap tightly, and threw it in the air.

"Yep! She always gets them!"

Lydia giggled.

There was a knock on the door, and Melvin appeared, dressed in one of the bright-colored shirts he favored, his eyes luminous, soft, his face quiet, relaxed.

"Hey!" Sarah said, glad to see him, hoping Dat had gone easy on him.

"Sarah! Why aren't you at home? You aren't even ready. Hi, Lydia," he added, turning to give her his full attention.

"Hello!"

Lydia looked up at Melvin, her smile wide and genuine, and Sarah told them both she did not want to go anywhere—not even to the Sunday youth supper. The air was cold and damp, and she was tired out from working at Enos Miller's. Besides, the following day was her first day of school, and she did not want to lose any sleep if she could help it.

Melvin nodded, then reached for little Aaron, who seemed completely at ease, being lifted from Lydia's lap and placed on Melvin's.

Melvin pulled on his hair, teasing him, and Aaron howled with delight.

CHAPTER 17

THE EVENING DISAPPEARED MAGICALLY, THE THREE of them talking, sharing thoughts, feelings, discussing the barn fires, Melvin showing a type of humility Sarah had never seen.

"All I can say is that if as much good comes to Enos Millers as I have experienced, I think they can honestly say the Lord has delivered them with a mighty hand," Lydia said shyly, her eyes averted.

"Yeah," Melvin said slowly. "I guess I have to keep my mouth shut. Davey really raked me across the coals. He's the only guy I know who can do that and make it appear as if he's not hurting you. That guy just has a way about him, he does. He sure did show me the error of my ways, got me back on the straight and narrow."

Lydia's eyes were a revelation to Sarah, the look she gave Melvin bordering on worship. "Oh, what I would have given, years ago, to hear Aaron say those exact words. He just...he couldn't see it."

"You've been through so much, Lydia," Melvin said, the emotion in his words thick, as if tears were pressing against the back of his throat.

"I have. But God has been more than good. I have so much. And I'm learning to say I am blessed and stop thinking I don't deserve any of it, as the counselors say."

Melvin watched Lydia, and when she met his eyes, there was so much tenderness in them, Sarah had to look away. She suddenly felt like an intruder and pondered the power of attraction for some people, but just not for her.

She and Melvin had helped Lydia clean up the kitchen after the children were in bed. Sarah watched as she hovered about him, two bright spots of pink on each cheek, her eyes dancing, laughing easily, even touching Melvin's arm when she needed his attention.

Oh, how Sarah longed for something that remained elusively out of her grasp. She knew it but was helpless to change the path she had made for herself. Her own stubborn refusal to let go of Matthew, when everyone she knew had tried to warn her, had broken her heart. Now he was gone, and when Sarah ignored Lee, he had started dating Rose.

Miserably, she shared this new insight with Melvin and Lydia, who both nodded wisely, agreed. They said they supposed the right one would step out of the woodwork one of these days.

But Sarah was sure now that the right one would never come, or come again. Lee had told her that he was in awe of Rose. Everyone was in awe of Rose, she'd wailed to herself later in the privacy of her room. She was just too awesome, apparently.

Now she spoke of it, of that insecurity, to her two dear friends, and was encouraged, lifted up. She ate another whoopie pie and drank way too much coffee and could not go to sleep when she wanted to, the caffeine, the conversation with her friends, and her anxiety about teaching keeping her awake long after she had intended.

She longed for a life companion but felt she needed to accept that it wasn't for her. And that was alright for now. She was on her way to making a giant leap right into spinsterhood anyway, embarking on her teaching career in less than eight hours.

Sarah had never experienced the word inadequate before, but that was the only true description she could think of as she stood behind the teacher's desk the next morning, stoked on more caffeine and false bravado.

The classroom was damp and cold, the colorless artwork peeling away from the walls, the gas heater stubbornly refusing to ignite.

She'd punched the igniter button so often, it was only a matter of time until the whole stove exploded in her face.

She didn't know who the caretaker was, vaguely remembering Lee mentioning Ben Zook. Well, she wasn't traipsing through the cold to fetch Mr. Zook, as she was pretty sure Lee would be in the barn and find her very un-awesome, unable, and stupid, not being able to light the gas heater on her first morning.

She jumped when the door latch rattled and was yanked open by a very small, very fat little girl, her round face red from exertion and protruding from her tightly-tied head scarf like a beet.

"Good morning!" Sarah trilled, too high, too loud, and a little too quickly.

When no answer was given, Sarah cleared her throat and tried again, thinking perhaps she hadn't heard.

"Good morning!"

The little girl yanked on her head scarf, jutted out her

chin, and said loudly, "It's cold in here!"

"I'm sorry. I can't get the heater started "

"Martha could."

"Well, I don't know how."

Instead of giving Sarah the satisfaction of an answer, the little girl placed both hands on her desk and glared at her, a belligerent little beet topped with unruly red hair.

The doorknob turned again, revealing a horde of head scarves, navy blue bonnets, straw hats, and multi-colored beanies, every last child wearing a black, homemade coat.

"Good morning!"

No one bothered answering, so she repeated her greeting, and was ignored again. Sarah immediately thought of the man in the Bible who sowed his seed and some fell by the wayside and withered in the hot sun.

"It's cold in here."

"That is because I can't get the heater going."

"Martha could."

Irked, Sarah said forcefully, "Yes, well, I'm not Martha. This is my first day, so how can you expect me to know how?"

A boy of about twelve gave her a look of surprise, turned to his classmates, and snickered, which started a wave of snorts and mocking sounds, which Sarah chose to ignore.

Two more boys entered, the one taller than Sarah, his face pocked with angry, red pimples, his glasses riding low on his prominent nose.

"What's wrong with the heater?" he growled, before Sarah had a chance to say good morning.

"I can't get it started."

Saying nothing, the boy padded to the stubborn heating unit, turned a dial, punched the igniter button repeatedly, and was rewarded by a low whoosh of flame.

"Oh, that's great! Awesome! Thank you!" Sarah said, meaning every word she said.

The boy blushed furiously, ducked his head, and shuffled back to the cloakroom, his hands stuffed nonchalantly in his pockets. His companions taunted him as he passed them.

The fourth time the door opened, the upper grade girls entered, and trouble walked solidly into Sarah's life.

Tall, pretty, wearing flashy colors, their arrogance showed immediately. Their postures spoke loudly of their possession of the entire school. All four of them.

Sarah felt the color recede from her face, and she swallowed as her mouth turned into sandpaper.

"Good morning!"

The girls looked at one another, raised their eyebrows, hissed behind the barricade of their palms, and snickered in a manner so annoying it set Sarah's teeth on edge.

"Good morning!" she said again.

"We don't say that at Ivy Run," the heavy-set blonde girl said, her voice commanding everyone's attention.

Sarah considered this statement for a few seconds, then asked how they did greet each other.

"We don't greet."

That brought hysterical giggles from her three companions and a braying from the older boys.

Wildly, Sarah looked at the clock, her courage slipping away by the minute. Time for the bell.

Would they go to their seats as expected, or would they say they don't sit down at Ivy Run?

Help me, please, she begged her Lord.

She stalked very firmly to the rope in the back of the room and gave it a hard yank, adjusted her cape and stalked back, placing her feet firmly on the tile floor.

Reaching her desk, she tapped the small bell repeatedly. Nothing happened, the laughing and talking and milling about continued as if they hadn't heard any bell at all. What would she do if no one sat down? Scream and cry and grab her new lunch box and book bag and go running down the road, toward home, blatantly admitting defeat?

Slowly, one after another, the children folded themselves reluctantly into their desks, eyeing her with different levels of curiosity or rebellion, depending where she looked.

"Good morning, boys and girls!"

Only the lower graders mumbled in response. The upper graders refused to greet her, sitting obstinately in their desks, all eyes watching this new teacher.

Taking a deep breath, Sarah opened the worn Bible to the ninth chapter of Luke, stood, and began to read, her voice low, carrying well, resonant, the shaking subdued by sheer force of will.

As she read, her voice gained more strength, and she looked around the classroom, her eyes catching the upper grade boys raising their eyebrows, followed by exaggerated eye-rolling.

Tap. Tap-tap. Paper crinkling. Rustling. Feet scraping. A book hit the floor with a loud bang.

Sarah stopped reading, said nothing.

Slowly, children sat up, their eyes questioning, watching, waiting.

"As soon as everyone quiets down, I'll resume reading from the Bible."

Nervous giggles were accompanied by more feet scraping, more crumpling of paper. A small boy flipped a book closed with a loud bang, his eyes challenging Sarah to do something about it.

She stood, relaxed, and said nothing.

Someone coughed. Another pupil dropped a pencil, then looked around for smiles of approval he was sure to gain by his lack of obedience.

The heavyset girl raised her hand, clearly intending to fix this new teacher with words of rebuke.

"Yes?" Sarah said.

"You can't expect the room to be quiet. Duh!"

It was the duh that provoked Sarah to the point that she spoke firmly, her nostril flared, her gaze withering.

"I certainly can expect the room to be quiet. When the Bible is being read, it is only respectful to ask for quiet."

There was no answer, only a shocked silence.

"Now, I have to ask you to place both hands on your desks, and keep them there until I'm finished reading this chapter in Luke."

The children looked around, checking with their peers to see if it was acceptable to obey this new teacher who spoke so clearly and forcefully.

A few lower grade students put their hands on their desks, hesitantly, their expressions bordering on fright.

The upper grade boys shifted from left to right, sat on their hands, smiling widely, their eyes challenging her.

The upper grade girls giggled dutifully.

The middle grade students copied the maneuvers of the older ones.

Slowly, Sarah closed the Bible, took a deep, steadying breath, and announced her intention in a clear, careful tone.

"Alright, then. We'll close for the day. You may put your things in your desks and prepare to go home to your parents."

A small, dark-haired boy raised his hand.

"I can't," he quavered, and then a heart-rending sob filled the air. "My...my...." His sobs cut off the words he wanted to say.

Waiting, Sarah watched the school's reaction. The sneers and raised eyebrows melted into uncertainty, leaving mixed expressions of half-hearted attempts at mockery. They were unsure how to handle this.

Going to the small boy, whose huge brown eyes filled with anxiety and the weight of being sent home to an empty house, Sarah put an arm about his shoulders, saying it was alright.

Sniffing, he put his hands on his desk. The lower graders followed suit, followed by a few of the older pupils.

"Thank you to those of you who are obeying. The remaining ones are dismissed."

A few more hands were placed on tops of the desks.

The older pupils remained in their seats, sitting on their hands, but they made no move to leave.

Sarah returned to her desk and stood behind it, still waiting. Again, the heavyset blonde raised her hand.

"We can't go home."

"Why not?"

"Well, just because. It's a school day."

"Will you place your hands on your desk then?"

"No."

One of the upper grade boys raised his hand.

"Yes?"

"Martha never made us do this."

"Martha isn't here. I am your teacher now."

"Really?"

The word was spoken with one intent—to make fun of her, and Sarah knew it. The blatant disobedience was far worse than she could have anticipated, and her heart pounded with fear. Was she taking this too far? Was it only a power struggle, her determination to prove her own superiority? She couldn't go back on her word now.

"It's up to you. If you will please obey, just this one small thing, I'll resume reading, okay? Then we'll go from there."

Her heart sank to a miserable depth as six upper grade pupils got up and went to the rear of the classroom. They noisily got down their outer wear, banged their lunch boxes in anger, slammed the door till the schoolhouse seemed to vibrate, and huddled in a dark group of rebellion in the schoolyard.

Steadying herself, Sarah finished reading the chapter, then stood with the now reduced number of children, steadily repeating the Lord's Prayer with very little help from any of them.

Sarah was no longer accustomed to saying this prayer out loud, so she stumbled over "Give us this day our daily bread," but she moved on, grateful to be able to remember just in time.

She passed out the homemade songbooks, brilliant plastic covers on sturdy binders, the pages encased in plastic, the songs typed neatly on the pages.

Someone had worked hard to supply the school with these good, strong songbooks. Perhaps it had been Martha, enthused, anticipating a successful year, only to fail so pitifully. Sympathy welled up in Sarah, and she realized she was as vulnerable, as unable to carry on successfully as Martha had been.

Sarah smiled now, as the pupils seemed hesitant, the singing class punctuated by empty spaces, leaving the class incomplete, little rows of strong white teeth with too many missing.

"Please stand together, share a songbook with the one nearest you, and let's sing page 47. I remember that song from my own school years."

The singing was pathetic, Sarah finally admitted to herself, after starting a clear rendition of "I'll Fly Away." She sang alone with only a few quavering, half-hearted attempts made by the lower grade girls.

Mostly, the pupils stood like angry little bees, their eyes bold, alert, watching her as warily as hornets protecting their nests and as ready to sting. The songbooks flopped in colorful disarray, some of them unopened, held belligerently to chests, clearly showing the students' unwillingness to participate in any form of song.

Well, she couldn't fix everything the first morning. She'd stood her ground about the Bible reading, so she'd pretend the singing class was not out of the ordinary.

After the children were seated back at their desks, Sarah introduced herself, then asked the children to wear the colorful name tags she had made with the number of each student's grade written in bold black beside their names, to make it easier to remember this first day.

No one seemed to mind, so Sarah pressed them to small shirtfronts and black pinafores, colorful dress fronts for the little girls who wore belt aprons pinned around their waists with sturdy silver safety pins.

"There!" she announced, smiling.

Ben Zook had two children in school, a little boy in third grade named Marlin, and Marianne in second grade. Sarah smiled to herself. Marianne resembled a much smaller version of Anna, her energetic little body as round as a barrel, propelled on two very small feet that were perfectly capable of carrying her swiftly wherever she needed to go.

Standing behind her desk, she told the children her name was Sarah Beiler, and she would be their teacher the remainder of the year, hopefully, if everyone would be willing to work together with her. There would be new rules, new ways, and she proceeded to read the twelve rules she'd set for the school.

A hand was raised, then another.

"Yes?"

"That's a stupid rule, about putting our hands on our desk when you read the Bible."

"You think so? Why?"

"It just is."

"Why?"

"We didn't used to have to do it."

The speaker was a fifth-grade boy named Chester, his hair as brilliantly inclined to a fiery, golden red as that of his sister Elizabeth—Liz for short—the fat, belligerent first arrival.

"I know. But it's very distracting to read from the Bible when all that noise is going on. It's unnecessary, annoying, and so I won't allow it."

"We gotta do it every morning?"

"Every morning."

Another hand was raised.

Roy, a sixth-grader, his straight brown hair hanging all the way into his eyes, shook his head as if to rid himself of the offending curtain of hair before telling Sarah that was when he learned his memory verse, when Martha read the Bible.

"Sorry, Roy. You'll have to learn the verse at home."

"I don't have time. I have to do chores, eat supper, and go to bed."

"Really? You must have an awful lot of chores, eat a long supper, and go to bed very early."

A few smiles accompanied this statement, a spark of interest shining from a number of eyes.

Arithmetic classes began with the first grade, the dark-haired little boy named Mark, a willing and eager student. Lena Mae, a small, thin girl with a perpetual frown and a pinched, weary look about her face appeared much older than her six years. Sarah wondered at the strain showing on the pale face.

Reuben and Kathryn made up the rest of the first grade, both brown-haired, quiet, and afraid to speak, which Sarah knew came from the lurking attitude of sarcasm that hovered over the classroom like a rotten stench.

Sarah had reached fifth-grade arithmetic when she heard a rapping on the front door and caught sight of two of the eighth-grade girls standing behind two older women, their faces boding no good.

Well, so be it.

Sarah went to the door, her knees almost losing the ability to carry her until her hand reached the doorknob, a much-needed source of support.

"Hello."

"Hi. Can you come out on the porch for a moment?"

The voice held no friendliness, but wasn't quite full of anger either.

Sarah stepped out, leaving the door open, the pupils turning in their seats to see what was occurring on the porch.

Ruth Stoltzfus was Rosanna's mother. She was short, squat, and clutched her sweater tightly around her waist, her brilliant red dress matching the high color in her cheeks.

"What is going on?"

Before Sarah answered, the taller, angular mother behind Ruth nodded her head, her eyes snapping, her mouth turned down in a stern frown. Sarah imagined a snapping turtle wearing a black bonnet but dismissed the thought immediately.

"I asked the pupils to stop making noise while I read the Bible for devotions. When that didn't work, I asked them to place their hands on their desks."

"Whatever for? I never in all my life heard such a thing. That's way too strict. You can't send children home from school because of such a little thing. I mean, who would listen to such a ridiculous rule?"

These words were forced from the angular mother's mouth, the frown bobbing up and down as she spoke, the nodding head of Ruth Stoltzfus accompanying the words of her friend.

The two eighth-grade girls watched Sarah, triumph an ill-concealed victory they claimed more fully with every word their mothers spoke.

"What should I have done?"

There was no answer immediately as the mothers looked at one another, then to the victorious daughters, before sputtering, shaking their heads.

Finally, the tall one with the black bonnet spoke. "Well, you wouldn't have had to go to such drastic measures. It's simply unnecessary. They wouldn't have HAD to put their hands on their desks. Being sent home is serious business."

"Yes, I agree. But if I'm supposed to teach Ivy Run School, we need to be able to understand each other. If you would like to know what needs to happen in this school, then we'll have a parent teacher's meeting on

Friday evening.

"If you won't attend, then you may as well take your girls out of school now. Putting their hands on their desks is only the tip of the iceberg, believe me."

After the last pupil had disappeared down the road, walking or propelling their scooters homeward, Sarah sank into the swivel chair, leaned back, and folded her hands on her stomach. She propped her elbows on the cracked vinyl arm rests with tufts of white fibers protruding from them, and she knew this day had been the beginning of the end.

She'd already failed, and it was only her first day. The mothers were right. She'd been too strict.

Love never fails, and she had reacted to disobedience with a hard, angry stance, a refusal to back down, and now all was lost. She'd be so ashamed. The only girl in Lancaster County who'd taught school only one week before having to give up.

Well, she also held the dubious title of being the only girl whose fiancé had run off to Haiti and married an English woman as well as the title of being the one caught in a web of intrigue as far as Ashley Walters was concerned. She'd failed her, too.

CHAPTER 18

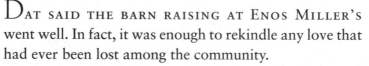

DAT SAID THE BARN RAISING AT ENOS MILLER'S went well. In fact, it was enough to rekindle any love that had ever been lost among the community.

It was the overwhelming number of men, the orderly manner in which things occurred when each one was willing to take instructions from the seasoned older men who had directed the raising of many barns before this one, that reduced him to a lip-quivering, tear-filled man of gratitude.

The weather had been unusually fine. The mud and debris had all been shoveled onto a blackened, odorous heap that would continue smoking for days.

The sun warmed them as they erected the skeleton of the building. The fresh, yellow lumber smelled of hope and faith yet again for Dat.

Opinions had been shelved for the day of the barn raising, as the charity among them built a shrine to love in action, a kind of holiness about the building that didn't allow gossip or hating or backbiting.

Dat was inspired, rejuvenated, his faith in his fellow-men firmly entrenched.

In his mind, he chose to look for the good in each one, tolerate the opinions that he didn't agree with, and live each day trying to look at the world through the eyes of a benevolent Savior.

"If God has so much mercy on us—each day it's fresh and new—then we need to acknowledge this same mercy for our *mit and neva mensch* (fellowman)."

As he spoke, the family was still seated at the supper table, Levi at his right, Mam at his left. The old doubleknit tablecloth covered the oak extension table and was laden with Mam's Corelle dishes. The serving dishes were now half empty, containing mashed potatoes and beef gravy and corn and buttered noodles. Smaller glass dishes held applesauce and coleslaw, and one had only a bit of red beet juice covering the bottom, the last red beet egg having been speared by Levi, salted well, and enjoyed with great relish.

The evening sun was casting deep shadows in the corners of the large farmhouse kitchen, so Mam got up and flicked a lighter beneath the propane lamp in the oak cabinet, illuminating Sarah's face and highlighting the misery that had been her day.

Levi, as always, trumpeted the news headlines, having head every detail from Sarah herself, as she wailed out her disastrous day, alternating between complete refusal to think her teaching career was salvageable to fighting for her own way, refusing to accept failure. It was alright for Dat to give this whole *schtick* (piece) about love and looking for the good in each person, but she simply couldn't run a classroom on love. That was all there was to it.

"*Die Sarah wahu un heila* (Sarah was crying)!" he

announced with importance, snapping his suspenders for emphasis.

Dat looked at Sarah sharply.

"You were crying? *Ach* my. And I completely forgot to ask you about your first day at school. Was it really that bad?"

"Every bit," Sarah said, nodding. She proceeded to relate her entire day in her own words, Dat listening carefully.

"So now you have this parent teacher's meeting Friday evening, right?" he asked finally.

"I guess. I don't know. Mrs. Turtle—oops!"

Sarah clapped a hand over mouth, her eyes already begging Dat's forgiveness.

"What?" he asked, grinning as he dabbed at a few spots of grape jelly on the tablecloth.

"Oh, one of the mothers looks like a snapping turtle."

Levi looked sharply at Sarah, then burst out laughing. Suzie snickered, then joined in, and Priscilla grinned widely, enjoying Sarah's description.

Dat remained sober, and Sarah was chastised by this alone. "You say the whole school is infested with mockery and sarcasm. I think perhaps some must have found its way home."

He told Sarah, then, that to expect perfection had been drastic. In disbelief, shame so acute she visibly squirmed in her chair, she listened as he told her in soft tones that he had experienced this type of uprising many times as a minister. He was expected to lead but often found that serving was the better approach.

"What you did, we would all like to do, but it was a huge bite for your first day. I wish you the best, having this parent teacher's meeting, but don't be surprised if not too much is accomplished. Your goal is to get those children to want to obey your rules."

"It's impossible!" Sarah burst out, on the verge of tears.

"Go halfway. Go to school in the morning, and see how many hands are placed on their desks, see how long it goes until they feel awkward, sitting on their hands. They can't do much, with their hands under their...um... backsides."

Mam shook up and down, her eyes twinkling.

"But Dat, they're so disobedient. So openly *fa-schput* (mocking)."

"That didn't start overnight, and it's not going to go away overnight. Try and win them. Stand firm."

"I just want to quit."

"I've wanted to quit many times. These past few years have probably been the hardest ever, with the differences in opinion where the barn fires have been concerned. Now a group of ministers thinks anyone who talks to reporters should be *schtrofed* (chastised), and I think that's a drastic measure."

"Like the hands on the desks."

"Afraid so."

Dat looked at the clock and rose to do the evening chores, whistling under his breath as he pulled on his boots.

"Oh, I forgot to tell you all. That Lee Glick that's helping the Widow Lydia's Omar with his Belgians? He was driving a mare double with that half-trained stallion. It was a sight, I tell you. Every head was turned when they drove into Enos's with a load of hay. I've never seen a neck on a Belgian like that. He sure does have a way with horses. I think he must be a special person, the way that Omar looks up to him. Not often you see such adoration."

Side by side, Sarah and her mother washed and dried dishes, discussing the school day as the land around them settled into darkness. Yellow squares of light appeared at the cow stable windows as the diesel purred into action, providing power for the milking machines and cooling the fresh, warm milk poured into the gleaming bulk tank in the milk house.

Levi sang loudly as he resumed shuffling his Rook cards, and Suzie came banging through the *kesslehaus* door, filling a bucket with hot water from the hose attached to the wall, faithfully doing her chores, feeding the new calves.

Mam shook her head when Sarah asked why Suzie didn't get her hot water in the milk house, so she let it go. Perhaps she was much more controlling that she knew.

She swiped viciously at a burnt pan, added a few sprinkles of dish soap, and attacked it once more, before rinsing it beneath the faucet and stacking it in the dish drainer. Then she leaned back, her hands propped on a corner of the sink, lowered her head, and shook with laughter.

"So, this is how my spinsterhood begins. I have to have you and Dat to set my priorities straight. Seriously, I'm so ashamed."

"Oh no, Sarah. Please don't be ashamed. You're so young. We learn by our own mistakes. Everyone does. Some learn faster than others, but we learn, eventually."

"What would I do without my parents?"

Sarah slid an arm around her mother's waist, leaving a trail of white suds, and her mother wrapped her in her arms, holding the red and white checked dish towel behind Sarah's back.

In the background, Levi sang, "We'll work, we'll work till Jesus comes, we'll work, we'll work till Jesus comes."

The clock struck six, steam rose from the teakettle on the coal stove, and Sarah knew she was blessed beyond measure.

As she packed her lunch the following morning, the world seemed like a better place, loaded with endless possibilities. It was amazing what a good night's sleep could do for her spirits.

She spread mayonnaise on a slice of whole wheat bread, layered Lebanon bologna, cheese, and lettuce on top, then added another slice of bread. She shoved it into a Zip-loc bag and turned to find a small container to hold some bread and butter pickles. Another bag of potato chips, a few carrots, and one small molasses cookie went into the insulated pouch, and she was done.

Today she was wearing a dress the color of her eyes, a deep sage green. She pushed up the sleeves as she prepared her lunch.

She'd wear her Nikes and accompany the children to the playground, if she could cajole them into playing an organized game.

She had never seen children huddled in individual groups without playing a single game at recess. She guessed it wasn't considered cool to play games, and some of those pupils surely could use some physical exertion.

The job was monumental, no doubt, but her energy motored along, fueled by a healthy breakfast of granola, vanilla yogurt, and a sliced banana. When her driver showed up, she ran out to the waiting vehicle, waving briskly at Dat, who stood at the door to the milk house.

One by one, or in groups, the children sidled through

the door, watching their new teacher with varied degrees of suspicion or curiosity.

No one answered her round of good mornings, but with Dat's advice intact, she could let it go. The upper graders slouched in various positions, their desks suddenly a place to display any outlandish way of sitting they could devise.

She chose to ignore that, knowing they were baiting the trap. Get the teacher mad and we have the upper hand, they seemed to say.

"Good morning, boys and girls!" Her voice quivered, straightened, steadied.

The murmurs were low, somewhat garbled, and came mostly from the first and second grade, as two upper grade boys flashed mirrors, combed their hair up over their heads, turning the mirrors to view the results of looking English.

Sarah began reading the Bible, as she had done the day before, asking no one to put their hands on their desks. Timidly, a few first graders placed them on their desktops, the little knuckles white from clenching them so hard.

Bewildered, unsure, the remaining students looked around, lifted eyebrows, mouthed questions. Their hands remained in their laps or hung loosely at their sides as they were unsure exactly how to proceed.

But it was quiet—clock-ticking-on-the-wall, beautifully quiet.

They stood and repeated the Lord's Prayer, Sarah stumbling over the same passage, a few more pupils reciting along with her than the day before.

Singing class was a study in disorganization. No one stood straight or even tried to put any heart into the song, so Sarah asked if they would like to learn new songs instead of repetitively singing the old ones.

No one bothered to answer, the girls' eyes half-closed with boredom, the boys much too cool to notice the fact that she'd spoken at all.

That set the tone for the whole day. Disinterest, rebellion, outright anger, refusal to accept rules, probably everything that could have gone wrong did.

At the end of the day, her shoulders ached from being held stiffly in place, her right ear was throbbing seriously, and the beginning of a major headache was hovering somewhere in the region of her right temple.

Not once had any child spoken respectfully to her.

The games at recess hadn't happened, the boys informing her the only game they played was baseball, and it was too cold for that.

Sarah suggested Prisoners Base or Colored Eggs, which brought such a display of mockery that Sarah dropped the whole idea.

Many students failed their lessons, scoring percentages below sixty-five, and refused to tackle the list of do-overs, so that at the end of the day, Sarah lay her arms on her desk and sobbed great tears of defeat and remorse. She wished she'd never started this impossible task. She wasn't cut out to be a schoolteacher. Unqualified—that was the word. And she still had that daunting parent teacher's meeting to live through.

When the doorknob turned, she wasn't afraid, figuring one of the students had forgotten a book or a paper. Then she seriously considered dropping on her knees and crawling under her desk, where she would stay till Lee Glick went away.

Why? How could he pop into her classroom unannounced? Her curly hair was completely out of control, her eyes were sore and swollen, her face blotchy, her nose red from wiping it repeatedly, and there he stood, dressed in clean, casual clothes. No work clothes this time.

"Sarah?" The word was a question, an inquiry with a polite, kind tone carrying it.

"*Ach* Lee. I…" Helplessly, her hands fluttered to her face. "I'm a mess."

He strode toward her desk, and she lowered her eyes. She felt him standing behind her chair and stifled a gasp as his hands came down on her shoulders.

"You look like you've had a rough day."

"Yep."

"May I massage your shoulders? Not in a …um…you know. I'm just a friend. Let me."

"Okay."

Whether it was right or proper was completely forgotten, the healing comfort in his hands restoring her sense of well-being.

She felt the headache dissipate, the sharp pain between her shoulders loosen, as his hands massaged away the frustration and hopelessness of the day.

"Feel better?"

He stepped back, flexing his fingers, and Sarah felt a sense of loss as sharply as any physical pain, accompanied by the absolute knowledge that he had no business being here in this schoolroom giving her a "friendly" massage. Lee was a two-faced deceiver giving her hope now, even though he was dating Rose.

She didn't answer, letting the waves of betrayal and anger take control.

He repeated the question.

Sarah faced him, her eyes golden at first, but they darkened by the first wave of unrest, then changed color again as the wave receded, leaving room for a swirling gray of emotion.

"No, I don't feel better, Lee. Just go away. Go away and leave me alone. You're Rose's boyfriend, and she's supposedly my best friend. You're in awe of her. You said so yourself. So just go. I'm sick of tagging after Rose Zook. I'm sick of…"

Her face crumpled, and she began crying quietly, her head lowered, her hands coming up to her face in one graceful movement.

Her future had been long and cold and barren before. She could take it again. If she just looked at it once and accepted it, gave herself up to it, in Mam's words, it would be alright.

It was just unfair to have Matthew living in Haiti with his wife, and Lee dating Rose, and Melvin finding far more than he had ever dared to hope, a situation turning into the sweetest love story Sarah ever hoped to attain.

But it was not alright that Lee was here. She grabbed a Kleenex from the box on her desk, turned her back, miserable and ashamed.

Again, she felt him behind her, his hands encircling her shoulders. She could feel his breath, like the wings of a butterfly.

"Sarah, I came to tell you, I broke off my friendship with Rose."

Sarah remembered seeing the words "broken arrow" on the blackboard, where she'd demonstrated the adjective broken describing the arrow. The feeling of rapture began in her feet, but it all came together, filling her entire being with music, subtle, soft, cymbal-crashing, drum-beating music, all at once.

She couldn't face him. Not now.

"I can't forget you, Sarah. I'm not being honest with myself or God if I continue dating Rose. Half the time, I'm thinking of you. It's been that way since the day I saw you at your barn raising. I know I don't have much chance. I think you are the kind of girl who loves only once, and you certainly..." His voice faded away.

So Rose had been right! She knew, too.

"Say something, Sarah. Anything."

The space of a heartbeat, the length of eternity—she didn't know how long she waited, until, slowly, she turned, her eyes downcast, standing before him, mysteriously unable to tell him everything she wanted to say.

"It's okay. I'll give you time. I probably should have waited longer. I know you're not ready. Maybe you never will be. You have this thing about spinsterhood."

In spite of herself, Sarah smiled, a small, trembling grin that slid away before she met his eyes.

His gaze was blue, so magnetically blue, and for long moments she was lost in the beauty of meeting his eyes without thoughts of Matthew wedging their way between them.

She understood the meaning of giving herself to a man. It was almost spiritual, the way they stood apart, allowing their eyes to convey what their spirits already knew.

"I'll wait," he whispered.

Sarah nodded. "Yes."

"We need to be sure. We need to...."

Brokenly, still saying words that made no sense, the music in her ears completely erasing any speech, he reached for her, brought her against his chest with a sigh of longing, a repressed love, and held her there, her heart beating against his, an ageless symphony of a love announced, examined, accepted.

"Sarah."

She was afraid that if she answered, the spell might break, so she said nothing. She wanted to stay in the safety of his arms, her heart beating in unison with his.

"Sarah?"

It was a question now, so she tried to step back to see the question in his blue eyes, that haven of safety, but his arms did not release her.

"Does this...does us being together mean anything to you?"

In answer, she lifted her face, raised herself only slightly, and touched her lips to his, to that wide, kind, perfect mouth.

Her touch was no more than a whisper, a breath, but it was her way of assuring him that, yes, he had a chance, that as long as their hearts beat strongly, she would be there for him.

When she pulled away, his grip tightened. He lowered his face, and his firm mouth sought hers again, until the room spun and she pulled away, a soft laugh breaking them apart, unthinkable to him, but so necessary she knew.

"Does that mean...?" He was smiling, but his eyes were dark with longing, tortured by the years she had always been just beyond his reach because of Matthew Stoltzfus.

"I should not have done that," she murmured, low and soft. "I don't know what got into me."

"Sarah, don't. Don't feel guilty."

"I don't want you to think I'm bold, or brazen, or... you know."

"I have never been as close to anything that I imagine

heaven to be, as when you kissed me. It was unreal. I still can't believe you just did that."

He touched his lips with his fingers, shook his head, and gave a soft laugh, barely loud enough for Sarah to hear.

Softly, her hands rested on his shirtfront, and she asked if it was alright to wait awhile. It wasn't proper for them to begin dating now.

"I can't wait. It seems as if the minute you're gone, this will be one long dream, and I'll wake up knowing I can never have you. How are we going to see each other? Just not get together, ever?" he asked suddenly.

The raucous honking of a car horn brought them rudely to reality, and Sarah searched wildly for her book bag and the red pen she wanted to take home.

"My driver. Oh my goodness. I wonder how long she's been out there."

Lee reached for her again.

"No. Lee, oh, we can't. Not now."

"When can I see you?"

"Don't come to my house. You just broke up with Rose. I…Melvin goes to play…um…Scrabble at the Widow Lydia's, so…you're there sometimes, right?"

"Yes! With Omar!"

"Don't let on."

"I won't."

"Bye."

"Bye, Sarah."

She locked the door behind them both, and he untied his cold, impatient horse. She rode away looking straight ahead, and he had an awful time of it getting into his buggy, his horse standing on his hind legs and pawing the air with his front hooves, coming down in a flying leap with Lee only half in the buggy, scraping his shin painfully on the cast iron step.

He decided he needed to spend more time with this crazy horse and less time with Omar Esh and his Belgians, until he remembered what Sarah had told him and his heart swelled with emotion. His head in the clouds, he pulled out in front of a gray Toyota with an irate driver behind the steering wheel, pumping his fist in the general direction of the buggy.

Mam had a fit. Only the second day of school and here was Sarah, her despairing daughter, suddenly bouncing into the house, her eyes alight, pink blossoms in her cheeks, her smile wide and genuine, her face glowing.

"Teaching certainly suits you today," she commented.

"Yes, Mam. It does. So much has gone better today."

Sarah began a vivid account of the Bible reading, the quiet, the newly acquired sense of accomplishment, completely pulling the wool over poor Mam's eyes.

Mam peeled potatoes, slowly gouging out any sprouts or black spots, and thought seriously that Sarah might actually remain an unmarried lady, an old maid, a spinster, choosing to live alone all her life and pour herself into her pupils.

Well, it wouldn't be too hard on Mam's pride. After all, single women were a blessing in a community—as schoolteachers, storekeepers, and they often helped out after a new baby arrived. The list went on and on.

Or she could marry a widower. She had a way with children. Imagining that, Mam cried furtive tears into the muddy water in the dishpan.

Wouldn't that be a touching day? she thought. Sarah so sweet, such a light to the community. Now that Priscilla was different. She liked her boys.

CHAPTER 19

THE NIGHT OF THE PARENT TEACHER'S MEETING arrived, in spite of Sarah's panic. Most of the parents attended, stepping through the entrance to the classroom with serious expressions, greeting one another gravely, brows furrowed.

This was serious business, a meeting called the first week of Davey Beiler's Sarah being the new teacher. They'd heard she was a go-getter, not afraid to speak her mind. Well, she'd better watch it.

The school board had come early and heard Sarah's grievances, which were mostly due to a lack of respect from the students. Then they opened the meeting with a moment of silence, stated the reason for the meeting, and allowed Sarah her time.

"I'm sorry for making everyone leave their work just to come here tonight, but I truthfully don't believe any of you have any idea how bad the attitudes of the students really are."

She let that statement rest where it might, before plowing through the stares of hostility, disbelief, and some of outright rebellion.

She described her first day in detail, her father's advice, and her willingness to work with the parents, but if she had no help from them at home, she may as well leave now.

All in all, the meeting was a surprise hit, the men especially agreeing with Sarah and the school board, the women whispering in the cloakroom afterward but coming to tell Sarah they wanted to know if their children were not behaving.

How could a teacher describe students who weren't really misbehaving but whose characters were soaked with the poison of rebellion and a lack of discipline, enabling them to freely voice their disrespectful opinions without conscience?

But it was a start.

Ben and Anna Zook stayed long after the last parent had gone through the door. They sat in the upper grade desks and shared their thoughts and opinions, the *frade* (joy) they'd felt when they heard Sarah would teach and the hopelessness of poor Martha Riehl, which hadn't been entirely her fault.

Anna was as little and round as ever, barely fitting into a school desk, her hair and covering neat as a pin as always, Ben smiling and nodding at all his wife's antics.

They were slowly coming to grips with the fire that had destroyed their old barn and were accepting of it now, although Ben had to see a doctor and take a good antidepressant for more than a year.

"He just couldn't handle some of the things, the financial part, mostly," Anna concluded, clucking like a protective little biddy hen.

"I couldn't have pulled through without Lee. Her

brother. He's something else. He has a talent for planning ahead, then seeing that the work gets done. He was a real pillar of strength for me."

Sarah acknowledged this bit of information with a dip of her head.

"Well, such is life," Anna remarked. "It goes on, gets better with time. Barn fires aren't fun, but you get a new barn in the end. It looks nice, our barn does. I like the color of the metal siding. It's cool."

She smiled a genuine smile of pleasure, including her husband in its brilliance, then announced the fact that she was hungry. Why didn't Sarah go along home with them and she'd make stromboli?

"At ten o'clock?" Sarah was incredulous.

"Shoot. I could eat stromboli, easily," Anna announced happily.

"Come along home, Sarah," Ben urged.

"No, I can't. Mam would worry. I'd have to call my driver, and there's no telephone here. No. Maybe some other time."

After they'd gone, Sarah was vastly relieved, in spite of the temptation. How could she and Lee have hidden their feelings from Ben and Anna? Could she have pulled it off?

She had asked the driver to pick her up at ten thirty, which meant she had another half hour to wait.

The night was warmer than the previous ones, so she turned off the propane lamp, locked the door, and sat on the cement porch steps listening to the night sounds, watching the half moon in the star-filled sky, listening to the whispering of the wind in the willow tree down by the fence.

She heard singing, didn't she? Or was it the willow tree playing tricks with her senses? There it was again.

High, a bit reedy, but a voice singing.

Headlights loomed of the darkness, putting the fence, the privy, the willow tree in plain sight. The singing stopped as the car slowed.

There were voices, a car door slammed. Then a high shriek, followed by a man's angry voice.

The wail of despair that followed tore at Sarah's heart, and she rose from her seat immediately and walked toward the sound before deciding it wasn't worth the risk. It would be foolhardy, putting her life in jeopardy.

A car door slammed again.

Sarah cowered by the brick wall of the school as a figure hurtled through the night, feet pounding the pavement, followed by desperate shrieks.

"No! No!"

How could she just stand against the wall and listen to that?

Sarah ran toward the open gate, calling, "Does anyone need help?"

The vehicle sped up again and then screeched to a stop. A dark figure leapt out and grabbed the fugitive, hauling him or her into the car as Sarah stood, afraid to intervene, afraid to step outside the boundaries of the schoolyard.

The small white car was not a Volkswagen. That was all Sarah knew for sure as it careened past, tires squealing, leaving her standing along the rural road watching it speed away.

It could have been Ashley. Who else would be in trouble around here, followed by a small, white car?

Another barn had burned to the ground, and the Amish still just sat, taking all the hatred and violence, bowing down, and saying, "Thy will be done."

Sarah was so upset when she walked into the kitchen at home that she strode purposefully to her parents' bedroom door and rapped smartly, her heart thudding in her chest until she heard her mother's muffled voice.

"Can we talk?" she hissed.

"Of course."

Bed springs creaked as her parents left their warm bed and appeared at the kitchen table where Sarah sat, the lamp lit, the teakettle heating on the gas burner.

Her parents slid into kitchen chairs, their eyes wide with worry, and Sarah immediately launched into a vivid account of the runaway person, the small white car, and the fact that they never did mention Ashley Walters to the police. What if she was in grave danger?

"Dat, you know she is!" Sarah burst out.

Dat nodded, listening, stroking his beard with a large calloused hand.

"But you don't know if it was Ashley, do you?"

"No. But I have a feeling."

"So you suggest we call the police and tell them everything we know?" he asked.

"Yes. Ashley knows something that bothers her terribly. I really do think she knows who is starting the barn fires. It's just an intuition, a hunch, but as time goes on, it becomes more clear. You know that rude guy who came to the door? When we were canning pumpkin? He warned us to stay away from Ashley. Her father, the man at the leather goods stand at market, said the same thing."

Dat pondered Sarah's words.

Mam rose when the teakettle's whistle pieced the air, unhooked three mugs from the wall, dropped a tea bag into each of them, and poured the hot water.

Long into the night, they reasoned among themselves,

Dat pulling in the direction of passivity, Mam steering toward finding out more of Ashley Walter's lifestyle, and Sarah leaning heavily toward Melvin's way of thinking.

"You know, Dat, someone is going to get hurt, or even killed. At first, everyone in the whole Amish community was afraid. After a while, we relaxed. Then there was another fire, we rebuilt, and the rage and fear and everything else just flooded in again. It's a vicious circle without an end. The barn fires are not going to stop until this person is caught. And I feel as if we know enough to try and do something about it."

"But is it right?" Dat asked, after a long pause.

"What do you mean, is it right?" Sarah asked.

"Our forefathers would not have fought in a war, neither would they have gone to court, or hired a lawyer to defend themselves. We are a nonresistant people. If a man smites one cheek, give him the other. If he asks you to go with him one mile, go with him twain," Dat quoted quietly.

"And if a man burns your barn, give him a bunch more to burn!" Sarah exploded.

Mam burst out laughing, and Dat smiled hesitantly.

"It's only common sense, Dat. This last fire just got my blood boiling. I mean, here is this humble couple, never hurt a flea, live their lives as best they know how, deny themselves anything wasteful or frivolous. You'd think God would smile on them always, but some lunatic creeps through the night and lights their barn. Why wouldn't we want to help them, Dat?"

"It's not our way, Sarah."

Mam raised her eyebrows, watched her husband's face, and kept her peace.

"I'm afraid if we try to put the law on Ashley, we'll be

raking in a whole load of trouble we didn't bargain for. We surely don't have much evidence."

Defeated, Sarah bade her parents goodnight and went to bed, frustrated, still committed to finding out what she could about Ashley. Dat was too old-fashioned, always bringing up that old forefathers thing.

Remembering Lee, she touched her fingers to her mouth, smiled softly, let the light of his eyes soothe her, and fell into a sweet and restful slumber.

A few days later, Sarah was shocked to see Ashley Walters when her school driver stopped at a Turkey Hill market for gas, the needle on the gauge of her old Chevy hovering just above empty.

Sarah's lips were chapped, a brand new cold sore popping up, so she ran into the small store to purchase a tube of Blistex. She stopped short when she saw the unmistakable profile of the thin, tormented girl behind the cash register, her hair falling forward as always, a curtain to shield her from the harsh realities of life.

Should she reveal herself? Or turn and leave?

Ashley was as shy as a wild deer, and Sarah desperately wanted to avoid spooking her. She didn't have much time, so she found the Blistex and walked boldly toward Ashley with what she hoped was a welcoming expression. Ashley's eyes met Sarah's before a wave of fright opened them wider, but she struggled to calm herself and remain professional.

"Hi."

"Hi, Ashley. How are you?"

"I'm okay. Back with Mike. We're good."

"I'm just so glad to see you. To know you're okay."

"Yeah. Well, that'll be a dollar and seventy-nine cents."

Sarah handed her two dollars, accepted the change, and was dismissed coolly when Ashley said, "Next," to the customer behind her.

"See you soon," Sarah said hopefully.

Ashley waved a hand while addressing the lady behind her.

Ivy Run School had turned into four brick walls of challenge, literally.

Once Sarah understood that the parents were not actually against her (except perhaps Mrs. Turtle), she caught her stride and dove headlong into each new day, making subtle changes that surprised her as the pupils allowed the changes to occur.

Bible reading remained a quiet, devotional time, and gradually more of the pupils spoke the Lord's Prayer. She introduced new songs, which didn't do much to increase the enthusiasm for singing class, but it was a start.

The first day she mentioned a game of baseball, the loud jeers and boos infuriated her, and she firmly told the intimidating upper graders that it was either baseball or staying in their seats.

"I'd rather stay in my seat," Steven Zook growled, slouched in his desk, his huge feet splayed disrespectfully in the aisle, a fine powder of brown dust surrounding them from the dried mud.

"Yeah. Who would, like, WANT to play baseball?" Rosanna chirped triumphantly, daring Sarah to challenge the rules Steven and she had created.

"Me," Sarah said.

"Well, good for you."

That day, Sarah made a deal. Whoever would participate in a game of baseball would get five points, and five hundred points would mean a field trip.

Of course, they all mocked the field trip. Who wanted to go traipsing across some farmer's pasture dodging cow patties to hear a few sparrows warbling?

Sarah swallowed the hot anger that rose like bile, threatening to choke her. She was terrified to feel a warm wetness in her eyes as a lump of defeat settled over her.

Unexpectedly, a quavering voice announced, "I'll play."

"Elam! That is seriously wonderful! Great! So, we have Elam and me. We can play batty in and batty out, unless we get more volunteers."

Hesitantly, two more hands went up—the sixth-grade boys, Christopher and David—followed by one fifth-grade girl.

That first day, there were seven players, and they played a dreadful game of Round Town. The students missed balls and struck out, not one of them skilled at the ageless game of schoolyard baseball.

The remaining pupils lounged around the porch or the horse shed, ate their endless snacks from Ziploc bags, jeered, tripped the little ones who dared venture close, and, simply put, did their best to make recess miserable for anyone who didn't hang out with them. Sarah chose to ignore them.

All through the month of November, recess remained the same. Sarah could barely control the urge to swat the two eighth-grade boys with the baseball bat.

The weather turned cold and damp, and still they kept playing. The lower graders established themselves, playing kickball with the good soccer ball Sarah had purchased, their cheeks rosy from the cold, their eyes snapping with excitement and good health when they crashed through the front door, whipped off their coats and scarves and beanies, and slid into their desks when the bell summoned them to their seats.

On the day when Sarah announced they had accumulated five hundred points, her eyes shone with anticipation.

"That is so exciting!" she said, speaking as if the entire school had participated.

"Our field trip will be a tour of the Strasburg Railroad Museum and a ride on the train!"

A great cheer rose from the pupils, especially the lower graders.

"For lunch, we'll go to my house, and my mother will make stromboli."

Another enthusiastic roar greeted this announcement, and Sarah dared peek sideways at the disgruntled upper graders who had refused to play and would not be joining the field trip. She found varying degrees of embarrassment, remorse, and a watered down mockery, perhaps.

"I have a brother, Levi, who has Down syndrome, and he will have a surprise for everyone as well."

"What's Down syndrome?" Reuben asked.

"He was born with a handicap. Years ago they called these people retarded, but he's just a little mentally and physically challenged. His mental capacity is about the same as an eight year old's. But he's so excited when the school comes to visit."

Rosanna raised her hand, her lower lip protruding petulantly. "What are we going to do?"

"You'll have to stay home that day."

Sarah actually felt sorry for those who had refused to play baseball. The jeering and rebellion suddenly felt as if it was running low on fuel, sputtering, dying but still gliding along, an airplane with no fuel gauge, unaware, above the clouds.

"That's against the rules. You can't make us do that."

"We'll see."

After third recess, Rosanna marched to Sarah's desk, leaned across it, and said briskly, "If we play baseball from now till you go, can we go, too?"

"What do you mean by we?"

"We. Everyone else. All the upper graders."

"Let me think about it."

Rosanna's eyes were a mixture of arrogance and shyness, which was so encouraging that Sarah burst through the door, threw her book bag on the table, and yelled for Mam the minute she got home.

Sarah missed two weddings in the month of November, refusing to allow a substitute access to the fragile foundation she had built so far.

The weddings were for distant cousins, relatives on her father's side who she wasn't well acquainted with, so she didn't feel too bad when she decided against going.

She thought of Lee constantly, wondered if he'd ask to take her to the supper table, the Amish tradition where the bride and groom coupled their friends for an evening of food and hymn-singing.

She saw him only from a distance on weekends, averted her eyes when he did come close.

Rose cornered Sarah, of course, one of the first weekends after Lee broke off their friendship, wailing unhappily about life's unfairness, and what was she supposed to do now?

They were seated side by side on the small sofa in Barbie Ann Smoker's bedroom. Her parents, Levi Smokers, had arranged to have the supper for almost 150 youth.

Sarah admired the solid oak bedroom furniture, the

double windows dressed in purple drapes, the matching floral comforter, and listened sympathetically as Rose rambled on.

Rose had lost weight. Her face was pale, her cheekbones etched sharply against the rich purple of the window coverings.

She was even more beautiful, her large, blue eyes limpid with sadness and misery. Her dress was a powdery blue, matching the color of her eyes, and Sarah could truthfully say she was astounding.

"I should have kept Matthew. I miss him now."

Sarah exhaled a derisive puff of air.

"Tell me about it." The words tumbled out before Sarah could recapture them.

"You really did love him, didn't you?"

"Oh yes. Definitely. I loved him all my life."

"I know. You loved him even when I dated him."

"No."

"Yes, you did."

"I know."

They burst into giggles and then became hysterical. Sarah held Rose's thin form as she cried pitifully against her shoulder. Sitting up, Rose sighed and blew her nose, before a fresh wall of tears tumbled down the porcelain face.

"We'll just be old maids. Buy a market stand. Sell doughnuts. Or make hoagies. Have a deli. Weight three hundred pounds and enjoy our lives."

"Immensely," Sarah nodded.

"No pun intended," Rose said sourly.

Then they became hysterical again, and Sarah decided a friendship like theirs was rare. It had withstood the ravages of unstable relationships with Matthew, gossip, and attractions to Lee. But would it be able to survive if Lee actually did begin a serious friendship with Sarah after allowing the proper span of time to elapse?

What if Lee was just another Matthew? Hadn't Matthew been fiercely attracted to her that day at the Beilers' barn raising? But nothing had come of it, really.

Sarah was consumed by fear and dread, the thought of Lee being untrue or insincere rendering her motionless.

"Sarah, did you know that your eyes turn dark when you think something deep or disturbing?"

"Do they?"

"Yeah. You have such a golden look about you. I often think of you that way. Your eyes and your skin sort of match your hair."

"You mean I look like a dog or a cat?"

"Oh now, stop!"

That day their friendship was cemented once more, the camaraderie between them a solid, binding thing.

Rose could not have known about the moment Lee found Sarah's eyes, and for long seconds, one yearned for the other, the attraction equal, complete, leaving Sarah in a fine misery afterward, pulled in two directions by her loyalty to Rose, her feelings for Lee. Why was life always so complicated?

Through the cold night air, Sarah walked alone, searching for Melvin's buggy after the supper. Suddenly a tall figure appeared beside her.

"Looking for a ride home?"

She stopped, turned.

"I'm Alan Beiler. I think I saw you at Enos Miller's, right?"

"Oh yes. Yes, I was there."

"Hello."

The hand that was proffered was large, firm, cool to her touch, and she looked up into two dark, dark eyes with a warm light in them.

"I'm Sarah. Beiler. Same as you."

"Yeah. Your dat's a minister. We're not related. Well, maybe fourth or fifth cousins. I checked the Fisher book."

Sarah was flattered. He'd checked the Fisher book. That announcement was pretty serious. Often, if a young man was interested or curious or attracted to a young girl, he only had to look up her family in the Fisher book, a recording of every family in Lancaster County and the surrounding areas.

"You need a ride?" he repeated.

"No. My cousin, Melvin, is around here somewhere."

And Sarah was suddenly relieved that he was.

CHAPTER 20

A BLEAK, WINDY SATURDAY IN DECEMBER FOUND Sarah walking into the Turkey Hill on Route 340, determined to talk to Ashley.

No one knew she had gone except Mam, who believed the story Sarah had given her about going to Country Cupboard for prizes, little objects to be handed to her pupils when they deserved a reward.

She tied Fred securely, blanketed him, and wrapped her coat tightly around her shivering body as she walked to the door.

It was better than she'd hoped. Ashley was on her knees, stocking shelves, and there was a glad light in her eyes.

"Sarah!"

"Hi, Ashley."

"It's good to see you."

"I came here to talk to you, Ashley. I really would like some information. Can you...do you have time?"

Ashley looked at the clock on the opposite wall.

"A few minutes."

They stepped off to the side, allowing a customer access to the coolers, and Sarah took stock of her friend's face, the healthy glow, the wide eyes, no longer hooded, frightened.

"You look good."

"I am. I'm in a good place in my life. Mike is really straightening up, and we're better. I'm better. Actually, Sarah, I want to thank you for everything you've done for me over these past few years. You saved my life, really. I want you to know I'm grateful. You know, like, appreciative."

"I didn't do anything," Sarah said.

"Oh yes. Yes, you did."

"Can I ask you one question, please?"

"Sure."

"How much do you know about the barn fires?"

Ashley stood still, her eyes averted, the shapeless sweatshirt hiding her thin figure, her fingers clutching the bands of the long sleeves.

The door opened and closed, the cash register whirred quietly, voices mingled, and still Ashley remained quiet.

Finally she sighed.

"A lot, Sarah. Way too much. It has to end, I know. In the past, I was afraid. I'm not anymore. It's weird, but I don't care anymore. He can just kill me. He threatened to many times. But his…"

"Ashley!" A large, buxom woman called from the register, her eyes snapping, her arm motioning Ashley over.

"You're needed on the other register!"

There was nothing to do but leave. Sarah walked by the register, waved, and was astonishingly rewarded with a genuine smile from Ashley who put her hand to her mouth, then flung it outward, a kiss thrown with a quick smile of love and friendship.

"Thanks!" Sarah mouthed, then hurried out of the market and dashed across the parking lot.

Deep in thought, she loosened the nylon neck rope and swept the heavy horse blanket off Fred's back with one swoop. She grabbed the reins and made a short turn, the steel rims of the buggy wheels grating against the cast iron roller on the side of the buggy, strategically placed to allow such turns.

Straining to see, holding Fred to a standstill, she waited patiently as the line of cars crept past. Then she loosened the reins and chirped, urging him out onto the busy roadway, the main route between Lancaster and the village of Intercourse.

Christmas wreaths, roping, holly, doors decorated for the season—houses everywhere were decked in holiday finery, Sarah observed. A wonderful time of the year, she thought.

Sometimes she wondered what it would be like to decorate a tree or hang a wreath or string bright lights along the eaves of a house. Keeping the Plain tradition, these things were viewed as frivolous, unnecessary, but Sarah enjoyed them on English houses, nevertheless.

She was always glad for the gifts they gave and received, the Christmas cards they sent, the cookies and treats they made, keeping the spirit of Christmas alive in their simple, Amish way.

Happiness was doubled for her, thinking of Ashley's recovery, the light in her blue-gray eyes.

Well, the problem wasn't Mike, her boyfriend, evidently. Who had threatened her? Surely not her father.

She watched absentmindedly as four mules pulled a manure spreader over the half frozen ground, their ears bobbing randomly, flopping up and down as their heads moved in time to their steps. The manure spewed out of the rattling spreader, inexpensive fertilizer for the fields, a boon for next year's corn crop.

Fred plodded along, slowing as they neared Bird-in-Hand, trying to veer off the roadway onto a side road leading toward home. Sarah had to open the window and slap his rump lightly with the reins.

"Come on, Fred. You're just lazy," she called, then closed the window and snapped it shut, satisfied when Fred changed his gait to a brisk pace.

She wiped the top of the wooden glove compartment with a gloved hand, opened the door only a crack, and shook out the accumulated horse hairs.

In winter, the horses' coats grew thick and heavy. The loose hairs somehow found their way into the smallest openings, clinging to lap robes and purses and gallons of milk or containers of food or plastic grocery bags.

At the Country Cupboard, Sarah greeted the cashier, then placed a few small tablets, packets of erasers, key chains, balloons, anything she imagined would please the children into her basket.

She thought wistfully of having a Christmas program but immediately changed her mind, knowing she had a long uphill road to travel before that was possible.

She picked up a package of clothespins for Mam and a few dishcloths, then stood in line at the cash register.

"Hey, Sarah."

Sarah turned to see Hannah, Matthew's mother, directly behind her, her eyes bright with interest, but a certain wariness in them as well.

"Hannah! My, it's good to see you. I miss you. You never come to the house anymore to see Mam."

"Oh, Sarah. I know. Too many things happened between us. Too many."

Sarah nodded as tears came unbidden.

"Matthew's coming home!"

Hannah leaned forward and whispered, her eyes shifting, making sure no one overheard, as if Matthew's appearance, his return from Haiti, would be heralded with the same welcome as a tornado or some other natural disaster.

"Really?"

"Yes. He's coming alone. His wife is ill."

"Why would he leave her then?"

"Oh, she has her parents, he said."

"I guess."

"Yes. She's really close to them."

"That's good."

"Come visit when Matthew's here."

"Why would I?"

"Well, Sarah, you're friends. You're good friends. He'll want to see you."

Sarah's face reddened. She said goodbye, exiting the store as quickly as possible, blindly loosening the neck rope, almost driving directly into a parked mini-van.

No, we're not friends. I am still Matthew's broken-hearted girlfriend, a recovering love addict. The sight of him would be enough to make me relapse completely.

Hannah would never understand.

It was on the front page of the *Intelligencer Journal*, the Lancaster daily newspaper. It was on the local radio station, on CNN and Fox News, but of course, the Amish people didn't know that. Only the ones who received the daily paper scanned the article, clucked, and shook their heads at the girl's young age.

Only twenty, they said. *Hesslich shaut* (Such a shame).

There were no alcohol or drugs involved. Ashley Walters had been flown to Hershey Medical Center, air-lifted after a horrible wreck, the small, white Honda she was driving folded like an accordion beneath the stainless steel tank of an oncoming milk truck.

She died there, alone, only a few minutes after she arrived at the vast hospital.

Sarah found out when she came home from school. She listened, openmouthed, as her mother brought her the daily paper. She crumpled immediately onto a kitchen chair, her head bent over the paper, one leg folded beneath her.

"Oh, Mam!" she wailed after she finished reading the article. Mam stood behind Sarah, a hand on the back of her chair.

"You don't think she did it on purpose?"

Sarah shook her head as tears streamed down her cheeks. "No, no. Absolutely not. The last time I spoke to her she was happier than I've ever seen her. I just can't grasp this."

Levi was saddened by Ashley's death, saying it really was *unbegreiflich* (unbelievable). He asked to be taken to her viewing, if Dat and Mam would take him.

Sarah wished Ashley had not been so alone when she died. She hoped fervently she had been conscious of nothing after the wreck. Sarah couldn't eat her supper, couldn't fall asleep, thinking of Ashley hitting the underside of the unyielding tanker, so small, so innocent, so alone.

She threw back the covers and got down on her knees beside the bed, cupped her face in her hands, and stayed there, praying, even though she knew Ashley had already died. What sense did it make praying for her soul? But it was comforting, instilling a certain peace throughout her.

What had Dat said about Ashley?

God loved her, too. She was important to Him.

Sarah figured God cared very much about Ashley's soul and would take care of her, *fer-sark* her.

Who could tell what upbringing the poor girl had had? Her mother living thousands of miles away, her father threatening. Or had he been? Would they ever know?

Three evenings later, the Beiler family dressed in funeral black. Dat and Levi wore blue shirts, crisp, homemade, ironed carefully, their high-topped, black Sunday shoes gleaming, their felt hats placed securely on their heads. Mam wore her black shawl and bonnet, the girls their woolen pea coats.

It seemed like such a short time since Mervin's viewing had taken place, and now they reached out to whoever had loved Ashley, broken family or not. Death was a universal bond, grief a language everyone understood. No culture was unique at the time of a death, the sorrow keenly felt by those who had experienced it before.

They helped Levi into the van, using a step stool and steadying his shaking legs, Mam's hand on his back, Dat holding onto the stool in the cold, December wind, his *mutsa* (Sunday coat) blowing up as he bent over.

Levi grunted, pulled himself up, and sat heavily in the front seat, his eyes alight with bird-like curiosity, before asking, "Who is the driver?"

The name was supplied—Randy Stover, a man who was fairly new in the business of driving the Amish.

"Well, good evening, Randy. I'm glad to meet you. I'm Levi Beiler."

Randy smiled, politely exchanged pleasantries with

Dat, and listened carefully as Levi informed him he was going to the city of Lancaster and not to a dentist or doctor.

"Nothing's going to hurt this round, Randy," he announced, giggling jubilantly. Then Levi turned to his father. "Can we stop at McDonald's, Dat?"

When Dat gave no immediate answer, Levi informed him that the last time he had had a Big Mac it was summertime, hot.

Dat smiled and said alright, Levi, which satisfied his inquiry.

The city of Lancaster was a frightening place on a dark December night, even if lights illuminated every sidewalk and street corner.

The funeral home was a lavish, stone building on King Street, a fancy canopy erected over the front stoop, brick pathways winding between exotic shrubbery and trees.

The parking lot was empty, or almost, and Sarah's heart felt dark and heavy for her friend. Surely someone was there for her. Someone cared.

They helped Levi down from the high van seat, explaining patiently that this was a viewing, like Mervin's, and he had to stay nice and quiet. If he obeyed, they would buy him a Big Mac at McDonald's on the way home.

Silently, they moved as one. A small group of Amish people dressed in black, going to pay their last respects to a new acquaintance.

There was no one standing in line. A handful of people were gathered at the end of a long corridor, an open book on a gleaming wooden stand nearby. Heavy carpeting muted their steps, and Dat stood respectfully aside as Mam bent to sign their names.

He took off his hat then, carrying it by his side,

whispering to Levi to do the same. Levi had a steady look of concentration on his face, so Sarah knew he would obey perfectly, his reward a calorie-laden treat.

The coffin was set in a warmly lit alcove, a few bouquets of flowers set at attractive angles around it. Surprisingly, the coffin was opulent, lined with white satin, lavishly carved and decorated, a cascade of white lilies spilling across the top.

Sarah recognized Mike, who appeared extremely nervous, wild-eyed, as they approached.

A handshake from Dat changed that, a hand to his shoulder altered the look completely, as his face crumpled and he turned away, his shoulders heaving.

Instant tears welled up in Sarah's eyes as Dat stayed with Mike, speaking kind words of condolence to the distraught youth.

They moved on to greet the man and woman standing at the head of the coffin, shook hands, introduced themselves. Mam was pulled into the elegantly dressed woman's embrace, then each of the girls in turn.

Dat repeated his kind gestures to the man, who was dressed in an expensive suit, his face openly curious.

Finally, the woman introduced herself as Ashley's mother from Fresno, California.

"My husband, Andrew."

Sarah stood and looked at Ashley, lying so still and lifeless, her face patched together and barely recognizable to her.

So young, she thought as tears slipped down her cheeks. As they talked, Sarah was shocked to discover the couple was named Andrew and Caroline Walters, Ashley's true biological parents.

"You, you aren't separated?" she asked softly.

"No. Oh no. Ashley came to Pennsylvania for college. She was estranged from Andrew and me."

Caroline was suddenly overcome with emotion, dabbing daintily at her tears. "I know this sounds lame, but she literally got in with the wrong crowd. We talked sometimes, but the sad part is there wasn't much we could do."

They talked for awhile, the Walters longing to learn all they could about their daughter's last years. Then the Beilers stepped aside as a few people from the farmer's market made an appearance.

Where was Harold from the leather goods stand? He was the one Ashley had claimed was her father. Confused, Sarah turned to greet Tim, the owner of the farmer's market.

Tim then said hello to Levi, who watched his face with curious eyes, both hands clutching the brim of his hat. But Levi would not open his mouth to acknowledge Tim's greeting.

Bewildered, Tim asked Sarah if Levi was mute.

"No. Oh no. He was told to be quiet at the viewing and then he'll be allowed to go to McDonald's."

Levi nodded, his eyes sparkling.

"Big Mac!" he mouthed, then checked hurriedly to see if Dat or Mam had overheard his breach of contract.

Quietly, the Beiler family moved on together, leaving the Walters to greet the handful of well-wishers and acquaintances.

Confused and sorrowful, Sarah walked back to the van.

"I'm just so glad she has parents to take care of her burial. It seems less devastating somehow," Mam mused quietly.

"But she said her parents were separated," Sarah said, her voice unsteady, troubled.

Dat was true to his word, and Levi enjoyed his sandwich, complete with the highly-regarded French fries and ketchup and a large Coke to boot, which he enjoyed to the fullest. Then he tossed and turned the remainder of the night, finally getting up and helping himself to a spoonful of Maalox and a long drink of water, keeping Mam awake until three o'clock in the morning.

Even Dat was grouchy at the breakfast table, drinking cup after cup of black coffee, his thoughts a thousand miles away. Finally, he spoke.

"It wouldn't be so bad, if we could only have obtained more information about these fires. Clearly, Mike is terribly afraid of us."

"I don't think he had anything to do with them," Sarah said.

"What makes you say that?" Dat growled, setting them all a bit on edge.

"Ashley as much as told me. I think he was mischievous about them, enjoyed scaring people, even wanted us to think it was him, but he was too immature, too childish. I don't think he'd be brave enough to do something like that."

"But the bottom line is still that our only source for information about the fires is gone."

"You didn't want to question her."

Abruptly, Dat left the table, which was completely unlike him. Sarah knew Ashley's death troubled him more than he would admit, which proved to Sarah that he struggled the same as everyone else, desperately wanting an end to the danger of yet another fire.

A heavy cloud of oppression hung over the rest of the

family. Suzie kicked the table leg, saying she didn't feel well and asking why she had to go to school if she was sick.

Levi ate oatmeal and bananas, belched loudly, and didn't ask to be excused until Priscilla reminded him sharply.

He said it was the Maalox.

Sarah went to school with a heavy heart, her face pale, her shoulders drooping.

She told her pupils about the accident, about knowing Ashley, and was gratified when even the older boys seemed interested. It was a small start at building a relationship with them, but it was at least a start.

At recess, the heavy, red-faced little girl named Leah came up to Sarah's desk, leaned across it, and watched her, the bright, beady gaze never leaving Sarah's face. Sarah put down the red ballpoint pen she was using and looked at her.

"What can I do for you, Leah?"

"Nothing."

Quickly, Leah swept away. Sarah raised her eyebrows and went back to work, checking the first grade's penmanship papers.

Five minutes later, Leah was back, watching Sarah's face.

"What?" Sarah asked.

"You know Ashley?"

"Yes."

"She got eggs from us."

"She did?"

"Yes. Her and Mike."

"Really?"

"Yes, they did. She gave me some bubble gum."

Quickly, Leah looked around to make sure no one

saw her.

"Here."

She thrust a small bag containing a very squashed chocolate cupcake in Sarah's direction. Her small bird-like eyes gazed steadily into her face before she opened her mouth, then closed it again.

"Don't tell anyone, but I pity you, because Ashley died."

Then she catapulted her round form away from the desk, shot out the door, and hid her face the remainder of the day.

Every small moment like that was a rosy victory for Sarah, making each day at the teacher's desk worthwhile. She ate every bite of the chocolate cupcake, finding it delicious, a symbol of the effort she put into each day, a small reward perhaps, but a huge accomplishment. What an angry little girl Leah had been that first day!

They made candy canes from red and white construction paper and hung them from paper chains, planning to stretch them from the center of the classroom to the four corners. Sarah decided to asked the two eighth-grade boys to do it.

"Sam, would you and Joe like to hang these paper chains?"

There was no response. Both boys slouched in their seats, reading tattered copies of old books brought from home, questionable paperbacks Sarah did not have the nerve to discuss.

No use opening that can of worms just yet, she thought wryly.

"Sam?"

Joe raised his hand.

"We usually don't help the teacher."

"This isn't usually."

No response.

Sighing, Sarah let it go but felt as if everything she'd accomplished had just slipped out of her grasp, leaving an oily residue that she could not wash away.

Teaching school was a trail with so many highs and lows, the highs like Mt. Everest, the lows an unexplainable abyss, a place full of hopelessness.

Six weeks, and what had she accomplished? Worse yet, five barn fires, and they were back to square one with Ashley gone. Sarah folded her arms on her desk, laid her head on them, and closed her eyes.

CHAPTER 21

SARAH SPENT THE FOLLOWING SATURDAY EVENING at the Widow Lydia's, her house cozy and warm, every corner lit with scented candles for Christmas.

There were wrapped presents on the old library table, and homemade bells hung from the window blinds.

They'd cut egg cartons apart, folded aluminum foil over the small cups, strung them on red and green yarn, and tied red ribbon around them.

They had just finished another batch of caramel popcorn, adding pecans to it this time. The house was infused with buttery, sugary smells. Lydia's face was glowing, her hair gleaming smoothly in the lamplight.

She confided in Sarah, whispering behind a hand raised to her face, that she felt guilty, but this Christmas she was simply going all out.

She had spent almost thirty dollars for a set of Legos for Ben, she confessed. Sarah stepped back, surveyed Lydia's face, and said that was fine, absolutely, not extravagant at all.

They made a double batch of Rice Krispie treats and

decorated them with green and red icing, for Aaron, the toddler.

Sarah was washing dishes, thinking how easily marshmallow succumbed to hot water, when someone spoke, directly behind her.

"Hello, Sarah."

Turning, her hands still in the dishwater, she found Lee Glick, his blue eyes conveying his gladness at seeing her there. Sarah wanted to fling herself in his arms, right then and there, but she slowly took her hands from the dishwater and dried them on a towel before she said, "Lee."

"How are you?"

"Oh, I'm okay. You heard about Ashley Walters?"

A great shout went up when Melvin suddenly appeared, his shirt the color of new grass in spring, his balding head shining like a freshly washed egg, his nose as crooked and dear as ever.

"Surprised you, right?"

Sarah laughed but acknowledged that yes, he had, while she blushed furiously. Melvin howled with glee, savoring her embarrassment.

Lydia stood shyly in the background, her eyes giving away the beating of her heart.

Melvin turned to her, and the look they exchanged needed no words, a rare and beautiful thing.

Omar had gone with his friends for the weekend, so Anna Mae and Rachel were thrilled to have company, making coffee, serving pretzels and cheese, obviously enamored with Melvin.

He held court with a kingly air, seated on a throne of his own imagination. To say he was in his element was an understatement, and Sarah watched him, marveling at the change in her cousin.

The candles flickered, the coal stove glowed, the smell of freshly-brewed coffee mixed with sweet smells from the kitchen. Sarah's happiness was complete when Lee turned and smiled at her, his face warm and filled with more than a welcome.

When they discussed the latest event pertaining to the barn fires, Melvin said there was no doubt in his mind that they had missed their chance by taking Dat's advice instead of allowing the police to interrogate that girl, and now look, she was dead.

Sarah mentioned the fact that Mike was still around. Lydia agreed. It might be worth a try.

Lee became somber, slouched in his chair only a bit, saying nothing as Melvin waved his hands for emphasis, explaining in his ringing voice why he thought the law should know about Ashley and Mike.

"You know, the police are a lot more intelligent than we are. They'll know which steps to take, which way to go. I don't know why your dat can't see that."

Sarah shrugged. "I thought he put you in your place."

"He did for awhile, but I got so upset at Enos Miller's it wasn't funny. They are the nicest couple, so simple and humble and God-fearing."

"About the opposite of you," Sarah teased.

Melvin made a face, while Lydia's eyes worshipped him.

Far into the night, they sat around Lydia's table, playing board games as the candles burned low in their glass jars. The coal fire needed stoking, and the children dropped off to sleep, one by one making their way upstairs to their soft beds to snuggle beneath thick comforters.

Melvin suggested they stay awake till four o'clock,

then all do chores together. He didn't have church this Sunday. Lee did, but he said it was alright to skip services, because he had other important matters to attend to—milking Lydia's cows.

Melvin really laughed about that, winking broadly, and Sarah slapped him, just for fun. The cousins exchanged a knowing look, and Sarah was rewarded by the warmth, the approval of Lee, in Melvin's eyes.

In the month of January, all of Lancaster County turned into a vast, arctic landscape dotted with white barns, farmhouses, and clusters of multi-colored homes forming quaint, homey villages.

Farm wives stoked the fires. Cornmeal mush sizzled in cast iron frying pans, liverwurst heated beside it in sturdy saucepans, fuel for shivering, hungry men when chores were finished.

In some of the new, more modern Amish homes, the husbands grabbed their lunch pails and thermoses, said good-bye to their wives, and were whisked away in diesel-powered pickup trucks, going their ways with framing or roofing crews to build townhomes, offices, garages, homes for a steadily-growing population centered around the Garden Spot of America.

It was called progress.

Others hurried off to welding shops or cabinets shops, manufacturers, builders of fine, timeless furniture or farm equipment. They wolfed down quick breakfasts of bagels or cold cereal, while the hungry farmers ate their fried mush and liverwurst, eggs and stewed crackers, and home cured bacon.

When the sun rose, spreading light and a thin warmth across the land, hundreds of Amish households were up and moving, making a living however they could, blessed to be dwelling in a land where freedom of religion was practiced and respected.

Almost every Sunday morning, a minister somewhere would mention the fact that the congregation could travel to church with their horses and buggies, freely and openly, worshiping without fear. Their forefathers in Switzerland had crept through dark fields at night, worshipped secretly in caves, were hounded, jailed, burned at the stake for this. This freedom.

And what were we doing with this wonderful, God-given thing?

That was the question that clung to David Beiler's conscience, wrapped tightly around it, never quite allowing him to let go in the face of a persistent adversary— the towering flames that had devoured too many Amish barns in Lancaster County over the past few years.

The forefathers, *die alte,* had ingrained in them the principle of nonresistance, taking the verses in the Bible quite literally.

They were Jesus's own words, weren't they? Love your enemies, do good to them that hate you, pray for those who use you and persecute you.

Liebe deine fiende (Love your enemies). There was no way around that.

He imagined that if spirits could be seen by the human eye, comprehended by the lowly understanding of mere mortals, a civil war of sorts would be raging in the frigid air today, on one of God's wonderful mornings.

For some reason, the burning of Enos Miller's barn had set off a fresh wave of indignant wrath. After coming together in unity for the barn raising, brother again rose against brother in fresh battles of opinion as verbal swords sliced through the air, and harmful charges and feints were executed.

Sisters days and quilting days and market stands became part of the darkness of verbal combat, as mothers, friends, sisters, and cousins voiced their opinions about the barn fires, the spirit of disagreement as thick as pea soup.

Bent and aged, their thin white hair almost completely hidden by their large white coverings, old *mommies* (grandmothers) shook their heads and said among themselves, "It wasn't always so."

Women were taught to be silent, obedient, and if they had anything to say, to say it to their husbands. And here were these young women, laughing uproariously, devising ways of catching the arsonist, including steel-jawed traps, among other outlandish devices.

They couldn't help it if their shoulders shook silently with mirth, though, could they?

David heard of these accounts from Malinda, who attended sisters days and quiltings all through January, coming home with her shoulders stooped with care, but often a twinkle in her eye as well.

For one thing, their two daughters, Ruthie and Anna Mae, were the works! Malinda just didn't know where they got their outspokenness. They claimed that if the Amish pooled their resources and paid for a private detective to follow Ashley Walter's boyfriend around, the fires would come to an end, and they meant it.

When Mam had protested, they said a private detective and a lawyer were two very different things. It was ridiculous, in this day and age, they said, taking this suffering like sitting ducks. No wonder he kept right on burning barns. Nobody even tried to do anything about it. And they were their own daughters saying this.

The next morning, David Beiler absentmindedly cut the baler twine on a bale of straw with his Barlow pen knife, then hung it carefully on the large nail pounded into the post for that purpose. He took up a block of straw and threw it into the horse trough. He was rewarded by a nicker from Fred.

The winter sunlight found its way through the dusty windows, and he reached up to turn out the propane lantern, then made his way across the cow stable, into the milk house, still wet with steam from the scalding, hot water Sarah had used to scour the milking machines.

The fact that she was still here on the farm, living in peace and harmony with her family, washed over him and infused his thoughts with gratefulness, engulfed his spirit the way the steam warmed the milk house.

God had delivered them with a great and mighty hand, as He had with the children of Israel in days of old, and it still had not ceased to amaze him.

But why was God waiting so long about the barn fires? Did He allow them to continue because of the *tzvie-drocht* (dissension)—the backbiting, the disharmony, the hateful attitudes? Have mercy on us, David begged as he stepped out of the milk house into the blinding light of the morning sun.

Seated at the breakfast table, smelling of the strong lava soap he'd used to wash his hands and face, David bowed his head. His wife and children followed suit as they clasped hands in their laps and thanked God for the good food spread on the table, then raised their heads and promptly began passing dishes and platters.

Levi was cold. He announced in grumpy tones that no one had *fer-sarked* the fire, and his toast was burnt.

"Just a little dark, Levi," Mam said gently around a

mouthful of sausage and egg.

"Don't talk with your mouth full, Malinda," he snapped.

Priscilla burst out laughing, spraying orange juice across her plate. She choked, coughed, covered her mouth with her hand, and went to the sink for a paper towel.

David Beiler smiled broadly, caught Sarah's eye, and winked. Sarah smiled widely, winked back.

Suzie said, "Don't boss Mam, Levi."

"Mam should swallow first, then talk. That's what she says to me."

Suzie looked at Levi without smiling, and he returned her look steadily, unblinking, before saying, "Did you hear what I said?"

Suzie nodded, and Levi tucked into his eggs and sausage, stopping only to tell Mam the toast was so burnt there were little black things smeared in the butter, and he didn't like that. She should be more careful, making toast.

Dat told Levi it would be a great idea for him to make toast. He could pull his chair over to the gas stove, put the homemade bread on the broiler, and keep checking it until it was just the right shade of brown, then turn the oven off and remove it.

Levi's eyes turned bright and cunning, and he saw the opportunity to show off his ability as a helper in the kitchen, latching onto the idea like a pit bull, never letting go. All day long, he begged Mam for the opportunity to make toast until she relented, and he ate perfect toast for lunch, as a snack, and for supper.

While Levi was either making toast, thinking about it, or eating it, Sarah was fighting her own private battle at school. Her courage fled completely when Hannah Stoltzfus brought her sister to visit the school, sitting in the back of the classroom, two sentries of disapproval, every bit as formidable as hungry vultures. Why had they come?

Sarah's hand shook as she called first grade to arithmetic class, attempting to hide the fact that she'd noticed anything amiss.

At recess, Hannah fluttered up to Sarah's desk, her face flushed, her sister firmly in tow. The color in her face was high, her eyes popping, as if her high blood pressure was actually pushing on her eyes, shoving them up against her glasses, which were spattered with grease.

Her old sweater was torn at the seam on one shoulder, and white lint clung to the front like dandruff. Her stockings sagged over her large, black Sketchers, so inappropriate for a woman her age, but Hannah's choice for comfort.

"Sarah! My, oh. I'm surprised how well you teach."

"Thank you," Sarah said coolly.

Her sister nodded her head in agreement, all her chins wobbling as she did so.

As Hannah leaned close, Sarah was subjected to a decided odor of something fried emanating from her sweater that had likely hung from a hook in her *kesslehaus* for years without being washed.

Mam did the same thing with her everyday sweater, that ratty old black thing that served a multitude of purposes, but Sarah often grabbed it and threw it in the washer with the last load of denim trousers.

"Did you hear about Matthew's wife?"

Just for a moment, Sarah steadied herself by placing her hands on her desk, before raising her eyebrows in question.

"Her name, you know, is Hephzibah, just like that

Bible woman. Sarah, she's such a good person. I feel as if Matthew has been rewarded for his life-changing conversion.

"Anyway, she is sick. She's *unfashtendich grunk* (very sick). Matthew calls every day. They are in the hospital, and they can't really find the cause of her fever. It just doesn't go away."

"Malaria?" Sarah asked.

"What do you know about that disease?" Hannah asked abruptly.

"Not much. I just know it's a common disease in tropical climates, a mosquito-borne illness."

"Are you telephoning Matthew?" The question was sharp, bitter, an arrow tipped with the poison of suspicion.

"Of course not."

Hannah's sister's eyes widened, and she drew back as if to gain a better perspective to watch this interesting exchange.

"Well, don't. He's married now, and I know it's very hard for you to give up. It always was. But you'll be alright, in time. But just don't call Matthew. It wouldn't be right."

Out of the corner of her eye, Sarah saw Joe push little Ben into the corner of the horse shed, heard the little boy's terrified howls from inside the sturdy walls of the schoolhouse, and quickly asked to be excused.

She met a shaking little second grader, blood pouring from a nasty gash on his forehead, his eyes showing the pain and fear of having collided with a sharp metal corner, his nose and eyes running.

Herding him into the cloakroom, she moistened a clean paper towel and held it firmly to the wound and sat him on a folding chair as she examined the cut.

It was deep but not very long. She felt sure a firmly applied butterfly bandage and some B and W salve would begin the healing process just fine.

Hannah, however, insisted he be taken to a doctor. She knew Ben's parents. She'd take him home, and his mother would want to take him. Why, that gash would leave an awful scar.

So she bundled up poor frightened Ben and trundled him out the door, clucking and going on all the while, her sister exclaiming and waving her hands, leaving Sarah with a discipline problem, a sour stomach, and a desperate need to run after Hannah and tell her to go home and stay out of her life, out of her business. And would she please never ever mention her son Matthew's name to her again?

Courage eluded her the remainder of the day, driven away by Joe's loud sneers, his swaggering shoulders, his demeanor challenging Sarah to try and do something about everything she'd seen.

He knew. He knew she'd seen him eating pretzels in class and pushing Ben on the playground. But her mind reeled from Hannah's visit, her senseless accusation. It robbed her of the ability to confront Joe.

By the time the afternoon arrived, Joe had tried her patience to the limit, laughing, whispering, flirting with Rosanna in an unthinkably bold manner. When Sarah finished her third-grade English class, she said "Joe Beiler!" very firmly and very, very loudly.

He jumped up, snickering.

"You need to stay in for recess, so we can talk."

A deathly silence folded itself over the classroom, the clock's ticking suddenly magnified.

They had never heard their teacher speak in such a terrible voice.

When the pupils were excused for last recess, Sarah was actually surprised when Joe remained seated, as she had been prepared to watch him openly disobey and follow the others out the door.

Seated, but slouched as low as possible, he fiddled with his ruler, scraping it across his desk with a grating sound that jangled Sarah's already harried resolve.

"Joe, you know you've been doing crazy things all day just to try my patience. What is up with eating those pretzels in class?"

He shrugged, became sullen, his eyes hooded.

"May I have an answer, please?"

"I didn't have any breakfast."

"Really?"

"Yeah."

"Why? Surely you had time for a bowl of cereal."

"Yeah."

"Why did you push Ben?"

"He made me mad."

"How? Joe, he's only seven years old."

"He's a pest."

"Not Ben. He's afraid of everything."

Suddenly, Joe sat up straight, his brown eyes flashing dark fire, and he burst out, his adolescent voice breaking into unmanly squeaks. "You sound exactly like my mam. 'Shut up, shut up,' she says. 'They're little. They're only three or four.' She hates me. You know why I ate pretzels? I had to finish hanging out the wash because she was fighting with my dat. So there."

Ashamed, he turned his face away.

Sarah was speechless. She had never known a mother

who would tell her son to shut up. Or argue so forcefully she couldn't finish the laundry. And get her growing son no breakfast?

For a long moment, she watched Joe, saw the bad skin, the acne engraved in his quivering cheek. She looked into the eyes that appeared rebellious, brash, sneering, curtains of dark brown hiding pain and a ceaseless yearning for love, patience, and understanding from two parents who were blind to their son's needs.

Sarah knew there were nine children in the Beiler family. Joe was the oldest at 13.

Still, he could have eaten the pretzels on his way to school.

"Joe, I'll tell you what."

Sarah sat in the adjoining desk and made him meet her gaze.

"Don't do it again, okay? And try and be careful on the playground. Ben was hurt pretty badly. And I guess we have to learn to get along if we're going to be stuck in the same schoolhouse until May, right?"

Joe shrugged, shifted his brown eyes.

She spoke to him about flirting with Rosanna, saying they were much too young for such things and was rewarded by a dark, painful blush creeping over his face.

"No speeding ticket this time, young man, just a warning," she said, touching his shoulder.

That day was a memorable one, a turning point.

CHAPTER 22

MAM PAGED THROUGH HER VAST ARRAY OF SEED
catalogs, clucked, licked her thumb, slurped the lukewarm tea by her side, cleared her throat, scratched her
arm, and did just about everything else Sarah could imagine that could completely annoy her.

She was seated at the kitchen table, towers of work-
books beside her, steadfastly plodding her way through
them. The lamp hissed, and the cold air swirled around
her legs as the mean January blast rattled the spouting at
the corner of the house.

Priscilla was curled up on the sofa, reading, and Suzie
looked as if she'd fallen asleep at the opposite end, a soft,
navy blue throw tucked securely over her shoulders.

Levi was in the shower and had been for the past fifteen minutes, singing a loud, off-key rendition of "Silent
Night," a fragment of the old song lodging somewhere
in his brain, a leftover from the holidays.

Dat was stretched out on the recliner, but the only
thing Sarah could see was an open newspaper, the tips of
his fingers, his legs, and stocking feet.

It was almost nine o'clock.

Sarah yawned, threw down her pen, shivered, and said loudly, "Priscilla, would you consider helping me check my books?"

Reluctantly, Priscilla lowered her book, eyed Sarah and the stack of books, and prepared to get off the couch. "I can, I guess."

Mam mused out loud. "I think I'm going to try a different kind of pea this year. Sam King *sei* Arie said Green Arrows are the best, but I disagree. And instead of zinnias, I'm going to plant hardy salvia. I'll start the seeds on the porch."

The porch was Levi's room. It was already decked out with Mam's geraniums, dropping brown leaves all over the shelves, tedious to clean around. All the porch needed was dozens of tiny, square pots full of soil and minuscule seeds, waiting to be knocked over by large bumbling Levi, muttering to himself in the dark of night.

When they heard a loud knock on the door, it surprised all of them, including Dat, who lowered his paper, raising his eyebrows.

"This time of night?" he asked, to no one in particular, then pushed back the footrest, got up, and walked to the front door, laying the folded newspaper on the table beside Sarah's stack of books.

When he opened the door, a whoosh of icy air was unleashed into the room, and Sarah drew her feet under the chair.

Sarah didn't recognize any of the three Amish men, all dressed in long, woolen overcoats and black felt hats, heavy boots on their feet, their faces somber, mouths pinched in grim lines.

The family knew without being told to exit the room,

except for Mam, who would be invited to listen if she desired.

The girls shivered their way through their showers, emerged steaming, and leaped into their cold beds, wearing soft socks and long flannel pajamas, homemade pieced comforters piled high on top of their blankets.

It was seriously cold at zero degrees with a brisk wind. All she remembered before falling asleep was the low murmur of voices, never changing, never stopping, a ceaselessly moving creek, a stream of opinions. She could gauge the nature of the visit by the looks on her parents' faces in the morning.

Dat was quiet while they milked, came in late for breakfast, his face inscrutable, nodding briskly at Levi instead of giving his usual hearty "Good morning." He picked at his food until he suddenly laid down his fork, looked around, and asked if anyone had overheard the conversation the night before.

Mam kept her face lowered. The girls shook their heads.

Levi stopped chewing, watched Dat's face.

"Except you, Levi?"

"Well, Davey Beila!"

Clearly ashamed, he turned his attention to his plate.

Levi had been stuck in the bathroom without his pajama pants, the path to his bedroom a wide expanse in full view of the visitors. Levi became more undecided and upset by the minute, brushing his teeth over and over, combing his hair, stalling for time, till he finally gathered enough courage to call Dat and, in typical Levi fashion, announced very clearly that he was stuck in the bathroom without his pants.

"Hop ken hussa kott (I had no pants)!" he said now,

justifying having had to ask Dat to leave the table, where his serious visitors were left trying to look as sour as they had before.

Dat chuckled, his eyes twinkling. "You could have gone to your room, Levi."

Levi shook his head vehemently, "*Oh nay. Hop rotey knee* (Oh no. I have red knees)."

Everyone laughted. Suzie giggled and snorted, rapping her spoon on the table. Levi looked around appreciatively, glad he could make his whole family laugh, especially on a cold morning like this.

Dat continued telling his family about the visit from the three men. Melvin had spoken to the local police, asking for night patrol between Bird-in-Hand and Enos Miller's in Georgetown. This had been picked up by the media, somehow, and became instantly blown out of proportion, followed by far-out assumptions and half-truths. A Philadelphia newspaper had run an article called "Non-resistant?" with Melvin's picture and his words in bold, black print.

Sarah's oatmeal turned tasteless, the thick creaminess sticking in her throat. Oh no.

So he had actually gone ahead and done it, this thing he'd long cultivated on his own, wagging a finger, threatening, the need to make his opinion known, overriding everyone's advice.

Dat sighed. "So I suppose all the words I spoke to him were pretty much worthless." Defeat was threaded through his voice.

Sarah felt a pity so keen it was physical. Her father had done so much for the community in the past years, treating his congregation with respect and kindness. He did not deserve this outright disobedience.

Anger welled up on the heels of her sympathy for Dat. "That Melvin!" she said, her eyes blazing green.

Dat shook his head. "Sarah, you agree with him sometimes, don't you?"

She felt the heat rise in her cheeks.

"I do. Sometimes. But Dat, do we ever really know one hundred percent of the time how we really feel? Do you?"

"I think I do. I can't move past turning the other cheek. Forgiveness. It's the whole, complete message of Christ. It is."

The last two words were spoken firmly, as if to reassure himself that this was really true.

Mam laid a gentle hand on Dat's arm, picked nervously at the button on his sleeve.

"It's hard, Davey. Truly hard to cling to a message of love when the fires have occurred, one after another. The verse in the Bible about forgiving your brother seventy times seven suddenly becomes almost impossible and hard to understand. How is it possible?"

"But it's necessary."

"Absolutely necessary."

Priscilla's eyes met Sarah's and flashed. "It's only going to get worse since Ashley's death."

"I don't know about that," Dat responded. "Remember the night of her viewing? I don't believe that Mike is a criminal. He was clearly devastated by her death. It was only when I spoke to him, touched him, that he began crying like that. My heart went out to him, as I would have felt toward anyone in a time of grief."

At school, the students spent recess sledding, playing snow games, building snow forts. Sarah joined her pupils during the lunch hour. The sun shone on most days, and icicles formed along the eaves, turning the brick school-house into a picturesque building nestled in a grove of leafless, winter trees.

Wet stockings, boots, beanies, and gloves surrounded the propane gas heater that whooshed dutifully to life, true to the temperature on the thermostat, a modern-day wonder in Sarah's opinion.

She clipped the smaller children's gloves to the home-made PVC ring that hung from its hook above the heater, allowing the wet articles to dry quickly and efficiently.

Joe and Sam, and Rosanna and her cohorts still refused to go sledding or participate in any running games. They opted to slouch against the wall of the horse shed, although the snickering had all but disappeared. Occasionally, they would trip one of the smaller children or roll one in the snow, but Sarah never let it go, always following the misdemeanor with words of rebuke or having them spend time at their desks.

Her days went by fairly well, although she constantly had to balance discipline with common sense, patience, and encouragement, working to instill that elusive ingredient into the school—a willingness in most of the children to want to obey.

There were small victories, the smashed chocolate cupcake, Joe's outburst of confession that day, Rosanna asking to go to the Strasburg Railroad, the long awaited trip that had gone very well without the stubborn upper grades after Sarah had refused to give in.

Not having a Christmas program had made Sarah sad at first, but she knew she had saved herself hours of frustration by giving it up.

Now she was secretly contemplating a spring program around Easter, waiting to see how the pupils would respond to discipline by the end of February.

Always, just when she felt she was gaining ground, some of the older pupils would get out of their seats to walk around without raising their hands, just to see how far they could go without Sarah calling them back to their seats.

Or their refusal to work on their scores would start all over again, leaving her in a black mood with no hope of ever changing anything.

Catherine, a sixth-grader, raised her hand just before school let out one day when Sarah's head felt like an overfilled balloon, ready to pop.

"Yes, Catherine?"

"What are we doing for Valentine's Day?"

Sarah stopped and thought.

"I forgot about Valentine's Day."

"We want to do something, don't we?"

"Certainly. Of course. Any suggestions?"

"Stay home, like, all day," Rosanna said loudly, looking around for any signs of approval.

When none were forthcoming, Rosanna slid to the side of her seat and leaned over as if she was searching for something in her desk. When she sat up, her face was red, and she was blinking self-consciously.

Sarah was thrilled, glad to see her discomfiture. It was, by all appearances, a good thing when no one acknowledged her wise cracks.

"So, any suggestions?" she asked, pointedly ignoring Rosanna.

"Pizza?"

"Hot lunch?"

"Valentine's Day party?"

The suggestions came thick and fast, assaulting Sarah's

headache, but welcome, nevertheless. It showed enthusiasm. Even if it was for something as frivolous as a party, it was still enthusiasm.

So Sarah traveled home, happily chatting with her driver, took two Tylenol as soon as she came within reach of Mam's medicine cabinet, and flopped on the recliner before she closed her eyes, breathing slowly, deeply, allowing the tension of the day to evaporate.

It was unusual to see Hannah striding up on the porch, her breath coming in short, hard puffs, her hair disheveled by the brisk wind, her coat pulled like sausage casing around her ample waist. As in former days, she didn't knock, just pushed the door open a sliver and yelled, "Hey!"

Quickly Mam turned the gas heat to low, checking the potatoes with a deft hand, and wiped her hands on her apron as she hurried to the door.

"Hannah."

"Malinda."

The words were unspoken questions.

Mam paused, then said, "*Ach* Hannah, you don't come anymore the way you used to. I miss that." The words were a healing balm, covering old wounds, cleansing them of harmful bacteria, the kind that fester and grow, turning a good, steadfast friend into a foe.

"Well, Malinda, a lot of water has gone under the bridge since Matthew dated Sarah. It's just awful, just awful now. His wife is dying. They say there is nothing more they can do for her. She has some sort of rare virus. They'll lose the baby, too. He is completely devastated. I want him to bring her home for better medical care, but he can't."

Sarah felt her mouth go dry. The room spun, tilted,

and righted itself as the blood drained from her face and her hands began a ridiculous quaking completely on their own.

What if Matthew's wife passed away? That would leave him free to marry again, to return to the Amish, come back to the fold, resume life as...as what? As it was meant to be? Or as her heart still yearned? Who was to know?

Her thoughts out of control, Sarah gripped her hands to still their shaking. She squared her shoulders and bent her head, noticing the intricate pattern in the linoleum, the perfection of the copied pattern, so similar to real ceramic tile with grout between the squares.

Which was real? When was love genuine and when was it counterfeit, only a replica of the original product?

She heard Hannah's voice, recognized Mam's answers as Priscilla's large green eyes watched them, as keen as a cat. But it was all secondary, as if in another realm. Would Matthew return?

"If she passes, I guess Matthew could return. But I can't see him coming back to us, to be Amish again. He knows so much more about the Bible now. He knows more than our ministers, I'm sure. He can talk about the Bible for hours. He's so interesting.

"Elam is afraid he'll mislead me yet, but I told him, *ach*, what would an old biddy like me want in another church? I'm about as Amish as they come. You know, Malinda. But Matthew is just something else, so he is."

Mam answered Hannah with only a polite nod of her head, her smile becoming fixed, lopsided, as she struggled to keep a hurtful opinion to herself, victory showing as her smile righted itself.

Mam knew Matthew was firmly glued to the pedestal

of his mother's pride, slowly turning from flesh and blood into various metals, hardening into an idol she would worship her whole life long. No mere words of advice would ever change that.

She listened attentively to Hannah's praise of her son, and when the potatoes boiled over, she was genuinely relieved to have Hannah glance sharply at the clock and say she must go as she had cornbread in the oven—nothing better in the dead of winter. She pulled her black men's gloves over her chapped hands and took her leave.

With a sigh of resignation, Mam sat down, shaking her head, as if a great weariness had taken up residence in her body.

"Sarah, what if Matthew returns?"

A blinding, fluorescent joy shone from Sarah's eyes, and Mam shivered in the face of it. "Do you think he will?" Sarah whispered, the hope still brilliant after the initial flash of rapture.

Mam shrugged, then got up from her chair, whipped the pot off the stove, and began beating the mealy potatoes with a vengeance, the potato masher clacking against the steel sides of the pot in harried circles. Mam's nerves supplied ample muscle power as she resisted the very thought of that cunning wolf showing up again on the front porch, opening up all the fears and sleepless nights yet again, just when they thought God had taken mercy and answered all their prayers.

Well, if she had anything to do with it, he wouldn't. Her eyes flashed, and her cheeks took on a color of their own as her arms pumped away at the potatoes. Turning, she snapped, "*Grick da dish ready* (Set the table)."

Sarah cast a frightened look at her mother.

"What in the world, Mam?" she breathed.

Mam's composure slid away as her shoulders slumped, tears leaking from beneath her sturdy glasses as she told Sarah in an unsteady voice of the fear in her heart.

"Matthew has such a strong hold on you, Sarah. I'm so afraid if he does come back, he'll want you, but not his heritage, not his Amish background, and he'll persuade you again."

That was how Dat found them—Sarah shocked, her face suppressing untold emotion, his dear, faithful wife in tears, which were not often seen, especially not without good reason.

Quickly, they tried to remedy the situation, and as quickly, Dat insisted on knowing what Hannah had wanted. When they had told him, he sat down heavily, the breath leaving his body, a furrow appearing on his brow as the only sign of his anxiety.

"Well," he mused, before his mouth widened into a grin. "This reminds me of a story in one of the old reading books—the one about the bride-to-be who went to the springhouse and found a hatchet imbedded in the ceiling. Till it was all over, the what-ifs, traveling from person to person, had resulted in numerous calamities and suspicions forming in the minds of the villagers. Don't you think that might be the case here?"

Mam nodded, shamefaced, but to save her pride, she insisted it was only she and Sarah, not a bunch of others, who had been speculating.

"I heard it!" Levi bellowed from his chair by the window, where he was identifying birds with his binoculars, the bird feeder stationed just outside for his enjoyment.

"These women act like the birds. Such a *ga-pick* (picking) and *ga-fuss* (fuss) they have!" Levi said, shaking his head.

In spite of vowing to keep everything in perspective, Sarah had a difficult time keeping her thoughts and emotions from spiraling to untold heights.

The only thing that remained to keep her anchored was Lee, the agreement they had to wait until the proper time to begin dating, and the love she felt for him. Or was that only desperation to relieve the hurt from Matthew?

Clearly, if Matthew returned, she would find herself in the most difficult situation of her life, a crossroad piled with insurmountable obstacles, all labeled with puzzling, life-altering choices yet again.

Priscilla entered her room late that evening, a towel twisted around her hair like a turban, her warm fleece robe tied around her waist, her feet cozy in woolen slippers.

"It's so cold in here, you can see your breath," she complained as she plopped on Sarah's bed, bouncing her and causing her pen to make a dash across her diary.

Leaning over, Priscilla raised an eyebrow.

"I'll give you five whole dollars to read your diary."

"More like five hundred, and then it's not guaranteed," Sarah muttered.

"You know, hopefully, you're just crazy." This sentence was spoken flatly, dryly, without emotion.

Sarah turned sharply, her eyes wide, as she found Priscilla's, the question hovering between them.

Not waiting for a response, Priscilla plunged ahead.

"What is it going to take? What will have to happen before you are finally shaken to your senses? Sarah, I can see it in your face. Matthew, or the thought of him, is still as precious to you as he's ever been. What about Lee? What about the sweetest, best-looking guy who would do anything he could for you? Are you just going to throw him away like a piece of trash, disposed of—CLUNK!—in the waste can? And he's already given up Rose for you."

"We're not dating."

"But you agreed to start as soon as the time is proper."

"Well."

"Well, what?"

Sarah shrugged her shoulders. "She didn't die."

"But she will."

"That doesn't say he'll return. Perhaps he loves Haiti and will stay there."

"And if he does, and if he calls for you, you'd swim the Atlantic for him."

When Sarah laughed, Priscilla unwrapped the towel from her head and shook out her long, beautiful, blonde-brown hair. She took a large, black brush to it, wincing as she did so.

"You disgust me." The words were harsh, accusing, hard stones of misunderstanding.

"Don't judge me, Priscilla. You've never been in love."

"You're not in love with Matthew."

Sarah laid her diary carefully on the nightstand and turned to look at her sister, holding her gaze without guilt.

"Sometimes, I'm not sure I know what love is," she said finally, quietly.

Priscilla nodded, then whispered, "I do."

Sarah raised her eyebrows. "At sixteen?"

"When I was still fifteen."

"Omar?"

Priscilla nodded.

"Love is not hard to figure out, for me."

Sarah nodded.

Outside, snow pinged against the window as

another snowstorm approached the county. The cold seeped between every crevice around the baseboards, between the window frames, sending a shiver up Sarah's back.

Was it the cold, or was it a premonition? Some strange dread of the future, an intuition that lurked around the perimeters of the farmhouse, finding its way into her soul?

CHAPTER 23

WHEN HEPHZIBAH DIED, THE UNBORN CHILD going with her, Hannah was one of the first people to know, and she lost no time in coming to tell the Beilers, her tears already streaming down her face, the gulping sobs coming without restraint as she reached the door. Mam ushered Hannah inside, putting a hand on her heaving back and a box of Kleenex at her disposal as she offered a gentle word of sympathy, her fear and foreboding tucked deep inside, where Hannah had no access to it.

Hannah's description of the situation took Mam to the primitive Haitian hospital, the heat, the rejoicing in the Lord as she passed into His arms, bringing tears to even Mam's eyes. Without a doubt, this woman had been a special person. The light of her Master's love had enabled her to serve selflessly, ministering to the poor and the needy, with a heart that was joyous in doing so, and Matthew's life had been blessed by her.

On and on, Hannah sobbed, bringing wadded tissues to her bulbous, red nose as more tears streamed from her squinted eyes. Over and over, she removed her glasses, wiped them, and replaced them, before a fresh onslaught of grief overtook her.

Mam realized, wisely, of course, that this was no ordinary grief. After all, Hannah hadn't even known the girl, this woman named Hephzibah. She put two and two together and decided Hannah was crying all the tears for another reason. Maybe these were the tears she had never cried for Matthew's leaving.

Malinda remained kind and sympathetic. She put on the coffee pot and brought out a tray of pumpkin cookies frosted with caramel icing and another plate of good, white sharp cheese. She added some Tom Sturgis mini-pretzels to the spread and a roll of Ritz crackers and some grapes they'd had on special down at Kauffman's Fruit Market.

Hannah grasped the hot mug of steaming coffee, laced it liberally with cream and sugar, and began dunking pumpkin cookies into the thick liquid as fast as she could break them in half and retrieve them with her spoon.

"*Ach* my, Malinda. *Ach* my. How can I doubt your friendship? You always know what I need, don't you?"

"You mean pumpkin cookies?" Mam asked sagely, and they threw back their heads and laughed until Mam wiped her eyes and straightened her covering.

She always did that when she felt guilty for laughing too much, as if the adjustment of her large, white covering could pay penance for her lack of holiness. Hannah knew this gesture well and had often teased her about it. So now, when Mam reached for her covering strings and gave them a good yank, Hannah shook her finger under Mam's nose and said ministers' wives were allowed a good laugh, now, weren't they?

Their friendship once again restored, Hannah poured

out her longing to have Matthew return to the fold. Wouldn't it be wonderful if he and Sarah could get together again, simply resume the friendship where it had left off? she asked.

Mam remained level-headed, agreeing, but clearly stating her fears. She told Hannah that Sarah had promised to serve Christ among her people, and she would be heartbroken if she broke her vows.

Oh, Hannah understood this. Indeed, she did. Halfway through the pack of Ritz crackers, the block of cheddar cheese dwindling rapidly, her stomach full and her spirits mellow, Hannah lowered her head, leaned forward, and confided in Mam. She admitted that Matthew made her so angry—just sometimes, not always—but he could come back and live among his lifelong friends and family and behave himself. Even if he was well-versed in the Bible, he better watch out or he'd be as bad as the person in the Bible who lifted his face and thanked God that he wasn't as bad as other people, and she meant it.

With that, she nodded, clamped her mouth shut, and said there was a very real possibility of Matthew being too big in his own eyes.

When Hannah polished off the last of the grapes and headed home, Mam's spirits were strangely uplifted, and she sang quietly to herself as she worked on her quilt, the light of the sun on the snow more than sufficient, her needle quickly rising and falling in and out of the soft fabric.

Who was she to map out God's ways? One simply never knew what He had planned, or what He was thinking, exactly the way Davey said.

At school the next day, Sarah sat down hard, the unforgiving wooden seat of the toboggan rising up to meet her backside before she was quite ready. "Ow!" she yelled, and the third-grade girls howled with laughter.

"Ready?" Martha Ann called.

"Ready."

Sarah gripped the narrow shoulders ahead of her and hung on, yelling with the rest of them as they careened down the icy trail that had been there for too long, the noontime sun turning the snow into a dangerous, slick path of pure, unadulterated terror.

The speed with which they shot down the hill was absolutely unsafe, but it was the thrill of each school day, the pupils arriving breathless, their entrance into the schoolhouse accompanied by their answers of, "Morning!" when Sarah greeted them. It was rarely "Good morning," just "Morning," but it was sufficient as long as her eyes were met, her presence acknowledged without hostility.

Constantly, Sarah reminded herself to be content with baby steps, little steps of progress, small differences in the children's attitudes, small changes, but changes, nevertheless.

In school, the turmoil in her heart was stilled, the challenges of the day occupying her mind as she focused her attention on the children and the work, constantly striving to be the best teacher she could be.

Dealing with the students in the one-room school, with all eight grades in such close quarters, was as challenging and nerve-wracking as it had always been. But, slowly, there were differences.

Geography lessons turned into discussions, in spite of the eighth-grade boys initially refusing to co-operate and instead tapping their fingers, fiddling with their pens, and making annoying sounds, which were all duly ignored. When Alaska was chosen as a project, with its vast expanses of unspoiled acreage, pipelines, and animals of the tundra, the lure of the exploration proved to be too much, and they were slowly drawn into the discussion. Their drawings and maps were truly phenomenal.

Joe proved to be an outstanding artist, although not without constant praise, words of admiration spoken whenever an appropriate moment presented itself.

The parents who occasionally took time off from their hectic schedules to visit the school were in awe of the artwork, the projects done so precisely, the pencil drawings and intricate designs done so well. And by their own children! My, oh, they said later. I didn't know Henry could draw like that.

Praise was hard to come by for the teacher, however. No one mentioned the artwork to Sarah, they just walked along looking at the drawings on the walls, their arms crossed around their waists. They sniffed, spoke in low tones to one another, and then changed the subject before approaching her.

That was alright. Sarah understood the need to withhold praise in order to keep someone humble, on the straight and narrow. She really did.

But a wee bit of affirmation would be nice, an unexpected ray of warmth on a chilly day.

When Lee's sister, Anna, showed up that week, she was so effusive with her loud words of admiration, it was as if the blazing summer sun itself had entered the classroom. Sarah's face grew flushed with heat as Anna repeatedly threw up her hands, squealing in amazement, turning to Sarah repeatedly, asking how she could get these children to draw like this.

Anna's youngest boy was entirely engrossed in cleaning out Rosanna's desk, books thumping on the seat, pens and pencils rolling across the floor, but it all went completely unnoticed by his awestruck mother.

Sarah winced when Rosanna spied the boy and pulled him away with an impolite jerk of his arm. This was followed by an indignant howling that brought his mother scurrying, flustered and apologetic. Her apologies were received coolly by the queenly Rosanna. Sarah felt like slapping her, but, of course, she didn't.

Anna settled herself on a folding chair, her son perched on her short legs, her hands holding him closer than was necessary, her eyes alert, eager, radiating good humor.

Sarah conducted classes as usual, and the children sang three of their favorite songs for Anna. At recess, Anna was close to tears, praising Sarah's teaching ability with a deluge of admiration, holding nothing back. Leaning close, she nudged her rounded shoulder into Sarah's and whispered, "I heard! Oh, I'm excited. I can hardly believe you are actually going to date. It's an answer to prayer!"

Sarah smiled, but her smile was followed immediately by a wave of horrible guilt, knowing that Matthew's potential homecoming had largely occupied her thoughts, enveloping her days with anticipation.

Perceptive, smart, Anna watched, her eyes like a bird. "What? Isn't everything okay?"

"Yes. Oh, of course."

"Good. Sarah, for real, you have no idea how thrilled I am, how thrilled we all are."

A smile that felt untrue, somehow, was all she could manage, but it would have to suffice. At least she hadn't spoken words that were not quite truthful. She hadn't said anything at all.

Sarah completely underestimated Anna's perceptive

abilities. She was taken by surprise, to state it mildly, when Lee knocked on the door of the schoolhouse late that afternoon.

Her heartbeats multiplied, skidded, steadied, but her face still showed alarm when she opened the door.

Ever since the night that car had followed the girl with Sarah watching the fight, hearing the heated exchange of words, she did not feel completely safe at school after the children went home.

She was jumpy, lifting her head at any unusual sounds, going to the window to be positive nothing out of the ordinary was going on, telling herself it was foolish. Was it, really?

"Oh Lee."

"I didn't mean to frighten you."

"I'm....No, you didn't."

"May I come in?"

"Of course."

Sarah stepped back.

She forgot how tall he was. She forgot how blond his hair was, how tanned his skin, how clean-cut his profile. His eyes were so blue they were ridiculous.

Before she could say anything, he found her gaze and held it with his own.

"Sarah, I came to ask if it's true. Is Matthew returning?"

Sarah lowered her head. Her eyes noticed the dust on the high gloss paint in the intricate pattern along the side of a wooden desk. She thought she should clean it.

"Yes. He....Well, his wife, um, died. I don't know if it's really true that he's coming back here. To stay. Hannah, his mother, thinks he might."

A silence hung over the empty classroom like a

suffocating blanket, cutting off Sarah's air supply.

Finally, Lee spoke.

"And when he does return, will things change between us, Sarah?"

Sarah answered too quickly.

"No. Oh no."

Still her head was bent, her eyes hidden from his, the top of her head the only way he could gauge her emotions, which was a lot like looking at a broken thermometer.

"Sarah, look at me."

It was impossible, and she knew it.

When he said nothing, the suffocation from the unbearable blanket of silence increased, and her desperation mounted until she knew there was no way out. The despair folded her into a child's seat. Her arms rested the desktop, her head on them, as shameful, terrible sobs shook her body. The sounds were muffled, polite, even, but they put a dagger through Lee's heart.

When he didn't place a hand on her shoulder, when he didn't crouch by her side to murmur condolences, the sobs became shorter, then weaker, then stopped entirely, before Sarah lifted her head long enough to look, search, bewildered. Had he gone?

He remained in the classroom, standing stiffly by the window, gazing through it at the late winter light, his hands clenched behind his back.

When he stayed silent, Sarah cleared her throat and said very softly and quietly, "Lee."

He turned at the sound of his name, his expression unfathomable.

"I...I..." Completely at a loss for words, her voice faded into silence.

When he spoke, his words were restrained, his tone soft.

"I thought Matthew's leaving was a clear, bold answer for me, straight from God. Now I'm not so sure. I guess perhaps if someone loves the way you loved him, there is never a time when that goes away completely. In other words, even if you choose to date me, I will not have you fully. A part of you will always love Matthew."

Sarah's denial began with a slow back and forth movement of her head, her eyes still lowered to the desktop.

Lee sighed, walked over, and stood so close to her, she could feel his presence. She could detect the odor of lumber and steel nails and strong hand soap, even the leather from his work boots.

"So Sara, I think the right thing to do in this situation would be to set you free. How does that old saying go? If you're not sure something—someone, in this case—is yours, set it free, and if it doesn't return, it never was yours to begin with. How does the rest of it go?"

She didn't think before she spoke. She just lifted her head and looked into his blue eyes and said, "If it comes back to you, it always was yours. Or something like that."

"Yeah. Something like that."

He walked away, toward the door, and Sarah opened her mouth to protest, then closed it again when he stopped.

"You're free to go then. Just forget about the fact that we had planned to begin dating, alright? When Matthew comes back, you'll be completely unfettered. You alone must choose."

Suddenly, the significance of that tremendous impasse loomed before her, a fire-breathing dragon of impossibility, hopelessness, coupled with the knowledge that she was clueless, holding a key to her future that was securely locked, and what if the key was all wrong? What if it didn't fit?

When Lee buttoned his work coat and placed a hand on the doorknob, her eyes took in the shape of his shoulders, the tilt of his head, as if she could store away the memory, a keepsake, something to hide in the deepest recesses of her heart. She had loved him, hadn't she?

Guilt made her cry out. "Lee?"

He froze.

"Don't. I mean...I..."

Without another word, he let himself out, closed the door softly behind him, and did not look back.

Sarah repressed the urge to run after him. What would she say if she did catch up to him? How could she begin to tell him she did love him, but she loved Matthew more? Matthew Stoltzfus's whole life was intertwined with her own. He was the missing piece of her, the way he filled up every loneliness, every moment of longing. She could not make Lee understand this.

Sighing, she stood and watched the road for a glimpse of Lee. When there was none, she simply didn't know what to do, so she sat back down, staring straight ahead, seeing nothing, until her driver arrived and pressed her palm against the steering wheel, emitting two loud honks. The sound brought Sarah quickly back to reality.

When Mam looked into Sarah's eyes and saw all the dark misery threatening to dissolve into tears, she wisely did not press the issue. She just turned away and said nothing.

Sarah mumbled something about not feeling well and went upstairs slowly. She flopped on her bed and wished there was someone she could confide in. Someone who understood.

Mam walked around with her mouth pressed in a firm line of denial, boding no good. Priscilla told Sarah unabashedly and repeatedly that she was crazy. And Dat was too involved in the meetings and goings on about the barn fires.

That was another thing. Sarah was completely fed up with all this talk of a dangerous person on the loose and people speculating about what to do. Men from the community just kept showing up in the kitchen, placing blame on Dat, on members of the community who clung to the old ways. What exactly was he supposed to do?

She felt a great pity for her father. He had aged many years in a short time. Over the winter, his cough would not go away, no matter how many different home remedies Mam spread on his chest or how many bottles of tincture or piles of herbal pills he swallowed. The cough wracked his body relentlessly.

He kept at his work, doing chores, hauling manure, oiling machinery, doing the things every farmer did during the winter, but he never quite got ahold of the rasping cough.

Even when he preached in church, he coughed, and it seemed to embarrass him. Perhaps he thought it was a sign of weakness and was ashamed.

Whatever the reason, Mam talked in hushed tones to Sarah, saying she knew why Davey coughed like that. He was under too much stress. There had never been a time like this for as long as she could remember. The way brother turned against brother, valuing his own opinion above everyone else's—it was turning into a battle of senseless speculation, and not one of them really knew anything.

Mam said that was the whole trouble with the world, the way no one could stay silent in the face of unexplainable situations. They all tried to figure it out, when in actuality, they were all helpless. Even the world, the *Englishe leid* (English people), did not know what to make of the repeated disasters.

As Sarah sat on her bed, staring into space, she heard Dat's cough in the kitchen below, then a murmur of voices, and she knew her mother would be clucking, fussing, hurrying to heat water for a bracing cup of peppermint tea.

She tried to imagine her life with Matthew as her husband, comfortably living in a house together, talking of ordinary, mundane subjects, the way they always had in school, at family get-togethers, their whole lives. They had been so close. Dating, seeing him every weekend, and often on week nights, living her dream.

He would have changed a bit, of course, which was only to be expected, living a different lifestyle. He had probably adopted different mannerisms, the way his people talked openly of their faith, freely expressing their beliefs, whereas Amish people preferred their worship in silence, their views often hidden.

But Matthew would return. He would come back to the Amish way. Sarah felt sure. If she couldn't believe in that, she didn't know Matthew very well, and she did. She knew him better than he knew himself, she told herself.

Sighing now, she leaned back on her pillow and let the anticipation of the future envelop her, seal her safely inside, secure, the doubts and fears kept outside. For now.

The candle on her nightstand flickered. Headlights beamed across the room as a car approached on the road, arcing across the ceiling as it turned.

Downstairs, Dat coughed again. A cow bawled from the barnyard, where the black and white Holsteins frolicked about, getting a bit of exercise in the still, cold air, their breath a whoosh of steam expelled from their warm nostrils.

Levi sat by the window, dressed in clean flannel pajamas, his hair wet, combed properly, his teeth brushed furiously. A jar of Vicks stood on the nightstand at his bedside for the long night ahead of him, when his sinuses would close, causing him grief and long hours of sniffling and honking dryly into piles of Kleenexes.

His eyes were tired, drooping at the corners, but it was only a quarter past seven on a cold winter evening. He'd finished his jigsaw puzzle. That one had been easy, and he didn't feel like playing a game with Suzie, so he thought perhaps he'd just go to bed.

He grasped the arms of his chair and started to get up, when he thought he saw someone, something.

He reached for his glasses, polished them on the tail of his flannel pajama shirt, and plunked them on his nose, squinting.

Slowly, he reached out and pushed a pot of geraniums aside, brushed off a brown leaf that fluttered to his lap. Aha. Some chap was walking up to the fence.

Tilting his head, he peered out the window between the leafy geraniums and watched. There. This chap sure was bold. Not ashamed of anything. What in the world? Was he just going to stand there and look at the cows?

It was too dark to see exactly what was going on, but Levi saw the animals stop and watch, their ears held forward, their wet noses held high, sniffing.

Levi's eyes slide toward the kitchen, where Dat sat hunched over his tattered German Bible, a cup of tea at his elbow. Well, he didn't need to be bothered. This was Levi's sighting. All his own. And so he sat, a still form peering between the geraniums.

CHAPTER 24

FOR SEVERAL LONG MOMENTS, LEVI SAT AS STILL
as the most experienced hunter stalking his prey, completely engrossed by the spectacle before him. As he tilted
his head one way, then another, he figured he'd have to
get rid of some of these geraniums if he wanted to know
what was going on.

He turned his head, saw Dat was alone as he read, no
Mam or Priscilla. Suzie sprawled in front of the black coal
stove, so he reached out with calculated precision and set
two coffee cans of geraniums on the sewing machine to
his left, soundlessly.

There, that was much better. He had a full view of the
chap by the barnyard. With snow on the ground and the
waning, half-moon's light providing illumination, Levi
could plainly outline the man's dark form, standing stock
still, looking up as if he was checking out the barn roof.

He figured the man was doing no harm. He certainly
was not driving a small white car, so it couldn't be the
man that had "struck the barn on," as the Amish often
said. Likely this man was out for a walk, maybe taking

pictures of the cows in the moonlight.

The man turned his head and looked at the house. Levi's breath came quick and fast. He could not tell who it was. Better tell Dat.

He had just opened his mouth to call Dat when a pair of headlights came slowly in the drive beneath the maple trees, their trunks inky black, lined up like sturdy sentries but allowing the car access to Davey Beiler's farm, the tires crunching quietly on the frozen snow.

Good, Levi thought. Now he'll be afraid and run across the field. Instead, the man turned, waiting beside the driveway, as the vehicle pulled up slowly. He looked toward the house.

Levi did his best, peering intently through the lenses of his thick spectacles, his breathing accelerated now. He looked like that other man. Not the man from California, the other one. That night they'd gone to Ashley's viewing, there where she had lain so dead in that great big fancy casket, with all those flowers.

Levi watched as the man opened the passenger door and lowered himself into the car. It moved off slowly, the crunching of the snow audible to Levi's ears.

Well, they were taking their time, he reasoned, so they weren't going to stick the barn on. And the car was not white. Levi couldn't really tell what color it was in the darkness.

When it turned around out by the implement shed, Dat lifted his head, coughed, and looked toward the window above the kitchen sink, as if he thought he heard something, but then he lowered his head and resumed reading.

Levi kept his eyes on the car as it drove slowly out the drive, turned left, and continued down the rural road.

Quietly, Levi replaced the geraniums, picked up the withered brown geranium leaf, and placed it carefully in the trash before shuffling out to the kitchen with his empty water pitcher.

David Beiler looked up as Levi approached, smiling at him absentmindedly, his thoughts on the verses he had read.

"*Bet zeit* (Bed time)?"

Levi nodded.

"*Brauch vassa* (Need water)?"

Levi nodded again.

"Did you take your garlic and echinacea?"

"No."

"You better would."

"Garlic stinks."

Dat chuckled.

"It does you a lot of good in winter, Levi."

"It still stinks."

Muttering to himself about his plans to hide the plastic bottle of garlic capsules, Levi took a tray of ice from the freezer, twisted it, and shook the cubes into the small plastic water pitcher. Then he opened the tap and filled the tray with water.

Mam emerged from the steaming bathroom, her face rosy from the heat, her navy blue bathrobe belted securely, a white *dichly* (head scarf) knotted around her head.

"Ready for bed, Levi?"

"*Ya. Vett an snack ovva* (I would like a snack)."

Mam's eyes twinkled. "We have good oranges."

Levi gave her a baleful look and shook his head from side to side.

"*Vill* (I want) shoofly."

"No, Levi, shoofly pie tomorrow morning, for

breakfast. Oranges tonight."

"I don't like oranges. They're sour. Hard to peel."

"How about an apple?"

"Apple pie?"

His face was so hopeful, his expression so woebegone, Mam's heart melted like soft butter, and she went to the pantry, got down the freshly-baked apple pie, and cut a sizable wedge for her perpetually hungry son.

Wreathed in smiles, Levi thanked her profusely, grabbed a fork, and enjoyed every bite to the fullest, then sat back and wiped his face very carefully.

"*Denke*, Mam," he said.

"You're welcome, Levi."

He thought he should tell Dat, the apple pie suddenly escalating his goodwill toward his beloved parents.

"Davey."

"Hmm?"

"There was a man standing by the barnyard tonight."

"Aw, come on, Levi."

"There was. I saw him."

Dat shook his head, "No, Levi."

Levi nodded. "A car came and picked him up. He looked at the house, then he looked at the barn."

"After he was in the car?"

Dat was fully alert now. He picked up his German Bible and took it to his desk with the rest of his German books, coughing again.

"No," Levi said slowly.

"Before?"

"*Ya.*"

"Why didn't you tell me? Why didn't I see or hear anything?"

"You were reading."

"Hmm."

Mam watched Levi's face intently.

Suzie rolled over, sat up, yawned, and said Levi told *schnitzas* (fibs) if he felt like it. She hadn't heard anything.

Levi said the man did not want to stick their barn on, and he was not driving a white car. He looked like that other man.

"What other man?" Dat asked sharply.

"Not the one from California. The other one."

"See? He's just making this all up," Suzie yelped.

"Hush, Suzie."

"Which man from California? When? Where?" Mam asked, bewildered now, hurriedly placing the apple pie back into the Zip-loc bag, keeping order in her kitchen even if other events in the world appeared unsolvable and disorderly.

"That dead girl. When we ate at McDonald's."

Dat looked hard at Levi, glanced hurriedly at Mam, went to the window, and looked toward the barn for a very long time without saying anything.

When he turned, his face appeared pale, and he spoke tersely, "Time for bed, Suzie, Levi. Where's Sarah and Priscilla?"

Going to the stairs, Mam called the girls, who appeared obediently soon afterward. They sat on the couch quietly as Dat reached from the German prayer book, nodding his head.

In perfect unison, they turned, kneeling as Dat read the old prayer, the evening prayer from the same *Gebet Buch* (prayer book) his father had read at the close of each day, his voice rising and falling as he pronounced the words, so dear to his heart, so comforting to Mam's.

As the rest of the family slept through the cold wintry

night, David Beiler could find no rest. He paced the kitchen floor, turning repeatedly to stare out the window, the one above the sink, gripping the countertop unknowingly, his shoulders tense, his mind tumbling with unanswered questions.

Was he putting the community at risk with his refusal to talk to the media and allow better coverage? What if Levi really had seen a suspicious person on their property that night?

Over and over, his anxiety led him to the window, his mind reliving the horror of his own barn fire, the terror, and poor Priscilla, losing Dutch, now not even caring whether she had a horse or not.

Cruel. It was all so cruel. And Priscilla had been just one victim of the arsonist. Still, it didn't hurt for children to give up their own wills. That was old knowledge passed down for generations, and it never failed to amaze him. Discipline served as a boundary of love, producing caring adults for society, over and over.

As long as there was love to balance the discipline, it worked. Traditions were dependable, safe. But always? Even now?

In the face of this fiery adversary, who was he to say? Old John Zook exhorted them over and over to forgive. God had allowed the barn fires to take place, so he would provide a way, if they stuck to their beliefs.

Christ had suffered so much more, and He without sin, and here they were, ordinary sinners, beset with flesh and blood, and they couldn't forgive without rising up in anger, insisting on vengeance.

In his heart and soul, he knew it was wrong.

Upstairs, lying beneath the heavy comforters, Sarah struggled with her own private battle, without confiding her fears to Priscilla, who had flounced out of her room after asking what was up with her sour mood and telling her she was crazy yet again.

Jagged edges of fear taunted her, restricted her from looking forward with a clear gaze, unable to decipher an uncertain future.

Torn between a great love for Matthew and an unexplainable misery about Lee, sleep eluded her completely. She lay on her back, staring wide-eyed at the dark ceiling as her thoughts chased away every last shred of peace.

What if Matthew did return and refused to acknowledge her? What if he denied the fact that he had ever cared for her?

He wouldn't. Would he?

Hannah told Mam he'd likely be home in the spring. Six more weeks! Not even two months.

Would he appear different? Older? Wiser? Ready to admit his mistakes? Would he grieve for his poor, deceased wife?

Suddenly, she remembered the Widow Lydia's words, a precise pinprick inserted into the magical bubble she had built around herself. She had bowed her head, Lydia had, in that way of hers when she was contemplating a weighty matter, as Sarah's words had rained around her, happy little dashes of anticipation, exclamation marks of joy punctuating every sentence. Matthew was coming home! That seemingly was all Sarah knew or cared about.

When Lydia finally spoke, she simply said, "Hopefully, Lee is an extraordinary man and understands this."

Sarah's face had flamed. Reaching up now, she touched the tips of her ears, remembering the searing heat of her discomfort. There had been no words to justify her anticipation of Matthew's return.

Melvin, of course, had his usual lack of tact, bluntly telling Sarah that he wanted nothing to do with Matthew, and he certainly hoped she felt the same. He said that if she didn't watch it, she'd be left high and dry, turning 40 and not being able to figure out what had happened.

"I can't think of it, but there's a word for girls like you," he finished.

Sarah looked up sharply.

"Fickle?" Lydia asked shyly.

"That's it. You can't be trusted, Sarah."

But what did Melvin know? He was one to talk. Going on 30 years old, unmarried, and now, by all appearances, completely enamored by Lydia. If he was a bit off the beaten track, why couldn't she be?

Besides, he didn't know if Matthew would return to the fold or not. Opinionated troublemaker.

Flipping onto her side, she peered at the numbers on her battery-operated alarm clock. 12:42.

Sighing, she resigned herself to a day of tired irritation at school. She began breathing slowly in and out, relaxing her shoulders, cleansing her mind of troubling thoughts about Matthew.

Just before she fell asleep, she thought she heard Lee say, "See you, Sarah."

Startled, she jerked awake, her heart hammering. Was she really losing her mind? When all else failed, she prayed fervently, asking God to direct her path and help her lean not on her own understanding.

She prayed for guidance, prayed for her pupils at school, for her ability to teach them with wisdom and understanding. Peace enveloped her, covering her softly as she fell into a deep sleep.

In the morning, a soft temperate wind moaned around

the house, whistling along the eaves, gently tossing the small branches of the bare maple trees in an undulating dance of promised spring.

Water dripped off the roof's edges, and icicles broke loose and crashed to the ground, burying themselves in the dirty snow. Everything melted together in a sluice of water, creating a fine, sticky mud anywhere there was bare earth.

Brown grasses huddled in sodden little heaps as the white snow around them dissolved into frigid water, slowly moving in little rivulets to join the large stream of water gushing from the downspout on the implement shed's corner.

Sarah jutted her chin comfortably into the confines of her dark head scarf, tying it securely as she walked to the barn to join Dat for the morning milking.

Ah. She lifted her face, felt the soft wind, heard the melting snow running along the eaves, and thought how lovely, how absolutely deliciously lovely, it was that spring was on its way.

Her eyes were dry and itchy, so Dat found her standing in the milk house, rubbing them with two fingers, blinking, then yawning.

"Didn't sleep?" he asked as his morning greeting. Just then a yawn caught him, his mouth gaping open tremendously, followed by a shaking of his head, a bleary look, and a grin of humility.

"No."

"Me either. What was bothering you?"

"Not much."

Time to start milking, Sarah thought wryly. Subject closed.

They worked together in silence, the cows munching

their silage, the milking machines chugging with a homey sound, just the way they always had.

Sarah fed the calves, her gloved hands getting wet as she laughed ruefully at the strength of the day-old calf's jaws as the little animal bucked and fought, ravenously hungry, willing the calf starter to come faster.

Stars twinkled overhead, and a thin streak of dawn appeared in the east, the promise of a beautiful day.

She rubbed the stubby black head of the last calf, withdrew the plastic bottle from its greedy little mouth, leaving it standing bewildered, wondering why the milk was already gone.

She washed the milkers and scrubbed the gleaming sinks, finishing just as Dat entered, hanging up an extra lantern for her.

"So, you didn't say why you weren't able to sleep," he said, leaning against the bulk tank, eyeing her quizzically from beneath his tattered chore hat.

Sarah lifted her hands from the hot water and wiped them on her bib apron before turning to face her father, shrugging her shoulders helplessly.

"Oh, just, you know, stuff."

"Same here. Stuff."

She caught the twinkle in her father's eye, and they laughed softly together.

Dat said, "Matthew?"

Sarah nodded, shamefaced.

Dat thought of all the things he would like to tell her to keep her from having to learn the hard way. Oh, how he longed for her to see!

"Just remember to pray each day, Sarah. Read your Bible, for in those inspired words lie wisdom. Remember that God comes first, and then earthly joys—guys, you call them, romance, whatever."

Did his face take on a reddish glow?

Sarah smiled genuinely at her father, encouraging him, knowing he was awkward when discussing matters of the heart.

"I'll be alright, Dat. I really will. Matthew will return in about six weeks, and then I guess I'll figure it out, don't you think?"

Dat nodded, placed a hand on her shoulder. "I think you will."

They walked together, splashed through the rivulets of icy water, the softness of the dawn caressing their faces, waiting for the first rays of the morning sun. They knew that each day is new, God's mercies as fresh as the dawn, renewed all over again as if each day was the very first day of creation.

Whatever lay before both of them—decisions, cross-roads, events, mountains that seemed immovable—they knew their faith would somehow sustain them.

Sarah bent swiftly, picked up a handful of snow, and squeezed it into a snowball of sorts. She drew her arm back, took aim, and fired a hefty shot at her father's broad, denim overcoat.

The resounding splat brought a surprised yell from her father, followed by a grand swoop, and a pile of snow landing directly in her face.

Spluttering, laughing, Sarah bent for another solid handful but was stopped by the sound of a window opening. Levi appeared, clearly delighted by Davey's antics, and he was yelling at the top of his lungs.

"Grick an, Sare (Get him, Sarah)!"

Dat cried, "Uncle! Uncle!" and Levi bounced up and down with genuine glee.

Laughing, they entered the *kesslehaus*, where the smell of frying mush greeted them, warm and crisp and cozy, the smell of home, tradition, and genuine happiness.

The End

A suspenseful romance by the bestselling Amish author!

LINDA BYLER

The WITNESSES

LANCASTER BURNING • BOOK 3

CHAPTER 1

HE WAS HERE.

She could see the sunlight glinting off the roof of his car. The new leaves were pushing out of the buds on the branches of the maples trees in the Stoltzfuses' yard. They threw dancing shadows of sunlight across the vehicle, but she could easily see it from her station at the living room window. She dusted the philodendron plant and clipped a few yellowing leaves from an ivy, attempting to hide the fact that she was unable to keep from longing to see him.

Would it be the same? Would her heart flutter in that same way, her breath quicken when he smiled? It had been so long.

When she could no longer justify her presence at the window, she picked up the yellow can of furniture polish and moved to the sideboard. She lifted the crocheted doilies, the candleholders, and the basket of greeting cards to dust beneath them.

As soon as she had that accomplished, the magnetic pull of Matthew's car began all over again. Quickly, she stole another glance. The same dappled sunlight on the glossy roof of the car. He was still there.

"Sarah."

She jumped at the sound of her mother's voice.

"Hmm?"

"When you're finished with the dusting, do you mind washing the floor? When Abram Miller's family was here yesterday, their children got a bit lively, and the grape juice was spilled more than once."

Mam looked up from mixing the Crisco into the mound of soft, white flour, deftly incorporating it for the flaky pie crust she could always turn out. She stopped and blinked, her mouth drawing into a tight line as Sarah turned to glance out the living room window yet again.

Mam knew.

The knowledge rested uneasily on her rounded shoulders and the capable arms that cooked and cleaned for her large family, some of them strapping sons who had married and gone off to Dauphin County, where property prices were more affordable.

Her large, white covering concealed her graying hair, or most of it. Her face was still smooth, though her glasses well worn. She was a comely older woman with years of compassion and hard work molding her features.

Mam sighed and resumed her mixing, absentmindedly now. She rolled a bit of floured Crisco between her thumb and forefinger.

So he was here.

He came to see her later that evening, when Sarah least expected him. He bounded up on the porch when she was washing dishes, and she had no time to fix her hair or her covering or have a quick look in the mirror. All she could do was lift her hands from the soapy water and snatch up a corner of her black bib apron, wiping furiously as her heart began its usual wild take-off.

His knock was the same. Rapid, eager.

Sarah flew to the door, her feet skimming the kitchen floor, color rushing to her cheeks as she reached for the doorknob.

Matthew Stoltzfus stood on the porch, his dark hair cut in a stylish manner, polished, in the English way. His eyes were still the same deep brown, but his skin was darker than she had ever seen it. When he smiled, those perfect white teeth dazzled her, and she became quite faint.

"Sarah?"

It was a question, a timid, quiet inquiry.

Her eyes found his, and she was at home. After a long, arduous journey of a million years, she was home. The glad light in his eyes peeled away the thin reserve she had been able to build up, and with a broken cry of welcome, she flung herself into his arms.

"Matthew!"

Her cry was no more than a whisper. She felt his arms gather her trembling form against him, felt the soft fabric of his cotton shirt against her cheek. She closed her eyes to the unbelievable sensation of being in Matthew's arms. Suddenly, the safety of those arms was pulled away as hard fingers closed around her forearms and pushed her away, firmly, cruelly.

"No."

That was all he said. That one small word meant she had been bold, presumptuous.

"I'm sorry."

Her head was bent as she mumbled the words.

"I'm a widower, Sarah."

"Yes, I heard. I was sorry to hear of it."

"Yes."

Matthew cleared his throat and looked around uneasily. He shifted his weight from one well-clad foot to the other.

"Will your mam speak to me? Is your dat around?"

"Yes, come in. Levi will be pleased."

Matthew smiled, and she had to tear her eyes away from his face.

When they entered the kitchen, Mam turned from the pantry door, years of training hiding her emotions. She smiled, greeting Matthew with genuine friendliness.

Matthew grasped her hand, saying, "God bless you," and continued holding Mam's hand until she gently tugged it away, and Matthew asked how she was doing.

She inclined her head and answered, still reserved, but friendly, remembering the Matthew of years past. Hannah's eldest son, the apple of her best friend's eye.

Levi sat at his window, his elbows propped on the arms of the swiveling desk chair, his narrowed, brown eyes alight with interest, his large body leaning forward with anticipation.

"There's Matthew!" he bellowed, breaking into a delighted laugh that bounced from wall to wall.

Instantly, Matthew bounded to Levi's side, one brown hand clapping his shoulder, another pumping Levi's plump hand, leaving him giggling with happiness.

Levi was a special character, the symptoms of Down syndrome endearing him to his family and the community. He often held court from his desk chair or the recliner, spreading humor and goodwill with his sometimes hilarious view of the world around him.

"Levi, old boy! Good to see you!" Matthew said, sincere in his greeting of an old friend.

Sarah stood rooted by the kitchen table, her large green eyes reflecting the worship she felt for Matthew. Tall, athletic, with curly brown hair, she carried herself with a finesse that she was completely unaware of.

"Where were you so long?" Levi inquired.

Matthew laughed easily. Having known Levi as a small boy, he was accustomed to his lack of restraint.

"In Haiti."

Levi nodded sagely, then looked up at Matthew with a cunning glance.

"Snakes didn't get you, huh?"

Matthew laughed again and shook his head.

"No, Levi, they didn't."

"But your wife died."

"Yes."

Matthew's features steadied, folded, the happiness now erased by his sorrow. His brown eyes turned liquid with the pain. Sarah had to grip the back of a kitchen chair to keep from going to him, running her hands over the beloved contours of his handsome face, replacing the pain with her love.

Mam had to turn away from the raw yearning in her daughter's eyes.

They sat together later, on the same swing beneath the grapevines, in the chilly spring evening.

Sarah wrapped her sweater securely around her body and drank in the words he spoke. She savored the sound of his voice, never tiring of hearing about his experiences in Haiti and his marriage to Hephzibah, the black woman he had loved, who had contracted a deadly strain of malaria.

When darkness hid the stark brown vines surrounding them and her teeth began to chatter, Matthew said he should be going as his mother would wonder where he was.

She could not let him go, not without knowing. She could not face the future without the assurance that he would stay.

"Matthew."

He became very still, the desperation in her voice assaulting him.

"You'll be back? You'll return to the Amish? You'll come back to us and pick up where you left off? I mean, quite obviously, God wants you to be here. He took Hephzibah. So now your work in Haiti is done. It was a learning experience, and now you'll be one of us again, right? I just need to know. Matthew, I have to know what you're planning for the future."

She was babbling, becoming hysterical, her voice turning into a thin, reedy whine, and she didn't care. This was her one chance.

Matthew exhaled loudly, then spoke with the patient tone of one far superior.

"Sarah, you just don't get it, do you?"

"What do you mean?"

"I can't come back to the Amish. Your beliefs are all wrong."

"Really?"

"Yes."

"Well, couldn't you believe what you want and still be Amish?"

There was a long silence, stony—hard, gray, and unrelenting.

"Dat says there are many levels of faith. Some eat meat and others dare eat only herbs. But the way of love is for the lion to lie peacefully with the lamb. He says you don't have to leave us to live as a Christian, the way you think."

Still Matthew stayed silent, which only increased Sarah's desperate desire to win him back—back to her, back to the faith of their childhood.

All her dreams were rolled into the vision of sitting beside him in a buggy, the warm summer air laden with the heady scent of flowers blowing gently through the open window. A good, sleek horse with a spirited head pulled them along, lifting his feet and making solid, ringing sounds against the macadam.

She would be his wife, secure in the knowledge that he loved her, that he wanted her there beside him, and that she was worthy. It was all she wanted.

"And Matthew, your parents would be so happy to have you return to the fold. You should think of them sometimes."

Matthew's words were clipped, harsh.

"My mother gave me her blessing the day I left, and you know it."

There was nothing to say to this.

"I chose to serve God the way I want."

"Yes. Yes, of course."

There was no use angering him further. If she argued, she would lose him, certainly.

"You really don't get it, Sarah. You're always going to stay Amish and not know any better."

Sarah bristled at the accusation in his voice, but she remained quiet.

"You didn't come to Haiti. You didn't come. It's your own fault that I married Hephzibah."

Sarah sat up very straight, the breath leaving her body in one quick expulsion, a sort of disbelief.

"You didn't want me!"

The tortured words burst from her, lava wreaking havoc as it rained from the still bubbling volcano of her heart.

The swing suddenly came to a stop. Somewhere an owl hooted, probably in the apple tree down by the orchard. Another one gave an answering call. A dog began a deep, anxious barking.

"I did want you, Sarah. I was just afraid that you wouldn't make the break with your parents. Your father is, after all, a man of God, a minister of the Amish church, and—I don't know."

His voice became quiet and trailed off, leaving Sarah hanging on desperately, searching the vertical wall of his voice for one more chance, one more fissure to pull herself up.

"You didn't think I'd leave?"

"No."

A song started in her heart then, the finely-tuned melody of repression and denial. She captured the knowledge that he had loved her, had wanted her, and still did.

"Matthew," she began, then choked and remained still.

"I wanted to go, would have gone."

"Would you now?"

"You know I would."

"I am a widower."

"I'll wait."

"You will?"

"Yes."

Again, he sighed.

"You must be sure."

"I love you, Matthew. I always have."

Victory was hers now, firmly in her grasp, the Olympic gold around her neck and lifted high.

"If you love me, you'll wait six months, and then we'll leave. Your job is to persuade your parents."

"I will."

The old wooden swing creaked. A lamp was lit upstairs, creating a yellow rectangle of light where there had been only darkness. Priscilla and Suzie were getting ready for bed. It must be later than she thought.

There was a woofing sound from the barnyard. The half moon rose above the implement shed, casting soft shadows across the newly tilled garden soil. Sarah thought of the insurmountable task she had promised.

In a very small voice, she asked if he loved her enough to come home to his Amish roots.

"Well, if that's how you're going to be, then just forget it," he said, without wavering.

"No, no, oh no."

She grasped his arms with nerveless fingers and implored him to have patience with her weakness. Then she gave up and threw herself into his arms, suddenly so aware of her need to feel secure, to grasp the fact that he did love her, without a smidgen of doubt.

He did not resist her, crushing her to him as his mouth sought hers.

Much later, she stumbled into her room and stood alone, her arms hanging by her sides, her senses reeling. A sob rose in her throat, then another. With steely resolve, she tamped down the tsunami of emotion, the quavering doubt and fear that threatened her.

The next morning she was red eyed but awake, making desperate attempts to act normal. She was kind to Levi, spoke quietly to Mam, answered Dat's questions honestly, but she was glad to escape when the school driver pulled into the driveway.

Entering the schoolhouse, she raised the blinds. The sunshine etched streaks on the glass, highlighting the small dots of residue the sticky tack had left after they removed the valentines, the colorful pink and red decorations the children had made the month before. She would wash windows today, throw herself into her work with renewed energy.

She greeted the children with a pale face, eyes that were brilliantly green, a smile that flashed a little too intensely. Rosanna lifted one shoulder, tossed her head, and said it must be that the teacher has a new boyfriend.

Little David in second grade raised his hand and said Sammy stuck a pin in his arm, whereupon that little person set up an awful howling of guilt and fear. He was duly punished, and quiet was restored.

They decided to begin decorating for Easter that afternoon. Sarah stood with her pupils clustered around her, discussing the artwork they had done for Easter in previous years. She was amazed at their ideas and the willingness to submit them without a trace of the former animosity.

At noon, she sat at her desk, opened her lunchbox, and spread the waxed paper carefully beside it. The thickly-cut baked ham drooped between the sliced whole wheat bread Mam had taken from the hot oven the evening before. The crisp lettuce was piled on top, and small streaks of mayonnaise clung to the golden brown crust. The scent of her sandwich mingled with the delicious smells that always accompanied the opening of twenty lunchboxes, and she could not imagine leaving the only life she knew.

Her classroom was dear and familiar, the only challenge she had faced, the small victories she won here serving as stepping stones to a new and different school environment. Even in the past month, the victories had come one after another as the baby steps of progress she had made developed into toddler steps.

Her reverie was broken by a blonde-haired, round form, eyes alight with pride, bearing a greasy wrapper.

"Here! My mother made these."

"Oh. Oh, my goodness! A doughnut!"

It was a soft cream-filled one, dusted liberally with powdered sugar, wrapped in brown paper.

Surely this was not the same belligerent, impossible child that had entered her classroom that first day?

Sarah's voice shook as she thanked her over and over, an arm hugging the soft, chubby body against her, quick tears filling her eyes.

When Rosanna offered to stay after school to wash windows, Sarah accepted happily. The extra help would allow a thorough job.

They raised the blinds and set to work, efficiently removing every trace of smudges and fingerprints, chatting as if they had always been friends, which Sarah knew had certainly not been the case.

Sarah was caught completely off guard when Rosanna eyed her frankly in that way only eighth grade girls can and blurted, "Hey, what was wrong with you this morning?"

As the heat rose in her face, she rubbed vigorously at one spot on a window, biding her time, desperately trying to hide her face from Rosanna.

"Well, aren't you going to answer?"

Feigning innocence, Sarah muttered, "Why are you asking?"

"Well, you looked different. Sort of shook up."

Should she confide in Rosanna? Should she tell an eighth-grade pupil that her whole world was spinning off its axis, thrusting her into outer space where she wasn't completely positive who Sarah Beiler really was?

No, she couldn't confide in Rosanna.

"Oh, now, why would you say that? I didn't feel different."

"You looked different."

Ah, the social graces of a thirteen-year-old!

Sarah tried to change the subject, but Rosanna maneuvered right back to what was wrong with her teacher.

"I bet you anything that Matthew Stoltzfus came back to visit his parents."

A streak of lightning could not have shocked her more. As it was, she stared open mouthed at the guileless face of her student, studying the blue eyes intently. How could she know?

"Yeah, well, if you're not going to answer, then I guess I'll know he came to see you. You know he really made a mess of my sister's life—Barbie Ann. She's married now. Thank goodness she had the nerve to step out of his clutches. He said he wanted her, but, well, bottom line, he didn't."

Rosanna sprayed far too much Windex on a window, vigorously pumping the sprayer, the painful memory of her jilted sister lending her strength.

"Whoops! Too much Windex."

Rosanna shrugged her shoulders and set to work, mopping up the excess window cleaner, saying, "You know every girl this side of Harrisburg wanted him."

Sarah nodded agreement, her face averted.

"Did you hear me?"

"I heard you."

"You know you're much too nice to waste your time on Matthew. My mother doesn't let us say certain words, but I could use one to describe him."

Sarah smiled but said nothing. Rosanna was always pushing against her mother's restrictions, which were few and far between as it was.

Sarah decided to conceal any further information she gleaned, cocooning it away to be safely brought out later in the privacy of her room.

She and Rosanna shared a cupcake someone had left in the cloakroom and drank cold water from a cup by the water faucet. They admired the shining clean windows and did not speak of Matthew.

Sarah did learn, however, that Lee Glick and Omar Esh had driven a pair of Belgians to the sales stables in New Holland, and it was the top selling team of the month.

Rosanna giggled and rolled her eyes and said she didn't know how old Lee Glick was, but she wished she wasn't only thirteen.

Sarah listened and smiled and thought of Matthew and wondered why the afternoon took on a dull quality.

When Rosanna left, Sarah sat alone behind the desk as a grayness descended, obscuring the yellow sunshine and puffy white clouds. It stilled the meadowlarks and the chirping sparrows and the warm brown branches of the budding trees, turning them black and gothic and frightening.

Outside the small, one-room schoolhouse, everything went on as before—the sun's brilliance, the moving white clouds, the birdsongs—but in Sarah's heart, a certain sense of despondency took over, a weight of discouragement.

Was it only Rosanna's prattle? What did she know?

Nothing. It was only Rosanna voicing opinions of her own concoction.

But what if Rosanna was right? What if God sent people like this girl to warn her? And what if she held herself in high esteem and pooh-poohed the warnings of one so young?

She would talk to a more mature friend, the Widow Lydia, the most fair person on earth.

CHAPTER 2

LEVI DIDN'T WANT HIS CHICKEN AND DUMPLINGS that evening and became quite ill later, so Sarah knew it was not a good time to visit with her friend Lydia.

Mam was busy making Levi as comfortable as possible, so Sarah washed dishes, straightened the house, and sat down with her schoolwork afterward.

It was a quiet evening, and even Dat seemed preoccupied, hiding behind an opened Lancaster newspaper, the *Intelligencer Journal*. Suzie went to bed early, and Priscilla sprawled on the rug beside the stove with another magazine.

When Sarah heard the rustling of Dat's paper, she looked up, her mind telling her before she actually saw Dat's hooded eyes and his concerned expression.

"Sarah."

"Yes?"

Still she could not meet his eyes.

"I guess Matthew was visiting here last evening."

"He was."

"How is he?"

"Good."

The old clock on the mantle ticked too loudly. Priscilla coughed, cleared her throat, and positioned both elbows so her hands fit over her ears.

"I guess we can trust you, Sarah."

"Yes."

"Did he ... mention your past?"

"Yes."

At this, Dat sat up, carefully folded the newspaper, and deliberately put it on the sewing machine beside his chair. He rose like an old man, painfully, unfolding his length as if each joint protested its support of him.

When he came to stand at the kitchen table, one large, calloused hand resting on the back of a chair, she could not look up. Blindly, she made a few red check marks, without seeing the fine black numbers on the page of an arithmetic workbook.

"I just want you to know that we are praying you won't be led astray. I know Matthew is a powerful influence in your life, but consider the promise you made to God the day you were baptized."

That was all he said, but his words were seared into her conscience, as red hot and painful as a branding iron.

She saw her father, old, bent, with white hair, years down the road, a silver stream of tears coursing deep ridges of pain in his wrinkled face. Our Sarah, he would say. Our Sarah left us. She stands *im bann* (in the ban, shunned).

Without rebellion, this was going to be impossible.

Sarah left the Widow Lydia a message on her voice mail and then waited to walk past Elam Stoltzfus's till it was fully dark. She did not want Hannah to catch sight of her, furtively scuttling past to dump all her fears and frustrations on the widow who likely had more than enough of her own.

She was cowardly, maybe, but this night she had to talk to Lydia.

It was Wednesday, an ordinary weekday, which was good. She did not want her cousin Melvin to see her either. He never admitted to courting Lydia, although he spent every spare minute within decency at her house, fixing doors or planting shrubs and doing other necessary little duties. He wouldn't be there on a Wednesday.

She tried walking as far off the road as possible, the headlights of oncoming cars an unwelcome intrusion. She did not want to be seen, so she half walked, half ran the whole way, speeding up as she passed Matthew's house.

She was welcomed warmly at Lydia's door and scolded sincerely for staying away so long.

A tray of fruit and dip, cheese and crackers, and a pan of Reese's peanut butter bars stood temptingly on the gingham tablecloth covering kitchen table, and a pot of tea steamed on the wood stove.

Little Aaron lifted his arms to be held, and Sarah eagerly scooped him into her arms. He was dressed in green camouflage flannel pajamas and informed Sarah immediately that he was an English man and he was going hunting.

Lydia laughed with Sarah, then shook her head. "I shouldn't let him wear them, but Melvin gave them to him."

The girls welcomed Sarah as warmly as their mother had, and she smiled back with sincerity and promised to come more often.

After nine o'clock, the children were put to bed, Lydia poured tea, and they settled comfortably by the kitchen table.

Sarah began to talk, her speech nurtured with the encouraging manner Lydia possessed, unfolding her story, bit by bit, leaving nothing hidden.

Somewhere during the course of the conversation, the exterior door to the *kesslehaus* (wash house) opened, and there was a great clattering, laughter, and talking heard through the closed door.

"Omar," Lydia said quickly.

"Who is with him?"

Averting her eyes, Lydia adjusted the tablecloth.

"It's Lee."

"Lee?"

Lydia nodded and sipped her tea.

There was no chance to get away, nowhere to hide, before they burst into the kitchen, their faces alight, flushed with success.

"She did it, Mam!" Omar burst out. "Penny had her colt! It's a filly! A little girl!"

Lydia leaped to her feet, and for a moment, it seemed as though Lee was going to hug her, but he didn't.

What he did do was catch sight of Sarah.

Slowly the elation left his face as he struggled to regain the former feeling of success, but he was clearly caught off guard.

"Sarah."

That was all he said. Not "How are you?" or "Hello" or anything.

She didn't answer, except for a small, frightened smile.

When Omar yelled up the stairs, a great commotion followed—a mad, headlong dash through the kitchen, out the *kesslehaus* door, and down the slope to the new horse barn. Sarah followed along, carrying Aaron a bit clumsily and then stopped to let Lee take him, his hand leaving a trail of awareness where he touched her as he took the small boy from her.

Together, they all huddled by the heavy timbers forming the box stall, as Omar held the LED battery lamp high, illuminating every corner.

Cries of awe went up as the blonde, spindly little creature wobbled around on new, unsteady legs. The great Belgian mare nuzzled her newborn, batting her eyelashes as if to remind the small group of people that she had accomplished this miracle all by herself, and they had better use the proper discretion — they were dealing with royalty here.

She was truly magnificent, and so was her colt.

"She's so huge!" Sarah said.

"She's a Belgian!" Omar crowed.

Aaron yelled that he was going to ride her as soon as he had breakfast the next morning, and Sarah looked at him, held high in Lee's arms, and smiled, her eyes shining.

Later, Lee would remember every perfect contour of her face, the beautiful green eyes, the generous mouth, and the hair that never quite succumbed to the efforts of a comb, hairspray, or hairpins.

Eventually, the children slowly returned to their beds after glasses of milk and large squares of the chocolatey peanut butter bars. Lee declined an invitation to join them, and Sarah was caught by surprise by the strong feeling of loss when he moved off across the driveway, riding his best horse through the night.

It wasn't safe, Lydia said, but Omar assured her Lee would ride in fields and along fence rows most of the time.

It was a bit after eleven o'clock when the propane tank ran empty, casting the kitchen into a steadily receding lamplight.

"*Ach*," Lydia said.

"I'll go," Sarah assured her.

"Please don't, Sarah. I still haven't told you everything."

Sarah laughed.

"Just light a kerosene lamp. Here, I'll get the one in the bathroom."

Sarah carried it out and set the small lamp with its cozy orange glow in the middle of the table, as Lydia replenished their tea.

"What I haven't told you is kind of hard now. I feel guilty, being so happy, when you are so obviously tormented with indecision," Lydia said, sighing.

"Just tell me."

"Melvin asked me to be his wife."

She said the words softly, as if they would not hurt Sarah if she spoke as lightly as possible.

Sarah gasped, the words filling her with surprise.

"Oh, Lydia. I am so happy for you. Congratulations!"

Lydia smiled and lowered her eyes, the humility that was so much a part of her so evident now.

They continued their conversation, both of them aghast when they noticed the clock's hands had moved another two hours.

"I'll walk home with you, Sarah," Lydia offered.

"Of course not. I'll be fine. No one's out at this hour."

They parted with a long hug. There were tears in Lydia's eyes as she promised to pray on Sarah's behalf.

"God does not want us to live in unhappiness or indecision, Sarah. You know, if we are a willing sacrifice, we are able to discern His perfect will."

But when the *kesslehaus* door closed and Sarah slipped out into the frost-tipped spring night, Lydia stood in the middle of her kitchen and clenched her fists. Then she picked up a small, square pillow and threw it against the wall with all her strength. Then she stamped one foot and growled a very unladylike growl and thought she had never wanted to shake some sense into anyone as much as she wanted to shake Sarah until her teeth rattled.

Sarah walked down the sloping sidewalk to the gate, opened it, and let herself out, then walked on down the driveway, the gravel crunching under her feet.

She waited in the shadow of the new barn, allowing a car to pass. She did not want to be caught alone in the middle of the night.

She shivered, stopped to button her sweater securely, and walked on. Lifting her face, she enjoyed the sight of the velvety night sky alive with the stars twinkling, winking down at her the way they always did, a reminder that God was up there in the heavens, the same as He always was, and things would be okay somehow.

Exactly what made her turn her head in the direction of the horse barn, she would never know. She did, however, and caught sight of an orange glow in the small window—the one under the eaves.

Surprisingly, at first, she was very calm. Reasoning, even. The moon was about half, maybe two thirds full. It had to be the glow of an orange moon.

Or perhaps her mind refused to accept what her instincts knew.

Not the Widow Lydia. Please, dear God. If You have to allow another fire, please, not her.

Is a prayer a thought, or a thought a prayer? Can anybody pray when monstrous knowledge slams into them with the force of a sledgehammer?

When the orange glow flickered, Sarah was immobilized. She was frozen to the macadam, as wave after wave of nausea attacked her.

She was only one person, a weak young girl, and who could blame her if she fled to the safety of her father's arms?

As she stood, her gaze riveted to the small second story window, the orange glow became decidedly brighter.

Then she remembered Penny and the newborn filly. She remembered Lydia's humility. This would beat her down so badly, she might never recover. Something had to be done.

Her feet unlocked as anger coursed through her veins. She did not utter a sound. She had no tears. She just clenched her fists and ran. She ran past the house, her only thoughts of Penny and her colt. She had to get them out.

She tore open the main entrance door, groped her way along one wall, trying to remember where Omar had taken the battery lamp. As she entered the row of stalls, there was an alarming roar overhead, gaining momentum by the second.

All her common sense told her to go to the house, but she knew every horse would be lost if she did.

Did she scream, or was it the horses?

She remembered Dat's words. Horses want to stay in their familiar home, no matter how terrified they become.

She whipped off her sweater, called Penny's name, opened the massive gate, called again, cajoled, coaxed, begged. Then, mercifully, her fingers caught the part of Penny's halter below her chin, and she tugged with every ounce of strength.

"Come on, girl. Good. Easy!"

Talking, she coaxed the horse as the crashing sound of hooves against heavy boards increased. She was so intent on coaxing Penny that the intensity of the flames overhead became lost on her.

Sarah was tall, but Penny was enormous, her head lifting repeatedly as Sarah tried to cover the horse's eyes with her sweater, only to have it slide down around Penny's nose.

Desperate now, Sarah slowly coaxed the great horse to the water trough and clambered up to balance precariously on its rim. With renewed effort, she threw the sweater over the great head, hanging on when Penny lifted her head and shook it.

The hours-old filly bounced awkwardly, its legs splayed out ungracefully like a baby giraffe.

Again, Sarah talked to the great horse, pulled with all her strength on the chain that opened the door facing the house, and with one final heart-stopping leap, they made it through.

Sarah was crying now, her relief was so great. Opening the gate to the pasture, she turned them loose, peeling the black sweater off as the panicked horse shot through the opening to safety, the squealing little filly cavorting along as best it could.

The barn was fully engulfed, although it was contained to the upper level.

Sarah raced up the driveway, through the gate, and pounded on the house door with all her strength, crying hoarsely now, then resorting to an otherworldly scream of fear.

When Lydia came to the door, it was as Sarah had feared. The defeat in Lydia's eyes was already evident.

She turned and ran back down the slope, leaving the

gate swinging drunkenly on its hinges, aware of only one purpose, to save the horses.

Behind her, she heard Omar cry out, warning her, but she ran, crashed through the door, yanked open the door to the stables, her black sweater clutched in one hand, her chest heaving, her breath coming in great, tearful gasps.

The horse stable was strangely quiet, except for a lone whinny at the far end. One horse remained. It must be the great stallion. They had likely turned the rest of them out to pasture.

She was aware of another presence.

"Sarah!" Omar screamed her name, again warning her.

Silently, she handed him the black sweater, then stood back, as he worked swiftly, efficiently, covering the massive head with her sweater, as the crackling roar overhead became a raging inferno.

Should she go? No, she'd stay. She wanted to be certain Omar and the stallion made it out safely.

"Get out!" he screamed, as the stallion plunged past, dragging him along.

Turning, she took one last look around, making sure there was nothing in the box stalls, as the roar overhead shut out all other senses.

Sarah was moving toward the door and could see the cool, clean night beyond, when a fiery beam exploded over her head. She looked through the opened door, wide, beckoning, and she knew she could make it out. When she heard the cracking, tearing sound, she was puzzled by it.

The great, blackened beam slowly tilted to the side, gathering momentum, and crashed to the cement floor below. The only object cushioning its impact was Sarah's bent form. When it hit her head and neck and shoulders, the sparks and flames from the burning wood ignited the soft fleece of her headscarf, which instantly caught on fire.

There was a moment of blinding, indescribable pain, and then nothing as Sarah's world turned darker than black.

Omar could not hold back Dominic, the great Belgian stallion, as he hung frantically to the thick leather of the halter. He had no regard for his own safety as the stallion reared, lifting him off the ground. He talked to the animal, he screamed out his fear, but in the end, he had to let go and watch helplessly as the enormous giant tried to return to his stall.

Horrified, Omar could only stand helplessly as the horse tried to crash through the opened door. Omar let out a desperate cry as a woman, skirts billowing, darkly clad arms waving, stepped directly in front of the plunging behemoth, turning him aside at the very last minute.

Snorting, eyes rolling in terror, the stallion wheeled, galloped down the driveway, and up the road in the direction of the Beiler home.

Omar skidded to a stop, panting.

"Mam!"

Lydia stood beside him, watching Dominic race out the drive.

"Where's Sarah?" Lydia asked.

"Where is she?"

"Don't you know?"

"No!"

"Omar! Oh, please!"

"She was in the barn!"

"With you?"

Omar didn't answer, he was already through the door, into the mouth of the roiling, smoking, crackling furnace that had been the proud handiwork of Lee Glick.

"Sarah!"

He screamed and screamed.

Smoke filled his eyes, his nose, and his mouth. He gagged, choked, couldn't breathe. Faraway, as if in a dream, he heard the thin, panicked voice of his mother, but he could not go back.

Somewhere, Sarah might have fallen, been overtaken by smoke inhalation.

He bent low and stumbled, falling headlong to the fiery concrete floor, aware of the dark still form beside a flaming timber.

Lifting an arm, he coughed into the inner elbow, the fabric of his shirt mercifully allowing him one more gasp for breath.

In one swift movement, he turned and found her, inert, the length of her completely engulfed in small flames.

Without knowing how, he rolled her, shoving, gasping, choking, until every devilish, dancing little flame was extinguished.

Disoriented now, the forebay spun around him as he staggered and fell to his knees.

It was the popping, cracking sound of the great timbers overhead that infused his veins with the adrenaline he so desperately needed.

In one swoop, his strong, young arms scooped up the charred, heated body that was Sarah. With flaming lungs bursting, he stumbled through the door and across the cold gravel to the frosty grass on the other side.

Lydia could not control her voice—hoarse sobs and cries emerging in unearthly wails as terror consumed her.

Omar lay face down, gagging, as wave after wave of nausea expelled his stomach's contents.

Her cries reduced to moans and sobs, Lydia bent to Sarah's charred form, tenderly laying her sweater over the burnt body. Then she removed her housecoat and covered her legs as well.

Lydia stood in her homemade, flannel nightgown, her large eyes pools of shock and incomprehension, as Elam Stoltzfus and Matthew came gasping up the driveway, Hannah's large figure behind them, crying, questioning, answering herself.

Immediately, they heard the high, thin wail of the vehicles from Gordonville Fire Company heading their way.

"What happened?" Elam gasped.

Matthew remained silent, surveying the almost fully engulfed barn before turning to look at the covered form on the grass.

"Who?"

Lydia, slowly entering the first state of shock, shivered, crossed her arms, and rocked from side to side, as small beads of sweat formed on her forehead.

Matthew yelled at her, not realizing what was occurring, "Don't act so dense!"

Grasping her arm, he lowered his face and yelled again, but Lydia's head wobbled on her shoulders, a rag doll now, as she slowly sank to the ground.

It was the brilliant, bluish headlights piercing through the orange, smoke filled night that illuminated Sarah's still dark form with Lydia sitting beside her, awake, but not aware. Omar sat up, tears streaming down his cheeks, and told Elam and Hannah that it was Sarah lying there, and, no, he did not know if she was dead or if she still lived.

CHAPTER 3

THE TRAINED INDIVIDUALS, BOTH AMISH AND
English, that answered the call of 911 that night all
agreed. They thought she had died and then wondered
why she hadn't. It was the worst case they had ever seen.

They found a weak, fluttering pulse and sprang into
action. Radios crackled, lights flashed blue and orange,
sirens wailed repeatedly through the early spring night.
The fire raged, roared, and crackled. The walls collapsed,
then the roof.

Neighbors came on foot. Men had thrown on their
clothes haphazardly and jammed straw hats backwards
on their heads.

Women left at home hovered on porches or at upstairs
windows with blinds rolled up, curtains held aside. Children pressed against them, and the mothers stooped to
answer childish questions as their hands dried frightened
little tears.

Davey Beiler was awakened by his wife, Malinda, with
a soft, repeated calling of his name. At first, he was bewildered, but then he knew with the assurance of experience.
Somewhere, there was another fire.

When Malinda told him it looked like the Widow Lydia's barn, he groaned within himself. Why her? Why a second time?

He fought back a rage so intense it filled his mouth with a metallic taste. He yanked on the strings of his brown, leather work shoes so hard that his ankles hurt.

Who was demented enough to return and do this same evil to Lydia a second time?

Davey pulled his broad brimmed straw hat down on his head, smashing it angrily. The rough straw beside the soft cloth lining inside of the crown scratched his forehead, but he was beyond caring.

"Take care of the girls and Levi," he said roughly, before lunging through the door.

His thoughts were tangled, his steps long, as he hurried up the road past Elam's. Cars were now vying for position to get near the fire, sirens wailing repeatedly through the night.

Men were directing traffic around roadblocks, their fluorescent vests gleaming in the night. Davey was glad. No use having all this traffic around.

As he neared the scene of the fire, he noticed the Gordonville ambulance at Lydia's gate. Had someone been hurt?

As he hurried, his mouth turned dry, and a premonition pushed its dark head into his mind.

Omar?

The Widow Lydia?

He remembered Sarah then. She had gone to visit her friend. Hadn't she returned?

He was fighting emotions as he walked up to Elam, his neighbor for almost thirty years, and touched his elbow.

"Who?"

That was all he could think to say.

When Elam looked at him and his mouth twitched downward, Davey knew it was Sarah.

When Elam's lips compressed in an attempt to check his emotions, and his great, calloused hand was clapped on Davey's shoulder, he knew it was bad.

"Iss noch laeva dot (Is there life yet)?"

"Ach, ich glaub (Oh, I believe so), Davey."

Davey nodded.

In the kaleidoscope of lights and sound, he singled out a member of the trained personnel and plucked at his sleeve. He pushed his white face towards the worker's and asked who it was, his capable fingers shaking, useless now, devoid of their usual power.

"I understand it's a neighbor girl."

"Sarah Beiler?"

The man inquired, returned, and nodded his head, affirming the premonition.

"I am her father."

Davey bowed his head then and let the tears roll down his cheeks. He shook like a leaf. He jammed his hands into the pockets of his broadfall denim trousers to still them, acknowledged the arm thrown about his shoulders.

He prayed silently that God would spare her life, but that His will might be done. He knew God ruled omnipotent, His ways so far above his own, and who knew if God would choose to take Sarah as well as Mervin, his beloved, towheaded six-year-old?

He could feel the submission come, the calming arrive, as he prayed on. Slowly, the night, the sounds, the smoke, and flames receded, and he focused on the interior of the red and white ambulance, where four people hovered over the figure on a stretcher.

He saw the tubes, the stethoscopes, the tanks, the lights, and knew there was nothing he could do. She was in good hands.

A driver came. He was ushered into the front seat of the ambulance.

"Remember to tell Malinda. Bring her."

Elam bowed his head, shook it. Matthew stood beside his father, his face waxy, white.

Hannah was illuminated in the lights of the ambulance as she knelt by her neighbor Lydia, a hand on Omar's back, the girls huddled around their brother.

The last thing he saw was the streams of water directed on the new dairy barn, keeping it safe from the overpowering heat from the burning horse barn. Then the ambulance crunched down the lane and turned onto the road, on its way to the emergency room at Lancaster General.

A sharp sense of reality made the night, the headlights, the two yellow lines on the road, the frosty grasses by the roadside, come into a clear focus.

When the driver turned on the siren and pushed down on the accelerator, Davey pressed back in his seat as they shot forward.

He sat immobile, as they raced through the night, picking up speed as they turned onto 340, the Old Philadelphia Pike, on their way through Bird-In-Hand and towards the city of Lancaster.

His lips moved in prayer, his shoulders slumped in submission, but his hands continued their weak trembling, so he stuck them both between his knees to still them.

As a minister of the Old Order Amish church, Davey was no stranger to the ER or the Lancaster General

Hospital. His duties took him there many times. The lights, the automatic doors that slid quietly open, the voices of doctors and nurses as they padded down glistening tiled hallways in professional footwear—it was all familiar.

The night air revived him, helped stabilize the feeling of defeat, but there was nothing he could do about his trembling limbs, so he stood, shaking, in the cold night air as the ambulance doors were flung open.

He cried slow, hot tears when the realization hit him.

A helicopter was standing by.

Men and women clad in pastel colors rushed out, swarmed the stretcher. Without thinking, acting solely on instinct, Davey rushed to the stretcher. He bent over, peering frantically between the doctors and nurses, trying to see until he was pulled gently away.

"I want to see her," he pleaded.

No one answered.

Inside, he sank to a chair in the waiting room and did as he was told. He answered questions, nodded his head, said yes or no, provided an address, a telephone number, her birth date.

No, he didn't know her Social Security number. He produced his own and felt like crying all over again because the small blue card was so old and worn, and he shouldn't carry it in his wallet, he knew.

He showed his ID, his wallet slapping against his knee as he tried to insert it back into the plastic sleeve.

He wished for Malinda intensely. She was quicker, smarter, better spoken at times like this. Small, stout, quick, she was so capable.

They didn't let him see Sarah. That was the hardest part. And he didn't know they'd taken her until she had already gone. He'd signed forms but wasn't aware how swiftly they would convey his daughter away from him.

Mein Gott (My God), he cried inside.

The Amish were forbidden to fly. They were not allowed to enter an airplane, small or large, so they didn't. Except when medical aid was needed.

It was hard to be alone, waiting, without knowing. He felt as though he was the one suspended in mid-air, dangling, fighting fear.

He kept his head bowed, his straw hat beside him, occupying a whole chair by itself. He should hang it on the steel hooks provided for that purpose, but he felt better having his hat close by, a familiarity, an old friend to wait with him.

He looked at the round black and white clock. Three eleven. Or twelve. Not quite quarter after three. He wondered when Malinda would come. Who would do the milking?

Panicked, he turned his head to the left, then to the right. The waiting room was fairly empty. A few weary people slumped in their seats, and a couple was having a quiet conversation in the corner.

Rising slowly, he went to the desk window and waited before asking if there was phone service available.

When he was led to the nurses' station, he followed instructions carefully, relieved to hear Malinda's greeting on their voice mail. He left a message, saying Priscilla and Suzie would have to milk as best they could, and the vet was coming in the morning for number 84 in the box stall.

He returned to the waiting room, his eyes filled with a new light when he found his wife standing hesitantly inside the automatic doors, wearing her black shawl and bonnet.

Quickly, he was by her side. They did not hug or touch at all, but their eyes spoke volumes. They understood each other's pain, the fiery trial, and the endurance that would be required. They were not strangers to suffering.

Together, they sat quietly, and Davey spoke in hushed tones as Malinda silently wept, her flowered handkerchief lifted repeatedly to wipe away the tears.

Finally she burst out, "But will she live?"

"I can't tell you. I don't know."

They sat, waiting, drawing comfort from one another.

When a doctor came to the door and asked for David Beiler, Dat almost leaped to his feet, but after shaking the physician's hand, he sat back down, weakly.

Mam lifted a white, ravaged face.

His name was Dr. James, and he was the specialist on call.

"Your daughter's injuries are extensive."

Mam caught her breath.

"We have what we call 'the rule of nines,' referring to the percentage of the body that is afflicted. The head and each of the arms make up nine percent, the back, front, and each leg eighteen percent, and so forth. We don't know the exact invasion on the epidermis or the deeper tissue, but most of one whole side of her body was in contact with the flames. For how long, we don't know. The actual depth of her wounds will be determined at the burn center near Philadelphia. That's at the Crozer-Chester Medical Center in Upland. There, she'll be given the best treatment possible."

The doctor paused.

Dat swallowed, his mouth gone dry, remembering horrific tales of children enduring the removal of dead tissue from a burned area. Debridement, they called it, the unusual term now springing unexpectedly to his mind. They'd once said no parent could stand to watch or to hear the cries.

Mam bowed her head, weeping quietly.

"Our first concern is the trauma. She was in shock and will need transfusions. Another big concern, of course, is the smoke inhalation with the risk for infection in her lungs and pneumonia. So far we can offer a fair evaluation. She's young and was seemingly in good health. Are there any questions?"

Dat shook his head.

Mam lifted her gaze to Dr. James and asked what percentage of Sarah's body was burned and how bad it all really was.

The doctor remained forthright, saying the evaluation would be much more accurate at the burn center. His answer seemed to satisfy Mam, and she nodded assent. They shook hands, thanked the doctor quietly, and turned to go.

Dat hadn't thought to ask who the driver was and if he was willing to drive them to the burn center at this time of the night.

It was Wendell, the good, dependable driver who knew every route in and out of Lancaster and the surrounding counties and states. A retired truck driver, he was competent and skilled at *goot zeit macha* (making good time). It was a term often overheard in Amish circles, an analysis of each driver's ability to efficiently get his load of people from point A to point B.

How could a night be so long? The sky was still pitch black as they travelled along on the interstate highway. The stars twinkled above them, and the half moon hovered to the west, yet it seemed the time moved twice as slowly at this nightmarishly early morning hour.

Davey hoped that the hovering, man-made wonder called a helicopter had landed safely. Would Sarah's burns be so severe she may be better off perishing because of them?

Just help us through, guide us, let us accept what You have for us.

His prayers kept him calm, centered, in the middle of this giant whirlwind that had whisked him off his feet and thrown him into a nameless land where nothing made sense, except to blame himself.

"You're going to keep this up until someone gets hurt!" Melvin's words rang in his ears now, and Davey laid his head against the van seat, drew a shaking breath, and closed his eyes.

He had not allowed it, in the end. No media or private detectives. God had allowed this, the spate of fires, barns burning at random, hadn't He?

Yes, it was wrong. But as Davey had said a hundred times before, the Amish were a nonresistant people. If a man takes your raiment, give him your cloak also. If he smites one cheek, give unto him the other. If he asks you to go with him one mile, you're supposed to go with him two.

But did it apply? If a man burns your barn, give him your house as well? The principle was insane when it came to personal loss. Or was it?

God's people were peculiar. They did things differently than the world, and it appeared a foolishness to many.

Davey Beiler knew God's people were everywhere, in many modes of dress, many cultures, and ways of life. Not only the Amish knew God's ways. Sometimes, in matters he kept to himself, he thought the English were the ones who came through with great, undeserved love and kindness, the spine of Christianity.

And now, his daughter, somewhere alone in a great hospital far from home, was severely injured. Was it because of his inability to "do something"?

Dozens of bishops and ministers agreed with Davey. The old way was best—the principle of forgiveness—even at a time like this.

Self blame edged out his conviction, causing an unrelenting torment in his breast as the van bore to the left, passing yet another tractor trailer.

Levi was awake.

He wasn't completely sure why he had been awakened, but when he heard a rapid pounding on the front door, he rolled over and opened one eye to peer at the alarm clock. He could see alright with only one eye if he wasn't wearing his glasses.

Two o'clock.

Throwing back the covers, he took his time pushing his feet into the corduroy slippers by his nightstand.

Checking the buttons on his flannel pajamas, he buttoned one that had come undone and pulled the fabric down over his ample stomach.

Shuffling to the bedroom door, he called for Dat, then Mam. When there was no answer, he shifted his gaze to the living room couch, then caught sight of the blaze beyond Elam's place and heard the thin wail of the fire sirens.

Ach, du lieva (Oh my goodness), he thought.

Another sharp rapping assaulted his slow senses, and

he snorted impatiently. Well, if Mam and Dat were not going to the door, he guessed he'd have to.

"Hang on!" he bellowed, exactly the way he heard his brother Allen say at his house.

He was not afraid, didn't even think of such a thing. He simply yanked the door open, stuck his great tousled head out, and peered into the youth's face. Levi asked, in a voice as English as he could possible make it, "May I help you with something?"

The tall, thin youth with the shaggy hair moved uncomfortably from one foot to another, his hands stuck in the pockets of his short jacket.

"Your dad here?"

"No. I'd say he's down at the fire."

"Oh, yeah. Guess he would be."

Levi checked his face for a full minute, thoroughly examining every angle, the plane of his nose, the way he held his head, the shaggy hair.

Yep, Levi decided. It's him.

"You can come in. I'll light the kitchen lamp. He should be here."

"Okay."

The youth moved through the door and stood awkwardly by the counter while Levi slowly lifted the lighter to the mantles of the gas lamp and turned the black knob. The tall youth blinked in the bright, yellowish light.

"Sit down," Levi said.

He sat down.

"Now, I have to go to the bathroom, so are you alright if I leave you awhile?"

"Sure."

"Alright, then."

Levi disappeared through the *kesslehaus* door, closed

it behind him, and instantly moved as stealthily and swiftly as his bulk would allow. Through the side door of the
kesslehaus, across the frosty lawn, and into the phone
shanty he sped, closing the door as quietly behind him
as possible.

Lifting the small LED penlight, Levi peered at the buttons, then deliberately punched in the nine, then two ones
in rapid succession. He told the dispatcher he needed a
policeman, or two, if she could, at the Davey Beiler farm
on Irishtown Road in back of Gordonville. He thought
he had someone they might want.

He replaced the receiver, swished through the cold,
wet grass back to the *kesslehaus,* and entered noiselessly.
He reached into the small alcove and flushed the com-
mode, then washed his hands, splashing and humming,
biding his time, before reappearing.

"Sorry about that."

The youth said nothing, his face working.

"You want coffee? Shoofly? Mam made whoopie
pies."

"No, thanks."

"Okay then."

"When's your dad going to be back?"

"Oh, I'd imagine before too long. He'll need something after while."

The youth cast a dark look at Levi and was greeted by
a look of childlike innocence from the narrowed brown
eyes.

When they heard someone on the front porch, Levi
knew it wasn't Dat, but he went to the door and said,
"Oh, you're here. Come on in. Your company is waiting
for you."

When the first policeman entered, the youth leaped to

his feet and made a mad dash for the *kesslehaus* door, but Levi had locked it from the other side. He crashed into it, swore, and tried an alternative route, straight into the burly officer's arms.

Levi hopped up and down with excitement, but then sat quietly as the youth was questioned.

When it was his turn, Levi answered the policeman's questions well. He believed this boy was "sticking on" (lighting) the barns. He had believed it ever since the very first night the small white car moved past their barn with no lights. He never told anyone that a teddy bear drove the car, because everyone in his family and the church would laugh at him. But his hair was shaggy, like a stuffed bear. Levi saw this boy at the funeral of that pretty English girl, and he thought his name was Mike.

The youth glared at Levi, then became quite somber. The boy leaned forward and lowered his face in his hands, and Levi knew without a doubt that he was *buze fertich* (repentant).

Too bad the policeman didn't want any shoofly either. It was pretty lonely eating it all by himself at such an early hour in the morning. He hoped Dat and Mam wouldn't return too soon. They'd be needed at the fire, he reasoned, as he cut his second wedge of shoofly pie. And he deserved a treat for his work that night. It had just been a matter of waiting till the time was right and knowing when to go to the bathroom.

CHAPTER 4

FINALLY, WHEN DAVID AND MALINDA BEILER thought they would go mad with impatience, another doctor appeared in the doorway of the waiting room and asked them to accompany him to a room where there would be more privacy. Their despair had become a steadily rising foe, and it was about to grow bigger.

In the private room, they were told the truth, bluntly. Nothing was held back, but in precise, physician's language, the doctor relayed Sarah's situation in a professional manner laced with empathy and kindness.

They were left examining the burden of information he dropped on them, an unwelcome weight dumped on their shoulders, impossible to carry. They tried to contain their emotions, but that, too, was an impossibility. Tears slid unheeded down their exhausted faces.

For now, she was stable, though her condition was critical. She had lost a lot of blood.

The burns covered roughly fifty percent of her body, the worst of the damage on one side, the right. It was centered on her upper chest, arm, neck, and face.

Mam gasped as the doctor said, "face."

The deepest burns had been caused when her head-scarf caught fire.

The biggest concern was the possibility of pneumonia and infection. They would need to take it a day at a time, the extent of skin grafting and surgeries depending on the severity of the tissue damage.

The recovery would be weeks, months. There were facilities provided for family within walking distance from the hospital, where they could stay free of charge.

They asked their only question, "When can we see her?"

He made a few quick phone calls, a nurse appeared, and, after shaking the doctor's hand and thanking him, they were on their way. Into the elevator and up to the third floor, they moved along behind the nurse with their heads bowed, avoiding gazes that were curious, kind, or puzzled.

They were joined by another nurse, a tall, angular woman with graying hair, who introduced herself as Junie Adams, the head nurse. She explained the tubes, machines, and monitors they would see, then asked them to don gowns and masks, remove their shoes, and wear only sterile slippers.

Quickly, they complied, then followed her into a cold, dim room, alive with clicks and whirs, lights, IV bags, poles, and a figure swathed in white bandages.

There was no trace of Sarah anywhere. Even her eyes were covered. That was the hardest part for Mam. If only she could see her eyes, she'd be able to find her Sarah.

As it was, they stood together, their clothes touching, the feeling of being joined at this hour absolutely essential.

"You may talk to her. She's on morphine, heavily drugged, as you can see, but she may respond. Her mouth is lightly covered, the same as her eyes, so go ahead, see what happens."

They could not speak, at first. It wasn't that they didn't try, but nothing would come except more tears, more pain, as they struggled together.

Finally, Mam said, "Sarah," and was instantly consumed with a flood of weeping so intense she sagged against her husband, and his arm went around her to hold her steady.

Then he spoke. He said her name. He told her not to be afraid; they were here with her now. Mam told her they loved her and were waiting until she could speak to them.

A long, hoarse moan came from the swathed mouth, then another. The nurse assured them it was okay.

They spoke again, but the first few moans were the only ones that came in response, and they had to be satisfied with the knowledge that perhaps she had heard.

It seemed more bearable now, somehow, since they had seen her.

They sat in the large room, after following a bewildering number of people to another floor and through an archway with a cafeteria sign above it. They had followed others, picking up plastic trays and silverware wrapped in white napkins, and chosen the food they would need to sustain them, for the forenoon hours, anyway.

Mam ate dry toast, without realizing it wasn't buttered, and Dat drank his coffee black, unable to find the creamer and not wanting to make his way through the crowd again.

It was alright, they could face each other, read the depths of one another's eyes, and drink greedily from the comfort and assurance they saw there.

When Dat reached across the tabletop and grasped Mam's hand, he told her she was all the support he needed and thanked her for being strong. And she knew her Davey was a man she still admired even after all these years.

Together, they were a mighty fortress.

Back in the waiting room, they leaped to their feet at the appearance of Ruthie and Anna Mae, their husbands in tow. Priscilla and Suzie followed them shyly, their eyes huge in their pinched white faces.

A clamoring ensued with talking, hugging, and crying. The girls needed to find out every single detail they could gather about Sarah.

Then Priscilla told them about Lydia and Omar's situation. The horse barn, of course, had been burned to the ground, but the dairy barn was saved, and not one horse was lost. Dominic, the crazy thing, ran clear out to Ben's Sam's in Gordonville and was being kept in the bull pen for now.

Melvin had stayed with Lydia, and so far, she did not seem to be sliding into despair, her spirits being bolstered by Melvin's unfailing optimism, which was good.

No one was allowed to see Sarah. Suzie sat close to Mam and would not leave her side. Priscilla stayed on the other. Ruthie talked and fussed on and on about what she knew about burns—the miraculous work of the B and W salve and burdock leaves. Dat nodded assent but said, "Not for now, Ruthie, not for now. This is way above our home remedies. Our Sarah almost died."

"Could she still?" Suzie asked, her terrified eyes large and intense.

"She could, yes. We'll take a day at a time—no, an hour at a time," Dat said.

Eli's Sam had stayed with Levi. They played game after game of checkers, and Levi did not say a word about the shaggy-haired youth or calling the police.

Priscilla and Suzie had slept through the ruckus, and Levi figured he'd not mention it until Sarah was better. Sarah was tough, he reasoned, but she was, after all, a girl, and you had to take care of them. Why, they screamed terrible when he took his dentures out of his mouth.

The Crozer-Chester Medical Center was a great earth-hued building, rectangular, seven stories high. It had an enclosure along the one side, a porch of sorts. Trees surrounded it and some newly planted shrubs and flowering bushes. They were dormant now, waiting for their time to join the greening of spring, the bark mulch around them weathered by the snows of winter.

The parking lot spread across acres of former agricultural land, the parking spaces painted white, like a crossword puzzle mapped out with signs—who could park where, this space reserved. Usually most of the spaces were occupied, the gigantic building a beacon of hope and caring for families whose loved ones were severely burned or burned beyond the realm of home care, in any case.

Hundreds of doctors, nurses, and other trained individuals worked within the tiled walls of the hospital, devoting their lives to the care and healing of unfortunate souls who had to endure one of the most severe forms of nature's suffering.

The Beilers' second night at the burn center was almost spent. The moon had descended far to the west, its bluish white glow turning the indigo blue night sky a bit silver. The parked cars took on the glistening luster of moonlight, and small shadows appeared on the east side of every object.

Inside, on the third floor, the figure in Room 312 moaned, sighed, then fell asleep, her limbs twitching after she attempted to verbalize her thoughts. Images spun through her head, but they made her too tired, so she let them go.

There was no use. The weariness was much too heavy. It lay on her chest like a fifty-pound bag of potatoes, slowly pressing out her will to live.

Those potatoes needed to be taken down to the root cellar. The garden must not have produced enough this year for Dat to have bought them in a fifty-pound bag.

She groaned, tried to roll out from beneath it. No use. She'd just have to breathe as best she could.

She was picking up potatoes now, the breeze soft and mellow, the earth still warm on her bare toes, although the summer was fast coming to an end, and most of the harvest was in.

There was still the cabbage Mam had planted late, and the celery, banked up with hills of loamy brown soil.

She stooped, felt the satisfying mound beneath her fingers, and brought up a big one this time. The biggest potato of the season. She tossed it into the wooden crate, then bent for another.

Mervin was with her, laughing, throwing small potatoes at her. She was puzzled that he was there, but the weight on her chest made it too tiring to ask.

Mervin sang, he laughed, he smiled, and all the

potatoes he threw at her hurt so badly, she wanted to
make him stop.

She cried out, "Mervin, *do net* (don't)!"

The more she pleaded, the harder he threw them, still
singing and laughing.

The pain was unbearable now.

She begged for mercy, asked him to stop.

Where was Mam? She had to have help. Someone had
to help her get out from under this weight. She called and
called, but no one would come to her.

Sarah's parents sat, one on either side of her bed,
with their heads resting on the backs of the vinyl-cov-
ered chairs. Their eyes were closed, mouths slack as sleep
loosened the muscles and tendons.

Rest had come suddenly for both of them. After almost
forty hours, there was no alternative. They slept.

While they slept, Sarah called, over and over. Or so
she thought.

Mam still slept with the trained senses of a mother of
ten, but there was no sound from the still, white form on
the bed. It was the swish of the nurse's scrubs that first
woke Mam. She sat up immediately, adjusted her covering, smoothed her skirt, and felt guilty for having dozed
off, away from Sarah.

The nurse didn't speak, just edged silently past Mam,
checked the blips and beeps on the monitors, inspected
the IV bag to check its level, then patted Mam's shoulder
as she moved past.

She was efficient and kind, even at this hour, Mam
thought. It was a miracle the way these people knew
exactly what they were doing.

A low sound came from the bed.

Mam turned, grasped the arms of her chair, and got to her feet. The sound was different this time.

"Mm. Mm!"

Quickly, Mam bent over Sarah, placing her hands lightly on her face, her shoulders.

"Sarah. Sarah. *Ich bin do* (I am here)."

Then, decidedly, from the thin confines of the white bandages, came a garbled sound, altered by a swollen throat.

"Ma-am."

"I'm here, Sarah. Can you hear me?"

Hoarse breathing, accelerated now, came rasping from her mouth behind the gauze. It sounded like fabric tearing as Sarah regained consciousness. The only form of expression her body allowed was a long, hoarse whisper of misery. A silent scream.

"Sarah. Sarah."

Mam was completely distraught now, afraid Sarah would choke. Forgetting the button she was supposed to press for help, she moved past the foot of the bed and out the door. Turning her head from left to right, she scuttled in the direction of the nurses' station.

The station wasn't there. Not where she thought it should be.

Oh, there was someone. She stopped the harried looking nurse.

"Can you help us? She's awake!"

The nurse, all six feet of her, looked down at the weary Amish woman plucking at her sleeve and resigned herself. These Amish were all the same. Inevitably, they all came looking for help, forgetting to use the call button.

Mam's feet slid across the tiles, following the long-legged stride in front of her, so befuddled she didn't even notice when the nurse stopped at a long, high enclosure and said, "312."

Instantly, the nurse—the same one who had checked the IV—rose and walked swiftly to Sarah's room, awakening Dat as she went to his side of Sarah's bed.

She pressed the button for help with one thumb, while her other hand reached for the thin gauze around Sarah's mouth. Mam stood by, her hands clasped in front of her, her mouth working, as the agonized sounds continued.

Another nurse, younger, with a tanned complexion and short, brown hair, joined the other one. Together, they began loosening some of the bandages around Sarah's face.

"If you would rather not be here, you can step out of the room," the first one informed them.

Dat's eyes questioned Mam, but she refused to budge. Sarah was "coming to," and there was no way she was leaving this room.

The pain was a white-hot, blinding force that took her breath away before she had a chance to finish it. She let out a small puff of air, drew one back, and then another, before the hoarse screams would stop them entirely.

Slowly, the light above her head came into focus. The doorframe, the track beside her bed, the sour green of the walls, the clashing color of the beige curtain.

Then the waves of pain pounded across her, a tsunami, a devastating wall that set all her nerves shimmering with unaccustomed intensity, like a razor blade drawn horizontally across her wounds.

As the nurses allowed a minimal opening, her eyes or the small, red swollen appendages that had been her eyes, opened far enough to search, desperately, for someone to help her.

A face, hands, voices, but not someone who would help.

"Mm. Mm." She strained to call Mam's name.

Stepping aside, the nurses allowed Mam into Sarah's line of vision. Mam never wavered. There were no tears. Her daughter was awake, she was calling for her, and she had a duty to perform.

Many nights Mam had nursed cranky babies. She had comforted her children after disturbing dreams. She had wiped vomit from their bedsides, gagging as she did so, bathed little ones smelling so sour she could taste it, poured baking soda on soiled mattresses, and tucked the sweet-smelling children back into beds made up with clean sheets—only to have the exact same scene repeated a few hours later. Those times, she didn't think of herself, her weariness. She just went ahead and did her duty, the same as she would do now.

"Sarah."

"Helf mich (Help me)."

"I will help you, Sarah. I will do everything I can."

Dat stood, helpless, his eyes pooled with tears, but calm.

"Voss (What)?"

The croak was barely audible, but the question, the plea, was known and recognized, the way it banged on Mam's heart.

"Sarah, the barn at the Widow Lydia's? It burned. Can you remember anything at all?"

"An drink."

Immediately, Mam understood. Of course, she was thirsty.

"She wants a drink," she said to Dat.

Mam asked the nurses for a cup of water, but they provided only ice chips, which made Mam breathe hard, the way she did when she was huffy inside, though she was trained to be quiet, submissive.

So she held a plastic spoon of ice chips to Sarah's swollen lips, lovingly, expertly. She held very still when Sarah gurgled, choked, and began a labored breathing that concerned the nurse. Mam figured that the ice was too cold and a cup of water would have been much better.

She needed comfrey tea and B and W salve and burdock leaves she had gathered from the fence rows and dried in the hot August sun. She needed the spring tonic she made with garlic and red pepper and aloe vera, but she knew all that would come later.

For now, they needed the care of professionals, the sterile environment, doctors with experience and knowledge far above their own.

"It hurts," Sarah moaned.

"Sarah, you'll need to be brave. You have to gather all your courage, every ounce of strength within you, to be able to heal. A beam fell on your head, and your clothes were on fire."

The only answer was another onslaught of ragged cries, and the nurse tugged gently on Mam's sleeve, drawing her away, then explained very gently about upping the pain medication, so Sarah would sleep for another few hours. The need to keep her quiet was explained in careful detail, and Mam folded her small form back into a vinyl chair and acknowledged their counsel, but the moment the door closed behind them, she turned to her husband and sputtered with indignation and suppressed emotion.

The morning sun made its appearance through the east windows on the third floor, as Sarah lay quietly. She was breathing in and out slowly, but then more shallowly as her breathing accelerated.

Over the course of the sun's ascent, she lay, as her parents spoke quietly, with furtive glances in the direction of their sleeping daughter. They both knew the weeks ahead would tax their strength to the breaking point, but with God's help, they would make it through.

When three doctors entered at once and stood gravely at Sarah's bed, then turned and introduced themselves, still grave, Dat's heart plunged within, and he felt physically ill from the feeling. Would she still not survive?

The oldest, with white hair in a semi circle around his shining bald crown, had square glasses and a goatee. He spoke first.

He addressed Dat as Mr. Beidler, and Dat did not bother correcting him.

"Her burns are severe, especially on the right side, where the beam hit. Her neck, ear, and right side of her face have mostly third degree burns, some second degree perhaps. We are still deciding about complete isolation in a room with laminar air flow, to keep her as free from microorganisms as possible."

The second doctor addressed Dat as Mr. Beidler as well, then stroked his dark moustache thoughtfully, lowering and raising his eyebrows, two perfectly matched black caterpillars.

"She's young, very healthy, and she may be okay here—strong enough to ward off possible infection."

Dat nodded.

Mam thought about vitamin C drops and capsules, and echinacea, but she didn't say anything. A woman was subject to her husband, and if she needed to know anything, she could ask him at home.

The third doctor was short and round, with a thatch of black, well-groomed hair lying flat along his crown. His Asian features were pleasant, his accent thick, his speech rapid. Dat nodded, his head inclined, but he did not understand a single word he said.

Finally, Dat spoke. He told the physicians that the decisions they made were theirs to exercise, and he would abide by them, and he wished them God's wisdom. He said, at times like this, he could only be thankful that God had imparted this learning to them, and he hoped they could communicate well and understand the process.

Mam nodded and smiled, but said nothing.

They were escorted through the door and walked like an aging couple to the waiting room, their steps slow, their heads bent, weary, defeated suddenly.

Why? Why had God allowed this devastation? Wouldn't it have been easier to let her die?

He didn't have the nerve to ask about the disfigurement. Surely, her face and neck would never be the same. She would carry horrible scars all her life, and folks would not be able to keep from staring at her. Davey and Malinda had been through all that with Levi.

The glances, quickly, then away, only to return—the pitying looks that came along with carrying her imperfect baby wherever she went. Mam knew the feeling well.

Yes, she had taken pride in Sarah's beauty. A nontraditional beauty, perhaps, but still. And now God had chosen to chastise her.

Together, they sat, side by side, three floors above the large parking lot, and stared through the immense glass windows without seeing, losing ground as they flailed themselves with harsh thoughts of self-judgment.

Because of my sin, my daughter lies in torture. Because of my sin, God is chastening me. Oh, I know that He loves me. But I have gone astray. Without knowing, my heart has turned to stone, and now He must bring me back.

Individually, but almost as one, they repented, asked forgiveness, prayed silently, separately, but found no peace.

The windstorm of self-blame had been efficient. It had wrecked their mighty fortress, leaving them both on high, bitter, arid ground, separating them as each sought to withstand the blows of fortune. Or of God.

CHAPTER 5

Back home in the area between Intercourse and Gordonville, the neighborhood buzzed with activity once again. Black exhaust poured from the smokestacks of great yellow earth movers as they cleared wet, charred beams and twisted metal. They formed a huge pile of useless, wasted material that had been the fine horse barn housing the Belgians. It had been the pride of the Widow Lydia's son, Omar, and his older friend and mentor, Lee Glick, the blond, strapping young man who lived with his sister Anna and her husband, Ben Zook.

Truckloads of yellow lumber made their slow, noisy way past Elam Stoltzfus's house, and Matthew was awakened by the sound, one he considered unnecessary.

His mood already foul. He dressed carefully, as he always did, in a white short-sleeved t-shirt with navy blue pinstripes and a clean pair of jeans. He pulled on a black leather belt and admired the buckle, thinking how much better it was to wear a belt than those elastic suspenders he used to wear.

Naturally, his mother was up at the Widow Lydia's, so he broke a few eggs in a bowl and beat them with a fork, set them aside, and searched the bread drawer.

No bread?

The door opened, and his mother walked in backward, holding the big plastic coffee container with both hands. Her black scarf was settled haphazardly on her head, her sweater closed with safety pins, as usual.

"Oh, Matthew, you're up!"

Her tone took on that high, desperate whine it always did when she wanted him to be in a good mood. Irritation welled up as he watched her slam the coffee container on the countertop.

"Matthew, Sarah is burned! She's burned bad. Oh, I think it can't be! Why did she ever go into the barn?"

"Mam, we went over all this before. She just wasn't thinking."

"No, she wasn't. She wasn't."

Bustling now, talking to herself as much as to Matthew, she chided Sarah for going into the burning barn, scolded Davey for allowing this to go on, scolded Malinda for letting Sarah go to talk to the widow that night. She was simply unable to come to terms with Sarah's suffering.

Matthew remained quiet, listening to his mother with an air of patience and understanding.

"Where's the bread?" he asked.

"Bread? There's no bread in the bread drawer? *Ach my!* I think there's some in the freezer."

Hastily, she ran over to the refrigerator, yanked the freezer door open, and searched frantically.

"Well."

Matthew watched from his perch on a kitchen chair.

"I don't know how I managed that. I'm out of bread."

"You manage that quite often, if I remember right."

"Now, Matthew. Don't be mean."

"Half the time, you're out of bread."

"No, not half the time."

"If you'd bake your own the way Malinda does…"

"You have a car. You could run out to Kauffman's."

"Nah. I'll just have scrambled eggs."

"There's sausage."

"Where?"

Hannah yanked open the refrigerator door, pushed containers aside, and produced a Tupperware bowl of ground sausage, her face alight, eager to make up for the missing bread.

Matthew lifted the lid, sniffed, slowly replaced it, and pronounced it spoiled.

"I'm not eating that stuff."

"Matthew. *Ach,* I just bought it."

"Where?"

"At Centerville."

"Hard telling where that junk comes from."

"We have bacon."

"What kind?"

"John Martin's."

"Is it fresh?"

"Oh, I think so. Surely. The package hasn't been opened yet."

Matthew found the bacon to his liking and proceeded to make his own breakfast, without toast. Hannah bustled about the kitchen, making more coffee, collecting sugar, milk, flour, and apple pie filling from the cellar. She was always hopeful that Matthew was pleased and not too put out by her poor management.

"Are you coming to help today?" she asked finally.

"Why would I? I'm not Amish."

"Oh, now, that doesn't matter."

"I don't want anyone staring at me or asking questions, okay?"

"Oh, alright."

"I'm going to have my devotions. My Bible is my strength now as I travel life's pathway alone."

"Oh, so true, Matthew. I'm so glad you have your faith, your Christianity."

Her hands clasped, her eyes lifted to her handsome son, the poor, hurting widower, the love of her life. She was so glad he was able to carry on alone, glad he was so well versed in the Bible. That was all that mattered.

Juggling her bags and boxes, only dimly aware of the fact that Matthew did not offer his assistance, she loaded the wagon, that ever-present and faithful conveyor of all things wagon-able, and was on her way, doing her duty at yet another barn raising.

Well, where there was life, there was hope. Sarah had not died, and Matthew might still be glad to make her his wife.

And they could be Amish, too, she decided, the very thought making her yank on the wagon handle energetically.

Lee Glick sat beside the coal stove in his sister's kitchen, his hands held to the warmth, as Anna stood by the gas stove, flipping pancakes skillfully, landing the golden brown orbs perfectly on her two-burner griddle.

Little Elmer walked over, lifted his arms, and smiled. Lee bent and picked him up, his chin nuzzling the top of the plump little boy's head, but he said nothing.

Anna slid a look in his direction, as tears sprang to

her eyes, and her nose burned. She bit her lower lip to keep from crying.

Lee was pale, he would hardly eat, his eyes full of unshed tears every time she dared look at him.

"Is Ben done yet?"

There was no answer, so Anna let it go, as she slid the casserole dish containing the fluffy pancakes into the oven to keep them warm. She plopped a pat of butter onto the skillet and began breaking eggs onto it, sniffing.

She hoped Lee could handle this.

When her husband, Ben, entered the kitchen, she looked up and gave him a smile, which he returned, saying over his shoulder, "Hear anything?"

"Not since last night."

"Is she awake?"

"Not as far as I know."

They sat together at the table, the two school-aged children subdued, hesitant to speak of Sarah, their beloved teacher, who was in a faraway hospital, badly burned.

Ben bowed his head, and the others followed, for the time of silent prayer that was customary before every meal.

When Ben raised his head, the ones seated around the table did the same. They raised their glasses of orange juice and set them back carefully, avoiding the eyes that bore too many questions and no answers.

Lee took a thick slice of homemade whole-wheat toast and reached for the butter, spreading it slowly without looking up, as if the concentration he devoted to this small task was absolutely essential.

He passed the plate of fried eggs without helping himself to one, bent carefully toward six-year-old Marianne, and raised his eyebrows.

"Want one?"

She nodded eagerly, anticipating the wondrous breakfast, her round little body already taking on her mother's proportions.

Lee sat back after helping Marianne, raked a hand through his short blond hair, and looked at his sister with blue eyes reflecting the misery he had been experiencing since the fire.

"How, I mean, how severe do burns have to be before they kill a person?" he asked, his wide shoulders leaning into the chair, as if to shrink away from the truth.

Ben was intently spreading homemade ketchup on his mound of steaming stewed crackers.

"Oh, I imagine it would have to be pretty bad. Sarah is young. She's what 20 or 21? She's a hard worker, healthy. I can't imagine it would actually take her life."

Lee nodded.

"Didn't anyone hear anything?"

Anna shook her head.

"At the barn raising, they'll know. Someone will have heard something. Aren't you going to eat, Lee? There are three eggs left."

He shook his head.

"Toast is okay for now."

Ben met Anna's eyes, raised his eyebrows. Anna shook her head only slightly, then looked at her brother.

"Lee, she'll be fine. With today's methods, they can work miracles."

He nodded.

"It's just so hard to understand why God would allow someone as kind and caring as she is to get burned like this. The only reason she went into the barn was to save that colt. I could see how she loved it, how completely taken she was after the birth." Lee shook his head. "She's a special girl," he finished, so soft and low that no one heard what he said.

At the barn raising, Lee lifted Omar's spirits by telling him to come with him to watch the new colt. They stood side by side, their feet propped on the aluminum gate, as the long-legged colt galloped around, cutting a ridiculous figure, its legs way out of proportion with its body.

"Now, that is a blessing, Omar. Our first colt, alive and well."

"Sarah...."

Omar looked desperately at Lee, then ducked his head. When he looked up, his eyes were dark pools of torture.

"She's not going to die, is she?"

Ashamed of his tears, his lack of "big guy" composure, he blinked miserably.

Lee put a hand on Omar's shoulder. When his back heaved and a sob emerged—a ragged cry of pain and inability to understand—Lee hugged him hard and said, "It's okay, buddy."

They stood. The black debris was rolled away now. The stench still hovered, but the bare earth was visible. Cement blocks and mixing machines and new lumber awaited the men clad in black, their varying shades of yellow straw hats bobbing amid the dark outer wear. The brown pasture showed a hint of green, a mixture of a remembrance of the past winter and of new life awaiting, a promise of spring just around the corner.

Word came via Hannah. Malinda had left a message.

The Widow Lydia waited with bated breath as Hannah relayed her friend's message, word for word.

"Hannah, this is Malinda. We are at the burn center. I think it's called Crozer-Chester or Chester-Crozer Medical Center or Burn Center—something like that. It's near Philadelphia. Sarah woke up, but they have her heavily drugged again, sedated. Her burns are serious, and they're going to put her in a special room with different air, so that she stays germ free. She's in pain, too much to bear, Hannah. Please *halted au in gebet* (pray for her)."

The word spread among the women and from the Widow Lydia to Melvin, her beloved friend, her betrothed. Sarah's garrulous, big-hearted, twenty-eight-year-old cousin—with a personality that was larger than life—immediately carried the long-awaited news to the men.

When it reached Lee's ears, he was bent over a cement block, cutting it with the edge of his block hammer. He stayed in his bent position, hoping no one could see, no one could gauge the intensity of the relief that flooded through him, leaving him light headed, his face blanched, his eyes dilated with feeling.

Melvin waved his hands and said he'd heard of Crozer-Chester. Wasn't that the place Abner's Joe was taken that time when he cut into an electrical cord and could have died?

Yes, yes, it was.

The sun was warm on their backs that day, the first serious promise of a gentler time ahead, and hearts swelled with gratitude that the winter would finally be over, without fail.

At lunchtime, Matthew Stoltzfus appeared at the doorway. His hunger drew him, and he was eager to fill his plate from the great kettles containing the variety of home-cooked dishes he had missed so much in Haiti. He didn't care if he never saw another piece of broiled fish in his life. He had been raised on good grass-fed beef and homegrown chicken, fried with flour and butter, with thick gravy on mounds of white potatoes. He considered it a privilege to join his mother now, at the lunch hour.

He figured seventy-five percent of the people he met would treat him respectfully, so he responded in a like manner. He met curious stares, smiled back when someone smiled at him, and answered inquiries in a level tone, being careful, wary, not disclosing more than he had to.

Hannah filled his coffee cup repeatedly, hovering close by like an annoying wasp. That was most of the reason for his being tight-lipped. He knew how desperately she wanted to sweep him back into the fold, and she wasn't going to accomplish it.

He watched the women and single girls, missing Sarah. She had always been at barn raisings, her bright expression and wavy hair a familiar sight, like a white fence freshly painted or a red barn beside fields of waving summer cornstalks, pleasant, a piece of home.

He wondered where Rose was, wondered how he'd feel if she was to arrive here, on this day, and find him back in his old neighborhood.

Digging into his second slice of chocolate cake with a mound of peanut butter icing on top, he chewed, then slid over on the bench to make room for Omar Esh.

Eyeing the Widow Lydia's oldest son, Matthew thought he was a looker with those black eyes and impressive height. He had grown at least a foot taller. Matthew remembered him as a pesky little eight-year-old, his father batting him around in church when he refused to behave.

"Hey, Matthew."

"Hey, yourself, Omar."

"Good to see you."

"You too."

"Sorry to hear about your wife."

"The Lord giveth, and the Lord taketh away."

Omar was unsure how to answer this, so he didn't. People like Matthew were *fer-fearish* (deceiving), and his mother had often warned him not to become entangled in a discussion with someone like him. He didn't fully understand what the big deal was, but he figured he'd better listen to the voice of his mother.

"Looks like the Lord chose to take from you as well. This second time around you really must admit you're doing something wrong."

Omar shifted uneasily, lowered his head, and slurped his coffee.

"You know you Amish should not be hiding the fact that you are being punished for your weak faith, which is a sort of disbelief in the Holy Scripture. If you took God at His word, you wouldn't need to justify your life by works, dressing that way and driving a horse and buggy."

Matthew stopped and looked up when there was a tap on his shoulder. Infinitely pleased, he scrambled up from the bench and walked outside with a blushing Rose Zook beside him.

Everyone saw it. The older women narrowed their eyes and compressed their lips. The younger ones whispered behind extended palms, "My, what a couple they still make."

Lee was chewing a toothpick absentmindedly. He heard the familiar high-pitched giggle and watched Rose talking animatedly with her former boyfriend. He showed no outward sign of emotion at all. He simply extracted the toothpick from between his teeth and threw it in the plastic garbage bag hanging from a nail on the porch.

Not much had changed, in his opinion.

When Friday's paper arrived at the David Beiler residence, Eli's Sam, or Sam King as he was known, brought it in with the rest of the mail, laid it on the counter by the sink in the *kesslehaus,* and forgot about it for a minute. Joe Kauffman, coming to do the milking, had distracted him with his speedy entrance into the forebay, his horse rearing and fighting the restraint on his bit.

Levi was by the kitchen window, mixing some powdered Tang with lukewarm tap water, and almost had a fit, the way Joe couldn't hold his horse. Joe was a bit of character, he thought, but Sam King was a good chap to have around, and Levi enjoyed his company immensely. An extra bonus was the fact that he was allowed to have that second slice of shoofly when Sam was there.

Levi pitied Sarah, felt sorrow for Davey and Malinda, and understood the events that caused their suffering. He was kind and considerate of Priscilla and Suzie, glad to see the arrival of his three brothers, and just as glad to see them go to the burn center. Davey liked those three— Abner, Allen, and Johnny. They'd make their father happy, for awhile.

So in his own simple realm, his life was upset, but not by too much, with Sam playing checkers with him and Priscilla to do the cooking.

Levi never bothered much about the mail. Unable to read, he sometimes looked at bright flyers and glossy advertisements and enjoyed the magazines, but deciphering the articles printed in the paper was beyond his limited ability.

Joe and Sam entered the house together. Sam scooped up the mail, unfolding the paper as he settled on a kitchen chair.

"Joe, you want a cup of coffee before you start the milking?"

"No, thanks. I'm a bit late as it is."

He turned, his kindly face breaking into a smile at the sight of Levi coming to join them.

"How's it going, Levi?"

"Real good, Joe. Real good. Sam is really good to me, a nice chap to have around. Priscilla made soft pretzels last night."

"She did?"

"Oh yeah. Were they delicious? Yes, they were. Did you know I don't use mustard to dip them in?"

"You don't?"

Levi shook his head, his eyes narrowing.

"I use ketchup!"

Joe opened his mouth to answer Levi when there was a decided yelp from Eli's Sam.

"What the world?! Joe, check this out!"

Spreading the newspaper on the tabletop, Sam started reading aloud, his gnarled forefinger following the newsprint.

There was a young man in custody—a Michael Lanvin. He was the suspected arsonist in the barn fires and was being held in the Lancaster County jail on $75,000 bail.

"Oh my goodness," Joe said, very soft and low.

Sam read on. He had been taken into custody at the David Beiler residence.

"Which David Beiler? There are dozens of them here in Lancaster County."

"Here!" Levi shouted.

They turned in unison, disbelief stamped on their features, mouths agape.

"What?"

"Here!"

Levi stood by the table, his wide girth lengthening as he pulled himself to his full height, hooked a thumb beneath his suspenders, and snapped them against his great chest.

"It was me."

"Come on, Levi."

Sam shook his head.

"Do you know this guy?"

Levi walked around the table, bent over, and cocked his head to peer closely through his thick bifocals at the paper. He began nodding his head.

"Oh yeah, that's Mike. That's the long-haired young man that cried at the pretty girl's funeral, and my dat, Davey, gave him a long hug, and he talked to him with nice words. He didn't know that Mike was the same man that drove his car in our drive that night, the time when our barn burned. I didn't either, for sure, but sort of. Then he came to our house, when the widow's barn burned. He wanted to talk to my dat, you know, Davey. And..."

Here, Levi paused for a moment, taking in the two men's undivided attention, reveling in his self-appointed position as conveyor of wonderfully astounding news. He leaned forward, his eyes narrowing with conspiracy.

"I told Mike to sit down, and he did. Then I told him I had to go the bathroom, which..."

His voice trailed off, making sure the two men were on the edges of their seats, as he played the drama to its fullest extent.

"I didn't really have to."

He almost hissed the words. Sam's and Joe's eyes opened wide in bewilderment.

"I just said so. Then I went quietly out the *kesslehaus* door and to the phone shanty. I ran. I can really run if I have to. I know my numbers. Did you know that? I punched the 9 and the 1 two times, and I told the lady I needed the policemen. They came, but not before I asked Mike if he wanted shoofly or whoopie pies. My mam had just made them."

"What happened when they got here?"

"Mike tried to get away, but he couldn't very easily do that. The *kesslehaus* door was locked."

Incredulous now, Joe Kauffman slowly shook his head.

"Levi, you are something. May God be praised."

"It wasn't God. It was me," Levi said, scowling at the thought of his rightful honor going elsewhere.

Eli's Sam threw back his head and let out a great roar of delight, and he and Joe laughed until they had to wipe their eyes with their navy blue handkerchiefs.

Clearly, that set everything right. Levi grinned widely, happy to be able to produce that sort of reaction.

"You know, they were saying at the barn raising that someone heard somewhere that they had caught the arsonist, but we've heard it dozens of times, and it's never been true—just a rumor," Sam said.

Joe nodded, then glanced at the clock above the sink.

"I have to begin milking right now. Levi, would you send Priscilla out to feed calves?"

"Suzie can help her."

"Alright."

Joe went out, the keeper of his neighbor's cows while they were at the distant hospital with their suffering daughter, and his heart twisted within his chest, keenly aware of their pain. He'd have to set up a trust fund at Susquehanna Bank tomorrow. They had some staggering medical bills coming their way.

But wasn't that Levi a corker?

Ah well, the least of these my brethren, and who would have thought he had it in him?

CHAPTER 6

THE NEWSPAPER ARTICLE SET UP A GREAT CLOUD of speculation, suspicion, and disbelief that hovered over the Amish community. It reached for many miles as housewives chatted at quiltings or sisters' days. Men working on construction sites tipped their hats, put down their nail guns, and gave their opinions. Many of them were likeminded, their voices laced with exasperation. They were just plain fed up, weary of the barn fires and their aftermaths.

What if someone was in custody? That didn't hold much clout, in their opinion. He'd lie his way out. No one had caught him actually setting fire to a barn. If the courts tried this Mike in a few months, who would testify? Who would press charges? Very likely the ministers would not allow it, so there was no point in getting excited about this guy's picture in the paper.

And now there was the minister's daughter, completely disfigured, some said, and Davey was the main one who had held back, not allowing the usual investigation.

Some said this would bring him round. Others said maybe this really would put a stop to the fires. And didn't Davey Beiler's Levi have Down syndrome? You just couldn't believe everything you heard.

Sarah was fully awake, her wits about her after that horrible battle to summon enough willpower to withstand the sensation hovering mostly on her right side.

She could not turn her head, and her vision was limited by that as well as the swollen lids of her eyes, but she could see the room and her parents' faces, briefly. She knew she was badly burned and had come to grips with it, sort of.

Each day, in the forenoon, they unwrapped the bandages, and the taking away of the dead tissue would begin—the debridement.

It was beyond anything Sarah had imagined the human body could withstand. She shook with uncontrollable spasms of fear and pain. She clenched her teeth to keep from crying out, but in the end, she gave up trying and begged them to stop. She cried and pleaded, thinking she would surely die.

Always, the nurses and doctors were kind, explaining over and over how absolutely essential this procedure was for the healing.

When she tried to tell her parents about it, after that first time, her hoarse voice caught on a sob, and she couldn't convey the overwhelming pain. Her father's face became grim, and he said he had to leave—he was going home to see to things.

His wife's eyes questioned him, and when she saw the raw agony in her husband's eyes, she became very afraid. Reaching out, she placed a hand on his trembling arm.

"Davey, are you alright?"

"No, I'm not alright," he whispered. "Who would be? Who could stand to think of their own children being tortured? Who?"

Turning on his heel, he left and stalked down the hallway, the soles of his high-topped black Sunday shoes ringing on the glossy blue and white tiles. His shoulders, clad in the black *mutza* (Sunday coat), were held stiffly, his face white and set, like granite.

The driver, Wesley, told old Dan King that he'd never seen Davey Beiler like that. He was afraid, so he was.

When Sarah woke up that afternoon after her father left, she found her mother dozing in the vinyl chair beside her bed. She called her name hoarsely, then cleared her throat and tried again.

"Mam."

When there was no answer, she lay back and closed her eyes as warm tears coursed down her cheeks, soaking the fresh bandages that covered her face. She felt alone, defeated.

How badly was she burned? Why wouldn't they let her have a mirror? Was she hideously disfigured, or could the doctors fix the worst of it? Surely she still had a nose and ears. And she had her eyes.

Sarah tried raising her left arm, but instantly felt a stinging sensation across the muscles in her upper back, so she let it go.

Every twitch, every slight movement sent shivers of pain through her body, like a million stinging needles pricking her skin.

She'd probably have to get used to that, wouldn't she? She'd have to work up some kind of resolve against the pain. She thought of her cousin who had a severe case of juvenile diabetes, plunging a needle into her stomach every day. She'd said that after awhile she hardly felt the *gix* (needle), and Sarah believed her.

She'd try hard to bear the pain the best she could, which wasn't the worst of it at all. The worst was the fear of disfigurement. The realization of it rolled into her consciousness like a fog on a wet spring morning, obscuring any hint of hope or encouragement.

She was accustomed to the stares of curiosity whenever Levi went somewhere with the family, but he was born with his disability. His features from Down syndrome and his tendency to be overweight drew looks, but his mind was immature enough to allow him to live among his beloved friends and family with a childlike innocence. Levi was genuinely happy.

Sarah felt trapped, not knowing her fate. She hung suspended between anxiety and acceptance.

And what about Matthew?

She groaned within herself, sharply aware of his dark good looks, his tendency to seek perfection in others. He'd never look at her again.

His perfect features were etched into her brain. She could conjure up any picture of him she wanted, anytime she wanted. Laughing, scowling, moving away, walking toward her, playing volleyball or baseball, or sitting beside her in the buggy, his profile was as handsome as that of any model she'd ever seen.

Oh, Matthew. You'll never want me now.

Closing her eyes, she prayed, asking God for one more chance, one more time to be with Matthew. Perhaps her injuries would soften his heart.

Alone in the confines of the small shed storing wood and coal, David Beiler fell on his knees, the rough bits of bark and chunks of coal biting into them through his denim trousers.

He reached up, removed his straw hat, and bent his head above his calloused hands, which were clasped in prayer, but nothing, not one word, could he utter. He felt infinitely alone.

Puzzled, he remained on his knees, the futility of being there slowly seeping into his mind.

He could not pray. The words, the lifting of his spirit, would not come, so he rose stiffly, brushed the bits of dust and dirt off his knees, and turned to go. Opening the door of the woodshed, he stopped. He leaned against the dusty doorframe and looked out across the night sky. The soft glow of lamplight from the upstairs windows, the neighboring lights, the silhouette of the new barn and outbuildings against the twinkling stars arrested him and he held himself still. Perhaps if he waited, God would come to him and peace would be restored, along with the ability to communicate.

The only emotion he felt, after a long while, was anger. Unresolved, boiling anger, as hot as the falling beam that had hit Sarah. It had scraped and burned her shoulders and back raw, like ground beef. Now, she lay in that hospital, tortured every bit as badly as the Anabaptists had been tortured, as told in *Martyrs Mirror*.

It was his fault. He'd clung to the old ways. How much of it was tradition, how much was pride, and how small was the slice of heartfelt conviction?

Was it really expected of him? This forgiveness? How could he forgive an arsonist who had burned his daughter at the stake?

He had no tears, only a pounding heart and a clenched jaw. He'd go, read his Bible, and try to get back on track.

Instead, he found himself sitting at the kitchen table, staring at the picture of Michael Lanvin, the shaggy-haired youth, looking at him from the photo above the article where he said he'd been the arsonist—was the arsonist.

Had he actually hugged that arrogant youth? Blessed him and wished him well? That had been pious of him, obviously. That was, of course, before Sarah had been burned.

Who knew? Did they really know he lit the barns? What was truth? Why? Why did a loving God allow his daughter Sarah to go through this senseless burning? Anger churned through his veins as his Bible lay unopened on the table, his breath coming in hard, frustrated puffs.

Did he believe in God? Had he ever been fit to be a minister? Outwardly, maybe, but had his heart ever been right?

The clock on the wall loudly banged out the seconds, and the refrigerator hummed quietly. Somewhere a wall creaked, and Levi mumbled in his sleep as the mattress beneath him groaned. David Beiler bowed his head as he wrestled with his demons—the purveyors of doubt and self-loathing, of discouragement and a lack of faith.

Suddenly, he sat up, drew back his fist, and slammed it into the black and white photograph of the man that was supposedly the arsonist. He tore the newspaper with the first assault. A coffee cup rattled, tilted, rolled off the kitchen table, and fell to the floor, breaking into dozens of pieces.

Again and again, he slammed the newspaper as great, hoarse sobs tore from his throat and tears rained down his cheeks.

David Beiler's Gethsemane had come.

Much later, he lay prostrate on the floor, his body convulsing as the force of his cries continued to shake him. His supplications rolled from him in whispers, cries, and questions as he railed before the throne of his God.

Slowly, peace and acceptance emerged, driving back the darkness and the void he had experienced in his place of anger and misery. Gradually, a quietness in his spirit led him to real communication with the One who resides in heaven, supreme. The way before him was clear.

There was no substitute for forgiveness, no question of its balance. But it first had to start with him. He could not allow himself to become short with his brethren. There would be a way. All he needed was the strength to face each new day, for now.

He felt deeply ashamed of his anger. It seemed so wrong, and yet hadn't Paul said the things he did not want to do were precisely what he ended up doing? David's human nature hung on his frame like an unbearable cloak, stifling, woolen, and extremely uncomfortable.

Rising, he went to the pantry, found the dustpan and brush, then lowered himself to clean up the broken coffee cup, sweeping up every bit of glass carefully.

Ah, yes, so symbolic was this mug. We need to be broken, again and again, to allow the waters to flow, those life-giving waters of love.

Before David went to bed, he checked on Levi. He adjusted the quilt and patted his son's shoulders as he did so. Sleep well, Levi, sleep well, he thought.

A love for his handicapped son welled up within him, and he turned, stumbling over the rug as tears blinded his eyes.

Yes, God did know, after all, exactly what He was doing. There were just too many knotty problems to understand the big picture.

After the morning milking, David sat at the breakfast

table. He ate the eggs that were fried beyond any hope of having soft, yellow yolks. He also had some burnt toast and the saltines swimming in hot milk, devoid of browned butter. And he praised Priscilla's attempts at cooking breakfast.

Suzie smiled up at her father.

"I made the toast!"

Levi was scraping anxiously at a blackened slice.

"You left it in the broiler too long."

"Nah, Levi. It's good that way," Suzie answered.

Levi chose to ignore her and asked instead when Mam was coming home.

"Soon, Levi. As soon as Sarah is moved into a regular room. Then you can go see her, and Priscilla can stay for awhile and let Mam come home."

"Nobody makes me anything to eat," Levi said so pitifully that Dat smiled widely behind his napkin.

As if someone had planned their lines, there was a knock on the door.

"Come in," Dat called, without getting up. He simply motioned with his hand, the way country folks living in rural Amish settlements often do.

Matthew was smiling, his handsome face alight with good humor. He was genuinely glad to see his old friends, especially Levi, who returned his sunny greetings effusively.

Matthew was laden with food. The cardboard boxes contained a casserole of lasagna and one of baked corn, loaves of homemade bread, pies, macaroni salad, sausages, and a quivering jello pudding, all leftovers from the ongoing barn raising at Widow Lydia's.

Matthew inquired about Sarah's well-being, his face serious, benevolent, and said anxiously that he needed to see her. When Dat told him about the isolation and the upcoming surgeries she would need, the skin grafting, he reconsidered but begged Dat to let him know the minute he could go and would be allowed in her room.

Dat remained kind and assured Matthew he would do everything he could, but he thought that the sooner he saw her, the better. He knew.

Matthew surveyed the now empty breakfast table, looked at Priscilla, and asked if she was the cook. Blushing, she nodded, her large green eyes lowered, the lids heavy with thick, dark lashes serving to enhance her prettiness.

Eyeing her a little longer than necessary, Matthew's face took on a smile of appreciation and something else that Dat labeled silently.

The surgery went well. The skin they harvested from Sarah's left side served as patches that they transferred onto the worst of her wounds on her right side.

A few days later, she was allowed to have a mirror, although the doctor counseled her wisely, preparing her for the shock of seeing the damage the fire had done.

Sarah insisted she was prepared. She had braced for the worst scene possible, she really had.

She searched the nurses' faces for signs of pity or horror, but they remained impassive, professionally trained.

She felt the bandages being unwrapped, the cool air frigid on the newly exposed skin, then took a deep shaking breath and held out her left hand for the mirror.

The skin on her arms and back still pulled painfully, but she moved everything she could, repeatedly, to acquaint herself with the sensation.

When the mirror was before her face, she squeezed her eyes completely shut and lowered it, courage eluding her.

The doctor encouraged her again, and this time she took the mirror and held it up unsteadily, but she did not lower it.

Slowly, a grotesque being came into focus.

Sarah's first impulse was to open her ruined mouth and scream and to go on screaming and protesting, raging against every force that had brought this bizarre accident into her life.

She was, by all accounts, truly hideous.

Determined, she kept holding the mirror at slightly different angles, examining, peering closely in the garish light from the overhead fixtures.

No hair, anywhere, although there was a slight fuzz on the left side, perhaps. No eyelashes or eyebrows. Red, peeling eyelids. A swollen forehead that was purple, red, and pink on one side. The only way to describe the other side was as some kind of meat, like ground turkey or pork. She guessed that would be sausage.

Well, she had a nose—a good sturdy one at that. The skin was just falling off of it in great peels, like a tomato skin in hot water.

Her lips looked as if she had at least fifty cold sores piled all over each other.

Her neck was barely burned on one side, especially on the underside of her jaw. The right side was where they had done the grafting, which looked much the same as she imaged it would. Skin from her back was adhered to her neck, and, incongruous as it seemed, it did look hopeful.

She smiled to herself. There was one good thing—if her back became itchy, she could scratch her neck.

When she lowered the mirror to her shoulders, she could not keep from crying, helplessly allowing tears to slide down the damaged skin on her cheeks. It was awful.

But she was alive. She was here. The doctors told her that the current methods at the burn center were just short of miraculous, and she was young and strong, something they had assured her repeatedly.

She clung to the words now.

She was taken out of isolation, and her family surrounded her. Allen, Abner, and Johnny must have made a no tears pact—joking and smiling, bringing her silly cards and balloons.

Their wives were less audacious, more reserved, so much so, in fact, that Sarah asked if she looked better or worse than they'd thought. No one provided a forthright answer, so Sarah knew they were shocked at her appearance. Well, so be it. They certainly weren't the last ones who would experience disbelief.

Maybe she should spend the rest of her life with a paper bag over her head, she told her brothers.

"Make sure it's one from a chain store that would pay you for the advertising, like Walmart or Target," Allen said, laughing.

"They use plastic," Abner said loftily.

Sarah's back hurt, trying to keep from laughing.

Anna Mae and Ruthie held nothing back, crying until their faces were blotchy and red. Their eyes were swollen, and Ruthie's glasses were messy with smudges. They said things that weren't helpful and lots of things that made no sense at all, but they were her sisters. And sisters are like good apples, even the cores and the little black seeds can be eaten and tolerated.

Anna Mae said her eyelashes would grow back. Ruthie said if they didn't, they'd take Sarah to a face place and have artificial ones sewn on.

Sarah couldn't smile, but she asked, why bother, a face

that looked like meatloaf was not improved by eyelashes. Johnny said if he had a choice, he'd definitely take the meatloaf with artificial eyelashes.

Then Priscilla came, along with Omar and Lydia, who had hoped they could gain entry to her bedside, but it was not to be. Not yet.

Priscilla walked over to Sarah's bed. Her face turned a sickly shade of green, and she folded up like a graceful ballerina as she drifted slowly to the floor. Allen caught her on the way down.

What a flurry then! Anna Mae and Ruthie had conniption fits, fanning her, sending Allen for Pepsi, saying her blood sugar was way down, she worked too hard, she was always dieting, and somebody needed to go ask a nurse for smelling salts.

No one did their bidding, and Priscilla woke up, blinked a few times, and was fine. She was accosted by her sisters for the next five minutes about protein and energy greens that come in powder form to be mixed with milk or water or juice. They insisted that if she took that, she would never pass out, no matter what.

After they all left, Priscilla and Suzie walked over to Sarah and told her she looked awful. Sarah said she knew that, but it wouldn't always look this bad.

Suzie, in all seriousness, said she looked like a catfish.

That time, Sarah cracked the skin on her lips. She couldn't help it, the laughter on the inside wanting to escape so badly.

After they all went home, Sarah slept the first deep sleep since the accident, relaxed in the knowledge that her family loved her, and for now, that was enough.

When she awoke, she was ravenously hungry, pressed the bell, and asked if she'd be allowed a snack.

Almost immediately, her favorite nurse, Alison, brought her apple juice, graham crackers, and peanut butter. She pulled up the blinds, letting the afternoon sun into the room. She told Sarah it was wonderful to hear she was hungry.

She made her spread the peanut butter on the crackers herself, even if it was painful to hold the graham cracker with one hand and spread the peanut butter with the other.

They got her out of bed again, for the third time, and there was nothing to do but grip the walker until her knuckles turned white, bend over as far as they'd allow, and shuffle along as best she could. She clenched her teeth, sucked in her breath, and kept going, refusing to admit defeat. If the hospital staff thought she was capable, then she was.

Tomorrow, the physical therapy would start. For now, Sarah was blissfully unaware of that additional form of torture.

The flowers began arriving then—vases of fresh-cut daisies and carnations and gerbera daisies and little white baskets of potted ferns and peace lilies and vines. They all came with attached cards of well wishes from neighbors and friends.

The largest, most flamboyant bouquet of flowers was from Melvin, and Sarah smiled. The card with a flowery verse written in small letters reminded her of him. He had no doubt driven the florist crazy, reciting these eloquent words for her. They had to be perfect.

So many greeting cards. Eagerly, she read each one, but none were from Matthew. And the phone did not ring, ever. Even if it did, she would not be able to answer it. She found herself gazing at it, thinking how it would be to have only one short conversation with him.

He probably wouldn't call.

She opened an especially large envelope containing homemade greeting cards from all her pupils at school. That was the highlight of her week. Over and over, she read the words, the innocent get well wishes, and traced the hand-drawn pictures with the tip of her finger, as if to permanently impress every outline in her memory.

Rosanna wrote that she cried for her every day, and Samuel said school was like an empty silo that had no silage in it if she wasn't there.

Well, now she was like silage. An improvement from a catfish. She grinned to herself.

When Alison poked her blonde head in the door, asking if she needed anything, Sarah said, yes, more graham crackers and peanut butter, but she wanted them with marshmallow cream and coated with chocolate.

Alison laughed and said, "No way, ma'am."

Before long, another skin graft was done, and Sarah become feverish and short of breath as she came down with a classic case of pneumonia, just when things were going so well.

It was a serious time, a setback for a condition that had been improving far ahead of schedule, the healing multiplying in leaps and bounds.

Rumors abounded, until some well meaning folks actually asked their friends in church which arm of Davey Beiler's Sarah had to be amputated—the right or the left?

Oh no, they said, nothing was taken off that they knew about. She just had pneumonia. Burn victims often do.

"*Vell, my oh* (Well, oh my)."

"Who starts this stuff?"

CHAPTER 7

Matthew Stoltzfus was the first one to come see her, after visitors were allowed.

She lay on her pillows, her bed raised to a comfortable position, with her eyes closed, half awake, still weak from the powerful antibiotics used to fight the infection in her lungs.

She wasn't aware of the fact that visiting hours had started and was shocked to see Matthew, alone, knocking softly on the door frame.

She wanted to pull the sheet up over her head and roll herself into a cocoon, a shroud, and never let him see her.

She could see him recoil, saw the nameless distaste, the horror, and his inability to conceal any of it.

Slowly, he walked closer, his hands clutching his belt, his shoulders hunched beneath his blue shirt.

But, oh, the beauty of him! The sheer wonder that he was here. He had come!

"Sarah. Sarah." The first word was stammered, as he tried desperately to right himself.

"Hello, Matthew."

Again, he drew back, and a hissing sound escaped his

lips. She was now accustomed to the croak that served as her voice, immune to the shock value of the sound that emerged from her swollen larynx and the tender walls surrounding it.

"How are you?"

She could only nod her head, the lump in her throat now causing an obstruction too painful to allow even one word.

"Are you in pain?"

Again, she only shook her head, realizing the effect of her croaking attempts at speech.

"Can't you talk?"

"Yes. But my throat is damaged."

"Always?"

She shook her head.

The visit fell so far short of her expectations that the pain of it was almost as bad as the physical pain of her wounds.

He volleyed questions at her, hard and rapid. Was she prepared to meet God? Was she born again, truly? Was she willing to confront her parents?

The wearying, mind-numbing questions sent her tumbling down a precipice, where she lay, battered, bruised, reeling mentally from the awful disappointment of his lack of empathy, his selfishness. She finally admitted to herself that that was his problem.

How long would she torment herself with Matthew?

One thing grew relentlessly in her understanding. It was a flowering seed and had lain dormant, but it was growing steadily in the sunshine of her family's love. She knew she could never leave them.

And the conviction that she wouldn't have to do that in order to be a Christian grew alongside it, like a sweet-smelling rose.

If God was love, then He was with her family. He was in the imperfect fuss of Anna Mae and Ruthie; He was in their tears and stupid advice. He was in the mood-lifting banter of her married brothers and their faithful wives. He was in the whole circle of them—Mam clucking and stewing and wanting only what was best for her family, and Dat's agony, his self blame, and Suzie's comparison of Sarah with a catfish.

As Matthew spoke, quoting endless Bible verses to justify his own desires, she heard only a small part of what he said. She silently nurtured the newfound wisdom that had been imparted to her since the fire as she had endured the agony of debridement, the surgeries, and skin grafting and pneumonia.

Wearily, she nodded or shook her head in response to Matthew's ramblings, but her heart was faint with fatigue, burned out with the whole deal.

"So, Sarah, what percentage of your hair do they think will grown back? I mean, seriously, you don't have any."

"I'll always be bald."

Why did she find such complete satisfaction in saying that if it wasn't really true?

Matthew snapped to attention.

"Ew. Really?"

"I'll wear a wig."

That clearly gave him the creeps.

Still, if he stayed quiet long enough, she could admire his good looks and hang onto the past, but she really just wanted him to leave.

Just go, Matthew. Go. You know you don't want me. She was surprised she hadn't said it out loud, surprised he still sat in that vinyl chair. For what?

"You think you'll ever look like yourself again?"

That was her undoing. That one unnecessary question that was brought on by his fear of having a less than perfect wife.

With all the strength she could muster, her voice a rough squawk, she asked him why he cared.

"You don't want me, Matthew. I won't leave my family. I don't have to. Just go, and stop tormenting me. Maybe God allowed me to suffer because I would not have given you up any other way."

Her voice turned to a whisper.

"You know there is nothing colder than ashes, after the fire is gone, just like that old love song Mam used to sing."

"You scare me, Sarah. You're losing your mind."

She looked directly at him.

"No, Matthew. You have it all wrong. I am finding my mind."

She began crying then and did not care that Matthew cast her a wild-eyed look and began backing out of the room. He would always remember a caricature of the former Sarah, misshapen, peeling, bandaged, hideous, but inside her a marvelous thing was slowly taking shape.

It was like a new barn rising after an arsonist's foolery, a beautiful thing, a symbol of caring, people working side by side, a whole community of love, including English, Mennonite, Hutterite, German Baptist, all following their Christ, all different, and all the same.

Strong and sure, grasping the truth handed down through the ages, Sarah's faith was alive and well.

Three weeks after the burning beam hit her, Sarah had made remarkable progress. Steadily, the healing process brought changes. Her hair was now a light copper-colored sheen over her scalp. Her eyelashes were short but coming in thick and fast, and the perfectly shaped wings of her eyebrows showed promise as well.

She walked the hallways, unassisted sometimes, enjoying an easy friendship with the staff, other patients, and the scores of visitors that entered the hospital daily.

She watched the red buds of the trees by the parking lot turn a beautiful lime green color. Then tiny leaves as big as quarters grew into small leaves of a darker hue. Lawn mowers appeared, landscaping companies mulched around shrubs and flowers, and she could only watch, her hands aching for the soil in Mam's garden back home.

Matthew never visited her again. It didn't surprise her. It left only a dull ache for a time remembered when he had been her utmost goal in life. The fact that he was the one who had brought all that yearning, the sweetness of young love to her life, always made her sad, but it was a fading melancholy feeling now.

When the doctor took the bandages off one day, he was pleased. In fact, he was so pleased that he forgot his professional manner, if only for a minute or so.

"Marvelous!"

Sarah smiled as best she could, a warm glow beginning to spread through her senses.

Would the time be close now? She eagerly anticipated the long-awaited moment when she would be dressed in her usual garb, the Amish colors and fabric she missed so much, and walk out the glass doors and never look back.

Her physical therapy sessions on the first floor went well after the first few times, when she had thought her skin would split open with the force of simple movements. She worked with the therapists, gritted her teeth, and kept going, pulling ropes attached to pulleys with weights on the other end, or simply lifting light weights, or raising and lowering her arms and legs.

She had started looking forward to physical therapy as she became acquainted with the therapists and those around her, other burn victims who shared their stories and formed a bond of closeness based on their shared experiences.

It was ironic, the way there were not Amish or English or Mennonite in a burn center. Each patient wore the exact same shapeless, colorless garments that tied in the back. Her bandages served as a covering, and no one could tell she was Amish.

For the first time in her life, she knew the feeling of blending in with other people with no distinctive dress or mannerism to set her apart. It proved to be very interesting.

The usual questions were always about school. Had she graduated? Was she in college?

In Sarah's culture, any young girl in her twenties would have been asked about her marital status, her situation as a dating or non-dating young girl. School was out of the question, except for being a teacher in a one-room parochial school.

There were no goals as far as a career was concerned. Marriage, managing a home, and motherhood was the only route, chosen for her by her parents' wishes. A rarity was the young girl who preferred to stay alone, becoming self-sufficient as a teacher or storekeeper.

Sarah walked the hallways wearing the light robe her sister Anna Mae bought for her. It was green, the color of her eyes, with a belt that tied around her waist, the hem reaching almost to the floor. She felt good when she wore it, sweeping along, her gait improving as each day went by.

She talked on the phone to well wishers, looked forward to her family's visits, spent hours with a small handheld mirror searching for all the small improvements she could find.

She grimaced as she checked the growth of the new hair sprouting from her head.

She'd even prayed it would be straight, wryly remembering Dat's words about asking God for selfish favors. Just let it be straighter. It doesn't have to be perfect, just not as curly as it used to be, she had pleaded.

Sadly, the new growth on top of her head looked a bit like steel wool, only a dark, copper color. She could not bear to look at it or touch it. What would she do if her hair was curlier still?

Sitting on the side of her bed, she pushed her feet into the slippers Mam had supplied for her, a pair of green and beige plaid Dearfoams that matched her robe.

The bandages were mostly gone, except for on her right shoulder and that side of her neck where the skin grafting had taken place. Her face was still discolored, scarred, but her eyes were open. The lids were a dark shade of red and still peeling, but so much better.

She walked down the hallway to the lounge area by the vast windows, to gaze out over the lawn as the sun sank below the horizon.

A sort of melancholy settled over her shoulders, and she sighed, crossed her arms at her waist, and stared unseeing, as distant lights came on, winking along the streets as folks warded off the night, turning homes into cozy, light-filled havens.

At home, Mam would be holding the lighter to the

mantle of the gas lamp, turning the knob, and infusing the kitchen in the homey hiss of the standard Amish source of light. Levi would lift the glass chimney of the kerosene lamp in the bathroom as he prepared for his nightly ritual of showering, teeth brushing, and gargling with his green mouthwash—not blue or purple or yellow. It had to be green.

A wave of homesickness washed over Sarah. She wanted to eat shoofly pie with Levi and tease him about the amount of milk and sugar he put in his coffee. She wanted to sprawl across her bed and play Yahtzee with Priscilla. The low IQ game, they called it, but they loved to roll the dice and say silly things and laugh with quiet heaves and great guffaws, the way only sisters can.

She stood in the dim light of the lounge, watching the twilight settle over the unfamiliar land, oblivious to those around her as tears welled up in her eyes.

No one had come to visit today, which was unusual, but she'd talked to her mother and understood. Allen and Rachel had become parents to a little boy named Samuel Lee, and Mam was going to Dauphin County while she had the chance.

Sarah tried to form a smile as she glanced at an older couple sitting on a sofa. She reached for a Kleenex and blew her nose, hating her own weakness, her moment of self pity.

The elevator doors opened, disgorging its occupants. Sarah paused, watching the people step out.

A head taller than anyone else, his blond hair shining in the yellow lights of the elevator, Lee Glick stepped out, looked to the left, then right, before his gaze traveled the lounge area.

He found her.

His gaze rested on her with a fleeting moment of recognition. He stood completely still, his hands at his sides. He was dressed in a navy blue polo shirt, his neat black Sunday pants, and a pair of black and navy blue sneakers.

His eyes found hers, and he moved toward her, as if in a dream, his gaze never leaving her face.

When he reached her, he stopped only a short distance away, but she could see the expression in his eyes.

What was she supposed to do when tears welled up and flowed unchecked down her discolored cheeks?

"Sarah," he whispered.

Then he put his hands on her shoulders, his touch so light she barely felt it. He leaned forward and placed his lips on her forehead, on the side that was scarred most. He kissed her cheek, the scarred one. He stepped back, his eyes searched hers, and he breathed out, quietly, and then pulled her close, so gently, she could barely call it an embrace.

But she felt the fabric of the navy blue shirt, the line of his suspenders, the muscle of his shoulder, and she closed her eyes. He held her, as the hand on the clock ticked away the seconds.

The old couple on the sofa bent their heads and whispered knowingly, then looked up, watching eagerly, remembering the time when their love was young.

Finally, he let her go, but he kept her hands in his. The blue eyes were intent on her face, examining, savoring.

"How are you?" he whispered.

"I'm doing well, as you can see," she said quietly.

"You're beautiful," he breathed.

She was surprised when he dropped her hands. He drew in his breath, then exhaled, almost a groan, before he gathered her back into his arms and held her there.

She had been crying before Lee arrived, the home-sickness unbearable, and now she wanted to stay here in this room and never leave the circle of his arms. She had come home, to a place where she belonged. Of this, there was no doubt.

Once more, he released her, stepped back, and searched her eyes.

"Sarah, you're alive. You're here. You did a very brave thing. You are an amazing person. No one but you would have risked her life to save a colt."

"The colt was not the main thing," Sarah said, very soft and low, embarrassment welling up, ashamed of the croak that was now her voice.

Bending his head, Lee questioned her.

"The colt...." Sarah began.

She placed a hand on her throat, grimaced, her eyes begging him, and whispered, "My voice sounds terrible."

"Your voice?"

Sarah nodded miserably.

"Let's sit down, shall we?"

Taking her hand, he led her to an alcove, away from prying eyes. They sat, side by side, and he did not relinquish his hold on her scarred fingers.

"What's wrong with your voice?" he asked as gently as possible.

"My throat was burned, damaged from the heat and smoke."

"It's okay, Sarah. It's okay. Just talk to me. Tell me everything."

And so she did, beginning with her first memory, which was waking up in the room at the burn center. He listened, rapt, as she described the pain, the hopelessness of the first look in mirror, the surgeries, the visitors.

Lee became very quiet.

"Was Matthew in?"

Sarah nodded.

A silence followed, as Lee separated the space between them. Suddenly, he got to his feet and walked away, over to the windows, his hands gripped behind his back as he watched the twilight.

The elderly lady sitting beside her husband raised her eyebrows and pursed her lips, while her husband lowered his head and whispered, "What do you think is going on?"

"Let's find out," she whispered back.

In complete agreement, they rose stiffly to their feet. He extended his arm, she placed her hand comfortably on it, and they shuffled their way back to the alcove. They gleefully found a sofa within earshot, where they settled. He produced a magazine to look at, and they both became cunningly absorbed in it.

When Lee stayed at the window a long time, Sarah slowly got to her feet. She felt unsure, but the need to be close to him overrode her hesitancy.

Placing a hand on his arm, she said, "Lee."

He turned, and she was alarmed at the bitterness in his eyes.

"It's…"

"Sarah, listen. I can't take one more minute of this, knowing you are going to throw your life away with Matthew. I should have never come."

Turning on his heel, he stalked away.

The old couple was left in the alcove, unable to see or hear the conversation. Like dominoes they leaned to the right, peered around the corner, their eyes wide, straining through the thick lenses of their trifocals.

"What do you think is going on?" she hissed.

"Mom, now hush," he hissed back.

Sarah followed Lee. Her pace was steady, her footsteps quiet, her heart swelling as the strains of love rose and fell in her heart, a rapturous symphony that swelled to a crescendo. She had never been more certain of anything in her life.

Her steps quickened.

"Lee?" she called, a question, a bewilderment.

He turned, his face a mask of pain.

"Sarah, if Matthew was already here, I'm just wasting my time, okay? I'll go now, and I'll talk to you later. Be careful."

"Lee, don't go," she said.

"I think it's for the best."

The elevator door opened, he stepped inside, gave a small wave, and was swallowed up as the doors closed. She stood, her entire being straining toward him, but it was too late.

Slowly, her hands fell to her sides. Sighing, she retraced her steps, without noticing the elderly folks examining the pages of their magazine, and returned to her room. She let the green robe slide from her shoulders, kicked off her slippers, and crawled into the high, narrow bed.

Well, he had come to see her. He was the polar opposite of Matthew. Even their hair color couldn't be more different. Where Matthew recoiled, worried over the future of her appearance, Lee had told her she was beautiful, which she obviously was not. And he had told her she was an amazing person, which she obviously wasn't either.

She blushed and put her cold hands to her warm face. Well, one thing was settled. The thought of it made her bounce a bit, shifting her weight from side to side the way a child does before opening a candy bar, so delighted with his gift.

Yes, it was a gift, this knowing, this undeserved reality check, this discovery.

She did not love Matthew. She was consumed by her wanting of him. For what? His good looks? The pride of having him? The winning of the race, beating every other girl that had ever wanted to be his girlfriend?

Sickened by her own human nature, she recoiled from the virtual mirror held to her heart. How long she had strained against the reins of her Creator! How long-suffering was her God?

She bowed her head, clasped her hands, and thanked Him for allowing her this one chance at true love. The future was still suspended, the question hanging in mid-air, but her heart was at rest.

When the telephone rang, she reached for it, answered quietly.

"How are you, Sarah?"

Matthew.

"Good. Tired. Ready for bed."

"Have any visitors today?"

"One."

"Who?"

She had a notion to tell him it was the man on the moon, but she didn't. When her answer was not forthcoming, he repeated the blunt question.

"Who was it?"

"A friend."

"Can I come see you tomorrow?"

For only a moment, the old anticipation crowded out her common sense, but it was instantly replaced by an anger that shook her to the core.

"Why would you want to, Matthew? You have nothing to say to me, and you know it. No, you may not come to see me."

"Wow!" Matthew answered.

Sarah didn't bother replying. She was plain down too mad.

"You still there?" he asked, his voice mellow.

"Yes."

"So this is it. Really it?"

"Yes. It is."

Firm and hard, her words were spaced, set in concrete. They were sure, sturdy, and full of conviction.

"Matthew, just go live your life. Forget about the gangly little eighth grader who thought the sun rose and set on you and you alone. You have wrung my heart for the last time. Let's just say the fiery trial I've been through has worked very well in producing a solid vessel, shining like crazy."

"Are you really losing your mind?"

"No, sir. I told you before, Matthew. I just found it."

"I'll be up to see you once you get home."

"Don't bother."

"You're serious, aren't you?"

"Yes."

"Goodbye, Sarah."

Gently, she replaced the receiver, then pressed down on it, firmly.

CHAPTER 8

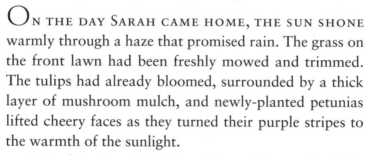

ON THE DAY SARAH CAME HOME, THE SUN SHONE warmly through a haze that promised rain. The grass on the front lawn had been freshly mowed and trimmed. The tulips had already bloomed, surrounded by a thick layer of mushroom mulch, and newly-planted petunias lifted cheery faces as they turned their purple stripes to the warmth of the sunlight.

Everything appeared dreamlike, with an air of the unfamiliar. Sarah was surprised at the lump in her throat, the heavy feeling of sadness in her chest.

The pink banner strung between the two porch posts that said, "Welcome Home, Sarah," dissolved the sadness and replaced it with anticipation. Then the front door burst open, and a horde of her family members appeared on the porch, all with varying expressions on their faces. They tried to produce wide smiles of happiness at her homecoming, but most of them didn't accomplish it, their faces contorting into all sorts of grimaces as they did their best to control the flow of tears.

Dat held her suitcase, and Mam stood by offering assistance, but Sarah unfolded her stiff joints from the backseat of the car and stood erect on her own. She breathed in deeply, savored the smell of the fresh-cut grass, the mulched flower beds, the cows, and yes, even the manure that had just been spread on the fields.

She was hugged, touched, fussed over, and leaning on her brothers' arms, taken inside where a huge brunch awaited them.

Her appetite was alarming, and Sarah swallowed as she asked Anna Mae to load up her plate with some of everything, please.

Her blue dress hung on her thin frame, and her black belt apron was pinned too loosely, but Mam said it wouldn't fit otherwise.

Sarah did not wear a covering. She didn't have enough hair to pin it to or hardly enough to consider it, her sisters said. Mam told her a *dichly* (headscarf) would suffice for now, until she had more hair again.

She sat on the recliner in the living room. Ruthie put warm woolen socks on her feet, Priscilla spread a soft blanket over her lap, and Levi brought a table leaf to put across the arms of her chair.

He stopped, looked at her gravely, and said, *"My oh, do gooksht different mit kenn hua* (Oh my, you look different with no hair)."

His brothers smiled, but they did not laugh, knowing Levi tried his best to say and do the right thing, earnest in his speech.

Sarah smiled up at Levi.

"Yes, Levi, I know. It's pretty easy to take care of."

Levi nodded seriously.

"Do gooksht ova shay (You look pretty, though)."

"Thank you, Levi."

Levi swelled with pride. His sister approved of him,

and that meant a great deal. He had done well on the day Sarah came home.

The brunch began. Plates were loaded with egg casseroles, sausages, bacon, waffles and pancakes, home fries, and applesauce. Homemade ketchup glugged from the narrow openings of re-used Heinz ketchup bottles, butter was spread thickly across the pancakes, and syrup was poured liberally over everything. The grandchildren sat at the small plastic picnic table brought in from Levi's room where it was usually folded and stored.

All except for a few bites of bacon or pancake remained on the children's paper plates. The eggs had green stuff in them, or tomatoes, so they remained untouched. Scolding mothers scooped up the plates, but they allowed the children their freedom for this one day, this celebration of Sarah's healing.

The children ran squealing outside to play on the swing at *Doddy's* (Grandfather's). Grown-ups slowly savored the shoofly pie and homemade cinnamon rolls frosted with caramel icing. They finished their coffee and began asking Sarah questions about her experience.

They showed her the newspaper article about Michael Lanvin and were surprised to find tears of sympathy in her eyes. She read the article and shook her head from side to side.

"I can hardly believe he actually is the real arsonist," she said finally.

Dat looked at Sarah, his gaze piercing.

"Why do you say that?"

"It just seems as if he is a weak, sniveling sort of person. He did not treat Ashley right, I know, but he often seemed scared of his own shadow. He just never struck me as someone who would intentionally kill harmless animals.

I think his bullying of his girlfriend was his portrayal of the weak person he is, same as his substance abuse."

Dat nodded soberly.

"You think they have the wrong person?"

"I don't know. If I said yes or no, I would only be surmising."

Levi drained his coffee cup, sat up straight, and said he was the one driving the little, white car though. And he had all that shaggy hair.

Allen said he believed Levi, but Dat said just because he drove the white car did not mean he actually lit the barn, which caused Levi to leap to his feet, one finger held aloft, and shout about another person hiding in the back seat.

This topic was a large, succulent bone for Levi. He'd chew on this subject for days, letting go of his captured suspect and honing in on another. He'd get it figured out eventually, sustained by his own ego, his sense of self-worth.

A serious conversation followed about the process in the court system for a case like this. Would Michael Lanvin be tried in court, and if he was, would any Amish person press charges? Would they testify against him?

David Beiler shook his head, his face grim.

"We are not supposed to go to court. We are not to take any part in testifying against another person. We are non-resistant people. That means exactly that. We don't resist. We don't believe in war. If someone takes your coat, give him your cloak."

Johnny, the youngest of the three married brothers, pulled at his short beard, his face turning redder by the second. Sarah could see the rebellion rising against their father and hoped the onslaught would remain reasonable.

"Dat, I disagree. What about Abraham Lincoln and the Civil War? He agonized over that, but he knew lives had to be lost for the greater good. Do you believe in slavery?"

"I'm not talking about slavery. I'm talking about someone doing evil against you. We are taught to return good for evil."

Johnny's face turned redder still.

"So when that overseer on his horse cracked the whip over the stumbling slaves, exhausted in the 100-degree heat, they were expected to turn the other cheek?"

Dat did not answer. Mam opened her mouth and closed it again.

"So when Michael lit your barn, the Bible instructs you to go out and tell him to light the implement shed as well? I mean, come on, Dat. Get with the program."

There was a long, tense silence as a gray cloud of discord settled over the happy family celebration. Dat blinked and took his time considering Johnny's words.

Outside near the swing set, a child was heard, crying in pain. Suzie took one look out the window, then ran outside to assist the victim who had fallen down the slide.

Finally, Dat spoke.

"I am with the program, Johnny. I understand your point of view. No, that would not have been feasible, the way you put it. But think. If a fellow was intent on burning my barn, and I would have gone out and offered the implement shed, he'd thought I was out of my mind. Would he have done it?"

"Of course! Without a doubt!" Johnny exclaimed.

Allen agreed.

Abner waited, leaning back in his chair, picking his teeth with a toothpick, one ankle propped on the other knee, his brown sneakers matching his brown shirt.

"A shot of lead in his britches would get him out of

here faster. He'd never return. He'd be GONE!" Johnny continued, bolstered by Allen's approval.

"Wait a minute, Johnny. He'd be gone, alright, but how would he reciprocate?"

"Talk Dutch," Johnny growled.

"Respond. Give or take."

"That would be up to him. At least my barn's safe."

Abner added his thoughts to the conversation.

"I can see Dat's point of view. In the long run, which would serve to make the guy lighting the barn feel as if he was in the wrong? He already knows that it's wrong, okay? And he doesn't care. He's out to hurt someone or something, full of rage and rebellion, just evil inside.

"So what if you shot his hind end full of lead? That's evil for evil. An eye for an eye, if you will. I think what Dat means is which response will help this person to accept forgiveness, which is, in the long run, the whole point. The person lighting the barn is perhaps a lost soul or someone gone astray, filled with hatred toward someone else."

"Oh, come on," Johnny growled.

"Hey, either you're Amish or you're not. Many in our generation do not fully understand the old ways. We think nothing of going after what is rightfully ours, in this dog-eat-dog world. But that's not really what it's all about."

"Some English people are kinder than we are," Johnny said, the wind fast dying out of his sails.

"I agree. Of course, Johnny. Good people are every-where, in every walk of life. Dat is just trying to remind us why we as a community shouldn't be determined to have our own way—to put the arsonist behind bars, the way we members of the younger generation would like."

"You boys have to understand what I went through when Sarah was burned at Lydia Esh's fire," Dat said quietly. "I wanted to literally beat up the person who did this. I am ashamed to tell you what I wanted to do. But there is only one way through this, and it's forgiveness.

"We don't need to *bekimma* (bother) ourselves about this Michael. We'll leave him in God's hands. He'll unwrap everything, and when it comes to the light, it will be done properly."

Johnny shook his head in disbelief, incredulous now.

"You're just going against common sense, Dat."

"We'll see."

The days turned warmer as the season progressed into summer. Sarah rested, ate, and slept. The hours of deep, restful slumber restored her spirits as nothing else had.

Mam had begun her home remedies the first day Sarah had returned, and she continued faithfully with her home-made salves and steeped burdock leaves. She used vitamin C in liquid form, an assortment of herbal capsules, and "body builders," as she called them, which conjured up visions of men lifting heavy weights, their oiled skin bulging unnaturally with muscles of iron. Sarah just shook her head and laughed and said they were not called body builders.

"What then?" Mam asked simply, slapping on yet another limp green burdock leaf as Priscilla stood by with the bandages.

Sarah did not visit her school, afraid her appearance would shock the pupils. If the healing progressed throughout the summer as well as Mam predicted, she'd be almost completely restored by September and could go back to teaching again then.

It was another lazy day in late June, and Sarah sat in the shade on the porch, shelling the last of the late peas. A bushel basket containing the oblong pods sat on one side of her, an empty box on the other. Her thoughts were dreamlike, resting on nothing in particular as she watched Dat cutting hay in the alfalfa field, the mules' heads bobbing in rhythm.

Why mules? she wondered.

They were the lowliest of God's creatures. They had to be. In fact, He hadn't even thought them up, they said in Dutch. She smiled, heaped another pile of pea pods on her lap, and wondered why Dat didn't buy a nice pair of Belgians from Omar Esh.

She wondered if Lee Glick had anything to do with the raising of the new colt. Or if he still existed.

She sighed.

Alles gutes nemmt tzeit (Every good thing takes time). It was an old saying, but tried and true.

Over and over, she'd relived Lee's visit to the burn center. Over and over again, she'd wondered at his mistrust of her. She had no one to blame but herself, obsessed with Matthew for too long.

A rich smell wafted through the kitchen window and circled beneath the porch roof. Sarah lifted her nose, sniffing. Mam was frying chicken. Fried chicken, mashed potatoes, new peas, and creamed lettuce with slivers of radish and onion and hardboiled egg. Mmm.

She had never appreciated her home the way she did now. It was so secure, so free from harm and pain and bright lights that hurt the eyes and attacked the senses.

And yet, she was grateful for the burn center. She still remembered to pray for the good doctors and nurses at Crozer-Chester. They had become her friends, mentors, a much-appreciated network of support when she needed it most.

She was surprised to see Hannah hurrying across the yard, her apron pinned with silver safety pins, unnamed bits of food clinging to her dress front, her covering strings flapping with each step.

"Sarah!" she called, throwing up a hand.

"Hannah. It's good to see you."

She stumbled up on the porch, fell heavily in a chair, and looked long and hard at Sarah's right side.

"You look amazing."

"I do?"

"You really do."

"Thank you. Mam has steeped tons of burdock and slathered gallons of homemade salve all over me."

"That's stretched," Hannah observed dryly.

Sarah laughed. "Yeah, it is."

"*Ach*, Sarah, you're a girl dear to my heart. I still wish that Matthew was different." Her voice trailed off, a wistful note suspended and hovering above them, echoing the sad repercussions Sarah knew came from her heart.

"What happened when he visited you in the hospital?"

Sarah told her, sparing nothing, and watched as Hannah bowed her head, then lifted it bravely to face her.

"You know, Sarah, I admire you. You see Matthew in the right way. Perhaps in the way I should. But he's my son, and a mother's love is unconditional. We love our boys, no matter what they do or who they become. But you know, I worry. He doesn't always have a nice way with me, and I'm afraid he'll treat his wife in much the same way. You know he's talking to Rose again?"

A familiar pang of jealousy tore through her mind, but she was able to quench it quickly, her new realization of the love she felt for Lee the only form of weaponry she needed to defeat it.

Rose had visited her many times, and she had never mentioned Matthew. Sarah wondered about it now.

"Is he?"

Hannah nodded.

"I'd be happy for him with Rose, but if he's not Amish, then he'd drag Rose along with him, creating bad feelings between her parents and us. Well, Elam says they're pretty liberal, so maybe they wouldn't care as much as we think."

"Hannah, I didn't know you were here." Mam came out on the porch, wiping her clean, wet hands on her black apron.

"It's just me, Malinda. Just me. I was chatting with Sarah."

"Doesn't she look good?"

"Oh my goodness! Yes!"

"Except for my hair," Sarah laughed.

Hannah laughed with her.

"You know what it looks like? I cleaned a house for an English lady once, and the hair on her poodle looked exactly like yours!"

Hannah shrieked with laughter after that remark, and Mam chuckled quietly, her rounded stomach shaking with mirth.

"Yes, Hannah. Just call me 'Poodle.'"

"Give me a handful of peas."

"Shell your own."

Hannah laughed again.

"They spoiled you at Crozer-Chester, didn't they? Your meals brought on trays, your bed changed every day."

"Her skin scraped off," Mam added wryly.

They joked, exchanged pleasantries, and laughed plenty. Sarah soaked up the camaraderie, keenly aware of the fact that all the ill feelings between them had gone away, proving their true friendship. The hurt was swallowed by the past, time healed the rift, forgiveness worked its magic, and life resumed its safe, comfortable routine of days past.

Here she was, exchanging barbs with Hannah. She could even joke about her horrific experience at the burn center, and she was glad. She was happy to be alive, grateful for her health.

Only God would have to know about her future.

That Sunday, Dat pronounced Sarah fit to go to church. She no longer needed visible bandaging, although parts of her right shoulder were bandaged, covered by a white t-shirt beneath her dress.

Mam said she could wear a colored *halsduch* (cape), as the stiff white organdy was too irritating against the tender new skin on her neck.

Sarah demurred at first, but Mam assured her everyone would understand. Sometimes the rules had to be bent to allow what was merely common sense in a case such as this.

Her hair was every bit as hopeless as she knew it would be. She plastered it down with gel as her hair spray was much too harsh for the delicate skin on her scalp.

She wore a new white covering and was pleased with the results, grateful her hair was now long enough to wear a covering. A navy blue dress and *halsduch,* and a black apron, shoes, and stockings, and she was ready to attend church services once again.

Sarah sat in the back seat of the carriage with Priscilla,

who was making all sorts of snorting sounds, trying to keep her white organdy apron from getting wrinkled.

"Things never change much, do they?" she observed, picking at her mouth to rid it of loose horse hair.

"Didn't you brush Fred?" Suzie shrieked, sticking out her tongue as she raked her handkerchief across it.

"Yes."

Dat never said much on the way to church, especially when he was prepared to preach the sermon. He remained stoic, spoke only when he was spoken to, and Mam sat devoutly by his side, as traditional as the special open-front carriage the preachers drove.

Sometimes the carriage seemed holy, or something close to it, and Sarah felt guilty for complaining or talking nonsense on Sunday morning.

"It will be warm today," Mam said, worrying about Sarah's bandage and the t-shirt beneath her dress.

"I wouldn't be surprised if we have a thunderstorm later in the day," Dat remarked.

Sarah took stock of their surroundings. Why were they going to Ben Zook's? She swallowed nervously but could not collect enough nerve to mention it. She was relieved when Priscilla spoke up.

"Why are we going to Ben's? I thought church was at Joe Fisher's."

"We were asked to come here. One of their ministers went to Indiana."

Sarah's heart beat harder, and she felt the color leave her face. Would Lee be at Ben's, at his sister Anna's house? Did he attend church services at all?

Well, she was being conveyed there at an alarming pace, with no alternative, and her face was as multi-colored and pieced together as a jigsaw puzzle, but so be it.

"What's wrong with you?" Suzie asked loudly.

"Me?"

Priscilla turned to check out her sister's face, grinned cheekily at Suzie, and whispered, "It's called Lee Glick Syndrome."

Suzie giggled, put her hand across her mouth, and hid her smile. They rode solemnly up to the shop on the Ben Zook farm, neat and prim and proper.

Sarah walked bravely to the side of the shop where the single girls were assembled, greeting others and smiling. She knew some of them, but was not acquainted with the younger ones.

She was completely aware of the curious stares, the pitying glances, but she feigned indifference, making it much easier for herself and those around her. Nothing was said, conversation resumed its normal tone, and Sarah relaxed and enjoyed the beautiful morning. She noticed Anna's yard and garden, tended to perfection.

"Sarah."

She looked around and saw her oldest pupil, Rosanna, dressed in a garish shade of green, her hair combed in the latest style, her covering sliding around on the back of her head.

"Rosanna. Why, of course, you'd be in this church district. It's so good to see you."

Rosanna shrugged her shoulders and tried to regain an air of indifference, but she looked again at Sarah's scarred and discolored face, stammered, and threw herself into Sarah's arms, bursting into little girl sobs. Sarah held her shaking form, patted her back, and looked at her through misty eyes.

"It's okay, Rosanna, really. It'll get better."

Rosanna was sniffling, wiping a finger viciously across

her nose, her eyes lowered, so miserably ashamed of herself.

Sarah looked around at the cluster of girls and found only sympathy and tears of pity for Rosanna. She assured her again, handed her a Kleenex, and slid an arm around her waist.

"I can barely wait till we have time to talk, okay? I have missed you so much this summer. I can hardly stand the thought of returning to school and you not being there. You're done with school!"

Rosanna nodded.

"You look awful," she said sadly.

"I know. But I won't always look like this."

"You think you'll need a helper this year?"

"I might."

Rosanna looked straight at Sarah, and they exchanged a look of confidence and trust.

"We'd have so much fun," Sarah said.

Anna came to lead the girls to their designated benches, and Rosanna left Sarah's side to follow the girls her own age.

Her eyes averted, knowing all eyes were on her injured face, Sarah walked slowly into the large building that would house the church service, gratefully sliding onto the bench, out of sight and away from prying eyes.

When the single young men filed in, there was a short, dark-haired youth leading them. So. He was not here. As Anna's brother, Lee would have gone first.

Bitter disappointment took her breath away, but only for a minute. She had the rest of her life, and this was the first day of it. Life was much easier when she thought along those lines, she mused and opened the black hymnbook after the song was announced.

CHAPTER 9

IT WAS GOOD TO BE BACK AT THE SUNDAY SERVICES, the traditional gathering of friends and family. In each district, a group of about twenty-five to thirty families took turns hosting church services at their homes.

The districts were areas agreed upon by the ministers and laymen, usually bounded by roads or other landmarks. When the district grew to more than forty families, causing challenges for hosting so many people, the murmuring would begin. The women grumbled to their husbands about baking forty pies and the necessity of having to make eight batches of homemade bread. It just took too much food, they said.

The women were to be keepers of the home, quiet, prohibited from speaking in church, but they carried considerable clout when the time came to divide a church district into two. They were the ones who fretted and stewed about hosting the ever-growing congregation in their houses or shops or basements, always concerned about the allotted spaces.

On Sarah's first Sunday back at church, Davey Beiler's family had gone to church at Ben Zook's farm, meaning they had gone to the district beside their own home church. They went because the lead minister had gone to attend services in Indiana and had asked Davey to preach instead.

Despite her earlier confidence, Sarah was suddenly not sure she should be there at all. She felt lonely, self-conscious, and now, noticing Lee's absence, a bit put out. But maybe he'd think she was running after him, coming to Ben's church service with her scarred face. Well, she wasn't. Most of her pupils went to church in this district, so what was wrong with that? Besides, her dat had been asked to come.

As the rising volume of the plainsong swelled around her, she opened her mouth and joined in. Few things could lift her spirits like the singing in church. The slow, undulating cadence sent chills down her spine. It was the sound of home, safety, and belonging.

Suddenly, she stopped singing, lowered her head, and kept it hidden behind the woman sitting directly in front of her.

Lee!

He'd just walked in.

Oh, my. Oh, my.

All thoughts of singing were completely erased from her mind. In fact, everything was. She hadn't seen him in church clothes since Susan and Marvin's wedding when he had selected Rose to take to the wedding table. His blond hair was cut short. She'd think he was an embarrassment to his parents, or to Ben and Anna, with hair like that, but it did look handsome. His shirt was so white, his eyes so blue, his vest and *mutza* (coat) fit so superbly, it actually took her breath away.

He was not yet a member of the church. He had never been baptized and taken Christ as his personal Savior. He was already 23, maybe 24. Suddenly, he seemed far away, unattainable. What had she done?

Why, if he was still so worldly, did his values and his attitude seem the opposite of Matthew's, who was born again, saved, without one doubt in anyone's mind? Matthew read his Bible endlessly and had a heartfelt testimony to back his knowledge of the Bible, but in so many ways, he still behaved like the same mama's boy he'd always been.

It was not her job to decipher the difference. It was God's. Dat had been very firm about that.

Over and over, she relived that last encounter with Lee at the burn center. Now the blinding fog of Matthew was completely gone, the warm sun of her understanding obliterating it, leaving her weak with gratification and the wonder of her love.

The difference was astounding. Where she'd felt desperation, heart-pounding greediness, really, with her desire to be Matthew's wife, this was slow, easy, secure. It was bliss borne of knowledge, knowing the wait was all a part of God's plan.

After the singing ended, there was a soft tap on her shoulder, and Sarah turned, meeting Anna's lowered face, her eyes bright with concern.

"*Komm* (Come)."

Sarah shook her head.

"Yes, Sarah, you can't sit on that hard bench. You're still weak. Come, sit with us. I have a chair for you with cushions."

Sarah waited until Anna left, then summoned all her courage and rose in one swift movement, flustered and painfully aware of the discoloration of her skin, the deep and angry scars.

Gratefully, she sank into the soft cushions placed on a patio chair, keeping her head lowered, her eyes on the bench directly in front of her.

How ugly she must appear!

A little girl turned around on the bench, gave Sarah a frank appraisal, and asked Anna innocently, "What is wrong with her?"

She was shushed instantly by her harried mother, who was holding a grunting infant over her shoulder.

When Sarah looked up, Lee's eyes were directly on her face. They both looked away, unanimous in their decision to avoid eye contact. Immediately, they both looked back, and just as swiftly, lowered their eyes again.

When the singing stopped, Dat got up, cleared his throat, looked around the congregation, and began to speak. His voice was deep and low, well modulated, a tone that carried well.

Sarah had never heard her father speak the way he did that day. He was kind and loving, but he firmly shared his new-found insights on non-resistance. He spoke of the test of his faith, when his daughter was burned, and said that on some days, he still wanted to testify against the man in prison. In fact, he'd imagined the hangings of old, the gallows, and any form of punishment man had ever devised, because he was human.

Human nature, he said, wants to slap back immediately. It's a natural response. Someone smites your cheek, and you want to hit back, but that is not what the Bible teaches us.

Christ's way is to turn the other cheek. If we return good for evil, it's like piling coals of fire on our enemies' heads. It becomes a misery, and it works.

He spoke with conviction, yet he remained gentle.

When Sarah began to feel faint, she put her head on the back of the cushioned chair and closed her eyes, but the room tilted and spun crazily. She gripped the arms of her chair and prayed the weakness would pass.

Recognizing the nausea that welled up in her throat, she got up, immediately grabbing the chair back for support as the room spun around her. She made it to the doorway, gulping as she headed to the house.

The fresh air and brilliant sunshine revived her for a moment. When she got to the kitchen, she sank gratefully on a chair, lowered her head in her hands, and closed her eyes.

She felt a presence, then a light touch on her shoulder.

"Bisht alright (Are you alright)?"

Startled, Sarah lifted her head. Two bright blue eyes peered at her from behind round spectacles, a kindly smile accompanying them.

The older woman was as round as Anna, shaped like a little human barrel, except much softer. Her face crinkled with lines that were likely formed by all the smiling she did.

Sarah nodded, weakly.

"You're that Sarah Beiler, *gel* (right)? I am Anna's mother, Rachel."

So. She was Lee's mother. That was interesting. She could see where he got the color of his eyes.

Clucking to herself, Rachel placed a soft hand on Sarah's face, turning the scars to the light, adjusting her own face to peer through the bifocals on her glasses.

"*My, my. My oh.* You really did go through something, didn't you? *Siss yusht hesslich* (It's too bad)."

Stepping back, she tilted her face, turned Sarah's cheek to the light again, and kept examining the burned area.

"You are using the salve?"

Sarah nodded.

"I still have one surgery to go through. The spot on my shoulder that was burnt worse than anything else."

"I guess you're thankful to be alive."

Sarah nodded.

"It could have been Lee, you know. It worries me the way he gets so involved with the people who have fires. I mean, that's why he's here at Ben's. He feels bad for Ben's loss and does whatever he can so Ben doesn't have to hire someone. And now he's so involved with that widow's boy Omar and his horses. I guess it's okay, as long as he doesn't do something foolish yet."

There was nothing to say to that, so Sarah merely nodded.

Likely, the busy little woman had no idea about Lee's relationship with Sarah. Or the lack of it now.

Rachel suddenly changed the subject.

"I'm hungry. You look like a bit of food would do you good. Let's sneak some cheese and *blooney* (bologna)."

Giggling like a schoolgirl, she searched the refrigerator, coming up with a plastic bag containing at least ten pounds of sliced sweet bologna. She proceeded to open the wrapper on a loaf of homemade bread and spread it with the cheese spread that was so much a part of the noon meal following Sunday services.

"I just didn't have time to eat breakfast."

Rachel handed a small plate of the bread and bologna to Sarah with one hand, stuffing a large portion of her own slice into her mouth with the other.

She turned her back, guilty now, as a young mother rushed into the kitchen with a screaming baby, a crying toddler hanging onto her apron.

Rachel polished off the slice of bread, then scuttled after the toddler and picked him up, saying, "Hush, hush, my goodness. Here, here. You want a slice of *blooney*?"

When the angry little boy's screams increased, she fished under her ample apron and produced a string of bright colored toys on key chains.

"Here. Look! Here. Now, now. Don't cry."

She pressed the button on a small flashlight, which did the trick. The cries dissipated as she clicked it on and off.

Sarah observed Rachel's motherly skills, the way she saw the helpless expression on the young mother's face and instantly bustled after the crying toddler. She thought of Lee being here, on this farm, for his brother-in-law, as well as helping Omar Esh.

She nibbled on the smoked sweet bologna, broke off a corner of the homemade bread, and appreciated the mellow taste of the cheese spread. Looking up, she saw Rachel with the toddler encircled in one arm, holding out a glass of orange juice to her.

"Orange juice. It's the best thing for low blood sugar. You're not hypoglycemic, are you?"

Sarah shook her head and accepted the juice. Then she moved to a rocking chair, where she leaned her head back against the cushion and closed her eyes.

No doubt about it, she was still not as strong as she would like to be, so she'd better stay in the kitchen and rest awhile.

The young mother fed the infant, turned her head to observe Sarah's face discreetly, then bit her lip and looked away.

Rachel fussed to the now happy toddler, showing him each trinket on the chain. She observed Sarah as well and pursed her lips.

The door was pushed open, allowing Anna's buxom form to enter. She was puffing slightly, the color on her cheeks high, her blue eyes alight with excitement.

Church was at her house, and everything had to be perfect.

"Forgot paper cups," she whispered to her mother, yanking on the pantry door with enthusiasm.

"Did you remember sugar this time?"

"Uh. No. I forgot."

Rachel's round form shook as she heaved with silent laughter.

"Best stop cleaning and remember you have church, Anna."

In answer, Anna swung the plastic packet of paper cups in her mother's direction, batting her eyelashes as she did so. Rachel ducked her head. The woman on the chair looked over and smiled. They all knew Anna.

Comfortable now, relaxed, Sarah smiled to herself. She savored the easy relationships passed down through the generations. There was a congenial acceptance of one another, at church services, quiltings, school programs, wherever there was a social gathering.

It didn't seem so long ago that she was a little girl dressed in a pinafore-style white apron, in a kitchen such as this. Her hand firmly grasped in Mam's, she was led to the bathroom or for a drink of water, as the singsong voice of the preacher rose and fell in the shop or the living room or the basement below.

Mam would meet a good friend, and they'd talk in hushed tones, only a bit, not too long. But they leaned in, touched a forearm as they quickly exchanged a community tidbit, swapped knowing looks, and passed on quickly.

It was rude to stay away from the service for an extended period of time, especially for a minister's wife. A baby that had to be put to sleep was an exception, however, so the kitchen or living room of the house was often a place where mothers put the little ones down for a nap, relieved to have a few free moments to absorb the sermon without squirming infants on their laps.

Motherhood was an eagerly awaited event for Sarah. She looked forward to cozily sitting together with other young mothers, comparing experiences about births and babies, raising children, the various ways of canning and freezing, cooking and baking. It was an objective for every young girl, and Sarah was no different.

She opened her eyes as the grateful young mother rose slowly from her chair, carefully carrying the sleeping infant into Ben and Anna's bedroom, where she laid a pre-folded diaper in the middle of the high king-sized bed, gently placed the sweet baby on it, covered her with a light blanket, and tiptoed out, closing the door lightly behind her. Going to Rachel, she bent over and held out her arms for the little boy, smiling as she did so.

"*Denke* (Thank you)."

"*Siss gaen schoene* (You're welcome)."

They exchanged smiles, and the young woman whisked her son back to the shop, where services were continuing.

Other young mothers milled about, changing diapers, getting their children cold drinks, sitting down with crying little ones—all a part of the usual church Sunday.

Sarah leaned her head back, closed her eyes wearily as the sounds ebbed and flowed, waves of laughter and talk coming and going.

"Did you hear about Anna's brother Lee?"

Instantly, Sarah's eyes flew open, before she caught herself and closed them, afraid someone had noticed.

A young mother folded a snowy white diaper across one shoulder, lifted her daughter, and draped her deftly across the cloth. She lifted her eyebrows and shook her head.

"They say he's going to Alaska."

"Whatever for? Is he going hunting or what?"

"I have no idea. He probably won't be Amish if he goes up there. He's pretty old and hasn't joined the church."

Sarah's mouth went dry. She took a quick breath to steady herself, then sat up to look for Rachel, his mother, but she had gone back to the service with her daughter.

Alaska. He may as well go to the moon.

"What happened between him and Rose Zook?"

"Who knows? The youth are always going through some sort of drama. Worse than we ever were."

Nodding righteously, the listening young mother inserted a pink pacifier into her sleeping baby's mouth, turning to address her friend.

"You know he won't be back. I pity his parents."

Sarah could not sit on the chair another second, so she rose, walked stiffly across the kitchen, looking straight ahead without acknowledging either woman, as if obliterating them from her vision would also dissipate the fact that Lee was going to Alaska.

She didn't believe it. He would not leave Ben and Anna, or the Widow Lydia and Omar. He was the most unselfish person she knew, as kind as her father, by all means. Why would he do something so completely out of character?

She entered the shop, her eyes downcast, and found her chair. She listened to the voice of the aging minister whose turn it was to speak as he expounded the Scripture in a meaningful way.

He spoke of faith, the essence of believing that which we cannot see, but Sarah's mind was churning with unanswered questions now, her attention diverted by the bit of gossip from the kitchen.

That was all it was. Two young mothers bored with their own lives who circulated rumors like that among themselves to make things more interesting. It simply was not true, Sarah told herself.

After the last hymn had been sung, services were over. The single boys and girls filed out in solemn rows until they reached the open door. The small boys pushed out between the young men, eager to grab their black felt hats from the back of the bench wagon.

The bench wagon was a large trailer built to carry the wooden benches from one service location to the next, usually pulled by a team of strong draft horses. As time went on and more Amish left farming for other occupations, the need to hire a pickup truck to pull the bench wagon became more and more apparent. It was frowned upon at first, but common sense eclipsed tradition, and the practice was accepted. A tolerant hired driver patiently traveled at a slow pace, the tongue of the bench wagon secured firmly to the pickup truck's hitch, rattling along from one Amish home to the next.

After everyone had left their appointed seats following the service, the murmurs swelled into a near roar as friends met and greeted one another. The men folded the

legs of some of the benches and set them on trestles to create long tables with the remaining benches set along side.

Women scurried out with white tablecloths draped
across their arms and snapped them across the tabletops
that had been benches only five minutes before. Plastic
totes containing plates, tumblers, saucers, knives, and
forks appeared like magic as many willing helpers scurried from the house bearing trays of sliced homemade
bread, plates of butter, and dishes of jelly. There was also
a delicious concoction that Sarah always anticipated. It
was made with boiled brown sugar and water that was
cooled and poured over great gobs of peanut butter and
marshmallow cream. It was a part of her life, a tasty tradition at church dinners.

Cheese spread, the smoked sweet bologna, dishes of
pungent little slices of bread and butter pickles, savory
red beets, seasoned pretzels, and *snitz* (dried apple) pie
completed the meal.

In years past, apples had always been dried and stored
in a cool place to be used later for *snitz* pies. Water was
added, and the dried apples were cooked, mashed, and
flavored with sugar and spices.

Somewhere along the way, a wily housewife had discovered an easier version for *snitz* pie. She mixed applesauce, apple butter, sugar, and spices with an almost identical result. It took only a few minutes, with no cooking
or mashing necessary.

Snitz pies were delicious, in Sarah's opinion, although
each housewife's version varied slightly. Sometimes a
wedge of pie proved to be almost inedible, leaving a sour
aftertaste when a well-meaning baker had spared the
sugar and cinnamon.

Crusts varied as well. In some pies, the crust was thick and hard where the *snitz* had boiled its way out between the crimped edges, leaving a dark, brown gluey covering along the crust.

When a crust was too inedible, it was usually hidden discreetly beneath the lip of a saucer. In some cases, it was left boldly on the saucer and dumped unceremoniously into the waste can. Then the saucer was handed to the dishwashers, who usually asked what was wrong with the crust. Eyes rolled or eyebrows raised, but never a word was spoken.

The men ate at one table; the women at another. They usually filled a second time with younger men and boys, young women and girls. The men always filed into services by age, as did the women, an orderly routine that was copied at the tables where dinner was served.

It seemed a bit unfair that the hungry boys and girls had to wait until their elders had eaten, but with their hungry children in mind, the older folks ate their meals quickly, without loitering or negligent conversation.

Sarah did not wait on tables. She remained in her chair, away from prying eyes, watching the swish of skirts, the colorful children dashing to and from the tables to snitch a salty seasoned pretzel if they could get away with it.

Sarah watched a two-year-old boy climb up on a bench, lean his rounded little body across the table, and grab a handful of bologna, knocking over a tumbler of water in the process.

Gasps went up as Anna dashed to clamp her capable hands around the errant little boy's middle and whisk him efficiently off the bench, the color in her cheeks giving away her impatience. The little boy stuffed a slice of bologna in his mouth, glared up at his abductor, and ambled off indignantly.

"People that don't watch their children!" she hissed to Sarah.

Rachel came scurrying with a tea towel extended, clucking and wiping, leaving Sarah in awe of these rounded women who moved with the speed of lightning, more or less.

She wondered if Lee would ever gain weight. Well, it was nothing to her, now that he was going to Alaska, if such a thing was possible.

She was summoned to the table, sat with eyes averted, enduring the open stares of the young children around her.

Rosanna, her former student, slid onto the bench opposite Sarah and smiled. She noticed the open stares of the children, Sarah's apparent unease, and spoke firmly, "Stop staring, girls. It's not polite. She can't help she was in an accident."

The response was immediate. Faces lowered, with color rising in their cheeks. The girls mumbled apologies, their eyes blinking.

Sarah immediately felt sorry for the girls, especially the ones that had been her pupils at Ivy Run School.

"It's okay, Rosanna. It really is. I know I look like a monster."

That brought a giggle from Katie Mae, a third grader, who shook her head and told Sarah she looked like a nice monster.

"When I go back to school in the fall, I'll look better, and we can really have an amazing health class with everything I learned about burns, right?"

Rosanna's eyes stayed intently on Sarah's face, until Sarah met them. The two raised eyebrows and exchanged knowing smiles.

A feeling of peace enveloped Sarah, a gradual sense of quiet, knowing she would go back to school, back to her teaching job, perhaps enabling her to help Rosanna find a sense of direction in the process.

There was so much more to life than finding a husband. First, she must heal, from the scars and burns, as well as the knowledge that she and Matthew were not to be. Not now, not ever. She knew it in her mind, but had her heart accepted it?

If Lee actually did go to Alaska, then she guessed that spoke of his character. Who did he think he was, anyway?

Sarah chomped down on a wedge of pie, and the sweet *snitz* filling fell to her plate. The girls opposite her covered their mouths with their hands to keep from laughing.

CHAPTER 10

IT WAS ON A HOT SUMMER'S EVENING THAT LEE rode down to Widow Lydia's for the last time, his schedule prepared, his Amtrak ticket bought, his future life as an Alaskan mapped out.

He wouldn't be back for the wedding, but it was alright. Melvin and Lydia could be married without him. He was sure they would have a very nice wedding, and the children would be happy to have a father again.

The hardest part was explaining his plans to Omar, without disclosing the truth. He tried to tell him it was a dream he'd always had. And now that Omar was old enough to take responsibility with the Belgians and his mother and Melvin were getting married in the fall, things would be just fine, Lee said.

Omar had squared his shoulders, believed him, and remained stoic, his young face showing strength, having weathered so much in his young life. He had survived the death of his abusive father, Aaron, two barn fires, and his mother's mental anguish. Lee believed his leaving was only a small thing, and Omar would accept it. He'd have Melvin now.

His horse raised his head, then lowered it, as Lee slid from the saddle. He led him into the newly finished horse barn, almost identical to the last one. The hooves clopped on the clean, white cement as Lee eyed the fresh lumber appreciatively. He'd have to tell Melvin to build a closet for the harnesses.

He tied his horse and turned toward the door. He leaned against the side of the barn, watching the insects wheeling and darting through the still, hot air. It wouldn't be long till the bats appeared, gobbling up their evening smorgasbord on wings.

The willow tree in the pasture was completely still, with not even a small shiver of the long thin leaves. Must be a thunderstorm brewing somewhere, as heavy as the air felt tonight.

Far away, the wail of a siren began, low at first, then more distinct. Likely a cop chasing someone out on the Old Philadelphia Pike. He'd miss this life, the hustle, the hurry.

Lee raised a hand to swat at a mosquito that was whining at his ear. The kitchen door opened, and Omar dashed across the porch and down to the barn waving.

"Hey!"

"I thought you might have gone to bed."

"Me? Why would I go so early?"

"Sleepy? Tired?"

Omar cuffed Lee's elbow.

"I am eighteen, not eight months old."

Lee laughed with genuine pleasure.

"Think it will storm?"

"It could. It's still."

"Yeah."

A comfortable silence lay between them, an easy,

velvety feeling, like the evening with the heat, the quiet of the willow tree.

The wailing siren grew in magnitude and was joined by another.

"That sound will never fail to give me the creeps."

"Yeah."

"Think the fires are over, now that someone's in jail?"

"I doubt it. I don't know."

Lee scuffed a heel against the edge of the cement, then lowered himself to sit on the edge, resting his arms on his knees.

Omar followed suit, and Lee looked at the youth's profile.

"How's your mam?"

"Good. Happy. Melvin makes her laugh."

"That's good."

"Yeah. She had a tough time of it, before."

"Did she?"

Omar nodded.

"Dat was not a nice person. I wouldn't know what a kind father is like, except for you."

"I'm not your dat."

"Closest thing to it."

Lee laughed, a derisive outburst, a mockery.

"Yeah, well, I'll never be a father. That's for sure."

"What? Why are you saying that?"

Lee shrugged his shoulders.

"You could be, if you weren't running off to Alaska."

"You can't change my mind, Omar."

"I know."

Suddenly Omar turned to face Lee and exclaimed loudly, "Why are you going? Really. If you want to see that state so bad, I'll get you a book."

"Omar!" Lydia called from the porch, her thin form upright as she leaned against the white post, her arm encircling it.

"Hey!"

"Come on up for mint tea and soft pretzels!"

Immediately, they were on their feet, moving toward the porch. Few things were as tempting as homemade soft pretzels, hot and buttery from a 500-degree oven. They were delicious dipped in warm cheese sauce or laced liberally with mustard, especially when there was ice-cold mint tea to accompany them.

They clattered onto the porch, joking, opened the screen door, and stopped short.

Sarah stood by the kitchen table, dressed in a soft shade of blue. She was wearing her covering all the time now, her hair growing fast, and a black bib apron covered her blue dress. She was pouring the tea in tall glasses filled half full with ice cubes.

She looked up, her eyes dancing, her wide mouth turned into an eager smile for Omar.

When she saw Lee, every attempt at self-control failed. She lowered the pitcher with a clunk, leaving two glasses unfilled. As the color left her face, her eyes became dark, as they did when she was confronted by surprise, or fear, or sadness.

Lee stopped, uncertain, as he struggled for composure as well.

"Lee!" Lydia broke the awkward silence with genuine welcome in her voice.

"Hello, Lydia. Sarah."

"You are just in time. Come, let's sit outside. Grab that tray, Sarah. You can put the tea on it."

Little Aaron toddled along, dodging feet. The two

older girls, Anna Mae and Rachel, hung shyly in the background as Sarah resumed filling the tall glasses, her hands shaking so that she needed both of them to steady the pitcher.

Why had he come? How could she survive this evening? She'd go. She'd tell them she was needed at home. She would not sit here and listen to Lee bragging about his upcoming Alaskan adventure.

But when she saw him leaning back in the wooden Adirondack chair, his golden head shining in the evening light, she hesitated. His wide shoulders exuded strength, the yellow shirt he was wearing a perfect backdrop for his tanned face. Her knees felt a slight loss of muscle tone, and she quickly set the tray of glasses on the wooden table, the ice clinking, the tea sloshing over the sides.

Lydia looked at Sarah's face, then dabbed at the spilled tea with a corner of her apron. She passed the platter of pretzels and small dishes of cheese sauce, noticing immediately when Lee waved them away and Sarah shook her head.

Lee was talking.

Sarah shrank back against her chair, her arms folded tightly around her middle, her knees pressed together, tense.

"I'll be back. I just don't know when. Six months, maybe a year. I came to say goodbye. I'm leaving Thursday."

Five days. This was Sunday evening. No. Three days. Four days.

"Where's Melvin?" Omar asked suddenly.

"He's late. Way late. You know, he's with the fire company, and I heard the sirens, so perhaps he's out on a call."

"Could be."

Sarah could only sip her tea, raising and lowering her glass, as if her arms were programmed like a robot, mechanical. As the twilight moved across the yard, enclosing the porch with a graying aura, she watched a light blink on in Elam's house, upstairs. Matthew must be home early.

As if Lydia had read her mind, she inquired about Matthew Stoltzfus. Was he dating yet? You'd think it was too soon, but someone had seen him down at Rockvale Square with Rose Zook.

Omar said people jumped to conclusions. Maybe she'd just needed a ride, and there wasn't a thing to it.

Lee said nothing, as the wall of tension between him and Sarah built itself up in the silence, sitting heavily, unseen, unspoken, but felt keenly.

"Aren't you going to say anything, Sarah?" Omar asked. "You surely know what's up with Matthew."

Sarah choked on a mouthful of tea, coughed, and wiped her mouth with a napkin. She shook her head.

"I haven't spoken to Matthew since I was at Crozer-Chester."

The silence exploded as Omar pumped his fist into the air, yelling something about I told you so, you big old skeptic, you. He jumped sideways, slamming a fist into Lee's arm with a smack. Lee grabbed his arm and grimaced in pain, before leaping to his feet as Omar took off down the porch steps and across the yard. Lee shot after Omar and easily overtook him, grabbed the waist of his trousers, and pulled him to the ground. They tussled a bit on the grass and then returned to the porch caught up in a new discussion about the Belgians.

As night fell, Sarah said she must be going. Everyone

protested, saying the night was still young. They'd go inside and play a game, but Sarah shook her head, remaining firm.

Why sit here on Lydia's front porch and prolong the torture of Lee's leaving when all she wanted to do was pound him with her fists? She just wanted tell him how disagreeable he was, how stubborn.

She was just getting up to return her glass to the kitchen when a team came up the driveway. It turned towards the horse barn, the blue LED lights raking across the porch, the glare invading their privacy.

Melvin.

Lydia, clearly relieved, began babbling senselessly and begging Sarah to stay, but Sarah was afraid. She feared Melvin's lack of restraint, his honesty, when she just wanted to cling to her pride, her silence the only hope of redemption.

She said goodnight, stepped down from the porch, and was ready to open the gate when she heard a frantic call.

"Sarah! What do you think you're doing? Get back there!"

A wide smile immediately spread across Sarah's face. He really meant it.

Hurrying up the slope from the barn, Melvin met Sarah at the gate.

"Just give it up, Sarah. Turn around. I'm here."

"I have to go," she answered.

"Why?"

"Because. I just have to."

"Sarah, I haven't seen you in ages. Come on. We'll play Upwords. Just for you."

She hesitated, weighing her options, but suddenly she had no choice as Melvin grasped her upper arms, turned her, and steered her back up to the front porch.

In the semidarkness, Melvin strained to see the occupants scattered along the width of the porch. He warmly greeted Lydia, his bride-to-be, then shouted overenthusiastically, "Lee! Long time, no see! What's up?"

"Not much."

"I hear you're going to Alaska! Boy, I envy you. Why don't you wait till we're married, and we'll go with you on our honeymoon?"

Lydia laughed and protested, while Omar yelled with delight. No one heard the telephone in the phone shanty when it began its incessant ringing—no one except little Aaron, who finally shouted, "Phone!"

"Let it go. They'll leave a message."

"I'll get it."

Omar made a dash for the phone shanty, slapped open the gate, and yanked the door open, catching the caller on the last ring. There was no sound from the phone shanty, only another siren wailing in the distance, then another.

When Omar stepped out of the shanty, he did not dash up to the porch. He walked, lifting the gate latch heavily, his steps leaden as he came. He leaned heavily on the porch post.

"Lee. It was your sister. You need to go home. I'll come with you."

Lee was out of his chair immediately.

"What happened?"

"It's Ben, your brother-in-law."

"What happened to him?"

"She didn't say how bad it was."

Lee leaped off the porch, ran down to the barn, loosened his horse, and was out the drive in less than a minute.

Omar followed on his horse, as Lydia and Melvin soberly cleared the wooden table on the porch. The children pitched in to do their share, but Sarah sat, immobile, unable to tell herself to do something, get out of her chair.

What had happened? She shivered. Surely not another fire, with the suspect incarcerated.

They sat together in the kitchen without speaking, the inability to understand robbing them of the will to make small talk. Lydia sat close to Melvin, his presence enabling her to get through this—whatever it was. It was a significant gesture she would likely incorporate repeatedly over the years, with her husband as the rock she needed when adversity emotionally disabled her.

After an hour had passed, they checked the phone messages to find nothing. They resumed their quiet vigil, until Sarah decided to check for a message again.

There was an ominous rumble in the distance. Heat lightning skittered across the sky, but the air remained heavy and still. Traffic could be heard plainly, the cars stopping and starting, changing gears, a horn tooting, then again.

There was a message this time. Sarah could tell by the beeping on the line, but she did not know Lydia's pin number or how to access her voice mail, so she called for her repeatedly.

Lydia came quickly, pressed the buttons, then listened, her head bent.

"No. Oh no," she breathed.

Sarah waited, frightened, afraid to know, afraid not to.

"What is it?" she whispered.

Lydia pressed the 3, then slowly replaced the receiver, a sob catching in her throat.

"A bull. A bull got Ben."

Sarah would never forget her friend's words. They did not convey the final outcome, only the immediate accident, but everything they had shared together already had schooled them in the art of acceptance.

Blindly, they clung together. Blindly, they broke apart and stumbled into the kitchen.

They told Melvin but could not remember, later, who had actually related the message. Melvin held Lydia in his arms and comforted her. Then he asked Sarah to stay with Lydia. He was going over to the Zooks' place. They sat side by side, the children around them, and stared unseeing at the opposite wall, jumping and afraid when the refrigerator hummed and clicked.

When a flash of bluish white lightning illuminated the kitchen, they squeezed their eyes shut like small children and cowered at the following clap of thunder. They allowed the children to pile a heap of sleeping bags and blankets on the living room floor, so they could stay close together as the storm approached.

Sarah closed windows upstairs, guided by the glow of the LED lamp she carried. When she went to close the downstairs bedroom window, a startling streak of lightning made her step back, stifling a yelp.

The rain came down in hard-driven sheets, sluicing down the west side of the house. It filled the spouting with heavy gushes of water that clattered against the inside of the downspouts and shot out the bottom, where it tumbled over the small path of rocks Lydia had built for just this purpose.

The wind howled around the eaves, and rain pounded against the windows as thunder roared and clapped overhead. The lightning flashed brilliantly, but the air became stifling in the kitchen with the windows closed to the only available breeze.

They sat around the table and comforted one another with words of hope, but they were unable to rest or relax. Lydia leaped to her feet repeatedly, searching wild-eyed for Melvin, but Sarah knew she was also in constant fear of lightning striking the barn. She ran from window to window, lifting, then lowering the sashes, always alert for any strange light from the barn.

As the storm slowly left, the lightning became weaker. The thunder grew muffled, and the rain fell gently instead of being pelted against the side of the house from the force of the wind. Lydia took a deep breath, sagged against the back of the couch, and said bluntly that she was so glad to be getting married again. She was eager to have a husband, a protector, a person stronger than herself.

Sarah nodded, a wave of longing taking her by surprise.

When Melvin finally came back, he found Lydia and Sarah, one at each end of the couch, asleep. When he woke Lydia, she sat straight up, her eyes wide with alarm. She shook Sarah to waken her, wanting her to hear what had happened.

Anna had done the supper dishes. Then they had worked together, she and Ben, weeding the watermelon and cantaloupe plants.

A cow was due to freshen, so Ben went to the pasture to bring her in, never thinking about the mild-tempered Holstein bull grazing with the herd.

When Ben did not return, Anna went to find him, calling and calling. She became alarmed when she saw the cloud of dust the bull was pawing from the earth. That was strange. He had never shown aggression.

Afraid to enter the pasture, she dialed 911. The dread washed over her repeatedly, yet she clung to the hope that Ben had not gone to the pasture at all.

They had to tranquilize the bull in the end.

They gathered up Ben Zook's broken body and carried him to his wife on a stretcher, these men dressed in navy blue outfits with EMT emblazoned across their backs in silver letters, with kind eyes and hands to help her sit down. Anna sat, but she did not faint. She remained alert as she gathered her children around her soft, ample body and wept endlessly into their clean, straight hair.

She was so glad they'd worked in the garden together on his last day on earth.

When Lee arrived, he was shocked, but they said his shoulders heaved with the force of his weeping.

The news spread like wildfire.

After hearing the details, Sarah went home to her bed, but she lay sleepless, wondering, her thoughts running rampant. What had God wrought? The taking of Anna's husband. Why? She was so lively, so full of life and energy and hope, no matter what the circumstances.

In the morning, a bit of sleep had been enough, and Sarah stumbled down the stairs at the first stirring of her parents in the kitchen.

She broke the news, which was received in a typically restrained manner. They wept, but acknowledged that the Lord giveth and the Lord taketh away, and blessed be the name of the Lord. Thy will be done, they said. The backbone of their faith was that highly esteemed acceptance of a higher power, and what God does, He doeth well, even in times such as this.

Sarah and Priscilla did the milking, knowing Dat

would be expected to go immediately to the Zooks' and Mam would accompany him.

Mam gathered a bag of potatoes, a container of jello from the refrigerator, a stack of white American cheese, and eggs. She filled her sixteen-quart kettle with bags of frozen corn. She had plenty, and this would come in handy, feeding all the relatives and friends during the three days before Ben would be buried.

She dressed in her black dress and pinned a fresh white covering to her head. As she sat beside her Davey in the buggy, she was thankful he was alive and well.

Sarah worked with Priscilla, milking the cows. They swept the aisles, fed calves, washed milkers, and hosed down the milk house. Sarah was grateful for her returning strength. When the milking was done, they returned to the house, just as the clock struck half past six.

Sarah missed Mam's breakfast immensely, but she got to work in the kitchen immediately, frying bacon, while Priscilla woke Levi and helped him get dressed and into his shoes.

As Sarah flipped the eggs, she heard a great shout from Levi, who did not want to wear his shoes.

"Levi, come on. I'm starving. You have to wear your shoes!"

"I'm not going to."

"I'm going to tell Dat."

"Dat does not care if I don't wear shoes. It's too hot."

"Alright, then. You're not getting any breakfast."

Levi lumbered into the kitchen in his bare feet and stepped on a pen that Suzie had left on the floor. He became so irritable that he threw the pen at Priscilla. It bounced off the side of her head and against the refrigerator.

"Levi! Priscilla!" Sarah scolded.

"She needs to sit down and read her Bible," Levi said.

Sarah told Levi about the events on the Ben Zook farm, blinking back tears of pity for her friend Anna, who would now be a widow with three fatherless children.

Levi could not fully absorb this awful news. He told Sarah that Ben wasn't really dead, that Dat said dead people went to heaven after they were viewed in *die laud* (casket). Did Ashley Walters? Did Mervin? If Ben Zook went up there with Ashley and Mervin, he was afraid there would be no room for him after he died.

Sarah assured Levi that heaven was very, very big.

"Bigger that Pennsylvania?" he asked.

"Oh my, yes."

Levi pondered this bit of information, then nodded his head, agreeing with Sarah. He was glad to be able to think of his own place up there.

"Did they shoot the bull?"

"I don't know, Levi."

"He should be ground into hamburger."

"He probably will."

Levi sat down to his breakfast and lowered his head with the girls for the usual silent prayer. When they lifted their heads, Sarah was surprised to see a trickle of tears falling slowly down Levi's cheeks.

He pulled out a red handkerchief, blew his nose, and shook his head solemnly.

"I wish Ben would have waited on me. It's not fun here anymore," he said. "Since you were burned, Mam never makes shoofly."

CHAPTER 11

WHEN THEIR PARENTS RETURNED, SARAH AND Priscilla were sent to work in Anna's yard, mowing grass, raking, tilling the garden. The women had cleaned the house and prepared the basement as a cooking and eating station. They would be feeding dozens of relatives, refilling the long tables over and over.

The girls were expected to wear their black dresses, with capes and aprons pinned over them, their white covering strings tied. They also wore their black shoes and stockings, even with the temperature hovering around 90 degrees.

Fred was lethargic. He was clearly displeased at the thought of returning the way he had just come. He would have preferred being turned loose into the green pasture to stand comfortably beneath a maple tree, swatting flies with his tail.

Sarah slapped his rump with the reins. Fred's ears laid back, flicked forward, and he broke into a halfhearted trot, allowing a cool breeze to flow into the buggy. At the slight incline on Old Leacock Road, he ambled into a stiff-legged walk, eliminating any hope of a breeze.

"Seriously, Fred. Make him go, Sarah. Fred! Come on!" Priscilla grabbed the reins away from Sarah, giving Fred a smart rap on his haunches.

"Come on!"

Fred lunged dutifully into his collar, and the breeze resumed.

"It's so hot," Priscilla groaned.

"Just wait till we have to start working in the yard in all this black," Sarah said.

"I don't think we should have to go help. We're not in Ben's, uh, I mean, Anna's church."

"So? We're friends. I used to work for her. Besides, lots of people came to help after our fire—church members or not."

"Whatever."

Priscilla leaned back against the seat and crossed her arms defiantly.

Fred slowed to a walk.

"Fred!" Priscilla shouted.

"How would you like to be hitched up in this weather? He's probably thirsty."

"I don't like viewings and funerals. Everyone is always crying and hugging and looking so awful and sour. I don't have to cry. I hardly knew Ben," Priscilla complained.

Sarah said nothing. She had been unable to share her deepest feelings with Priscilla since she had been burned. Sarah never even mentioned Lee's name to her sister. She was afraid Priscilla would think her too sure of herself.

How could she tell Priscilla about the anticipation of seeing Lee? She couldn't. So she looked straight ahead, stopped at stop signs, turned the buggy, and prodded Fred some more. She wondered what Lee would be doing now—if he'd be there, if he'd see them drive in, and if this unexpected turn of events would prove his undoing.

She did not have long to wait. When they drove up to the house, Lee appeared, dressed in his Sunday clothes—a blue shirt, black vest, and black trousers. He stopped when he caught sight of them. "Want me to take him?" he asked reaching for the bridle.

"You may."

Priscilla smiled widely. Sarah became painfully aware of the discoloration on her right side. The angry, red scars had ruined her creamy complexion and the perfect symmetry of her face.

The realization stung. Priscilla's smile was the most irritating thing she had experienced in a long time.

Sarah didn't look at Lee. She imagined her stubby lashes, the dark scars, the skin taut like red Saran Wrap pulling her cheek and slanting her right eye down on the outside.

She walked away.

Lee spoke to Priscilla, who gazed up at him and then came running after Sarah, gushing on and on about his blue eyes. And what in the world was up with her, she wondered, walking away from him like that.

"Pris, hush. This is a viewing. Or going to be."

Meeting Anna was almost more than Sarah could manage, but she held the short, soft woman in her arms as tears of sympathy coursed down her face.

"I am so sorry, Anna. He was a good man."

"Oh, he was, Sarah. He was."

Stepping back, she swabbed viciously at her swollen eyes, blew her nose, and shook her head from side to side.

"He was never the same, though, after the fire. Remember how he had to take anti-depressants, the Zoloft? It seemed as if my Ben never quite returned. He had his struggles, and I was the only one who really knew."

Suddenly, she grabbed Sarah's hands. "But who am I to stand here and pity myself? You have gone through so much."

"But I am here, disfigured maybe, but grateful."

Sarah stepped back, allowing others to shake Anna's hand and offer condolences as she moved on to talk to Rachel and Anna's sisters. Then she set to work, mowing grass, weeding, working side by side with girls from the church district where Ben's lived. They were not strangers, only acquaintances, but they were all united now because of the death of a young husband and father.

The sun beamed down, its strength like an oppressive hand, large and heavy with the heat. Admitting defeat, Sarah leaned against a tree, lifting her apron to mop her brow. She had regained a lot of her strength, but she still couldn't do everything she had been able to do prior to the fire.

When she became overheated, her scars thumped painfully, and she knew it was time to stop. Lifting a hand to her cheek, she was shocked to feel the heat.

"I probably look like a tomato under the broiler, so hot it's ready to pop," she said ruefully.

There was a deep, masculine chuckle behind her. She recognized Lee's laugh, so she kept her back turned, hoping he'd go away.

She sighed with relief when he did.

The day of Ben's funeral was not quite as humid. The black clothes were much more bearable, and the tall, green corn stalks waved in a perfect summer breeze.

Priscilla did not "have word," meaning she was not invited to attend funeral services, so Sarah rode with her parents, dressed in her lightweight black outfit.

Why was it that sewing a new dress, cape, and apron made her feel so much better about herself? That morning, she had discovered the unscarred side of her face matched the scarred side better now that it was tanned by the summer sun. Her hair was sleek and neat for once, in spite of being thin, and the covering she wore was brand new and very white. For the first time since she had been burned, she felt a real sunbeam of hope.

The large shop was filled to capacity. The mourners endured the heat stoically. Heavy women flapped crocheted handkerchiefs for the slightest whisper of a breeze, while men's faces turned ruddy as the shop's temperatures escalated. The sea of people dressed in black endured together, for Ben.

After the short service, they filed respectfully past the wooden casket. The tradition was expected of them, and they turned their faces for one last look at Ben Zook.

Many spoke of the disfigurement, the likeness not even close to the friendly face they remembered. But they must have done the best they could, considering the circumstances. They just hoped he hadn't had to suffer.

The bull probably caught Ben in the right side, the way every rib had been broken. His chest had caved in, they said. Perhaps the bull crushed his heart instantly, and he felt no pain after the first pounding to the ground.

His face was a mess, though, so they couldn't bear to think too much about Ben's death—alone in the deepening twilight on a midsummer evening, a thunderstorm rumbling in the distance, the fear of the charging bull.

Like a magnetic force, the death of Ben Zook drew the local farmers to face their own livestock and the dangers on their properties. It was not just a seemingly docile bull in the pasture, but also the uncovered squares upstairs on barn floors, broken gates, and loose ladder rungs. Many repairs were completed in the following month, and more than one massive two-thousand-pound Holstein bull was sent to auction.

They all said it was time to sell—the bull was too heavy. However, in the back of their minds, they cringed as they pictured the lowered, wide, hard head of the angry creature, coming at a terrible pace. They envisioned the impact, the crushed bones as poor Ben was ground into the dry earth of his own pasture, and they were relieved to sell.

Halt uns, Himmlisher Vater (Keep us, Heavenly Father). Ben's death just after the Widow Lydia's second fire and the Beiler girl getting so burned—what was God trying to tell them? Everyone had better sit up and take notice. It was the end times, for sure. The fires, the danger still among them—where would it end?

After the service, a giant circle of buggies stood waiting. Numbers had been written in white chalk on the gray canvas of each buggy. Solemnly, the plain wooden casket was loaded into the carriage designed for that purpose, and the driver was seated on a plain wooden chair. Anna and her children rode in the buggy marked with a large number one and followed immediately after the carriage containing Ben's coffin. Lee drove the horse. Relatives of Ben's—his parents, brothers, and sisters followed—then Anna's family and then their uncles, aunts, nieces, and nephews.

Slowly, the first carriage started, followed by the buggy Lee was driving, then numbers two and three. One by one, they fell into an orderly line, wending their way down the drive, turning onto the road as the director from the funeral home signaled for the traffic to stop.

After the buggies had all gone, a flurry of activity resumed as the church members prepared the traditional funeral meal and set up the long tables made with benches.

Sarah did not go to the *begrabnis* (burial). She opted to stay and help, filling the tables with great platters of cold, thinly sliced roast beef, slices of Swiss, Longhorn, Farmers, and Provolone cheese layered beside it.

Bowls were heaped high with mashed potatoes, and silver gravy boats filled to the brim with thick, savory beef gravy.

Pepper slaw, chilled and pungent, applesauce, and dinner rolls completed the meal.

Dessert was cake and fruit. The women of the district each baked a cake and brought jars of canned peaches or pears, applesauce, or whatever they had on hand.

There was plenty of chatter as the members of the church and Amish community worked together. Everything ran smoothly, the way they had been taught. Their parents and their parents before them had done things in the same manner.

There were always the older ones, with bent backs and graying hair turned mostly white, who would have their say.

"We didn't used to have cake."

"Prunes. We always served prunes at a funeral."

"Should still be that way."

"Ah well, changes come. May as well enjoy the cake."

"Sure tastes better than *gvetcha* (prunes)."

Younger women would stop to listen and ask, why prunes? Shoulders were shrugged, eyebrows raised, hands lifted. A mischievous smile played around a stout little grandmother's features, her round shoulders shook.

"Maybe to offset all the cheese?"

Yes, if they took time to *unna such* (search), these traditions had reasons, usually based on common sense. Yes, indeed, prunes were a wise choice, they thought, eyeing the mounds of sliced cheese.

They assigned each person to their tasks. Three couples cooked and mashed potatoes with mounds of butter, gallons of milk, and plenty of salt and cream cheese at their elbows. The men, dressed in traditional Sunday garb with white aprons tied about their waists, straddled benches, kettles of steaming hot potatoes in front of them. Their sturdy arms were put to good use, as the women stood by with the hot milk, salt, and butter.

As the potatoes were beaten to creamy masses by the potato mashers, piles of cabbage were grated across hand held graters. But no one thought of the hard work. The companionship they shared was a labor of love.

Sarah leaned against the cupboard in the basement, her eyes filling with tears as she watched Anna return from the graveyard. Her face showed the strain of the trial laid heavily on her ample shoulders, but she was brave. She was holding up the way Sarah knew she would, her pleasant, can-do attitude serving her well at a time like this.

Sarah caught her breath, watching Lee follow his sister. She groaned within herself, etching his profile in her heart, remorse taking away all ability to breathe, to go on living.

Where had she been? What had possessed her? It was too late now. He really was leaving for Alaska tomorrow. Tomorrow. He had changed his tickets to stay for Ben's funeral, but now he was really leaving.

Lee bent, picked up Anna's youngest, Elmer, and set him on the bench beside him. When Elmer couldn't reach his plate, Lee picked him up and set him on his knee. Immediately, one of the girls that was serving rushed over with a booster seat, and Lee placed Elmer on it carefully. He looked up at Lee, a bright smile spreading across his handsome face.

"*Konn do sitza* (Can sit here)?"

Lee nodded, smiled back.

When the table was full, heads were bowed in silent prayer, and the meal began in earnest. Anna filled her plate well and ate hungrily. Sarah filled their coffee cups, consumed with longing to touch Lee's shoulder for just one second, his nearness sending her into despair.

Numbly, she served, washed dishes, and served another table, feeling as if she had one more day to live. It was a hard sentence, flung rudely in her face.

Her future stretched before her, a hot, gritty, wind-blown desert devoid of joy or purpose. Her spirits plummeted down and down, until she knew if she kept this up, there would, indeed, be consequences. Depression would rear its ugly head, crippling her life.

Gepp dich oof (Give yourself up). Mam always said those words, regardless of the dilemma. They were her mantra, a cloak she wore like a royal garment, enabling her to face life unafraid.

Sarah knew she must do this, deep down, in her spirit. But oh, why was it so hard?

Because it's my own fault. Now I'm all messed up, my face hideous. Who will ever look at me or want me for his wife?

You're beautiful, Lee had said. That was before he knew Matthew had been to visit her.

She went upstairs, suddenly filled with purpose. She'd stay.

Grabbing the hamper in the bathroom, she lugged it to the laundry room and began to sort clothes. She closed the drain on the wringer washer and turned on the hot water, then hurried upstairs for Lee's hamper.

She had never been in his room.

The afternoon sun shone through the sparkling windows. A warm breeze toyed with the beige linen panel curtains at each window.

His bed was high and wide, made up neatly with a brown plaid quilt and extra pillows. She touched it with her fingertips. On his dresser, there was an expensive-looking world globe, a chest, and some carved shore birds.

She reached out a hand to straighten the red placemat beneath the small, wooden chest, irritated when a square, white paper fell to the floor.

Bending, she swooped it up, the glossy feel of it a realization. A photograph.

She had to hurry. She had the hot water running in the wringer washer. A gaggle of noisy girls was coming up the stairs, brooms and dust mops thumping. Quickly she flipped it over. She gasped. A younger version of herself smiled up from the glossy photograph, her skin tanned, her hair disheveled, as usual.

When she heard the girls coming down the hall, she slammed the photo beneath the mat, turned, and grabbed the hamper as the girls reached the doorway. Just in time she turned to face them guilelessly. She smiled and said quietly, "I'm washing."

"Good!"

"Good for you."

"This must be Lee's room."

Giggling, they all voted to clean it. Sarah gritted her

teeth and lunged towards the stairs heading for the laundry room at breakneck speed.

Well, the despair would have to go. She'd stay until the last chore was completed. If God gave her one last chance before tomorrow, she'd take it. If not, she'd go home, prepare for a new school term, and settle in for the wait.

Gepp dich oof. Alright, Mam. I will.

Opening the lever on the air hose, she was rewarded with the loud er-er-er-er of the air motor turning beneath the machine, swirling the water as the agitator swished steadily back and forth.

On the shelf, instead of Mam's Tide with bleach, there was an odd-looking white Melaleuca box. So, Anna was one of those women who stuck like a determined leech to her choice of off-the-wall products like Amway or Shaklee or the new eCosway. Everyone who was someone had to be introduced to the cheaper and apparently far superior products, which, in Mam's opinion, left the men's socks gray, but she told only Sarah.

Mam would listen with great interest and pour over the literature. Then she would smile, give back the catalogue, and never order a thing. Absolutely nothing could beat her Tide.

Well, there was always the possibility of trying to beat Mam, Sarah thought. She carefully measured white soap powder into a rather small plastic cup and dumped it into the steaming water, followed by a load of white tablecloths.

"Sarah."

Turning, her face flushed from the heat of the swirling water, she looked up into Lee's blue eyes.

"Oh. Oh. you sc...surprised me."

Flustered, she reached for the corner of her apron to

dry her hands.

"Do you need the diesel started?"

Sarah checked the pressure gauge on the air line.

"Eighty pounds. Yes, you'd better."

She met his gaze. The blue eyes were pools of kindness that washed over her, erasing every thought of despair or remorse. She did not want to look away, but the intensity in his eyes was almost more than she could manage without flinging herself into his arms and begging him to stay, to reconsider.

She must have been leaning toward him, when Marlin came into the laundry room. Sarah was embarrassed to find she had to grasp the edge of the washer to catch her balance. She got her hand wet and had to dry it all over again.

Lee left, and Marlin got a pair of boots from the closet.

She'd stay. She didn't care if the whole place was put back in order, every piece of laundry hung on the line, the driveway raked, the cows milked. She'd stay.

She had one day. One evening.

Humming under her breath now, she counted her options, bolstered by the photograph, and…. She smiled. She'd call it "the look."

How was it possible? Perhaps he was just happy to find her doing laundry, sparing his grieving sister the mundane chore.

Going to the mirror above the small sink where Ben had always washed his hands, she turned her face slightly to the left and tentatively ran the tips of her fingers across her neck and cheeks. The red Saran Wrap had definitely turned to pink. A bit better.

Turning, she began to feed the sweet-smelling table-cloths through the wringer. She watched as they sank into the rinse tubs and settled in the blue water containing the odd-smelling Melaleuca fabric softener.

She added a load of towels to the washer and put the tablecloths from the rinse water through the wringer. Then she took the laundry basket through the door to the back porch to hang them on the wheel line.

The afternoon sun was headed towards the western horizon, the heat shimmering from the macadam drive and the tops of the gray and black buggies. Men stood in huddles, their identical black felt hats reflecting a sameness that spoke of contentment, of unison and brotherly love.

Women clad in black, their white coverings bobbing, moved across the lawn. They bundled boxes of leftover meat and cheese, pepper slaw, and plastic containers of gravy into the buggies of the Zooks' relatives, gifts to take along home.

They would be told that they could "make use of it" and given a kind pat of sympathy on shoulders drooping with grief.

Sarah hung the last white tablecloth on the line, secured it with wooden pins, and pushed on the bottom cable, sending the tablecloths flapping high across the lawn. A pulley wheel attached to a steel post at the other end served to pull out the loaded lower line and return the empty upper clothesline. The wheel line was really an ingenious device, allowing busy mothers to stay on a protected porch and send laundry high across the lawn, without lugging heavy baskets of wet clothing into the blazing sun or through a foot of snow.

Sarah watched Lee emerge from the door of the diesel shed and experienced a strange thrill, an intuition, or was it only her imagination? Would he feel it, seeing her there by the wheel line, hanging out his laundry?

As if he read her thoughts, he looked her way. He lifted a hand and gave a thumbs up to signal he had started the diesel.

She lifted her own thumb for only a second, then turned away. She picked up the basket, overcome by shyness, feeling the blush spread across her face. She hoped no one had seen them.

Then, a wild thought. What did it matter? Who would care? They were two mature adults, no longer silly teenagers shamelessly flirting.

She had only tonight.

CHAPTER 12

THE DIRTY WATER SWIRLED DOWN THE DRAIN AND gurgled in the pipes of the sink as the last pair of denim work trousers squeezed out from between the rollers of the wringer. Reaching across the washer, Sarah turned the lever, shutting off the air valve. Silence reigned as she lifted the heavy basket holding the last load.

She tried to imagine how Anna would feel later today as the sun slid its way toward darkness. Night would arrive, and with it, the necessary act of going to bed. Now, Anna would sleep so completely alone. Tears stung in Sarah's eyes as she imagined Anna's mourning. Surely a mother or a sister, perhaps both, would stay.

On her hands and knees, she wiped the laundry room floor clean, hung up the rag, and went in search of her friend Anna. She found her sitting on the living room sofa, her head on her mother's shoulder, crying quietly, a group of sisters and sisters-in-law crying with her.

When she saw Sarah, she sat up, dabbed her eyes, and honked furiously into a sodden Kleenex.

"*Komm*, Sarah."

"Is there anything you need done yet?"

Was it only her imagination or were there a few knowing looks being exchanged, a thread of cunning glances she thought she was seeing?

"They're going to be starting supper and the milking soon. I was wondering if you'd like to take leftovers to Old Mommy King. Maybe Lee could take you. I asked Benuel *sei* Rachel to take them along, but they already left. It's about six or seven miles. Do you mind?"

Warily, Sarah was slow to answer.

"Could he do it on his own?"

"No. He....Well, no."

Their faces were poker straight, their noses red from weeping, their eyes blue and guileless, devoid of strategy.

"Where do I find him?"

"In the basement."

Anna immediately turned and began to show her mother the angry red rash on the back of Marianne's knees, thereby abruptly excusing Sarah. There was nothing to do now, except head for the bathroom with its mirror and all the demons of insecurity and fear that lurked within its frame.

A cool washcloth. Some soap. With shaking hands, she washed her face gently, swabbing it clean. Then she opened the vanity drawer to search for a bit of face cream.

She unpinned her covering, took her hair down. There was only a bit of it to make up the tiny bob on the back of her head. She found Anna's hair gel, her hairspray, and thanked God for allowing these wonderful supplies. It was necessary that her hair looked okay.

She smiled to herself, her eyes bright with wondering, longing, and something else.

There. That would have to do.

Her knees threatened to buckle as she ran down the

basement stairs, almost bumping into Lee as he carried a box away from a plastic folding table.

"Oh, there you are."

"You going?"

"I guess. Anna says I should."

"Yeah. Mommy King will be more at ease with you."

He smiled, and his smile stayed for a long time, which was a good sign that he was actually pleased that she had agreed to accompany him.

The buggy was clean, the horse spirited. Sitting beside him, the late afternoon sun's rays had no mercy through the opened window. Sarah withdrew into the corner, attempting to wrap a protective shell around the right side of her face. All the words she had wanted to say slipped out of her mind and disappeared, leaving her mouth dry, her tongue thick with anxiety. Now she wished she had not come.

When Lee guided the horse out on the main road, he asked if she wanted to go the long way around, since it was such a gorgeous evening. They could stop at the park on Buena Vista Road and feed the ducks.

"I will if the sun isn't too bright."

She had nothing to lose, so she figured she may as well tell him exactly what she felt.

Astonished, Lee looked at her.

"Whatever is that supposed to mean?"

She did not meet his eyes.

"My face."

"Your face. What about your face?"

"It's—you know, Lee. Don't make this hard for me."

When there was no reply, she stared miserably out the window, to the left, away from him. When the silence continued and stretched out before her with painful intensity, she caught her breath when he suddenly picked up her right hand and held it very lightly in his own. Still he did not speak.

Barely daring to breathe, Sarah turned her head slightly to the right and was shocked to see a wet trickle of tears washing over Lee's tanned, chiseled cheek.

Well, yes, of course. It had been a tough day. He had buried Ben, his beloved brother-in-law, and soon he would be leaving his dear sister Anna. He needed a hand to hold. The human touch has great power, she had read. Her hand was just that, a comfort on this troubling day of mourning and anticipated farewells.

He pulled his hand away then, and Sarah left hers in her lap. It lay there, feeling obsolete, helpless, cast away.

Lee had to use both hands to guide the horse down a gravel road. A pond stretched before them, with geese and ducks of different colors swimming and milling about on the freshly mowed grass.

There were trees and rustic pavilions with weathered picnic tables. Several cars were parked in a designated area, and children played on the swings as mothers watched from their perches on lawn chairs.

To Sarah's surprise, Lee drove to the far end of the park before he stopped the buggy. The horse immediately stretched out his nose, raising, then lowering his head, attempting to relieve himself of the neck rein that kept him from stretching his neck comfortably.

Lee climbed out of the buggy and loosened the rein. Then he stood facing her, a hand draped across the shaft.

Hesitant, Sarah was unsure what he wanted to do, so she remained seated.

"Would you like to walk for awhile? We'll stay out of the sun."

He smiled. Sarah would not look at his eyes.

When she alighted from the buggy in her black funeral garb, Sarah moved in one swift, graceful movement. She was unaware of her elegance, the ease of her movement. Lee imagined many girls had to train themselves to move like that.

He stood very still, and Sarah hesitated, wondering at his stillness. Throwing the reins across the horse's back, he led him to a tree, then got the neck rope from beneath the seat, tied him securely, and turned to look at Sarah.

"Ready?"

She nodded.

The park was a lovely place, but the small adjoining woods was far more restful for her, the leafy, green shadows giving her more confidence.

Crickets and cicadas were noisily lending their voices to herald their walk, creating an uninvited, deafening harmony of clamorous sound. Sarah remembered the woodland insects from her childhood, when she and her siblings had played on the wooded hillside at her grandparents' home.

Sarah wanted to tell Lee about these sounds from her memories, but he seemed so aloof and remained so stone silent that the words would not come.

They walked toward a small, decorative bench made of cement. The seat was wide, comfortable, inviting. He stopped, looked down at her.

"Do you want to sit for a while, to talk?"

"Yes."

Sitting side by side with her shoulder touching his, but barely, she was completely aware of him, and her speech left her again.

She knew then, that she could not do it. She should have gone home the minute everyone was fed. Instead she had come up with all these grandiose presumptions about the possibility of Lee staying here instead of going to Alaska, when in reality that was a dream swiftly coming true for him.

Overhead, the leaves fluttered and rustled, the sound accented by the chirping birds, heralding the evening as they called their offspring to bed, or at least for an evening snack.

A goose honked on the pond, and another answered. A child's high squeal came from the swings.

It all seemed unreal. Here she was with Lee, on his last night, and the longer she remained seated beside him, the less she could think how to go about asking him to stay.

Lee cleared his throat and turned to look at her.

"Sarah."

The word was woven through with so much kindness, her throat tightened.

"Look at me."

The courage to do his bidding came slowly, but finally she turned her head and lifted her eyes to his. Always, the color of them amazed her. There was sheer pleasure in the blue depths, but now, in the shadowy green of the trees, they were electric with emotion.

"Sarah, you know my tickets are bought, plans made. You know—Alaska, new life, here I come."

He laughed derisively.

"Can you figure out my life for me?"

Sarah's hands were in her lap, the fingers twisting, turning. She clenched them together to still them, straightened her shoulders, drew a deep breath, and opened her mouth, but her courage fled.

She closed her mouth again, bent her head, and said nothing.

Lee waited. He thought he heard something, but he

wasn't sure. He turned again to look at Sarah.

"Don't go," she whispered again.

He heard.

"Did you say what I thought you said?"

Sarah nodded.

"You don't want me to go?"

She shook her head.

Then he did something she would never forget. He reached across her lap, picked up the scarred hand, and pushed back the sleeve. He let his fingertips trace the scars and the ridges where the sutures had been. Softly, he stroked her arm, then stopped and looked at her, tenderly.

"I can't go. Every bit of my conscience, every pore of my body knows I have to stay here on Ben's farm. It's a moral obligation, the only right thing to do. Ben was in debt, of course, as every young farmer is, and now that Anna is alone, the place will have to be sold. It's a shame. I am attached to the place."

Lee paused but kept Sarah's hand in his. Then he continued, "I could sell my roofing and siding business—I think I could swing it—to buy the farm. Anna could stay. We could add an addition for her living quarters maybe. Or else we could just live together. She's so easy to get along with."

Lee was talking quickly now, the words tumbling over each other.

"I think I could be happy as a farmer, but I'm not too sure about being a bachelor. Anna's a wonderful cook, but there are things in life I need other than just food. You know, Sarah, I get the feeling that you and I are two people with the same mind set. We want what we want, and nothing is going to change our minds."

Sarah listened to the beauty of his voice, his words,

and tried to grasp the true meaning.

"Then God comes into our lives and says, look here, it's time you sit up and take notice."

Sarah nodded.

"After I was burned, I knew what Matthew had become."

"You mean, what he always was. You just looked at him through rose-colored glasses before."

"Yes. I was kind of stuck in tunnel vision."

Lee laughed.

"But Sarah, are you sure this time? Are you certain no love stays in your heart for Matthew?"

Sarah shook her head.

"No, Lee. My eyes were opened, after I went through all the pain of my burns. There was nothing I needed, as far as Matthew was concerned."

"I couldn't stand it, Sarah. I couldn't bear to think of you suffering. I'd end up pacing my room in the middle of the night. No human being should have to endure what you did. I'll never know how you came through it."

Sarah shrugged her shoulders.

"You do what you have to do."

"And now, Ben is gone. And it torments me. Did he have to die so my pride could be extinguished? I was going to Alaska because of you. Your sad eyes, your scars. And then Matthew living down the road, asking you to leave your family. I could not take one more week, one more day of it."

"Lee, don't blame yourself for Ben's death. You know the Lord truly does end our lives according to His will. When our time on earth is finished, we're done."

Lee groaned.

"Oh, Sarah. You will never know what I've gone

through. I tried to give myself entirely to God's will, but I could not bear to think of the possibility of you drawing your last breath, never to have you as my own."

Sarah couldn't move. Was she hearing Lee correctly? Was he speaking from the heart?

"But I'm burned, scarred," she whispered.

In answer, he stood, reached for her hands, and pulled her to her feet. Slowly he let go of her right hand. His fingertips explored every fissure, every riddle of her scars, along her cheek, her ear, the side of her neck. He stepped back to smile at her. He looked deeply into her eyes that changed color with the rustling of the leaves overhead, stormy with her own discovery of this new and certain love.

He bent his head, his cheek brushing hers, as he placed his lips delicately on the side of her jawline where the scarring was worst.

"I love you with all my heart. I have always loved you, this way and before. I love you, Sarah, your scars, your burns, everything. These scars are a testimony of God's will for our lives. I believe in my soul we are meant to be together, here on earth and in eternity."

When Sarah's tears overflowed, he kissed them away. Then he pulled her into his arms and crushed her painfully against himself, shocked when she let out a soft cry.

"I'm sorry, Sarah. I didn't mean to hurt you. Can you forgive me?"

Sarah laughed.

"No, no, it's okay. It's just my shoulder. It's the worst. I'm.... Well, Lee, are you sure you want me? I'm probably scarred worse than you know."

Lee searched her eyes. He saw the anxiety, the genuine doubt, and he wrapped his arms around her gently this time. He lowered his face, inches from hers, and whispered again, "I love you."

From the depths of her heart, Sarah replied, "Lee, I love you more."

He kissed her then, softly. It was a pact, an agreement of a budding consent, cementing a love between two people that would stand the test of time. The years would bring changes, more trials, days of happiness, sorrow, and shared concern, but their love would see them through.

This knowledge flowed between the sweetness of their lips, the wondrous sense of having found the good and perfect will for their lives.

Lee sighed, trembling, his hands on her shoulders.

"Do you think you can stand to be a farmer's wife?"

She gasped.

"What?"

"I'm asking you to be my wife."

"But we never dated!"

"I dated you a lot—in my head."

Sarah's laugh rang out, and she reached for him, put her arms around him, and said, "This year?"

"Sarah, oh yes. This fall. I will have a whole herd of cows and the harvest, and, well, everything."

"You won't have time to get married."

"I'll make time."

Smiling up at him, Sarah breathed, "Yes, Lee, I will be your wife."

His lips sought and found hers, and they became part of the wonder of the nature around them, created by God, designed so that man should not live his life alone.

Darkness was falling as they walked out to the pond. The mowed grass, the pavilions—everything took on a new appearance as the grayness descended.

They found the horse, patiently snoozing by the tree

where he was tied. He lifted his head when he heard their approach, ready to go home to his stall and box of feed.

"Oh, Lee, what about Mommy King's leftovers?"

Lee stopped short.

"We forgot."

"She'll be in bed."

"What should we do?"

"Have a picnic?"

The horse had to wait another half hour, and Mommy King told Anna's mother, Rachel, that it was a shame the way these old practices were becoming lost. Since she had been unable to attend Ben's funeral, she should absolutely have gotten some cheese and sliced roast beef. The older generation did not get the respect they deserved.

Rachel bought a nice pound of meat and cheese and told her they had saved it for her, which repaired the rift quite nicely. Especially since Rachel sent along some cupcakes as well.

They would wait to tell their parents, but only for a few short weeks. They had to think of Sarah's mother, the one who would be organizing the wedding.

Lee told Anna that very night, after he took Sarah home. His sister hadn't been able to sleep. She was lying on the recliner, weeping, her poor face blotched with the depth of her grief.

"Anna, is it a help to you to know that I asked Sarah tonight?"

"You're not going?"

"To Alaska? Oh no. I can't, Anna. Not with Ben gone. I'll buy the farm. We'll build an addition. Don't worry, Anna. I'll *sark* (care) for you."

A storm of weeping ensued, but it was a relaxed, gentle crying. Over and over, she thanked her brother, told him it was a dream.

How she had dreaded having to leave the farm, and now she wouldn't need to. She wished she could tell Ben.

"When is your first date?"

"No, not dating. I asked her to marry me."

"But what about joining the church? Lee, you can't get married this year. What are you thinking?"

Far into the night they talked, planned, and remembered Ben. Lee got up to do the milking and felt as if he hadn't slept at all, which didn't make much difference. He could live on fresh air and the thought of being Sarah's husband.

When Sarah did tell her parents, they were shocked, then ecstatic, unable to hide their wide grins of approval. The anticipation made their faces young, the surprise proving a veritable fountain of youth.

It had been a long time since Anna Mae was married, almost five years. Having a wedding would be something to look forward to.

Over at Elam's, the news was received with far less enthusiasm. Hannah stated the news, said she was supposed to keep it a secret, and they better not say anything.

Elam grunted behind his paper and said he'd not tell. He was one hundred percent trustworthy, as everyone knew the length of time that elapsed between him ever opening his mouth about anything. A cow could be dead for a week before he'd bother telling his wife. The time the milk tested for high bacteria, he silently and sourly let it run down the drain and never said a word.

Hannah fussed for weeks about the pathetic milk check, but he told her the hot weather was hard on milk production. She clamped her mouth into a solid line and didn't believe him.

Matthew, however, lay in his bed, full of frustration. He could guarantee Sarah didn't love that Lee. He knew she had always loved him. She still did.

Suddenly, he knew without a doubt that he wanted Sarah for his wife. Who else would he marry? Her scars would improve.

Knowing she was betrothed to another man made her twice as desirable. He lay on his back, his hands clasped behind his head, and schemed, his heavy black brows drawn down, his mouth curved in the same direction.

He'd go Amish again, if that's what it would take. He'd tell her that for now, and perhaps after they were married, she'd again agree to leave.

The thing was, he didn't think Rose would take him. She was starting to act the way she always did—grouchy, bored. Yes, Sarah would be just right for him.

Thinking of the challenge, he smiled. All it would take was to announce his desire to be Amish again. He'd do it.

Down in the kitchen, Hannah berated her husband for just sitting behind his paper. She thought he should be admonishing Matthew, the way other fathers did. It was no wonder he wasn't Amish, and now it was hard to tell who he would marry.

Elam harrumphed behind his paper and rustled the pages. He crossed one stockinged foot over the other, snagged the hole in the sock with his big toenail, and resigned himself to the fact that his toenails need clipping.

Getting up, he headed for the desk drawer and began his task as Hannah stood over him and finished her tirade. She went to bed without him, so upset about Lee and Sarah.

Elam finished his toenails, shook his head, and was glad for Sarah.

He'd hate to be married to Matthew.

CHAPTER 13

MICHAEL LANVIN WAS RELEASED ON BAIL, HIS court appearance not yet announced. He maintained his innocence, and since there was no proof and no one willing to testify, the case was left undecided, likely to be placed on the back burner. For one thing, Michael had no money. He was assigned a public defender, rendered helpless for lack of prosecution.

David Beiler, one in a group of ministers, stayed true to his convictions, despite the visitors who entered the house on many week nights, quietly assuming Levi and the girls would be in bed or at least out of ear shot. One late-night group of visitors accused Davey of being hard-hearted, unfeeling. How could he stand to see his daughter injured so badly? If he'd use some common sense, they'd be glad to testify and get these fires stopped. Levi had all the information they needed.

Davey argued quietly, sensibly.

This situation could be resolved with forgiveness, he felt—so strongly, in fact, that he quoted Scripture to justify his actions. And that was something he did not condone, depending on the circumstances.

Davey's eyes became weary, underlined by dark circles, as he lay sleepless night after night, endlessly pondering the viewpoints of his distraught laymen.

Sarah moved through the remainder of the summer on wings, her feet skimming the ground as she ran to the barn, skipped across the yard, or swung on the tire swing attached to a limb of the maple tree. She was full of life, nearly fully recovered despite her lasting scars.

Matthew began to show up at the most inopportune times, cheekily rapping on the screen door and asking for Sarah. Sometimes, he simply spent time with Levi, who promptly produced a checker board, proud that his English friend Matthew wanted to stay.

One evening, the leaves on the maple tree stirred restlessly as an east wind bore smells of an oncoming rain. Dat asked if all the girls could help unload the remaining bales of hay stacked on the wagons by the barn.

Mam said she'd clear the table and do the dishes, so the girls went out to the barn and watched as Dat started the engine on the elevator. It would carry the bales to the bay already stacked high with hay for the horses and cows.

When it popped to life, the belt on the long elevator began to move. Sarah hopped up, grabbed a heavy bale, and heaved it onto the moving belt. She watched as it righted itself and began its slow ascent to the top, where Suzie and Priscilla helped Dat stack the bales tightly, making a good solid pile.

Steadily throwing the bales, she stopped to scratch her shoulder, the healing places itchy so much of the time. Shrugging her shoulder, she shifted her apron strap into place, bent to lift another bale, and looked up to find Matthew staring at her, his face uplifted, a half smile playing around his mouth.

Sarah could feel the heat rise in her face, but she kept working. The noise of the rattling engine drowned out the possibility of any conversation, though she was aware of his eyes steadily watching her.

When the wagon was empty, Dat came down to turn off the engine. His face was red, perspiration dripped off his chin, and his shirt clung to his back. It was a warm evening. Up under the metal roof with no ventilation, it was probably well over a hundred degrees.

Matthew shook his head.

"You're never going to change, Davey. Still doing everything the hard way, aren't you?"

Sarah drew a forearm across her face, her eyes burning with perspiration. She could tell by Dat's unhurried answer that he needed time to compose himself. Hot, itchy, uncomfortable, he would have to measure his words.

"Probably," he said finally.

Matthew laughed, a short superior snort.

"I figured you'd say that."

Dat nodded.

"Need any help?"

"Well, we have one more wagon load. If you want exercise, help yourself."

"If Sarah will let me."

Sarah jumped down from the wagon in one swift movement, pushed back her hair, and smiled at him.

"Feel free."

"Aren't you going to help?"

"I'll help Dat in the haymow to give Suzie a break."

Before he could protest, she scrambled up—up to the top and into the stifling heat under the metal roof, away from the sun and Matthew. She knew it was infinitely better there despite the temperature.

There was no avoiding him that evening, however. Matthew was determined to have her alone, so she stayed by the wagon in the fading evening light. She was itching all over from the hay, her legs a maze of scratches, her hair a mess, her face red and dusty and scarred.

Matthew gazed off across the cornfields, the tall stalks rising high above the fertile soil, the yellow ears already formed with the kernels filling out from the heat of the midday sun. He shook his head, solemnly eyeing her with a sad gaze.

"You know Sarah, it's times like this that I want to be about 14 again. We were so young, so innocent, so untouched by the world."

She pushed her bare foot beneath a small pile of loose hay. She picked it up with her toes and let it drop, but no response came to her mind, so she chose to stay quiet.

"You're going to marry Lee, then?"

Sarah nodded.

"Why?"

Why, indeed. Good question, Matthew. Thoughts filled her head, dissolved, reappeared. Some she understood and let go. Others she examined again in a constant shifting of ever-changing emotions and memories. Why do people marry the ones they do?

All she did was shrug her shoulders.

They stood beside each other, leaning against the now empty wagon, neither one daring a glance at the other.

The scene before them had remained greatly unchanged from the time they were teenagers. Seasons had come and gone. Corn and alfalfa and soybeans were rotated. The earth was replenished with manure and lime and fertilizers, and crops planted. Rains came, and the sun coaxed the seeds into high-yielding crops.

What was the final deciding factor in her choosing Lee over Matthew? Did God reach down from heaven with His great, unseen hand and set Matthew in Haiti with Sarah away from him, now with Lee?

Matthew cleared his throat, becoming uncomfortable in the quiet that surrounded his question. Taking a deep breath, Sarah lifted her head. She looked out across the cornfields and the trees along the fence rising above the moving sea of green and began to speak.

"All my life, Matthew, I loved you—a devoted sort of worship, a feeling stronger than any love I have ever experienced. I never doubted we would marry, spend all our days together, always. Then, there was Rose. You chose her. Still I clung to the high ideal of you. You left the Amish—you left us, our way of life. I would have been excommunicated for you. I would have left everything I believe is right, for you. But you didn't want me."

Matthew's sharp intake of breath stopped her.

"I did. I was afraid you wouldn't leave your parents."

"I question that, Matthew. You married Hephzibah."

"I wanted you first."

"If you did, you would have waited, obviously. Still, I loved you. I felt God had taken Hephzibah because of our love, our destiny to be together. I clung to my desire for you, desperately willing us to be together, just the way I had always imagined. Then..."

Sarah spread her hands, palms up.

"There was the fire. I was burned. I endured pain that I didn't know a human being could take and live through. I feel now that I literally went through the fire spiritually, as well. My eyes were opened to God's will. You were my will, my way. You were a magnet that drew me irresistibly."

Matthew stood straight, took a few steps, gripped her shoulders, his eyes dark with rekindled passion. Without a word, he drew her roughly toward himself, his face lowered, and placed his lips roughly on hers. There was no gentleness.

His fingers dug into her shoulders. She threw herself back, away from him. His touch was offensive to her, repugnant in its power, like a charred beam, dead and black, soaked from the fireman's hose.

The action left him standing awkwardly, his hands slowly going to his sides.

"Sarah."

"Matthew, you have no right. You never let me finish. I think when a love of such magnitude dies, it is completely dead. Ashes, cold, lifeless. I'm sorry. I really am, but I wish you the best."

"Shut up!"

Sarah gasped as his words rang out, feeling as if he had slapped her. She was caught completely off guard.

Trembling, his breath coming in spurts, he spat out, "If you were any sort of Christian, you would see I am the one you want. But since you're not born again, all spirituality makes no sense to you. You're as blind as you always were."

When Sarah faced him, her green eyes were tempestuous, churning with feeling. The dark colors surfaced, then receded, leaving a yellowish light, a gladness.

"Yes, Matthew, oh yes! I was blind. That's one thing we agree on."

He began to cry, his face crumpling, his features twisting, as he begged her forgiveness. He hadn't meant to lose his temper.

"Just go. Goodbye, Matthew."

Quietly, her words sank in, and with wide-eyed disbelief, he backed away.

"You really mean it, don't you?"

Sarah nodded, her eyes on his, and he could not bear to look at the victory in hers.

He lowered his head.

"Sarah, I'll come back. I'll be Amish for you. I love you. I always have, just like you have loved me. We are meant to be together. You knew that. You still know it."

In response, she turned and walked slowly down the slope, away from the empty hay wagon, away from the power she felt and knew she must resist.

He may do that—return for her sake—but that was pathetic. What a pitiful attempt at redeeming the years of treating her as second best, which is what she would always be in his eyes.

Suddenly, she could see the future with Matthew. She would have to take the blame for everything that went wrong, accept the responsibility as fact. She envisioned a houseful of babies, little children, and her attempting the impossible, trying to keep him happy, be perfect, be what he wanted her to be. He would always expect absolute devotion and perfection, without taking any responsibility of his own.

She slammed the *kesslehaus* door, causing a few clay flowerpots to rattle on the shelf above the sink. She washed her hands and lowered her head to wipe her mouth, erasing any trace of Matthew's presumptuous moves.

Mam was in the kitchen as usual, looking hot, tired, and short-tempered. Her face was a brilliant shade of pink, her nostrils distended, her mouth a straight, thin line.

"Where were you?" she burst out.

"Unloading hay."

"No. No, you weren't. I watched Matthew walk right past this kitchen window on his way to see you, and here you're getting married, and that man is going to mislead you."

"We talked, Mam. He wants to come back to the Amish now. He says he wants me."

Mam's eyes were fiery with disdain.

"He won't."

"Mam, please don't get upset. I am marrying Lee. I love him with all my heart, truly, with the real love that God gives. I'm going to be a farmer's wife, Mam, just like you. And I was never happier, never more sure of anything in my life. Lee is a special and absolutely amazing person."

Mam was not an emotional person. Her feelings were always well contained, her demeanor stoic, as reserved as anyone Sarah had ever encountered. Now, she threw her apron over her head and burst into tears. She let out little girl sobs of fear and worry, catching Sarah completely off guard.

"Mam!"

Sarah was incredulous.

From behind the apron came a muffled wail, as the rounded shoulders shook. A hysterical laugh emerged, and the apron was lowered, producing a red, sheepish face changed by the force of her feelings.

"Sarah, I'm only a human being, and a silly mother, at that. But I think if you would run off with that spoiled..."

She clapped a hand over her mouth, her eyes round with shock.

"I almost said brat."

Sarah threw back her head and laughed uproariously.

It was an unladylike, belly laugh that was so infectious, it caught Mam and tugged her along. Mam lamented her total lack of restraint but finally conceded to it, sitting down and laughing till she had to remove her glasses, wipe her eyes, and take a deep breath.

"*Ach* Sarah, *ach my.* We mothers are a pitiful lot. We only want what is best for our children, and so often we see it long before they do."

Darkness was falling rapidly, but Mam said it was too hot to light the gas lamp, so they'd sit on the porch. Dat would be in, and he'd want his mint tea and pretzel.

Sarah hadn't seen Levi in the house, so she asked Mam about him. Mam shook her head, saying the warm temperatures were hard for Levi. He had gone to bed.

Relaxing on the wooden porch rockers in the still evening air, a companionable silence settled between them. They watched the bats emerge from under the eaves of the old shed by the corncrib. They wheeled and darted on their wide wings, snatching up the night's winged delicacies.

Finally Mam asked, "Have you decided on the color of your wedding dress?"

"I'd love to wear a rich green—a sage color, because of my eyes. Or maybe brown."

"You know that isn't traditional."

"I know."

"I suppose some girls would wear it."

"Yes."

"But I would like for you to remain traditional. Blue or purple."

"Do you think a dark gray, a charcoal, would be alright?"

"I wouldn't know why not."

"Too dull?"

"I think very neat and very in the *ordnung* (rules)."

"Oh, good. Is it too fancy to have the little girls wear a light shade of teal? Sort of aqua?"

"Plain fabric, no. That would be alright."

Dat came up to the porch, lowered himself on the porch swing, and sighed contentedly. When the silence continued, he spoke softly.

"You didn't have to stop talking because of me."

"Oh, we didn't. Just making sewing plans."

"Sewing? That's right, Sarah. You're getting married! We'll be making a wedding. Is that what Matthew wanted this evening?"

Shamefaced, Sarah nodded.

"I saw everything," her father stated calmly.

Horrified, Sarah glanced at him.

"You didn't!"

"Not everything, but enough."

Sarah was so ashamed. She stared at the floor of the porch, noticed the way the evening shadows painted the floorboards black.

"I'm sorry."

"You have nothing to be sorry about. He owes you an apology."

"Dat, it's okay. I can live the rest of my life without his apology, or anything at all from him, for that matter."

"Good girl, Sarah. I'm proud of you."

Then he asked, "How is Anna holding up? We should visit her again."

"She has her times. She had a close relationship with Ben and can hardly bear the *zeit-lang* (missing him)."

"And the children?"

"They miss him, of course, but children are so resilient.

They accept things, without question, much easier than we do. Anna is an outstanding mother, providing so much for them. It's hard, but she's doing her best."

Dat nodded.

Priscilla and Suzie joined them, freshly showered and in their pajamas, chattering happily about mundane, teenage affairs. They plopped down on the porch steps, comfortable being with their parents on the farm on a warm late summer's evening.

"Is Levi in bed?" Dat asked

Mam nodded.

"He's just not himself. I can't put my finger on it. He hardly says a word, walks around muttering to himself. I think he suffers because of the heat."

"Could be."

From the opened window, Levi's voice bellowed out from the confines of his bed, "You're discussing me. Don't you know we're not supposed to talk about other people?"

"*Ach* Levi, we were just worried about you."

"Well, I'm coming out there. I have my pajamas on. Did you make something to eat?"

"Just pretzels."

Levi shuffled out on the porch, his flat, white feet glowing in the semidarkness, his blue cotton pajamas hanging loosely on his great body.

His hair was still damp, and he smelled of medicated body powder. He loved it, saying it made his skin feel cool and slippy when it was warm. He settled himself on the porch swing beside Dat, his hulking figure dwarfing Dat's thin frame.

Reaching over, Dat slapped Levi's wide knee.

"How's it going, Buddy?"

"Not so good."

"Why?"

"Well, how do you expect me to get a good night's sleep if I have to have *kalte sup* (cold soup) for supper?"

"*Ach* Levi. We go through this every summer. We also had fried chicken. Did you forget?"

"But nothing for dessert."

Mam patiently explained how it was better to abstain from overeating when it was so hot, saying he would stay more comfortable when he ate less.

"We need air conditioning."

Dat's frame shook silently, as he tried to hide his laughter from Levi.

"Now, Levi, if we had air conditioning, you might not hear things—like strange cars coming in the driveway at night. It was a brave thing you did, watching, remembering. And now, you helped catch Michael Lanvin. That was also a courageous thing to do."

Levi shot his father a contemptuous glance.

"That didn't make a difference. I heard Melvin talking to Ez Beiler on Sunday. He said if no one charges Michael, he'll go free. So there are going to be more fires. And don't blame me, Davey Beiler. I did all I'm going to do."

"You did a lot. That was the beginning of the end, mark my words."

"*Vee maynshnt* (What do you mean), Davey?"

"To me, it seems insignificant whether or not Michael is jailed. If he did start the fires and he's living in anger, he'll try it again. Eventually, he'll be caught. They always are. But we really don't have enough evidence now."

"I caught him, though."

"Oh yes, Levi. You did."

Satisfied, Levi squared his shoulders, leaned back. The

chain on the porch swing creaked as he pushed one foot against the porch floor to set it in motion.

Priscilla smacked Suzie's shoulder playfully, and Suzie leaped off the porch steps. Priscilla chased her across the dark lawn, caught the tail of her pajama top, and yanked. They fell in a helpless heap of girlish laughter by the petunia bed.

Sarah smiled, remembering to cherish this last summer at home as one of Davey Beiler's girls. Soon she would be Mrs. Levi Glick. His name was Levi, a traditional name from the Bible, just like hers. A generation before them, there had been a Levi and a Sarah. Would they continue the tradition, or would there be a Justin or an Abigail or a Caitlyn, a "fancy" name?

Sarah wanted a whole houseful of children to run up and down the stairs, swing on a rope swing in the haymow. They would play with calves and kittens and baby goats and run barefoot along field lanes lugging a red and white Rubbermaid thermos filled with the spearmint tea she had learned to make from her mother. They would take it to their dat, who was mowing hay in the alfalfa field, hot and thirsty, just like her dat.

She wrapped her hands around her knees, rocked back, suddenly ecstatic now.

She didn't hear the first part of Levi's unhurried speech, but his words penetrated her thoughts eventually.

"That Michael Lanvin needs a haircut. He'll have to get one when he goes to jail, right?"

Absentmindedly, Dat said he would likely get one.   .

"Yeah, Michael told me that night. He told me he's not the one starting the fires. He told me that. He said he knows who it is, but he was afraid of him.

"He said the real arsonist is not him, but if he told

me, and I told someone, he could get shot. What did he mean by that?

"Then he said this. He said that years ago that man of Widow Lydia's, what was his name? Her husband?

"Michael said he didn't pay this man for a lot of money. Did he mean Lydia's husband didn't pay? Or what?"

Dat stopped the porch swing, his body tense as his breath whooshed out.

"Levi."

"Hm?"

"Are you positive you're not making this up?"

"Why would I? Michael would not want me to do that. He said he thinks Ashley Walter's father is the arsonist."

Dat gasped, and Mam said sharply, "Levi!"

"Well, what?"

Sarah said very quietly, "Harold. Harold Walters."

The man at the leather goods store, the stand at the farmer's market. He had been in a dispute about money. Apparently with Lydia's husband, who had not been a stable person. He had struggled with old grudges and a mental instability and sometimes became quite violent.

Sarah knew Harold Walters as a friendly man though brusque, a good business person. But then, there was the suspicious mistreatment of Ashley.

Dat said, "We'll wait and see what happens, alright?"

"Why?"

"We have no proof. Even if we summoned the police and Michael spilled everything, they could both deny all of it. There were never any fingerprints."

Levi shook his head and said Michael hadn't spilled a thing. He drank the whole glass of water Levi had given him.

CHAPTER 14

Wᴀᴇɴ Lᴇᴇ ᴄᴀᴍᴇ ᴛᴏ ᴘɪᴄᴋ Sᴀʀᴀʜ ᴜᴘ ᴀɴᴅ ᴡʜɪꜱᴋ her away to Anna's house, in Suzie's words, she was ready, her cheeks flushed with anticipation, wearing a new green dress the color of a cornstalk. She remained barefoot, the heat stubbornly draped across Lancaster County, a stifling bubble of high humidity creating uncomfortably warm nights and sending daytime temperatures to a high of 95 degrees or more.

Lee greeted her from the buggy, dressed in a cool, white short-sleeved shirt, his teeth flashing as white as the shirt, his tanned skin a dark contrast. She climbed up and seated herself beside him before he had a chance to step down and help her up.

Their eyes met, and they smiled and continued smiling, both unable to wipe the ridiculously happy emotions from their faces.

He reached for her hand and said, "Sarah, tell me I won't wake up from the best dream I have ever had."

In response, Sarah squeezed his hand, laid her head on his shoulder, and said happily, "You won't."

Few things can compare with driving along country roads in a horse and buggy, she thought. Especially on a night like this. Both doors were pushed back, both windows held to the ceiling of the buggy by a metal clasp, allowing the air to circulate freely. The horse trotted at a brisk pace, knowing he was going home.

She breathed in the aroma of summer as they passed a field of tomatoes, one of corn, and yet another with freshly cut alfalfa, infusing the air with its heady fragrance.

Oncoming traffic was heavy, so the train of cars behind them grew increasingly longer, until one revved its engine with impatience.

Lee looked in the rearview mirror and pulled steadily, easily, on the right rein, drawing the buggy off the main road and onto the wide shoulder beside it, allowing the cars to pass, one by one. Sarah smiled.

"Lee, pulling off to the side of the road and allowing cars to pass—that puts you in the same highly-respected category as my father. Thank you. Not all men will do that."

Lee grinned at her.

"So you think you made a good choice?"

"Definitely."

Their smiles became slightly idiotic once more, and they stayed that way as they pulled up to Ben Zook's farmhouse.

Not Ben's anymore, Sarah corrected herself. Anna's. And not for long. This farm would be Lee's. And hers. She could hardly bear to think of it. The disbelief, the joy of this great and perfect gift was almost more than she could contain.

Anna greeted her at the door. She threw her soft, ample form into Sarah's arms, laughing, then crying and becoming completely hysterical, as Sarah held her, laughed, and cried with her.

"Sarah, oh Sarah! I told Lee we have to build a patio between our two houses, so you and I can meet every summer morning to talk and drink our coffee. Do you think we'll get along? I promise you, I will mind my own business. I will not meddle in your affairs. Ever. I can't believe you're going to be my sister-in-law."

Sarah was drawn into the kitchen, and for the first time, she viewed the house with eyes of ownership.

The walls were painted a soft white, and the trim and doors, as well as the kitchen cabinets, were a softly gleaming golden oak. There were double windows above the sink and behind the table, allowing plenty of light and air into the large kitchen.

The linoleum mimicked dark ceramic tile. Sarah thought it was very tasteful, as was the hidden alcove containing a small sink and a round ring to hold a hand towel.

The cabinets contained a large number of deep drawers and doors that contained evenly spaced shelves. The large EZ Freeze propane gas refrigerator was built into the cabinetry, as was the gas stove beside the double sink.

Sarah had been in this house many times, but never like this. Her mind tumbled with possibilities—furniture, colors, things she would have on her countertop or her table.

She did not want to be materialistic or greedy, but she overflowed with ideas, thinking of things she wanted to buy, items she would need.

Anna's three children, Marlin, Marianne, and little Elmer, all clamored about her now, asking for attention. She had to focus on the needs of the fatherless children, her heart aching for them as she gathered them on her lap and around her on the brown tweed sofa.

She stroked Elmer's squeaky clean hair, answered Marlin's rapid fire questions, listened patiently as Marianne talked about her new kittens in the barn. She showed Sarah where she had been scratched, and Sarah clucked properly over a proffered hand, which Marianne held to the light, the band-aid removed, so the scratch could be examined and fussed over.

She was not aware of Lee's entrance or of the light in his eyes as he stopped, watching Sarah with the children.

Anna was perspiring freely, mopping at her face with a clean washcloth, complaining about the intense heat.

"You know, Sarah, there's hardly a nice, Christian way of complaining about the weather. But what's the difference—that or snapping at everyone all day because you're so hot and tired of it? I can hardly take one more day of this stickiness."

"I think a thunderstorm is on its way, later tonight," Sarah said.

"Yup, paper says that," Lee agreed.

"Well, good. I hope it's a doozy. It better clear the atmosphere and lift this humidity. Did you know it was ninety percent yesterday? It was so humid. I had a glass of water setting beside me on the sewing machine, and it condensed so much there was a puddle all around it."

Sarah smiled. She knew exactly what she meant, having tried to sew and given up herself.

They talked for over an hour, remembering Ben and making plans for the future. Then Anna went to the pantry and refrigerator, producing armloads of food, enough for a dozen people.

There was cold, freshly squeezed lemonade that was so refreshing the temperature seemed to drop ten degrees, Sarah told her.

There was cold, chunked watermelon, red and seedless and mouthwatering, squares of golden cantaloupe, piles of cheese and ham and sweet Lebanon bologna, mustard and dipping sauces, stick pretzels and potato chips. She'd coated strawberries with a combination of milk and dark chocolate, and there were two different kinds of whoopie pies individually wrapped in plastic wrap, moist and soft with a heavy layer of vanilla frosting in the middle.

Sarah had never tasted better whoopie pies. Never. She told Anna, who laughed heartily.

"I bought them, Sarah. You won't catch me baking when the whole house is like an oven. Forget that."

Sarah eyed Anna's plate, then Lee's, and wondered if she would be Anna's size in a few years. Their appreciation for food was contagious. She found herself chiming in with praise of the texture of the watermelon, the chocolate, everything.

They took food very seriously. She was alarmed at the amount Lee consumed. She eyed his wide shoulders, muscular arms, his flat stomach, and decided he likely had a terrific metabolism, plus he did an enormous amount of physical work each day.

As if he read her thoughts, he smiled.

"We Glicks like to eat, Sarah. I can hardly wait for you to get to know the rest of the family."

"I met your sisters at the funeral and your mother before. She's terribly nice. So friendly."

They all sat up, silenced, as the rustling of leaves began and quickly turned into more than a rustling. An opened newspaper lying on an end table flapped, then slid to the floor, blown by the increasing force of the sudden gust of wind.

Anna ran to the window, flapping her round arms as she went.

"Air! Air! The wind is coming!"

The children were trundled off to bed, and the table was cleared before the faraway rumbles of thunder began.

"Nothing to worry about yet," Lee announced, returning from a short vigil on the front porch.

Anna produced a pink spiral bound notebook and wrote across the front cover in bold, printed letters: Levi and Sarah's Wedding.

They sat together at the kitchen table and planned, writing names of grandparents, uncles and aunts, cousins, friends, co-workers, an endless stream of relatives and acquaintances until Sarah's head was reeling with the immensity of it all.

Who would be the corner waiters to serve the bride and groom's table? Who would be *fore-gayer* (managers)? Who would have the *babeyly* (paper)? Where would Levi sit? He might be better off in a wheelchair that day.

Lee was too easy, saying anything they decided was okay. Anna told him he could say that now, but he'd come up with a few clunkers later. He always did. He'd just wait till a few weeks before the wedding, and then he'd throw a monkey wrench into the works.

She assured Sarah that Lee was bossy. Look at him, running his own roofing crew. He was used to being the boss, and she'd better start preparing to live a humble life of servitude. This thing of sitting there saying anything was alright was just till Sarah married him and she couldn't get away; then the real Lee would show his true colors.

Lee grinned, relaxed, completely unruffled, as Anna's harmless banter continued.

Sarah watched him, as he raked a strong, brown hand through his sun-streaked blond hair. She noticed the way his shoulders were propped against the chair, took in his steady, smiling blue eyes, and her knees became quite weak, her heart accelerated. The love she felt for him was growing into a steady, consuming flame.

She was grateful, humbled, to have this man in her life. Only God's infinite mercies could have enabled her to safely make this choice. Deep in her heart, she knew Lee would be the kind of man that would never cause her a moment's grief. Like Dat, he existed on a bedrock of kindness.

Dat's description of others was almost always, "He would do anything for anybody." That was his way of relating the goodness he saw in most people. This phrase could truthfully be applied to Lee, she knew. It showed in how he had worked for Ben, became a mentor for Omar, and all while he ran his roofing crew during the day, working long, wearying hours to help others.

In his heart, Lee felt he didn't know much about God or the Bible, choosing to remain quiet when others had long, heated discussions about theology, Scripture, whatever. But the fruits of being inhabited by the Spirit were all there. Lee knew God, or how could he have had this natural inclination toward kindness?

Dat said that was a great mystery, but it was all around us, every day, in mundane things, often unnoticed by others, but very important.

She wondered if Matthew had found a job, or if he would be returning to Haiti. She didn't think he knew what he wanted. He really didn't. Right now, he wanted her, she knew. But wasn't he just acting like a spoiled child who wanted a toy only because it was held by someone else?

And yet, she would always remember Matthew as someone who had flavored her life with sweetness, the first stirring of young love, the reason for living at times. She would always be grateful for him, for his friendship. But that was all.

"A penny for your thoughts."

Lee smiled at her, and she returned it gladly, but chose to keep her thoughts to herself. Someday, she would tell him.

The thunder rumbled, louder, closer, and Lee turned to watch out the window as another streak of lightning cut across the night sky.

"Think it'll be hard this time?" Anna asked.

"I don't know. Seems pretty powerful all of a sudden."

The wind tore at the trees surrounding the house and ripped across the lawn as lightning illuminated the landscape around them. There was a particularly loud boom. Anna grasped her head, her hands clapped across her ears, her eyes widened.

Inevitably, the high wail of the sirens followed. Soon a car's headlights came up the drive and stopped. The door opened, and a figure splashed through the rain. The heavy front door was flung open, and a neighbor stepped inside, dripping.

"Samuel Zook's barn!" he shouted.

Instantly, Lee was on his feet, following the neighbor out the door and away.

Anna sat, staring morosely at the remains of her delicious snack, shaking her head.

"I hate these fires. I'm sick of them."

"It was probably the lightning, Anna. That crack had to hit something, didn't it? I don't think the arsonist is loose, at least not doing that anymore."

"You always say that. You know what I think? I think we should have stocks, those wooden things they used to hold criminals, you know, thieves or mischief makers. We used to see them in our history books in school. Men or women were stuck in there, and other citizens, the good people, were allowed to throw tomatoes or eggs at them. That would be perfect."

Sarah laughed.

"In the Bible, they just stoned them, got rid of them."

"That's sick."

"I know. But still, it would be nice to be rid of these fires. I know how it was for us."

Anna's face became hard, rigid, with the intensity of the memory.

"You know, Ben suffered more than you'll ever know. He had days when he could barely drag himself out to do the milking. I milked alone more than once. I can't tell you the fear I experienced, the heart-sinking feeling of knowing my husband was lying in bed, crying with despair.

"I think the night our barn burned was honestly more than he could handle. He tried, Sarah, he tried so hard. He took his anti-depressants, talked to counselors, but I'm not sure he always felt as good as he let on. I'll tell you, Sarah, if you promise to keep this a secret."

Sarah nodded.

"I'm not sure he was thinking as he would have in former times, the day he went to get that calf. He knew the bull was there. He often told me never to trust him."

Anna sighed. She winced at the sound of the thunder and the rain and the wind moaning about the house.

"We never know, the day we get married, how wonderful God's gift of a sound mind can be. Another thing we never know is what God has in store for us. The important thing is that we live fully, trusting Him, and experience all that joy along the way."

Sarah nodded.

"For sure, Anna, for sure."

"I may spend the rest of my life as a widow now, living with you and Lee."

"No, you won't, Anna. You're young. You're attractive."

"I'm short and fat. You know men don't like big women. Besides, I won't talk about it. Ben is still in my heart, and he'll stay there."

They did dishes, listened to the strength of the storm abating, and read a few articles to each other from a magazine. Then they took off their coverings and stretched out, Anna on the recliner and Sarah on the couch. They closed their eyes and relaxed, but they kept on talking, the way sisters often do, of everything and anything, comfortable confiding life's joys and sorrows, their fears and failures.

Finally, at two o'clock in the morning, Sarah wondered out loud if Lee was alright. Did Anna think he was?

"Oh yes, he's old enough to take care of himself," she said. "He probably just thinks the whole night's outcome depends on him. He takes too much on himself."

They must have dozed off and were awakened by a shrill cry from the bedroom. Elmer was thirsty, so Anna stumbled to the kitchen and got him a cold drink. She crooned and fussed to her baby boy, before settling herself on the recliner, with plenty of grunts and snorts of discomfort.

The night was still warm, but Sarah tried to remain positive, imagining a cool morning breeze to greet her.

Suddenly, the footrest of the recliner slapped down. Anna sat up and announced loudly, "I'm so miserable. I cannot take one more minute of this heat. I'm going to take a shower. It's too hot on this itchy recliner. I guess if something bad happens, you'll have to call me."

With that, she stomped off toward the bedroom. Sarah heard drawers open and shut. The bathroom door slammed, the water turned on, and peace returned.

Sarah watched the remains of the storm, the ripples of blue heat lightning, and listened to the distant rumbles. She was glad the storm had gone through, giving hope of cooler temperatures tomorrow.

Her eyelids became heavier and heavier.

She was awakened by someone softly calling her name. Her eyes fluttered open, looking straight into Lee's blue eyes, his face blackened, his gaze weary.

"Oh."

She sat up immediately, all her senses keenly aware of him.

"Sarah."

Reaching up to fix her hair, her eyes remained on his face.

"They, we, I...we caught the arsonist."

Unable to comprehend Lee's words, Sarah looked at him blankly.

"We caught him. We have his lighter, the newspapers, the car, everything."

His voice was hoarse, strained, exhausted.

"Tell me," she said.

Evidently, Harold Walters had taken no precautions that night. The lightning was so sharp, the fire could have been blamed on it handily, so he got bold and drove up to Samuel Zook's barn without trying to cover anything.

In the flashes of lightning, they'd watched. When the barn was hit by a bolt of lightning, it was soon extinguished, most of it saved. But there he was, crouched beside the silo on the barn hill sloping up to the haymow, stuffing newspapers in the door, igniting them.

Lee, the neighbor Amos, and the driver—the three of them jumped him and wrestled him to the ground. They were surprised when they saw he was an older man. It wasn't Michael.

They subdued him, called the police, and spent the rest of the night listening, watching, answering questions.

So now a lot depended on the arsonist's willingness to tell the truth and the Amish people's ability to prosecute. Without pressing charges, they were back to square one.

Sarah listened, then stated that this was not a whole lot different than Michael Lanvin being taken into custody. It still depended on the Plain people's prosecution.

"Dat will not do it."

"Perhaps others will."

"Which one is right, Lee?"

He sat beside Sarah, leaned back against the cushions, and closed his eyes.

"We'll talk at breakfast. I need a shower, then I may as well start milking. Anna's asleep, right?"

Sarah nodded.

"Let her sleep. Poor thing, she minds the heat so much. I can milk."

"I'll help," Sarah offered.

"No way. You hardly slept."

"I want to."

And she did. Secretly, she wanted to see how it would be to milk cows in the stable that would be hers and Lee's. Her feet skimmed the wet sidewalks, she was so excited. She knew cows and could hardly wait to show Lee her expertise. Without any instructions, she assembled the milking machines, washed udders, fed cows and calves, and swept the aisles. She was a regular cyclone of energy, leaving Lee duly impressed.

Afterwards, they washed the milkers together, and Sarah swept the cement floor, carefully rinsing it with clean water. She smiled at Lee and said, "Let's go make breakfast."

But Lee was staring at her with a strange look on his face. And he stood rooted to his position by the bulk tank.

"What?" she asked innocently.

"I am in disbelief. Besides being beautiful and kind and sweet, you're a real workaholic."

"Oh no, Lee. This is the first time I ever helped you do the milking. I was trying to make an impression. It might not always be this way," she laughed.

"But do you like milking? Farming? It's terribly hard work for a girl."

"Oh, it's not. I love it. It's all I know. I've been a farm girl all my life."

He closed the gap between them, folded her gently, with a sort of reverence, into his strong arms, and held her.

The milk house door was suddenly yanked open, and Anna stuck her head in.

"Whoopsie! Sorry! Hey, if this is how it's going to be, and I run into this kind of situation all the time, you're going to have to set up a beeper or something. Like a flare at an accident, some kind of warning."

But she was laughing, and Lee introduced Sarah to her as the new Mrs. Lee Glick, outstanding farmer of the year. Sarah smiled, then laughed, and said, "Oh, come on." But the pleasure of his approval stayed with her all morning, creating a smile that fairly glistened, until Anna said she had never known her teeth were so white. Sarah replied that Anna had just never seen them for such an extended period of time.

CHAPTER 15

As always, when everyone was least expecting it, a small white car drove up to the house. No one
could predict exactly who the caller was, although Levi
said his heartbeat was getting heavy—that car was
the same one that drove in the lane the night the barn
burned to the ground, or would have if the firemen hadn't
soaked it.

Dat listened halfheartedly, watching warily. Sarah
scraped a residue of meatloaf from the supper plates
and leaned over to catch a glimpse for herself. Priscilla
said that—sure enough—it was the car Levi had always
described, and Suzie said perhaps they should all run to
the basement—what if he had a gun?

They all tried to make light of the white car's arrival,
but even Dat's face blanched when the car door opened.
A gangly, unkempt youth unfolded his long limbs and
stood uncertainly, one hand clutching the door handle,
as if he would rather reopen the door and fold himself
back inside.

He was dressed in torn jeans and an old sweatshirt
of a nondescript color with the sleeves hacked off. A cap

sat low on his forehead, stray hair erupting around it like brush bristles.

Levi said this was too scary for him and he was going to his room. But as soon as he saw all the windows in his room, he felt exposed and shuffled back to the safety of the recliner. He sat down solidly, watching with a stony expression.

Finally, when Dat wondered if he should go out and invite him in, the young man began a wary walk up to the porch, his focus mostly on the sidewalk.

At the first rapping sound, Dat went to the door, opened it, and stepped outside, perhaps to protect his family, perhaps for privacy. Sarah couldn't tell. She was surprised when Dat opened the kitchen door and ushered the visitor inside.

Quickly, Mam pushed aside a few empty serving dishes and wiped the tabletop swiftly, murmuring excuses, casting furtive glances at the visitor with the intense black eyes.

But here was Dat, asking him to sit, so if Davey did that, she assumed he knew what he was doing. But Mam still felt so ill at ease that she scrubbed all the pots and pans so vigorously that they shone like a mirror the remainder of the week.

Sarah went to the sink, finding safety in turning her back. She concentrated on the simple task of helping Mam with the supper dishes. Her ears, however, were fine-tuned to words spoken by the two men.

Dat kept up a friendly conversation, until that ran out, sputtered, and died. Mam cleared her throat and cast a sideways glance at Sarah, who coughed involuntarily.

A steady thumping ensued as the youth bounced his one knee in furious repetition, his large gray sneaker steadily whacking the linoleum. He raked his soiled cap off his head and ran a hand through his unkempt hair.

Sarah turned halfway around and observed him closely. Yes. It was. He was the guy at the funeral home. Michael Lanvin. The arsonist?

His mouth was working, painfully. He ran a hand across the back of his neck, tugged at the neck of his sweatshirt. Beads of sweat appeared on his upper lip. He wiped them off with a shaking forefinger.

"Um, yeah, I'm like."

He stopped, searching Dat's face.

Dat remained steady, his gaze unknowing, calm, and unfazed, waiting for the youth to reveal what was on his mind.

Hadn't Davey dealt with many youth, recognized guilt and its unfailing disciple, its lack of trust? So he waited.

"Yeah, um...." Again, he stalled, unable to continue. "See, I, like, met you when she ... Ashley ... my girlfriend died. It was you, right?"

Dat nodded, a half smile of reassurance evident now.

"That was you, right?" he repeated.

"Yes, it was. I remember you," Dat answered. "You seemed quite upset."

"Yeah, I was, I guess."

Another pause.

"Which one's Sarah?" the youth asked suddenly.

Sarah stopped, motionless, and slowly put down the plate she was washing, watching the suds cover it. Drying her hands on her apron, she stepped forward, smiled slightly, and introduced herself.

"Hi," he responded, "I'm him. Ashley's boyfriend."

Sarah nodded.

"I'm, well, how much did she tell you?"

"About what?"

"The fires."

"Nothing. She was concerned about each family, cared about them."

"She never said nothing about, you know?"

"No."

Suddenly, he slid down in his chair so far Sarah thought he would slide off, but he splayed his feet, stopping himself.

"It wasn't me."

Sarah looked, found Dat's eyes. His face was frozen, a granite profile.

"It was her dad. That guy at the leather goods place at the market. Not her real dad. I drove him around, but he lit the barns. He hates a guy named Aaron. Or he did. This guy died, but he's never gotten over it."

Dat nodded. "They caught him."

"I know. But they think it's me. He'll lie. He won't care if I go behind bars, as long as he can save his own skin."

"I see," Dat said quietly.

"Will you come to my hearing?"

Dat pondered the question without answering.

"I know you guys don't do court appearances, but would you help me out? I'm...I don't want to go again. Jail is not a good place."

Finally Dat said, "I don't know what to tell you."

Sitting up straight, he leaned forward, pleading. "I'm in trouble, either way. What do they call it? I'm responsible as long as I hauled him around some of the time. Look, I got in too deep. I owed him money, lots of it. I couldn't pay him back. I got into trouble, lost my job. It's a mess. I'm scared. I don't know what to do."

"Is this Walters person in custody?"

"I doubt it. He has money."

"Is he dangerous?"

"No. He's a...." Michael caught himself, sputtered, and looked pleadingly at Dat. "If you'd just come to my hearing, testify."

"But all I have is your word."

"No! No!"

Desperate now, Michael spoke rapidly. "You gave me a hug, at the viewing. You said God should bless me. Well, He didn't. He can't on His own, the way I figure, but if you were in the courtroom, God would be there, too."

Dat shook his head. "No, Michael. I am not the go between you need. There is only One that came to earth, died for you, and is in heaven on your behalf. He's the One you need in the courtroom, not me."

Bewildered, Michael lifted his eyes. "Who?"

"Jesus."

"Oh, him."

Embarrassed, Michael's eyes slid away.

"Yeah, I remember my Sunday school teacher. I remember all that stuff."

"You do?"

"Yeah."

"So all you have to do is ask Him back into your life. He'll come. He'll be there for you."

"Yeah, but...." His voice trailed off.

"Are you sorry for what you did?"

"Well, of course. I wish I had never met Walters. Now Ashley's dead, and I...I treated her wrong."

There is nothing quite as shocking as the first ragged sob from a man who is truly at the end of his resources,

Sarah thought, as the initial battered sound tore from his throat.

"She's dead, and I can never fix it."

He flopped against the tabletop, folded his arms, and dropped his head onto them, his shoulders heaving.

Silent as wraiths, Priscilla and Suzie left the room. Levi began crying, as he always did when he heard the sounds of a distressed person.

Sarah stood, uncertain. Dat laid a hand on the youth's shoulder, his great calloused hand beginning a slow massage, an assurance of his presence.

"You are forgiven," he said softly.

Still, Michael's face remained buried in his arms, and his sobs did not lessen. If anything, they intensified.

"I can never make it right," he repeated between hiccups.

Patiently, Dat explained the plan of salvation, urging Michael to accept forgiveness, share the yoke of sorrow with Jesus. He would carry it for him, relieve him of the shame and guilt. How much of it got through to him, Sarah did not know, but Michael's crying ceased. Mam brought him a clean paper towel, which he accepted shamefacedly, muttering a garbled thanks.

In the end, he accepted the fact that Dat would not come to his hearing.

"You may not have much of one," Dat said. "If the Amish people show their forgiveness, which I believe they will, you will have fines and penalties perhaps, but hopefully, no jail time."

"I will. I deserve it. You know that."

"We'll see."

When he rose to go, Dat did not shake hands, he simply pulled the young man into an embrace and released him. Keeping a hand on his shoulder, he said firmly, "We forgive you. Be a man now, and change your ways. You'll come out of this a better person."

"You think?"

"I think, definitely."

"I need to....I don't have a Bible. I used to, you know, read it."

"I'll see that you get one. Stop by tomorrow night."

Unbelievably, he did.

Sarah looked up from weeding the lima beans to find the small white car driving up to the house. She straightened, shaded her eyes with her hand, then laid down her hoe. Walking toward him, she smiled hesitantly.

"Michael. Good to see you!"

"Hey."

"You came for the Bible?"

"Yeah."

"I'll get it."

"Where's your dad?"

"He has a meeting tonight."

"What meeting?"

Immediately, his eyes became hooded with suspicion.

"A meeting about the fires, the arsonist."

David Beiler had known before he hitched Fred to the shining, freshly washed buggy that this would be the last meeting as far as the arsonist was concerned. He was in custody. And it was likely that Michael Lanvin would serve some time as well, although he couldn't be sure.

The meeting would be fraught with argument, he knew. It would be like walking in a war zone, stumbling onto hidden land mines. Dangerous to the hearts and souls of men.

Always, church problems were the same. Maneuvering between the liberals and the conservatives required the wisdom of Solomon. Or more, he concluded to himself.

The leader of the liberals was Melvin, his own nephew, outspoken, charismatic, able to bend other men's wills because of his ability to talk. He could make an expert salesman, selling innocent folks things they certainly did not need.

Melvin and his followers wanted revenge. They called it justice, which was only a nice word for it. In David's opinion, to wish anyone ill, punishment, pain, anything, was a form of revenge. That was an eye for an eye, a tooth for a tooth, the Old Testament teachings of the law.

When Jesus came, He brought a better way, but so few understood or trusted the form of love the ministers struggled to keep alive within the churches as well as without.

To forgive was the epitome of Christ's message. So near to forgiveness, Davey had almost given up the whole gospel when Sarah was injured.

Never, as long as he lived, would he forget the pleading look in her eyes as she begged her father to help her, to free her from her pain. Watching as the doctors scraped the dead tissue from her exposed nerve endings left him weak and drained, completely helpless. That emotion was followed by a bitter wish for revenge, wanting to make the arsonist endure exactly what Sarah had gone through.

It was only human nature.

Tight-lipped men sat on benches around the long table in Sam Esh's shop. They were dressed in colorful shirts with back vests and trousers, their straw hats on pegs along the wall. Some of the younger men wore shirts with a stripe and no vests, their patterned suspenders in stark relief against the distinctive shirts.

Those in the more modern, youthful dress, most of them asking for justice, would gladly enter a courtroom, testify, and press charges.

David was surprised to see Melvin dressed in a plain shirt and wearing a vest, his normally tousled hair combed down over his ears in a modest fashion. He felt a tug of amusement at the corner of his mouth. No doubt Lydia's influence was taking hold already.

Good. That was good. She would be a grounding influence in his life. She was quiet and stable and would bring him back to earth if he went off on a far-flung rant, the way he tended to do.

The meeting opened with a silent prayer, time well spent as David laid his heart open for God to examine. Thy will be done. Amen.

Sam Esh was the main speaker, having had more interaction with the law and the media than anyone else.

He began quietly, a humble man. It was hard to stand up and face the prying eyes of men who were in disagreement.

He was a man of common sense, and as he spoke, this quality emerged, his voice gained momentum, and assurance broke through as his voice carried well to the far reaches of the room.

"We all want this man behind bars, for our own safety. As of now, he'll go there, whether we testify or not. He was caught, doing the grisly work he's been doing for a couple of years, and there's not much we're going to do to change that. The law is the law. I spoke to the local police, and they're guessing he'll get between five and ten years."

Immediately, murmurs erupted, hands were raised.

"He'd get more than that if we testified."

"Is that all?"

"You know he'll be out in two, the way court cases go."

"Bunch of crooks."

"It ain't right."

David Beiler sat and listened, his heart dropping with a sickening thud. So this was what he'd be up against. This thirst for revenge.

"Two years from now, the barn fires will start again."

Sam Esh stood, silenced by the outrage, his face flaming with discomfiture.

Melvin raised his hand. Sam nodded toward him. Melvin stood.

"See, this is our trouble. We're gullible people who don't understand the law. Anyone can feed us anything, and we believe it. I talked to a lawyer and got the real deal."

David cringed at his arrogance, his superiority.

"If we testify, he told me, we can change the course of the court's decision."

Melvin paused for emphasis.

David noticed the worshipful demeanors on the faces of the younger men and wondered anew at the necessity of God telling the children of Israel to support the arms of Moses in battle. As long as Moses's arms were held up by his people, their armies had the victory.

Here, tonight, it was the same scenario, but in spirit. When Godly leaders had the support of the people, there was a blessing in the land.

He inhaled deeply, steadied himself, kept his silence, and allowed Melvin to ramble on, using words from his lawyer's book that very few of these simple, Plain men understood. Perhaps this was good.

After Melvin sat down, there were murmurs of agreement.

Samuel Riehl stood and elaborated on Melvin's views.

Old Dan Dienner asked for time, was given it, and David took another calming breath. Dan had never been known for patience and often lacked forbearance. He was a mighty little warrior carrying the spear of his own highly esteemed opinion.

Dan's words were scathing, his bushy gray eyebrows drawn down like angry caterpillars. His mouth snapped open and closed as if elastic controlled his jaws after every hurtful sentence had been released. His words swirled about the room bringing each rebellious nature to fruition.

David watched sadly as a few younger men stood up, grabbed their hats, and strode smartly from the room, angered by Dan Dienner's fiery words.

The meeting stalled when the old minister sat down. Unease crept beneath the chairs. Men settled themselves in different positions, feet scraped fitfully on the cement floor, throats were cleared, and here and there a self-conscious cough erupted.

They called on *Davey Beila*. His limbs were heavy, burdened by the fractious atmosphere. Slowly, like a sorrowful old man, he stood.

"Would someone ask the men that left the room to return, please?"

That was his first concern. They were the church of tomorrow. Personal opinion was meaningless, when it came to *fer-sarking* (caring for) the church of the future.

After a moment of bewilderment, someone nudged Melvin, who hurried out, returning with the young men in tow.

David shared what was on his heart. He could speak no other way. He told of his own fire, the loss, the hard work, but also the overwhelming gratitude in the end, when he viewed the members of the Amish church in a whole new light.

"For we have something. We have an upbringing, a tradition that teaches us to reach out, perform duties born of brother love.

"After the new barn stood in its place, I was as changed as the barn. I have never known gratitude the way I do now. I can never stand in the forebay, throwing a harness on a mule's back, and not be thankful for the mule, the harness, the roof over our heads. I think God wants that gratitude from us.

"So how can He teach us better, besides allowing fiery trials, in this case, literally, into our lives?"

Heads nodded, faces contorted in all sorts of ways to keep emotion from rising to the surface.

"Yes, it was hard sometimes. The hardest by far was when our Sarah was burned. I couldn't forgive then. I couldn't forgive the arsonist. I railed against God. I wanted revenge, any form of torture. I wanted the arsonist to experience debridement, just once. Let him feel what Sarah had endured."

Clearly, Davey had the attention of the liberals. Now he was talking. Sarah was burned so this preeminent minister would stand in the courtroom, his voice carrying well in the great room. What a grand testimony he would have! Their moment of glory was at hand.

"I hardly slept one night," David continued. "Like Jacob, I wrestled with the angel of God. I knew what was right, but just this once, I wanted to be exempt from doing the right thing.

"Toward morning, though, I knew I had to let go. I had to let go of all those thoughts of revenge, of justification and hatred. 'Vengeance will be mine, saith the Lord.' Forgiveness is the only way to peace. The only way.

"Now, before you decide to speak against me, let me finish. The young man who drove Harold Walters to some of the farms where he lit the fires came to visit us. He's sorry for what he did. He wants our forgiveness. He did not start the fires, just drove the car."

"He'll get jail time anyway," Melvin barked.

"Let me finish. He said this Harold Walters held a personal grudge against the Widow Lydia's husband, Aaron. They had some business dealings in the past, not very honest ones, I presume.

"Aaron is dead, may he rest in peace, and it would not be uplifting to speak of his faults now. But, in a sense, because of the misdeeds of one our brethren, we suffered. In a sense, it was brought on our own heads."

"That's ridiculous!"

The words were harsh, cutting, spoken forcefully by a young man in a striped shirt.

Slowly, one by one, in ripples, heads turned from side to side.

"Yes, I know. It might sound ridiculous, but I'm afraid it's true," David continued. "One bit of spoiled dough will ruin the whole loaf. If we want to live righteously, separating ourselves from the world, then we have a responsibility to live up to what we profess. God sees this long before we do and sends chastening. He *schlakes* (punishes) us, like naughty children.

"After children are chastened, don't they come climb up on our laps and lay their sweet heads on our chests? And we cuddle them, our love for them multiplying and theirs for us. Same with God. We are His children. We have been chastened, and this *schtrofe* (punishment) we will accept, take it upon ourselves. Mind you, the fruits of it will follow. Already it is visible."

Heads nodded, eyes misted, glasses were removed, cleaned. Even the young men understood perfectly the picture of a young child who was punished. They fully accepted the theory, and their heads bowed before the wisdom of David Beiler.

"What about Sarah?"

Like the last sputter from a dying engine, Lloyd Fisher had to throw one more barb.

"Sarah was my Gethsemane, my finish, so to speak. But in ways that are of a personal nature, her outward suffering brought an inward acceptance of God's will for her. I can't call her injuries wrong."

Everyone knew what he was talking about. Eyes twinkled, knowing looks were exchanged.

She'd be published—her engagement officially announced—after communion. That Lee Glick was really something. Good for Sarah.

So Dan Dienner's eyebrows leveled off and smoothed out. The young men acknowledged their leader's wisdom and gave themselves up to it. And Melvin stuck his lawyer's book in his jacket pocket, where it bulged uncomfortably and made him feel lopsided the remainder of the evening.

CHAPTER 16

As THE SUMMER DREW TO A CLOSE, THE CICADAS and crickets set up their symphony outside Sarah's bedroom window. A breeze billowed the sheer panels at her windows, and she flung her arms above her head and clasped her hands, a sigh of happiness and contentment escaping her lips.

A farmer's wife! Why had she never imagined it? It was the fulfillment of a dream she was never aware of, until it turned into reality.

Beside her, Priscilla was reading a book by the light of an LED battery lamp.

"Pinch me, Priscilla, to make sure I'm real," Sarah said laughing.

"Gladly."

Reaching over, she pinched Sarah's arm between her thumb and forefinger, producing an excruciatingly painful sensation worse than a bee sting.

"Ow!" Sarah yelped, leaping off the bed. "Ow! I didn't say you had to pinch that hard."

Laughing out loud, Priscilla lowered her book, her face lifted to the ceiling, her eyes squeezed shut in laughter.

"It's not funny."

"Uh...oh my! Shoo!" Priscilla gasped.

Suddenly, she caught sight of Sarah's shoulder. Her laughter ended abruptly.

"Sarah," she whispered, horrified.

"What?"

"Your shoulder."

Turning her head to the right, Sarah lowered her eyes, then looked at Priscilla, a sad question in her eyes.

"Is it so bad?"

Shaken, Priscilla nodded.

"I just never realized, I guess. My goodness, Sarah. In this glaring light, it doesn't look very good."

"I know. And I'm getting married. It scares me."

"Does Lee know?"

"I told him. But still. I mean, there's no guarantee he won't be repelled. Priscilla, what should I do? Really?"

"Well, what does he say?"

"He says the scars are beautiful. They remind him of God's answer to his prayers, His will to blend our life into one. After Matthew, he means."

Priscilla's eyes turned soft and liquid.

"Aw. He's so sweet. He's a special guy, Sarah. You're blessed."

"I am. This is first time in my life I can understand that overused word—awesome. Lee is truly awesome."

"Tell me, was Matthew easy to forget?"

"I couldn't let go of him, until I was burned."

"I know."

Sarah lay down on the bed again, and a comfortable silence followed. Finally Priscilla crawled off Sarah's bed, said good night, and padded to her room. Sarah heard her turn off the lamp and sigh. She could soon tell her sister was fast asleep.

Sarah turned on her side, facing the window, thankful for the cool breezes. She listened to the clamorous sounds of summer's insects and wondered at the thought of her upcoming wedding.

They'd chosen December 6, a Thursday. It was smack dab in the middle of the Lancaster County wedding season.

That was fine with Sarah. Everything else in her life would be traditional, being a farmer's wife, living with a relative at the "other end." *S'ana ent.* It was a vague description of a double house, with an addition—the "other end"—built for parents or sisters or brothers on the home place, the family co-existing in peaceful harmony as much as they were able.

Would she always get along with Anna? Already, Sarah looked forward to having coffee with her every morning. Anna was the funniest person she knew. Her sense of humor was outrageous but so deliciously spirit lifting, so light and sweet to the senses, like cotton candy.

With Ben's death, that had changed a bit. Now her grief was a gray shroud that hung about her much of the time, an aura of unbelievable sadness, though her humor still broke through once in while. She had loved her husband with a love that was true and strong, in spite of the many ways he exasperated her.

Sarah smiled to herself, picturing Anna canning peaches with the oversized stainless steel bowl balanced precariously on her short lap while she related the story of the calf chasing incident.

In spite of herself, Sarah's shoulders shook, remembering Anna's outrage.

"There I was, big as a barrel, my arms waving, my legs pumping, running as fast as I could to keep that calf out of the peas and onions. What does that Ben do but start waving his pitchfork in the wrong direction, sending the calf straight through the garden, crossways, while he continued waving that stupid fork! Dense!"

That was the typical Anna, who found the humor in almost any situation. Now though, her sunny disposition had begun to fail her as the reality of her situation sank in. She spent whole afternoons lying listlessly on the recliner, getting up only to care for her "littles"— changing a diaper, getting a drink. The immaculate house became cluttered. Little fingerprints were etched on the windows, and dishes lay unwashed on the countertop. Even the laundry piled up, and when she did wash, it stayed on the line till suppertime, as she lacked the energy to bring it in.

Lee's blue eyes became pools of worry about his sister. His mother assured him this was common. She'd seen it before, and they'd just have to do things for her for a while.

True to her word, Rachel came and scrubbed and swept and polished. She stripped the beds and hung clean sheets on the line. She got down on her hands and knees and flipped the switch on the gas refrigerator, turning it to "defrost," then heaved herself back up and proceeded to empty it of its contents.

She cleaned the shelves, the drawers, and the freezer. She made chocolate chip cookies for Lee and graham cracker fluff for Anna. She put little Tom Sturgis pretzels in a huge bowl, dribbled olive oil and a blend of cheddar cheese powder, sour cream and onion powder, and ranch dressing mix all over them. She stirred and mixed and mixed and then ate them, one by one, all afternoon.

She melted white American cheese in milk and butter and made *smear* cheese as a dip for the seasoned pretzels. She made gallons of *vissa tae* (meadow tea) and set it in the spotless refrigerator. Then she kissed Anna's cheek, hugged her and patted her, and said, "My little girl, you'll be fine."

Then off she went, perched all alone on one side of the spring wagon, for all the world like a plump little badger, leaning forward and slapping her slow horse with the reins. She had to get home. She had work to do.

Sarah lay in her bed and thought she could always love Lee's mother. Then she couldn't help comparing her to Hannah with her slovenly sweater, her plodding pace, and the grayish whites on her wash line. Oh, Hannah's heart was in the right place, and her talents were distributed differently, but…well, there was much to think about.

Matthew and Hannah.

It was interesting, the way she thought her good-looking son incapable of making one misstep. Pure unconditional love. Sarah couldn't say if that was right or wrong, but ninety-nine percent of the time, Matthew would likely expect that same kind of unvarnished idolatry from his wife. What if he didn't receive it?

Sarah shook her head, remembered his pouting and the stone cold silences that froze her soul, her will, her very being. She had not loved him or approved of him, somehow, somewhere along the line. And yet, if he had remained Amish and married her, could she have had a good life? Some questions are never answered.

Would she ever feel the same kind of love for Lee that she had experienced as a young girl with Matthew? The love for Lee was different. It was slow and steady, comfortable and easy. There were no doubts or heart thumping moments of passion or drama. Within Lee's arms, she was safe, secure, loved, accepted.

Could she include her scars? As a young, innocent bride, would she revolt him? Already, she knew deep in her heart that the answer was no. Lee loved her with a pure and Godly love, and with this assurance, she dropped off to a restful slumber, as the cicadas outside her window kept up their frenzied calls.

The next morning, Mam was in a dither, a fine one. Lizzie Zook's store had only one bolt of the blue crepe fabric they needed for the wedding. They had sent for two more bolts, and it was positively not the same color. Even the shine was different.

Mam hired a driver, fabric sample in hand, and went to Belmont Fabrics. She came home so frustrated she was almost crying and said they might have to start all over again. She could not match Sarah's dress.

"We can't do that, Mam. My wedding dress is finished, and I love it. I found exactly the shade of cornflower blue I want. I'm not going to change it."

Mam tried to put all her good virtues to use. She closed her mouth and attempted serenity, but her eyebrows shot straight up, and she said tightly, "Sarah, now listen to me. You have to have the same color for the other girls!"

"Why?"

"Well, because!" Mam sputtered.

And so they were off to Georgetown, to Fisher's Fabrics and Housewares. They paid the driver an exorbitant fee, as he charged for waiting time, but Mam emerged triumphant, carrying two bolts of the exact shade, texture, and quality she wanted. Along with the perfect blue fabric, she found the black she needed as well.

The white organdy capes and aprons had been sewn a few weeks prior, pressed to perfection, and hung in Mam's downstairs closet. One for Sarah, one for Priscilla, and one for Rose, who would also be part of the bridal party.

Normally, Rose's mother would have sewn Rose's dress, but Mam offered, knowing she was *fit* (capable). Rose's mother was only too happy to allow Malinda that chore.

They painted the kitchen, the downstairs bathroom, and Levi's room, leaving Levi rocking all alone on the wooden porch swing, dragging his feet across the painted floor, singing dolefully under his breath.

They wouldn't let him paint. He couldn't drive the mules. He felt as if there was not one thing he could do to help with the wedding. He was hungry for shoofly, but no one baked that or whoopie pies or chocolate chip cookies anymore.

Every day they had *kalte sup* for supper, which he refused. He had to eat Corn Flakes or Wheaties, and even if he sliced a banana into his cereal, it hardly filled him up. He sneaked potato chips or Ritz crackers into his bed, but they left a lot of crumbs that made him itchy during the night when he was so tired. Then he had to get out of bed, brush the crumbs off the sheet, and then climb back into bed and settle himself, which was a bit of a chore.

He was hungry for a hot dog with onions and pickles and cheese and ketchup. He lifted his head and listened at the window, wondering if Mam was happy enough to ask her for a "doggie." Singing at the sewing machine usually rated pretty high, like two cookies or cheese and pretzels, sometimes even a grilled cheese sandwich.

Cleaning windows on a cold day without singing rated only an apple, but maybe he would get some peanut butter, if he was lucky.

Painting meant a pretty slim chance of acquiring anything at all, by the sound of the clipped sentences coming through the kitchen window.

He sighed and flapped a hand in front of his face to cool himself. Maybe he'd be allowed some chocolate milk, if he made it and didn't ask Sarah to do it.

Rising slowly, he lumbered across the porch, letting himself in through the kitchen door.

"Watch it! Watch it!"

Immediately, Mam swooped over, stopping him in his tracks. "Don't step on that pan of paint."

Levi wrinkled his nose, looked dolefully at Mam, and then turned to see what Sarah was doing.

"We're almost finished, Levi. Why don't you go out and sit on the porch a while longer?"

"I'm hungry."

"It's almost suppertime."

"Are we having *kalte sup*?"

"Probably."

"I want a hot dog."

"Wait till supper."

Levi shuffled back out to the porch obediently, flopped on the porch swing, and resumed his mournful singing. His stomach was growling, tumbling about with nothing in it, and he had no hope of anything to eat till suppertime.

A cloud of dust on the horizon slowly came into focus revealing a line of mules pulling a wagon. The steel wheels rattled across the handmade wooden bridge that spanned the small creek by the orchard. It was dried up in late summer, becoming an unhandy little ditch that was no good at all. Levi knew just how the dry creek felt.

Suzie sat on the hay wagon, her skin tanned a dark brown, her hair curling about her face like Sarah's. Her feet were bare and browned by the sun, her pale green dress soiled, one sleeve ripped up the side, exposing her white upper arm. Catching sight of Levi, she waved.

Levi waved back excitedly, cheered by the sight of his youngest sister.

The mules' harnesses flapped, and the chains on the traces jingled. The hoof beats were muffled on the gravel, as the mules' ears flopped up and down, their heads bobbing in time to their footsteps.

Dat stood on the front of the wagon, his darkened old straw hat pulled low over his forehead to keep from blowing off in the hot, dusty air.

"Levi!" Dat called happily.

"Hey, Davey!" Levi shouted, sliding off the swing to stand on his bare feet, waving both hands, his broad face wreathed in a great smile.

Dat hauled back on the reins, stopping the team of mules.

"Levi, tell Mam we want ice cream and hot dogs for an early snack. Elam and Hannah want us to come down for a late evening cookout."

Beside himself with joy, Levi moved towards the door at a rapid pace. Dat clucked to the mules, and they continued on their way.

Levi told Mam he could chop onions, but then his burning eyes watered so profusely that the streams turned into genuine tears. Then, because he was so terribly hungry, he began sobbing in earnest, howling and crying and saying it wasn't right that no one allowed him something to eat when he was hungry.

Sarah brushed the last of the paint onto the wall beside the door to Levi's room, hid her smile, and brought him a package of dried apricots from the pantry.

Levi roared with indignation.

"Sarah! Now you know I don't eat dried apricots! They look like earlobes. They even feel like the bottom of my ears!"

Sarah laughed and laughed. She hugged Levi with both arms and smeared paint on his best everyday shirt, but he smiled and was glad for Sarah's hug. She brought him a Nutty Bar. Oh, how he loved those Little Debbies from the store!

"Don't tell Mam," Sarah whispered. Levi bowed his head humbly, put his hands under the table, and said, *"Denke, Goot Man, fa my Nutty Bar."*

Sarah told Mam that Levi was getting lost in the shuffle, getting ready for this wedding, but Mam was so hot and so tired, she gave Sarah a look of impatience and told her to go clean her brushes. Why in the world were Elam and Hannah having a cookout on a Wednesday evening when it was ninety degrees, she wondered. And if that Matthew was going to try and worm his way in here again, why, she had a notion to shun him good and proper.

Sarah laughed so hard she had to sit down. She wiped the sweat from her forehead, looked at Mam, and shook her head. "Are you going to be so … well, dumb, from here on?" she asked.

"Go clean your brushes, Sarah," Mam said, but there was a smile twitching at the corners of her mouth.

Mam was still a bit abrasive on the walk to Elam's, saying she didn't know why they wouldn't trim those maple trees. They looked so *schloppich aufangs* (sloppy now).

Dat cast a pitying glance in her direction and caught Sarah's eye. They both looked in opposite directions, their mouths twitching. Planning a wedding was taking its toll on Mam's good nature.

Hannah met them at the door, wearing a soiled purple dress. The sleeves had been whacked off too far above the elbow, revealing pearly white forearms with distinct tan lines below the sleeves. It was just about the most unattractive thing Sarah had seen in a long time. She decided it was just like Hannah to cut the sleeves without measuring, creating results that were less than appropriate. But for her, it was alright, good enough.

When Matthew entered, Sarah caught the scent of his overpriced men's cologne before she actually saw him.

He was dressed in a thin white shirt and spotless clean jeans. He was wearing a pair of sandals with his short hair crisp and wet. Sarah had to look elsewhere, the look in his eyes a remembered temptation.

"Good evening, folks!"

His voice was hearty, confident, full of energy. In spite of herself, Sarah's knees turned weaker as she looked at him.

"Ready to start the grill?"

Hannah immediately lowered her head, rambled on about getting the steaks out of the "stuff," and yanked open the refrigerator door, dumping a square Tupperware container of applesauce all over the floor. Putting both hands to her cheeks, she screeched loud and long about the applesauce, then hastily got down to wipe up the mess. Sarah saw that her dress was so old and faded that where the pleats pulled apart in the back, the dress was two completely different colors.

"What did you marinate them in, Mother?" Matthew asked.

Cool and suave, such a man of the world, Sarah observed.

"Well, Matthew, you said French dressing, didn't you?" she asked over her shoulder, straightening and going to rinse the cloth under the faucet.

Sighing in exasperation, Matthew rolled his eyes, shook his head, and said, "Italian, Mother," with practiced patience.

"Well. I don't have any. We don't eat it. It's not good," Hannah said simply.

"Whatever. We're not going to eat these steaks if you have them in French dressing."

"*Ach* now."

But that was the end of the discussion. There were no steaks.

Matthew grilled hot dogs—they'd all eaten one an hour before—but no one said anything. Hannah's scalloped potatoes were amazing, as always, and her green beans laced deliciously with bacon and cheese.

Levi was in his glory. A Nutty Bar and two hot dogs in one evening was more happiness than he could contain. He became so jovial that he turned into the life of the party.

Matthew genuinely enjoyed Levi's sense of humor and laughed uproariously when Levi described the evening snacks that he hid away from Mam.

Sarah sat in a patio chair under the shade of the huge maple trees and watched Matthew's enjoyment of Levi.

She thought maybe his self-righteousness was already diminishing. He seemed so much more like the Matthew of old, joking, comfortable, at home here on the farm with his parents.

Elam, as usual, had very little to say. He was quiet, a slow smile spreading across his weather-beaten face and a slight twinkle in his dark eyes. His hand was slow to pass the salt or the ketchup, but he was always friendly.

Sarah thought Elam had to be the most mild-mannered man she had ever encountered. He was completely overridden by his condescending wife but was happy to let her be that way.

Elam knew there was nothing he could do to change the situation with Matthew, so he made peace with co-existence. Matthew lived in the farmhouse with them, doing as he pleased. It made life easier to just go along with it.

They drank cold grape juice and ate Moose Tracks ice cream as the sun settled below the horizon and the heat of the day faded with the setting sun. Robins chirped, calling their children to bed and hopping about on the lawn before flying into the fluttering leaves of the maple tree.

Elam's collie, Lassie, romped on the gravel driveway with Suzie. Sarah sipped her juice, her eyes on Matthew. When his eyes met hers, she looked away hurriedly.

As twilight fell softly, the conversation turned to the two men who were responsible for the barn fires. Elam said, in his slow, wise manner, that the absence of the Amish in the courtroom wasn't going to make much difference, that the Walters man's goose was pretty much cooked either way.

Dat observed Elam, a slow smile of understanding spreading across his face. He knew Elam well, had lived beside him most of his life, and understood his pureness of heart. There was no hidden animosity, no hatred. He was only stating a fact. He'd forgive the arsonist his mischief, acknowledge the wrong-doing of Aaron, accept events as the days brought them.

Elam watched his wife shoveling ice cream into her mouth and wondered why she didn't get a headache, eating it that fast. He smiled at her and thought she still was the amazing young woman he'd married. He had a heart of gold.

He never could figure out what had gone wrong that Matthew didn't want to be Amish, but he guessed that was his son's business, and none of his own. Matthew was an adult now.

Tomorrow was another day, another chance to plant his late rye seed, milk his cows, and spray the weeds along the fence. He really should get to trimming those maple trees, they looked so *schloppich aufangs.*

Then Matthew got up, stretched, and asked Sarah if she wanted to go for a walk for old times' sake. Maybe they could go visit the Widow Lydia and see if Melvin was there. Elam watched Sarah's face and thought of Daniel and the lion's den. She'd need the courage of Daniel, that was one thing sure. Hannah choked on her ice cream, and Malinda looked as if a thunderstorm had settled over her head.

Davey caught Elam's eye, calm, unperturbed, trusting. It was all that was necessary.

CHAPTER 17

THE TWILIGHT TURNED SLOWLY INTO A WARM SUM-
mer night as Matthew walked beside Sarah.

He turned to her and said, "Let's not visit Lydia." His
voice was husky, breathless. Sarah stopped and looked
at him.

"Where do you want to go?"

"Anywhere we can be alone."

"Matthew, listen. I am going to be married to Lee. In
two and a half months. I am not going for a walk with
you if you are...."

Embarrassed, her voice trailed off.

"I just need advice, Sarah. You were always a true
friend. How should I go about winning Rose?"

Taking a deep breath, Sarah looked into Matthew's
eyes, those black pools she had gazed into so many times
before, when she was always seeking, hoping, wondering. Now here she stood, back to square one, back to the
beginning when he had chosen to ask Rose for his first
date.

This time, however, there was a difference. Matthew's
dark eyes did nothing for her. Instead, she compared them

to Lee's blue ones and the purity of the love she found in them. He gave her strength, happiness, an objective for life.

Suddenly she blurted out, "You really want to know?"

"Yes, I do."

"Grow up."

Clearly startled, Matthew drew back and stopped walking. They were in the field lane, between fields of freshly mown alfalfa and waving corn. The dust under their feet, like sifted flour, rose up with every footstep, leaving soft puffs.

"What do you mean by that?"

"Exactly what I said."

"Boy, you're being mean to me, Sarah. Just because you're going to marry someone else doesn't mean you can get all high and mighty on me now."

"Rose is my friend. Or was. I seldom see her now, since I'm no longer at market. Lee and I rarely go to the supper crowd. I taught school, you know, until the accident—when I was burned. I planned to teach again, but Lee asked me to marry him, and I accepted. I feel bad for Rosanna, my eighth-grade girl last year. We had been looking forward to teaching together.

"But that's not really answering your question. I think you could win Rose if you chose to be Amish, and if you had a steady, full-time job, and made a commitment to stay at that job for at least a year."

"You think I'm lazy, don't you?"

"No. Yes."

"What does that mean?"

"Yes."

"Sarah, I'm not. I'm just not interested in farming. It's an endless and repetitive thing, over and over and over.

My back isn't good enough to be a roofer, and framing houses is dangerous work. I could landscape, start my own business, but it's too much like farming. I don't have any money saved up either."

Sarah nodded.

"You could always work at McDonald's, flipping burgers, making fries. You always enjoyed cooking. I remember the first barn raising, that whole roaster of French toast you made. It was delicious."

"I bandaged your hand that day." Matthew shook his head ruefully. "I should have taken you when I had the chance."

Sarah saw her life with Matthew. It appeared before her like an empty ship, bobbing on uncontrolled waters. It was impossible to guide and had no destination, no rudder to control it, no way of predicting if it would reach a harbor.

Here was Matthew, twenty-three years old, no job, no money, no goal, no roots. The one single thing in life that he was concerned about was himself. Doing anything he did not want to do was quite out of the question. Every excuse he uttered was rife with the old unwillingness to bend his back and perform the duties expected of him, the one true source of every man's happiness.

At the end of the day, a man or woman who had worked, performing physical labor of some kind, was tired, content. The sun had risen and shone on their labors. When it set, they rested and thanked God for their sound bodies and their blessings.

Paychecks at the end of the week were distributed, used for mortgage payments, utilities, food, clothes, and if there was anything left over, small luxuries. For almost every family, there were sacrifices to make, giving up things they could not afford, learning to live frugally, the sacrifices no big thing.

Matthew had no paycheck. Where was his money coming from? Sarah knew Hannah would try and keep Matthew with them, eagerly handing him cash whenever he required it. Her love for him provided the monetary funds, and what did she receive in return? No respect, none of her feelings taken into consideration. Poor, misguided Hannah.

Without a doubt, she felt superior to Elam. He was too quiet, didn't do his *dale* (share). Why would he even try when he knew any attempt at reining in Matthew would be met by the unyielding brick wall named Hannah?

So they existed peacefully together, but so far out of God's order. They lacked that priceless, perfectly structured family with God at the head, then Elam, and then Hannah in her place below them, the white covering on her head an outward symbol of subjection to God and her husband.

Brought back to earth by the cloying scent of Matthew's extravagant cologne, Sarah shifted her weight on first one foot, then the other, her hands clasped firmly in front of her.

Softly, Matthew spoke again.

"Aren't you going to answer?"

"There wasn't a question."

"No, I guess not."

Matthew gazed out across the dry fields of Lancaster County, his expression unreadable. Sarah looked at him, this man handsome enough to be a model in a worldly fashion magazine, and felt the familiar tug at her heart.

"I should never have broken up with you."

A sadness seemed to erase the evening's light, a

melancholy fog settling over them, wrapping them both in the stillness of a mournful remembering.

"But you did."

Suddenly, Matthew grasped Sarah's shoulders, his breath coming thick and fast.

"Sarah, you're just marrying Lee to forget me. It's not going to work. After you're married, you'll wake up and discover you don't even like him. Your future will look long and unhappy, and it will be too late. You know you love me."

Shrugging her shoulders, she stepped away from him.

"Matthew, listen. I love Lee Glick, not you. I told you that before, but you're not giving it up. You don't want me. I am like the carrot dangling from a stick in front of the proverbial donkey. The only reason you think you love me now is because you can't have me. I think there's another old story about the fox that leaped endlessly after a cluster of delicious-looking grapes. After he finally did manage to get them, they were sour, and he spat them out and knew he'd wasted his time for nothing."

"Sarah, stop comparing yourself to carrots and grapes."

"A carrot. Not carrots."

They laughed together, their sense of humor fine-tuned over the years.

It was dark now, their closeness turning into an intimacy. How many evenings had they shared, just like this?

"Sarah, let's sit down, shall we?" Matthew's voice was husky with feeling. "I want to tell you a few things before you marry Lee, okay?"

Realizing the slippery slope she would be descending, Sarah found a soft clump of grass a safe distance away from him. Matthew folded himself close to her. She shrank away from him and the warm, beguiling sensation of nearness.

"I always liked you. Even in ninth grade, I liked you, the way a fourteen-year-old boy does. It was my mother's fault that I asked Rose Zook that first time. She had a fit about what a nice girl Rose was. Then Rose broke up with me, but by then I couldn't have you. It was Mother's fault. She messed up my life, not me.

"And I'll tell you another thing. It's my father's fault that I don't have a job. Everything I did at home was wrong. I could never please him. Mother used to pity me so much."

His martyrdom wrapped securely around him, he rambled on, but Sarah was not listening. She was thinking of Lee, her beloved man. Yes, man. He was a man, so grown up, always thinking of Anna and her "littles," of Omar and the Widow Lydia's plight. He was so busy caring, nurturing, loving others, she doubted whether he ever had a minute to think of himself. And if he did, she thought— oh, if he did!—he would fill that time loving her.

She was the blessed recipient of the love of a man that was so fine and so good, she was sure she did not deserve him, not even for a minute. All his life, Lee would work, till the soil the way his brother-in-law had. They would prosper, endure life's trials, rejoice in the blessings, working side by side, the way their Swiss ancestors had. And then their children after them, and their children after them, on and on, they would hand down the treasured tradition of hard work and love of the land, raising generations in the same order.

Silently, humbly, Sarah bowed her head with this knowledge. She was blessed among women, like Elizabeth and Mary and many other women who came after them.

God had granted her the wisdom to make a difference. Blindly, He could have allowed her to marry Matthew.

Why hadn't He? She supposed God was a mystery, and she simply had to hold the goodness of Him to her heart. That was just the way it was.

She sighed.

"Matthew, I don't think it's fair to blame your parents. They did the best they could."

"Who then?"

Should she tell him? Her heart thudding, she said, "Try blaming yourself, Matthew."

"Myself?"

He was completely bewildered, at loss.

"You make your own choices, Matthew. You are an adult now. You chose to leave the Amish way of life. You chose Rose. You chose Hephzibah. You chose Haiti. You did. Not your parents."

"But maybe I would have chosen differently, if they had acted differently. Parents are a huge influence on their children's lives."

There was nothing to say to this. The futility of her words, the sheer helplessness of them, struck Sarah as being so sad she could not bear it.

Matthew was comfortably held captive in the grandiose imagining of his own martyred state. He was innocent of any wrongdoing, firmly entrenched in this misguided belief.

Born again, in his own eyes, he was oblivious to the fact that he was reveling in life's greatest trap—that of laying blame on others and being comfortable with it.

By your fruits, ye shall know them, Sarah thought. Matthew would learn and would mature. She just wouldn't be there to take the punches in the process.

Inevitably, someone like Matthew would be sent head-long into fiery trials but delivered by God's hand, so that when he was old, he would be a vessel of God's handiwork.

But Sarah was free. Matthew was God's job, not hers.

They parted as friends. This was made possible only by Sarah's ability to stay quiet and allow Matthew his rants of injustice. He whined about the unfairness of life, and his words fell like rain around them. The sentences started like a soft summer mist, then turned to droplets that came down in earnest, soaking Sarah, leaving her exposed to something she wanted to avoid, but couldn't. She had to give him this evening to unburden himself, she felt. It was all she had to offer.

Bright and early the next morning, Sarah was still enjoying her final cup of coffee. The breakfast table was laden with sticky syrup-covered plates, bits of pancake, and a leftover fried egg congealed on a greasy plate. As Levi was swallowing his vitamins and blood pressure medicine, Hannah burst through the door without knocking, threw herself on a chair, and told Mam a cup of coffee would be *hesslich goot* (awfully good).

Her hair had been freshly plastered to her head, dragged back with a wet, fine-toothed comb. Her round face shone from a washing with the soap she kept at her *vesh bengli* (washbowl).

She eyed the remaining fried egg and cold pancakes and looked at Mam, who nodded and pointed. They knew each other so well, no words were needed.

"*Ach* Malinda, I haven't eaten yet. Matthew often cooks breakfast, but he didn't get in till so late. Then he was restless, walking around, going to get pills. I guess he had a headache."

She turned towards Sarah.

"What happened last night?"

Ducking her head and squeezing the syrup bottle as if her life depended on it, Hannah avoided meeting Sarah's eyes.

Mam choked on a hot mouthful of coffee, got up, and coughed over the sink, wheezing and hacking.

"Malinda, *geb dich an acht* (be careful)," Levi said gravely.

Mam straightened, a hand fluttering to her chest, and smiled. She said she got some hot coffee in her Sunday throat, the way she always said.

"Uh, not much," Sarah answered Hannah.

"Did you talk?"

Hannah inserted a huge forkful of pancake and egg into her mouth. Syrup dripped on her dress but went unnoticed. Sarah watched the gob of stickiness elongate, then drop onto her stomach, where it soaked into the gray fabric.

"Um, yes. Yes, we talked."

"Did he say what's on his mind?"

"Yes."

"So. What's happening then?"

Anger lurched through Sarah. The nerve of her! Assuming that the minute her Matthew wanted her, Sarah would literally leave Lee at the altar and come racing back to him. Knowing she would cause an uncomfortable situation, as she had done before, Sarah opted to keep the fiery retort to herself.

"Probably not much."

"But Sarah, he'd go Amish for you! He said he would!"

Hannah's voice was plaintive, whining, begging.

"Hannah, I am engaged to Lee. He is the one I love. I would never leave him."

What she wanted to say and what actually came out of her mouth were two completely different things, and she spoke in a way that was entirely distinct from the way she felt.

What she wanted to do was to tell Hannah to heave herself off down the road with that syrup all over herself. She would tell her to go let her husband raise that spoiled son of hers (or at least help), and if she had an ounce of insight, she'd remember every painful day Sarah lived through with Matthew's rejection of her.

Delighted with Sarah's deliberate stand, Malinda's face shone with the sheer relief that flooded through her. Immediately, her hospitality increased fourfold. She hovered over her neighbor with the coffee pot and brought the leftover bacon she had put back to use in a salad, placing it at her elbow.

She touched Hannah's shoulder and said, "Hannah, let me make you some toast. I'll heat up these pancakes. You want a few more eggs? It won't take long to fry up a couple."

Levi saw his opportunity and seized it.

"Malinda, if you're going to make more eggs, I could use another one."

Hannah's defeat was not accepted or acknowledged, the grumpiness in her voice holding it at bay.

"I don't know why you let Levi call you Malinda. He should know enough to call you Mam."

She swallowed a mouthful of scalding coffee, grimaced, shook her head, and said now her taste buds were cooked for the day.

"I'm sorry, Hannah," Mam trilled, whirling to the refrigerator, lifting a carton of eggs, and using her foot to close the door behind her. She had basically done a pirouette, Sarah observed, hiding a smile.

Well, that was alright. Let her longsuffering mother enjoy that flashy little dance to close the refrigerator door. Sarah had put her parents through enough as it was. Let her whirl all over the kitchen, her arms held high, her skirts billowing around her, her face lifted in praise to the Creator. She deserved to let her spirits soar.

At that moment, Sarah fully understood the depth of her love for her mother.

Hannah cleaned up her plate, swabbing viciously at the orange yolk with the well-buttered edge of her toast, and shook her head mournfully about Matthew's future.

"What is he supposed to do now, Sarah?"

"I'm sure there are many, many young girls who would be more than pleased to have him. Rose is dating him now, sort of. Maybe they'll get serious, and he'll return for her."

Eyeing the syrup on her dress, which had been joined with egg yolk, Hannah heaved herself from the chair and went to the sink. She yanked a dish rag from the drawer, wet it, and began to steadily clean up the remains of her breakfast.

"But you don't know how it's going with those two. Just like the last time. She's all giddy and happy to begin with, but then, sure enough, something turns her off, and she pouts. Matthew said they ate at the Olive Garden, and it cost them sixty dollars! I'm suspicious that they ordered an alcoholic drink. You know they serve them there. Amish people shouldn't even go in there.

"Well, I guess Matthew would be alright, he's not Amish, but still. Matthew says it's a good place to eat. I said I like McDonald's or Wendy's. It's good food and cheaper. Sixty dollars! Imagine! *Unfashtendich* (nonsense).

"Anyway, he said they were eating, and Rose didn't talk, just turned her head to the side and pouted. Now he's afraid to ask her out to dinner. Matthew says if you're English and classy, you say dinner for supper, and dinner is lunch. I guess breakfast is still breakfast, or what does it mean when they say sunrise service? Maybe that's breakfast."

Malinda coughed, sputtered. She could not meet Sarah's eyes, or they'd each lose their composure.

Innocently, Hannah lowered her eyebrows.

"What is a sunrise service if it isn't breakfast?"

Sarah told her it was an early morning Easter service. Mam's back was conveniently turned.

"Oh, is that so? Well, now that would be touching, *gel* (right)?"

Mam nodded as she turned, and Sarah said, yes, it would. Thankfully, Hannah dropped the subject.

"Well, then, I guess if you're going to marry Lee, you're going to marry Lee. I just have to give up. But *ach my oh*, it would certainly have been nice to see you two together. I think you would have been good with Matthew."

"We could have been, perhaps, Hannah."

When her chin wobbled and fat tears welled up in her eyes, Mam patted her friend's shoulder and asked if she wanted to make the scalloped potatoes for the supper at Sarah's wedding. That seemed to placate Hannah entirely, although she said sadly, "I should be sitting right up there with you, Malinda, side by side, as the parents. And there I'll be making scalloped potatoes with the rest of the church women."

She went on to say how long and hot the day stretched before her, with all the corn she had to do. The whole patch had ripened over the weekend, and here it was Thursday morning and not an ear pulled.

Sighing, she said she'd likely have to cream every ear. Dragging those big yellow ears of corn across the creamer gave her a crick in her neck and made her shoulder blades hurt.

Mam, in her newfound happiness, immediately offered her assistance, along with that of the girls. Levi could help shuck. He loved to sit beneath a tree and shuck sweet corn. All he needed was a brush, a paring knife, and two containers—one for the clean ears and one for the husks.

Hannah was so overwhelmed with gratitude that she told Mam if they helped her, she'd donate all the corn for the wedding. They were planning on having peas for the vegetable, but Mam told Hannah that would be just fine, they'd have corn for supper.

So Hannah let herself out the door, casting a worshipful glance at Mam. They smiled, and then Priscilla told Mam she wasn't going down to Elam's if Matthew was there. Mam raised her eyebrows in question, and Sarah stopped clearing the table, listening.

"Why ever not?" Mam asked.

"Mam, he wrote me a letter! He asked me for a date! I'm only seventeen. Is he crazy?"

Sarah stood stock still, chewing her thumbnail. He was desperate, this was very clear. Is that all his passionate pleas had been? A desperation?

Mam gasped. Suzie looked up and said dryly that Matthew was English. Did she want English?

Sarah washed dishes, tightlipped now, angry thoughts swirling about her head. It was time she spent a weekend with Lee and got away from the upheaval that Matthew always created.

Saying nothing, she left the kitchen, walked across the lawn to the phone shanty, and dialed Anna's number. She left a message, asking Anna to call if she needed help with corn or tomatoes.

That was how Mam and Suzie and Levi found themselves at Elam's, knee deep in corn. Hannah was eternally grateful for their help, and Mam smiled and joked and laughed, that was how light her heart was. She lifted heavy bowls piled high with golden ears of corn, creamed them endlessly, and retained her exuberant spirits.

Hadn't she heard from her daughter's own mouth the stand she had firmly taken, and the right one, no doubt?

Yes, there was a *saya in die uf gevva heit* (blessing in sacrifice). This Malinda firmly believed, as her mother had before her. In matters of the heart, this was best, especially after Sarah's burning and the pain afterward.

Over at Anna's, Sarah and Priscilla picked two wheelbarrow loads and one garden cart full of corn. They shucked it, cooked it in the outdoor cooker, cooled it in huge plastic totes, and cut it off the cob for chicken corn soup. Anna buttered, salted, and ate so many ears of corn that Priscilla said it had to be ten. Or at least nine.

When Lee put the team of Belgians in the barn and came in for lunch, Sarah's heart became all fluttery, followed by a rush of genuine love. There was a sense of caring, a gratitude even, that proved to her, without a trace of uncertainty, that Lee was the real love of her life.

CHAPTER 18

Amish weddings are usually held after the fall communion services, sometimes the last week in October, but mostly in November and December. However, when a widow remarries, the service can be held at any time that is convenient, but preferably not in the hot summer months, because of the possibility of food spoilage.

Secrets are highly esteemed where second marriages are concerned, so in Lydia's typically quiet way, the announcement of the upcoming wedding for her and Melvin was a genuine surprise for many. Sarah figured it would be in the fall, but a September wedding was earlier than even she had thought.

Lydia's parents offered to have the wedding, saying they were not too old at 62. They only asked that not too many guests be invited. Perhaps 200 would be a good number. Perhaps 220, but no more than 230.

Lydia blushed and beamed like a schoolgirl. The children seemed to be as pleased as their mother. The new dresses were brought out and showed proudly to Sarah that Sunday afternoon. Navy blue, plain fabric.

Sarah folded it between her fingers and told Lydia it was very pretty. She admired the black cape and apron that would be pinned neatly on top.

When Lee drove up to Lydia's barn with his black Dutch harness horse, the spokes in the wheels flashing in the September sun, Sarah ran down to meet him.

He climbed out of the buggy, his teeth gleaming white in his tanned face, and reached for her. Hearing the sound of horses' hooves on the gravel, he stepped back politely, his eyes never leaving her face.

It was Melvin, red faced and exuberant, his spirits in high gear, his energy level off the charts, in his own words. No, Melvin was definitely not humble. He was talked about all over Lancaster County and in the sister settlements, and it suited him just fine. He reveled in the happy banter, the teasing, all the attention he garnered.

Well-meaning older men would reverently place their hands on his shoulders, telling him quietly what a *saya* (blessing) he would acquire, becoming a father to those dear fatherless children.

What a Godly thing to do, people said. So unselfish. So generous. He will make a good father. Lydia deserves this. Lord knows she suffered enough with Aaron.

Old Dan Dienner's wife, Leah, said Aaron wasn't all bad. People were just bringing a curse on themselves, talking that way about him after he was dead and buried beside his parents. She knew his mother well, and she was one of the most likable women around.

The Widow Mattie Stoltzfus said, so what, just because his mother was likable didn't make him that way, and Leah gasped and said she better watch it. Mattie didn't sleep very well for awhile, but in her heart, she knew she was right. Leah just tried to sugarcoat everything. That whole family did.

Talk swirled and circled, as these events tend to bring out people's opinions. There was praise from the generous of heart, and caution expressed and trials predicted from the more pessimistic, but all in all, people wished them well.

It didn't make any difference to Melvin what people said. He felt pretty sure he was Lydia's knight, come on a mighty steed to rescue her from her sad existence, and he set about making her happy.

True to his melodramatic fashion, an enormous ornate grandfather clock showed up in Lydia's parents' plain kitchen on the day of the wedding. It was adorned with a huge lime green bow and the largest, most garish card Sarah had ever seen. It was completely out of character in an Amish home. Then two dozen red roses were delivered during the service, the likes of which Sarah had never seen.

Lydia was dressed as neat as a pin, completely flawless, her eyes shining with a glad light that touched Sarah's heart. She was so slender, so youthful in her appearance, especially considering she had an eighteen-year-old son. Melvin sat beside her, his reddish brown hair not quite right, a small section sticking out on back of his head, where he couldn't see. He, however, would never have imagined anything wrong with his own appearance. His white shirt collar was meticulously fitted with a black bow tie, his new *mutza,* vest, and trousers were immaculate, and his new shoes squeaky clean.

The position of his abundant eyebrows spoke of his anxiety, though, and only Sarah knew him well enough to pick up on this. After all, he did have to stand in front of the minister and the crowd and pronounce a *"ya"* at each of the proper times. With hundreds of pairs of eyes on him, it was enough to rattle even the heartiest ego.

The singing rolled in waves across the freshly painted shop, ministers spoke, and everything went as planned, as tradition required.

When it was time to be married, Melvin did a good job, holding Lydia's hand tenderly, steering her to the proper position beside him. He answered at the expected times, in a low well modulated voice, although not necessarily a humble one. Lydia's voice was only a decibel above a whisper, but it sufficiently bound her to Melvin as his wife.

However, when it was time to leave the minister, Melvin turned the wrong way, and Lydia had to turn twice to accommodate his incorrect turn. She did it so gracefully that not everyone noticed.

Melvin knew though, and he blinked at least a dozen times, his eyebrows lifted another quarter of an inch. He sniffed and cleared his throat self-consciously, and then it was over.

Sarah could see the cloak of well-being return and settle across his shoulders, as his status as a married man sunk in.

She also knew if she ever wanted to rile him, she need only mention the fact that he'd made a misstep on his way down from the preacher. She had no intention of doing it, but you never knew when it might come in handy, she decided.

What a theatrical gift opening, Sarah thought. Leave it to Melvin to add drama to everything he did, but her admiration for him resumed as she watched the gentle manner he had with the hesitant Lydia. Melvin was smart enough to know she thought very little of her own ability to handle life, so in spite of his excessive smiles and tears and gesturing, he always thought of her.

Yes, Melvin would, indeed, be a genuine benefactor for his new bride. He would treat her well, as he would treat the children, especially little Aaron, who was his constant favorite.

So it was on that clear September evening that Lee and Sarah rode side by side in Lee's buggy after Melvin and Lydia's wedding. The black horse, Lino, moved along at a brisk pace, his shining mane and tail lifting and flowing as he trotted along.

The air was infused with late afternoon sun, a perfect ending to a golden day. The dust rose from a hayfield, where horses plodded, pulling a baler behind them. They dropped squares of newly baled hay, depositing them at neat intervals along the perimeter of the field.

The heavy cornstalks were turning brown, at least the ones left standing after the silage cutters had gone through, Sarah thought.

Suddenly, she slipped a hand behind Lee's arm.

"Lee! Imagine! I'll have to cook for silo fillers when we're married. I don't know how to make gravy now."

"You'll learn, hopefully. I love gravy. That gravy we had at the wedding today was absolutely unreal."

Sarah burst into laughter.

"You and your description of food! You really do love to eat."

"I do. I take it very seriously."

He grinned at her and placed his hand on hers.

"You better learn to make gravy, Sarah. I can be pretty mean when I'm hungry."

Sarah went to spend the evening with Anna and was surprised to find her scrubbing the front porch. She was using a broom and a hose with a nozzle attached to it, taking on her task with a renewed vigor. The three children were soaking wet, and Marianne's dress clung to her chubby form. Their hair was plastered against their skulls, and water dripped in rivulets down their faces as they ran and splashed across the wet floor of the porch.

Sarah helped Lee unhitch and waited while he checked on the cows. Then she watched as he fed his horse, closed the door of the cabinet where he kept the harnesses, and turned to accompany her to the house.

"My goodness, Anna. What ambition!" Sarah greeted her soon-to-be sister-in-law.

"I was hoping Lee would bring you!" Anna shouted, her face beaming from the confines of her *dichly*, which was tied behind her ears so securely it seemed to pull her eyebrows outward.

Sarah thought of Aunt Jemima on the box of pancake mix. Dear, dear Anna.

Anna shut off the water, coiled the hose on its rack, and swished the broom across the remaining bit of floor. The three children were ushered into the bathroom for soapy baths and their pajamas, before returning to the kitchen.

Lee sprawled on the recliner, picked up *Lancaster Farming*, and was soon engrossed in an article. Anna and Sarah poured tea and cut cheese in neat slices. They put crackers, a plate of Rice Krispy Treats, and a container of chocolate ice cream on a tray to carry to the porch.

"I didn't bake. I hardly have anything in the house to eat. Sorry. Now tell me all about the wedding. Please do."

Leaning in, Anna began eating the cheese. She shook her head, clucked, sighed, and clapped her hand on her breast, as Sarah described the service and meal afterwards.

Finally, Anna sat back and rolled her eyes toward the sky. She clasped her hands across her ample stomach.

"But, you know, Sarah. I don't mean this in a bad way. Lydia's doing pretty good, marrying Melvin. But seriously, he just — you know — turns me off with his crazy ways. Nothing is calm and restful with him. To be honest, my eyebrows go straight up — and so does my blood pressure — the minute I see him. It's like, whoa!" Anna spread her arms, her feet thumping the floor.

Sarah jumped, then burst out laughing, Anna joining in with her.

"So now, you're feeling better, aren't you?"

"I'm getting there. Every day is a challenge, but every day I can rise to it better."

Sarah nodded, understanding. A silence enveloped them in its calm, providing a sense of rest, allowing them both space to contemplate the past and the future.

Finally, Anna spoke, her blue eyes twinkling with humor.

"Just do me a favor, Sarah. Don't let Melvin within a mile of my house for at least a month."

Despite the twinkle, Anna was so sincere, so genuine in her desire for avoidance that Sarah promised solemnly. She tried not to laugh, but it burst through despite her attempts. She and Anna both exploded into whoops and hollers that brought Lee to the door. Anna was wiping her eyes, her face in a grimace that was almost painful to watch, as they gasped for breath, and Sarah emitted a few more ungraceful guffaws.

Lee sat down and watched, laughing just to hear them, chuckling again as Sarah tried to stop.

"Sorry, Lee," Sarah said, placing a hand on his knee.

"It's okay, my love."

Anna's eyebrows shot up, her eyes widened.

"My love? Isn't that a bit much?"

Lee and Sarah shrugged their shoulders, and the three all smiled at each other. As the evening flowed along, they enjoyed the time together. And each was inspired to help the others along the way as they realized the time was swiftly approaching when they would co-exist on this farm.

This home place, Sarah thought. That is truly what it is. My place to call home for the rest of my life with my handsome, kind, and loving Lee.

On the Beiler farm, Mam was trying to grow the celery for the wedding. She was a great traditionalist and remembered her own mother carefully tending to the long rows in her garden, fertilizing, watering, and finally bleaching it — covering everything but the tops with heavy layers of newspaper.

Mam fretted and stewed, worried and watered the stuff. Meanwhile, the heads of cabbage grew enormous, as that robust vegetable required very little care. The carrots were every bit as easy to grow as the cabbage. The tops were thick and heavy, the oblong orange roots below truly huge. They were amazing, for ordinary carrots.

Dat wanted to raise chickens for the wedding, but Mam said, no, they weren't going to put their *roasht leit* (people who make chicken filling) through that. Too many folks were unaccustomed to the fine art of beheading a chicken. Even if the men braved that gruesome act, the women would still need to scald and pluck them, not to mention remove that nauseating coil of, well, chicken guts. If Mam wasn't willing to do it herself, she was not going to make others do it on their behalf.

Dat said too many of these old traditions were being lost. Lots of young couples were no longer able to do their own butchering or smoking of meats. They no longer made cheese or churned butter. All of the old ways were being left behind, and Dat thought it was *shaut* (a shame).

"We still have so much, though," Mam said. "We want to be glad for what we do have. All in all, Sarah won't look much different than I did the day I became your bride, Davey."

Dat nodded.

"Yes, and I have to remember that we men use air-powered tools, milking machines, and generators to run electrical tools. You know, the list goes on and on. Times change, and so do we, very slowly. Change does come."

It was the end of a late summer day. There was still a bit more than two months before the wedding, and tension was building. They had to finish a thorough housecleaning and paint the shop, among many other things.

But for this evening, the time went by slowly. The air was mellow, their moods matching the quiet, peaceful time.

Levi was cracking peanuts, one by one. Suzie grabbed the shelled ones before his heavy fingers could retrieve them. Frustrated, he yelled at her, then drew his heavy arm back and fired a peanut against the side of her head. Suzie giggled and made a face at him.

A rooster crowed somewhere off in the distance. The caw of a crow answered the poorly-timed noise from the rooster.

The train zoomed through Gordonville, sending a rumbling across the fields as it always did. A dog barked. A siren sounded, far away.

"We won't be doing this too much longer, will we?" Mam asked.

"Listen!"

Dat held up a finger. Everyone snapped to attention, their ears fine-tuned to the sounds of wailing from the fire sirens. They faded off into the distance.

"You think we'll ever get over those sounds completely?" Sarah asked.

"Oh, I think so. This will all be a distant memory someday. Our children will talk about it to their children, until it's only a passing thought. The nights of terror, the fear, the rebuilding will all become lukewarm memories, then hardly worth mentioning, then forgotten. And that's as it should be. Why would you want to remember? What good could come of it? It'd certainly be of no help where forgiveness is concerned," Dat answered, his voice soft, relaxed.

Continuing, he told them that some things in life are best forgotten—the evil of fellowmen, the sins of others, the misdeeds of anyone around them, English or Amish, Mennonite or whatever. "But we will always remember the good, won't we?" he said.

His eyes were soft and liquid, bluish green and flecked with gold, like Sarah's. She could have watched the changing colors all evening, when Dat spent precious time with his family.

Levi threw another peanut at Suzie and said he would never be able to forget Suzie stealing his peanuts.

"I work hard to crack these, and she gets them all. It's just horrible."

Levi began to cry, and Suzie cast a guilty look in Dat's direction. She was sent to bed immediately with a stern reprimand.

Priscilla watched her younger sister go, her face soft with empathy. Discipline was a way of life in every Amish household. It was to be respected, especially when Dat doled it out.

Levi sniffed, then bent to his peanut cracking, his glasses wet with tears. Laboriously, he took them off, grasped his shirt tail firmly, and began wiping the heavy lenses methodically. Then he replaced them, sniffed, and went back to his chore.

A figure walked up to the house in the semidarkness. He was unseen until he was almost at the porch.

Dat's head turned swiftly, clearly shaken.

"Omar!"

Relieved, Mam sat back in her chair. Sarah breathed out.

"Hey, Omar!"

"Hi, everyone. Priscilla, want to come for a walk?"

"Sure. I'm barefoot, not cleaned up at all."

"That's okay. Just come on."

Priscilla rose, rushed off the porch, and together they walked down the drive, their faces turned toward each other, talking.

"I never saw anyone who can talk endlessly the way those two can," Mam observed.

"I look forward to the time when we all stop snapping to attention every time someone shows up unexpectedly," Sarah said.

Dat laughed.

"Whether we admit it or not, we're still extremely jumpy. Even with the arsonist in jail, it'll be like this for a while."

"Has anyone heard what's going on?"

"It can take months. Even up to a year or two."

Mam nodded and wondered if any of the Amish would show up at the hearing.

"Probably," Dat answered.

"Who would?" Sarah asked.

"There are always the few disobedient among us," Dat said.

Mam drew her breath in sharply.

"There! Something is out in the rows of celery. It's not a cat. I think it's a rabbit. No wonder my celery isn't doing well."

Grabbing the stiff straw broom, Mam hopped off the porch, moving fast and waving the broom.

Dat yelled the same time that Sarah screamed.

"Mam! No!"

It was a skunk, and a very defensive one. He turned his backside, lifted his tail, and sprayed the garden, Mam's broom, the celery, and everything else within a ten-foot radius.

Levi roared with glee as Mam pivoted and made a stumbling dash for the porch. The evening came to an abrupt halt as they all scrambled to be the first one in the door, laughing and gasping, Levi shouting that he'd seen a skunk, a real one.

Mam took a shower and used her best talcum powder, but Dat said she smelled mildly of skunk all night. He shook with laughter at her indignation. Suzie said that's what they deserved, getting sprayed by a skunk, because they made her go to bed early.

Levi said he had spilled all the shelled peanuts. But the next morning, there was not a single one left on the front porch. He bet that skunk was up on the porch during the night, eating them.

Since the celery now smelled like skunk, Mam finally admitted defeat, much to Sarah's relief. They bought crates of celery the day before the wedding.

CHAPTER 19

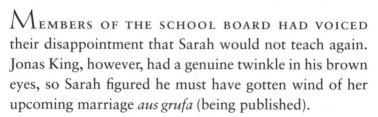

MEMBERS OF THE SCHOOL BOARD HAD VOICED their disappointment that Sarah would not teach again. Jonas King, however, had a genuine twinkle in his brown eyes, so Sarah figured he must have gotten wind of her upcoming marriage *aus grufa* (being published).

It was good to know her efforts had been appreciated by the school board. It was rewarding to understand the ways she had made a difference, for girls like Rosanna and for Joe, all the sullen eighth graders who had become her friends.

Suzie had gone back to school the last week in August, and Priscilla worked several days a week in the bakery at the farmer's market as Sarah had done. Mam and Sarah worked side by side through the busy fall days in anticipation of the approaching wedding season.

The organized, relaxed atmosphere in the quiet house allowed Dat a deep and peaceful nap after dinner. His glasses slid down his nose, and *Die Botschaft* (a weekly Amish newspaper) lay open across his stomach. With his head lolling to one side, he started softly snoring, enjoying a genuine, restorative power nap.

Mam yawned and yawned after dinner, but she always said she had to keep going. They were "making wedding."

Sarah read a few lines of a book and dropped off to a deep, restful snooze. She woke with renewed energy and started in again.

Today, it was pears. Four bushels of the odd-shaped, green fruit were purchased from the fruit peddler at a whopping sum of fifty dollars a bushel. But Mam refused to do without her *beer* (pears). You could not buy the taste of home-canned pears, and that was all there was to it, she said.

Dat nodded vigorously as he wrote the check for the peddler. Yes, indeed. There was no better dessert than a heavy chunk of chocolate cake with rich caramel frosting and home-canned pear juice ladled over it, two succulent halves of pear beside it. Nothing better, not even vanilla cornstarch pudding.

It was the first real disagreement Sarah had with Mam. Pears and peaches were traditionally served at every wedding dinner. The golden yellow peach halves were mixed with the pale pears, and the juices combined. It was wholesome, delicious, and should be served, Mam insisted.

Sarah cringed at the thought of that common, everyday fruit being dumped into Melmac serving dishes and set on the wedding tables. Nowadays, many of her friends did not have fruit. They only served pies, or jello or tapioca dessert, and cookies and doughnuts at their weddings. If they didn't serve fruit, why should she?

Mam was firm, unmoving. She'd never heard of a wedding without home-canned fruit. Sarah told her it would be different if they didn't have to be served in those *koch-shissla* (serving dishes). Why, she, her own mother, would never serve fruit to company in plain old serving dishes like that.

Mam's lips tightened, her eyes narrowed. She said in rigid, clipped sentences that what had been good enough for her was good enough for her daughter. Sarah could either accept it or make it hard for everyone, and then they'd all be miserable just because of fruit.

Grimly, they sorted the pears, discord hanging between them like Plexiglas.

Pears were different than peaches. Peaches were spread on newspapers on the *kesslehaus* floor. Each day they were squeezed gently. The soft ones were chosen, put in large stainless steel bowls, and peeled. They never ripened all at once.

Aunt Lydia King had taught Mam, only a few years before, to leave pears in their bushel baskets and cover the tops and sides with heavy comforters or sleeping bags. Then they would check them each day, and eventually, they'd all ripen at once.

Today, they had all turned yellow, soft to the touch, every one of them, except a few tiny ones that had been picked off the tree way too soon.

They filled their bowls and washed the pears. Then they spread clean towels on their laps to absorb the juice that never failed to drip off their elbows. They took up their paring knives, cut the pears in half, expertly gouged out the centers, and began to peel. The heavy outer skin came away easily. Sarah popped the first peeled pear into her mouth, her senses infused with the perfect, autumnal taste of ripened fruit.

One by one, the pear halves made soft thudding sounds as they hit the bowls, and nothing was said. Sarah coughed. It was forced and unnecessary, but at least it was something. She ate another pear half and glanced sideways at Mam, whose stony features remained unchanged.

Levi shuffled out to the kitchen, helped himself to a pear from Sarah's bowl. He sat down heavily in the chair beside Mam, took a large bite of the fruit, chewed, swallowed, and looked at Mam.

"*Vell*, Malinda."

Mam raised her eyebrows.

"Why aren't you talking?" Levi inquired.

"Oh, we're relaxed, busy with the pears."

He looked into Sarah's face, his small brown eyes cunning, sharp.

"*Bisht base* (Are you angry)?"

Sarah shook her head.

"*Bisht an poosa* (Are you pouting)?"

"Stop it, Levi."

Levi grinned cheekily, turned to Mam, and said Sarah was both angry and pouting.

Eventually, Sarah told Mam it was alright to have peaches and pears if they put them in glass serving dishes. Mam thought that was completely unnecessary, but she did not want to be too set in her ways, so they reached a compromise. Pears and peaches would be served in glass "company" bowls.

As they worked, Levi was allowed to spear the pear halves with a fork and place them—every single one of them—in the wide-mouthed jars.

Mam scooped a half cup of sugar over the pear halves, then added water. She wiped the rim of each jar, placed a lid on top, added a ring, and tightened it. After she had filled fourteen jars, she set them in the heavy, water-filled canner, turned on the burner, and sat down to continue peeling pears.

The pears would cook for fifteen minutes before they were preserved, or cold-packed. Then each jar was wiped clean with soapy water. They would be taken down and set on the shelves in the basement.

They did 102 quarts that day. Levi speared every pear half, and Mam praised him with warm words of affection. He had done well.

Levi said he knew what Davey and Malinda should do with their boy since he had worked so hard. They should take him to the Tastee Freez in Smoketown for a large swirled cone, the kind that had chocolate on one side and vanilla on the other.

Mam said she'd ask Dat, but Sarah watched her mother's shoulders droop with weariness and knew she needed a good long rest, not to have to get dressed up. Mam would never go away without a *halsduch* (cape).

So Dat took Levi and Suzie down to the Tastee Freez with Fred hitched to the buggy. Mam and Sarah stayed behind to clean the kitchen, wash the supper dishes, and sweep the porch.

Mam surveyed the rows of sparkling clean pears, the jars shining, ready to be taken down to the cellar in the morning. She sat, rocking slowly, eyeing the day's work. She knew it had been a day well spent.

Oh, it was a restful thing, going about her work, knowing the family would no longer have to live in fear now that the barn fires were a thing of the past. She thought of the troubled youth, Michael, and her lips began to move as she prayed for the teenager, who was so obviously misled. He had made bad choices, perhaps, but still.

He was always so terribly ill at ease, as jumpy and frightened as a newborn colt. Malinda prayed God would *fer-sark* (care) for his soul, show him the way, the truth, and the light. She wondered if he read the Bible they gave him. She hoped so.

As for that other one, that older man—she forgot his name—he ought to know better, so he should. At his age, to be hanging onto that silly grudge against Aaron Esh, who was no longer even alive, was simply beyond her grasp.

It did serve him right to be sitting in jail, at least for a while. She guessed she should pray for his soul, but she wasn't sure she could just yet, at least not in the right way. Davey was much faster to forgive than she was. Sometimes, it felt pretty good to know that the arsonist was confined to jail. She'd heard the food was nothing to brag about in there.

Ah, yes, they'd all come through it, God be praised.

Well, the wedding was about seven weeks away, but she had enough time to manage things. If Levi stayed healthy, and nothing unforeseen came up, they should have everything in top shape by the end of November.

She lifted her hands, sniffed them, and thought of the skunk spraying her, or very nearly. My goodness, she thought. She could still smell that awful scent and almost feel that choking sensation that had accompanied it. And there went hours of labor, worry, and effort, the celery ruined by that odorous little creature.

Ach, so gates (it goes), she thought.

Upstairs, Sarah had showered, her shampooed hair rolled into a towel. She lowered her right shoulder in front of the full-length mirror, the late evening sun slanting across it.

She bit her lip, and quick tears formed in her eyes, trembled there, and dropped on her cheek for only a second, before sliding off.

It just wasn't good. The skin looked too tightly stretched across her neck and shoulders. It was colored pink or white, depending where the lines zigzagged into each other. It was hideous. There was no getting away from it.

The side of her face was still discolored and uneven, but not like this. This ugliness was shocking.

The truth of her disfigurement hit her, caught her off guard. She couldn't marry Lee this way. She was too revolting. Her heart hammered in her chest, and her breathing became shallow as her eyes widened with fear.

She had to talk to Lee. She had to make him understand that he didn't want her. He would not be happy to live with an imperfect woman, one that was disfigured with a hideous scar all along her side.

Oh, he said he loved her, but he didn't know how bad it was. Perhaps she should show him, to make sure he knew. It would be like purchasing a team of horses. They checked their teeth, their hooves.

Surely somewhere, there had to be a miraculous cure for scars such as these. She had used so many different homemade salves and lotions, burdock leaves, vitamin E capsules, oils, and all sorts of tinctures. Still, the scars remained, imprinted on her body, the mark of the arsonist.

Why me, she thought? Why do I have to carry the map of all the Lancaster County barn fires? Truly, it was like a map with all the rural roads and the ashes of barns that had stood for centuries. Like them, her skin was ruined, destroyed.

Suddenly, she couldn't understand how Dat could be such an advocate for forgiveness. When she saw her body at times like this, she was glad Harold Walters was in jail. Sometimes people had to reap what they sowed. That was all there was to it.

Anger churned through her, and self-pity descended, pushing her into the quick sand of despair.

When Priscilla came home from market, there was a light in Sarah's room, but by the time she got upstairs, Sarah's room had been darkened. It was a clear sign that her sister did not want to talk, so she went to her own room and figured she could wait to hear the local gossip till tomorrow evening.

On Saturday evening, they all loaded into a fifteen-passenger van and traveled to Dauphin County to spend the weekend with the married brothers and their families.

Abner had complained to Dat that he barely knew Lee. How was he expected to take charge of the wedding if he never met this guy?

Sarah laughed when Dat told him, and they made immediate plans to go with Sam's Danny's *freundshaft* (family). They packed their bags, and asked Omar Esh to do chores.

Lee was happy, joking with the men, courteous to Sarah, but only for the first hour of the drive. Sensing Sarah's detached manner, the tense position of her eyebrows, his stomach turned over with the same sickening flip-flop of former days, when Matthew had come around.

No, it couldn't be that. Not now. Not less than two months before their wedding. In spite of trying to reassure himself, he became increasingly skeptical until the evening stretched before him like an unattainable height, a slippery slope of doubt and fear.

They both laid their troubles aside when they arrived at Abner's home, a palatial one that spoke of well-managed finances. The yard was cut to perfection, the garden and flower beds immaculate.

Abner and his wife, Maryann, greeted them warmly, their curiosity shining through their polite smiles of welcome. Their two small children were already in their pajamas, peeping shyly from the folds of their mother's dress.

The evening flew by with board games and delicious food. It was late when they were shown to their rooms, and quiet settled over the house.

Almost as soon as Maryann went back downstairs, there was a soft sound on Sarah's door, a tapping.

"Yes?"

"Come. We'll go for a walk," Lee whispered.

She hadn't undressed, so she said, yes, she'd go. She followed him down the stairway and out the door, closing it softly behind them.

They walked down the drive and turned left onto the road. Lee's hand sought hers, and when he found it, he held it lightly in his own.

The night air was cool but not uncomfortably so. There was a woods, fields. Beyond them was the dark indigo color of the mountain. Overhead shone stars and a crescent moon, the same ones shining above Lancaster County.

Here, though, the houses were far apart, the farms dotting the countryside across much wider spaces. It was a younger settlement and smaller, but the ways and lifestyles were much the same.

Lee stopped. "Can we find someplace to talk?"

His voice was strained, the words short and almost clipped, lacking his usual warmth. Lee was terribly afraid, desperately sick at heart, but there was no use trying to avoid Sarah's pitiful attempt at covering up her feelings, so he plunged ahead.

"Here. We may as well sit on this little hill. There's a lot of soft grass."

He led her to a comfortable spot, then sank down beside her. She could feel the moisture forming on the grass, the dew that would be sparkling by morning. Her skirt felt damp already.

Headlights approached, the tires of the car making a dull whooshing sound as it passed by, the lights stabbing into the darkness as it continued on its way.

"What's wrong, Sarah?"

"Why? Nothing. Nothing's wrong."

"Don't lie."

"Lee! What do you mean? I seriously do not understand."

"You're not being your usual carefree self."

"Of course I am."

She couldn't speak to him now. Courage failed her.

"It's Matthew, right?"

"What?"

"Matthew. I know it's him. Our relationship has always ended like this before. You're just in too deep this time. It's okay, Sarah, if you can't go ahead with the wedding. I mean, it's not okay, but I won't make it hard for you. If you want to be set free, just say it. Don't marry me if your heart belongs to Matthew."

His voice was choked now, a near sob in his throat. In the darkness of the night, Sarah could plainly see the outline of his head, dropped low on his chest, a picture of abject misery.

She took her time, pondered her words.

"It's not Matthew."

His sharp intake of breath almost scared her.

"What else? What single thing on earth can make you feel so far away from me? Sarah, I do not want you to become my wife if you cannot love me. I've been selfish, inconsiderate, demanding. But I think I honestly love you so much that I want only your happiness. If I have to give you up for you to find true happiness, I will. It won't be easy, but I'll do it. For you."

Sarah had never been bold, certainly not with Lee, but now there was only one thing to do. Words were inadequate. Slowly, her hands gripped his arms, went around his shoulders. She lifted her face to his, found his lips, and conveyed her deepest feelings with the touch of her mouth to his.

The night became magical. The stars seemed to applaud and cast bright little sparkles all over them. The moon fairly skipped and whirled, before settling back into place with a happy sigh.

The Creator made this wonder, the love of a man for a woman. He created the ties that bind them until death parts the union ordained from the beginning.

She whispered, then, her deepest fears to him, and Lee listened in total disbelief.

Shocked, he shook his head, over and over.

"Sarah, you don't understand," he choked. "When I say I love you, that means you, exactly the way you are."

She broke in, quickly, desperately.

"No. But you don't know how bad it is. I panic, Lee. I look at my shoulder, and it's so hideous. You can't know how bad it really is. It will disgust you."

"But Sarah. That has nothing to do with love. If a man truly loves a woman, he accepts her just the way she is. Her size, her looks, what she wears, scars, whatever — it's all insignificant."

"Lee, I simply can't believe that."

A moment passed, as Lee pondered her response.

"I guess I'll just have to tell you that after we're married.

Maybe then you'll be convinced. Look at my sister Anna. She's not every man's ideal of the perfect woman, but to Ben, she was. He deeply loved every pound of her."

Sarah took a deep breath, inhaling all the happiness she could hold, greedily grasping it.

"You see, Sarah, I can't look at your scars now. But I imagine what they look like. And I've told you before. For me, they represent God's will for our lives. And if you really do love me, and...."

He broke off as a deep rumbling laugh emerged, and he said, "I really think you do, Sarah, and I almost can't contain my happiness."

"I do. Matthew is just simply no longer there for me. I can talk to him, and everything's changed. He has begged me twice now to marry him. Can you imagine?"

Lee shook his head. She heard a deep breath as he jumped up from the hill. Suddenly, she was lifted to her feet in a crushing embrace. Then he held her tenderly, for so long, time was forgotten, until another pair of headlights appeared behind them. They sank back on the grass, giggling like schoolchildren as the car rumbled past, its headlights slicing through the night.

Sarah slept a deep and restful sleep, blinking awake to find brilliant sunlight shining through the sheer burgundy panels. The curtains made the whole room cozy. It was like wearing rose-colored glasses. Well, her world was not just viewed through those glasses. It was rose-colored without them.

She stretched, smiled to herself, and flung her arm across the pillow beside her, imagining being married to Lee, waking with her husband beside her, in his rightful place.

What had he said? Was that really how it was?

She thought of Anna's wide back, the ample legs, the rounded arms, her full stomach. Yes, she probably weighed more than 200 pounds, but to be with her, her weight was not what counted. Her pretty face, her neat hair, and her white, always ironed covering along with the energy, the quick smiles, and ready sense of humor— that's what made up the whole aura that was Anna. And her off-the-wall humor as well.

Sarah grinned and looked around at her brother Abner's wife's guest room with the neat bed and dresser, handmade, no doubt, but burgundy curtains? Pink artificial roses in cut glass vases?

A plastic cat stared at her from a pink doily, and two red roses protruded from a pink ceramic urn. My goodness.

She sat up and pulled the quilt up to examine it. She saw it was a Lone Star pattern done in brilliant red, white, and pink.

On the floor, lying on a decidedly magenta rug, were two pink crocheted accent pillows that had tumbled off the bed. Definitely rose-colored—her whole world, literally.

Maryann cooked them a huge breakfast with many different dishes to taste. And each one was delicious.

Abner made waffles, perfect ones, which Lee raved about. He wrote down the name of the heavy cast iron waffle maker, followed by instructions, step by step. He folded the paper and gave it to Sarah, saying that was one of the things that was a requirement for their marriage.

They sat around the breakfast table with second and third cups of coffee, talking comfortably, like old friends. In fact, it was as if they'd always known each other. Abner even tried to persuade Lee to buy a farm in Dauphin County.

"Look at what your place is worth!" he finished.

That was the moment when Sarah saw Lee's genuine humble attitude.

"Nah. Not more than this beautiful home."

He continued, saying Abner must have a special talent, the way this house was built. He diverted all attention away from himself, focusing on Abner instead. Sarah knew full well the farm Lee had purchased was worth three or four times the amount of this home, but Abner was very happy to accept Lee's praise.

Again, she reminded herself that she was not worthy of Lee.

Back home, Anna burst into tears the minute they walked into the house. She laid her head on the table and cried so heartbrokenly, they both rushed to comfort her. Sarah rubbed her back, Lee patted her shoulder. Then they made her a cup of tea and talked far into the night.

Her buddies, the married couples that she and Ben had run around with, had all visited. She knew they meant well, but the awful ache of missing Ben had only intensified as the day wore on.

She mopped up her tears and blew her nose, honking loud and long, then started shaking her head.

Omar had brought Priscilla to do the chores. Anna had watched them with so much longing. She could see the intensity of their attraction, the easy way they could talk about any subject. They were simply so cute.

"Don't ever go to Dauphin County again," she concluded. "I can't handle it. You have to realize you have a dependent, fat, widowed sister who is going to be the biggest pain in your lives."

Sarah could only hug her soft, lonely body.

CHAPTER 20

AND THEN, WHEN EVERYONE HAD FINALLY
relaxed, glad to be free from the fear of another barn
burning, the fire sirens wailed from every direction. The
undulating, deafening whistles rose and dropped off, only
to have another, sharper one pierce the air.

Windows were closed that night, warding off the
fall's chill. The call came towards dawn, when the bright
October moon hung low in the sky. The same sickening,
quaking feeling rudely roused slumbering households.
Men stumbled around in the dark, shouting questions
that made no sense.

Voss in die velt (What in the world)? Had they let him
out of jail?

Half of them didn't even know his name.

Old Danny Dienner said to his wife, "*Grund da lieva*
(grounds of love), Mam!"

She said it *was* grounds for love. Somebody was going
to have to come up with some forgiveness again, if that
man was out of jail and back to his *umleidlich* ways.

"*Unleidlich* (mischievous)," Danny corrected her, but
she was bent over, searching under the couch for her

slippers. She was holding a flashlight that was barely usable, the batteries were so low, and she didn't hear what he said.

Sure enough, another barn was on fire.

Now what?

In stunned disbelief, families huddled on couches in the early morning hours, little ones wrapped in blankets, their eyes huge and dark in their faces. School-aged children cried like babies, imagining the devil himself breaking out of jail and lighting every barn in Lancaster County.

No one was safe. Locks on door were laughable. Someone was out there and would certainly come to get them. They quoted little German prayers, climbed up on their fathers' laps. Surely Dat would not let "the man" get them.

But where was the fire?

Men dressed hastily, held goose pimply vigils in phone shanties and unheated shops. The disobedient who owned cell phones talked plenty. Word spread rapidly, crackling through the air. The fire was close to the Vintage Sale Stables, at Aaron Zook's.

Ach, poor man. Poor family. But relief also flowed like a healing wind, a veritable chinook of comfort.

Aaron had been out at 3:30, helping a cow with a difficult birth. He saw he really needed a veterinarian's assistance, so he left his naptha gas lantern on the hay-strewn walkway and ran to the phone shanty. He had forgotten the LED flashlight, so he got it from the *kesslehaus*, and called Dr. Simms. He smelled the smoke the minute he opened the door and remembered the lantern.

Evidently, one of the barn cats had been chasing a mouse or another cat—who could tell? The lantern was knocked over, the mantles broke, and the little jets of blue flame continued to spurt out, igniting the hay. The gas leaked out, the flames roaring to life in seconds.

Aaron had tried bravely to beat out the flames with plastic feed sacks, but he saw he was only worsening a dire situation. He ran for the hose from the milk house, saw it was futile, and started loosening cows before he remembered to dial 911.

Poor Aaron, everyone said. He always had a struggle, scrambling to meet each monthly mortgage payment on his small farm. His crops were always a bit inferior, his thin mules working the fields until they all but collapsed. The animal rights people had turned him in once. He had borrowed money to pay his fine and then humbly paid it all back in weekly twenty-dollar installments. But he continued to feed the same poor quality hay and meager amounts of grain to his mules.

His wife, Nancy, was small and thin. She was a hard worker, who had faithfully borne her husband nine children, so far. Nancy never blamed Aaron for the overturned lantern. She never blamed him for anything. He was the head of the house. It was her duty to respect him, and respect him she did. He did the best he could. *Die guava sinn net gleich* (Talents are not alike), she said.

She kept her old farmhouse shining, scrubbed the cracked linoleum with Spic and Span, washed the old glass windows with cotton sheets and vinegar water. She washed countless loads of laundry in her old wringer washer, hung it all on her wheel line. She grew an enormous garden and canned well over a thousand quarts of vegetables and fruits each year.

She cried when the barn burned. She held her children to her thin breast and let the tears flow. When the neighbors came to stand with Aaron and watch the jets of water from the fire trucks hit the leaping, dancing flames, which were fanned by an unhandy October wind, her tears kept flowing.

When her mother and father came, they had to leave the horse in the neighbors' driveway, because so many fire trucks were parked all over the driveway. Nancy stopped crying, and no one ever saw her shed another tear, as far as the barn was concerned.

Perhaps relief that this fire wasn't arson brought the great outpouring of love. Whatever the reason, the response was overwhelming.

The family couldn't handle all the food. Some of it was given to the poor people at the homeless shelter in the city of Lancaster. A man came with a white minivan and loaded canned goods and pies and cakes and noodles and potatoes into cardboard boxes and drove off with them.

So many men showed up on the first day of the barn raising, they took turns working. The frame of the barn was up, ready for metal roofing, in approximately six hours.

The Lancaster paper ran an article titled, "Practice Makes Perfect." It said that with all the recent barn fires, there was a new expertise and better management at barn raisings than before, which was probably true.

Sarah was serving coffee again. It seemed unreal to be at another barn raising, after everyone thought the whole nightmare was over. But here they were, the same black, stinking, smoking piles shoved into a field. There were piles of the same yellow lumber with that sharp odor of freshly sawed wood. The trucks came and went, the sound of iron tracks clashing and rumbling as dozers cleared the remaining debris, even as the new barn took shape.

Hungrily, Sarah bit into a filled doughnut. She grabbed a napkin when the filling squished out each side of her mouth. The 10X sugar rained on her black sweater, creating a mess that the napkin was completely worthless to remove.

Anna rushed over, her eyes wide. "Seriously! Did you taste these?" She held out a raisin-filled cookie, the sugary top held high by a generous mound of creamy raisin filling.

Rose Zook—this Aaron was her uncle—came up to the two of them. She squealed and hugged them, praised their sweaters, their coverings, and ooh, where did you get that doughnut?

Sarah enjoyed Rose's antics as usual, hoping she'd quiet down long enough for her to ask a few questions about her own life.

When Lee came for his coffee, Sarah smiled at him, reveling in the security of having Lee, being engaged. She caught Rose's eye and looked away.

They did get some time to be together, peeling potatoes, before others arrived.

Everything was great, Rose said. Single was the way to go. She had the chance to manage the restaurant at the farmer's market, so that was her latest thing. She was a regular career girl, she said, giggling at her own audacity.

"So!" she said pertly. "You're getting married, Sarah. Tell me the truth. Does it even seem real?"

They shared feelings, just like old times, laughing, talking fast, remembering times with Lee and Matthew, the insanity of it all, Rose said.

She didn't know if she wanted Matthew. He was so English, so ungrounded, like a dandelion seed, just floating along with no direction.

"But Rose, think about it. The restaurant at the farmer's market! Perhaps Matthew just never found his calling."

"Yes, he did!" Rose snorted. "He's next to God."

"But he's doing better. Lots of young people, who come to the light and understand God's love, become a bit carried away. I don't think he's as airheaded, or whatever you call it. Why don't you see if Matthew could cook at the restaurant? I still think he would be okay once he found his niche."

"I can't stand his smarmy ways."

"If he'd cook at a busy restaurant, his smarminess might disappear. You'd have the old Matthew back pretty fast."

Rose tilted her head to laugh, and Sarah admired the porcelain doll prettiness of her friend all over again.

Yes, they'd make the perfect couple.

"Why don't you ask him?"

"Maybe I will."

Rose threw a large, peeled potato into the container of cold water, splashing Sarah's sleeve. They were joined by more women, who greeted them, but neither Rose nor Sarah had any idea who they were, so they gave up their paring knives and went back to check on the coffee.

At home that evening, they sat around the kitchen table, reviewing the day. Dat was in a pensive mood, remembering conversations with the members of the Amish church, men raised in the same culture, the same *ordnung,* and way of life.

He could only conclude that in the vast realm of God's earth, human nature didn't vary a whole lot. All goodness was a gift from the Father of Lights, exactly the way the Bible said.

Dat said Ammon's Amos's Eli thought all the barn fires were an act of God, whether they were caused by an arsonist or a lantern. Mam's eyebrows shot up, but she nodded, saying she could see his point.

They discussed Nancy's old house, the torn flooring and rattling old windows, and how nice it would be to help them remodel.

Mam shook her head. She said, No, Nancy is happy that way. She keeps that old house spotless, makes do. The children are clean and happy as larks. That home is blessed, she said. And if Aaron is a bit of an *aylent* (slow one), so what? That family is happy.

Dat nodded his agreement. Levi said he was happy, but he'd be a lot happier if he was allowed a *blooney brote* (bologna on bread).

Dat looked at the clock, then raised his eyebrows at Mam.

"What about a piece of fruit, Levi?" she asked.

"Alright."

Obediently, he ate his apple, slice after slice, chewing methodically, his glasses bouncing up and down slightly, jarred by the movement of his cheeks, his bright eyes intense as he concentrated.

Levi loved his food, easily weighing 240 pounds now. But he was having difficulty breathing. He coughed relentlessly even in the summer. He would soon turn thirty-three years old, so the family knew they would not have Levi much longer, since his heart was weakened as much as some eighty-year-olds.

Dat's reasoning was to let Levi enjoy the foods that made him happy. Dat would have allowed the homemade bread and the slab of homemade bologna, but Mam maintained her vigilance with Levi's diet.

Their sleep that night was deep and restful, relief being the comfort in their dreams. No, another arsonist was not starting fires. It had been an accident this time. And so they slept.

About 10:30, Levi's bed creaked loudly. He stopped, held his breath, listened. Slowly, stealthily, he rolled over, swung his legs over the edge, found the wooden step stool, and lowered his great body to the floor, shoving his feet into his slippers.

Three steps and he was at his oak chest of drawers, pulling slowly at the drawer pulls. One hand crept inside, but he froze when a loud crackling escaped.

Eventually he managed to ease a bag of potato chips up through the opening, carrying them carefully between one heavy thumb and forefinger. He laid them on his bed and kicked his slippers off. Pushing the potato chips aside, he crawled into bed.

Opening the bag, he thrust a hand inside, clutched about four potato chips, and stuffed them into his mouth, chewing rapidly. These chips were delicious. They were a very good kind of potato chip. Because he couldn't read, he remembered the colors on the bag—red, white, and blue.

Humming contentedly, he lay on his side, munching the greasy, salty chips, waves of happiness accompanying the steady, unrestricted supply. Potato chips were his favorite.

He slowed his chewing to savor them, then stopped. He heard something. It was a roaring sound, a dull, distant rumbling. He heard the leaves rustling in the maple tree, heard the wind pick up, bending the branches, and went back to eating potato chips. It was only the wind, and he was used to those sounds.

The bag was starting to feel weightless now, and he had to put his hand farther inside to find another handful.

Without warning, a brilliant, bluish-white light ripped through the room, followed instantly by a loud clap of thunder. Levi's eyes flew open, and a great shout of fear tore from him. He forgot the chips, and the fact that he was not supposed to be eating them, as he squeezed his eyes shut and called for Mam.

"Fire! Fire!" Levi shouted.

Mam appeared almost instantly, her face white with shock.

"Levi! Hush! Hush! What fire? There's no fire."

The flashlight in her hand was trained directly on the potato chip bag. The beam moved to the crumbs and then the salt and grease on his heavy cheeks. All she said was, "You're probably thirsty, Levi." She said it in a dry, tightlipped way that Levi recognized very well, and he knew poached eggs and dry toast would be his breakfast.

Dat called from the bedroom door, and Mam told him Levi was fine. She got him a drink of cold water and made him get out of bed while she cleaned it, but she didn't say a word.

"They should not allow flashlights," he said. "*Sie sinn aus die ordnung* (They are out of the *ordnung*)."

Mam's face stayed tight, her features buttoned into place by her anger at Levi's disobedience. But when she crawled back into bed, she began to laugh so hard the whole bed shook, and Dat rolled over and asked what in the world was wrong with her.

She gave up and let out a long guffaw. It was ungraceful, especially coming from the normally composed Mam. Between gasps, she told Dat what Levi had said, producing the same response in him.

As the lightning ripped across the sky and the thunder bellowed and crashed, Dat and Mam lay in bed and laughed long and hard at their erring son.

How they loved him! How many hours of pure delight had he brought into their lives? Indeed, the shock and sadness of having a baby born with Down syndrome had been great, but in the end, he had brought them much more happiness than they had ever dared to hope.

Dat reached for Mam's hand, squeezed it, and said, "Goodnight, Malinda."

They both fell asleep with smiles on their faces, as the thunder and the lightning roared above them. The rain beat against the house, filled the spouting, and sloshed out over the edge.

Levi burped quietly, said, *"Mude bin ich* (I'm tired),*"* and fell into a restless sleep, his stomach busily digesting all the carbohydrates, salt, and fat from the chips.

In the morning, the whole farm looked freshly washed. The grass shone with the wetness that clung to each blade, and the chrysanthemums burst into shades of red, yellow, and gold. The pumpkins in the garden were growing an inch every day, especially boosted along by the two inches of rain the thunderstorm had brought.

Sarah was in the milk house, banging milker parts against the stainless steel tubs, her curly hair creeping out beneath her *dichly* as she worked vigorously.

The sun cast a golden shaft of light through the steam. Her heart answered the sunbeam, a gladness she could not explain suffusing her entire being.

Thank you, God, for everything. Thank you for all You have given me. Because of You, I can feel joy again, feel Your love around me.

She spun on her heel and plunked the heavy milker on the rack to drip dry. She pulled the plug in the sink, grabbed the broom hanging on its rack on the wall, and swept the floor of the milk house thoroughly before heading to the house for breakfast.

She stopped to peer at the rain gauge mounted on the post by the bird feeder. Two inches. A little more. No wonder the rain had woken her.

Well, maybe they wouldn't be canning pumpkin after all. They'd sink to their ankles, carrying those cumbersome things out of the muddy garden. But knowing Mam's dosage of wedding preparation adrenaline, she'd probably find a way to get them off the vine.

Mam showed no sign of stress, however, standing by the stove flipping golden squares of cornmeal mush. The sizzling increased each time she flipped a slice, but she stood back, away from the small spits of hot vegetable oil. The kitchen smelled heavenly, the air permeated with the crisp, golden flavor of the fried mush.

Levi sat in a kitchen chair close to the gas stove, making toast. He had learned to set a timer for three minutes, then open the bottom broiler drawer to check the slices. If the bread was not toasted to his specifications, he'd slam the drawer shut and set the timer for one more minute, before placing the toast carefully on a small plate.

This morning, however, he was scowling, his eyes hooded, his glasses sliding far down on his nose. The timer was nowhere to be seen.

Mam laid down the spatula, sighed, and let out a mighty, long, drawn-out yawn. She tapped her mouth with four fingers and said, "Shoo."

Levi sat glumly, staring at the broiler.

Mam wiped her eyes and sniffed the air.

"Levi, your toast."

Slowly, Levi pulled open the broiler drawer and glanced at Mam. He opened his mouth, then closed it again. He took up six slices of blackened toast, burning his fingers and shaking them against his knee, and silently stacked the slices on the small plate.

Getting to his feet, he shuffled to his place at the table, his face set in stone, completely silent.

Dat appeared at the *kesslehaus* door, looked at Mam, and smiled a good morning at her, before taking his place at the head of the table. Priscilla and Suzie both slouched into their chairs, yawning, rubbing their eyes. They smiled sparingly at Dat's resounding, "Sleepyheads!"

Levi didn't give his usual response.

"Two inches of rain."

Dat's comment was met by a mere nod from Mam, as the silence clung to the room.

Sarah cracked eggs onto the two-burner griddle and turned the gas heat on low. She propped a closed fist on her hip as she leaned against the counter, watching the eggs sizzle and waiting till the whites lost their gelatinous look so they could be flipped successfully.

Mam scooped the sizzling slices of cornmeal mush onto a platter topped by two folded paper towels.

Levi swallowed.

Mam poured scalding hot milk into the Melmac serving dish containing saltine crackers. Then she set the fried mush platter on top to steam the stewed crackers.

Levi watched with grief-stricken eyes, then swallowed again. He bent his head low when they put "patties down." The family paused for a time of silent prayer, and Levi's mouth moved as he prayed fervently.

Dat lifted his head first, then Mam, followed by the girls. Levi was last. With a deep sigh of resignation, he folded his thick hands across his protruding stomach.

Mam helped herself to a fried egg and passed the platter to Dat, who had served himself four slices of fried mush.

When the platters reached Levi, he passed them on without putting anything on his plate. Sarah looked at him.

"Aren't you hungry?"

"Yes."

"Then why aren't you eating?"

"I'm not allowed."

"You're not?"

Priscilla stopped salting her fried egg and looked questioningly at her brother.

He shook his head sorrowfully.

"Why?"

"*Die Malinda iss base* (angry)."

Mam was totally caught off guard. A mouthful of hot mush came flying out as she choked and sputtered, her shoulders shaking as she laughed heartily.

The crow's feet at the corner of Dat's eyes deepened and spread outward as he watched his wife, but he did not laugh, seeing Levi's cheerless countenance. The girls smiled, waiting for Mam's response.

Wiping her eyes, then her mouth carefully, she dabbed at the tablecloth, shaking her head.

"Tell them, Levi. Tell them what you did."

"*Ich farich ich grick schlake* (I'm afraid I'll be spanked)."

Dat's eyes danced and twinkled, greenish pinwheels of merriment.

"What? What did you do?" Suzie asked.

"*Hop chips gessa* (Ate chips)."

Dat and Mam burst into peals of laughter, remembering the night before. Their laughter was as infectious as a yawn, and the girls joined in, not understanding completely what had occurred.

Still Levi did not smile. He admonished them all in firm tones about the boys who had mocked the prophet in the Bible. A bear came out of the woods and ate them, which set everyone into fresh gales of mirth.

"No, Levi, we are not making fun of you. It was just funny, the way you said Mam was angry," Dat said quietly.

Hope was rekindled, and Levi met his father's twinkling eyes.

"If Malinda isn't angry, can I have mush and eggs?"

"Yes, Levi, you may," Mam said, still smiling.

Sighing happily, Levi tucked into his breakfast. He polished off a wide wedge of fresh shoofly and told Dat that he imagined this family had *der saya* (a blessing).

CHAPTER 21

THE RAIN DID NOT DETER THE PUMPKIN CANNING.
Sarah took off her shoes and socks and stepped into the
garden in her bare feet. The cold, clammy earth sucked
at them, hindering her steps.

Cold chills crept up her back, but she slogged on, bent
over, and snapped off the first of the ripe pumpkins. They
were dull golden neck pumpkins, shaped like oversized
gourds in varying U shapes.

They were heavy, slippery, splattered with bits of wet
earth. Their weight caused grunts of effort, as Sarah staggered from the pumpkin patch to the sturdy cart parked
at the edge of the garden.

Mam stayed in the house to give Levi a haircut—after
she had shampooed his hair. That was a job he usually did
himself, but not always to Mam's specifications.

Back and forth Sarah went, her feet numb with the
cold. Grimly, she bit down on her lower lip, determined
to get every last one of these pumpkins out of the cold,
muddy garden.

A pickup truck drove up the driveway and stopped
near the house. The passenger door opened, and a man

got out. He stood watching Sarah as she staggered along with the heavy pumpkins in the garden.

She dumped two of the awkward vegetables into the cart, then turned when she noticed someone approaching.

"Lee!"

A glad smile crossed her features, a light came into her eyes.

"What are you doing in your bare feet?" he asked.

"Can't you see?"

"In your bare feet?"

"It was that or have my shoes sink to the ankles."

"Sarah, our wedding isn't very far away. What if you got sick?"

"Oh, I'd get over it in a week, hopefully."

He looked deeply into her eyes, smiled, and asked if she could accompany him to the outlet stores in Rockvale Square sometime this week. She blushed, unexplainably embarrassed.

Yes, she could go, but her heart raced, thinking of the fine china, the tableware, the stemware—all the beautiful dishes he would be required to buy. Because of tradition or out of love, either way, he'd do it.

"Perhaps I'd better stay here now, help with these pumpkins."

"No, no. We'll get them done. You know you don't have time."

"Not really. We're starting on Anna's addition today."

Again, Sarah's heartbeat increased. Her mouth went dry. She smiled a wobbly smile, her cheeks heating up again.

Lee looked down at his bride to be, the unruly curls springing from her white headscarf. She was wearing an old, torn sweatshirt, but her cheeks were rosy with health, the scars on the side of her face noticeable, but better. A mere discoloration, a constant reminder of God's hand leading them together.

He stepped forward.

"I love you so much, Sarah."

Her eyelashes swept her cheeks, as her eyes fell shyly.

"I love you, too," she whispered.

He reached out and tucked a stray curl behind her ear, straightened her headscarf, and said, "See you Wednesday night?"

She nodded and let her eyes find his, the message between them a complete story of love, anticipation, and joy.

The hard work of peeling pumpkins was definitely energized after seeing Lee. Sarah tackled the wearisome task with renewed vigor.

Pumpkin pies for the wedding dinner. She knew better than to try to argue against Mam's reasoning about pumpkin. All canned, store-bought pumpkin was inferior, even the best brand. The taste of home-canned neck pumpkin could not be replaced.

Sarah knew Mam's pies were a creamy testimony to her theory, so she gripped the knife handle and sliced through the heavy, unyielding skin of the pumpkin, her mind churning with possibilities.

Why Rockvale Square? It was such a worldly, expensive place.

She was afraid Lee could not afford fine china. She had heard that Steven Stoltzfus gave his girlfriend Lenox china and paid close to a thousand dollars for service for sixteen. Oh, my goodness.

Well, Lee would never. He bought the farm and was building an addition. She'd be happy with serviceable stoneware or dishes from an Amish store. That price was bordering on sin. One thousand dollars.

"Mam," she blurted out.

Mam was at the sink, cutting the pumpkin into sizable chunks, filling a giant twenty-quart pot. She was preparing to set it on the stove to cook the pumpkin to a mashing consistency.

"What?"

"Lee wants me to go to Rockvale Square with him. That means expensive china. What should I do?"

Mam set the stainless steel pot on the stove with a clatter, turned, and asked Sarah what she meant.

Sarah thought expensive china would be a sin. Not really a sin, but sort of wrong.

Mam smiled a secretive, indulging smile, as if she meant to stay humble but couldn't quite carry it off.

"*My oh*, Sarah," she said. "Well. I guess if he wants to buy expensive china, that's his business. And, no, it's not wrong. How much do you think our ancestors paid for their china from England? It wasn't cheap. Not at all. I guess in the Amish heritage, dishes are cherished by the women. We don't have other things, like diamond rings or bracelets, whatever it is English men give their friends, their girlfriends. So, no, if he wants to give you fine china, that's his choice. Remember your great grandmother's? That pink and white?"

She pointed to the hutch cupboard, where the antique dishes resided with the more inexpensive set Dat had given her.

Sarah nodded.

Yes, she knew what Mam was saying. In each culture, there are cherished objects handed down from generation to generation, treasures of the past. Dishes were valued. They were taken carefully from cupboards made by Amish craftsmen to be used on special occasions and then washed and replaced with absolute care, these china dishes used by *de alte* (the old ones).

Sarah was relieved. She didn't need to worry about shopping with Lee. She and Mam then discussed the colors Sarah had chosen for her table, the corner table. The bride and groom would be seated on either side with the four attendants—two on each side—beside them.

Sarah had chosen white. All white. Her dress was blue, her cape and apron were white organdy, so that would be very different, unique, a touch of class. Sarah smiled at the thought.

She would need to wait, though, to plan the details until after she had the china.

Her hands were getting tired, her fingers stiff, refusing to slice through the thinnest skin, so she laid down her knife and washed her hands at the sink. She had to use a scrubbing brush as the pumpkin left a sticky, wax-like film on her hands. Cucumbers did the same thing, only that was lime green and this was yellowish.

She turned the burner on beneath the pot of coffee left out from breakfast and went to the pantry to look for a snack. Popcorn, oatmeal, noodles, flour, sugar, chocolate chips, baking cocoa, rice.

She lifted the aluminum foil that was covering a pie and found half of a peach pie covered with fuzzy, green mold. She set it on the counter. She'd allow Mam the pleasure of discovering that one for herself.

Sarah snapped open the lid of a Tupperware container and found a half dozen chocolate chip cookies. She squeezed one, and it broke into crumbs immediately. Hard as a rock. Taking the container, she set it on the counter beside the moldy peach pie.

Returning to the pantry, her gaze skimmed across the shelves. Peanut butter, honey, olive oil, grape jelly, graham crackers, saltines. Suddenly, she wanted a bowl of puppy slop—that mushy, milky dish from her childhood.

Taking the graham crackers, she broke five of them in half, placed them in a cereal bowl, and added milk. With a spoon, she broke the crackers into smaller pieces, soaking them well in the cold, creamy milk.

Mam smiled at her, watching her enjoy the dish.

"Nothing like puppy slop," Sarah grinned through a mouthful.

"I have a big notion to have some, too," Mam remarked.

"Who gave it that disgusting name?"

"If I remember correctly, it was Abner that started it. He was five or six years old."

Sarah nodded.

"You think that will turn into a tradition, too? Will my children also call it puppy slop?"

Mam nodded happily, her mouth closing over a large spoonful.

On Wednesday evening, Sarah dressed carefully, pinning her black belt apron with precision, settling it comfortably around her waist. The green of her dress matched her eyes perfectly, the black sweater around her shoulders carrying the black of her apron.

At Rockvale Square, Lee asked the driver to park close to the Lenox place. Sarah felt the color leaving her face. When he opened the door for her, she cast him a wild-eyed look, which he answered with a wink.

Two hours later, she was the stunned recipient of a large set of the most beautiful china dishes she had ever imagined.

It was white all over, except for a slightly off-white spray of wheat, or a fern, she wasn't sure, splayed along the right side. It was as if an artist had drawn it there, impulsively, as an afterthought.

She murmured about the price, which she wasn't sure about, and Lee would not reveal.

The knives, forks, and spoons to match it were so beautiful, she had to catch her breath. They chose a pitcher, clear crystal, and a dozen water glasses, a set of stemware, two white tablecloths, and cloth napkins.

Such a dizzying variety, but Sarah knew her mind, completely stealing Lee's admiration yet again for the quick decisions she made. She obviously knew what her tastes were and never wavered, once she saw what she wanted.

The evening flew by like a dream, albeit a real one that never faded away. At home, the dishes were taken from the box, admired, and fussed over. Then they were put away to be taken out the day before the wedding, when the *eck-leit* (corner people), the couples whose job it was to serve the bride and groom, would wash and prepare all the dishes needed for that special day.

Steadily, through the remainder of October and into November, the work continued. And on the weekends, Mam and Dat attended different communion services in neighboring districts.

The silos had been filled, and long, round snakes of white plastic covered the excess silage layered behind the barn. Fourth-cutting alfalfa was already in the haymow. The garden was cultivated, and a good cover crop sowed for the winter.

The cabbage remained undisturbed like squat, round little sentries, standing guard all alone after the celery was cultivated into the ground, including the newspapers that had been used to "bleach" it. Mam said she was glad to see the celery cultivated under, her failure now well hidden.

Melvin and Lydia came one Saturday to help paint the shop. Melvin had a fit that they were using rollers and not a sprayer.

If anything, marriage had only increased his chattiness. The expounding of his viewpoints reached new heights, the smiling Lydia swelling his already well-developed self-worth.

He eyed the good quality rollers, the metal pans, and gallons of white paint with a certain condescending weariness, resignation setting in as Lydia said rollers were fine. They didn't need to do the ceiling, she added, and this would be fun, working together with Lee and Sarah, the soon-to-be newlyweds.

She pronounced newlyweds as two separate words, putting grins of pure happiness on Sarah and Lee's faces. Melvin's face softened to a state of high emotion, his bushy eyebrows went straight up, and his nose became red as he began to speak in a most holy manner.

"You just have no idea what God has for you. I never thought I would be so happy on this earth. I mean, I was happy before, or I thought I was, but I wasn't. I lived for myself. Now I live for Lydia and the children."

On and on, Melvin spoke of his exalted position as stepfather, reveling in the assumption that he was counted as one of the best that ever held this position of such honor.

Lee opened the paint, stirred it with the wooden stirrer,

dumped it into the metal pan, and began to spread it on the drywall. His grin was lopsided, listening to Melvin.

Sarah couldn't hold it against her cousin. He was so obviously just being Melvin, genuine and sincere in his own belief in his abilities. She knew he wasn't blatantly blowing his own horn. He was just telling Lee and Sarah something he thought they needed to know. That was how harmless he was.

Lydia had acquired a bit of spirit as well. She chattered like a busy magpie, her roller moving steadily across the vast shop walls as she talked.

She had to make new trousers for Melvin. He had already gained ten or eleven pounds, and he said it was her cooking.

She made the best fried chicken and meat loaf he had ever tasted. And her chocolate cake with peanut butter icing was unbelievable. Who would eat salad and apples if she cooked like that? Lydia beamed and dimpled, smiled and talked, until Sarah was completely in awe.

What a transformation! Remembering the sad, thin, cowering Lydia of old, Sarah felt the quick sting of tears in her eyes.

She could still see her the night the original barn had burned. That night she stood there, too thin, her face immovable, showing no emotion. Her feelings were hidden away, where they festered, damaging the thin hold on the emotional health she had left.

Her faith had been trampled as her first husband's harsh words had torn at her. She truly believed she had been what he chose to call her. Miserable, hate-filled man that he was. But he was gone, and he had had a chance to repent. The judgment of his soul was God's duty and none of theirs, the way they had been taught.

So there was a positive thing. Good had come out of evil. Sarah became Lydia's friend, introduced Melvin, and here they were.

It was an intricate design, this web of life. The good came with the evil. It just had to be sifted through, and the priceless lessons kept, while the rest was discarded.

"Where's your dat?" Melvin asked suddenly.

"He went to a farm auction."

"He just wanted to get out of painting these shop walls."

"I doubt it."

"No. I was teasing. He's a good uncle. Good guy."

Again, Melvin went off on an emotional bluster, exalting the many merits of Davey Beiler. He lectured on forgiveness then, reminding them all that in the end, Davey was right. Even if that Walters guy sat in jail for a hundred years, they still, in their hearts, needed to forgive.

Leaning against a door post, his elbow propping up his now slightly fuller frame, he informed them that they didn't have to go further than the Lord's Prayer to know about forgiving.

"You know, guys, it doesn't say how someone trespasses against you—if he walks across your property or burns your barn or shoots someone you know. We're still supposed to forgive."

"That's requiring the superhuman, right there," Lee broke in, stopping to adjust his roller handle.

"Oh, absolutely. But Lee, how can we be forgiven if we don't forgive? We can't."

Lee nodded, went back to work.

They discussed Michael Lanvin, who seemed to be doing alright. He was a work driver for Sam Fisher in Leola. Sam said he was punctual, always on time, no matter what. Michael now had an apartment in Leola, above the laundromat. He had just gotten in with the wrong bunch before, and Ashley had known all along what was going on, poor girl.

Sarah nodded.

"It's over now. May that pitiful girl rest in peace. She was in an awfully hard place, between that violent Harold Walters and her boyfriend, Michael, who was under his influence as well."

"Did the trial ever come up?"

"Oh, I think so. Surely."

They became aware of another presence in their midst. One by one, they turned to see Matthew Stoltzfus standing in the doorway.

"Hey."

He said it quietly, with reserve.

"What's going on, Matthew?"

Effusive as ever, Melvin hurried over and shook his hand, pumping vigorously.

"It's been awhile. Sorry about your wife's passing."

Melvin rambled on, asking questions about Haiti, his church, his future plans.

Sarah cringed when Matthew's words became short, clipped, the questions answered halfheartedly or not at all.

"So," Matthew said finally. "Preparing the wedding chapel."

Lee had his back turned, rolling the paint furiously. He didn't stop or bother answering. Sarah became ill at ease, hurriedly acknowledging his words with a quick smile, a nod of her head.

That subject sputtered and died at take-off, so Matthew found an old folding chair and dropped onto it, stretching his legs and crossing his feet at the ankles, hooking his thumbs into the belt loops on his jeans.

"Go ahead, keep working. I don't want to hold you up."

"You're not," Melvin assured him.

They all continued with the job at hand, but with a note of discord, a certain tenseness making them do unsettling things. Sarah tripped over the metal pan, spilling paint on the newspaper, and some of it soaked into the concrete. Lee broke the broom handle that was screwed into the roller, and Lydia hurried off to find another one.

Matthew then informed them that Rose had asked him to be a cook at the restaurant where she worked. He was duly congratulated and went on his way, a smile of satisfaction on his lips, a new purpose to his step.

Lee watched him go and glanced at Sarah, but he said nothing.

Melvin began barking immediately, like an excited dachshund.

"Did you ever hear anything more perfect? He always liked to cook. He always wanted Rose. He'll be cooking with Rose!"

Slapping his knee at his own hilarity, Melvin went to fill his roller, chuckling to himself.

Straightening, he had to say what was on his mind and burst out, "I'm so glad that guy is out of the way. He used to irk me so bad. I could hardly stand how he treated you, Sarah."

Lee didn't answer. He just kept painting. Sarah watched the rise and fall of his wide shoulders, the blond hair above them, and she was filled with gratitude, and so much more.

Carefully, she laid down her roller, walked over to

Lee, and slipped an arm around his narrow waist. On her tiptoes, she whispered in his ear, telling him of her love. Then she gently kissed his cheek, blushing to the roots of her hair.

Melvin blinked back genuine tears and could find no words to enhance the moment. Lee propped his roller along the wall and gave Sarah a look that could only be described as worshipful as he pulled her into a quick embrace.

They ordered pizza and sat in Dat's office to eat. They took a whole pepperoni pizza to the house for Levi and Suzie, and Levi was clearly beside himself at this wonderful opportunity. Mam wasn't even at home, so if he ate four or five slices, nobody would know, except Suzie, and she'd never tell.

Lydia finished her first slice of pizza and reached for another, shaking her head in wonder.

"You know, there was a time in my life when I didn't have enough money to buy five pounds of flour. Not even enough to make this pizza crust. And here I am, wolfing down pizza delivered to our—I mean, your—door."

"Oh, Lydia!" Melvin cried. "My dear wife! My darling girl!"

Gladly, Lydia accepted the unrestrained endearments, smiling at her exuberant husband. She ate three slices of the good, hot pizza and said it didn't seem right, being so blessed. That sent Melvin into an account of the day he met her, that very first time when she stood in her kitchen surrounded by all those women, her heart so burdened, her situation so dire. Through the dark valleys we walk through, he said, we become blessed.

Lee chimed in then, telling a bit about his own life, which hardly had any dark valleys, except for Sarah's tendency to leave him for Matthew. Lydia reassured him. She said he lived a life of unselfishness, always giving his time and energy to others. Trials were often withheld from people such as him, she told him.

He shook his head, humbled, but Sarah knew Lydia's statement was true.

A contentment, a unifying silence floated among them like golden fog. It comforted them with the knowledge that they had come through so much and had been blessed just as much.

"Look at us," Melvin chortled, "We'll still be friends fifty years from now, old and fat, sitting together drinking peppermint tea. Or, no—what is it old people drink?"

"Ovaltine?" Lydia asked quietly.

"That's it!" Melvin shouted. "Ovaltine!"

"We'll know every Nature's Sunshine product from A to Z," Lee said dryly.

Melvin slapped his knee and reached for his sixth slice of pizza.

CHAPTER 22

THE DAY BEFORE THE *RISHT DAG* (DAY TO PREPARE before the wedding), Levi came down with a terrible sore throat. His hacking cough tore through him, and his fever rose steadily, requiring all Mam's resources. She mixed a poultice of steamed onions and salt, plastered it on his chest, and tied a heavy white cloth around it. She almost drenched him with a dark, bitter brew of black tea laced with Southern Comfort whiskey. She put his feet in lukewarm water containing vinegar and red pepper, then massaged them with quick, sure strokes of her thumbs and fingers.

In between *fer-sarking* Levi, she barked orders. She sent Priscilla for the groceries she had planned to buy herself, wrote a list of jobs for Sarah, and did what had to be done for Levi, saying she didn't know how long they would have him. She would do what she could for him while he was here.

The weather was surprisingly mild, for the first week in December. The forecast in the daily paper predicted moderate temperatures with plenty of sunshine. It looked like at least the weather would cooperate for the big wedding day.

All through November, they had attended weddings. Lee was not always able to stay the whole time. He had his herd of cows to tend, the addition for Anna to build, and the fall work to finish up. He never complained and was always cheerfully on time to escort Sarah to yet another wedding. But by the time November came to a close, he appeared tired with a weary look around his eyes.

That was when Sarah decided to spend a weekend with her sisters Anna Mae and Ruthie, leaving Lee to a long, restful weekend of much needed sleep and plenty of Anna's calorie-laden snacks.

Now, on this day before the *risht dag*, the memories of the weekend with her sisters kept her smiling as she went about her duties.

They had been seated around Ruthie's kitchen table until four o'clock in the morning, drinking coffee and Pepsi. They made unhealthy buttered popcorn loaded with salt and sour cream and onion powder and Brewer's yeast. That strange but delicious mixture gave the popcorn such a unique flavor.

Anna Mae told Sarah in advance that they were preparing her for marriage with words of well-seasoned wisdom coming from them—women of substance, wives of experience. If she listened to them, she couldn't go wrong.

They weren't very far into the evening before her sisters decided Lee wasn't normal.

"You mean, he never says no?" Ruthie shrieked.

"I wouldn't know when."

"He never gets angry? Not even when he's stressed? Snappy?" Anna Mae asked in disbelief.

"I have never seen him that way."

Sarah's eyes narrowed, contemplating what to say next. Should she tell them?

"Okay, listen. Once Lee told me that if he knew I would be happier with Matthew, he'd let me go. My happiness is all that matters to him."

Ruthie placed both hands over her face and said she couldn't stand it. It was too sweet. Then she began sobbing hysterically, her shoulders heaving. She snorted, got up for a Kleenex, and said that was the single most unselfish thing she'd ever heard of. They decided then, for sure, that Lee wasn't normal.

Usually only sisters enjoy the bond they shared that night. They talked of their deepest fears, their greatest joys. They discussed life—all of it. They cried, they shrieked with hilarity, and then spoke in hushed tones of reverence, as the subjects changed.

Anna Mae gave Sarah a book to read about love and marriage with something about respect in the title. Sarah thanked her wholeheartedly and said even though she knew Lee was extraordinary, she was sure they would have their times. Everyone did. Simply everyone.

Ruthie added some extra salt to her popcorn and poured a handful into her open mouth. She nodded and chewed vigorously, before repeating the maneuver all over again. She wiped her mouth, chugged away at her Pepsi, and burped quietly. Then she opened her mouth and belched unrestrainedly, her eyes opening wide with surprise, her nose turning red as tears formed in her eyes.

"You are excused," Anna Mae said, sending a baleful glace at her.

Ignoring the stab at her lack of etiquette, Ruthie leaned forward and wiped her mouth with the sleeve of her housecoat. It was a ratty old blue thing she had had when she was a young girl at home.

"Hey, but you know what?"

Sarah was picking unpopped kernels of corn from the bottom of her bowl, crunching them between her teeth.

"Would you stop that?" Ruthie asked.

"Pure fiber."

"Salt and grease."

"Remember what Mam used to say? You'll get appendicitis. One of those kernels will get stuck in your appendix."

"That's an old wives' tale."

"Huh-uh. No, it's not."

"Hey, be quiet. I was going to say something," Ruthie paused. "Oh, I know. Love is never perfect. I wish it was, but it isn't. That wonderful, good looking, amazing guy we fall so in love with will eventually become the same person who sprawls on your new couch with feet that smell like road kill, snoring away, while you are feeding the baby with a whining toddler at your knee. Meanwhile you have a pile of unwashed dishes and a flabby stomach, and the best way you can think of to express your love is a quick thump on the head with a baseball bat."

Ruthie howled with glee at her own description.

"He'll be the same man that invites his parents for supper and forgets to tell you until Sunday morning, when you have a good book stashed away—one that you finally, finally planned on reading that day. And his mother is so *piffich* (meticulous), and you gave your Friday cleaning a lick and a promise...."

"You mean you licked the floor and promised it you'd scrub it next week?" Anna Mae broke in, and they all burst into peals of laughter again.

"Then they arrive, and right away she says, '*My oh,* looks like I should send Rhoda to help in the garden.' You know exactly why she says it. You know the garden is not pristine, mostly because it was too hot, and you plain down didn't feel like weeding it."

Ruthie sighed. "And you know, Rhoda goes tearing through that garden, thrashing around with my hand cultivator. Not one vegetable is safe. She doesn't want to be there, so she plows through in double quick time so she can go home again."

"Sounds like marriage!" Anna Mae trilled, shaking her head from side to side.

"Lee wouldn't do either one of those things," Sarah said stoutly.

"Oh, but he will!" Ruthie sang out.

"He surely will!" Anna Mae chimed in.

Sarah laughed and looked at the clock.

"I have plenty of advice to last me for a long time. It's past one o'clock, and I'm going to bed now. I'm tired. There is still work at home to get ready for my wedding, you know."

Her sisters would hear nothing of it. They still planned on making soft pretzels.

Sarah groaned as Anna Mae leaped to her feet and began throwing yeast, salt, and water into a bowl. But the sisters talked and joked while they baked the pretzels and savored their salty goodness. There was not much sleep for any of them that night.

The weather was perfect, for December, on Sarah's *risht dag*. The air was nippy, but so clear you could see all the surrounding farms etched against the green of fall rye crops, the dark brown of bare trees in stark relief against the colorful backdrop.

Mam had been up since three o'clock, when she could bake her own pumpkin pies with no interference or well-meaning advice from sisters or mothers-in-law. Mam knew what she was about when it came to pumpkin pies.

For one thing, the egg whites had to be beaten until stiff peaks formed and stood up to a point, all by themselves. They couldn't be folded over in the least bit, the way they had when Davey's mother did them for Ruthie's wedding. She could still feel the dismay that came over her, sitting at the special table with the close relatives, when she cut into the pumpkin pie that had not met her standards. A thin telltale line of *bree* (juice) had formed around the crust, spoiling it and making it soggy.

She remembered the quick stab of irritation, though she had quenched it just as quickly, the smile on her face folding for a mere second before being put back into place.

She had seen it. Those peaks had not been stiff. They had folded over easily. Plus Davey's mother had taken the pies out of the oven a few minutes too soon. Yes, she had. Malinda had seen the centers jiggle. Centers of baked pumpkin pies do not jiggle. She had told her mother-in-law that, but she was snapped off with quick tones of reassurance. The tops were golden brown, and she didn't want dark tops on pumpkin pies for a wedding.

Well, Malinda knew what she wanted, but Davey's mother wouldn't listen, so it was up and out of bed at three o'clock for these wedding pies.

She giggled a bit, a quiet burst of mirth. She felt very much like the little pig that got up especially early and beat it to the apple orchard before the cunning fox appeared. No one was going to bake these pies but her.

And another thing, the oven had been about twenty-five degrees too hot when Davey's mother made them for Ruthie's wedding. That was why the tops would have been too brown. But you couldn't tell Davey's mother one thing, so here she was. Well, no use spoiling this *risht dag* with thoughts like that. She'd just make her own pump-kin pies. That was all.

So at five o'clock, when the first couple, Sam Kings, arrived, Malinda had just put the first of the pumpkin pies into the oven. She wiped her hands on her apron and turned to greet Mary, the energetic, very large woman who entered her kitchen.

"Malinda."

"Mary. Good morning."

Mary's kindly brown eyes sparkled from her smooth, tanned face like wet acorns. Her cheeks were puffed up and smiling.

"*Ach* Malinda, I'm just going to come over there and hug you."

This she did, wrapping Mam into a pillowed embrace. Then she stepped back and said with tears sparkling from her dark eyes, "Such a blessed day. Oh, I felt so much joy as we drove in the lane. I told Sam, these people have been through so much. It gives me goose bumps to think of the blessings pouring out on you now. God has truly brought you through."

"Oh my, yes!" Mam answered, her own tears reflected in Mary's.

"This is a special day. I can feel it in the air. The new barn standing there as if nothing bad has ever happened and was never going to again."

Mam nodded, smiled.

"Well, I came to make *roasht* (chicken filling). I guess everything is ready for us out in the shop?"

"Oh, yes. If you need anything, just give us a holler."

Mary nodded, eyed the pumpkin pies, and shook her head as she voiced her admiration. No one made better pumpkin pies than Malinda.

Smiling her acceptance of Mary's praise, Mam said, "Well, now."

Sarah awoke a bit after five o'clock, long before her alarm went off. Then she lay in bed for only a minute, embracing the day's wonders. This day, the *risht dag*, was every bride's anticipated day of joyous preparation for the actual wedding day.

She dressed carefully in a bittersweet-colored dress, a black bib apron, a clean, fairly new covering. Her eyes shone back at her from the bathroom mirror as she applied the concealing lotion on her scars. She turned her head to assess them carefully, willing herself not to panic.

He'd said it was okay. She had to accept that. She ran down the stairs, finding Mam bristling with tension, leveling the top of a pie crust before crimping the edges. Her huge bowls of pumpkin pie filling stood ready, and the smell coming from the oven announced that pies were already baking.

Mam stopped, smiled at Sarah, and said, "Good morning, Sarah," but her face was flushed, her eyes puffy from lack of sleep. Her hair wasn't combed quite right, her large white covering was a bit off center, and she had one shoe lace dragging from her sturdy black shoes.

"Good morning, Mam. What time did you get up?"

"Three."

"What's wrong with you?"

"Davey's mother, Mommy Beiler, is what's wrong with me. Remember Ruthie's wedding? The pumpkin pies?"

Sarah poured a mug of good, hot coffee from the pot, splashed a dollop of creamer into it, and sipped appreciatively as Mam recounted step by step what she considered the failed pies. Sarah hadn't remembered that there was anything wrong with them, but there was no use saying this to Mam now.

Sarah wouldn't give her mother a hug this morning either. It would be the same as hugging a porcupine, with her quills of irritation and tension sticking out all over. A lot of weight lay on Mam's shoulders this morning.

"Sarah, when you've finished your coffee, you should go check to see if the celery was placed in the washhouse. Just make sure it's there. There's not very much laundry, but wash what's in the hampers. And Sarah, you better hurry. It's later than I like it to be. Oh, and don't forget, the rinse tubs Dat brought in? Be sure and scrub them well, with a splash of Clorox before Lee comes to wash the celery. I'd sure feel bad if the taste of Downy fabric softener was in the celery."

Sarah nodded, set down the mug of coffee, and ran back up the stairs for the hamper of dirty clothes. She was bent over the rinse water at six o'clock, when she felt two strong hands on her shoulders.

Lee. Her bridegroom.

She turned and went straight into his arms, placing her own snugly around his waist. The closeness of him was a homecoming, a place she felt loved, secure, safe.

"Good morning, my lovely girl," he murmured against her hair.

"Good morning, Lee," she answered, her arms tightening momentarily.

They stood together by the washing machine, sharing this moment of closeness before the rush of the day.

Neither of them heard Mary King open the door and peer inside, looking for a plastic bucket. Her brilliant brown eyes lit up at the sight of them in an embrace of true love. Her eyes filled with tears, her shoulders shook with emotion, and she snorted a few watery sobs outside the door as she felt another set of chills across her heavy arms.

She bit down on her lips and got control of herself, reaching under her black apron for a handkerchief. She honked loudly into it, sniffed, replaced it, and went back out to the shop to make *roasht* without the plastic bucket. She'd tell them she couldn't find it. They didn't have to know what she'd seen. It was too precious.

The job of washing celery was to be done by the bride and groom, along with the four people who would be their attendants, their *nava sitza* (beside sitters).

Priscilla would be seated with Omar, Lydia's son, who was closer to Lee than anyone else. He was like a brother and was chosen to be in the bridal party because of that. Priscilla radiated high excitement, being chosen to *nava sitz* with Omar. It was a long-awaited event, a wonderful duty in her life, being Sarah's sister. She was chosen by tradition but felt extra fortunate to be allowed to sit beside Omar.

A cousin of Lee's, Marvin Stoltzfus, would be seated with Rose Zook, Sarah's special friend. To her knowledge, they had never met, but, hopefully, it would work with them being seated together at the bridal table for one day.

Lee and Sarah broke the celery into individual stalks, washing them well with cold water, and stacking them into large plastic dishpans. The full pans were whisked away by happy aunts and sisters. Ruthie and Anna Mae descended on them, furiously animated into whirling dervishes of excitement, teasing, and laughter. They splashed Sarah with cold water, batting their eyelashes at Lee and acting like twelve-year-olds who had a crush on him.

The *risht dag* was something, wasn't it?

The kitchen was alive with happy chatter, punctuated with peals of laughter. Mam's sister Emma was cooking "cornstarch," a creamy vanilla pudding cherished by the Amish.

Mam acknowledged Emma's skills at making cornstarch. She just had a way of producing the creamiest pudding, not too thick and not too thin.

The celery chopping began as the two grandmothers seated themselves at one end of the extended kitchen table, wooden cutting boards in front of them, paring knives flashing as they sliced and chopped their way through the mountain of celery. They talked quietly, their shoulders periodically shaking softly with laughter.

They needed three sixteen-quart kettles full.

"*Unfashtendich, vee feel leit henta* (Nonsense, how many people are invited)?" Emma asked, adding that there would be way too much celery.

Mam informed her tersely that a few more than four hundred were invited, but they wouldn't all show up.

Emma turned her back and stirred her cornstarch pudding. She thought that Malinda was as crazy as ever when she planned a wedding, but she'd better keep her mouth shut. Well, three sixteen-quart kettles of *tzellrich* (celery) was too much. She didn't care if four hundred people showed up or not. She'd be canning celery till January.

Two of Malinda's brothers came in to cut celery, since the grandmothers weren't doing the job fast enough. The *roasht leit* needed celery out in the shop. They promptly sat down and cut in double quick time, and Aunt Barbara joined them. The brothers began a heated discussion about politics, voicing their conservative Republican views. They predicted doom and gloom, citing the ineptitude of the president, and the two grandmothers nodded in agreement.

Barbara, however, became stone silent, her lips compressed, listening to her brothers. They thought she'd brought outright sin into her life, arguing with them before and leaning much too far towards the Democratic view of things. She only upset other members of the family when she voiced the left wing's opinion. Her own husband had shunned her for a few days for being the rebel she was. She was politically incorrect, everyone thought.

So she'd learned to be quiet, being a woman and Amish and therefore subject to her husband and men in general. It was all, in her opinion, a lot like in Iraq, or wherever it was that they wore those burqas, the long, loose coverings with just little screens to see out. The only difference was Henner never beat her, the way those men did—some of them, anyway.

When Grandma Beiler became tired of the political blather, she quoted Scripture, saying all rulers were ordained by God, even if we don't understand it. Barbara began to smile again, even if it was only halfheartedly.

Anna Mae and Ruthie, along with two of their brothers' wives, were *eck leit* (corner people), meaning they would serve the bride's table. It was a high honor, one with prestige on a day when they were trying to achieve perfection.

One corner of the shop was partitioned off and filled with tables and chairs. It was decorated with Sarah's colors—mostly white with little accents of blue—and the fabulous china, silverware, and stemware were brought out. Everything was fancy and elegant, for this was a wedding, even though there were no candles or flowers on the bridal table as neither were allowed in the *ordnung*.

Sarah was not allowed to see anything the *eck leit* prepared. It was all a surprise for her after the ceremony.

Carpet was unrolled across the cement floor of the shop and duct taped at the edges, ensuring a smooth floor for the many guests and servers. Propane heaters purred from corners, doing their best to heat the chilly shop, as doors continually opened and closed. The bench wagons were emptied of their contents, as the men set up tables along every wall and a long one through the middle. They marked them with pieces of freezer tape and placed corners of duct tape on the carpet, ensuring they would be arranged in the same way after the ceremony on the following day.

There was lots of banter and well wishing as the whole shop transformed into a place lit with warmth and high anticipation. This was the *risht dag,* as exciting as the wedding day itself.

The tables remained until after lunch was eaten. It was a sort of trial run for the wedding day. The lunch was provided by two helpful ladies from Davey's church district. At precisely 11:30, they delivered lasagna, creamed peas, and a lettuce salad with cake and fruit salad for dessert.

Lee and Sarah sat at the head of the long table, as tradition required, flanked on either side by their parents.

After lunch was eaten, the tables were taken down and the benches set for the actual service. Hymnbooks were distributed, and a last polish given to the windows by anxious women. The yard had been raked to perfection, the driveway cleaned with the leaf blower, and the cow barn was immaculate.

Upstairs in the house, Sarah and Priscilla dusted and swept. They put the new quilt on Sarah's bed, the one Mam had bound only a few weeks before. It was a solid off white and quilted with thousands of tiny stitches with two pillow shams to match. It was absolutely breathtaking, the pattern so fine and intricate.

Mam told Sarah if she thought that was a lot of work, she should see how they used to embroider and crochet the edges of the pillowcases to put in their hope chests. Then, when the couples visited every wedding guest as newlyweds, the women would make pillow tops out of yarn, pulling it through latticed plastic to create pillows with colorful designs. These pillows often went on the seat of a rocking chair in their formal living rooms, *die gute schtup.*

Mam shook her head, keenly feeling the sadness of lost tradition and telling Sarah the Amish homes appeared more and more *vee die Englishy leit* (like English people). No one had a *gute schtup* anymore, a closed room that would only be opened for important company on Sunday.

But Sarah did cherish her quilts. All four of them. She just did not want to embroider pillowcases. Or make those yarn cushions. They were stodgy and old fashioned, but maybe someday—who knew?—they would be more important to her again.

She was happy to have all her packaged sheet sets from Walmart or Kohl's or JCPenney, wherever Mam found them on sale. She even had a stack of Ralph Lauren towels that Mam bought on clearance at Park City. A kindly neighbor lady had alerted her to the sale.

Life and times move on, tastes change, and styles come and go for the Amish or English or whatever culture. Traditions are precious, indeed, but some things just didn't make a whole lot of sense in this day and age.

CHAPTER 23

TRUE TO THE FORECAST IN THE *INTELLIGENCER Journal*, the next day dawned perfectly with a sunrise of gold, yellow, lavender, and deep blue heralding the arrival of Sarah's wedding day. The Davey Beiler farm was bathed in a glow of blessed light.

Even Levi's throat had improved quickly, aided by Mam's adrenaline-fueled ministrations. She had heaped his chest with steamed onions and spread copious amounts of Unker's salve on a clean white cloth, pressing it to his throat and kneading the salve into the bottoms of his swollen feet. She gave him cup after cup of tea laced with whiskey, as well as vitamin C, echinacea, and goldenseal tablets. The poor man was overwhelmed with home remedies, complaining loud and long to anyone who would listen.

On the morning of the wedding, this had all paid off, and Levi sat dressed in his new suit, his shirt collar big enough, finally, that it felt comfortable. His hair was washed and combed, his teeth brushed, and he smiled eagerly as he greeted guests from where he was seated in a comfortable chair just inside the door. He had breakfasted well on rolled oats and the breakfast casserole Aunt Emma had brought.

Sarah's hair behaved better than usual, as if it somehow knew that this was not the time to be out of control. Priscilla said she'd never seen anyone spray so much hairspray. She claimed Sarah would get lung cancer from the fumes, but Sarah only smiled tightly and told her to watch what she said.

The blue dresses were worn by Sarah, Priscilla; and Rose. They were covered with immaculate white capes and aprons, pinned to perfection. Their white coverings were placed carefully on the much-sprayed heads.

Rose was as blonde and beautiful as ever, giggly and nervous, elaborate in her praise of the good-looking Marvin. He acted like a typical guy where Rose was concerned, completely enamored, appearing extremely pleased to be *nava sitzing* with her on his cousin's wedding day.

Omar was groomed to perfection as well, his dark hair cut nicely in the *ordnung*, as was required on a wedding day. He had eyes only for the radiant Priscilla. His heart was worn on his sleeve all day, the hope of having her for his bride some day carried within and shining from his eyes.

Lee appeared relaxed, but Sarah noticed a certain tightening of his jaw, a twitch in his cheek, as he shrugged on his new *mutza* and ran a comb through his thick, blond hair one final time. Sarah adjusted his black bowtie and stepped back to admire him, her eyes conveying all the love she felt on this perfect, beautiful morning of her wedding.

Anna wore blue as well, choosing to dress for Lee and Sarah, instead of the usual black worn long after a close relative or spouse passes away. She looked radiant,

her pretty face wreathed in smiles of congratulations, but
Sarah knew there was a shadow behind the happiness, a
cloud of grief and loneliness that was ever present.

"I can't hug either of you," she remarked as a greeting,
indicating the easily wrinkled organdy fabric used for
Sarah's bridal cape and apron.

Mam appeared to have settled down after the *risht
dag*, but she didn't waste very many smiles on anyone. She
spoke in short sentences, giving orders she expected to be
carried out immediately. Sarah knew she had swallowed
every herbal concoction meant to calm the nerves — vitamins B12 and 6 and something called Nature's Calm,
which was likely supposed to provide exactly what its
name implied. She squirted a vile-smelling tincture called
Ladies' Formula, a blend of herbs from Dr. Schultz's,
into a glass with a bit of water and swallowed it. She
rinsed the glass, banged it back into the cupboard, and
went briskly on her way. She always ate a few pretzels
or crackers soon after, so Sarah knew it must have tasted
absolutely horrendous.

When guests began arriving at 7:15, there was no
doubt about it. Mam's management skills had paid off.
She had missed nothing. The two large meals planned
for 400 people were both taken care of to the last fork
and pie.

Out in the shop in the room sectioned off for *die shoff
leit* (work people), potatoes were being peeled by helpful
church ladies. The *roasht leit* were finishing the preparation of the forty fat roasting chickens with the cubed
bread, celery, eggs, and seasonings. Cabbage was being
grated for huge dishes of cole slaw. Dat had made sure —
his own management skills also apparent — that there
were five gas stoves with working ovens set up at different

places throughout the work area. One was for potatoes, one for coffee, another for gravy, celery, or whatever.

Aunt Emma and her sister Barbara were the ones with "the paper," the important piece of tablet paper stating each person's job. As the helpers arrived, Emma and Barbara told each one who would make gravy, who would cook the celery. That lowly piece of tablet paper was what kept the whole work area going, with every last job assigned to someone by Mam's sisters.

Lee and Sarah sat on a bench, side by side, flanked by their attendants, greeting guests as they arrived. They smiled, shook hands, and acknowledged the beauty of the day.

Through the shop windows, Sarah could see the brilliance of the December sun, the yellow glow it cast across the prepared shop. The *fore gayer* (managers) scurried about, ensuring last minute details were taken care of.

Then they began seating people in earnest—ministers, parents, grandparents, other family members, workers or co-workers, and on down the line, the way people had been seated for many generations at Amish weddings. The men were on one side of the room, and the women on the other. The last ones to be seated were the single youth, all dressed in their very best, for this was a wedding day.

The announcement of the opening song was swallowed by the vast number of people, but everyone knew the hymn sung first at a wedding, so after the first line was sung, a crescendo followed with the second and third lines.

Sarah's heartbeat accelerated when the first minister stood up, followed by ten others. They watched them file out, then Lee stood, reached for her hand, and led her after them into a small area set aside as a conference room.

After they were admonished, blessed, and given spiritual advice, they were free to rejoin their attendants. They filed slowly into the middle of the large shop, where six additional folding chairs now stood, three facing three, waiting for them to be seated in the row of ministers as the singing went on.

Sarah took a deep breath, concentrated on relaxing, and kept her eyes downcast as a demure bride should. There were no smiles, only slightly bent heads, signs of true humility and obedience. Around them, the singing rose and fell, a comfort Sarah had been used to all her life. It was now especially beautiful, this well recognized wedding hymn.

Someone coughed. A throat was cleared. A baby set up an earnest howling. A frustrated mother got up and edged her way carefully past the bent knees of others, as her tiny infant continued to wail. Color appeared in the mother's cheeks, embarrassment setting in from having to get up and move among all these people. She wondered if her baby truly had colic, as little sleep as she got every night.

When the ministers returned, the singing stopped. David Beiler stood, rubbed his hands together, and cleared his throat. He lifted his eyes to the large shop filled with his daughter's wedding guests—his guests and Malinda's.

A great swell of emotion took away his ability to speak. He stood quietly, lifted his eyes to the shop ceiling.

When Sarah realized Dat was unable to speak, she felt the sting of emotion in her eyes and nose. She knew her tears would spill over, so she reached as delicately as possible for the folded white handkerchief in her pocket and lifted it discreetly to her face.

Finally, Dat spoke in the deep baritone she was

accustomed to hearing, with the roughness of emotion changing it only slightly.

He spoke from the heart on his daughter's wedding day. He recalled the barn fires and Sarah's deliverance from death by God's hand. He spoke of the men who had done this and the insignificance of the jail term. The only necessary thing was the genuine forgiveness in each individual heart.

He spoke of past trials and the mighty hand of deliverance that allowed Lee and Sarah to be together and to live in a land that was blessed with religious freedom, allowing them to have their horses and buggies, their Amish lifestyle. Sarah bent her head and held her handkerchief to her nose. She sniffled as tears plopped on the white organdy of her apron. She felt Lee shift in his chair and heard him pull out his own handkerchief, blowing his nose quietly, not wanting to draw attention.

Lee's bishop, Amos Esh, was the one who would "give them together." After the short prayer and the reading of the Scripture, he stood, a small man with a mighty voice, and rattled off every story in sequence. He told all the required stories for wedding sermons—Naomi and Ruth, Samson, and many others. They were all Old Testament tales that were filled with good advice and precious lessons of love and marriage.

How many young brides had the love for their mothers-in-law that Ruth did, wanting to dwell with her and worship the same God she did? Sarah thought of Mam's pumpkin pies and doubted if she ever felt like Ruth. She had to stifle a smile that threatened to surface.

Indeed, how many women were guilty of cajoling and seducing their husbands by their own foolish whims, thereby robbing their husbands of their power, the way

Delilah did to Samson? Women could be devious creatures, propelled by their own wills, depleting strong men
of their strength.

Sarah shivered and covered her forearms with the
palms of her hands. She loved the Old Testament stories; she always had. She had usually been the preacher
when they played church. She loved to get up and wave
her arms and tell Priscilla and Suzie and Mervin about
Moses in the basket and Pharaoh drowning in the Red
Sea and manna falling from heaven. She had even stolen a
few slices of white bread from the drawer in the kitchen,
broken it into pieces, and said they were the children of
Israel eating their manna.

Her heartbeat thudded against her ribs when Amos
Esh launched into the story about Tobias, a revered story
from the Apocrypha and the one used at every Amish
wedding to unite two people as husband and wife.

The bishop wasted no time, and when Sarah thought
she just might faint from her rapid heartbeat, she heard
him say their names, Levi Glick and Sarah Beiler. Then
Lee stood, reached for her hand, and walked with her to
stand in front of the bishop, who was dwarfed by Lee's
height.

Obviously undaunted, his mighty voice continued,
asking them the required holy questions. They each
pledged their commitment in the age-old union of marriage with a soft *ya* (yes).

They received the bishop's blessing and turned to go
back to their seats. Lee maneuvered the correct turn flaw-
lessly, though Sarah would not have noticed if he did it
all wrong.

She kept her eyes properly downcast through the
remainder of the sermon, but when the rousing swells of

the last hymn rose to the confines of the ceiling, she dared one furtive glance at Lee. Her eyes connected with the blueness of his, and she wondered if she had ever known that love was a color.

The remainder of that day was as close to perfection as possible. The corner table was every girl's dream. The china dishes Lee had given her were so gorgeous that Sarah was hesitant to put food on the plates, let alone eat from them.

The cakes and dishes set all over the table, given as gifts in the traditional way, were enough to inspire awe. The array of gifts and food was endless, and Lee stayed by her side as they opened and recorded each one.

In the afternoon, Priscilla led the old German hymn "Wohlauf" about the church being Christ's bride. Her voice was rich and steady as the remainder of the people seated around them chimed in. Omar sat beside Priscilla, his heart in his eyes, his gaze never leaving her down-turned face as her eyes followed the German words of the hymn.

On the other side of the newlyweds, Rose kept up a string of witty conversation topics, and Marvin was obviously enamored, but no one could tell if anything would come of it. Rose later gushed about Marvin continuously, but who knew? She had also just asked Matthew to be the short order cook at the restaurant where she worked, giving Matthew hope that she would take him back. But would he come back to the Amish for her sake? That was obviously a huge question, carrying a doubtful answer.

And there was Sarah, Mrs. Lee Glick, with her manly husband of approximately four hours by her side. All the doubts and fears, all that senseless heartache, erased, gone. Or had it been senseless? Did everything, including mistakes, all add up to a richer, more enduring maturity in the end?

Suddenly, she noticed Matthew, tall, handsome, his dark good looks accentuated by his smartly cut gray suit. He was watching Rose, a confused look in his brown eyes, a sort of embarrassed bewilderment, as if he wasn't sure what he was seeing.

He had come to her wedding, and Sarah was glad of it, but seeing him this way tugged at her heart in spite of the pain he had caused in her life. He still loved Rose. He always had, always would.

His love for her had likely been the driving force that caused him to leave the Amish and the sole reason he had ever lowered himself to date Sarah. Everything in his life had revolved around his desire for the lovely Rose, who, it seemed, was happily embarking on another flirtatious fling.

What would happen to Matthew?

Suddenly, Sarah realized that it wasn't up to Rose to fix Matthew. No one could blame another person for their situation in life. It was up to Matthew to find the resources to learn to give up his own will. Sarah realized Rose was Matthew's will but not necessarily God's.

Poor Hannah, having thoroughly spoiled her son, now lived on antacids and anxiety medication. She lay awake at night, praying and worrying about his life.

Sarah looked at Matthew with his puzzled stare. She smiled at him and looked away, but not before he had returned her smile. It was a small, unsure widening of his lips, with a hesitant, almost humble expression in his eyes.

So the world kept spinning, Sarah thought, and only life's trials would help to mature the charming Matthew.

It was simply the way of it.

At nine o'clock that evening, the string of well wishers filed past Lee and Sarah at the corner table. They shook hands and wished them well, giving their congratulations and goodbyes. There were promises to visit as the bride and groom gave away the trinkets with their names and date of the wedding day. Sarah's head spun with weariness.

Rose and Priscilla had gone off with their guys. Anna Mae and Ruthie sank onto their chairs, their shoes kicked off, and said if they had to walk one single step more, they'd collapse, and someone would have to bring in a skid loader to move them.

Lee said he would; he was pretty good with a skid loader, which sent them into shrieks of glee. Sarah thought they still acted like kids when Lee was around.

Levi came to wish them a goodnight at their table. It was past his bedtime, and he was sleepy. They gave him a large Ziploc bag filled with all sorts of candy, which he hastily stuffed into his vest pocket, his eyes darting back and forth, making sure nobody saw him hide it away.

He said he was glad he had a new brother-in-law and wished them *Herr saya* (God's blessing).

He lumbered off, one hand on his vest pocket and a smile on his face, heading to tuck the candy in a bureau drawer and settle himself for a long night of rest. The next day promised to be a good one with all the wedding leftovers to eat.

At last, Lee and Sarah could leave the corner table. They found Mam and her sisters clattering dishes in the work room. Dat was reclining on a folding chair, a steaming cup of coffee in his hand, his hat pushed to the back of his head, smiling contently as he listened to the ramblings of his wife and her sisters. Emma shrieked some nonsense about the amount of *roasht* they had packed into gallon Ziploc bags and carted off to the freezer.

"Malinda, you do it every time. Way too much food."

Mam set her mouth determinedly, shook her head, and said she would be happy to have all that *roasht* and *tzellrich* for quick meals all winter long.

Emma grumbled about the work she put on everyone, making all that extra food, but Mam threw an apple at her, missing her completely. Barbara giggled like a schoolgirl, and Dat leaned over to pick up the apple. He lobbed it at Emma, and she whirled and said, "*Unfashtendich*, Davey, *doo bisht kindish* (nonsense, you are childish)."

Such goings on were completely common. The tension lifted, the pressure released. Everything had gone well, and now it was time for fun.

Mam delicately put a finger through a corner of a half-ruined wedding cake. She thought no one had seen her until Dat called loudly, "Malinda, I'm surprised at you!"

She jumped, caught red handed, then looked up and laughed with the abandonment of a teenager.

The wedding was over.

Lee and Sarah stood together, taking in this whole scene of carefree release. Lee slipped an arm around Sarah's waist and pulled her close against him, under Dat's warm gaze.

"Well, Mrs. Glick, how does it feel to be an old married woman?" he asked, smiling at Sarah.

He had barely finished the sentence, allowing Sarah no time to reply, when the door burst open, and six rowdy young men charged through it. They whooped and yelled, grabbing Lee by his arms and legs, in spite of his fervent yells and his flailing and kicking. They carried him out the door, as Sarah clapped a hand to her mouth to keep from crying out.

Dat laughed out loud.

"He may as well give himself up!"

"Over the fence," Barbara chortled.

"That's so ignorant," Emma snorted.

"I hope they don't hurt Lee," Sarah said.

"He'll be alright. The more he resists, the harder it will be for him. If he quiets down, he'll get dumped over safely," Dat said.

And sure enough, as Sarah later found out, the youth had also placed a broom across the doorway to the upstairs. Sarah tripped on it, catching Lee's arm to stay upright, as they headed to her bedroom.

Well, they'd gotten her good and proper, too, so now she and Lee were traditionally fit to be husband and wife. They'd thrown Lee over the fence (Sarah detected the smell of manure on his shoes when they left them in the *kesslehaus*), and now she had "stepped across the broom," enabling her to be a true wife. Old wives' tales, traditions, myths—whatever one called them—they were all done in the spirit of fun. They were endearing pranks that tied them all together as one culture, the way English people threw bouquets and removed garters.

Sarah's bedroom was strewn with red rose petals and a sea of white balloons, decorative and romantic. It had all been done by her sisters and best friends, bringing a lump of appreciation to her throat. The room was lit by soft candlelight, making it ethereal, almost heavenly in appearance.

They would spend their first night together here in Sarah's room on the home farm, following tradition. And

they would live with Sarah's family until they had visited
most of their wedding guests. Then they would move to
their farm, making a life of their own. That would be
soon, Sarah knew, with the chores to do and the whole
farm to look after.

Now she looked around the room, taking it all in. But
what was that in the corner?

Softly, the magnificent grandfather clock bonged eleven
times. The sound was rich, muted, and elegant, the
golden glow of the oak finish luminescent in the candlelight.

Shyly, her eyes wide, she turned to her husband, questioning him with her gaze, speechless.

"Your clock," he said.

She could only shake her head in disbelief, as she went
across the room to touch the smooth oak wood and listen
to the great pendulum swinging slowly back and forth.

"You never did give me a clock," she said softly.

His answer was his strong arms around her, as the
white balloons bobbed and floated, and the candle flames
sputtered. Sarah did not know this much happiness was
possible.

It was so much like Lee to keep this clock hidden from
the guests at the wedding. He had chosen, instead, to
have it delivered late in the day as a secret, a surprise for
her alone. It somehow made it seem almost sacred, this
wonderful gift.

"Sarah, you'll be a farmer's wife, and who knows if
we'll be poor someday, but at least we'll have a beautiful
clock, won't we?" Lee said, as they watched the pendulum's movement together.

Sarah nodded.

Yes, time moved on, the great clock ticking it off with

every movement of its second hand. Life would be measured in seconds, minutes, and hours, with days turning into weeks. The weeks would turn to months, and the months to years. Through time, they would live together, evolve together. Their love would grow into a sturdy tree, swayed by winds of adversity, storms, and trials, but the foundation of their deep roots would hold.

Hadn't they experienced firsthand the fires of life? One after another, the arsonist had set fire to men's hard labor, their very livelihoods, and one by one, they had overcome, growing stronger in faith, understanding forgiveness as never before.

Lee placed the palm of his hand on Sarah's scarred face, then bent his head to the dearest sign of God's will for their lives, to be together always.

EPILOGUE

THE STURDY GRANDFATHER CLOCK STOOD IN ITS corner of their home for many years, faithfully recording the time. It was wound by Lee at the end of every week on Saturday evening.

Sarah polished the oak wood, wiped the glass clean. When housecleaning time arrived every spring and every fall, she would take down the great gold weights and the intricately engraved pendulum. She polished them with great care, lovingly rubbing them with a soft cotton cloth.

The clock bonged out the hour when their first child was born one stormy winter night, when the local midwife had to use her four-wheel drive and every skill she possessed to maneuver through the cold and the wind and the drifts. It chimed joyously when Lee carried his newborn son across their living room to show Malinda. They named him David Lee, for Sarah's father and for Lee.

When Levi died and was buried in the cemetery at Gordonville, both Sarah and Lee neglected the usual winding of the clock. It stopped, the motionless pendulum paying tribute to Levi, the great and beloved man who had brought joy and simplicity to the whole family. He was 38 and had lived a happy and blessed life, his memory living on in their hearts.

The ticking of the great clock witnessed the sight of Lee with his head bent, his elbows on his knees, his shoulders heaving with the weight of having been ordained into the ministry the day before. Far into the night, he wrestled with fear and doubt and his own insignificance, for he was a humble young man and could not imagine why the lot had fallen on him. Sarah was his loving helpmeet, his staunch, unfailing supporter, having been raised in a home where they always expected their father to expound God's word.

The sun shone again for Lee. It glinted off the gold pendulum as it swung steadily back and forth one bright summer morning when he realized his joy had returned as he learned to again give himself up to God's will.

As the contours of the land were filled with crops, the cycle of life moved on. Corn and alfalfa were planted, grew, and were harvested. There were seasons of plenty, of rain and of sunshine, of storms, and always the beauty of sunrises and sunsets.

Changes came, as they are bound to do. More children were born to Lee and Sarah, filling the table in the kitchen.

The glass on the grandfather clock was smudged by sticky little fingers, the sides beat upon by sturdy little fists, and yet it continued chiming out the hour, day after day.

The clock could not speak; it only ticked away the minutes. Every evening after the *gebet* (prayer) was said, Lee bent to the rhythm of the ticking clock. He kissed his wife goodnight and touched her still scarred face. Time had not completely removed those reminders of the hard times they had been through and God's continuing presence with them.

The End

THE GLOSSARY

aus grufa—A Pennsylvania Dutch dialect phrase meaning "being published."

ausre gmayna–A Pennsylvania Dutch dialect phrase meaning "other churches."

aylent—A Pennsylvania Dutch dialect word meaning "slow one."

babeyly—A Pennsylvania Dutch dialect word meaning "paper," particularly a paper with a list of duties to be done the day before a wedding.

bann—A Pennsylvania Dutch dialect word meaning "ban" or "shunning."

base—A Pennsylvania Dutch dialect word meaning "angry."

beer—A Pennsylvania Dutch dialect word meaning "pears."

begrabnis—A Pennsylvania Dutch dialect word meaning "burial."

bekimma—A Pennsylvania Dutch dialect word meaning "bother."

bet zeit–A Pennsylvania Dutch dialect phrase meaning "bed time."

bisht alright—A Pennsylvania Dutch dialect phrase meaning "are you alright?"

blooney—A Pennsylvania Dutch dialect word meaning "bologna."

bree—A Pennsylvania Dutch dialect word meaning "juice."

bupplish—A Pennsylvania Dutch dialect word meaning "childish."

buze fertich—A Pennsylvania Dutch dialect phrase meaning "repentant."

chappy—A Pennsylvania Dutch dialect word meaning "boyfriend."

chide—A Pennsylvania Dutch dialect word meaning "right."

dale—A Pennsylvania Dutch dialect word meaning "share" or "portion."

Dat—A Pennsylvania Dutch dialect word used to address or refer to one's father.

de alte—A Pennsylvania Dutch dialect phrase meaning "the old ones" or "ancestors."

denke—A Pennsylvania Dutch dialect word meaning "thank you."

dichly—A Pennsylvania Dutch dialect word meaning "headscarf."

die alte–A Pennsylvania Dutch dialect phrase meaning "forefathers."

Die Botschaft–A weekly periodical in which volunteer "scribes" report on the events of their communities. Its name is a Pennsylvania Dutch term meaning "The Message."

do net—A Pennsylvania Dutch dialect phrase meaning "don't."

doch veggley–A Pennsylvania Dutch dialect phrase meaning "carriage."

Doddy—A Pennsylvania Dutch dialect word used to address or refer to one's grandfather.

eck leit—A Pennsylvania Dutch dialect phrase meaning "corner people." They are the ones who serve the bride and groom's table at a wedding.

Englishe leid–A Pennsylvania Dutch dialect phrase meaning "English people."

ess mocht sich—A Pennsylvania Dutch dialect phrase meaning "it will be alright."

fa-schput—A Pennsylvania Dutch dialect word meaning "mocking."

fer-fearish—A Pennsylvania Dutch dialect word meaning "deceiving."

fer-sark—A Pennsylvania Dutch dialect phrase meaning "to take care of."

fit—A Pennsylvania Dutch dialect word meaning "capable."

fore-gayer—A Pennsylvania Dutch dialect word meaning "managers," usually for a wedding or funeral.

frade—A Pennsylvania Dutch dialect word meaning "joy."

freundshaft—A Pennsylvania Dutch dialect word meaning "family."

gaduld—A Pennsylvania Dutch dialect word meaning "patience."

ga-fuss—A Pennsylvania Dutch dialect word meaning "fuss."

ga-mach—A Pennsylvania Dutch dialect word meaning "to do."

ga-pick—A Pennsylvania Dutch dialect word meaning "picking," as in picking on someone.

geb acht—A Pennsylvania Dutch dialect phrase meaning "be careful."

gebet—A Pennsylvania Dutch dialect word meaning "prayer."

Gebet Buch—A Pennsylvania Dutch dialect phrase meaning "prayer book."

geduldich—A Pennsylvania Dutch dialect word meaning "patient."

gel—A Pennsylvania Dutch dialect word meaning "right."

gepp—A Pennsylvania Dutch dialect word meaning "give it."

gix—A Pennsylvania Dutch dialect word meaning "needle."

gook mol—A Pennsylvania Dutch dialect phrase meaning "look here."

goot zeit mach—A Pennsylvania Dutch dialect phrase meaning "making good time."

gros-feelich—A Pennsylvania Dutch dialect word meaning "proud."

gute schtup—A Pennsylvania Dutch dialect phrase meaning "formal living room."

halsduch—A Pennsylvania Dutch dialect word meaning "cape." It is part of the traditional attire worn by Amish women, covering the upper part of the body.

helf mich—A Pennsylvania Dutch dialect phrase meaning "help me."

herr saya—A Pennsylvania Dutch dialect phrase meaning "God's blessing."

hesslich goot—A Pennsylvania Dutch dialect phrase meaning "awfully good."

himmlisch—A Pennsylvania Dutch dialect word meaning "heavenly."

ich bin aw base—A Pennsylvania Dutch dialect phrase meaning "I am mad."

ich gleich dich—A Pennsylvania Dutch dialect phrase meaning "I love you."

ivver vile—A Pennsylvania Dutch dialect phrase meaning "soon."

kalte sup—A Pennsylvania Dutch dialect phrase meaning "cold soup."

kesslehaus—A Pennsylvania Dutch dialect word meaning "wash house."

kindish—A Pennsylvania Dutch dialect word meaning "childish."

koch-shissla—A Pennsylvania Dutch dialect word meaning "serving dishes."

komm—A Pennsylvania Dutch dialect word meaning "come."

kopp-duch—A Pennsylvania Dutch dialect word meaning "head scarf."

laud—A Pennsylvania Dutch dialect word meaning "casket."

Mam—A Pennsylvania Dutch dialect word used to address or refer to one's mother.

mein Got—A Pennsylvania Dutch dialect phrase meaning "my God."

mitt leidas—A Pennsylvania Dutch dialect phrase meaning "sympathy."

mit-leidich—A Pennsylvania Dutch dialect word meaning "understanding."

mutza—A Pennsylvania Dutch dialect word meaning "Sunday coat."

naits—A Pennsylvania Dutch dialect word meaning "thread."

nava sitza—A Pennsylvania Dutch dialect phrase meaning "beside sitters," the members of a wedding party who sit beside the bride and groom.

nay—A Pennsylvania Dutch dialect word meaning "no."

ordnung—The Amish community's agreed-upon rules for living based on their understanding of the Bible, particularly the New Testament. The *ordnung* varies from community to community, often reflecting leaders' preferences, local customs, and traditional practices.

phone shanty—Most Old Order Amish do not have telephone landlines in their homes so that incoming calls do not overtake their lives and so that they are not physically connected to the larger world. Many Amish build a small, fully enclosed structure where a phone is installed and where they can make calls and retrieve messages.

piffich—A Pennsylvania Dutch dialect word meaning "meticulous."

risht dag—A Pennsylvania Dutch dialect phrase meaning "day to prepare before a wedding."

roasht—A Pennsylvania Dutch dialect word meaning "chicken filling."

roasht leit—A Pennsylvania Dutch dialect phrase meaning "people who make chicken filling."

rumspringa—A Pennsylvania Dutch dialect word meaning "running around." It refers to the time in a person's life between age sixteen and marriage. It involves structured social activities in groups, as well as dating, and usually takes place on the weekends.

s'ana ent — A Pennsylvania Dutch dialect phrase meaning "other end."

sark — A Pennsylvania Dutch dialect word meaning "care."

saya — A Pennsylvania Dutch dialect word meaning "blessing."

schadenfreude — A Pennsylvania Dutch dialect word meaning "pleasure at the misfortune of others."

schlakes — A Pennsylvania Dutch dialect word meaning "punishes."

schloppich aufangs — A Pennsylvania Dutch dialect phrase meaning "sloppy now."

schnitzas — A Pennsylvania Dutch dialect word meaning "fibs."

schtick – A Pennsylvania Dutch dialect word meaning "piece."

schtrofe — A Pennsylvania Dutch dialect word meaning "punishment."

sei — A Pennsylvania Dutch dialect word meaning "his." In communities where many people have the same first and last names, it is customary for the husband's name to be added to that of his wife so it is clear who is being referred to.

shaut—A Pennsylvania Dutch dialect word meaning "a shame."

shoff leit—A Pennsylvania Dutch dialect phrase meaning "work people."

siss net chide—A Pennsylvania Dutch dialect phrase meaning "it's not right."

smear—A Pennsylvania Dutch dialect word meaning "cheese spread."

snitz—A Pennsylvania Dutch dialect word meaning "dried apple."

tzellrich—A Pennsylvania Dutch dialect word meaning "celery."

tzimmalich—A Pennsylvania Dutch dialect word meaning "humble."

tzvie-drocht—A Pennsylvania Dutch dialect word meaning "dissension."

unbegreiflich—A Pennsylvania Dutch dialect word meaning "unbelievable."

unfashtendich—A Pennsylvania Dutch dialect word meaning "nonsense."

unleidlich—A Pennsylvania Dutch dialect word meaning "mischievous."

unlieve—A Pennsylvania Dutch dialect word meaning "hatred."

unna such—A Pennsylvania Dutch dialect phrase meaning "search."

vassa—A Pennsylvania Dutch dialect word meaning "water."

vesh bengli—A Pennsylvania Dutch dialect phrase meaning "washbowl."

vissa tae—A Pennsylvania Dutch dialect phrase meaning "meadow tea."

voss—A Pennsylvania Dutch dialect word meaning "what."

Wohlauf—A traditional German hymn sung after the meal at Amish weddings. It is about the church being Christ's bride.

ya—A Pennsylvania Dutch dialect word meaning "yes."

yoh—A Pennsylvania Dutch dialect word meaning "yes."

zeit-lang—A Pennsylvania Dutch dialect word meaning "missing/longing."

Other Books by Linda Byler

Available from your favorite
bookstore or online retailer.

"Author Linda Byler is Amish, which sets this book apart both in the rich details of Amish life and in the lack of melodrama over disappointments and tragedies. Byler's writing will leave readers eager for the next book in the series."

–Publisher's Weekly review of *Wild Horses*

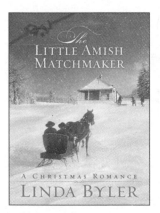

THE LITTLE AMISH
MATCHMAKER
A Christmas Romance

THE CHRISTMAS
VISITOR
An Amish Romance

MARY'S CHRISTMAS
GOODBYE
An Amish Romance

Lizzie Searches for Love Series

BOOK ONE   BOOK TWO   BOOK THREE

TRILOGY   COOKBOOK

Sadie's Montana Series

BOOK ONE   BOOK TWO   BOOK THREE   TRILOGY

Hester's Hunt for Home Series

BOOK ONE   BOOK TWO   BOOK THREE

ABOUT THE AUTHOR

Linda Byler was raised in an Amish family and is an active member of the Amish church today. Growing up, Linda loved to read and write. In fact, she still does. Linda is well-known within the Amish community as a columnist for a weekly Amish newspaper.

Linda is the author of the *Lizzie Searches for Love* series, the *Sadie's Montana* series, the *Lancaster Burning* series, and the *Hester's Hunt for Home* series. She is also the author of *The Little Amish Matchmaker*, *The Christmas Visitor*, and *Mary's Christmas Goodbye*, as well as *Lizzie's Amish Cookbook: Favorite recipes from three generations of Amish cooks*!